THE
ADVENTURES OF A
GOOD AND DECENT MAN

A Mark Davidson Anthology

HELLMUT EDELMANN

The following stories are works of fiction. Names, characters, places and incidents are the products of the author's imagination, or are used fictitiously. Any resemblance to actual events, locales, or persons, living or dead, is entirely coincidental.

Ausgabe Letzter Hand 2017
Herausgeber: Paulovia Verlag

ISBN: 13: 978-0692931974
10: 069293197X

Cover design by Cover Design Studio

Print layout by booknook.biz

Contents

REMEMBERING
285

A DEATH AT SEA
371

COLLABORATION
467

DARK JOURNEY
575

Character is Destiny.

Epictetus

DEDICATION

To Maya, Sandy and Dieter
For their encouragement, support and love.

A Mark Davidson Story

LOVE AT FIRST SIGHT

PART I:
A WINTER ODYSSEY

Hellmut Edelmann

Love at First Sight – Part I:
A Winter Odyssey

Pronunciation Guide

Aja (Eye – a)

di Sogno (Dee – sewn – yo)

Hui (Hoy)

Jaroslav (Yar – o – slaf)

Jiřina (Year – zhee – na)

KaDeWe (KahDayVay) (Kaufhaus Des Westens = Dept. Store of
The West)

Košice (Ko – sheet – sa)

Malcesine (Mal – chey – zina)

Pavliček (Pav – lee – check)

Škoda (Sh – koda)

Staříková (Star – zhee – kovaa)

Székely (Seck – hey)

Tibor (Tee – bore)

Tomáš (Toe – maash)

Večer (Vech – er)

Vesnicka (Ves nyi-tska)

Zdeněk (Zden – yeck)

Žilina (Zhil – eena)

A Winter Odyssey

Chapter One

1991

Mark Davidson, Ph.D., dean of a college and everybody's 'good guy', was, well, flirting – flirting with a nun! Sitting in Charleston's modest international airport on a bench in a long row along one side of the waiting room, somewhat absentmindedly scanning the rows of seats arranged perpendicular to his own, his eyes had momentarily locked onto a pair of female eyes that was mated to a most beguiling, disarming, and innocent smile, which brought forth an involuntary and equally natural response from the slightly embarrassed academic. Mark hadn't intended to stare at the lovely peaches-and-cream countenance framed by the incongruously severe white crown band and under-veil of her habit, but he simply couldn't help himself. He had merely looked up from his *Charleston Post and Courier* for an instant to ascertain that the waiting room was beginning to fill up, and there it was, a vision of divine beauty. Looking up once again, only to note that she, too, was peeking in his direction, albeit discreetly, they exchanged smiles and both looked away. *This is most unusual,* thought Mark. He resumed his survey of the waiting room, to determine, if by chance, anyone he knew might be there. No one, as far as he could tell.

The early morning air had been slightly chilly. The driver of the Honda Civic didn't mind. It was normal for late October and he was a morning person. Although Bob Holland, a fellow Midwesterner, who headed the Medical University's Forensic Pathology Department, had extended a standing invitation for him to park in his extra garage anytime he wanted, Mark opted for the airport's overnight parking lot. After all, he was leaving Friday and returning early Sunday. *No sense making Bob break up his weekend by having him drive me to the airport and back to John's Island twice just to save a few dollars.* Some of Mark's friends, had they heard him utter that thought aloud, might have been surprised, for he had a reputation as a tightwad, not only with his own money, but also with the College's budget.

Even though he had only his weekend luggage, a small overnighter, Mark had decided to check it. The pert uniformed agent behind the counter seemed unusually friendly for such an early hour. *I'm going to take that as a good omen. Maybe she has a big date planned.* The waiting room was relatively small at Charleston International Airport. The name was something of a misnomer, since international destinations generally required travel to Atlanta, to Dulles or some other intermediate departure point. Setting his laptop down beside him, Mark had unfolded his copy of the Low Country's major newspaper, and started to check the local, national and international headlines before boarding. *Same old, same old. Local politicians campaigning for next month's elections. The last weeks of October can be counted upon to churn up some nasty rhetoric and lots and lots of promises. As usual, the candidates are struggling to come up with an issue that might resonate with the electorate, looking for a favorable photo opportunity or a sound bite to give themselves an edge. Generating a little scandal around your opponent is never completely ruled out either.* Mark noted that a few pundits were hinting at a change in Spoleto leadership. *Sagging revenues seem to be a problem. Or still a problem. Oooohh!* AN ATTEMPTED ROBBERY THWARTED YESTERDAY NEAR THE BATTERY. YOUNG FEMALE JOGGER WITH MARTIAL ARTS TRAINING DISABLES ATTACKER. *I'll bet that was a surprise!*

Mark again lowered his newspaper slightly and surveyed his fellow travelers. *Looks like more tourists than business types.* A briefcase or laptop here and there gave away the salespeople and executives heading home after a business trip to South Carolina's bustling port city. Mark nonchalantly turned a page and continued reading.

The temptation was too great. He glanced again towards the seat occupied by the charming smile. She was reading a small book she held in her right hand. Her hair was covered, but her hazel eyes gleamed from a well-scrubbed face. Her tunic was dark gray. Sensing she was about to look up, Mark focused again on his newspaper. He didn't quite know what to make of this unusual 'encounter'. He read a few minutes more, only to be interrupted by the pleasant voice on the loudspeaker inviting passengers to board Delta's first flight of the day to the Big Apple.

Professor Mark Davidson had been perfectly happy as a popular member of the History Department at Marshland State College, his second teaching position following a satisfying and successful period of study at a prestigious, private Midwestern university, and an assistant professorship at a small college in Missouri. Fate, however, had intruded on his peaceful routine and introduced an abrupt change in his life. Traditionally, at MSC the dean was elected by the faculty. Two factions among the faculty failed to elect their favorite candidate to the deanship opened unexpectedly when Cordellis Lee Johnston, who had held the position for over twenty years, fell asleep at his desk one day and never woke up.

After several painfully protracted and unsuccessful ballots at a faculty meeting to choose his successor, the wrangling among disparate points of view had become distressfully contentious. The early spring rain pounding on the roof of ancient Ashley Hall paralleled in intensity the ongoing verbal battles inside. Southern gentlemen were in danger of drawing their swords, as one old-timer in the English Department had put it. The lateness of the hour compounded the fatigue of many members, who were eager to retire to the peace and quiet of their comfortable homes. Suddenly, a disenchanted colleague in the Biology Department, not without facetious intent, nominated Mark. After several further ballots had taken their toll on faculty patience and the stalemate had assumed ugly overtones, Mark was elected by his somewhat exhausted and exasperated peers to be the new Dean of the Faculty. Many of them were as shocked as Mark by this strange turn of events. Mark's comfortably routinized bachelor existence metamorphosed almost immediately. At twenty-six he was the youngest dean in the college's history.

Being among the youngest at almost anything was not new for Mark Davidson. The only grandparent he ever knew, old Jake Davidson, constantly bragged about his grandson, the prodigy. Mark's mother, more of a realist, attributed his rapid progress through school to unusual motivation and extraordinary diligence. He was barely 16 when he entered college, and just a few months past the legal age when he received his doctorate. The more he thought about it, the more natural it seemed to Mark, that he should be named dean at age 26.

An interesting coup had solidified Mark's new stature in the college and local community. Triggered by a tip from one of his former professors, Mark had aggressively pursued a special grant opportunity that resulted in the creation of an international Wetlands Research Institute at the College. Attracting Harriet Crawford, a Nobel Prize winner and one of the nation's foremost environmentalists and wetlands authorities to head the institute, was regarded as much, much more than mere icing on the cake. MSC was now officially 'on the map', as they say. The real respect from knowledgeable colleagues and townsfolk, however, stemmed from Mark's diplomatic and political finesse. He graciously allowed the Governor and several top legislators to garner all the credit. Thus was a campus hero born. Henceforth, whenever Mark called Columbia for help, his voice was heard.

Now beginning his third year as Dean, Mark's evenhandedness and ability to effect convenient compromises on thorny issues, to stroke fragile egos and put petty interdepartmental turf battles to rest had earned him admiration and respect from even the most skeptical and hostile among his colleagues and would-be detractors. On the negative side, his personal social life was virtually nonexistent. The never-ending committee meetings, the trips to Columbia to lobby for appropriations, the *de rigueur* speaking engagements and a myriad other official duties and responsibilities left him with little time for himself. The prolonged illness of Judge Harmon Willinggate, the College's affable president, had exacerbated Mark's creeping exhaustion, because he had been obliged to assume many of the president's duties as well.

This visit to New York for the annual meeting of the Overseas Studies Consortium was an item Mark had circled on his calendar back in May, knowing a break, however brief, would be most welcome once the new academic year was underway. *Too bad Jeff Horton had to back out of our planned evening at the Met!* Jeff, an old college buddy and fellow opera buff from Indiana, had called last night to tell him that family matters were forcing him to delay his arrival in New York until Saturday. *So what am I supposed to do with this ticket? This expensive ticket? Maybe I can find someone at this afternoon's leadership session who would like to join me.*

Professor Davidson was a handsome, sandy-haired, athletic-looking young scholar, whose lithe, energetic step was nicely balanced by his mature, thoughtful demeanor. Davidson had enjoyed but two Sundays at the beach near Savannah this summer. Developing a faculty evaluation project, redesigning the automated registration program, hiring new faculty and riding herd on the construction of the new Science Center notwithstanding, he had also squeezed in time to play the role of Shylock in Beaufort's Summer of Shakespeare Festival. Local reviews had been quite favorable. Acting, especially character roles, was a pastime from which he had drawn much pleasure ever since taking the plunge on a dare as a high school senior. He was Tevya in *Fiddler on the Roof* in an amateur production. Parts in a few college plays, including the lead in a short run of Rostand's *Cyrano*, had helped him develop his talent further. During this time, he mastered make-up and costuming. Whenever he could, he helped back-stage with lighting and set building. A visit to New York always represented a golden opportunity to attend the theater, take in an opera, and, if he was lucky, to just generally catch his breath.

Mark had been a 'Spätling', as his German-born mother often referred to him. She was over forty when he was born; his father, a mill executive, over fifty. Both had died while Mark was in college. He had no siblings or close relatives. An only child, Mark had been a precocious, active boy, who demonstrated considerable self reliance and maturity for his age. As an adult orphan, he quickly learned to fend for himself. He adopted a permanently positive outlook and was determined to maintain his equilibrium, no matter what obstacles he might face. This simple philosophy had served him well as his young career developed.

Offsetting his lack of congenital relationships, Mark, with a naturally outgoing personality, cultivated his college friendships and was immensely popular with all with whom he came into contact. He kept in touch regularly through letters, and occasional phone calls and visits. The OSC meeting in New York was a 'must do' on his calendar, especially because so many of his college chums shared his international interests.

Gentleman that he was, Mark let most of the passengers file past him. He was in seat 18B. *No reason to hurry.* His eye caught sight of the gray and white veil and crown band that had so nicely framed the face of the mysterious nun in the waiting room. She was already seated.

Actually, he thought, as he peered up the aisle to the approximate location of his row, *I believe she's sitting right next to me.* It crossed his mind that destiny was playing with him once more. Was he being moved about like a puppet? *Is fate manipulating my strings again?*

Chapter Two

Mark looked at his boarding pass, then at the row and seat number, then again at his boarding pass. Yes, his seat was next to the nun. Not usually at a loss for words, Mark bought a few seconds of time before sitting down by opening the overhead and stowing his briefcase. His was the aisle seat. He made room for a passenger who needed to move to a seat further back. Leaning over slightly, he addressed the nun, who was in the process of squeezing her oversized handbag under the seat in front of her. "Would you like me to put that bag in the overhead for you?"

His seat mate turned with the most charming smile. "Thank you. I don't seem to have much room here." She handed him the bag. It was black, most likely plastic, and fairly heavy.

As Mark seated himself and fastened his seatbelt, she spoke again. "Thank you. These seats are so close together there's barely enough space for one's feet much less a carry-on."

Mark agreed. *She's absolutely lovely*, he thought. *And quite friendly. Completely at ease.* "We're lucky we don't have to fly further than New York. Is that your final destination?" He didn't know what else to say. After all, how often do you meet a nun, an exceptionally beautiful nun, at that? It didn't matter. Sister Catherine introduced herself. She described her order, a non-denominational Christian group, the *Paulian Sisters*, with headquarters in New York. The order's mission involved teaching and health care, both in the United States and abroad, with a special focus on orphaned children and displaced persons. She went on to say that the order had a more autonomous structure than most religious groups. For Sisters past the novice stage, wearing the traditional habit was not always mandatory, and dress was often at the discretion of individual members. She, however, found it useful when traveling alone to don the habit.

Sister Catherine soon had Mark giving a capsule history of his *Werdegang,* from a happy, rather carefree childhood and youth in the Midwest to a position of responsibility at a small southeastern state college with aspirations for broader recognition of its academic legitimacy. If it had been Mark's aim to lay back with his eyes closed and to relax *en route* to New York, which could be considered his customary traveling mode, his new-found loquaciousness, driven by a subconscious desire to continue the conversation *ad infinitum,* completely transmogrified his intention. Although he was not immediately aware of it, Mark was smitten by the beauty and vivacious charm of his fellow traveler. Her intelligence and obvious dedication to her calling struck a chord. He, too, could be considered an educational leader. He felt a profound kinship. *I can't believe we have so much in common.* He envied her self-assurance, admired her commitment to her mission, was inspired by the way she embraced the vicissitudes of life.

For her part, Sister Catherine found Mark to be, well, handsome. After all, nuns are human too. He had a quality of wholesomeness about him that was very appealing. He was strong and determined. She appreciated his politeness; found his shyness attractive. He was educated, sensitive, modest, quietly masculine. *If I... Uh, no!* She didn't allow herself to go there. She had chosen her vocation after a prolonged period of painstaking reflection. She broke a slight lull in their conversation. "I've been called to New York for possible reassignment. It may be abroad. I have a bit of a reputation for solving problems. I hope and pray I'll be able to handle the challenges I'm sure to face."

"Somehow," Mark said with great certainty, "I know you'll be successful, regardless of the difficulty of the circumstances."

Without any particular forethought, it was Mark who interrupted another brief period of silence in their conversation by mentioning that he had two excellent tickets to the opera at *Lincoln Center* that evening. He wondered aloud, if she would consider attending with him.

"I'd love to! It may be the most extraordinary date you'll ever have," she chuckled.

Mark experienced a surge of adrenaline like none he had ever known before. They agreed, it would suit both their schedules best, if they met at the entrance to the *Metropolitan Opera* about fifteen minutes before the curtain. Sister Catherine related how much her mother wanted her to be a ballerina. As a good daughter, she had taken lessons for years, but ultimately decided it was not a compelling interest and gave it up. Mark described how three fingers on his left hand, jammed in a pick-up basketball game in a high school gym class, had ended his violin lessons. "My teacher telling me I'd never be another Paganini didn't help either."

When the plane landed at La Guardia, Sister Catherine's small suitcase was among the first to appear on the carousel. She claimed it and vanished. Mark's frustration brought color to his cheeks. His overnighter finally bounced out of the chute in the company of the last half dozen or so to emerge from his flight. Baggage from another flight was already attracting an unruly group of arriving passengers jostling for position.

One of OSC's senior planning committees, of which Mark was Co-Chairman, had an afternoon session scheduled. Mark dropped everything off in his hotel room. Fortunately, most of the meetings were being held in the hotel's own meeting rooms. Refreshments had been ordered to obviate the need for a lunch break. The agenda was full. Mark played his role as facilitator well, getting each item to a vote after a reasonable period of discussion. He was not only a gifted conceptualizer, but was known as a master implementer, a demon for detail. The atmosphere was cordial and the group finally adjourned, satisfied that it had been one of the most productive sessions in recent memory. Mark had a few minutes to exchange friendly banter with some of his old acquaintances before excusing himself and dashing upstairs to run the electric razor over his light beard and take a quick shower.

Dark suits and dresses were no longer part of the unwritten dress code at concerts, the opera and plays. Nevertheless, Mark was wearing a dark blue blazer and medium gray trousers, both of which had survived the trip virtually wrinkle-free. A white dress shirt and a blue and red striped silk tie completed his attire for the evening. As he looked around the lobby at the arriving opera goers, he felt comfortable with his choices. The cool air outside was confirmation that autumn had indeed arrived in the Northeast. It was still quite balmy in the Low Country. The size of the crowd milling about in the lobby was impressive. A good sign, Mark decided. *Should be a good performance.* He had only seen *La Bohème* once before, in London on a student holiday. Standing to one side, he enjoyed watching the early arrivals, while keeping an eye on the entrance to catch Sister Catherine as she arrived. He slid his sleeve back to check his watch. *Well, I thought she might actually be here by now.*

"Hello, I hope I'm not late." Mark's eyeballs nearly popped out of his skull. The beaming face before him was none other than Sister Catherine's. She had shed her habit for a high-necked black dress that came fashionably just below her knees. A jacket in the same color and style completed her tasteful outfit. She wore no jewelry or ornamentation. Her shoes, also black, had low heels. Her sandy blonde hair, not previously visible beneath her habit, was cut short. It shimmered in the brightly lit hall. Sister Catherine had the healthy look of an athlete. Make-up would have been superfluous. Her skin radiated good health and gentle care. Mark was sure she must think him stupid or something close to it, because a long pause developed, until he finally blurted out a response.

"You're… you're absolutely stunning!" He thought she was blushing. "You haven't run away from the convent, have you?"

"No, nothing like that. Remember, I told you we weren't always required to wear a habit in public. This seemed like a good evening to borrow something different from one of the Sisters stationed here. I'm glad you like it." Although she tried not to show it, she was inwardly pleased her femininity was capable of evoking an appropriate response. She had, of course, no intention of exploiting it. Still, she felt good about herself as Mark escorted her to their seats.

The performance is all Mark hoped it would be. His peripheral vision is strained to the maximum. He is joyous beyond measure that Sister Catherine shares virtually every reaction of his, whether it be the glorious romantic music, the outstanding voices, or the unfolding of a tragic love story whose ending can be no mystery to any opera fan. They turn slightly to face each other as they rise to applaud the cast, the final scene still locked in their emotions, each noticing the misty eyes of the other. They share a warm smile. The chance nature of Rodolfo's first meeting with Mimi doesn't escape Mark. Leaving the theater, Mark takes Sister Catherine's arm and leads her through the noisy throng crowding the Center's courtyard. For a long while they say nothing.

"It was really marvelous. Thank you for asking me. Thank you for having the courage to ask me, I should say. What man would ask a nun to go out with him? You are quite extraordinary, you know."

"I'm glad you enjoyed it. It was a truly fine performance. One for the memory bank. I'm certain Signor Puccini himself would have been pleased. Would you like something to drink? Coffee, perhaps?"

"A cup of hot tea would be welcome. It's a bit chilly. Fall arrives here about three weeks before it drops down to South Carolina. Are you warm enough?"

Mark's biological thermostat was out of control. He realized it must be cool by observing the quickened pace set by other pedestrians. As for himself, he felt no wind, no chill, just an unusual warmth in his chest. "I have an idea. Let's take a bus a few blocks in the direction of your Order's headquarters. Then we can walk the rest of the way. I believe there are some nice places near there to stop for something to drink."

"Great. Here comes a bus now."

The bus is full. They stand and ride in the direction of upper Manhattan. A few blocks later they alight and begin walking. On a quiet corner they pass *Kurt's Rot/Weiss Enothek*, an attractive looking wine bar. It looks a trifle trendy, but they decide to enter. Seated at a cozy corner table, they order two glasses of a robust Bordeaux and begin to talk by recalling, in turn, events from their past involving concerts, pleasant meals in strange places and people who influenced them. In the course of the conversation, Sister Catherine reveals that she has already received her new assignment. She is to be the headmistress of a girl's school operated by the Order in Hong Kong. The school has severe financial difficulties and declining enrollment. Although its history in the Crown Colony has been a rather distinguished one, it is now confronted with the possibility of closing. The government is unsympathetic to its problems and outside sources of assistance have not sufficed to reduce the school's debts.

In spite of himself, and in spite of their unusually brief period of acquaintanceship, Mark is losing his heart, knowing that before the evening is over it will be broken. He offers some words of encouragement. They seem bland and terribly trite. He wishes he were not so powerless, that he could provide some tangible help, for he would intervene in an instant and wave his magic wand to ameliorate Sister Catherine's predicament, if only he could. He delivers his 'unusual date' to the door of her temporary residence on a darkened side street of once majestic homes still dominated by the elegant staircases and entrances of an earlier heyday in the great metropolis. "How soon do you have to leave?" asks an anxious Mark.

"Possibly tomorrow" is the answer. The odd couple, both with lumps in their throats struggle to master their emotions. Suddenly, Sister Cath erine steps closer, kisses Mark and runs up the stairs. The door is unlocked. She steps into the building, disappears, and the door closes.

With a profusion of emotions, Mark, who is unaware how his almost monastic, workaholic *modus operandi* has rendered him unusually vulnerable in the presence of a lovely member of the opposite sex, heads back towards his hotel on foot. He is crushed by the realization that two people had found a soulmate under the most remarkable and improbable circumstances. Each had known deep down from the beginning the situation was hopeless. Initially distraught, Mark wanted to scream and release his anguish. The more he thought of the beauty and purity of the incredibly endearing creature the fates had sent along his path today, the higher his heart soared. Like an apparition, she entered his life abruptly, and as quickly, she was gone. It was so complete, had an aspect of utter finality, like death. It was a powerful blow. As he walked, totally unaware of his surroundings, Mark gradually accepted his loss. *After all, I only knew her for a few hours.* In his mind it was transformed into a feeling of exuberant joy. He had been touched by an angel. It was an ironic thought, for Mark was not particularly religious.

His path led Mark past many stately homes. Some now housed the successful in the Big Apple's high tech, high achieving international set. He also walked past a few run down shops and seedy storefronts, dead businesses out of synch in the unceasing chain of change and transformation in a city that truly never sleeps. A string of clichés flowed through his tormented mind. A few lines from an old Sinatra song about '*Strangers in the Night*' even mingled there for a while, tarried, then drifted off into the darkness.

The autumn air was growing cooler. A gentle breeze had become a bit brisker, announced by the flutter of leaves and the movement of trash in the gutters. A few enterprises had evidently failed. Their show windows were either bare or cluttered with obsolete store fixtures, mostly cloaked in dust and cobwebs. From the old-fashioned indented entrances wafted the smell of stale urine. Accumulations of discarded newspapers and flyers, crushed cigarette packs, an occasional wine bottle, a hypodermic needle, even a rusting grocery cart or two filled with black plastic bags holding some poor soul's worldly possessions could be seen.

Just as Mark was on the verge of a profound philosophical breakthrough regarding the nature of infatuation and love and the significance of the most unusual romantic night he could recall in his twenty-nine years, these unsavory sensations of sight and smell were assaulting a memory he did not wish to disturb. *I should be dedicating myself to the service of this heaven-sent vision. I'm being silly! Am I a victim of some sort of 'Ivory Tower Syndrome'? Hmmm. Yet, I wonder what might be behind all this. Doesn't everything happen for a reason? Is it possible that some greater force or purpose is at work here?*

The ruminations of a love-sick fool were suddenly interrupted by a moan Mark thought he heard coming from the indented storefront of an abandoned business he had just passed. He continued on a few steps, listened, heard it again, a muffled cry of pain. *Probably some wino, a homeless basket case.* Sister Catherine insinuated herself into his thought processes. He knew he had to go back and investigate.

Peering into the filthy opening between the placard-covered display windows, Mark could barely make out a seated figure, the figure of a person leaning against the door some fifteen or twenty feet away. He called out: "Are you O.K?"

Another moan sounded like, "Help. Please help me." The voice was weak; the strangely accented words unclear.

Mark was more than a little hesitant. It was getting darker. He was, after all, in New York just for a short, professional meeting. Still hesitant, Mark ventured haltingly into the passage between the display windows. He saw what appeared to be an elderly man in the shadows. As he drew closer, he tried not to inhale. The smell was not pleasant. The man was wearing a dirty coat. He had a shirt and tie on. As he helped the man to his feet, Mark noticed no odor of alcohol. The elderly man, disoriented and dazed, continued to mumble: "Please help me." He had difficulty standing unaided.

The stranger spoke English, albeit with an accent, possibly German or East European. "Can I call an ambulance for you? Are you injured?" The stranger seemed confused. Mark was struggling to think what steps to take. "I could call the police. They'll take you to a shelter."

The stranger's words and gestures protested. He was able to explain he had been mugged by some young thugs who took his money and dumped him here after delivering a few gratuitous blows and hurting his hip and leg. He clearly didn't want the police and said he didn't want to go to a hospital. Unfortunately, he wasn't able to suggest any alternatives. Mark had no idea what to do. *What would Sister Catherine do? She would step up to the plate, show compassion and common sense.* It was past midnight. The sidewalks were virtually deserted. Street traffic was very light. It was cooling down very rapidly. Mark's blazer was proving itself woefully inadequate. The stranger at least had a coat, even if it was soiled. Mark saw a taxi approaching slowly. He made an instantaneous decision. He would handle the situation. *What if this man were my father? How would I want someone to treat him?* He stepped onto the street and hailed the cab. It stopped. Mark helped his companion in and gave the driver the name of his hotel.

This has been some day! The thought ran through Mark's mind over and over. *First, that fateful encounter at the airport. Then the wonderful evening at the Met. I was kissed by an angel I'll probably never see again. Now I'm sitting next to a confused old man in dirty, rumpled clothing. How is all this going to end?*

The elderly man next to him, in spite of the coat, had been uncomfortably cold, not shivering, but pleased to be out of the chilly autumn drafts – and off the inhospitable pavement where Mark had found him. He gently rubbed his hands together and stuck them in his pockets. He sat silently. Pity, compassion, concern were sentiments ricocheting in Mark's mind. *What would I want someone to do, if this man were my father?* The question was asked again and again, as Mark searched for an answer. He ruminated rapid fire about possible solutions. At Marshland State he had earned a reputation as a quick study and a solid problem solver. *I need to be rational, but this is all so irrational. Well,* Mark was summing up the situation as his brain worked overtime, *he seems to be European in background. He claims his wallet was stolen. He has a formal air about him. He is clearly out of his element. He has been the victim of some rough play, but not badly injured. It's late. It's cold. Heck, neither of us needs any unnecessary hassle right now! I've got an extra bed in my room. He can clean up and crash there for the night. He'll be in better shape tomorrow and we can sort things out then.*

Upon their arrival at the hotel, Mark's plan, if it could be so termed, was still not completely formulated. His appraisal determined that this rather forlorn stranger was not a bum, but someone, maybe a tourist, dazed and confused, who had unwittingly become a victim of big city crime and was desperately in need of a safe haven for the night. The cab disgorged its odd contents. Mark gave the driver the fare and a good tip. The lobby was crowded with several foreign tour groups, probably returning from a Broadway show, or just arriving from JFK. There were stacks of luggage off to the side near the elevator bank. A Japanese tour group, replete with a guide sporting a blazer in the vilest green Mark could remember seeing, was led by a little lady holding a similarly tinted pennant aloft as the group snaked through the crowd and lined up on one side of the lobby. Everyone seemed to be jabbering at once and totally preoccupied with luggage, documents and keys. Mark discreetly guided his companion through the melee to the elevators. They quickly ascended to his floor. No one had taken notice of his seedy-looking sidekick.

Chapter Three

It was late. Still not tired from his long, busy day, due no doubt to the adrenaline high his evening with Sister Catherine had produced, Mark helped his "guest" with his coat. He next turned on the shower, adjusted the water temperature and handed a weary, but grateful old-timer a bath towel and his own fresh pajamas, indicating he should refresh himself and change into sleep wear. While the shower was running, Mark prepared one of the twin beds for his "guest" and ordered hot tea from Room Service.

Accepting the proffered tea eagerly, Mark's "guest" uttered a barely audible "Thank You." and appeared quite overwhelmed by his bene-factor's sensitivity and generosity. Then, traumatized by a possible mugging and physical mistreatment on a dark, cold evening, the "guest" set his empty cup down on the side table, lay down, pulled up his blanket and almost immediately dropped into a deep sleep. If it hadn't been for some gurgling sounds emanating from his "guest's" throat, Mark might have thought him a cadaver, so still did he lay there.

Partially dreaming, Mark's unconscious/semi-conscious nocturnal wanderings transported him through time and ancient civilizations. Visions of Sister Catherine floated in and out of his dreams. She was at once a voluptuous, earthy, coquettish flirt set on seducing him and luring him to destruction; next a noble princess, a queen, a woman of exquisite beauty and grace, granting him knighthood and sending him forth to slay the enemy, to perform good deeds, and to bring truth, justice and enlightenment to her troubled empire.

Fortunately, Mark had set his alarm clock upon his arrival at the hotel. Its gentle vibration eased him from his strange reverie. He shaved, showered and dressed, for he had committed to leading an early seminar at the conference. The "guest" was still resting soundly, obviously secure and comfortable between his sheets. On his way out, Mark took his "guest's" clothing to the concierge and arranged for rush dry-cleaning and a full breakfast to be delivered to his room in about an hour. Catching a cab in front of the hotel, Mark zoomed off for his duty, which was in a hotel across the island. Now the question was, should he share his adventures with his colleagues? *Maybe I had better keep this tale to myself.*

The coffee and orange juice, the bagels and doughnuts worked their magic. The milling academic types slowly overcame jet lag and general lethargy with the aid of the caffeine and sugar. The chatter halted only when Jim McGuire of Boston College tapped his cup with a spoon and announced that the first seminars and presentations were about to begin.

Jeff Horton grabbed Mark by the arm from behind. "Sorry I had to miss the opera last night. One of the kids got sick and we had to ride out the flu with her for a couple of nights. How was it?"

Mark struck Jeff as a bit absent-minded. It took him a few moments to collect himself and remember that Jeff was supposed to have been in the seat next to him. "Oh, it was very good. Very, very good!" A girlish giggle rang in his ear.

"*La Bohème*, right?"

"It was truly a night to remember." Savoring the unintended double meaning of his response, he continued, "I sure missed you. Maybe we'll have better luck next time. By the way, how's your daughter now?"

"Doing much better. Hope I didn't catch the bug myself. I wouldn't want to send my colleagues home exercising all their orifices at the same time." A chuckle tripped off his lips as he moved to the rear of the room to take his seat.

The session went smoothly and everyone left feeling good about the mission to help young Americans study and travel abroad as part of their collegiate learning experience. Mark avoided getting involved in any post-session chit-chat, as he wanted to drop by the hotel to see how his "guest" was doing. *I guess, I could have looked to see if he had any documents, an ID or something on him. I don't even know his name.* Mark was a bit perturbed with himself for not being more inquisitive.

When he reached the hotel he went straight to his floor, knocked on his door and, hearing no response, unlocked it. The room had not been made up yet; it was just shortly after noon. The trolley covered with empty dishes, a glass and a cup and saucer was parked near the door. Not a crumb was left on it. A small piece of paper from the obligatory telephone notepad was lying next to the steel warming cover; scribbled on it the simple message: "*Thank you. Z.S.*" The pajamas Mark had lent his "guest" were lying neatly folded on the pillow. The mysterious stranger and his clothes were gone. Mark opened the door, checking the hallway to see if any of the hotel personnel were around who might have seen his "guest". Not a soul anywhere.

Well, I have to assume he was O.K. Otherwise, he'd probably still be here. I certainly wish him well. A cursory check of the room satisfied Mark that none of his things had disappeared. The hotel would also be pleased to discover all their towels and ashtrays were present and accounted for. Mark refreshed himself with a steaming-hot face cloth and left for lunch and the afternoon sessions.

Saturday afternoon. Cool, but sunny weather predicted. Mark dressed casually, that is, no tie, a thin crew neck sweater over his sport shirt, a tasteful British-tailored tweed sport jacket and brown loafers. He dutifully participated in a round-table discussion on African study programs, said his good-byes to the "regulars" and dashed to the airport, having decided to head home early. He wanted to be back in the Low Country for Sunday to catch up on any correspondence that might have arrived during his absence. Besides, he felt a little empty. Anything he might do in New York now would be anti-climactic. He had lost any desire to take in another theatrical performance. By evening he was home thanks to direct flights to Charleston from the Big A.

As he drove home, he wondered silently where Sister Catherine was. *Probably over the Pacific somewhere.* In his mind he recounted every detail of the past two days. *Imagine, me, Dean of the Faculty, infatuated… with a nun. It has definitely been a most unusual weekend.*

Chapter Four

Thelma, as many who knew her claimed, was "a jewel in the rough." She had been a fixture in the Dean's office at Marshland State since its earliest incarnation as the *Beaufort Bible Institute*. A true workaholic, Thelma was always "on duty" and never showed her previous bosses anything less than total reliability and loyalty. One did have to overlook, however, the fact that she was addicted to the worst-smelling cigarettes on the market. The air-conditioning system notwithstanding, most staff members in the Dean's wing of antebellum Live Oak Hall, Marshland's main administration building, kept a window cracked, regardless of the weather outside, hoping for an occasional breath of fresh air. Thelma had been discreetly lectured on the dangers of smoking by all who knew her. She understood, but lacked the will to give up the habit.

The Thanksgiving break was coming up soon and many faculty members as well as students were determined to make of the extended weekend a somewhat longer holiday. Mark, on the other hand, was looking forward to a simple holiday at home, probably with a turkey sandwich and a beer. He had politely declined a number of invitations. His old house needed a few minor repairs and his modest garden was overdue for a fall sprucing up. The seasons were in transition. Summer had faded gracefully and was changing slowly to something most Northerners enviously wished was their winter.

It was Monday morning and Mark was alternately calling influential legislators to remind them of the upcoming dedication of the new Science Center and day dreaming about the lovely, charming and mysterious creature he had met while in New York.

Just two more calls. Mark turned towards the large windows in his office. Both faced the tree-studded expanse of dormant lawn that extended from the front of Live Oak Hall all the way to the street. As he was about to pick up the receiver and begin dialing, he suddenly got up and strolled over to see what activity might be creating the noises he heard coming from that direction. Ahhh! Professor Satterthwaite with his Botany class examining the live oaks that provided the shade in summer that helped keep its namesake comfortable, as well as the year-round umbrella of green so admired by visitors from the North. The old prof, one of the gems on MSC's faculty, was a dedicated arborist. An MSC graduate who hadn't taken at least one of his courses, would be hard to find. The class wandered off in pursuit of the flowing white lab coat seeking another specimen.

Mark stayed by the window. Much of what he surveyed on the campus was the result of his efforts. He was too modest to brag or boast, but it was a fact. His colleagues and some townsfolk who made it their business to know what those who wore the gown were up to understood the remarkable campus transition of the past three years was largely due to the vision of one man and his ability to marshal the forces and resources required to effect change. Probably the most telling compliments were the feelers Mark was getting from two prestigious institutions, one on either coast, looking for a successor to retiring presidents.

Mark was happy at MSC. He was pleased and proud. Yet, he couldn't deny that the price of his success had been high. Knowing from the outset that many colleagues considered his election a fluke, even spreading rumors that he would soon fail, Mark had seen the gauntlet at his feet and had felt compelled to prove himself over and over and over again. Leading by example, he had courted, cajoled and convinced the governor and the legislators who held the purse strings to sign on to a grandiose plan of growth and improvement for the only viable institution of higher education in this part of the state. Influential members of the community as well as key faculty got on board. Mark outplanned and outperformed his critics. Yes, he had reason to be happy. Nonetheless, as his interlude of introspection continued, his mental assessment of his accomplishments inevitably turned to the flip side.

An involuntary sigh accompanied his acknowledgment of a nonexistent private life. Since meeting Sister Catherine, actually long before his trip to New York, subtle signs of 'burn out' had begun to manifest themselves. Soon to be in his thirties, Mark regretted sacrificing so much of his personal life, characteristically withdrawing from strictly social events to concentrate on his agenda for the College. *Low Country charm*, he thought, *might be slowly, almost imperceptibly, losing the battle with a restlessness of spirit approaching from behind.*

He found his way back to the desk and the telephone. He dismissed an inexplicable feeling of unease. He was about to hum his rendition of Frank Sinatra's *Strangers in the Night*, when a knock on the door, followed by a busy Thelma, a smoking cigarette concealed behind her back, handed him a thick envelope marked 'PERSONAL AND CONFIDENTIAL'.

Mark accepted the envelope. It had been sealed with packing tape. At first, he was inclined to set it aside to open later. The white cross on a red field on the larger of the three stamps drew his attention to the cancellation stamp. *Hmmm. Zürich. Now who could be sending me something from Switzerland?* He hung up the telephone receiver he had just raised for the final calls on his list. His name, address, even the zip code – all correct, yet obviously penned in haste by a shaky hand.

A letter opener quickly released the contents, which Mark placed carefully on his desk. The airline ticket with the Swissair logo caught his attention. Round trip, business class, departing from Atlanta on Wednesday afternoon. Arriving early Thursday, return date: open. Next, two thousand dollars in Traveler's Checks. Finally, a slightly smudged piece of paper with a hand-written message:

* * *

Dear Dr. Davidson,

Please excuse my English. It has grown weak from disuse. Excuse also, please, this abrupt interruption of your busy schedule. I am the person you helped last month in New York. I am sorry I left without thanking you personally. You were very kind to a tired and confused old man. I desperately need the aid of an honest, resourceful and compassionate person. You accepted risks to help me once. I beg you to visit me in Zürich. I need your help again. Time is of the essence. I have arranged a reservation for you at the *Hotel garni Drei Linden* in the Gottfried-Keller-Strasse. I will leave a message for you there.

Danke. Zdeněk Székely

* * *

Standing once more by the large window facing east, Mark took a deep breath. He looked out onto the fading Zoysia, the creeping ivy, the huge oaks, and the moss-covered brick wall along Beauregard Avenue, thinking about the disheveled stranger he had helped just about one month earlier, when Sister Catherine's spirit had so invaded his heart and filled it with joy and love for all humanity. Had he been foolish? He had taken a complete stranger to his room, nursed him, fed him; then the stranger had silently slipped away like a ghost. Now, this unusual appeal. *Risks? What might that mean? Zdeněk Székely... sounds a little Slavic and a little Hungarian to me. From Switzerland? Hmmm!* "Sister Catherine, what did you get me into?"

"Sir, did you call me?" Thelma had cracked the door and stuck her head in.

"No, Thelma. Sorry, I was thinking out loud." Thelma hovered for a moment in the doorway with a strangely quizzical look.

"Wait a minute. I do need you."

Removing the ever-present cigarette from between her lips, where she often let it hang while typing, Thelma stepped back into Mark's office. "Sir?"

30

"Could you call the travel agency and get me a flight to Atlanta that will have me there by noon Wednesday? Oh, please use my personal credit card. This isn't Marshland business. And please connect me with Judge Willinggate on line 2. He should be at the President's Residence for morning coffee by now. Thanks."

A couple of minutes later, Judge Willinggate, the college's tenth president, a long-term state representative whose political influence and good connections paved the way to his appointment following a narrow defeat at the polls, was on the line. He was a stately figure many claimed was a dead ringer for Colonel Harland Sanders.

"Mark, what can I do for you today?" The Judge, who had been seriously ill for the past six months, was very fond of Mark. Mark had taken over many of the president's duties, especially those involving public speaking, travel and legislative liaison, allowing the Judge to concentrate on his recuperation.

"Sir, I've decided to accept an unexpected invitation to visit someone in Switzerland. I'm hoping to be back early next week, but it might be a few days later. Just wanted you to know. I'll call to give you my schedule, as soon as I have it pinned down. Please give my regards to Mrs. Willinggate and your family for the holiday."

On his way to the library for a staff meeting, Mark made a mental note to drop by *Warstein's Clothing Emporium* to check out a new winter parka. *It will probably be chilly in Zürich at this time of year.*

* * *

Neighbors, Hugh and Molly Shoreham, old friends from the Midwest, drove daily to Charleston, where they owned a prominent antique gallery. They had offered many times to take Mark to the airport, whenever he planned a longer out-of-town trip. "Why pay for airport parking when we're up there nearly seven days every week?" Being frugal at heart, in spite of the $2000 in Traveler's Checks he wasn't completely sure he could accept, Mark decided to take his neighbors up on their standing offer.

Following a hearty breakfast in the Shoreham's cozy sunroom and the hour-long drive up the coast to Charleston, Hugh dropped his friend off at the main entrance in time for a 9:00 am flight to what many called the country's busiest airport.

In Atlanta, Mark checked his overnighter, but was carrying his favorite piece of luggage, a slightly worn rucksack, a holdover from student days, slung loosely over his shoulder, as he entered the 747 for his non-stop flight to Switzerland's largest city. He noted, he hadn't seen a single nun in either Charleston or Atlanta.

Chapter Five

Late November in Zürich was vaguely reminiscent of New York a month or so earlier, cool, blustery, trees denuded by Mother Nature as she gradually turned most flora dormant for the approaching winter. As in the Big Apple, the Christmas season was already manifesting itself here too. Festive window displays were everywhere in the shopping areas in the heart of the city. Retail inventories were replete with colorful wares designed to entice even the most disciplined shoppers.

Mid-morning crowds moved along the streets with purpose. Some shoppers were content to stop and imagine themselves wearing that exquisite watch, the beautiful necklace, the finely knit Cashmere sweater, this handsome leather jacket with matching shoes. Others were entering or leaving the many coffee shops, perhaps to mull gift options for Oma or Tante Berta and others on their shopping lists. Had Mark seen the freshly baked delectables filling the glass cases, he might have allowed himself a brief detour into a busy *Stehimbiss* or *Konditorei-Café*.

Mark had taken a bus from the airport to a corner he determined was about a block from the *Hotel drei Linden*, preferring to approach it on foot to better familiarize himself with the surroundings. He easily spotted the building as he drew nearer on the opposite side of the street, but looked in vain for the three trees in the hotel's name. *Perhaps they had succumbed to old age. Perhaps they had never existed.* At any rate, the only vegetation visible in front of the hotel was to be found in three window boxes on the second floor containing red and white geraniums that had thus far evaded the ravages of early morning frosts. *Maybe they're plastic.*

In his musings Mark reminded himself that things are not always what they seem.

The hotel, a sterile looking B & B, was in a narrow building sandwiched between two similar structures, differentiated only by their gables. The street was relatively busy. Small offices and shops predominated: a shoemaker, a *Chemische Reinigung,* an apothecary, a bakery, a florist, and an insurance agency prominent among them. Mark's light packing made his overnight case tolerably easy to carry, but he was glad to set it down in the tiny lobby.

A graying, yet spry woman in her sixties popped up behind the reception counter. "You must be Professor Doktor Davidson," she said with a slight British accent.

"Ja, ich bin Herr Davidson. Herr Székely hat ein Zimmer für mich bestellt." Mark was pleased that he had remembered so much of his college German.

"Your German is very good," replied Frau Scherli, "but you may speak English here, if you prefer. Your room is Number 34. I regret that the lift is not working today. If you need help with your luggage on the stairs, my husband will be glad to assist you." She handed Mark a bulky key attached to a large knob-like object, clearly intended to discourage guests from accidentally walking off with the key. "Oh, I almost forgot, Herr Székely asked me to hand you this note. Have a pleasant visit. Please do not hesitate to call upon us, if we may help you with anything during your stay."

"Thank you very much," was Mark's enthusiastic response, as he shook Frau Scherli's plump, pink hand.

Unpacking took all of ten minutes. Breakfast on the plane hadn't been especially filling and Mark noted that it was Thanksgiving – *time for my turkey sandwich and a cool one*. He slowly opened the envelope Frau Scherli had given him. He read a neatly printed message:

* * *

Dear Dr. Davidson,

Willkommen in Zürich! Thank you for coming. I realize you must be weary from the long flight, but I must see you today, if at all possible. My assistant, a nephew, is usually away Thursday afternoons. Frau Scherli can give you directions. My residence is nearby.

Try to come about 3:00 p.m. Thank you.

Zdeněk Székely

* * *

Székely's *Wohnung*, a condominium flat, was just two blocks from the hotel. It was not difficult to find. Mark found it readily on a largely residential street. The building in which the condo was located had seen better days. It was a tad on the drab side, although architectural details on the exterior of the building were evidence that it had once deservedly commanded admiration and respect.

So I'm going to see Mr. Székely again. In New York he had been too weak, too tired and too scared to talk much. He had left, the traveler recalled, while Mark was attending a meeting, and had returned to his home here in Switzerland, leaving only a hastily-scribbled note saying, "Thank you. Z.S." Talking to himself, Mark asked out loud, "Why am I here? Am I expecting some kind of reward? I didn't act with anything like that in mind. Is it, perhaps, some morbid curiosity about a mysterious figure, a stranger, whose path intersected mine in the dark of night? Oh God, am I being foolish, or what?" A woman passing by stared. Mark didn't notice.

Mark entered the lobby of the residential building. It revealed a simple elegance, muted, unfortunately, by rather dingy paint that begged a fresh coat. Next to the mail boxes were nameplates for the building's residents. *Ah yes, Székely, Z., fourth floor.* Mark pressed the button adjacent to the name. He thought he perceived a faint auditory impulse.

"Wer ist da?" Inquired a rather coarse-sounding male voice through a small speaker next to the bell.

"Ich heiße Herr Davidson. Ich komme aus Amerika und möchte gern Herrn Székely sprechen, wenn es ihm recht ist." Mark chose to pretend his was an unexpected courtesy call.

After a few silent moments, the coarse-sounding voice returned. "Warten Sie am Lift!"

A few minutes later, a tired elevator opened in the lobby. A large man, whose features were – to be kind – homely, exited the elevator and approached him. He looked older than he probably was. He had a full head of longish dark hair and a permanent case of five o'clock shadow. Pock-marked cheeks, a large nose and deep-set, dark eyes evoked thoughts of a lunar landscape. He gave Mark a quick visual once over, then spoke in a gravelly voice. "Good Day! I am Gregor Mukhachevo, Mr. Székely's secretary and chauffeur. You must be the American Mr. Székely met in New York." Mukhachevo's voice was deep and rough. The language was a fair attempt at schoolbook English, but the accent sounded Russian to Mark. His words expressed a begrudging welcome, but his demeanor suggested he was not happy to see the visitor. He made no real effort to conceal his displeasure. A mean glint in his eyes registered high on the list of negative observations dancing in Mark's head.

Mark, about 5' 11", felt small standing next to the taller escort in the poorly lit lobby. "The air is quite invigorating this afternoon; a genuine autumn day." There was no response. Mukhachevo, seemed caught up in his own thoughts. He stared straight ahead. Trying to be civil and polite, Mark continued. "My name is Davidson. As you mentioned, I met Mr. Székely in New York recently. He suggested I call on him, if ever I was in Zürich. I happened to be on a short trip to your country and decided to stop over in Zürich. I hope I'm not interrupting." Mark didn't know how much, if anything, his employer had shared with his tall escort about the incident in New York. Gregor's facial expression told Mark his white lie was not totally convincing. Mark wondered why his greeter was here.

Herr Székely's note had said Gregor was usually away on Thursday afternoons.

"It is not really convenient." Mukhachevo was disinclined to cooperate. There was a momentary pause, then the sullen giant acquiesced. "Please to follow me. He is not well and can only see you for a short time." Gregor motioned to the elevator. The door was open. Mark entered first. Gregor stepped in behind him and pressed the button. The smell of recently imbibed alcohol quickly reached Mark's nostrils. *Gregor likes to drink during the day,* he thought, as they ascended slowly to the fourth floor. Sizing up his escort, Mark estimated Gregor to be about 6' 4", maybe 260–270, strong, but not necessarily very agile.

The fourth floor landing was generously sized, boasting enough space for a velvet love seat, a small side table with a bronzed lamp and, on one side of the entrance, a mahogany credenza. All probably qualified as antiques. Mark, who occasionally visited Low Country antique dealers, made a hasty assessment: *Neat workmanship, Good condition. Exquisite detail. Probably pretty valuable.* Gregor guided the visitor into a large sitting room. A gentleman Mark recognized immediately as the man he had helped in New York rose with difficulty from a large armchair, whose heavy upholstery was worn and drab, extended a frail, wrinkled hand, which Mark took in his and shook gently, but warmly.

"Dr. Davidson, it is an honor to see you again. I trust your trip across the Atlantic was not unpleasant." Székely sat down again, attempting to mask the discomfort caused by advancing arthritis.

"Please call me Mark, sir. I have been to Switzerland before, but not to Zürich." As Mark spoke, Gregor took his jacket. "You have a lovely apartment." Struggling to find something positive to say, Mark told another white lie. The apartment actually seemed old, dark, foreboding. It hinted of a musty smell. The faded curtains were partly drawn. It was not an inviting scene. "Have you been well?" Mark inquired solicitously.

"I am sorry to say, my health is declining. But then, I am an old man and accept the realities associated with mortal life." Székely paused for a moment and coughed into a handkerchief he had been holding in his left

37

hand. "Gregor, could we have some tea, please? Do you take it with milk or lemon, Mark?"

"A cup of hot tea would suit me fine, sir. With lemon, thank you." As Mark finished, Gregor, who had been silent, but whose eyes continually expressed hostility and irritation with his employer, left the room for the kitchen.

When Gregor was out of earshot, Székely leaned towards Mark and motioned him to do likewise. Half whispering, he said, "Meet me tomorrow morning at 9:00 in the small coffee shop at the south end of Münsterstrasse. It is not far. Be careful that no one follows you!" Gregor's heavy footsteps, muffled only faintly by the carpet in the hallway, signaled his return with the tea. Székely straightened up abruptly, saying in his normal speaking voice, "Autumn here was quite pleasant until a few days ago. Since then there have been reports of snow falling in many alpine villages. Cool winds have stripped the trees hereabouts of any leaves that sought to cling to their branches. Winter can't be far away."

Between sips of the warm brew Mark and his host exchanged small talk, while Gregor hovered nearby. Mark looked at his watch, suggesting he had other things on his agenda this afternoon. At last, he stood slowly, thanked his host, nodded to Gregor and walked towards the door. Gregor assisted with the new jacket. Székely coughed slightly. "It was kind of you to come and see an old man. Zürich has much to offer. I hope you will have time to see the museums and take advantage of the other cultural offerings while you are here."

"I intend to, sir. Thank you. I'll call you before I return to Atlanta." While Gregor was preoccupied with a corner of the carpet that had accidentally flipped over, Mark winked at Székely in an attempt to acknowledge their meeting the next day. Leaning on an ornate cane, the elderly gentleman responded with a discreet and barely perceptible nod.

Once outside the building, Mark breathed freely, finding the cool, fresh air invigorating. He walked briskly to the corner, crossed the street and continued in the direction of the river, away from his hotel. His dual intention, to enjoy the antithesis of the strained meeting in Székely's stuffy apartment and to determine whether anyone might be following him. Gregor had not been overly rebellious during his brief visit, yet Mark sensed a strange, unhealthy tension between uncle and nephew, employer and employee. A tension that had dark overtones. Purposely doubling back a couple of times, entering and exiting a book store and a *Drogerie*, Mark was almost certain he wasn't being followed. *Why am I acting so paranoid? Stupid of me to think I might be followed. After all, Gregor must know where I'm staying.*

Although tired and suffering a mild case of jet lag, Mark slept fitfully. In a weird dream he pictured himself as some kind of insect grasping at threads in a carpet, as a vacuum cleaner headed in his direction. He rose early, had a continental breakfast in the *Frühstückszimmer* on the first floor, looked at the headlines in the local newspapers and set out around 8:45 for his rendezvous in the coffee shop with Mr. Székely.

The skies had adopted that shade of heavy, dull gray that would be in vogue until spring. Men and women who worked in the city were walking to their places of employment. Some were alighting from trams, others were stepping gingerly from autos parked at curbside with that skill Europeans have for fitting midget-sized vehicles into the tiniest spaces. Mark marveled at the energy demonstrated by this virtual army of workers determined to be on time, to produce or perform whatever it was they did for a living and finish the day satisfied with a job well done.

As Mark caught sight of the coffee shop Mr. Székely had mentioned, he thought he saw him moving through the entrance in the midst of a cluster of seven or eight office types, male and female, all seeking a sudden caffeine boost before settling into the routine of the day. Instinctively, Mark stopped briefly, looked discreetly around and ascertained he was not being followed. He then managed to slide in, so to speak, within a group of about six men, who had the look of mid-level paper pushers.

Székely spotted him and motioned for Mark to join him at a small round table that stood about elbow height on a single metal pedestal. Mark noticed that except for a few patrons at a long shelf on the shop's interior perimeter, most were standing in twos and threes at these mini tables drinking coffee and munching on a sweet roll or croissant. The din of the early morning banter made conversation difficult. Mark and Székely shook hands. The latter whispered to Mark to eat and drink quickly. Székely had ordered a cup of coffee and an *Apfeltasche* for each of them.

Mark surveyed the room, which was shaped like a large L. As he did so, his eyes met a remarkably lovely pair of brown eyes belonging to a young brunette, whose hair was hanging in neat curls just above her shoulders. She was alone. Her shy smile was absolutely intriguing, enchanting. She seemed to be studying him. When their eyes met she looked away momentarily, as if caught in the act. Her complexion was Mediterranean, her flashing eyes had lovely dark lashes and eyebrows. She was strikingly beautiful, even sexy, thought Mark. He felt a slight bump on his left arm. Politely, he turned to his host, who had wolfed his pastry and was finishing his coffee.

"Komm schnell, wir gehen hinten hinaus! Quickly, the back way. Follow me!" Székely spoke softly, but his tone was nevertheless commanding. Mark involuntarily scanned the section of the room where he had seen the beautiful woman with the unforgettable smile. Gone! His eyes searched the front of the shop, hoping to catch a glimpse of her leaving. Nothing! Székely was displaying more energy than Mark had given him credit for. He tugged on Mark's jacket. They slipped hastily past the restrooms and out a rear door. Then they moved with hurried strides down an alley to a neighboring street. From there, they walked three blocks to a small park, a green oasis in the urban landscape. Székely's determined urgency prevailed over his arthritis.

The park, an elongated rectangle, was rather compact. Cinder paths, edged by low-cut hedges, bisected the green space from corner to corner. A few trees had been planted. The flower beds were bare, apparently in seasonal transition. Traffic signals prevented certain mayhem, as vehicles of all types converged on the area in the morning rush hour. Starting, stopping, honking, idling noisily, the background cacophony was not conducive to serious conversation, although voices didn't carry far and privacy was guaranteed.

Székely, after looking furtively about and struggling to catch his breath, spoke first. "Ich spreche lieber deutsch, wenn es dir recht ist, denn ich muß dir vieles ganz schnell erklären."

Mark nodded to indicate he understood the German. He strained to follow. Continuing in German, Székely said, "Please listen carefully because time is of the essence. Gregor was drinking with his friends again last night and, as usual, was too hung over to crawl out of bed this morning. I usually take a walk to begin the day and I hope he doesn't suspect I am meeting with you."

"Is your relationship with your nephew not a good one?" Mark inquired, likewise speaking German.

"Actually, Gregor is not really a nephew, but the son of my niece Branca, who was living near Kiev. Following the break up of the Soviet Union, she was suffering from a serious illness. She begged me, as her only living relative, to take him in and serve as a kind of mentor. I had misgivings from the beginning and I can tell you now that I have not only failed to have any positive influence on him, but also that I have grown to fear for my life in his presence."

"Can't you get help?" Mark interjected, genuinely concerned. "Has he hurt you physically? Can you report him to the police or have him returned to... to...?"

"...to Ukraine?" Székely finished the question. "He would resist that. He was conscripted into the Soviet Army at age 17. He fell in with a rough crowd, soon became involved in criminal activity and was discharged early after spending several months in an army prison. All this I learned after I arranged for him to come to Switzerland. It is rumored that he still has contact with some of his old buddies, most of whom are *Mafiya* types up to no good." Székely paused to compose himself. "Word from the East," the East being a term he used to refer to the area from which his family had fled prior to World War II, "is that this group is wanted for burglaries, car theft, drug activity, even murder. I believe him to be potentially very ruthless. Because I am technically responsible for him, as his sponsor, I even arranged for an investigator to follow him. The names of his associates," Székely's eyes rolled upwards as he uttered the word 'associates', "are in an envelope I will give you. They're very unsavory characters. Watch for them! They are capable of anything."

Mark wondered to himself, why these admonitions and cautions were being addressed to him. "I'm just an academician, an educator, sir. My mission in life to date has simply been to help educate young Americans. How can I possibly help you? Where do I fit into this picture?" Mark was beginning to sense something developing that would embroil him in a situation far beyond his normal realm of activity. *Was this trip to Switzerland a mistake?*

"Let me give you a capsule lesson in history, my young friend. My father, Tibor, was born shortly after the turn of the century in Hungary. With his parents, who were successful business people, he moved to a region known then as Podkarpatská Rus. In 1919, the area became part of Czechoslovakia. Later, it was ceded to the Soviet Union. Currently it is in western Ukraine. The family bought land there and over the years built a large estate. Part of the land was farmed, part was used to raise horses. My father married a handsome Slovak woman, Lene Domková. They had two sons, my older brother Ottakar, who died in a Slovak concentration camp, and myself. Our first names are Slovak in origin, our family name Hungarian."

"How did you end up in Switzerland?"

"In 1935, my father, who was an astute student of politics, sensed that times were irrevocably changing and that he could not stay in Sub-Carpathian Ruthenia, as you called it in English. He broke the estate into three parts and sold them. Through acquaintances, he was allowed to emigrate to Switzerland with my mother and me. I was eleven at the time."

Székely cleared his throat and continued. "My mother fell ill and died in 1944. Ottakar, regrettably, had stayed behind in the East and involved himself in political activities. He chose poorly the side to support."

Székely stopped again to compose his thoughts, all the while looking around carefully to assure himself no one was watching or listening.

"Please continue, sir. The loss of your mother and brother must have been a terrible blow. You were just twenty, if I'm not mistaken." Mark was becoming absorbed in the story.

"It was indeed, for, in addition, we were receiving bad news from the East on a continuing basis. Many relatives and former friends had died or were missing. The causes were varied, but all quite distressing. In a neutral Switzerland we were safe. My father was employed by a major bank, the *Cantonal Kredit Anstalt*. He was a wizard with numbers and had risen quite high in the bank hierarchy. Suddenly, in late 1945, while returning by plane from a banking conference in Barcelona, the bank's entire upper management was wiped out in an alpine crash that stunned the country. The surviving board members named my father, who was the senior remaining bank officer, the new General Director, a position he held until he retired at age 75."

"Were you also involved in the banking business?" Mark thought he could propel the story forward by asking a question.

"Yes, I was. Back to my father, however. Upon taking his new position, my father personally conducted a thorough audit of all the bank's holdings, scrutinizing every single account, no matter its size. To his amazement, he discovered five large accounts that had been kept completely secret by the bank's managers. A discreet and exhaustive private investigation covering nearly two years revealed no details regarding the exact source of the funds involved, nor their ownership. They were numbered accounts." Székely took a deep breath.

The noise in the adjacent streets continued unabated. Mark scarcely noticed it, so engrossed was he in Székely's tale. Pulling his collar up against a slight breeze, Székely continued. "What was clear, was that the funds for the accounts had been surreptitiously deposited by Nazi and Slovak officials in the late Thirties and early Forties, probably the proceeds from the sale of confiscated properties, art objects, furniture, livestock, safe deposit boxes, jewelry, bank accounts and the like. The sums involved were definitely substantial."

Mark pondered a moment, then asked, "Did no one ever come forth to claim these accounts?"

"No one!" There was a certain finality to his response. Székely paused again. "This was a great dilemma for my father, who is the most honest man I have ever known. He is completely without any avarice. He desperately wants to see this treasure, now increased beyond imagination, to be used to ease pain and suffering, to deal with the turmoil and destruction man has caused his fellow men. Unfortunately, he felt he could not trust his own board of directors and at the time he didn't consider any of the existing governmental or international organizations as appropriate for the kind of philanthropy he envisioned."

"Why didn't you step in to do this? You are the obvious choice."

"It may be difficult for you to believe, but as a young man I was a dissolute and angry person. I disgraced my father several times. We had a severe falling out. The death of my wife and the loss of our unborn child a year and a half after our marriage was a shattering experience. I did not deal with it well. I drank heavily. I had one woman after another. I continued to work, but my life was fraught with reckless and irresponsible behavior. Eventually, I adopted a reclusive lifestyle and did not speak to my father for years. I understood why he could not ask me to undertake his mission. We reconciled shortly before senility, some call it Alzheimer's disease, clouded his mind. Until two months ago I visited him every few weeks. He is quite old and is living in a hospice operated by a religious order in a monastery north of Riva in northern Italy."

A wistful expression crossed Székely's countenance as he stared for a moment at a nearby tree about to release its last leaves to a gust of wind. "On my last visit he embraced me." Székely began to choke up. Mark, who pitied him, also had a lump in his throat, as he felt the older man's pain. "On my last visit," he continued softly, "my father forgave me. He swore me to his complete confidence and charged me with a great responsibility. It is all the more burdensome, because I, too, am old and frail."

Székely, obviously tiring, went on, "I promised him that I would find a person or an organization that would see to it that the funds, now increased vastly in value, would be used wisely and compassionately to help mankind." The speaker cleared his throat quietly. "To get to the point of our meeting." He looked nervously at his watch. "My father helped found a private bank in the western part of Switzerland, in Vevey in Vaud, the Swiss Canton on the north shore of Lake Geneva. He created two special numbered accounts. They can only be claimed, in person, by someone using the ten-digit numbers he established. I do not have these numbers, but I do know where they can be found. If you accept the challenge, that will be your task." These words were uttered in a voice that was both somber and hopeful.

Mark, mesmerized by Székely's tone and intense focus, looked deep into his eyes. This was not a decision one would normally make on the spur of the moment. Székely was, after all, a man he barely knew. *Indeed*, Mark thought, *Székely barely knows me.* There was obviously considerable danger in this undertaking. The lure of vast sums of money was, in and of itself, not something that really excited Mark. He had often insisted that less was better. He could afford a Jaguar, but was perfectly content with his Honda Civic. His current home was an aged "fixer-upper", not the ocean-side condo that would have been well within his budget. *What business do I have going after a fortune? A fortune of dubious origin?*

"If I understand correctly," Mark continued to gaze into Székely's eyes, "these accounts would legally be mine in their entirety, if I obtain the numbers and claim them?"

"Yes, that is true. I have no need for wealth. I am too old to contemplate riches." Again, Székely returned Mark's gaze. The two men were, in fact, positioned eyeball to eyeball on the park bench. "I have taken the liberty of having you investigated rather thoroughly. I consider myself a good judge of character." He paused slightly. "I have had a lot of practice. I have made many, many mistakes. Some would call it a coincidence, others might use expressions like "God's will", still others could term it an act of fate. No matter. When I met you, I knew I had found a man of principle, an honest man, a truly good and decent person with the character and capacity to carry out my father's desire to help those in need, regardless of their nationality, their religion, their politics. I trust you. You are...," and here Székely took Mark's hands in his own and held them firmly. In a tone, both fervent and hushed, he said, "You are the son my father always wanted. You are the son I never was."

Mark swallowed hard. For a moment his mind returned to New York and Sister Catherine. *What would she do in these circumstances?* Mark's own parents had preached and practiced honesty and personal integrity. Mark was uncomfortable with major decisions made impetuously, based primarily on emotion. This, it seemed to him, was not an occasion when he had the luxury of time for slow deliberation. "Sir, I accept this challenge. I will help you and your father." Somehow he felt like a knight setting off on a quest for the Holy Grail.

"Mark, you are a person who possesses the wisdom, the imagination and the will to fulfill my father's wishes." Looking about discreetly, Székely pulled an envelope and a canvas money belt from his coat and slid them across the bench towards Mark. "Take these quickly. The envelope contains instructions for finding the account numbers. My father gave me the details on my last visit to the hospice. He had one of his moments of fleeting lucidity. I gave him my solemn word that I would do everything I possibly could to right a terrible wrong. After you memorize the contents, please destroy the letter. There are $5000 in Swiss and German currency for expenses. Be ever watchful and resourceful." The pair stood. Székely kissed Mark on both cheeks. "Now walk away. God speed!" They shook hands, turned and each went his separate way. Straightening his coat, Székely pulled his hat down, then shuffled off in the direction of his residence.

The envelope securely in his breast pocket, Mark strolled to the corner of the park, caught a green light, crossed nimbly and walked to the Rudolf Brun Bridge, turned left on the Limmat Quai, and strode energetically north in the direction of the Bahnhof Bridge, seeking a roundabout path to his hotel. Occasionally, Mark stopped or hesitated, carefully checking the street behind him. He was unable to identify anyone following him. About an hour later he reached the *Hotel Drei Linden*.

Wow! What have I got myself into? This is not the weekend visit to Zürich I assumed when Székely's message reached me back home. Mark was sitting at a small table in the corner of his room. He still had not removed his jacket. He was just beginning to absorb the import of this morning's meeting. His brow was damp from perspiration. He reviewed it in his mind: the *Apfeltasche* he had not fully digested, the strange behavior of his "benefactor", the hauntingly beautiful woman, the enchanting smile, the brown-haired princess with whom he had exchanged glances, and who had disappeared so suddenly, so completely. Then there was the rather complex story Székely had shared with him, and his promise to… to take control of a substantial sum of money. *How much is it anyway? Székely omitted that detail.*

Taking off his jacket, Mark retrieved the envelope. The letter was hand-written. The shaky penmanship of Mr. Székely he recognized immediately. He had written in English.

* * *

Dear Mark,

I write in haste. Gregor is drunk again. Please destroy this note after you memorize the contents. I failed my father by being a poor son to him. I wish now to realize his dream through you. The numbers for the two accounts at the *Banque sociale de Léman* in Vevey can be found as follows: #1. Carved in the inside frame of the side or front entrance to the large barn on the old Székely estate approximately four kilometers north of Uzhny in what is now Ukraine. (My father returned there secretly while on a business trip about five years ago.) The barn was part of a collective farm. I heard recently it is under extensive renovation. #2. Somewhere in the monastery, where my father has been living in Italy. The monastery belongs to an obscure Franciscan order located near the *Lago di Tenno.* It is not difficult to find, but the numbers may be, as my father's memory for certain details was a complete blank.

I have arranged for some identification documents for you. Go to Hermann Runzli. He is the son of a trusted colleague. He is located in a small warehouse in Tödi Strasse between Dreikönig and Gotthard. It's a print and photo shop. Mention my name and he will know what to do.

Mark, Gregor and his cronies are evil. Be alert at all times. No act of violence is too great for them. Make no assumptions. They have ways and means of gaining access to information. A short time ago, I accidentally left my safe unlocked and I found Gregor going through my papers. There was a vague reference there to the secret accounts. He knows no details.

Führ' Di Gott!

Zdeněk

P.S. Gregor has four cronies that he sees on a regular basis, according to the investigator I hired. They are:

Ivan Pustarov. He served in the Soviet Army with Gregor. He is a ruthless thug and has much influence on Gregor.

Vassily Karchenko. Reported to be a wild, trigger-happy, ex-soldier, who served time in prison with Gregor.

Günther Uebel. Uebel is a "skinhead" from Berlin. He is wanted by German police for a variety of petty crimes, for arson, and for attacking foreigners.

František Veselý. A former Czech commando, Veselý has a girl friend in Zürich. He reputedly runs a ring of smugglers and prostitutes out of a base in Pilsen.

* * *

Mark read and re-read the letter, noting the locations mentioned. *Not exactly very specific. Sounds like they could be difficult to find. It could take a while. I need a map.* He re-read the names appended to Székely's note. *Hey, I'm in way over my head already. I don't need to mess with characters like these.* Another read-through left him even more disturbed.

He tore the letter into as many small pieces as he could. After flushing a few down the toilet, he left the hotel and distributed a few pieces at a time into waste receptacles on the next three street corners. Hunger pangs prompted a visit to a café frequented by locals. He ordered *Gegrillte Putenbrust, Rösti* and *ein Helles.* Time for his belated Thanksgiving treat and a call on Herr Runzli.

* * *

Runzli was a youngish man, probably early thirties. He wasn't much over five feet tall and appeared to walk with a limp. Mention of Zdeněk's name prompted a wave of the hand directing Mark into the back room where a press was busy printing flyers for a holiday concert. Mark had already decided he might find an extra passport and a couple of driver's licenses handy for crossing international borders. As an occasional amateur actor, assuming another *persona* was a challenge he enjoyed. Runzli took a few instant photos and within half an hour had produced passports for the Bundesrepublik Deutschland, the Republik Österreich, and the Confoederatio Helvetica, as Switzerland is officially known. Each had accompanying driver's licenses and credit cards. *Pretty clever little chap!* An offer to provide a small firearm was turned down without a second thought. Mark eschewed personal firearms. His parents had always been vocal in their opposition to guns. He had adopted their position. He knew how to handle them, but felt it might actually turn out to be a liability in his case.

Walking along the Limmat, Mark decided he'd go first to Slovakia and explore the possibilities for getting into Ukraine. Later he would work his way back to the west and go to Italy. It just so happened, a college roommate lived in a small town on Lake Garda. *First things first,* Mark thought. *I'd better call the Judge and ask for six weeks off so I won't lose my job.* The call was made; permission granted.

* * *

Mark thought he had made up his mind. He was already in an implementation mode. Before turning in for the night his mind retraced its journey of the previous twelve hours. A kissin' cousin of something like buyer's remorse bullied its way to the forefront. Sleep? Rest? Not this night. Mark tossed and turned, rolled from side to side, to no avail. His mind was hyperactive, gave him no respite. He sat up in bed suddenly. Dawn was beginning to caress the landscape. His head was damp with light perspiration, his body cool. Involuntarily, his hand applied pressure to a stomach complaining of indigestion. Half of the badly rumpled down cover was on the floor. The oversized down pillow had been compressed into a ball. It looked as though Yin and Yang had engaged in a battle royal on his mattress. The sheet had come loose and lay there creased and lumpy.

Was I too rash in accepting Mr. Székely's challenge to search for the account numbers? What does he expect to get from all this? Will his story hold up? It seems so far-fetched. Yet, his honesty, his earnestness are utterly convincing. Am I doing this out of pity? For him? For his father? Have I been suckered somehow? Shouldn't this be someone else's fight?

Reflecting on his career in the Low Country, Mark acknowledged that he enjoyed what he was doing. It was satisfying and he was good at it. He knew people called him a workaholic behind his back. He, himself, realized the all-consuming nature of his position and his perfectionist approach. The night he was named Dean he had made a list of goals and objectives for his own personal guidance. He had accomplished virtually all of them. There were, naturally, lots of other things he wanted to do for the College. But, he admitted to himself, someone else could do them too.

Much of what Székely stated or alluded to held such a mix of conjecture, of guesswork obscured by the haze of history in a time of turmoil and upheaval involving people long since departed. If he should be right, and Mark wanted desperately to believe he was, then some sort of moral imperative was operating here. *I don't need some bewhiskered philosopher to come down from his tower to lead me by the hand! My gut, my heart, yes, my mind, know what I must do! Still, I need a few more answers.* Mark, who could hardly be called a wimp, was, nevertheless, uneasy about the "dangers" to which Székely had referred.

While freshening up and dressing, Mark decided he would drop by Székely's place on the pretense of a brief call to wish him good-bye before returning to the States. *Maybe Gregor the Ugly won't be around and I can chat privately with Herr Székely.* As he went down to the *Frühstückszimmer* to grab a bite to eat, he thought about the questions he would ask. *I wonder if Sister Catherine, under her calm exterior, harbored trepidations about going to Hong Kong?* Perhaps something with caffeine would get his brain on track again. Things seemed to be moving too fast in a direction and in a way over which he felt he had little control. Mark left the hotel on foot.

The walk took all of ten minutes, slowed only by the early morning traffic, both vehicular and pedestrian. As Mark approached the building where Székely had his flat, he saw a crowd of people that had gathered at the entrance. At the curb stood a white van with a revolving blue light and CARITAS NOTWAGEN painted on the sides. Mark picked up his pace, arriving just in time to see the rear doors of the van close. *An ambulance!* A dark thought was denied expression. The vehicle pulled away from the curb. No siren! The onlookers, most with that 'Glad it isn't anyone I know' look, gradually dispersed. Gregor, whom Mark spotted about to enter the building, stopped briefly when Mark asked loudly: "Ist Herrn Székely was passiert?!"

Gregor, little emotion discernible in his expression, barked, "He died suddenly this morning while dressing." The sturdy Slav then pointed to his heart, suggesting to Mark that it was a heart attack. Gregor disappeared hastily into the lobby.

Mark was frozen. He stood alone in disbelief. Seeing that there was nothing to be gained by sticking around, he walked, slowly at first, then much faster, in the direction of his hotel. *He had been frail, but… a heart attack? I didn't notice any signs of circulatory problems. Hmmm. Was it natural causes, or…? Mr. Székely had said Gregor was capable of anything. But this?* Leaving Zürich – and fast – struck Mark as his best course of action. He went to the hotel, got his gear together, checked out, and left by taxi for the railroad station. There, he placed a call to *Caritas Krankenhaus* inquiring about a Herr Zdeněk Székely, who had apparently died of a heart attack and had been transported to the hospital in an ambulance approximately one hour earlier. The call was transferred three times before a young man with a strong Swiss German accent came on the line. "We have no reports of a person by that name being brought to our emergency room this morning. You must be mistaken. Auf Wiederhören!"

Mark was puzzled. Perhaps the ambulance took its passenger to another hospital, to a mortuary or funeral parlor. *What's going on? I'm in the middle of something I don't really understand.* At the railroad station, he bought a ticket for Vienna. Not easily frightened, Mark noticed he was constantly looking back, wondering if someone might be following him. Gregor, was, to be sure, a shifty looking character. Then, too, Székely had mentioned Gregor's unsavory buddies. Mark, who in spite of his high school wrestling background, with many a trophy to prove it, abhorred violence. He would avoid a physical confrontation, if he could. An evasive tactic might be prudent. Pressing his left hand against the cash in his hidden money belt, he was beginning to think he should use some of it proactively to distance himself from Zürich as fast as possible.

In the men's restroom, he slipped into a stall, stuffed some of his more essential clothing items from his overnighter into his backpack, a college-days' relic with high sentimental value.

From his make-up kit, he used gum arabic to attach a neat dark brown mustache. He abandoned the overnighter, carried his parka, put on a black Greek sailor's cap he had purchased his first day in Zürich, and walked confidently to the first cab in a waiting row of Mercedes taxis. Hopping into the rear seat, Mark said, "Zum Flughafen, bitte!" He had opted to fly. Not only had he chosen a different mode of transportation, he bought a ticket for a new destination: Prague.

Chapter Six

Swiss Air's flight to Ruzyně Airport in Prague was, thankfully, uneventful. Mark's temporary facial hair began to itch somewhere above the Bavarian Forest. He managed to suppress his natural instinct to scratch and concentrated instead on reading virtually every word printed in today's *Zürcher Tageszeitung*, a gratis copy of which had been in his seat. Burying himself in the newspaper was the perfect excuse for not engaging his neighbor in conversation. Thus, he maintained his *incognito* transit to the former Soviet block nation, now emerging as a good partner for the West.

With no luggage to claim, Mark quickly passed through customs. In a men's room off a large concourse he removed the moustache and gum arabic, added a tie and reversed his sweater. He stowed his Greek headgear in the rucksack and took a cab to the Main Railroad Station, where he bought a train ticket to Žilina. It would be a six hour ride. He decided to go Second Class. Before boarding, Mark grabbed a bite in a snack bar in the railroad station. He had exchanged a few German *Marks* for Czech *Koruny* and paid cash for as much as he could.

The view from the window was much like any other ride through the visually impaired track-side milieu when leaving any big city and heading out to more open countryside. As usual, the less desirable apartment blocks were near the tracks. Graffiti-marred factory and workshop walls, a mixture of political slogans and obscenities, scarred the exteriors of too many structures. The train rumbled on, occasionally parallelling various highways and byways, slowing only slightly when passing through smaller venues. The fields and forests were hunkering down for the inevitable snows of winter. Mark's mind was in overdrive. *Guess I'm heading to Eastern Slovakia. I could turn back, but… Naw, I gave my word.* He dozed for a few minutes now and then. He checked his watch. *Let's see.* Žilina coming up in about thirty-five minutes.

It was late afternoon in Žilina. Mark was reasonably certain he hadn't been followed. Looking pretty much like a graduate student touring Europe, he checked into a *pension* a block away from the railroad station. Not unlike other commercial establishments in the former Soviet satellites, the exterior of *Pension Nový* had recently been painted. The wooden stairs leading to the front entrance also appeared to have been replaced. Since late November was considered a "transition period" between seasons, Mark was able to have a double room with a private bath for a modest price. As he surveyed his temporary quarters, he felt the "modest" price more than adequate for a "modest" room. It was clean, however, and a hot shower proved refreshing. He napped for an hour. It was dark outside when he got up to answer the call of nature. Snacks had been his primary sustenance since leaving Zürich. It was time to begin thinking about a hot meal.

A short stroll in the neighborhood revealed two pub-like eating places. The interior of the one with the more presentable exterior had a warm, cozy appeal. The few diners present were likely locals. The posted menu was in the local language, but had German translations. Mark found that the *Knedliky shovězí,* dumplings with beef, if the German was reliable, sounded like an appetizing choice. Indeed, together with red cabbage, a hearty gravy and two bottles of *Prazdroj*, the perfect Pilsener, he was very satisfied. He paid in German Marks. It was not far to his *pension.* Slowly, he walked, belching occasionally, as the dumplings underwent heavy duty processing by his digestive juices.

The mattress was a bit lumpy, but Mark slept well. There was little, if any heat in the room. Mark shaved and washed up in double time. Good bread, homemade sour-cherry preserves, a bowl of yogurt with something resembling cornflakes and a mug of strong coffee constituted breakfast. Mark was raring to go. When he returned to his room, one of the windows was open. The bed linens felt cool to the touch. Mark could see that the sky was overcast. *Tough for the sun to break through those clouds.*

For every passport he had created, Herr Runzli had also provided, per instructions from Herr Székely, a matching *EuroKarte*, that was automatically billed to one of the latter's accounts in Switzerland. Székely knew Mark would probably have to rent a vehicle at some point. It was difficult to do so without the means to guarantee payment. All this Mark realized when he was looking for a car hire service in Žilina. Milena, the middle-aged proprietress of the *Pension Nový*, sent him back towards the railroad terminal. On the other side of the station was a small office of the *GloboRent* agency, which, in spite of its name, did not allow its cars to be driven outside Slovakia. No problem. Mark only wanted to get closer to the Ukrainian border area.

The highways in northeastern Slovakia were not in very good condition. Mark found them narrow, full of potholes and in use by too many farm vehicles: tractors, horse-drawn wagons, and small utility trucks. His *Lada*, of indeterminate vintage, probably attractive when new, had a dull blue coat of well-worn paint, was underpowered and, unlike the Fiat prototype, did not shift well. The highway map the rental agent had given him was out of date, but seemed to include the salient details required to locate towns and villages in this sparsely populated corner of the country. To the north, the *High Tatras*, patiently waiting for winter sports' enthusiasts, dispassionately observed his progress.

In light of its recent transition from member status in the Soviet Union to independent republic, Székely had implied dealing with Ukrainian officials with regard to a visa might be problematic. Mark construed the offhand remark as a suggestion that an unauthorized visit over an unguarded portion of the border might be best under the circumstances. Roaming back mentally through his own experiences, Mark had to admit that he had on occasion broken a rule or two to achieve a solution, that, once put up for discussion, might have engendered a host of unwanted and insurmountable objections and obstacles. Dobson Armitage, aging Chair of the Philosophy Department at MSC, apparently did not know of these 'indiscretions', otherwise he might not have called Mark a "latter day Jack Armstrong".

Ahead he saw a sign – **Vesnicka, 2 Km.** *Yes, here it is on the map. In a small valley fairly close to the part of the Slovak-Ukrainian border where the old Székely estate is supposed to be.* Pointing the *Lada* in the right direction, Mark cruised along at about 60 kilometers/hour. The sky seemed grayer now. Sticking a hand out the window, he noted a marked lowering of the temperature that definitely was of some concern. He was glad he had brought along a warm jacket and a baseball cap. His canvas off-trail walking shoes were warm enough for the moment. Unfortunately, he had neglected to bring gloves. *Got to pick up a pair*, he thought, rubbing his hands to promote circulation.

Vesnicka was a smallish town, a village really. Virtually no traffic. What passed for the main street wound past ramshackle homes, a few basic shops, a couple of taverns, a wooden church and a small hostel. Peering down the few side streets, Mark detected what was probably a school, a combination town hall and police station and more residences. *Well, maybe I have to reassess. I guess by Slovakian standards it's a genuine small town.* In the interests of accuracy, Mark quietly corrected his earlier impression.

The first tavern he saw boasted a butcher shop. Mark pulled into a parking area next to the tavern, noting in the short walk to the entrance that rain was on its way. An ominous stillness brought to mind some nasty winter storms he had experienced in his Indiana days. *A great ham and cheese sandwich would really hit the spot now.* Using his German, Mark asked for *"ein Schinken-und-Käsebrot, bitte."* The waitress, probably the butcher's wife, was a portly *Hausfrau*-type, rosy cheeked, wearing a slightly soiled apron, but undoubtedly fresh from the hairdresser's, as her "do" was incongruously elaborate. She pointed to the menu: 'Šunka y emmentalský sýr'. It was served open-style on a large, thickly sliced piece of rough, hearty, farmer's bread. Although he would have preferred a cold beer to accompany his fare, an inner voice dictated freshly-brewed *čaj*.

Looking out the window as a gust of wind blew a sheet of cold rain across the parking area, Mark knew hot tea was a wise choice.

Hunger pangs assuaged, Mark dashed through the rain to his waiting transportation. He prayed that the *Lada* had a pair of windshield wipers that functioned effectively. He was relieved and delighted when they squeegeed the windshield of the rain, which was rapidly changing to sleet. The *'thunk-thunk'* noise was easily overlooked. Not quite ready to settle down for the day, Mark urged his steed on; heading southwards roughly parallel to the border. The terrain was more hilly than truly mountainous. The peaks looming up on either side of the valley were no match for the Alps or the Tatry, but still looked formidable against the darkened sky. Mark estimated them to be under 5000 feet. It was becoming windier. The *Lada* felt light on the slick pavement.

Uh ooh! The sleet was gradually giving way to snow. The wind seemed to blow in gusts. It was almost impossible to see out the rear window. Mark used his cap to clear his side window so that he could try to use the rear view mirror. He thought he had spotted a car drawing closer from behind. The road was climbing slightly and passing through a thickly forested section. He had only driven a couple of miles south and east of the town. Traction was a concern. The *Lada* fought to hold on to the edge of the slippery knoll on which the road was located.

Suddenly, a car was beside him. It lurched ahead, forcing him to the shoulder of the road. Not content merely to occupy the left half of the highway, the vehicle was crowding him to the right on the narrow shoulder. Intentionally! Mark had no choice but to jerk the wheel to the right. He slid into a shallow ditch. He shut off the engine, shouting some choice language he seldom used in public. There were four men in the car. The two in the rear seat jumped out, opened the driver's door on Mark's vehicle and pulled him out, pinning him against the car. One had a small revolver; the other a hunting knife. Neither bothered to mask his identity. Both were brandishing their weapons recklessly. *Oh my God,* thought Mark, *they're going to kill me on this… this damned, desolate road to nowhere!* He tried desperately to stay cool, figure a way out of this predicament. He was outnumbered. He had no weapon. The wind hurled snow in his face. From the trees on the other side of the highway two shots rang out, bullets whistled overhead. Someone in the car parked at an angle in front of the *Lada*, shouted a command Mark couldn't understand. The knife-wielding man, dark-haired with long sideburns and cold, dark eyes, snarled an epithet in a strange tongue. He swiped at Mark with his weapon, striking his left shoulder, then the two assailants ducked, ran forward at a crouch and leapt into the opened doors of their car, firing a couple of shots blindly into the woods. The car pulled away, swerving dangerously to and fro on the icy asphalt.

A figure in snug-fitting dark blue ski pants appeared out of the woods, a rifle with a scope slung over its shoulder. A gentle, but authoritative voice shouted, "*Pojd' jsem! Rychle!!!*" The words were incomprehensible to Mark, but the beckoning hand signal was quite clear. He grabbed his rucksack and crossed the highway into the forest in three giant leaps. Had he looked, he would have seen the blood that was on his jacket. Sensing that Mark did not understand either Czech or Slovak, the figure asked, "Sprechen Sie deutsch?"

"Ja, Danke!" Not knowing what else to say, Mark stared at his rescuer and began to follow. *By golly, it's a... I mean, she's a woman!* His guide moved swiftly, half walking, half jogging deeper into the woods.

"Sie kommen bestimmt zurück," she said, negotiating her way through the densely growing trees, mostly conifers. Indeed, they did come back, for Mark could hear some shouting from the highway, as he and his mysterious benefactor lunged up a rather steep hillside beneath a canopy of frosted green. A shot rang out. Then another. Neither seemed too close. Both Mark and his saviour stopped momentarily behind large trees, then quickly resumed their rapid pace.

The rain had dampened the needles under foot and had made them slippery. The snow was beginning to collect on the upper boughs, but had yet to penetrate to the floor of the forest. Agitated sounds could be heard behind them. Multi-lingual cursing! Unclear what was being said. The wind, held at bay by the densely wooded hillside, nevertheless whistled and whined, carrying voices away. Mark struggled to keep up with his guide. He was sure now, she was a woman. When he caught a glance he could see that she had handsome features. Her short-cropped auburn hair peeked out of a blue woolen knit ski cap. She was about his height. She leaped and bounded gracefully like a gazelle through the underbrush.

There were no longer any sounds from the highway somewhere back in the distance. Now they were descending into a deep declivity between hills. Mark fell twice. His hands were cold, but he needed them for balance. Every twenty meters his guide stopped briefly to be sure he was still with her and to discover whether the attackers were on their trail. She seemed to be adept at making it difficult, if not impossible, for anyone to track her. Her moves were silent. She zigged and zagged across difficult terrain. *Highly unlikely,* thought Mark, between gasps of air to fill his aching lungs, *that anyone will find us if we keep this up. And I thought I was in reasonably good condition. Ugh!* His nose was running. His eyes were watering up. His fingers were nearly numb.

They reached the bottom of a ravine. Mark soon found himself wading in ankle-deep ice water. A brook was gurgling beneath him, carrying leaves and pine needles over a rocky bed as it raced for the valley below. Mark's feet were soaked. He began to shiver in the cold. His shoulder ached. He wanted to stop, but continued on. After about fifty meters they started to climb again.

Behind them only the swirling of the wind could be heard. The snow was falling with greater intensity and showed no sign of letting up. His guide was once more leading an ascent at an impossible pace. She seemed to revel in speed. They came upon a path of sorts. It was strewn with rocks. To their right appeared a large meadow, likewise covered with rocks that now had a coating of white.

The grass, probably a foot long, was lying prone, cowering under a blanket of snow; snow that was swirling into drifts, which in some places were already over a foot in height. Mark's thighs were on fire. He began to cramp up. He was ready to collapse. All he could think of was stopping to rest, but he knew that if he did he might not be able to get going again. The pain reminded him of the first week of high school football practice, when, as an exhausted freshman, he could scarcely walk home from school he was so tight and stiff. His feet were frozen. His hands had lost sensation. His guide was flowing effortlessly up the incline, urging him on. Before them, at the edge of another, smaller meadow bordered by a number of scrubby trees, a rustic mountain hut came into view. Snow had been blown by the unrelenting wind, now wailing a lament across the barren soil and stone, against the north side of the building. It was a grayish, weathered structure, rather small and nondescript. The tiny windows were covered with shutters. Wood split and cut for use in a stove or fireplace was stacked against two sides of the building. It reminded Mark of his college travels in Bavaria and the Tirol. His head was spinning. He felt dizzy.

His guide unlocked the entrance and helped her breathless charge to a table. Mark sat, gasping to inhale through a parched, fiery throat. His lungs were burning. His clothes were soaked with perspiration from the inside, with rain and snow on the outside. The temperature inside the hut wasn't exactly warm. Mark was so completely drained by the incident on the highway and the perilous escape that he hardly noticed.

Still speaking German, his angel of mercy, her cheeks a rich crimson, said, "My name is Aja. I see you were wounded. I am a doctor and I'm going to check your injury." So saying, after first throwing a coarse blanket on it, she helped her patient onto the large oaken all-purpose table in the single room that was kitchen, bedroom and living room. Simultaneously building a fire in the great iron stove, placing a kettle of water on it and stripping Mark of his damp clothing, she noticed how handsome he was. A shivering Mark was virtually unconscious.

Aja stoked the huge black iron stove that comprised the heart of this unusually simple mountain refuge. She heated the water to the boiling point, poured some into an enamelled basin and sponged Mark, cleaning his cut. Luckily, no stitches were required. She applied a salve, covered it with a bandage, dried Mark with a towel and slid a flannel nightgown over him. After helping him to a sitting position, she gave him a couple of tablets to swallow with a cup of warm tea. In the weak light Mark saw her take a vial of medicine from a small refrigerator. He felt nothing, as she injected the Tetanus vaccine. She placed his right arm over her shoulder and half walked, half carried him to a niche in the wall that served as a bed. A wooden base, approximately one meter off the floor was covered with a thin mattress. Pulling back the down comforter, she laid him on his right side and tucked him in. Before retiring herself, she straightened out the kitchen, banked the fire, placed a pot for night soil near a door at the rear of the room and peeked out the window after dousing the small overhead light she had used as illumination. This done, she checked Mark again. He was still cold and shivering. She climbed over him, pulled up the bed covers and slid in behind him, using her body heat to increase his temperature. A few minutes later both were sleeping soundly.

* * *

Mark was still on his right side facing the large open room. His eyes opened to a bright white light. It turned out to be the glare from a layer of snow on the mountain invading the room through the opened shutters. Aja was at the stove preparing breakfast.

"Good morning, Mr. Davidson!" Her slightly British-accented English was very good. "You are American, aren't you?"

"Yes, I am. How did you know?" Even slight movements revealed muscle soreness he hadn't experienced in years.

"You have a laundry tag in your shirt and you were talking in your sleep. I couldn't understand everything. Something about calling Thelma. Is that your wife, or a lady friend?"

"Thelma? Oh, no." He smiled slightly. "She's my secretary. Ouch, my shoulder is sore."

Mark could barely stand, much less walk. His legs were very stiff.

"You'll feel better in a few days. We had a strenuous climb. Very difficult, if you're not used to it. You also had a knife wound on your shoulder. Your jacket has a hole, but it protected your shoulder. The cut is not deep."

Mark was looking about him. *This place probably has an outhouse. Don't relish stepping out in that cold right now.* Aja read his mind. "If you need to relieve yourself, take that white vessel next to the back door, and step out into the stall area. When you're finished, leave it there."

Mark had already found the worn felt slippers by the bed and was at the door. He stepped out into an attached barn with eight stalls. There was some hay strewn about, but no sign of any animals. When he was finished he returned to the "kitchen" and the warming aura of the stove.

"You can wash up here." Aja pointed to a basin of warm water in a wooden sink. A towel lay on the counter.

Breakfast featured porridge with buttermilk, two boiled eggs, a large heel cut from a huge loaf of dark bread with a chewy crust, a slightly shrivelled apple and a mug of coffee. On the table was a container of goose fat. He spread some of the fat on the bread, tore off a chunk with his teeth and started to down spoonfuls of the warm oatmeal.

"I've laid out a few pieces of clothing from my father. He was your size. They are all clean and will keep you warm."

While Aja was working near the stove, Mark quickly slipped out of his nightgown thinking, *Wow, this is a first.* A heavy canvas work shirt and blue coveralls fit perfectly. Mark found the woolen socks just right too. Bending over to pull them on required painful stretching of recently abused muscles. After donning his new clothes, he asked, "Well?"

"Now you are beginning to look like a Slovak farmer," she said with a wide smile. She hesitated a few minutes, then asked, "Do you know who attacked you, and why?"

Mark had just finished looking at the diplomas and certificates in cheap frames on one of the side walls. A Doctor of Medicine degree from the University of Kiev for Aja Lasková, a certificate of successful completion of a one-year residency in the Prague City Hospital trauma unit, a diploma from Central Birmingham Mercy Hospital in England for Internal Medicine and Orthopedic Surgery. Mark approached Aja saying,

"I don't know. It was a complete surprise. I've never seen those men before. I guess it was just an unfortunate coincidence that they chose to attack me. Perhaps they thought I had a lot of money." Actually, he was wondering privately if Gregor's buddies were involved. *How could they have found me?*

"I think the man with the pistol was Ivan Pustarov," continued Aja. "People around here claim he is Russian *Mafiya*. He is a trouble-maker, very ruthless and suspected of robberies and burglaries in the villages in this region. My fiancé, Sergei, was robbed and murdered last spring. He owned an auto repair shop. One night, when he was going to the bank to make a deposit, he was robbed and shot. Pustarov was seen drinking at a local tavern that evening. Sadly, there were no witnesses to the crime. He couldn't be charged. Still, most people feel certain he did it."

"I'm terribly sorry." Mark could hear the sadness and bitterness in her tone. "And your father, is he...?"

"He died three months ago. In the same bed where you slept. In the same nightgown you were wearing." Mark's eyes widened. Aja continued. "He loved this mountain and this hut. He built it himself. It was used by the milkmaids in the summer, when cows were brought up to the high-land pastures to grow fat and make good milk from the grass and wildflowers that thrive here. My father wanted to die here. He knew his days were numbered. He lingered for several weeks. Finally, the cancer took him away. I cared for him. He was my idol. There was no cure. Unfortunately, even a doctor has limitations." There was a tinge of regret and resignation in her voice.

"You have had a hard year. Now I have come along to bring you more trouble. I should leave now."

"Please don't. You need to recuperate, rest. I think you are safe here, besides the early snow storm has blocked many of the roads. By now the police have surely towed your vehicle to a repair shop."

"How did you happen to be in the woods near the highway yester-day? With a rifle?"

"I am training to qualify for the Slovak National Ski Team. The

European championships are in late February. The qualification trials start in four weeks. My event is the Woman's Biathlon. When there is no snow, I run and shoot at targets I have set up in the forest and in the fields nearby. My father was a *Langlauf* skier; cross country skiing I believe you call it. Yesterday, I was running the hilly part of my training course and doing some marksmanship training. The snow was a big surprise."

"Lucky for me! You saved my life." Mark spotted the trophies on a small shelf near a window on the other side of the room. *Viktor Laskov, 2. Platz, 20 Km Langlauf, Zell am See, 1930.* "Your father was a pretty good athlete. From what I've seen, you're bound to be successful." Mark had observed, with some embarrassment of course, that Aja was a truly magnificent specimen of womanhood. At about five foot ten, she was relatively tall. Her shoulders were broad, her posture erect. She had powerful thighs that would be the envy of any NFL wide receiver. "With your professional credentials you could have a thriving practice in one of the big winter sports resorts. I'm sure it would be more…"

"…comfortable there? More lucrative?"

"Well, yes. Is that so bad?"

"I stayed here initially because of my father. Then for the training. Now I stay for my patients. The people in the villages here are not wealthy. They pay me with chickens, a basket of fresh eggs, a wagon load of firewood, potatoes, cabbages, whatever they can spare. I feel that I am truly needed and appreciated. There is little room for vanity and fancy airs. These are real people, down-to-earth folk, in a largely forgotten corner of the world with a long history of suffering."

Mark listened attentively, but silently. *What a marvelous woman!* His thoughts wafted back across the mountains and oceans to Sister Catherine, who also understood the needs of those too weak to survive without outside help. Aja's words echoed those of Zeněk Székely.

Chapter Seven

Except for occasional flurries, little snow accumulated the following four days. The temperatures remained low and the skies heavy with threatening cloud cover. While Aja skied almost daily into the villages and hamlets in the valley below, tending to her patients, Mark exercised to loosen his sore muscles and to regain full use of his left arm. He regularly undertook responsibility for a major meal. The compliments forthcoming from Aja were flattering. In the evening, she often played an old accordion and sang Slovak folk songs. *Měla jsem chlapce* became all the more poignant when she translated it into the English 'I had a boy'. From Smetana's *Bartered Bride* she sang *Proč bychom se netěšili? Indeed,* thought Mark, *Why shouldn't we be happy?* At one point, Aja's eyes welled with tears. She translated a melancholy melody's lyrics, *Loučení, loučení* (Good bye, my love!) and stopped for a few moments to regain her composure. Mark was touched. Aja showed him her marksmanship medals. He was impressed. He watched as she cleaned her weapons. They traded stories about their travel experiences. Their friendship grew. Aja Lasková was an admirable woman.

As the end of their first week together approached, Mark, who was feeling stronger, realized it was already December. He waited for a suitable opportunity to broach the topic that had brought him to Slovakia. "One of my reasons for coming to this region was the hope that I might be able to cross into Ukraine to get some personal information for a friend from the old Székely estate. Do you know of it?"

Aja digested this news for a moment before responding. "Oh, yes. You must mean *Golden Harvest Kollektiv #2*. It's a huge farm, once a thriving enterprise during the better years of the Soviet Union. It is perhaps fifty or sixty kilometers from here. I've heard it fell into disrepair and is now under extensive renovation, essentially closed down until spring."

"Is there someone who could take me there… ah, unofficially? I would be glad to pay the person. I can assure you no international intrigue is involved. I simply promised a friend I would do some private family research for him."

Without hesitation, Aja said, "Tomáš Kučera! He's a real mountain man. He's retired, but I'll call on him tomorrow, when I go to see Milada Staříková. Tomáš is in his seventies, but hale and hearty, and he knows the area better than anyone I can think of."

Mark's eyes lit up. "Great! About fifty to sixty kilometers away you say?"

"At this time of year, especially with the weather being so bad, the distances are not so critical. It's the time needed to cover the distance, the terrain, weather conditions, and the timing and duration of the visit. Tomáš is definitely the one to take you. I believe, he'll like the challenge."

* * *

Two days later, a short, compact, sturdy-looking man with a full head of thick dark hair and a leathery face punctuated by piercing brown eyes, a thin nose and a prominent, manly chin stomped his boots at the door and entered the hut. He followed Aja into the light, and, while pulling off his parka, shook Mark's hand with a steely grip Mr. America would like to have claimed as his own. Mark sensed immediately he was being scrutinized thoroughly as Tomáš assessed his fitness and determination to cross the mountainous boundary separating the two states without the formalities of passports, visas and border checks.

Speaking Slovak laced with a few German words, Tomáš Kučera, the one-time partisan dropped behind German lines as a teenager to organize resistance fighters, indicated on a well-worn map he carried in his pocket, precisely where the collective farm was situated. He noted that few locals knew of its former incarnation as the Székely estate. Many of the structures, he claimed, were being renovated or replaced. Poor maintenance and general neglect during the past three decades had taken their toll. "The property is guarded, but only lightly, I am told, by small patrols housed in an out-building near the old highway. They are there mainly to prevent vandalism and theft of building materials." Tomáš added, "The guards are lazy. New winter storms are predicted for at least the next couple of weeks. They'll be hocking around their stove trying to keep warm. We'll take advantage of the cover provided by the bad weather. The *Kollektiv* used to be located directly on a highway. Last year, the highway was straightened, leaving the farm on a little-used arc. Can you ski well?"

Mark, although naturally modest about his athletic accomplishments, knew he'd better be completely frank with Tomáš. After all, this would be no sleigh ride and Tomáš deserved an accurate estimate of his ability to deal with the rigors posed by rugged terrain, lousy weather and the dangers presented by illegal nighttime travel. "Most of my skiing has been recreational downhill skiing. And infrequent at that. However, I have done some cross-country skiing and I'm confident I can follow wherever you lead."

If he was skeptical, his mien did not reveal it. Tomáš nodded. He spoke quietly in Slovak with Aja, promising to return the next afternoon with some equipment. First, Aja fished about in a large wardrobe in the rear corner of the hut and brought out several items of clothing suitable for outdoor activity. Tomáš surveyed the items, then donned his parka and cap. He left with a simple, "Dobrý Večer!"

Two days later, Tomáš reappeared. He brought some skis and poles for Mark. A training schedule was established. Tomáš carved out a loop, approximately two kilometers long, around and through the meadows and inclines near Aja's hut. For ten days, Mark followed the tracks for two to three hours at a time. "To toughen him up," as Tomáš expressed it.

Finally, one evening as news of new storms was coming over Aja's emergency radio hookup with the Volunteer Fire Brigade in Vesnicka, Aja sat down next to Mark. Her tone reflecting some apprehension, Aja revealed the plan Tomáš had given her. "You will leave tomorrow in the late afternoon. Tomáš aims to cross one elevation that is about 1800 meters. It will be necessary to ski around two other peaks nearly as high. Snow is expected. It will be very dark. These are important factors Tomáš believes will work to your advantage. You will bivouac in a wooded area just inside the timberline on the east side, the Ukrainian side, of the mountain range until dusk the next day. Do you follow?" Mark nodded. "From there you'll ski through a long valley that is only slightly inhabited. Once you reach the old farm, Tomáš can show you the large horse barn you are seeking. You will only be able to spend a short time there, as a return through the valley to your bivouac point must be accomplished before sunrise, even if the storm continues. Is that clear? Tomáš is insistent."

The plan sounded logical. Mark, masking his grim reaction to the notion of a "forced march" under trying conditions, allowed as how he was clear about his obligation. He understood, he would be placing himself and Tomáš in great jeopardy, should he falter. Aja suggested he try on some more of her father's cold weather gear. This he did, choosing a combination he thought would keep him warm, yet not restrict his movements. A wrestling champ and junior varsity football player in high school, a good swimmer, and occasional skier in his youth, Mark's adult sports' interests had shifted to tennis, cycling and running. He participated in a few 10K's every year, often finishing in the top dozen. Now he was facing one of the biggest physical challenges of his life. He tried not to show his concern, while acknowledging the seriousness of the undertaking.

Early the next morning Mark was outside next to the hut splitting logs into kindling. The air was cold, very cold, damp and still. *Ominous,* thought Mark, glad the exertion of chopping was keeping him warm. Aja had departed earlier on skis. She hoped to reach all her patients and return before the impending storm broke loose.

Only minutes after noon, Aja came into view, pushing hard on her skis. Mark envied her powerful stroke, the ease with which she moved, whether on foot or on skis. Tomáš joined them within minutes. There were three places set at the rough-hewn wooden table. While Aja was away, Mark had prepared a delicious mushroom soup for lunch. The entrée consisted of roast pork and gravy with boiled potatoes and a side dish of sliced apples cooked in a brown sugar syrup. Hot tea was the unanimous choice for a beverage. Mark's culinary skills were lauded. Aja cleared the table. Tomáš studied his map, outlining for Mark the route they would take. Mark waxed his skis according to Tomáš' instructions. For the journey, Aja packed snacks: long thin tubes of hard salami, chunks of farmer's bread, apple juice in plastic flasks, some nut bars wrapped in butcher's paper of some sort, and a small bag of dried apricots. Both skiers had an insulated canteen with water.

As four o'clock approached, new snow began to fall, slowly at first, then more intensely. Lacking any appreciable wind, the big, fat, juicy flakes of wet snow began to build up fast. Tomáš rose from his seat, went to a window, where he watched the snow for several minutes, then turned back into the room and beckoned Mark towards him. He checked Mark's skis and bindings, nodding approval. Aja helped them both with their parkas. Tomáš, in addition to his rucksack, was carrying a compact two-man tent. A clever attachment on their rucksacks allowed a pair of light snowshoes fashioned from a frame of aluminum with canvas webbing to be fastened to them. Aja translated Tomáš' directions on their use at places along the trail that were too steep or otherwise unstable for skis.

A cold blast of winter air laced with damp snow slapped their faces as they slipped out of the hut. Mark, who preferred to be in total control of his life, pushed off on his skis, realizing he was almost completely dependent for his life and well-being on this taciturn "old timer". *This strange odyssey began with Sister Catherine and Zdeněk Székely. I can't believe I'm about to shove off for a destination I couldn't have dreamed in my wildest fantasies I'd be visiting. I can't blame them, though. I made the choices. Or did I?* Mark hoped and prayed his guide truly knew the route well enough to proceed into what seemed virtual zero visibility.

Going on an east-southeasterly heading, the two skiers first followed a road bed that tended to involve more descents than ascents, stopping briefly to traverse a couple of large meadows and to climb over low fences erected to prevent summer-grazing cattle from wandering beyond control. The going was difficult due to the heavy snowfall. The landscape, Mark acknowledged silently, was actually quite beautiful. The serenity and purity of the pristine white blanket before him brought a fleeting memory of Sister Catherine to mind. Tomáš' hand, motioning him to pick up the pace, betrayed a tinge of annoyance with Mark's gawking reverie. Reading the body language, Mark regained his focus and the duo pressed on, Tomáš leading the way. Both men were clear that their adventure had just barely begun.

To note that Mark's muscles were already beginning to feel the strain would be an understatement. He struggled diligently and consistently to let his mind, which was determined to be successful, maintain mastery over his body, which could only hope to succeed by over-achieving. Tomáš plowed ahead resolutely. His younger companion marveled at the elder's incredible sense of direction and his unrelenting progress through the challenging terrain. Tomáš motioned Mark to a halt. He checked his compass and, map in hand, tried to show Mark that the next part of their journey required some uphill travel. Specifically, they would have to carry their skis for a while and use the snowshoes until they reached a ridge he pointed to in the distance. It was primarily a blur to Mark's eyes, squinting through the falling snow. Fortunately, the accumulation of snow on this stretch of the trail allowed them to use snowshoes, for buried not far underneath the thin, slippery layer of white were rather large rocks, unwelcome obstructions in any season. At last, attaining the peak of a rather substantial mountain, Mark and his guide stopped, shared a chocolate bar Tomáš had in his pocket, and drank a few swallows from their canteens. A hasty glance at his watch informed Mark it was eight o'clock. It was dark, really dark. Both men were sucking air. Mark was beginning to feel a bit clammy. His undergarments were soaked with sweat. Tomáš set off again pointing to a narrow path between large out-croppings of boulders. The snow was letting up slightly. Visibility improved. The two skiers, controlling their speed, descended cautiously.

As the trail leveled off, they stayed on good snow along the edge of a forested area. Ahead and to the right, still a good distance away, were two or three cabins right at the foot of the eastern slope of the range they were crossing. Smoke wafted upwards from the chimney of one cabin. No lights were visible. Mountain folk often retired early. The barking of dogs could be heard faintly. The skiers barely slowed their pace, continuing steadily on the trail that was leading them to yet another ascent.

Mark was slogging along a few meters behind Tomáš. The path on which they were laboring was a quarter of the way up a fairly steep incline. It was narrow, but level. It passed through a wooded area consist-ing mainly of beech trees. *A beech forest*, Mark thought. *In German, Buchenwald. I suppose that's how the notorious camp got its name*. He bent his knees and pushed off with his poles, trying to catch up with 'Mr. Irre-pressible' ahead of him. *Funny, or should I say, strange, how a random thought can serve as a grim reminder, however oblique it may seem, of the serious purpose behind my mission for the Székelys*. Mark pushed hard again. He was catching up to Tomáš, who had eased his pace slightly. Tomáš pointed with a ski pole to a 'family' of four deer crossing off to their right side.

The climb was substantially more arduous than those accomplished earlier. Mark, now enjoying a second wind, held his own. Ascending slowly on the eastern slope, well inside Ukraine, Tomáš signaled to stop at a point roughly ten meters from a patch of scrub trees that would not provide much cover. He checked his watch. It was after midnight. Snow was falling again. Moving further down the slope to a large stand of con-ifers, Tomáš removed his skis. Mark followed suit. They trudged through the trees, finding a small natural clearing. They brushed some of the snow aside. The two-man tent was quickly erected. Mark unrolled his sleeping bag and got in out of the elements. After reconnoitering, Tomáš returned, and he also slipped into his sleeping sack. Both consumed some of the salami, a chunk of bread, which Mark savored for its thick, chewy crust, and sipped on some apple juice. Tomáš, speaking in his halting German, indicated that there was a large, long valley immediately below them. Several small villages or groups of houses were observed. They would stay here in hiding until the next evening. As the wind began to howl through the trees, the weary travelers drifted off to a much deserved sleep.

Chapter Eight

Snow continued to fall. The air seemed dry. Gray, heavy skies made dawn seem like dusk. Mark, wriggling in his sleeping bag, noticed his clothing had dried almost completely as he slept. Salami, bread, an apple and a few swigs of water comprised their morning fare. After relieving themselves, both flexed their weary bodies, trying to stretch and soothe muscles and sinews taut from the previous night's exertion. They rested much of the day in their camouflaged tent. Tomáš engaged in some reconnaissance in the afternoon, looking for the best approach to the *Kollektiv*, which was positioned at the south end of the valley. He reported seeing two hunters and a few children playing on a small hill near their cabins. Heavy clouds and occasional flurries constituted the day's weather. The wind chill was palpable.

By five, the forest was dark. Tomáš wrapped the sleeping bags inside the tent. Then he strapped them to a tree. Now unencumbered by extra baggage, Mark and Tomáš could move swiftly to their target. They glided silently down smooth slopes to the valley floor. Tomáš led the way, sticking very close to the lower edge of the tree line. He stopped periodically to be sure no one was out and about. His field glasses were pretty old. They fogged up frequently. Mark decided, if he survived this weird excursion, to buy Tomáš a new pair. The wind had grown in intensity. It was especially noticeable the further they strayed from the protective cover of the trees.

Visibility was miserable. Neither skier had goggles. Snow was still falling. What little moon there was hid behind thick clouds. They squinted and moved on. Drifts piled up wherever the wind deposited the snow.

Although they passed within four hundred meters of two tiny villages, even closer to some isolated wooden farm houses, not even the dogs detected their passage.

Just ahead, after negotiating a rusting two-meter steel fence, Mark could make out the outlines of several farm buildings scattered over approximately five acres of relatively flat farm land. They skied on. Tomáš pointed with one of his poles to his left. "Pferdeställe!" he said. *Horse barns,* Mark repeated to himself, in English. *Yes, Zdeněk had said, I should find the first of the two secret account numbers inside an old barn.* It was, in fact, an old pre-WWII structure that had undergone several stages of rehabilitation as a Soviet collective operation in the years following the war. Although Mark didn't know it, it was a large barn where the prize studs were kept in 'the old days'. Mark picked up the pace. Tomáš had tried to impress on him the urgency of conducting and completing his investigation with little wasted motion, for they had to return to their forest camp under cover of darkness. To himself, Tomáš also prayed the snow would continue, until they were safely back across the border. Ukrainian authorities did not appreciate illegal border incursions.

As if on cue, the storm suddenly grew fiercer, at least temporarily approximating white-out conditions. Looking back, Mark noted that their ski tracks disappeared almost as soon as they were made. The largest barn also had the appearance of being the oldest and the most used. Mark was leading now. He felt certain they had located the building Zdeněk had described to him. They approached a side door. It was a sliding door, but was secured by a large, cheap-looking padlock. Tomáš slipped his rucksack off, fished about in a pocket and pulled out a tool. He extended the handles for more fulcrum and easily snapped the lock. The door slid open with little effort. Both men entered. They closed it and removed their skis, which they leaned against the wall.

Mark had a flashlight. He first guided the light to the left. On the stone floor between two long rows of stalls were piles of lumber and boxes and bags of building materials. Playing the light beam to the right, Mark saw a larger entrance some dozen meters away. Before they could move in that direction, Tomáš grabbed the flashlight and switched it off. Holding his finger to his mouth to signal silence, he tip-toed to the door used for their entrance. Both men could hear a rough-idling automobile engine. Peeking through a crack in the wall, they spied a jeep-like vehicle, partially open on the sides, with two uniformed men. They had stopped on a road bed about twenty meters from the door. One of the men was apparently in the process of coming over for a routine check of the lock, when the driver raced the engine a couple of times, and hit the horn twice to show his impatience and elevated state of aggravation. He then shouted in Russian, **"Come on! I'm freezing my balls off!!"** His agitation with his colleague was unmistakably at the breaking point. The vehicle rolled forward a couple of meters. Waving his arm in disgust at the barn door, the dutiful guard turned abruptly and strode back to the jeep-like vehicle. He could be heard muttering some vile invective. The vehicle then moved off toward a dimly lit out-building about three hundred meters away in a corner of the complex near a roadway.

Tomáš and Mark, with raised eyebrows, looked at each other, sighed softly and played the flashlight beam on the side door. There were no discernable markings. Mark pointed to the larger door they had seen. They trotted in that direction. Again, Mark pointed the light towards the door, but noticed nothing unusual. As his light hit the lintel above the door, he thought he saw something. Motioning for Tomáš to help him, Mark was boosted up to get an eye-level view of the markings. He traced them with his finger: **2437 x ENEL.** He shone the light on his discovery. What he saw corroborated his finger tracing. He got down, ran the numbers and letters through his mind once more, and indicated he had what he wanted. Tomáš shrugged an anticlimactic shrug and followed Mark back to the place where they had stashed their skis.

Both men decided to take a swallow or two from their water containers. Tomáš reached in his rucksack and offered Mark a large round cherry-flavored candy ball. *A celebratory treat*, Mark thought to himself. They opened the sliding door noiselessly, just wide enough to exit comfortably. Once closed again, they looked at each other for a moment, stepped firmly into their bindings and began the perilous return, the younger of the pair hoping he would have enough strength left to keep up with the elder, who came as close to being perpetual motion as any human he'd ever met.

Tomáš peered in all directions, then motioned for Mark to fall in behind him. The snow was lighter now and the wind had abated somewhat. Mark was quietly mouthing the numbers and letters he had discovered in the barn. For the training on the loop near Aja's, suggested by Tomáš and directed by Aja, Mark would be eternally grateful. Without that practice he never could have endured Tomáš' relentless forward movement. Skiing skills long neglected by academic duties had been partially regained on the isolated upland meadows with Aja's patient help and stern discipline. If it hadn't been for the ever present danger of being caught by the border patrol, Mark began to think he might actually enjoy a demanding exercise such as this. When he suddenly realized that he was only halfway through his journey to the *Kollektiv*, his spirits dropped a few notches.

Following essentially the same path taken on the outward leg, Tomáš, grinding away in front, as usual like a well-oiled machine, and Mark, trailing a few meters behind, managed to slip past a few small groups of farm houses. Residents appeared to be hunkering down, fireplaces generating needed heat, until the storm subsided. Near a small bridge across a swift moving river, that Mark thought was possibly a tributary of the *Uzh*, the two saw three other skiers about sixty meters away on the opposite side of the river. They waved. Tomáš and Mark waved back, bent forward and pushed onwards. It was near dawn. Fortunately, there would be no sun again today. The cloud cover was simply too dense. The snow, still falling lightly, showed signs of stopping.

As they reached the base of the mountain, where they had earlier spent the night, Tomáš stopped and removed his skis. Mark followed suit. The climb up through the trees would require snow shoes. They elected to move slowly under the green canopy of the conifers, trying to avoid leaving any footprints. Much of the brush at the lower levels had been removed in the autumn by local peasants to use for starting fires. Eventually, they recovered their sleeping bags and the small two-man tent. They set up housekeeping and lay down to rest. Mark, for one, needed the break. He ate another of his apples, drank some water and, physically exhausted, quickly dozed off.

By mid-afternoon the snow had stopped. The air was crisp, and cool. Mark was snoring lightly. Tomáš sat up abruptly. He held his head still, listening. Gradually growing louder, coming closer and closer was the familiar 'thunk – thunk – thunk' of a helicopter. '*Border patrol*', thought Tomáš. Mark woke up. Tomáš put his finger to his lips and motioned upwards with his head. The chopper passed overhead, then banked slowly to the left and made a second pass. Tomáš and Mark remained motionless. Satisfied that nothing out of the ordinary could be spotted below, the chopper continued north along the border. In German, Tomáš said: "Just a routine patrol. Maybe assessing the storm damage."

"Good," replied Mark, also speaking German. "We had better get across the border and proceed back to Aja's place." *Lucky we were in the trees! There's really no place to hide once we move into the open.* The helicopter had left Mark a bit unnerved. Tomáš, however, was already rolling up the sleeping bags inside the tent. He strapped the bundle onto his rucksack, attached his snowshoes on top and, carrying his skis, led the way out of the thick stand of evergreens that had served as their refuge during the day.

An hour later, at a low point between two hills, challenging even for experienced hikers or skiers, the twosome passed a metal post with an engraved plate on each side. Tomáš pointed to the sign that marked the official border between the two nations and made a gesture with his hand to show relief at crossing back into Slovakia. Mark was also relieved. The next phase of their journey involved climbing about three hundred meters higher to clear a rather formidable peak. It was either that, or ski about five kilometers around the base of the mountain. Fortuitously, the heavy snow had blanketed the pesky boulders that had caused them diffi-culty two days earlier. Now, using a combination of snowshoes and skis, they traversed this section with relative ease. The skies cleared somewhat and a partial moon illuminated the way. Around three in the morning, Mark recognized the terrain as a hilly area east of Aja's upland retreat. His spirits were lifted. He quickly caught up to Tomáš, who was surprised to note his companion's sudden burst of energy.

They raced the final hundred meters to the hut. Mark was drained, but, oh so happy. *Home at last,* he thought. *Funny, how this place has grown on me.* Aja was waiting for them. Hot soup, hearty brown bread, cheese, dried fruit and a mug of beer disappeared with equal rapidity on either side of the table, as two famished men gulped their food and brew like half starved wolves. Mark would like to have "showered" first, but knew he could bathe later.

Aja watched the two thoughtfully, filling empty mugs and bowls, bringing more butter and fruit preserves for the bread. The adventure was described in great detail. Mark heaped profuse praise on his guide, who steadfastly refused all offers of money and other material rewards. Two weary travellers and one proud hostess slept well in their respective niches. Hugs and handshakes marked Tomáš' departure early the next day. He skied quietly out of sight, heading for his home in a valley north of Vesnicka. A widower, he lived alone.

Living on the mountain for over three weeks now, Mark had lost track of time. A warm sponge bath and a three-hour nap saw a revitalized young man, proud of his accomplishment. He knew he had found the first set of ten digits, although he was aware they were probably scrambled somehow. He put on one of Aja's father's flannel work shirts and joined Aja outside next to the hut. She was wielding an ax. Nearby was a chopping block and a stack of logs to saw and split into pieces for her huge iron stove. Mark pitched in. He cleared a wider path and helped stack the kindling.

They worked well together, side by side. Aja hummed Slovak folk songs. Then she sang a familiar tune. "Oh, my god!" Mark blurted out. Hearing Aja hum 'Stille Nacht, Heilige Nacht' reminded him that tomorrow was Christmas. "This is Christmas Eve. I don't have a thing for you!" He was obviously distraught. "You have been so kind and generous and I didn't even remember the holiday. Can you forgive me?"

Aja smiled. She was pleased simply to be alive, out-of-doors, breathing in the cool, fresh air, happy at the prospect of sunshine after three weeks of dark, dull, snowy weather. "You don't need to give me anything," she said. "Your company has been a real tonic for me. It has been the best gift I could have had. Our talks have helped me to come out of a kind of fog. I shall always treasure them."

Mark had developed strong feelings about Aja. *What was there not to like?* She was a handsome woman. He admired her and felt enriched by her selfless humanitarianism. Her work ethic was exemplary. He thought of Sister Catherine. *They would make an incredible team,* he thought. If he had had a sister, he would have wanted her to be like Sister Catherine or Aja. He began to consider that there was some sort of link between these two extraordinary human beings and his "mission".

Aja found Mark funny, yet thoughtful. He revealed to her a depth of understanding, a level of compassion she had known before in her father and her fiancé. She appreciated Mark's willingness to help without ever being asked. He was a brother and a friend, a valued addition to her simple existence here in this remote rugged area with its unique pleasures and concomitant hardships. In her heart she knew his stay would be brief. He would have to move on soon. It would most likely be after the holiday. She had accepted it, but a tear formed in her eye anyway.

When Aja went into the hut to prepare the noon meal, Mark said he wanted to split a few more logs. Instead, however, he took out his pocket knife and went to a small piece of soft pine, he had set aside. It took him about half an hour, actually until Aja called him to come in and eat, to finish his whittling project. That night they sat at the table, a red candle flickering in a tiny crystal holder their only light. A fresh evergreen bough hanging by the door introduced the scent of the season. Aja had poured each a glass of red wine, a gift from a patient. She presented Mark with a small package wrapped in red tissue. In it was a nut pastry she had baked while he was napping. From his pocket, Mark produced a small wooden angel that he had carved. They embraced and sat quietly, sharing the wine and sweet baked goods. Aja marvelled at Mark's ability to create such a lovely carving in such a short time. She was genuinely touched. She sang '*Stille Nacht, Heilige Nacht*'. Mark joined in softly. He couldn't recall any Christmas Eve that had moved him more.

The hut was not totally isolated. An emergency radio had been installed at her father's insistence. She rarely used it, but the police in Vesnicka, the largest village in the region, could contact Aja whenever a medical emergency made her presence in the area desirable. Early Christmas morning such a call came. A local midwife anticipated a need for assistance with a potentially difficult childbirth. As Aja prepared to ski down into the town, Mark asked if there was someone who could help him get to Košice. He planned to take the train from there to Bratislava, the Slovak capital. Aja said she might know of a person who could be of help.

Chapter Nine

Aja was gone most of the day. When she returned she was nearly exhausted. The birthing had been successful, but there had been complications. The mother was not one of Aja's patients. The midwife involved should have contacted her sooner. It was fortunate that Aja was able to respond so quickly. While in town, she had met with Jaroslav Pavliček, a local farmer who served on the area's volunteer fire fighting force. The fire fighters had attended a routine meeting in the police headquarters. Jaroslav participated in the same emergency radio network as Aja and had heard the call that morning too. He was familiar with the young mother's family and he and Aja discussed the case. Up to this point, some members of the community suspected that Aja might have a "guest" up on "her mountain". She confirmed this to Jaroslav, a friend from her youth whom she felt she could trust.

Pavliček raised chickens and also had a thriving egg business. His small farm was located about seven kilometers southwest of Vesnicka. Once a week he made a run to Košice with a load of live chickens and eggs for the weekend outdoor market. Initially, he balked at the prospect of concealing a stranger on his new truck and "smuggling" him to Košice. Aja won him over and it was arranged that Mark would come down to Pavliček's farm, situated on the outskirts of his hamlet amongst other farm houses in a row of about eight buildings backing up to a heavily forested hill. Mark was to ski and walk down from Aja's to the nearby highway, cross over into the woods and follow the trail until he was immediately behind Jaroslav's farm house and chicken sheds. Once there, he could slip quietly through the rear gate and come to the kitchen door in the rear of the house. If this was agreeable and other conditions permitted, Aja was to contact her friend by radio the night before by asking about driving conditions on the secondary roads in the area. Jaroslav understood that discretion was a necessity. He did not question why this was so.

Apprised of the arrangement, Mark quickly agreed and decided to spend the next two days chopping more wood, making a picnic table and benches from wood he found stored in the barn attached to the hut, and widening the path to the outhouse. Aja spent her time in the nearby hills and valleys. She alternately practiced cross-country skiing and sharpshooting on the loop that began in the meadow next to the hut, and tending to her patients. Being busy helped time pass. Evenings she would tell of her time in England or Prague, of her studies in Kiev and her aspiration to improve her skiing and marksmanship enough to qualify for the next Olympics. Often, she sang Slovak folk songs she had learned in school. In turn, she encouraged Mark to talk about his youth in Indiana, his college days and his career. She was surprised to learn he was still somewhat uncertain about his future, unclear about his goals.

Thursday evening, Aja made contact with Jaroslav, saying she planned a trip and wondered if the highways were clear enough to drive without snow tires. Reception was poor and the conversation dragged on for several minutes. She stated a time the next day when she planned to leave. The reply was slightly muffled by static. Never mind, she thought, he knows Mark will be there at the appointed time.

The skis from Mark's escapade across the border had been lent to him by Tomáš. When he had returned to his home following that demanding adventure, Tomáš hadn't wanted to deal with the extra pair of skis, so he left them, promising to collect them later. Meanwhile, Aja notified Tomáš she would arrange to drop them off at his cabin. Thus, Aja suggested that Mark use the skis to reach the highway near Jaroslav's farm. He could leave them strapped to a tree in the woods near one of her fixed targets and she would claim them on Sunday and arrange to get them to Tomáš.

Late the next afternoon on a rather gloomy day, Mark, choking slightly, wished Aja good bye, thanked her for her understanding and unquestioning help. She would accept no money for anything, not even for her father's clothes, which, while perhaps not in style in the cities, fit Mark well and protected him from the elements. After a protracted, heartfelt hug, Mark pushed off and headed through the forest for his rendezvous with Jaroslav.

The trail turned sharply to the right after about two kilometers. There, evidence of other activity was apparent. Well worn tracks, now somewhat frozen, generated a humming sound as Mark sailed downhill, bending his knees and carrying his poles tucked under his arms. The final three or so kilometers to the highway whizzed past in a flash. On a narrow trail off the rough mountain road Mark saw the number **6** Aja had painted at eye level on a tall pine on his left. He pulled up, then turned into a foot path between a stand of closely packed conifers. Roughly fifty meters later, Mark stopped, stepped out of his bindings and, using a leather strap Aja had given him, strapped the skis upright on a large pine two rows in from the highway. From there he had only to walk another thirty meters south along the highway before crossing over to approach the little hamlet where the Pavličeks resided.

State Highway 31 was a relatively new, two-lane stretch, completed within the past few months. It passed through a rather isolated wooded area. At the point where Mark was instructed to cross over and follow a trail on the opposite side, the highway made a long, gentle curve on a moderate slope. Steep drainage ditches about a meter deep had been carved on both sides of the highway. On either side a flat grassed area of approximately ten meters had been cleared to allow for better vision of the road ahead.

Peering out of the trees, Mark spotted on the other side the beginning of the trail he was to take to reach Pavliček's house. The road was clear and Mark jumped over the first ditch with ease. Just as he stepped on the pavement, where most of the ice and snow had been plowed and was now melting away, two men brandishing weapons emerged from the trees ahead of him. They ran towards Mark. Almost simultaneously, a black Škoda sedan raced around the curve and headed right for him. He leaped backwards, slightly off balance. The vehicle slid to a halt. The two tough looking men who had moved from the woods to the highway, grabbed Mark and flung him against the trunk of the car. It was a flash-back to the incident that brought Mark and Aja together. This time, however, there seemed to be nothing coincidental about it. Both men were dressed in dark clothing. One wore a knit cap. The other had a mop of greasy looking black hair. The latter, holding what appeared to be a Kalashnikov, was twisting Mark's left arm. The former held a pistol close to Mark's head. The abruptness of the attack took Mark totally by sur-prise. Both men were shouting at the same time, demanding he tell them why he was here and what he had found out in Ukraine. *How could they possibly have known he would be here at this time? How did they know he had crossed the border?*

Neither of the two assailants was known to Mark, although he thought they resembled the men who had attacked him when he first arrived in Vesnicka. Perplexed and helpless, absolutely stunned, he was unable to respond. Struggling to free himself, he drew the anger of the assailant in the knit cap. The barrel of the pistol was pressed ominously against his temple. Mark feared for his life.

From behind, **a sharp crack** resounded in the clearing formed by the highway. The 'knit cap' dropped the pistol and slid down onto the pave-ment behind the car. A second shot broke the brief interval of silence that followed. 'Grease Top' fired blindly in a reflex action, aiming into the woods from which Mark had emerged, then shuddered, doubled over and hit the pavement. In the distance, Mark heard the faint wail of a police siren. The car that had intercepted him sped away, two men in the front seat ducking down, as if expecting a hail of bullets. Mark took two giant steps and dove into the ditch he had crossed minutes before. He fell onto a body. Aja lay there staring into the sky, a hole oozing blood in the middle of her forehead.

Mark turned snow white. *This is the sort of thing you read about in the news or in cheap novels. But it's actually happened!* She had saved him again! She had obviously followed him. Had she suspected foul play, or was it a matter of a woman's intuition? Mark might never know the truth. In the process she forfeited her own life. Tears welled in his eyes. He froze. His legs were jelly. He wanted to vomit. He screamed an obscenity. His pulse was pounding like a hammer. The wail of the siren was closer, though no vehicle was yet in view. Instinctively, Mark lunged back across the highway, avoiding the two motionless bodies on the damp pavement. He was swallowed by the woods. He ran full tilt for about 100 meters, then slowed to a jog, running nearly a kilometer before stopping. He spied a row of houses to his left through the tall, straight trunks of stately conifers. He counted one... two... three... four and *there's the fifth house, must be Pavliček's.* He braced himself against a tree. Breathing heavily, he needed to catch his breath and compose himself. *I see the chicken sheds.* He lost part of his breakfast. He coughed and spit, trying to rid himself of the bilious taste in his mouth. He struggled to collect himself and see if he had been followed. He wiped the perspiration from his brow. The ache in his heart persisted. He would need all his acting skills to mask the dreadful horror of Aja's death. A loving soul lay lifeless in the melting ice and snow, a victim of ruthless greed. *Were these secret accounts a curse or a promise?* Mark was beginning to think the former.

"Oh, Aja, why did you follow me?" The trees offered no answer. "Why did this have to happen?" No echo, no rejoinder, just a sullen silence. *She saved my life twice and I did nothing for her. Did Székely know this might happen? I had better not mention this to Pavliček,* thought Mark. It was getting dark. Mark surveyed the scene before him. No one in sight. He cut through the trees on a small path leading to Pavliček's rear gate. It wasn't locked, but did not readily open. Mark vaulted over the low fence. He found the rear door of the residence and knocked quietly.

A round, wrinkled face framed by a *babushka* smiled a friendly greeting. A warm hand took his and guided him into the light of a kitchen. Compared to Aja's, this was a modern kitchen: gas stove, oil-fired space heater in the corner, florescent light overhead. Mark was trembling slightly when Jaroslav Pavliček entered the room. He was talking to someone out of sight, probably a child, telling her or him to go upstairs to read. He came forward and shook Mark's hand. "You feel cold. Matka, give him some *čaj!*"

Mark welcomed the mug of hot tea. The heat radiating from within soothed his cold, chapped hands as he clasped the porcelain container with both. The hot liquid calmed his nerves. In German, Jaroslav said, "We have to leave in a few minutes. The merchants in the open air market insist on early deliveries so they can set everything up before their clients arrive in the morning. I tried to check the weather again on the emergency radio, but it is temporarily down."

"Good, I'm ready." Mark fell in behind Jaroslav, who kissed the elderly woman, giving her instructions in Slovak, mentioning several names as he did so. A covered building behind the house and next to the chicken sheds housed a new-looking Isuzu three-quarter ton truck with an extended bed. The truck bed had a heavy canvas tarp draped over an aluminum frame. The bed was loaded with crates holding live chickens on the left. These were stacked about a meter and a half high. The remainder of the truck was filled with corrugated cartons labelled *Vejce.* Handing Mark a thick blanket, Pavliček pushed a few cartons aside and helped him up, motioning with his hands as he did so, to impart to Mark he was to find a comfortable spot and hide behind the cargo. Satisfied that Mark got the message, Pavliček closed the tailgate and tied down the canvas flap in the back of the truck. Minutes later, the Isuzu was moving cautiously through the darkness down the bumpy main street headed for the highway to Košice. As it did, Matka was listening in disbelief to the emergency radio that had just as suddenly begun to function normally.

Huddled in his blanket, Mark wept silently. He was filled with guilt. Aja had followed him to provide protection and had lost her life. He, who owed her so much, had run off and abandoned her body. *Those men. Who were they? How did they intercept him so readily? Who told them when and where to look?* Mark's mind was rushing around in circles.

Could men truly be so utterly evil? They didn't know him. He didn't know them. What do these secret accounts hold? Hundreds of thousands? Millions? It must be far more than Zdeněk revealed to him, if men are willing to kill for it. The emotional strain of the past few hours coaxed him into a fitful sleep.

Chapter Ten

The trip to Košice took an eternity. Or so it seemed to Mark, who was substantially bounced about. Not that Jaroslav was such a poor driver. There were numerous detours, where sections of the road had either suffered frost damage or simply had repairs delayed. Although the streets were fairly quiet, after all it was very early in the morning, Mark sensed they were somewhere in the middle of a good-sized city. Because some of the cartons and crates had shifted slightly enroute, Mark could not see anything through a slight gap in the tarp closing off the rear of the truck. Eventually, the truck made a couple of slow left turns and then began to back up gradually. Jaroslav apparently enjoyed driving in silence, for he had not listened to the radio during the entire drive. He knocked gently on the rear window of the cab, that had been obscured by a shade. Mark barely made out a hand signal that said all was OK. The cab door opened and closed. Mark heard someone fumbling with the ropes that kept the tarp in the rear taut. He was quite stiff, not having been able to stretch much for the past few hours. He said a silent prayer for Aja just as the dim light of some street lanterns slithered its way past the cargo in front of him.

"Hoppla!" said Jaroslav, as Mark jumped down onto the pavement. "Komm her!" he whispered, pointing to the side of the large stone building he had backed up to. The sound of railroad cars being shifted about in a rail yard and a couple of short whistle blasts all served to confirm the proximity of increasing activity.

"Ich kaufe Karten für dich. Warte hier!" So saying, Jaroslav held out his hand. Obviously wanting the necessary money for the ticket. Mark handed him some *Koruny* that Aja had obtained for him. Jaroslav disappeared around the corner.

Great! If he buys my ticket, I'll be able to slip onto the train without attracting too much unwanted attention.

Jaroslav returned in about twenty minutes. Mark had become a bit anxious, not understanding why the transaction should require so much time at this hour of the day. He had even wondered, if somehow, by accident or by design, Pavliček had betrayed him. Jaroslav handed Mark a booklet with the winter timetables for all of Slovakia. He showed Mark which trains to take, first to Bratislava; then on to Vienna; gave him his change, shook his hand and said, "Viel Glück!!"

With his familiar rucksack slung loosely over his shoulder, Mark watched the Isuzu pull away. He was grateful for the help, but wondered what Jaroslav would think when he learned of Aja's death. *He gulped hard as the memory of her lifeless body screamed through his mind. I must not let these hoodlums beat me!* He wanted desperately to avoid falling victim to paranoia, but knew now, more clearly than ever, that he could be in mortal danger, anywhere, at any time.

In the station, all was quiet. Janitors were sweeping the floors. Mark found the lavatory. *Not bad*, he thought, *for Košice!* He realized this was not the end of the earth, but actually a bustling central European hub, Slovakia's second largest city after Bratislava. Sitting and lying all night on a cold truck bed hadn't been the kindest treatment for his bladder. The pressure relieved, Mark washed up, rinsed his mouth vigorously and combed his hair. He contemplated adding his moustache again. Decided instead to take his borrowed jacket off and carry it. Once back in the large lobby, he scouted out a coffee shop and opted for a small pot of black tea and a sweet roll with some kind of fruit filling.

On a wooden bench in a corner of the large waiting room Mark found an abandoned newspaper. It was two days old, but he used it mainly to help him blend in. He hoped to recognize a few key words that would let him deduce what was happening in the world. Glancing up at the large clock in the waiting hall, Mark reckoned he had about ninety minutes to kill before his train was to leave. He looked around. *Everything seems to be normal – whatever that is.*

Between dozing off for a few seconds or minutes at a time and watching some of the early arrivals, both trains and passengers, Mark checked his watch to assess how much time remained before his train was scheduled to depart. An electric sign showed all trains operating as scheduled. He had about twenty minutes more.

Some passengers were very well dressed; scurrying about with briefcases, tailored overcoats or leather jackets. Others clearly came from more modest backgrounds, probably small town and village people. Four nuns passed by and sat down not far away. They were quite animated. Two were engrossed in a serious discussion, *or were they simply exchanging schoolgirl gossip?* One was fingering her rosary. Mark thought of Sister Catherine. *What motivates a woman to renounce the attractions of modern life to serve a religious cause?* He reflected on his own life. *Am I too isolated from reality? Is académe a refuge from the real world, as some critics have long maintained?* Mark glanced at the large clock. He jumped up quickly and headed for the platform indicated on the electronic sign. He had just five minutes to board. Travelling light had its advantages. He found a car marked Bratislava and swung aboard.

He had no seat reservations. Walking down the narrow passage in his second class car, he peered into each compartment. Virtually all of them full. Finally, he found a compartment with an empty middle seat, slid the door open, pointed to the seat and was relieved when an elderly woman next to the window, simultaneously invited him by hand signal to be her guest and motioned a corpulent elderly man opposite her to scrunch over and make room. His ample rear end gave up a half inch or so. A young girl in the seat nearest the sliding door also moved a bit and Mark wedged himself into the middle seat with a nod of thanks to his unofficial hostess. In the process of seating himself, Mark's olfactory nerve promptly reported that the odor of stale tobacco and garlic breath were not able to mask his male seat mate's aversion to regular bathing.

Before putting his rucksack on the overhead luggage rack, Mark looked once more at the winter schedule Jaroslav had thoughtfully furnished, and noted that he would have only about fifteen minutes to change trains in Bratislava. He had already decided to use his German passport for the border crossing.

The teenaged girl next to him engrossed herself in a French fashion magazine most of the trip. Her brother, likewise a teenager, sitting in the other door seat, was absorbed in a soccer publication. The overweight seat mate constantly emitted a low decibel snore, periodically punctuated with a snort worthy of the porcine species he so closely resembled. Occasionally, he farted audibly. The elderly woman was especially solicitous of the male seated to her right just opposite from Mark. He appeared to be twentyish-thirtyish, had a slight beard and the vacant gaze of someone whose mental faculties were impaired. Mark dozed, too, his head bobbing up and down, serenaded by the clickety-clack rhythm of the rails.

After a brief stop in Zvolen, Mark felt a hand on his knee. Looking up, he saw the elderly woman offering him a sandwich. Coupled with her friendly smile, the food was welcome. She followed the rather fatty, salty salami sandwich with a few sections of an orange she peeled on a piece of butcher paper in her lap. The young boy and girl ate the same fare. The chubby one, presumably the dominant male among his fellow travellers, slept on.

A vendor came by, opened the door and offered bottled soda and cups of beer. The beer looked inviting, but Mark, using hand signals, offered everyone a lemon-flavored soda. They all accepted gratefully and Mark was pleased to be able to reciprocate. A discreet glance at his watch indicated two hours to go. The vendor looked back at Mark, probably wondering his relationship to the others.

Chapter Eleven

As the train pulled into Bratislava, Mark helped the elderly woman get her family's luggage down from the racks on either side. During the trip, it had occurred to him that Aja's body, as well as those of his assailants would have been found by now. Perhaps Jaroslav would have heard about it. *Would he have mentioned Mark to the police? Given them his description and his destination?* Although his own much-used rucksack showed its history of wear, the bags and valises Mark lifted off the racks were even more tattered and torn. The young ones put their magazines away, treating them like prized possessions. The heavy-set man brushed past Mark as he stepped into the passageway. The odor took Mark's breath away. Sadly, the heaviest bag had been left for the elderly woman to carry. She seemed to take it in stride. Mark shook her bony hand warmly. Without her noticing, Mark slipped a folded bill, a hundred-Mark note, into her purse. *She surely deserves a pleasant surprise.* He smiled slightly. *For Aja, for Sister Catherine*, he thought to himself. Spotting a few uniformed police on the platform, Mark took the woman's heavy suitcase in his hand, grabbed the girl's valise in the other, after slinging his lighter rucksack over her shoulder, and exited the train with 'his family'. The uniformed police on the platform appeared to be on the watch for someone or something. They took no notice of Mark.

Signage was excellent in the railroad station. Mark spotted a sign with an arrow showing the way to trains for Wien. With just minutes to make his connection, he rushed off, saw the train, walked down the platform and sought out a car that was not too full. *This evening train must be quite popular*. Once aboard, Mark found only one vacant seat. At the last

93

minute, a woman with an infant in her arms climbed up the stairs. Seeing her, Mark rose and pointed to his seat. The woman acknowledged quietly and with a smile of gratitude sat down. Mark, surveying the passengers, moved to a spot where he could lean against a window. Luckily, Vienna was only about an hour and a quarter further west. He bought his ticket from the conductor.

Of the passengers Mark could see, none appeared the least bit interested in him. *So far,* he told himself, *I haven't gotten the impression that I've been followed while in transit. Of course, I've tried to be circumspect and cautious. Yet, somehow, in the area near Vesnicka, Gregor and his cohorts picked up my trail. They knew about the trip into Ukraine. They also seemed to know I'd be going down to Pavliček's. How did they do it?* Mark couldn't explain it. He couldn't imagine that anyone had betrayed him.

The *Südbahnhof* in Vienna was crowded. People carrying bags and suitcases everywhere. The heavy coats, caps, hats, gloves and scarves told Mark it was cold outside. Reaching into his rucksack, he took out the jacket he had stuffed there to alter his appearance. He saw a bulletin board with hotel information. A small, neat advertisement for the *Hotel Wieden* caught his eye. He read aloud. "Wayringergasse 35, five minutes on foot from the railroad station." *Perfect!* Mark checked an orientation plan nearby, chose the main exit and walked briskly, stopping to look back a few times. The hotel was not very distinguished looking from the street. Its lobby was small; the reception desk dark mahogany and well scratched. A Black man wearing a green apron stepped out of a tiny office off to one side behind the desk. Mark asked for a single, preferably with bath or shower and toilet for two nights.

The Black man was in his early thirties, Mark estimated. His German rang clear and melodious. A small stack of opera flyers for a performance of Verdi's *Othello* lay on one side of the counter. All the rooms had toilets, but rooms on each floor shared a combination bathtub/shower. Advised that there were no other guests on the fourth floor, Mark decided that would be his best choice. He showed his German passport, signed the register and took his key. Since there was no elevator, Mark walked up the four flights of stairs and found his room. The bedding was crisp and clean, but the room was in dire need of renovation. *Oh, well. All I really need for two nights is a simple flop house and this fits the bill admirably.*

Besides the toilet, there was a sink with running hot and cold water in his room. Mark spruced himself up. He changed into a woolen sweater under his coat and headed out to find something to eat. Being near the railroad station, he expected to find a variety of dining establishments. Sure enough, half a block away on *Prinz-Eugen-Strasse* was a small restaurant. The lighting was 'romantic', that is, rather dim. A few wall sconces and candles on each table created a cozy atmosphere for couples. Mark found a corner table. Sitting there, he decided, he'd be less noticeable. *People will probably figure my date didn't show.* Mark was not only alone, he was lonely. Subconsciously, he envied the couples dining together.

There were only three other tables with patrons. From the menu, which he struggled to read in the weak light, he selected, in honor of his visit to Vienna, *Wiener Schnitzel* with *Bratkartoffeln, Rotkohl* and a *Stein of Schwechater Export*. The food was outstanding. The gray-haired waiter was attentive, yet unobtrusive; a real pro. On the way back to the hotel Mark crossed the Wredner Gürtel and went into the railroad station again. Among the shops still open was a drugstore. He picked up some toiletries and a chocolate bar. *Dessert*, he thought. A men's shop further on had a dark knit shirt, a pair of gray trousers and a black beret. Mark bought them. Next door was a leather goods store with a luggage display in the window. Mark went in and found a small pullman type suitcase. He put his rucksack in it, along with his new acquisitions. Satisfied that he wasn't being followed, he inquired at a travel office near the entrance about flights to Milan. Seats were available on a 6:00 am flight Monday morning. His irrepressible college roommate Luigi Nardini was going to get a call soon.

* * *

Sunday brought a break in the weather. It was still cold, but the sunshine and lack of wind created good walking conditions. After Continental breakfast at the hotel: the coffee was first rate; the sweet rolls were at least a day old, the orange juice was watery and the hard boiled egg much too soft, Mark strolled around the neighborhood drinking in the sun and enjoying the exercise after a day of cramped rail travel. Images of Aja lying in the ditch returned repeatedly. Finally, he found a quiet dining establishment in a side street away from the noisy buses and streetcars. Roast chicken, dumplings, bean salad and a glass of the house white wine satisfied him. He continued walking and arrived again at the *Südbahnhof*. Inside, at the telephone office, he placed a call to "Nardini e Figli, Immobili" in Torri del Benaco, Italy. The phone rang and rang. No answer. Mark asked the operator to try and find a number for the residence of Luigi Nardini in Torri. Zdeněk had told Mark that his father, Tibor, resided in a hospice in a monastery north of Riva. Mark knew Riva was on Lake Garda. His old roommate often bragged about the beauty of his hometown on the same lake. If he could get help from Luigi, Mark figured he might locate the monastery and obtain the second account's code without any hassle.

The operator waved to Mark, holding up three fingers to indicate Booth Three was where he could get his call. "Hello, Luigi, is that you?" A slight pause. Silence. "Luigi, it's me Mark. How are you?"

"Hey, buddy, where are you calling from?" Luigi's inflection rose dramatically. Surprise gave way to genuine enthusiasm.

"I'm in Vienna, but I'm heading for Lake Garda. Can you help me find a place to stay for a few days?"

"That's great. I hope I can see you here in Torri. Unfortunately, I'm packing now for a business trip to Rome. Leaving early in the morning. A hot real estate deal. You may not know it, but I took over the business from my father and I've expanded big time into development projects."

"You always were a hustler. Can you make any suggestions?"

"Sure." Mark could almost hear Luigi's brain cells. "Look, here's what we'll do. My cousin Toni will work out something for you. Will you be coming from the south or the north?"

Mark was planning to fly to Milan, then drive east, turning north on the east side of the lake. "I'll be coming from the south."

"O.K. Here's what you do. Our office in town may be closed tomorrow when you get here. Once you go past the *Scaliger* fortress you'll see the post office on the right. A few doors down on the same side is a tobaconnist shop that stays open at night until about 9:00 in the winter. Signor Fraumeni, the proprietor, will have an envelope for you with keys and instructions. Toni will take care of everything. O.K.?"

"*Grazie*, Luigi. Thanks a million. By the way, I'm trying to be, …uh, inconspicuous, if you know what I mean?"

"Gotcha! *Ciao*!"

Mark didn't know what to expect. He did remember Luigi talking about the dozens of great rental properties they had. Most rented, he had said, to German tourists. Sometimes, he added, the same people return year after year. *I guess I'd better get back to the hotel, pack and get ready for tomorrow.*

First thing, early, very early the next morning, Mark shaved and showered. He had already laid out his wardrobe for the day. A moment or two in front of the mirror convinced him he'd pass for just another busy traveller; a well-dressed one at that. He was too early for breakfast, however, the rosy-cheeked young woman setting up the Breakfast Room managed to bring him some coffee, a fresh roll with butter and marmalade. Neatly wrapped in a napkin was a shiny, red apple. Mark slipped it into his coat pocket with a "*Danke vielmals*!" to Jarmila, as indicated by a name tag on her apron. He settled his bill with a credit card and walked to the railroad station carrying his new suitcase. Actually, he had dragged it around the floor in his room a few times to mute the newness.

A rail shuttle to Schwechat Airport required only a few minutes. He was not too early and moved promptly to his departure gate. An announcer informed those waiting there would be a thirty-minute delay.

Mark took a seat across the departure hall in a section reserved for passengers taking a later flight to Rome. As he did so, he spotted two elderly nuns, dressed in gray and black habits, who were standing on the side of the long corridor stretching down the middle of the hall. They looked at their tickets and boarding passes, then at each other, then at the flashing and constantly changing list of destinations and departure times. Obviously bewildered by the overwhelming energy of a modern international airport experiencing peak traffic, the two somewhat rotund and diminutive figures appeared completely helpless. Noting this, Mark got up, stretched his legs, and walked slowly up to the ladies, whom most passengers easily overlooked or ignored.

"Darf ich Ihnen behilflich sein?" he asked. Two pairs of eyes reflected surprise at first, then delight. Rarely had such a handsome young man asked if they needed help. Mark listened attentively. Sorting through the confused chatter, the girlish giggles and sighs, Mark checked their tickets and determined they were flying to Madrid and directed them to the appropriate gate. Waddling off at great speed, the two proceeded down the hall, continuing their breathless chatter. Upon reclaiming his seat, Mark looked around carefully. Nothing unusual, as far as he could see. The flight, too, was smooth and uneventful.

The New Year had arrived with a nasty cold spell. Milan did not escape. Chilling temperatures slid off the southern slopes of the Alps and rolled all the way onto the *Po* plain. Relatively speaking, however, Mark found the air friendlier than in the *Vyhorlatské Vrchy* mountains he had traversed in Slovakia.

In a toilet stall, Mark organized his papers. He had a driver's license to match up with his Austrian passport, also a EuroKarte credit card. *Hmmm, Rudolf Schmidtke, St. Gilgen, Austria. I have no idea where that is, but it sounds interesting.* He applied a little gum arabic and pressed a slim dark moustache in place.

The econobox Fiat he chose, courtesy of Avis, handled well and was guaranteed not to attract undue attention. Keeping his speed about ten kilometers an hour below the posted limit took effort. The little Fiat was a perky pup that wanted to romp with the big dogs. Mark's discipline reined in any urges to pull into the fast lane and see how far to the right the odometer needle would really go. The *Autostrada* might be a racetrack for the majority of drivers, but not for Mark, alias Rudolf Schmidtke.

Sunshine warmed the winter landscape by early afternoon. Constant glances in his rear view and side view mirrors reassured Mark he was not being tailed. *Strange,* he reflected. *Someone was able to intercept me when I left Aja's, yet I never felt I was being followed. So far, no signs I'm being tracked.*

Flags on a manufacturing plant Mark passed as he approached *Brescia* were hanging straight down. *Sun, no wind. Maybe I should try another mode of transport, as an extra measure to throw someone off my trail. Just in case.* Mark was trying to think like some character in a typical movie thriller. He took the second exit into Brescia. His Fiat was from the Avis stable, so he stopped at a gas station and found someone who knew where the nearest Avis office was located. Navigating around town was a challenge, especially when every other driver is intent on getting to his destination first, at all costs. The Avis clerk on duty, a business-like young man, gave Mark a map showing where he could find a motorcycle dealer and rental agency nearby. One of the maintenance crew offered to drop him off there on his way to deliver a car.

As a teenager, Mark had the use of an old *Enfield 250cc* cycle one summer in Maine. When his mother found out about it, he abruptly shifted to vehicles with four wheels. He never lost his love for the motorcycle, though. At *Motocicletti Domenico,* Mark spotted a real beauty, a red *BMW*. It was used and the price was reasonable. The shop also sold motor scooters. Mark had seen them by the dozens, both on local streets and on the highway. A black job, an *Aprilia,* lured him back to touch and feel a few times. He was intrigued. He had enough money to buy it without excessive damage to the bundle Zdeněk had given him. The scooter was also a used model. The shop owner personally gave him a technical rundown in English. He himself had planned to use it, until he came across a great deal on a used *Harley*. He looked around, nobody was listening. Then, as if in a confessional, the dealer, speaking *sotto voce,* admitted he had "modified" the scooter's motor, but "just a little". Now, it could do about 140 kilometers an hour on a flat stretch, he claimed. The price sounded like a bargain. Mark was sold. He bought a heavy duty luggage strap to secure his suitcase on the rear. From the accessory department he purchased a black leather jacket (*de rigueur,* he thought), and got two helmets, both matching the *Aprilia's* shiny, black paint. Insulated gloves, a scarf and a knit cap rounded out his outfit. The second helmet for the *sozius* seat was a gift from the dealer, who had three cousins living in Brooklyn.

The half dozen men cheering and waving good-bye on the curb, as Mark zoomed off, heading back to the A4 highway to Verona, constituted more attention than he considered prudent under the circumstances, but he understood their joy at such a hefty cash transaction on an otherwise slow business day.

Mark rode comfortably on his new steed. Before he knew it, the exit for Peschiera del Garda was a mere 1000 meters away. Mark turned off and headed to the town on the lake's southeast corner. The riding characteristics of the scooter were only vaguely reminiscent of those he recalled from his holiday in Maine. Mark stopped at a small roadside *Trattoria.* After a meal of *lasagna, insalata mista,* a cup of coffee and a few *biscotti,* Mark continued, following the road that hugged the lake to his left. Traffic was light. Most people were enjoying their evening meal. Darkness fell over the lake. Mark's gaze swept fleetingly left to right as he headed north towards *Garda* and *Torri.* In *Bardolino,* he stopped at a gas station, where he checked his tires and lights before tanking up. He hadn't used much fuel at all.

A January evening in the resort towns on the southern half of the lake was a lonely experience. Shops, for the most part, were already closed. A few stragglers were scurrying to find comfort indoors by the kitchen stove. Mark remembered the cozy warmth of Aja's stove, the flames greedily consuming the crisp, dry logs. His heart skipped a beat. Entering Torri, Mark was pleased to see the fortress, then the post office Luigi had mentioned. Next came the tobacco shop, a tidy kiosk with a myriad items for sale from cigarettes to souvenirs. Lights shone inside. No customers were visible from the limited parking area in front. Mark parked his scooter. Stepping inside, he shook off the chill he felt. "*Fa molto freddo!*" The voice came from the back of the store. A pleasant fellow of about fifty years came into the shop carrying a stack of newspapers he had tied together.

Freddo meant cold, Mark knew from his four years as Luigi's roomie. "*Si, molto freddo,*" he responded, returning the friendly smile as well. Switching to English, Mark asked about the envelope Luigi said he would leave here for him.

The shopkeeper's smile grew larger yet. Quite animated, he shook Mark's hand vigorously and produced a sealed brown envelope from a drawer next to the cash register, all the while rattling off rapid fire in Italian a burst of comments, of which Mark understood only the names Luigi and Nardini, to the accompaniment of gestures suggesting a close and admiring relationship between the tobacconist and the Nardinis. Mark found himself nodding actively in agreement.

Mark opened the envelope. Inside were three keys of varying sizes and a sheet of paper with a hand-drawn map and a set of directions printed in block letters in English.

* * *

Welcome to Torri.

Continue north along the lake about ten kilometers. When you see a small sign saying *Pasola*, take the first right turn. You will see a row of three tall poplars on the corner.

(Should you see a sign for *Castelletto*, you have gone too far!) Watch for traffic. It is a one-lane road with a few deep potholes. Follow the steeply winding road to the second right turn. A sign on the entrance says *Villa Diana*. The steel key is for the iron gate. You may park in the carport or under the large tree next to the stone wall on the left side. Please lock the gate after you.

Walk around the front of the building to the far end. There are stairs leading to a huge wooden door. The over-sized key opens the main door. The small key with the red mark is for Luigi's closet.

The shutters are closed and locked. You may open them, if you wish. I stocked the small refrigerator and the wine cabinet. Help yourself! Luigi says you are (or were) about the same size. You may borrow anything you want from his closet. Enjoy!

Toni

P.S. There are four other units in this complex. They won't be occupied until March.

Chapter Twelve

Mark's trusty steed seemed a bit loud in the cool night air. The highway north was his alone. Two trucks heading south passed him as he pulled out of town; otherwise only the waves of *Lake Garda* lapping gently on the deserted stony shore and the throaty hum of his *Aprilia* interrupted the calm. A sliver of moon sufficed to silhouette the three poplars standing sentinel in the chill winter night. Toni had selected a great landmark.

The odometer showed he had travelled exactly ten kilometers since leaving the tobacco shop. He hadn't seen any signs yet for *Castelletto*, the next political entity up the road. *This has to be it.* Mark grimaced slightly at the noise from his robust motor, when he gave it enough throttle to climb the steep, narrow road to "Luigi's Lair", the name he had assigned to his temporary digs. The wrought iron gate was rather imposing; obviously not an inexpensive creation. The key worked. The gate opened with nary a creak. Mark strained for a couple of minutes to make out his surroundings. The carport Toni mentioned was empty. The tree was huge. Its umbrella protected a wooden bench standing against the wall. Facing west, the bench offered a splendid view of the lake and the mountains whose peaks could be seen, even in the weak glimmer of a first quarter moon.

Concerned about his personal safety, now that he had witnessed the extremes to which Gregor and his partners would go to obtain what they wanted, Mark decided to roll his scooter into a space between the villa and the free standing carport, a kind of narrow alley partially blocked by three large trash cans. In the shadows there it would not be likely to attract any attention.

A stone path led him around the front of the building. He counted four numbered entrances before reaching the south end of the structure. None of them showed any signs of life. A stone staircase terminated on a veranda hosting a number of hardy plants in large ceramic pots. A wrought iron railing surrounded the tiled veranda. Partially hidden behind a tall shrub were two good-sized propane tanks. Two windows, covered by thick wooden shutters, faced the lake. Between them was what appeared to be another door, that was also secured by a heavy shutter accessible only from inside the dwelling. The large key was easy to locate in the envelope without any light. It looked and felt like an antique. Mark inserted it in the keyhole. He turned it once. Nothing! He turned it a second time. The door wouldn't budge! A third turn of the bulky key was similarly without results. Mark twisted the key once more and it turned a fourth time. Success! The door opened inwards. Mark closed it slowly behind him and felt the inside wall, where he thought there ought to be a light switch. Of the three switches, Mark flipped the first. Two lamps blinded him at first. He surveyed the room. Attractive leather furniture arranged around a handsome stone fireplace, a built-in wall unit housing a sophisticated audio system, including a television. A generous coffee table with a floral arrangement in the middle and a few magazines carefully arranged in two piles formed part of the decor. *Almost too tidy for Luigi*, Mark mused, recalling what a disaster their room at college would have been, if he hadn't been such a diligent housekeeper himself.

Beyond this living room space Mark saw a rustic wooden table with chairs forming a separate dining area. He locked the entrance from the inside and explored further. He found a small efficiency kitchen with fridge, stove, oven, microwave and an enamelled sink, a huge bathroom with an elaborate whirlpool tub and a shower only an Italian master could have created from marble tiles and space-age technology. *My old buddy has built himself the grand daddy of all bachelor pads*, thought Mark. There were two bedrooms. One had twin beds. The other featured a king-size bed and had been made up with fresh white sheets and a damask-covered down comforter. Mark assumed this had been done for him.

As he sat in the living room sunk deep in an exquisite burgundy leather lounge chair quaffing a *Spaten Oktoberfest* he found in the refrigerator, Mark looked at a note taken from the dining table. It was from Toni's prolific pen.

* * *

Mark,

Luigi deeply regrets he could not rearrange his meeting in Rome in order to greet you. In his place, I welcome you. I am happy to help make your stay a pleasant one. Please excuse the weather. Luigi insists you make yourself comfortable. The smallest of the three keys is to his closet. Wear anything you want. You will find some snacks in the refrigerator, also beer, and in the wine rack some of Luigi's favorites. I recommend the *Bardolino Classico*. For special occasions, the *Brunello* will not disappoint you.

Luigi says you wish to be inconspicuous. I suggest we meet Wednesday. If you drive north along the lake for thirty minutes you will come to the town of *Malcesine*.

Follow the signs to the cable car. Enter the underground garage and park there.

The cable car will take you to the *Monte Baldo* station. From there walk about 500 meters to the *Refugio Gustavo Martini*, an inn with boarding facilities for skiers and hikers. You'll see it on the left when you exit the cable station. Take a seat at the west end of the restaurant and order an *espresso*. I will be there at noon.

Ciao,

Toni

* * *

"Whoa, Toni, I'm no secret agent or CIA operative! Hey, I've got to straighten you out." Mark was beginning to express his thoughts out loud. *This guy has the wrong impression. Still, there is danger attached to me. If it hadn't been for Aja, my corpse would be back in the Low Country now and people probably would think I really had been up to some international intrigue.*

A long soak in the tub sounded great, but the opportunity to test the engineering marvel awaiting in the over-sized shower was irresistible. The dials, knobs and buttons got the ultimate consumer test. The water was adjustable to the perfect temperature. Sprays in every imaginable pattern and intensity soothed and invigorated. *Luigi ought to put an "X-Rated" sign on the bathroom door.* A thick, white chenille bath towel hung dry and ready. A new blue toothbrush, a squirt of *BlancoDent* and his mouth felt fresh again. A long look in the mirror gave Mark pause. He looked more weathered and tired than he had since cramming for his dissertation defense.

Although he still felt a little saddle sore, the shower had worked a miracle. Mark headed straight for bed. Within minutes he was asleep. He woke up a few times, mostly with Aja on his mind.

* * *

With the shutters open, sun poured through the windows and drenched the dining nook with light. A warmly dressed Mark sat at the table. *Toni, you're a gem*, Mark thought, *this is the best breakfast I've had in a long while. Maybe I should get you a box of cigars.*

Mark gorged himself on the fresh fruit in the fruit bowl. The corn flakes and cream took him back twenty-five years to his Indiana home. He passed on the coffee; choosing instead to drink a glass of milk with his poached egg and toast. The west-facing veranda off the dining area exten-ded an invitation. Standing at the railing, Mark revelled in the sunshine and cool fresh air. The view across the lake was everything Luigi had ever claimed it was – a treat for the soul of man. *Tomorrow I'll drive up and meet Toni, see what help he can give me. Today, I'm going to catch up on my sleep and wash some clothes. Good thing, Luigi has a washer and dryer. Better thing, my stuff doesn't need any ironing.* Mark completed his homely chores and, relaxing on the sofa with a warm blanket, dozed off for what seemed an instant, but was in fact, three hours. Hungry again, he heated a can of soup, made some toast and sipped on a glass of *Bardolino*. Before retiring in mid-evening, Mark reflected on his situation and began to formulate a plan of action. First, of course, he had to discover the next set of numbers. Would Herr Székely be able to help. He was not convinced that old Herr Székely simply left them to be found by anyone without first scrambling them somehow. *And Gregor? What about him?*

* * *

Wednesday mid-morning, Mark opened the shutters again. Sunny, though still cool and windy, it was a day that summoned to action. Two delicious bananas, a South African navel orange and a fistfull of dates, followed by coffee yoghurt, a microwaved breakfast roll and a glass of hot tea later, Mark zipped up his black leather biker's jacket, rolled his *Aprilia* through the iron gate and coasted downhill to the highway. The scooter started smoothly. He let the engine warm up for a couple of minutes and slipped deftly into the stream of traffic that was building rapidly. The ride to *Malcesine* was without incident. There were numerous signs pointing the way to the cable car station. As Toni had suggested, Mark pulled into the underground parking facility. He found a slot in a remote corner designated for small vehicles. He had his rucksack with him. In it was an emergency change of clothes, his theatrical make-up kit and two apples from the fruit basket.

Looking westward out of the ascending cable car, a beautiful panorama greeted Mark. Immediately below were the lakeside buildings of *Malcesine*, including a substantial fortress and the winding streets lined with shops and homes, enjoying a respite from the tourists who crowded the narrow alleys in the warmer seasons. *If my memory serves me, Johann Wolfgang came here once. Had some kind of problem with the authorities.* The lake was narrower here than further south. The sun reflected lovingly off its glistening surface. Before him the cable car passed over a few farm houses perched precariously on the steep hillside. Snow covered the fields below. The higher the elevation, the deeper the snow. The cable car reached an intermediate station and the passengers disembarked. After a few minutes' wait, a second car appeared and loaded for the last leg up to the mountain top station. In all, only twelve passengers; four carrying skis.

Mark and another male passenger stopped outside the cable station. They both looked around a couple of minutes to survey the scene and orient themselves. The stranger went to the right. Mark started in the direction of the *Refugio Gustavo Martini*, to the left. A middle-aged German-speaking couple, bundled against the constant cold breeze from the west, walked unhurriedly a few meters behind him.

The *Refugio* was, in fact, a rugged looking building of logs and stone that served as a restaurant for tourists and outdoor enthusiasts year round. Simple overnight lodgings were available. The boots he had bought with his biker's garb in *Brescia* kept his feet comfortable. Two pairs of hiking socks borrowed from Luigi's wardrobe helped.

Mark scraped as much snow as he could off his boots before entering. The vestibule was wet. He removed his jacket and a thin woolen cap belonging to Luigi. His helmet he had locked in a compartment of his motor scooter back in the covered carpark. Seating was informal; long wooden tables with benches, no table coverings. Centered on the back wall facing the kitchen and serving area was a large fireplace.

The roaring wood fire acted as a magnet for the majority of patrons. They could be seen talking animatedly, while rubbing cold hands to warm them. Mark climbed into a bench at an empty table at the west end of the dining room. There didn't seem to be any waitresses or waiters, so after a few minutes he went to the serving counter and ordered an *espresso*. Seated again, he drained his cup in a single draught. As he set the cup down, he heard a charming female voice behind him say with a slight English accent, "Hello, you must be Luigi's friend, Mark. I'm Toni, welcome to the *Lago di Garda*."

Mark turned and stood. He was looking into the blue eyes of a lovely, petite blonde. She held out her hand. He took it and returned the brightest, friendliest smile he had seen in a long while. "Can I get you something to eat or drink?" The words came out of his mouth, yet he heard them not at all, so taken was he by the perky charm of his rosy-cheeked hostess.

Toni looked down at her hand. Mark noticed that he had not released it. Embarrassed, he uttered a hasty, "I'm sorry."

"I'll have an *espresso* too," she replied. Mark rushed off to fulfill her request.

Upon his return with cups, saucers and small napkins for two, she asked, looking about to see if anyone might be listening, "What brings you here in the winter?"

"I'm engaged in a research project. It's rather private. Perhaps you can help me."

"Oh, I'd love to. I'm taking a few days off this week. I'm available."

Mark thanked her for the housing arrangements. He assumed Luigi had explained who he was and had provided enough background information to satisfy her initial curiosity. She sensed he wanted to know who she was. Concisely, she gave him a brief bio. She, Antonia di Sogno, a native of Verona, had attended the university in Milan. Had spent summers learning French in Lyon and English in London. Her father, Luigi's uncle, was a veterinarian with large practices, both here on the lake and in Verona. She had thought about becoming a veterinarian because she loved animals. Instead, she had studied Jurisprudence and considered joining a law firm. That was until she helped Luigi one summer with his real estate dealings. She got the bug, so to speak, and invested in a failing boutique, turned it around, and now had three, one in Garda, another in Sirmione on the south end of the lake, and a third in Verona. Now she was a full-time shop owner and entrepreneur. She had been delivered to the *Refugio* by a lady friend with whom she had stayed overnight. The friend lived in a villa on the east slope of the mountain. An access road and four-wheel drive had conquered the snow.

Both laughed, when Mark revealed, with some embarrassment, he had expected Toni to be a man. Mark was captivated by this bubbly, vivacious woman with short blonde hair, and an air of adventure about her. He estimated she was about 5' 5", not over 110 pounds. A white turtle-neck sweater accentuated her well endowed figure. She was wearing black pants similar to his own. Her bright red parka with a fur-trimmed hood was hanging on a wall hook next to the table.

They decided to have lunch at the *Refugio*. The special of the day struck both as a good choice. Thus, *risotto,* chicken marsala, spinach and fried potatoes, washed down with a glass of Bardolino sated both hunger and thirst. The myriad conversations occurring in the *background* combined to create a pleasant din, penetrable only by sitting closer. The intimate *tête-à-tête* continued longer than either noticed. The time was spent pleasantly by both.

During the meal, Mark told Toni he was trying to find a man who was a patient at a hospice, in a monastery somewhere north of *Riva.*

"*Il Convento San Vigilio!*" she exclaimed. "I have been there once many years ago. It is near a tiny lake in the mountains, rather isolated, I would say."

"Is it far from here?" Mark wanted to know.

"Not too far. It's a bit late to go today, but," looking at her watch, "is tomorrow all right?"

Toni seemed interested in finding out more about this 'research'. "Who is the patient?"

"Toni, I must be honest with you. The information I seek is innocuous enough. No international secrets are involved. Nevertheless, a small group of desperate men with evil intentions is also after the same information. Since arriving in Italy I've been checking very carefully to see if anyone is following me. Either I've thrown them off my trail, or they're far more clever than I realize. I don't want to endanger you."

"If you think you have come this far without being detected, you should be O.K. I see no danger in accompanying you to the monastery. I believe it is still operating." She paused for a moment. "I know, let's go to

Luigi's place for the night, then we'll get off to an early start in the morning." Toni explained that she occasionally stayed there and kept a closet full of clothes in the guest bedroom.

"Toni, I just don't know!" Mark was genuinely concerned. He had dreamed of Aja and the hole in her forehead the night before.

"No need to worry. I can take care of myself."

"Would you mind riding on the passenger seat of my motorscooter?"

"Of course not. I have a scooter of my own at home. I grew up on a *Vespa*."

Having noticed a ring on Toni's left ring finger, Mark inquired in an off hand fashion, "Will your husband mind?"

Toni laughed. "No. I'm not married, just engaged. In Europe, engagement rings are often worn on the left hand and switched to the right hand when married." Mark looked slightly embarrassed.

The cable ride down to lakeside went swiftly. This time at least two dozen passengers were aboard. Roughly half carried skis. The *Aprilia* was waiting obediently in its peaceful corner of the garage. Mark and Toni donned their gloves and put on the matching black helmets. They fit fine. On the way back towards Torri, Toni, ensconced on the *sozius* seat, hugged Mark tightly. She motioned for him to stop at a small mom-and-pop grocery store in a village north of their destination. She rushed in and returned shortly with two plastic bags full of edibles. Sliding onto her seat, she shouted, "Avanti!" and urged their steed to take to the pavement.

* * *

Unapologetic about using a prepared spaghetti sauce instead of making one from scratch, Toni's meal was fast, but eminently flavorful and satisfying. After clearing the table, they sat next to each other on the large leather sofa gazing first out the picture window at the sun setting over the mountains above the Val Sabbia behind the western shore of the lake. Mark built a small fire in the fireplace. They continued to sip *Brunello* while looking at some home videos featuring Luigi and his family. They took turns telling stories about Luigi and his humorous escapades; she invoking his childhood; he Luigi's college years in America. They shared lots and lots of laughs. The tone was merry and congenial. They made a splendid couple. A new wine bottle replaced the original. Toni told of her fiancé, an officer in the *Carabinieri*. Mark, avoiding mention of his own recent adventures, talked about his activities in the Carolina Low Country. This had been a busy day, a delightful day, but it was decided mutually it was time to retire.

After freshening up, they met in the hallway between their bedrooms. Toni told Mark how nice it was to finally meet the man her cousin had so often praised as a god. She embraced him suddenly, planted a big kiss on his lips and slipped into her bedroom, saying "*Buona Notte!*" Mark heard the lock on her door as it clicked shut. His mouth opened simultaneously with the raising of his eyebrows. He stood silently for a second, then entered his room and gently closed the door.

* * *

While early morning commercial traffic was humming busily on the lakeside road below 'Luigi's Lair', Mark, ever the early riser, prepares a fruit salad and sets the table for breakfast. Toni, freshly made-up and dressed for their outing, is blushing slightly as she approaches him. "I hope you weren't offended that I locked my door last night." Mark nodded a silent negative. Toni continued, "I wasn't concerned about keeping you out. I was actually locking myself in." They looked at each other, smiled warmly, and without another word, sat down to breakfast, realizing full well that fate was on their side and everything was just as it should be.

The *Aprilia* took them comfortably north along the lake to Riva. Toni showed Mark some of the sights. The sun had long since burned off the morning chill. They decided to lunch at a café adjacent to a boat dock at the edge of the lake. From there they easily found their way north towards Tenno with Toni's help. At the conclusion of the traditional mid-day pause for dinner and a catnap the day's work was resumed and traffic on the highway became somewhat more intense. The terrain was more mountainous than Mark had imagined. The scooter had enough power to negotiate the hills and curves. The air cooled considerably as they achieved more altitude.

Finally, at a fork in the road between steep hills, Toni directed Mark to turn right onto the access road to the monastery. They had passed several private dwellings, a couple of bed and breakfast inns with 'For Rent' signs and now on the corner was a small vegetable stand and convenience store. They continued up the hill to a wide plateau. Before them was the monastery.

Surrounded by a high wall, the monastery consisted of a small chapel and several other buildings constructed of stone, brick and concrete. An olive grove occupied the southeast corner of the grounds. Behind the main building was a large field, likely a garden, now under a thin blanket of snow. The hillside above the monastery was covered with neat rows of vines, patiently awaiting the advent of spring. The gated entrance was open. An off-road vehicle and a small Fiat were parked to one side of the chapel. Mark parked the *Aprilia* on the well-worn cobble stones next to the building's entrance.

Chapter Thirteen

Over the entrance to the monastery compound was a sign: *Convento San Vigilio*. Immediately beneath the name in much smaller iron letters the Italian phrase: "Comfort Every Sufferer". Both riders strode towards the door next to which was a small enamelled plate inscribed "*Ufficio*". Each had removed his helmet and was stretching arms and legs stiffened by the ride into a cold wind.

Inside the entrance they heard a male voice in a nearby office humming a popular Italian song. Peeking through the open door, they saw a monk in a dark brown cloak, its attached hood hanging on his back. He appeared to be organizing files in an old wooden cabinet. Hearing footsteps, the bushy-haired monk turned.

Toni spoke first. "*Buon Giorno, Signor*! My name is Antonia di Sogno. My companion, Professor Davidson, is an American who wants to make an inquiry about a patient here."

"*Buon Giorno!* I am Brother Benedetto, the abbot here. Welcome to *il Convento San Vigilio*. Visitation here, I regret to say, is most infrequent. Whom do you wish to see?" Brother Benedetto, mid-fifties, robust looking, friendly and outgoing, shook his visitors' hands cordially as he guided them to some chairs near his desk.

Mark, speaking English and looking to Toni to interpret for him, asked, "Is a Herr Tibor Székely living here? His son, Zdeněk, who lives in Zürich, asked me to stop by and visit with his father, if ever I should be in this area." Mark felt it wise not to mention that Zdeněk had died just a few weeks ago.

"Yes, I know Herr Zdeněk. He used to come every few weeks before

114

his father's senility worsened. Herr Tibor, alas, barely recognized him when he visited last summer. I wrote to Herr Zdeněk three weeks ago. It was, I regret to say, to inform him that his father had passed away. I have received no reply."

"We are sincerely sorry to learn of Tibor Székely's death." *This could complicate things,* Mark thought. "Were there burial expenses? I would be glad to pay them."

"Signor Tibor was dearly loved here by all the brothers. He was a kind and gentle man, a very gifted artist, and generous, very generous to the monastery. His gifts were more than adequate to defray all funeral expenses. Would you like to see his room?"

Mark was silent; still processing this unexpected turn of events. Toni spoke up, "*Grazie,* Fra Benedetto, we would be pleased to see his room." Realizing that Mark had come to obtain some information from Tibor, Toni added, "Did he leave any personal effects?"

"*Si,* follow me!"

The threesome exited Fra Benedetto's office. The door was left open. They walked down a long wooden-floored hallway and went through a wide, heavy door onto a covered portico. A large tiled courtyard with an inactive ornate fountain in the center separated this end of the convent from another larger section. The air nipped at their noses. At the end of the portico was another door leading into a hallway with numerous doors, most were at least partially open. They passed a few cloaked monks pushing elderly men in wheelchairs. Peering into a room here and there, Mark and Toni noticed bald and gray-haired men lying in bed or sitting quietly in wooden armchairs. Some were mumbling to themselves. In one room two men were playing checkers. All obviously patients, old, fragile, frail, waiting to die.

Fra Benedetto stopped in front of a room. He unlocked the door. Light was still coming through a window facing the southwest, although it was now afternoon and dusk waited impatiently for the sun to finish its descent below the mountains to the west. The furnishings were spartan. Besides a simple cot bed, there was a dresser, a wardrobe, a night stand, two wooden arm chairs and, in one corner, an artist's easel. On a wall facing the bed and the lone window was a rather large painting: a lake scene viewed from an elevated position. Rooftops could be seen in the foreground. Beyond was a lake cradled by rather high mountains. Done in oils, the painting was quite appealing, especially the treatment of late afternoon sunshine on the water and the mountain peaks.

In response to Mark's inquiry about documents Herr Tibor might have left behind, Fra Benedetto opened a drawer and laid a cardboard portfolio on the desk. "You may look at these," he said, heading for the door. "By the way, two men came here days after Herr Tibor's death and asked to see him. When told of his death, they wanted to take his belongings, but were told he left nothing. They complained, but left without incident. Oh, yes, you might want to know that Herr Tibor made that painting in his lucid days. Shortly after coming here he spent a week in Riva. While there, he painted several lake scenes. This one he gave to the monastery." The monk stepped into the hall, exchanged a few words with a passing colleague and receded back to his office.

Mark thumbed through the papers. "Nothing of great import," he said. "A couple of letters from his son, a certificate and letter upon his retirement, an out-dated passport and a few pencil sketches." Mark checked to see whether Tibor had a Soviet visa stamped in his passport. Indeed, he had visited Ukraine when Zdeněk said he had. *Swiss citizenship has its advantages.*

Toni was studying the painting. "I think I know approximately where he set his easel for this painting. It's been painted many, many times, by many artists, but this is particularly well done. Look, he signed it in the corner and dated it, too, I think."

In the lower right hand corner, Mark read: *T. Székely,* **AVIR** $_x$ **3825**. "The numbers don't make sense as a date," Mark mumbled. "I wonder what their significance might be?" Toni, who was checking the drawers in the nightstand, made no response. Memorizing the notation, Mark went back to the papers on the desk. He knew the notation was a code and that it was related to the one he'd found at the *Kollektiv*. He pretended it was of no interest or value. After another twenty minutes looking through the papers and checking other articles in the room, he suggested they return to Fra Benedetto's office.

They retraced their steps, noting that the sun was beginning to set and the moon was already inching up slowly on the horizon. Upon hearing them in the corridor, Fra Benedetto approached them. "Find anything worthwhile?" he asked.

"No." Toni volunteered. "Grazie! You were very kind to help us."

"I'm so sorry," replied the monk. "Your journey here has been in vain. Will you join me for a late afternoon snack? We have good bread, baked in our own ovens, fresh butter and *prosciutto*. Also, a fine red wine we produced in our vineyards."

Before Mark and Toni could respond, a young monk from a room across the hall poked his head in the door. "Fra Benedetto, telefono!" His voice and demeanor conveyed a sense of urgency. Fra Benedetto excused himself and followed the young monk. He returned a few minutes later.

"Brother Marcello has gone down to the little shop at the foot of the access road to purchase some food to supplement our humble fare. He says that the shopkeepers, Signora Frascati and her cousin, report that two strange men, possibly the ones who came here inquiring about Herr Székely, have been camping in a parking area on a small knoll nearby where several hiking trails begin. They can be seen from the store. They have been observed studying the monastery through binoculars. Activity there apparently picked up considerably about the time of your arrival earlier this afternoon."

Mark and Toni exchanged glances. *This is more than a coincidence,* Mark thought to himself. *Someone always seems to show up when I appear at one of the places Zdeněk told me to visit.* He kept the thought to himself, not wanting to alarm either Toni or the abbot.

"Mark, did you see anything here that will help you with your research?" Toni looked deep into Mark's eyes as she made her query.

"Possibly." He didn't want to come right out and tell her the letters and numbers under Tibor's signature could be significant, and he didn't want to lie to her.

"Well, we've done all we can do here, right?" Toni was temporarily lost in her thoughts. "Fra Benedetto, may I use your telephone?"

"Of course, *Signorina*! The one on the desk across the hall is an outside line."

Toni excused herself. Mark and Fra Benedetto speculated coldly about the strangers. Mark suspected they were up to no good. His conversation partner, not knowledgeable about Aja's tragic end, postulated several scenarios, all of which assigned harmless motives to the strangers and their actions.

Several minutes later, Toni burst into the room. "Mark give me your leather jacket! Fra Benedetto, could I have two old towels? Here's my plan." Both men, open mouthed, marvelled at her decisive, take-charge attitude. They listened intently.

"I'm very suspicious of these two strangers," she offered candidly. "Professor Davidson has fulfilled an obligation he undertook for a friend. There is no need to stay here any longer. I am going to leave on the scooter wearing his jacket and a helmet with a visor. The towels I'll stuff in the shoulders of the jacket."

"That's too dangerous," Mark interjected solicitously. "I can't let you do that!"

"It's all arranged. My fiancé, Vittorio, is a Captain in the *Carabinieri*. He's stationed in *Malcesine*. I'm assuming these strangers will follow me. When I reach *Riva*, two plainclothes officers on motorcycles and an unmarked police car will pick me up and follow at a slight distance. When I enter *Torbole*, they'll drop off and be replaced by *Carabinieri*, again two on motorcycles, two in a small off-road vehicle."

Mark was frowning. The abbot strained to understand Toni's British English.

"In *Malcesine*, I'll suddenly pull into the police headquarters' parking lot, which is just off the main road, and whoever is following me will be apprehended. In the meantime, perhaps one of the Brothers can get Mark to *Trento*. From there he can continue his trip."

"But…"

"No buts, Mark. This plan will work! Let's go before it gets any darker. If you leave here about fifteen minutes after I do, all should be O.K." She hastily recapped the conversation in Italian for Fra Benedetto's benefit, adding, "please call Fra Marcello and ask him to remain at the grocery store to report on the two strangers."

The monk, flushing slightly, was caught up in the excitement of the moment. His English was more competent than his visitors assumed. "Agreed. An excellent plan. Brother Angelo will drive you to *Trento*. He is our mechanic and our best driver."

Mark helped Toni fill out the leather jacket with the towels. In the twilight the black outfit and black-helmeted driver on the *Aprilia* could easily be taken for a male, for Mark. Mark hugged her, beseeching her to be careful and waved good-bye.

Shortly after her departure, Marcello called to confirm Toni's hunch that the mysterious pair would follow her. They were driving a dark-colored *Alfa Romeo* sedan. They were keeping a respectable distance behind her.

With the coast clear for his own departure, Mark donned a ski jacket Fra Benedetto gave him and slipped into a heavy brown monk's cloak. He pulled the hood up, threw his rucksack onto the back seat and Brother Angelo eased the off-road vehicle through the gate and onto the narrow winding road that would take them to *Riva*, then across the A22 *Autostrada* that connected the *Brennero* with *Verona*, finally through *Roveretto* and on to *Trento*, a major city in the *Alto Adige* region.

It was 5:30 in the afternoon. Two hours later, the rough, drafty ride was concluded. Mark had opted to try and catch a bus north to *Innsbruck*. According to Brother Angelo there were several departures every day. Should be one around 8:00 pm, he guessed. Sure enough, the next to last departure was scheduled to leave, half full, as it were, at 20:35; arrival in *Innsbruck* shortly before eleven pm.

In the rest room, Mark disrobed, squeezing the monk's robe into a sack Brother Angelo had brought for the purpose. The ski jacket, body in dark blue, sleeves and collar in red made Mark look and feel younger. He found a knit cap in the inside pocket and pulled it on at a jaunty angle. He carried his rucksack in his hand. Claiming a seat near the rear of the bus, Mark put his legs up and drifted off into dreamland, but not before reflecting on Toni's courageous act to divert attention from his departure. Aja's fate was also on his mind.

Chapter Fourteen

Consciously holding her speed in check, Toni managed to stay close behind a delivery truck also headed for *Riva*. She assumed the two strangers, who pulled out to follow her right after she passed the grocery store and made her turn onto the narrow highway leading to the largest community at the northern end of the lake, would be unlikely to overtake and attack her with other vehicles nearby. The roads in *Riva* were busy with what constituted evening rush hour in this laid-back "metropolis". The traffic signals presented an opportunity to assess her situation in the rear view mirror. So far, everything was going according to plan. At the second stop light, one motorcycle with a tall, muscular rider dropped behind the vehicle following her. Just as she turned south to drive through *Torbole*, she noticed a black *BMW* two-wheeler with *Verona* plates joining the flow from a side street on her right. A Jeep Wrangler pulled up behind the *BMW*.

As she left the town limits of *Torbole*, she detected two different cycles nonchalantly keeping tabs on the *Alfa Romeo*. A blue *Volvo*, possibly another unmarked car, came into view. It had cut into traffic from the left side a few cars behind her. The driver of the *Alfa* was wearing sunglasses in spite of the fact the sun was nearly over the horizon. The passenger was bald and had a cigarette dangling from his lips.

The nature of the highway, punctuated as it was with tunnels and blind curves, did not lend itself to passing or overtaking easily. Her tail had to content itself with reasonable proximity. There would be no possibility to force her motor scooter off the road, at least until they had left

Malcesine behind them. The two-lane, lakeside highway had essentially two directions: north or south.

From *Navene* to *Malcesine* Toni noted that the lakeside camping sites that were always so crowded in the summer vacation period, were now totally deserted. A strengthening breeze was crashing waves against the rocky shore below on her right. Approaching *Malcesine*, she glanced at the dials before her. Plenty of fuel left. She slowed slightly, although traffic did not require it. She was caught by the town's first traffic signal and rolled to a stop. On green, she proceeded smoothly. Suddenly, she banked sharply to the right, zoomed down a short hill, leaned to the left like a race rider, and pulled into the parking lot of *Carabinieri* headquarters. Captain Vittorio Albesano, waiting near the entrance to the building, spoke forcefully into the radio strapped to his left epaulet, "*Grazie,* Leoncarlo! Julio! Vittorio! Gianni! Apprehend them!"

Taken completely off-guard, the vehicle trailing Toni swerved to the right and began to follow. Her deft swing into the parking area and the prominent *Carabinieri* sign on the building combined to produce such a shock that the driver knocked off his shades and barrelled ahead, aiming to regain the lakeside highway south. Two motorcycles and three police vehicles took chase. The rapid acceleration of so many vehicles at once left a cloud of exhaust fumes hanging over the road. Blue lights and wailing sirens prompted oncoming traffic to pull over. Most of the oncoming traffic, that is. The *Alfa*, reaching speeds of 100 miles an hour between occasional heavy breaking to avoid immovable obstacles, evaded the police pursuit. Until it reached *Cassone*!

In *Cassone*, the highway retreats slightly from the lakeside. Below the highway some seven to eight meters, protected by a low stone wall at the edge of the highway and a huge wrought iron fence surrounding a few parking spaces below, was a row of three small bed and breakfast hotels clinging precariously to a plot of level land at the edge of the lake. All claimed four-star status. As the *Alfa* drew close to this point, the rear end of a tour bus loomed in front. The *Alfa* driver floored his accelerator, intending to pass the bus. In the same instant, an impatient truck driver coming from the south likewise wanted to pass a car in front of him. See-ing the truck mere meters from his front bumper, *Alfa*-man hit his brakes and attempted, unsuccessfully, to slide back behind the bus.

Later, officers, who had witnessed the accident, described how the *Alfa* had gone airborne, vaulted the low stone wall and performed a *salto mortale* onto the wrought-iron fence approximately seven meters below. They reported that hotel guests had become quite ill when, upon hearing the crash, they ran out to discover two men hanging upside down in their smashed vehicle. Both had been impaled on the sharply pointed spikes of the massive wrought-iron fence.

Calling from a booth outside the bus station in *Innsbruck*, Mark learned from Toni that neither man had been carrying any identification. The driver was wearing clothes manufactured in Russia. The passenger with the shaven head had a pair of shoes made in Germany. Thus far, no additional information had been generated. Toni's fiancé had sent their fingerprints and a request for information to Interpol.

The events of the day had left Mark physically and emotionally drained. Relieved that Toni was safe and her pursuers neutralized, per-manently at that, Mark found a small hotel in town, took the last room available, "the bridal suite" as he called it, because of the mirrors every-where, and fell asleep immediately.

* * *

The next morning, the luxury of a shave and hot shower was enjoyed to the maximum extent possible. Fortunately, Mark had enough clothes rolled neatly in his rucksack to present himself as a travelling academic again. A green turtleneck, a worn, but clean pair of jeans and clean socks and underwear. It was his last pair. *Better work in a shopping spree before I check out. I'll have to re-pack and I also need a new coat or jacket.* The sojourn on Lake Garda hadn't required any major expenditures, thus Mark knew he still had a sizeable amount left from Zdeněk's thoughtful and generous "travel allowance".

Continental breakfasts weren't actually Mark's preference, as he would normally opt for a more substantial morning meal. He came down to the *Frühstückszimmer* shortly before it was due to close. Two middle-aged *Hausfrau* types were sipping their coffee and two young people Mark pegged as university students on early break were surreptitiously preparing sandwiches for a snack on the way to the slopes. The cold cuts and cheese, the *Brötchen*, butter and preserves that had not been claimed found their way onto Mark's plate. He helped himself to two small glasses of orange juice. A kitchen helper brought him a steaming pot of coffee and a hard-boiled egg. Having decided to take his time, Mark enjoyed his repast, all the while mulling over and over in his mind the letters and numbers he had retrieved both from the *Kollektiv* and the monastery.

Thinking quietly as he tanked up for another busy day, Mark thought to himself, *Tibor, as smart as he was, was an unlikely crypto-grapher. He would certainly want to keep any code he might use relatively easy for himself to remember, and not necessarily impossible for others to decipher. Therefore, a simple, almost childishly simple code would involve the substitution of letters for numbers. Perhaps even in rudimentary A, B, C, 1, 2, 3 order. Or, quite possibly, reversed.* He had picked up a pen in his room and was about to write on his paper napkin the letters and numbers he had found. *This is not the place to make a stupid mistake. I'll work on this later.* He finished his breakfast and left, nodding to the waitress, while mouthing a quiet "Danke schön!"

The *Goldenes Dachl*, or golden roof, Innsbruck's beacon to visitors, was a substantial tourist draw, even on a cool winter day. Mingling with the strolling out-of-towners, Mark dropped in and out of several of the shops in the area adding to his wardrobe for the next phase of his odys-sey. The familiar double arches of a McDonald's were spotted on *Herzog-Friedrich-Strasse.* Casual observation suggested they were effectively luring a steady stream of people with a hunger for hamburgers. For just an instant, Mark thought about going in for a double cheeseburger. *Never can tell whom you might run into in a place like that.* The idea was promptly rejected. Instead, he detoured a few blocks for some exercise on the way back to his hotel. Along the way he frequently checked, as had become his habit, to determine if he was being followed.

A small storefront *Reisebüro* across the street caught his eye. In the left window he saw a display of ski boots, skis and poles. In the right hand window was a model of a cruise ship with a Caribbean poster behind it. He went in. His next destination had to be *Vevey* in order to fulfill his promise to Zdeněk. Radio reports before breakfast discouraged highway travel through Switzerland. Mark knew the main roads were generally clear. Regardless, he felt that flying to *Bern*, then going to *Lake Geneva* by car was best. He purchased the ticket. In spite of the inconvenient routing through Vienna, the flight would obviate a long drive. His afternoon would be devoted to further thought about the account numbers and some risk assessment, now that four of Gregor's cronies had been eliminated. Mark posed a question, *Are there more?*

What about this "promise" to Zdeněk, Mark wondered to himself. *Is a hastily made commitment, a "promise", made to a person who is, when you think of it, a stranger, actually valid? I know I grew up in a family where personal integrity, giving one's word, was a cornerstone of character, but....*

Waking up only moments later after the most restful thirty-second nap he could recall, Mark's brain cells became suddenly hyperactive. *Yes, yes, that's got to be it. The subscript and superscript x's are intended to indicate that either the words or the numbers are supposed to be exchanged. Each then still gives a total of ten digits. The difference is that the numerical dates now make sense. Thus, we have Lene's, Tibor's wife's, birth date and the approximate date of what must have been Tibor's first visit to* Riva. *The words RIVA and LENE were merely written backwards. Now, how am I going to work this out at the bank?* Mark closed his eyes again.

The window of Mark's room faced west. Afternoon sunshine warmed his face and woke him. The thought that accompanied him as he fell asleep was still on his mind as he rolled out of bed to splash some cool water on his face. *Got it!* he smiled into the mirror. *Gordon will know what I should do.*

Gordon, the European name he chose for himself before going off to the States for college, was another of Mark's college buddies. Hui Chen-Li hailed from Hong Kong. He came from a large, well-connected family, influential in Hong Kong's social, economic and political circles. Gordon's father, a world-famous surgeon, owned one of the Colony's most prestigious private hospitals. Deep mutual trust had developed between them when Mark saved Gordon's life in a boating accident on a lake near the campus. The two of them had collaborated to organize numerous all-night tutorials for Luigi, without which the happy-go-lucky Italian might not have graduated. Now 34, Gordon was an influential banker and business leader in his home town.

On the way to find a quiet restaurant for dinner, Mark stopped at the post office just before closing time to place a call to Gordon. It was midnight in the East Asian colony. Gordon was still up. Flabbergasted to hear Mark's voice, Gordon's manner, inscrutable to some, became curiously serious. How to handle secret accounts? Possibly a large sum of money? Where to keep it secure until Mark could decide what further steps might be necessary? Gordon's curiosity was definitely aroused. After some discussion, Gordon recommended transferring control of the accounts to his bank for possible dispersal to safe havens in Mark's name, should he choose to do so. Mark should then fly to Hong Kong to take possession of the appropriate documentation. Mark agreed and made note of the procedures to follow to effect smooth transfer of all funds. A specific timetable for the completion of the technical aspects of Gordon's recommendation couldn't be made. Mark wasn't sure exactly when he would get to *Vevey*, how soon he could make arrangements at the bank there, and when he might reach Hong Kong. Then, too, there was Gregor to worry about. Mark wondered to himself, *What would he do now without his cronies to help him?* It was decided that Gordon should wait for Mark to contact him further.

Gulyas and *Tokayer* with pleasant zither music in the background in a cozy Hungarian restaurant, *Das Zigeuner Paradies*, seemed a fitting tribute to Tibor Székely's heritage. Mark finished off a huge plate and raised his glass to an invisible companion: "I shall not forget the source of these accounts," he whispered.

Only the waiter noticed this imaginary toast. "Möchten Sie noch etwas, mein Herr?"

"Nein, danke. Zahlen, bitte." Mark was eager to settle up, get a good night's rest and proceed to Lake Geneva.

Chapter Fifteen

In what might be termed casual business dress, Mark boarded an Austrian Airlines flight to *Bern*. Unavoidably, many of AUA's flights first go to its Viennese hub before continuing to the desired final destination. The stopover in Vienna was mercifully brief. Mark passed the time in the terminal and on board reading a news magazine and a few pages from a newspaper he purchased at an airport kiosk. He managed to discourage conversation with his fellow passengers, preferring to be as inconspicuous as possible. *How different,* he reflected, *from that flight to New York in October, when I sat next to Sister Catherine. I hope and pray that everything has gone smoothly for her in Hong Kong. Maybe I'll see her again, if I get to go there.*

Although these intra-European hops were relatively short, and in spite of his lack of a large piece of luggage that required checking, it was well into the afternoon by the time Mark made arrangements for a rental car in *Bern*. This time it was a SEAT, a Spanish VW the clerk told him. Smooth shifting and peppy in traffic, *and not likely to attract undue attention,* Mark thought, as he aimed his silver sedan in the direction of the east end of Lake Geneva on highway number 12. He only had to cover about a hundred twenty kilometers, so he drove at a moderate speed, not wishing to arrive too early.

Negotiating the streets of *Vevey* was a cinch. The city was smaller than he expected. He dropped off his 'Spanish VW' at the rental agency in town. In *Bern*, he had specified *Geneva* airport as the drop-off point. The clerk in *Vevey*, a harsh-looking woman, probably in her forties, was on the verge of creating a scene, claiming a fee was required because the agency would have to transport the vehicle to *Geneva*. Mark capitulated without a fuss, paid the fee with his *EuroKarte*, and exited the agency in haste. He walked down a hill a couple of blocks, looked to his right, saw what looked like a vacancy sign on a small hotel and homed in on the sign, which grew dimmer and dimmer as the sun set over the lake and the mountains to the north and west.

A reluctance on the part of the stooped figure behind the counter in the hallway that represented the hotel's lobby to utter any language but French, forced Mark to resurrect his college *Français*. Undismayed by the clerk's negative facial expressions, Mark was pleased that his accent sounded reasonably authentic. *Madame Perreaux, my old French teacher, would have given me an A-, or at least a B+, Bien sûr!*

* * *

Up early the next morning as was his habit, Mark was systematically walking the streets of *Vevey*. His olfactory nerve detected a hint of chocolate in the air. The priority today was to locate a used clothing outlet. In a shop with a hand-printed sign in the window at the end of a deserted street, that was half residences and half undistinguished street-level shops, Mark found exactly what he was seeking. He eagerly stuffed his purchases into two old paper sacks. On the way back to the hotel his mind raced at double speed. *Yes! He would go to the bank this very day*, he concluded.

Mark alternately munched on an apple he had taken from a basket in the lobby and applied make-up from his ever-present theatrical kit. He put on a wig that sent thick gray locks down the back of his head and over his ears and sideburns. Careful shading made his nose look larger and his eyes older and more deep set. The dark brown trousers, worn knees and shiny seat rather prominent, were held up with suspenders. Over this he put on a brown tweed sport jacket in a hounds-tooth pattern. It was about three sizes too large and had worn leather elbow patches. Taking a cue from Toni's disguise, he had pinned a towel inside the rear of the jacket to suggest a physical deformity. A Greek sailor's cap in dark navy blue, Mark's favorite headgear, and a pair of well-scuffed boots completed his *tour de couture*. Discarding the leather valise he had arrived with the day before, he crammed his belongings into a large plastic bag he had liberated from a trash receptacle on his way back to the hotel. On the dresser next to the valise, Mark left a Fifty-Franc note to cover his bill. The most difficult decision involved his rucksack. Considering it 'out of character', Mark sadly left it behind.

The hotel clerk was answering the phone in the lobby, when Mark noiselessly passed by on his way out. The clerk looked up to see the door close and an elderly man limping his way down the street. He shrugged and continued his conversation.

Mark was anxious to give his disguise a test. He stopped at a small *croissanterie* and ordered a *"croque monsieur et un jus d'orange, s'il vous plaît."* He paid when his sandwich arrived. The waiter seemed not to take any particular notice of him and Mark was quite pleased.

In the telephone directory Mark had checked the street address for the *Banque sociale de Léman*, the institution where Tibor had his numbered accounts. The bank was uniquely situated at the narrow end of an oddly shaped plot of land that formed an elongated scalene triangle. The front of the building featured a stately classical façade on a broad avenue near the lakeshore. The building was also accessible from the rear where it backed up to a smaller, one-way commercial road. A shallow parking area and an entrance for bank personnel was found in the rear. Off to one side was a huge trash bin, dumpster-like in appearance, hidden from view by large shrubs strategically placed on three sides.

After the customary noon business recess honored universally by traditional banks, but before the early mid-afternoon closing time that often irks Americans seeking banking services in Europe, a down-and-out senior citizen stood for a few minutes on a corner a block away from the bank. He waited patiently, leaning on his walking stick, while his faithful dog, a Yorky pup that had not protested being named Foux-Foux a short while earlier, when it had been liberated from a cage in a pet shop, applied liquid fertilizer to a small plot of grass in front of a building that seemed to house a legal aid society. Unobtrusively glancing up and down the broad avenue with sidewalks on both sides, the elderly man appeared to scratch his short, bristly, salt and pepper beard before signalling with a gentle tug on the leash that it was time to move on. He scooped up his tiny pup, crossed the avenue somewhat gingerly, limping and steadying himself with his cane. Once across on the bank's side of the street, he set Foux-Foux down. The latter insisted on checking every one of the trees and poles en route, as dogs are wont to do.

The beard was scratched again. It was itchy and the gum arabic was irritating its bearer's skin. The elderly gentleman had made note of a black *Mercedes* strategically parked to obtain maximum surveillance of the bank's entrance, which involved an imposing staircase spanning the entire width of the building. The dog lover gauged there were approximately fifteen steps. When he reached the steps, he stopped, coughed into a handkerchief, picked up the Yorky and, carrying it under his left arm, painfully negotiated the stairs, seemingly struggling to open the heavy glass entrance door.

Inside the building, the pup was gently placed on the floor. *Le Vieil* pretended to search for something in his jacket pocket. Thus engaged, he discreetly looked back to ascertain whether the lone figure in the *Mercedes* was stirring. Nothing! He emitted a soft sigh.

A second set of heavy glass doors was traversed. Here on the right was a rich walnut reception desk with accents of glass and stainless steel in a lobby that was eerily silent. The marble floor was accented with a thick hand-made Finnish carpet, the walls had attractive fabric art extending well up towards the ceiling in the two-story high foyer. An attractive woman behind the reception desk asked politely in French, if she could be of assistance. Responding slowly in his flawed French, the man indicated that he wanted to access his accounts. The receptionist pressed a key on her intercom and asked for Mme Chounard. That wonderful evening at the opera with Sister Catherine immediately popped into his mind. *Strange*, he mused, *how he always prefaced her name with Sister.*

Through the large glass doors there emerged a neatly attired woman.

She was probably no older than 35, short, well fed, wearing a wine-red dress. She introduced herself as Mme Chounard and, not recognizing him as a regular client of the bank, inquired what type of account he had and under what name it was registered. The client drifted away from the desk, gazing absently at a copy of a Greek statue on the opposite side of the lobby. When he felt he was out of earshot of the receptionist, he moved closer to Mme Chounard, who had wandered with him, thinking him to be an eccentric, for whom she might need to call security. In a half whisper, he said that his were numbered accounts. He would like to speak privately to the manager.

Mme Chounard asked him if he would mind leaving his dog with the receptionist. The old timer limped over to the desk and looped the leash around a post behind it. With a gesture, he reassured the receptionist, who was already petting the pup, that it would behave until he returned. She, for her part, was fascinated by the gentleman's heavy eyebrows and bushy salt and pepper beard.

Escorted beyond the third set of doors, the client huffed and puffed as he followed the stocky young woman down a long hallway. In front of a door that led to a number of smaller rooms from which there emanated typical office clatter and the glow of innumerable computer monitors, the client was asked to take a seat on an upholstered bench that was placed there. After a few minutes, that seemed much, much longer in the silence that reigned in the long hall, a woman in a fashionable, probably very expensive, tailored two-piece gray suit strode gracefully out of the office complex and approached him. She extended her hand saying, "*Bonjour, je suis Mademoiselle d'Entremont.*" The elderly client, leaning on his cane, rose slowly, ostensibly favoring bones aching from the ravages of age, grasped her hand meekly and mumbled, "Jean LeClair", a name that just leapt effortlessly from his lips; an act of complete spontaneity. Mlle d'Entremont was a lovely woman. Her skin, the color and texture of honey, possibly not from exposure to the sun, was marvellously smooth in appearance. She wore no lipstick; actually needed none, so naturally red were her lips. Her dark brown hair was combed back neatly in a kind of bun. She was wearing gold rimmed glasses. Behind them were dark eyes that searched his soul. She was wearing medium high heels and her height was about 5' 6". She was the epitome of professionalism.

"You have numbered accounts with us, Mme Chounard has told me, is that correct?"

Something about this woman is strangely familiar. The client struggled to place her. *"Oui, Mademoiselle."*

Still speaking the most mellifluous and seductive French he had ever heard, Mlle d'Entremont asked the gentleman to follow her. Another lengthy walk down one hall, around the corner and down another hall to a small elevator. Mademoiselle pressed the number three. The man accompanying her had observed, when approaching the bank, that it had four floors. The third floor would be the top floor, as Europeans figured it. Mlle d'Entremont did not speak, but had a most enigmatic smile.

What is it about her? No answer was forthcoming.

The halls were done in hardwood parquet. Each was covered with a custom woven Persian runner in rich hues of red and blue. Doors to the rooms they passed were heavily carved wood with huge brass handles. Mark recognized some of the artwork covering the halls as originals, mostly modern, by renowned artists. Thinking it unbefitting his current persona, the client tried not to stare at Mlle d'Entremont's shapely figure and gorgeous legs as she led the way. Near what would be the right rear corner of the building, she unlocked a door and invited him to enter.

The room was large. It looked like a room set aside for board meetings. In the center was a huge mahogany conference table sitting on a magnificent hand-woven carpet. Ten leather armchairs were placed around it; one at each end, four on either side. At the end nearest the door was a handsome burled walnut credenza, apparently an antique. A silver bowl was in the middle, a silver candlestick on either side. A huge portrait in oil in a handsome gold frame, no one the client recognized, hung above the credenza. He was ushered to a seat at the rear of the room. Behind him was a second oil painting in an elaborate gilt wooden frame. It represented an historic battle scene with rearing horses, a panoply of fluttering military banners and the glint of myriad flashing swords. There was sufficient blood and gore depicted to nullify any glory the artist might have intended to imply. Mark felt rather insignificant, given the over-sized oil painting behind him. Mlle d'Entremont stood beneath the portrait above the credenza. "Monsieur Renard, the Director of the bank, will join us momentarily. Is there anything I can bring you, **Dr. Davidson**?"

Mark didn't know whether to hyperventilate, utter a cry of relief that he no longer had to continue the ruse, or bolt for the door. "I, I, I, how did......???"

Taking off her glasses and involuntarily sporting the smile of a cat that has just surprised a mouse with one paw on the cheese, she gently let her hair down. Her light olive skin was framed by soft, luxuriant, brunette curls hanging to shoulder length. Mark's eyes were glued to her lovely countenance. Continuing in French-accented English, she said, "Please forgive me. Your disguise is truly outstanding. If we hadn't been expecting you, we might never have guessed your identity." Her enchanting smile was inextinguishable.

Mark blurted, "**The café in Zürich!** You were the... *are* the woman with the unforgettable smile, those wondrous eyes. You disappeared so quickly. I looked back to see where you had gone, but..."

"I know. I was hiding behind another patron." She smiled.

"But, I don't quite understand the connection."

"Here at the bank we have had a very special relationship with Herr Tibor Székely and his son, Zdeněk." She paused. "I hear Jean-Luc, ahh Monsieur Renard, coming. I will let him explain everything."

Renard was a prematurely balding forty-seven. He made no effort to conceal a slight paunch. His banking uniform was international in nature, blue pin-striped suit, white shirt, conservative tie, light blue with a few silver accents. He came down the room towards Mark and held out his hand. Mark's firm grip was obviously not that of an aging senior citizen.

"Elli, that is, Mademoiselle d'Entremont, has told me about you. We are glad that you have finally arrived. Where have you been for the past two months? I believe it was in late November when Herr Székely called to ask Mlle d'Entremont to come to Zürich to see you in person, in the eventuality your identity required corroboration."

"Well, I've been collecting the information required to claim the two numbered accounts in accordance with Herr Székely's, that is, Herr Zdeněk Székely's instructions. There were some difficulties and impediments along the way." Mark coughed slightly. "Including some attempts on my life."

Elli had moved to a chair on Mark's left opposite Jean-Luc. She looked at Jean-Luc, who was fascinated with the rumpled appearance of his guest, a guest who did not appear to belong in the board room of a large Swiss bank. Jean-Luc acknowledged the glance. "Dr. Davidson," he began, "before we continue I will need to have the two account numbers."

Mark asked for a piece of paper. Elli produced one from the credenza. Mark printed the two ten-digit codes from memory in large block numbers on the sheet of paper.

* * *

2437122918   5145123825

* * *

Jean-Luc studied them, then asked to be excused for a moment. When he returned, he was carrying a *Leitz Ordner*. Opening the thick file, he matched the numbers Mark had given him with some in his file. He pushed back his chair, stood ceremoniously and again held out his hand.

"Elli has verified that you are Dr. Mark Davidson, whom Zdeněk wished her to see personally. These numbers match perfectly those on the two accounts. Dr. Davidson, you are a rich man! Far richer, I suspect, than you might ever have imagined."

"Well, how much money is there in these accounts?" It seemed like a logical inquiry. Mark blushed, however, embarrassed at his display of interest in the money. His raw curiosity had trumped his usual class.

"If I may, let me recount the history of these funds. You may have been told by Herr Zdeněk that his father was catapulted by fate into the directorship of a major bank in Zürich not long after WW II. He discovered several secret accounts that had been established early in the war by government officials and military figures operating in parts of Subcarpathian Ruthenia, Eastern Slovakia and Eastern Hungary. No one came forth to claim the monies. The banks deceased directors had excluded the accounts in question from all bank records. There was no official explanation for this action. Why they did so is a matter for speculation. Herr Tibor devoted much time and effort, also personal expense, seeking to learn the exact sources of the funds.

While he ultimately assumed they came from looted bank accounts, stolen property, the illegal sale of *objets d'art* and monies extorted from persons 'unwelcome' in those areas, he produced no concrete evidence to that effect." Jean-Luc paused for a minute, before continuing. "Herr Tibor had little faith in his own government or any international organization to return these monies to those from whom they had presumably been taken. Nor did he fancy that the various schemes broached publicly regarding other unclaimed booty would be a satisfactory solution. He believed the dilemma he faced could only be resolved by extraordinary means. He founded, together with a small group of friends, the *Banque sociale de Léman*. Its initial reserves included these funds. He transferred them here."

"Did no one know about them?" Mark was attempting to comprehend.

"My grandfather, you see his portrait there," he pointed to the oil above the credenza, "was the first General Director of this bank. He was a *confidante* of Herr Tibor. His successor was my uncle, Monsieur Francke, my mentor. They had to be privy to the information. They were sworn to secrecy. When my uncle died fifteen years ago, I was promoted and likewise sworn to secrecy. Herr Tibor's son, Zdeněk had a rather wild and rebellious youth. Perhaps he has told you. He constantly disappointed his father with his escapades and scrapes with the law. It is true, that as he grew older he settled down and became a respected banker himself. However, while he did reconcile with his father, Herr Tibor stipulated in his will that Zdeněk could not inherit or gain control over these funds. Herr Tibor, realizing that senility was gradually robbing him of his reason, did acquiesce somewhat, however. He charged his son with the responsibility of searching for and finding a person, or an organization that would discover the account numbers and, most importantly, would oversee the charitable use of the accumulated resources. You are that person."

Following a brief pause, Renard continued. "My reason for relating this story of the bank's origin and of my family's role is to impress on you the intimate connection between Herr Székely senior, his son, and the present management of the bank. We have always taken great pride in our stewardship of all the funds invested with us, regardless of size. It should be clear to you, nevertheless, that our relationship with the Székelys transcends ordinary banking arrangements. I hope you understand what I am trying to tell you."

Mlle d'Entremont listened very intently, looking alternately at Renard and Mark. She had developed a crush on Mark when she first saw him in Zürich. He was *simpatico*. His sudden wealth, the shear magnitude of it, she recognized as a potential complicating factor in her life.

Mark slipped off his wig and peeled off the beard. He took off his tweed jacket. Standing, he was tall, erect, strong. The remaining make-up could not conceal his handsome features. He looked first at Monsieur Renard, then at Mlle d'Entremont. "I still do not understand fully, why I, Mark Davidson, am here. I cannot begin to grasp the ramifications of what has happened. This may be the most humbling moment of my life. I can only promise to do my best."

"I still haven't answered your question," Renard interjected. "You wanted to know how much money was involved. That's understandable. Perhaps you should sit down again. It is impossible to be absolutely accurate, because these accounts grow literally by the second. At Herr

Tibor's direction, two accounts were created. One of these has been an investment account that includes stocks, mutual funds, precious metals, bonds, real estate holdings, negotiable securities and a variety of other liquid assets. I supervise this account which is split into over a dozen sub-accounts managed by specialists in seven different countries. I estimate its value at well over 7.5 billion dollars." Mark blinked. Renard continued. "The other account evolved into a holding company. You have probably never heard of *White Cross Holdings*. It owns all, or a substantial portion of, or controlling interest in large-cap, mid-cap and small-cap companies on six continents. You will automatically become the General Director of the holding company, presently worth, on paper mind you, somewhere in the vicinity of 29 billion dollars. A most striking example of the growth of money through careful investing and compounding."

Mark took a deep breath. "Your patience and kindness are exemplary. We have just met and I cannot tell you how impressed I am with both of you. You have undoubtedly not heard yet of the deaths of both Herr Tibor, who died of natural causes in his hospice in Italy, and Herr Zdeněk, who died at his home, ostensibly of a heart attack, as I was told by his nephew, Gregor." Renard and Mlle d'Entremont, gasping, were both visibly shaken by the news. Mark continued, "Frankly, I don't really know, if I should be grateful or fearful of the honor that has been bestowed on me. I beg you not to take personally what I am about to propose. I will do everything in my power to insure that your bank does not suffer. A very dear and trusted friend of mine, a person, who like you, has a wealth of knowledge of banking and investments, has advised me to transfer, on a temporary basis, control of all funds to my account in his bank until I decide best how to deal with them." Mark paused. He looked at Renard and Mlle d'Entremont.

"I intend to fulfill Herr Tibor's wishes," he went on, "but I need some time to think through an appropriate policy, as well as the vehicles necessary to accomplish it. I hope you will understand. I wish in no way to show either of you or your colleagues any disrespect or ingratitude. The *Banque sociale* will continue, of course, to receive its customary fees and commissions until I've decided on a final plan of action." Having spoken, Mark looked at both again and awaited a response.

Chapter Sixteen

Jean-Luc and Elli both expressed shock upon learning that the Székelys had died. If Jean-Luc was hurt by Mark's proposal, he masked his feelings well. Elli understood that Mark would want to move swiftly to take control over the assets involved. She admired his decisiveness, his tact and his commitment to abide by Herr Tibor's wishes.

"I understand and I have no objection," offered Jean-Luc, speaking reassuringly in a calm voice.

"It is a natural thing you do," Elli added. She looked at her watch. It was almost four. "We close at three on weekdays. Usually, we have completed our bookkeeping and other tasks by four. I must confer for a few minutes with the staff. Please excuse me."

"Oh my! I forgot all about the dog!" Mark felt embarrassed that he had neglected Foux-Foux.

On her way out the door, Elli stopped, looked back, and said, "Don't worry. I asked Mme Chounard to look after her. It's a female, you know. She may take it home to her nieces and nephews, if you have no objection."

"None. That would be great." Mark was pleased such an easy solution was found so readily.

Jean-Luc interrupted, "I will prepare for the transfers. There are a few key documents to sign. The electronic transfers will occur first thing in the morning. I will need the name of the bank in Hong Kong, the designation of your master account there, and the name of your contact at the bank."

"Why don't you come down to Jean-Luc's office?" Elli was still standing near the door. "Marie, Jean-Luc's secretary, is waiting to assist you. I'll join you in a few minutes."

Mark brought up the rear, as all three left to complete their tasks. With the help of his diligent and efficient secretary, Monsieur Renard completed within an hour the documents required to authorize transfer of Mark's liquid assets to the *Senghai-Macao Banking Corp.*

Elli, her beautiful brown hair framing the exquisite features of a face no plastic surgeon could ever emulate, entered the office. "Herr Bergmann, our security officer, has seen a suspicious vehicle circling our block several times. The street behind us is a one-way thoroughfare. The car, he says, drives by slowly and the driver, a rather tall man, appears to be studying our rear entrance. Because the bank is closed now, there is no client traffic at the main entrance."

"That could be Gregor Mukhachevo, Herr Zdeněk's aide. Herr Zdeněk was afraid of him. I was told he read some of the private papers from Herr Zdeněk's safe and was aware of these numbered accounts, although he was not familiar with any particulars."

"Should we be concerned?" Jean-Luc chimed in. "We could call the police."

"There is no question that Gregor is dangerous. I know for a fact, four of his cronies are dead. They were responsible for the death of a woman who helped me in Slovakia. I think I can elude him."

The mention of death definitely struck a note with Elli. "No, wait. I have the solution." Elli inspired confidence. Without soliciting agreement, she reeled off commands like a lieutenant in the field preparing to storm an enemy position. She quickly dispensed with the formality of titles. "Jean-Luc, let Mark borrow some clothing items from your closet! Mark, wash off your make-up in the rest room! Take Jean-Luc's clothes and change! I'm going to leave by the rear entrance when some of the other staff members depart. Jean-Luc will also leave. Your 'Gregor' will think he simply missed you. Then, I'll return in twenty minutes, pull into the parking area, where you will be hiding behind the dumpster. When you're in the car, we'll head into the hills."

"Into the hills?" Mark wasn't sure, whether this was just an expression or something meant to be understood literally.

"Yes, my sister Dani and her husband have a villa north of *Lausanne*. They are away in America on a combination business/pleasure trip. I am house-sitting for them. It's the perfect place to go."

Jean-Luc nodded. "Good plan. Be careful!"

Still processing the information about the incredible sum of money for which he was now responsible, Mark's countenance bore the vacant stare of someone striving to conceal his intoxication. He looked into Elli's dark eyes. His heart fluttered and turned to marshmallow. *How could one not trust anyone so sweet and charming?* "OK, I'm game. I'll be ready in a minute."

Mme Chounard, waiting in the rear lobby for the planned exodus, had difficulty keeping her eyes off Mark. She observed how Mark and Elli frequently looked at each other, not realizing how deeply Mark had been impressed by this remarkable woman when he first saw her beautiful eyes in the *Stehimbiss* in Zürich. Her smile then spoke volumes. In retrospect, cupid's arrow had struck him in that momentary exchange of glances. Could it be possible? Mme Chounard felt a tinge of jealousy. She was attractive too. Why didn't he see that? She studied him carefully. "Here's a real man," she thought. "Polite, courteous, masculine without any necessity to run about flexing his muscles and thumping his chest. If rumors are correct, he may also be quite rich." Her eyes undressed him. Without his make-up she admired his handsome face. "I need a man like this more than Elli," was the banner-like message whirling through her brain.

Only Renard, Elli and, to a lesser extent, Marie, Jean-Luc's private secretary, knew the whole story of the secret accounts. Nevertheless, there had been silent rumors spread for years. Because the staff was so well treated, there was a universal reluctance to bring up the issue. Many a person, however, had wondered to himself, how a small local bank could occasionally wield such financial clout well beyond the immediate community.

Elli, wearing a stylish coat, left in her vehicle, together with three female members of the staff, each driving alone in separate vehicles. Just as she had said, she returned in twenty minutes. No other traffic was visible on the vacant street behind the bank. She drove a *VW GTI*. It was red in color and made a throaty sound as she throttled down and turned neatly into the parking area. The passenger door flew open and Mark jumped in. He was wearing Jean-Luc's tan raincoat and a matching hat with a plastic rain cover. He had discarded his dark-rimmed glasses. Elli looked twice. He seemed even taller and more handsome now.

With one hand on the wheel and the other on the shift lever, Elli propelled her 'rocket' forward and joined the busy afternoon traffic. Not long after, she spoke. "Uh oh! A black *Mercedes* is tailing us. It's two blocks back. How did he pick us up so quickly? Hang on, we're going to see what kind of a driver he is."

What Jean-Luc knew and didn't mention in the office as Elli spelled out her plan, was that she had a spiritual kinship with two Formula I drivers from her mother's homeland, Brazil. Indeed, Nelson Piquet and Ayrton Senna would have been proud of her skill behind the wheel. She went north, skirting the foothills of *Mt. Pèlerin*. The vines on the surrounding slopes, through which Elli maneuvered corniche fashion, were bare. She knew the roads well. Doubling back and descending to the old road between *Vevey* and *Lausanne*, Elli sped toward the latter. Luck was on her side. She managed to make virtually every traffic signal and was able to execute 'California stops' at every stop sign. Still, the black *Mercedes* eventually returned to maintain the pressure. The sun was setting and visibility ahead was less problematic.

Chapter Seventeen

Mark had no idea where they were or where they were going. Elli was concentration personified. Mark had little choice but to trust implicitly her knowledge of the roads and her ability to handle the sprightly *GTI*. From the changing position of the sun Mark was able to discern they were now heading south. He caught himself holding his breath a few times. He didn't have to look to realize his knuckles were snow white. His grip on the door handle was unbreakable. It was necessary to reduce speed shortly before Elli turned onto a corniche road that was north of the main highway connecting *Montreux* to *Geneva*. Mark turned and looked behind them. The driver of the car in pursuit was taking advantage of a paucity of traffic on the access road Elli had just taken to steer with his right hand and to shoot with his left.

"Watch out! He has a gun and he's shooting at us!" Mark, looking back, was alarmed.

A spark on the right side of the hood just as Elli made a sharp right hand turn prompted a concerned exchange of glances. They had become targets. Another bullet whizzed past. Elli accelerated and pulled quickly into the passing lane. Two of the vehicles she passed sounded their horns angrily. A phalanx of heavy traffic ahead threatened to bring the *GTI* to a screeching halt. Elli let the vehicles in front of them run interference, then like a fullback slicing through a narrow opening in the line, she boldly gained a more comfortable separation from the persistent tail. Mark had determined it had to be Gregor. Zdeněk had named four possible accomplices. Four had been eliminated. If his math was correct, Gregor was now doggedly working solo.

Lausanne was coming up fast. Without warning, Elli ducked onto an exit ramp and roared down off the highway into the early evening melange that characterizes every vital, lively city, regardless of location. Lausanne was no exception. The evening rush hour was in full swing. Mark's admiration for his gifted driver was boundless. She darted and dodged her way in and out of dozens of streets, avoiding the most congested, finding those that allowed faster movement. Doubling back on occasion, she employed every trick she could think of to separate the GTI from the Mercedes. *This woman has nerves of steel.* Mark was reluctant to distract his pilot. "You certainly know your way around Lausanne," he ventured, while they waited for a light to change.

"I went to school here. I read economics at the University in Basel. When I had worked at the bank for three years, I was given a leave of absence to attend IMD here in Lausanne."

"IMD? It doesn't ring a bell. If you know what I mean?"

"*The International Institute for Management Development.* It's actually world famous. I earned my MBA there. In Finance and Banking."

"I'm impressed. You're a woman of many talents." Elli was illuminated by the street lamps and the headlights of oncoming traffic, which had temporarily become rather dense. Mark stared at her profile. "So young, so talented and so beautiful."

"Don't get fresh, Professor Davidson" A certain irony was detectable in her voice. She had a faint smile, but looked straight ahead. To Mark's right was a large, forested park. He was trying to make out some of the signs. "*Sacre bleu!*" Lips pursed, chin jutting out, Elli was looking into her rear view mirror. "Pardon my French. I don't want to believe it, but..."

"The Mercedes again?"

"Yes! It has Zürich plates. It must be him!"

The GTI had worked its way systematically north as Elli executed numerous detours and cutbacks, and was now passing through a more residential area in the hills above the city. Traffic thinned. Mark saw extensive plantings of vines. Hedgerows of tall shrubs divided many of the vineyards. The area was dotted with houses tucked in between rows ands rows of sleeping grape vines. The sun had set and dusk was transitioning to dark. The highway was virtually empty. A new moon reduced visibility. Elli checked her gas gauge. Her eyebrows rose. Mark noticed. He sensed some ultra fast calculations were underway.

Elli's control of the *GTI*, especially around corners was enviable. Mark also enjoyed driving fast. The double nickel limits at home put a crimp in his preferred driving style. Then, too, as a college official, he felt pressure to observe all the rules and signs religiously, lest he create an inadvertent scandal. If he were honest, he thought, he would have to concede, Elli was a superior driver. The MB had temporarily disappeared from view.

His musing was abruptly disrupted, as Elli shouted, "Hold on!" Deftly dousing her headlights, she simultaneously geared down drastically and pulled on the hand brake. In the same instant, she spun the *GTI* ninety degrees to the right, brushing gently the first of a long row of shrubs. They were over two meters tall, Mark guessed. Mark's seatbelt tightened noticeably. Hugging the hedgerow, they rolled along slowly and quietly. Elli was depressing the clutch and employing the hand brake to control her speed. She dared not hit the brake pedal for she didn't want her rear lights to give away her location.

While the black *Mercedes* sped on and Gregor committed extreme blasphemy by uttering every curse word he knew in Russian, Slovak, German and French, Elli nursed her VW past four villas on the left side of the road. The first fifty meters had been asphalt. The hard-top gave way to hard packed dirt and gravel. In the first two houses, lights glowed in the kitchens and living areas. The third house was dark. The fourth had security lights at the entrance and garage area. A sigh of relief escaped Elli's lips as she turned and rolled to a stop beside the fifth house. To the right, facing the house and separated from it by a huge open courtyard was a structure much larger than a conventional garage.

"The garage here is actually under the house," Elli whispered. She flipped a switch extinguishing the map and door lamps. "Get out quietly. We're going to roll this car into the warehouse." She exited the car,

146

moved swiftly to a huge door on the outbuilding and, *voila!*, unlocked it with a key on her key chain. Mark helped her open the doors. With Elli reaching through the open driver's side window to steer, both pushed the car into the shed. Elli jumped in and pulled on the hand brake. It was pitch black outside. Soundlessly, they closed the doors and Elli locked them.

"Hurry!" Elli grabbed Mark's hand and pulled him behind the warehouse building. They crouched, scarcely breathing, behind a tractor parked there. It was attached to some weird looking trailer. "For harvesting grapes," she whispered, anticipating his question. The crunching sound of a vehicle inching down the cinder road they had just left was a cause for anxiety. It stopped in front of the house. A spotlight flashed, illuminating the driveway. The night was still. The bright beam scoured the house systematically, especially the doors and windows. It played for a few moments on the warehouse, painting the entrances and outlines with light. Satisfied there was apparently no life there, the car moved on slowly to the next villa.

"We must stay here a little longer." Elli's lips were just an inch away from Mark's ear. "This is a *cul-de-sac*. There are two more villas beyond this one. Normally, only residents and service vehicles come down this road. The car will have to return. And very soon." The thin covering of cinders and gravel on the access road running past the Denis-Breuer villa ruled out surprise approaches. Elli squeezed Mark's hand hard as they heard Gregor's car creeping back up the road. When it was even with the house and the large outbuilding, the car turned so that its high beam headlights lit up the courtyard area brightly. Mark sensed that Elli was frightened. When Gregor's spotlight began again to probe the shadows, Mark was scared too. The spotlight beam lingered just around the corner from their refuge. The two felt like defenseless prey, squatting as they were behind a tractor parked adjacent to the backside of the warehouse below the rows and rows of dormant vines. Probably two or three acres, Mark estimated. He strained to see if he could find a rock or stick, in the event he had to take action. Nothing but signs of careful raking in the area. *This guy is almost too tidy for my taste.* Mark figured the only thing that he might use as a weapon was his belt.

In the reflected light coming from Gregor's frantically searching spotlight, Mark saw Elli's face. Strangely, his inner ear heard Rodolfo's tenor voice singing '*O soave fanciulla*', *o dolce viso di mite circonfuso alba lunar in te, vivo ravviso il sogno ch' io vorrei sempre sognar!* as he looked at Mimi, a vision of loveliness in the moonlight penetrating their humble Bohemian lives. Indeed, before him was the dream he had always dreamed.

Fortunately, Gregor was too lazy to get out of his vehicle. The spotlight was extinguished. The car backed up and continued its retreat towards the main road, halting for a minute or so in front of each house. The still night air carried the sound of the MB turning onto the highway and accelerating. Mark wanted to hug Elli and kiss her. His reverie was broken, when Elli, seeing that the coast was clear, pulled her companion out of their hiding place and, taking him by the hand, darted across the open area to the house door at ground level. She listened again for a moment to see if her evasive move had lost Gregor for good. The door opened easily with Elli's key. They slipped up a flight of stairs to the first level. "The living quarters are on this floor. The bedrooms are upstairs. I don't want to invite attention by turning on any lights right now. Follow me!"

"You're the boss. Oops!" Mark bumped into a table near the stairs. "Sorry! Do you come here often?"

"Dani's husband, Roland Denis-Breuer, is an industrialist and scientist, who is very well known in this region. He manufactures medical instruments and owns a bio-medical research facility outside *Lausanne*. He and Dani are attending a medical convention in Aspen, in Colorado, this week. They own a condominium there and plan to stay on another week to ski."

"And that's why you're house-sitting for them?"

"Yes, Dani, her name is actually Danielle, mine is Michèlle. Our parents called her Dani and me Elli. People often assume we are twins because we look alike. Dani is two years older than I am. Our parents are no longer alive. My mother was a teacher in Brazil, when my father met her in São Paulo, while he was supervising an engineering project there. He was a civil engineer. Dani takes after our mother. She loves house plants. Their house-keeper usually comes by to water them, but she's on vacation herself this week."

"So you volunteered to take care of the plants?"

"And to check on the security. In the morning you'll see some of their artwork. It's quite valuable. My reward comes in two weeks, when I go to Aspen. I plan to learn to snowboard there."

The couple made a left turn at the top of the stairs. Elli's hand felt cool to the touch. *Che gelida manina.* Mark would like to have held it indefinitely. She opened a door and they padded across the thick carpet to a huge wardrobe. Mark could just barely make out the outline.

"Here. Dani keeps their pajamas in this drawer. Hers on the left, Roland's on the right. See if you can find a pair."

"Yes, this seems to be a pair. Is he my size? Roland, that is?"

"Maybe a little taller." She pulled him gently towards a doorway. "Be careful. Don't hit your head!" They entered a spacious bathroom. "I'm going to close the door. When I do, turn on the light. You can shower first. The warm water will help ease the tension. That was pretty harrowing."

So saying, Elli closed the door.

The bathroom was very modern. White marble tiles on the floor and walls. Stylish fixtures, towels and facecloths, along with matching area carpets, in a rich, deep magenta. The shower was very large. Mark turned on the water, adjusted it to suit himself, and stepped in. The hot water soon enveloped him in steam. He hadn't realized how tense his muscles had become, until now.

Mark soaped up, then rinsed off. He heard the bathroom door open and close. Next, a slight draft on his legs as the shower door also opened and closed. Mark wiped his eyes and blinked as he strained to see. Two arms embraced him firmly. He felt damp hair on his chest. It was Elli.

He put his arms around her. She was sobbing gently. He felt her flesh against his and a heart pounding in unison with his own. Looking down, his eyes met hers. The warm water cascaded over them and formed an invisible cloak. He heard her voice. "We had a very close call. I was so worried that something would happen to us,… to you. I, I…" She pressed her body against his. She needed say no more. They had known each other for just a few hours, yet they acted as if they were sharing a moment with a lover with whom each had long ago transcended the need for words.

Sitting side by side in their matching magenta robes on the edge of the bed, Elli broke the silence in the dimly lit bedroom. "I hope you'll understand. This was the first time I have felt this way since my fiancé died."

"I didn't know." Mark's eyes widened. "I'm so sorry." Astonished, he spoke in a solicitous tone, unsuccessfully concealing his surprise at this revelation.

"We met at the university. We fell in love and were engaged after graduation. His name was Armand Vautrain. You may have heard it. He was a world-class mountain climber. His first love, his obsession, was climbing. Just five months after our engagement he had an accident while on an expedition in Pakistan. It took two months to recover the body." Elli was becoming mildly distraught. Mark held her in his arms. They were both silent for a few minutes.

"Elli, you don't need to explain anything. I understand. I have to be honest with you. I have strong feelings for you. Most of my life, as far back as I can remember, I've always subjected everything to a logical examination. Tonight, my heart took over. I've never known anyone like you." They embraced and sat there in semi-darkness a few minutes longer.

"Mark, give me five minutes. I'm going to close the blinds in the kitchen and make some supper for us. I'll call you." She pressed his hand to her mouth and kissed it, before slipping silently out the door and going downstairs in the dark.

A few minutes passed. "O.K." She called upstairs in a subdued voice.

"I'm coming."

Mark hugged her upon reaching the kitchen. A candle flickered on the table. Elli's eyes sought approval as she pointed to the soup steaming in two bowls. Crackers, slices of cheese and a bottle of red wine completed the spread. "I wish there was more," Elli blurted out, apologetically. "This is all my dear sister left in her cupboard."

Mark sipped a spoonful of soup. "Delicious! My compliments to the chef!"

"It's a chantarelle soup. Unfortunately," she said, giggling, "I have to pass the compliments on to *Maggi*. It came from a package." They both smiled. She poured the wine. They clinked glasses, sipped, and exchanged glances.

"You know, when I first saw you in Zürich, even though it was only for an instant, my heart almost melted. It made me a believer in love at first sight. When I look into your beautiful eyes my brain tells me to surrender. You are absolutely irresistible." Mark was speaking from his heart.

Leaving the dishes in the sink, they retired, locked in an embrace. They slept soundly, hardly moving the entire night.

* * *

Mark stretched. A streak of light penetrated the narrow crack in the shutters. Night was making room for day. He heard a familiar tune. *Could it be? Indeed. 'O, mio babbino caro'* wafted up the stairs and caressed his ears. He was alone. He jumped out of bed, rinsed his face in the bathroom and rushed downstairs in Roland's robe.

Elli broke off her singing. "You'll have to leave that robe here. Dani claims it's Roland's favorite." Her smile gave her away. She was merely joking.

"*Gianni Schicchi*, Puccini! I love that aria. Your voice is truly lovely. You didn't tell me, you could sing like an angel." Mark hugged her and kissed her. She was relaxed and reciprocated his welcome ardour.

"I studied singing until I went to the university. Economics, in more ways than one, pushed the music aside."

Elli blushed. She pointed to a chair. "You've got to hurry. I found some strawberry preserves for the crackers. I fried a couple of eggs and some slices of hard salami. It's all they have in the refrigerator. Coffee is almost ready. While you eat, I'll tell you what I've been up to." Devouring everything in sight, Mark listened and made careful mental notes of everything Elli said. "We're going to dress you in some of Roland's clothes. They should fit you. The ferry to *Evian* on the French side of the lake leaves from *Ouchy* in an hour and a half. My plan is to deliver you just minutes before it embarks. In the winter there is only one crossing each day. Once in *Evian*, you must cross *Quai Paul*, then walk up the hill next to the thermal spa. When you reach the main commercial street, the *Avenue des Grottes*, go to your right. The fifth or sixth storefront you see is an auto rental office. I called and reserved a compact vehicle for you."

"Where is *Ouchy*?"

"It's a part of *Lausanne*. On the lakefront."

Mark nodded.

Elli resumed her instructions. "From the car rental agency, drive east on the *Rue National*, then on the *Avenue Anne de Nos* until you reach *Route National #5*. I advise you not to go to *Geneva*. The person who followed us may assume you'll leave this region from *Geneva* and stake out the airport."

Mark repeated the instructions. "Where should I go, then?"

It's about ninety kilometers, say fifty-five miles, to *Annecy*. If you want to fly to Hong Kong, you will be routed by *Air France* through Paris no matter where your flight originates. From there, you can go via Rome, Istanbul, Tehran, Karachi, or Bangkok. Choose your route as you go. Do you have enough money for tickets?"

Mark put his hand on his money belt. "Yes, I'm sure I have enough." He had been listening attentively. "And I have several credit cards."

When Mark returned to the bedroom, Elli had a small pullman suitcase from Roland on a bench at the end of the bed. "Here, pack the clothes I've laid out for you in the suitcase. Perhaps you can pick up a couple of other things you may need somewhere along the way. The small plastic case has toiletries."

"Are you coming back here tonight?" Mark asked, as they went downstairs to the garage.

"No, I'm going to ask Mme Chounard, if I can spend the night with her. She lives ten minutes away from the bank." They reached the garage. "Get in the back and stay low." Elli was opening the door to a *Land Rover*. "Roland loves this clunker. I wouldn't take five of them for my *GTI*."

Mark lay on the back seat, warm in Roland's tan peacoat and a maroon head band. Elli had combed her hair into a bun again and was wearing a pair of sun glasses. She chose the most direct route through *Lausanne* to *Ouchy*. Nothing unusual to report in the rear view mirror. *Ouchy* was a fairly busy port this morning. Several modestly-sized motor launches, apparently private, could be seen departing for various destinations, either across the lake in France, or eastward in the direction of *Montreux*, or to the west, possibly heading for *Geneva*. The large state-operated ferry to *Evian* was boarding. A few stragglers rushed to avoid missing the only trip of the day. Mark also rushed to make it, after leaning over and giving his chauffeur a big kiss.

"I want to see you again," he said earnestly.

"Meet me in Aspen and I'll teach you to snowboard."

Her words still rang in his ears as he dashed down the dock. He waved back. An attendant pulled up the gangway. A man on the dock cast off the last rope tethering the ferry. An unfriendly breeze whipped across the bow. Mark watched the *Land Rover* leave the parking lot and head for *Vevey*. He went inside to warm up.

Chapter Eighteen

Inside the ferry, Mark, who hadn't considered taking a ferry today until Elli presented the idea at breakfast as possibly the best way to slip out of Lausanne unnoticed, concluded on entering the main passenger cabin, that most of the people on board were probably regulars going to work. A few, like himself, were crossing *Lake Geneva* as tourists. The nearest empty seat was in the front row. He sat down, placed his suitcase between his legs and folded his arms. He lamented leaving his old rucksack behind. *That's life,* he decided. The peacoat was soft and warm. *Cashmere,* he guessed, *or a very soft camel hair. Roland goes for quality.* The wind outside was whipping up whitecaps. The ferry plowed on, maintaining an even keel.

Upon landing on the French side, the crew efficiently assisted the off-loading of motor vehicles. Passengers passed quickly through the stiles. The custom's check of Mark's Swiss passport was perfunctory. He turned down several taxi drivers seeking fares and crossed at the traffic signal on *Quai Paul,* and immediately spotted the dormant gardens on the grounds of the thermal spa. His suitcase was light, just a couple of underwear changes, a sweater, his toiletries and the ever-present make-up kit. He had used it this morning to lighten his hair a shade. Halfway up the hill to the *Avenue des Grottes,* he stepped to the side, set his suitcase down and wiped the sunglasses he was wearing. No one anywhere near him. Nothing suspicious. He continued, following Elli's directions. The staff in the auto rental agency expected him. His car, a *Renault,* was ready. He signed the forms.

He wanted to pay cash, however, company rules demanded credit cards, so he used the appropriate credit card to make an advance payment. Mark was glad he had coordinated his passport, driver's license and credit cards during the drive to *Ouchy*. *A slip up could invite real trouble*, he told himself.

The *Renault* proved to be a good performer. The leg room might have been more generous. Mark's back and butt were sore. He tanked up at a gas station near the airport in *Annecy*. Snow covered the mountains. The sun played peek-a-boo with the clouds throughout the ninety minute drive. Mark had a mild headache from the glare. Booking a flight to Rome went smoothly. Elli was on target; no direct flights abroad from the smaller airports. Almost everyone is required to fly through the Paris hub. Mark opted to get a ticket only as far as Rome. Once there, he would assess his situation and purchase a fare on another airline for his onward travel. Final destination: Hong Kong. Gordon Hui had shown him countless dias of the Pearl of the Orient, his family and the cabin cruiser they used for weekend outings to the lesser islands in the Colony. Mark was excited about seeing it all in person. Sister Catherine was on his mind, as well. And Elli too.

Air France has outdone itself, ran through Mark's mind, as he found his seat on an afternoon flight from Paris to Rome. The connection from *Annecy* involved a minimal wait at *Charles de Gaulle*. Although not the most convenient airport, he had managed to get to the international departure terminal with little difficulty.

Fiumicino, by way of contrast, was bedlam in the early evening hours. People moving in haste in every direction. An *Alitalia* agent, short, stocky, sporting a thin black moustache, exhibited the most charming attitude. A last minute cancellation released a first-class seat on a flight departing within minutes for Bombay, with a two-hour stopover in Tehran. Mark thanked him profusely and jogged most of the way to the gate. Luckily, he had no baggage to check.

From Bombay, an Air India flight transported the now weary traveller to Bangkok. Later, *Thai Air* delivered a body, both mentally and physically drained, to Hong Kong. The landing at *Kai Tak Airport* was hair-raising. The aircraft flew so close to some apartment buildings Mark could actually see their interiors.

Gordon had told him to stay at the *Mandarin Hotel*, because it was not far from his office. The taxi driver, grinning from ear to ear, was elated when he heard the destination, hoping that the 'European' would give him a big tip.

As instructed by his college roommate, Mark mentioned the name of Hui Chen-Li at the reception desk. Immediately, wheels began to rotate at top speed. The manager was called to the desk where he personally arranged for a suite on the top floor. Somewhat surprised by the lack of much luggage, the bellboy, nevertheless, carried the small pullman proudly to the elevator bank. Taking care of Mr. Hui's friends was generally a lucrative assignment.

Travelling as a representative of Marshland State had meant pinching pennies on government *per diem* allowances. The tasteful opulence of the large suite he entered with his small suitcase nearly caused his jet-lagged eyes to bulge. He fished a five-dollar bill, obtained at the airport, from his pocket and handed it to the bell hop. *How can I afford a room like this? I can't expect Gordon to pay for it!* Mark was about to telephone the desk and ask for more modest quarters. "Oh my God, I'm a millionaire! I'm a multi-, multi-millionaire!" Mark covered his mouth and looked around to see if anyone might have heard him. *Yes, I'm a millionaire, actually, a billionaire,* he said under his breath, expressing his thoughts calmly and deliberately. *But then, I'm really not. This money is not really mine. I didn't earn it. I was perfectly happy without it.* He continued this rambling in his mind. *Elli is the only woman who knows about the money. Could the money influence her feelings for me? Everything between us seemed so natural and spontaneous. How will I ever know?*

A call from Gordon jolted him from his inner thoughts. Mark picked up the phone, "Hello!"

"Mark, welcome to Hong Kong. I can't wait to see you. Is your room O.K? I told them you were a VIP." Gordon's mid-western accent completely concealed his ethnic origin.

"If this is an example of Chinese hospitality, I can only hope to be equal to the challenge. I'm awfully tired. I've been on the road, so to speak, for over thirty-six hours. I'm headed for the shower right now."

"Take your time. Freshen up. Nap a little and enjoy the fruit bowl that's on its way to your room as we speak. Maybe we can get together tomorrow morning around ten. How does that sound? Whoops! I have a staff meeting at ten, come by the bank at eleven. Is that O.K.?"

"Great! I'm looking forward to it. I'll be there at eleven. Bye."

"Bye! Say, can I arrange some… err… 'companionship' for you?"

"You're a rascal, Gordon. What would your mother say, if she heard you now?"

"She'd probably say, I shouldn't bother to ask, just arrange it. But I respect your wishes. See you tomorrow."

Mark unpacked. The task took all of two minutes. He suddenly felt like a housewife invited to a formal dinner at the boss' house. *I don't have a thing to wear!* He rifled through the drawers of the handsome lacquer desk in his room. *A Gideon Bible. A few sheets of writing paper. And a handy street guide! Just what I need.* Mark thumbed through the guide. An advertisement for *Lane Crawford* on *Des Voeux Road. Men's clothing? Well, it's a department store and it should be right down the street.* There was a knock at the door. "Come in!"

A short, slender Chinese in black trousers, a white shirt, black tie and a crimson vest stood smiling at the door as Mark opened it. "For you, sir, compliments of Hui Chen-Li and the management. May I set it down here on the desk?"

"Please. Thank you very much. It's the loveliest fruit bowl I think I've ever seen." Mark scurried to find another five dollar bill for the diminutive messenger.

Two bananas, an orange and a kiwi later, Mark soaped up and let the vibrating spray of hot water play on his back. He recalled the shower at the 'Vineyard Villa' in Lausanne. *I've got to contact Elli at the bank.* Dressed for the street, Mark felt he didn't fit in well in these elegant environs. *Well, let's see what I can find at Lane Crawford.*

157

Before leaving to upgrade his wardrobe, Mark placed a call through the desk to the *Banque sociale de Léman*. No answer. *Darn, they're closed now! It's still the middle of the night in Switzerland.* He left a short message for Mlle d'Entremont, giving his hotel and room number.

The salesman, a British expatriate, he dealt with at the department store was so unbelievably proper. At first, Mark resisted some of the clothes the salesman recommended. Gradually, he gained confidence in the salesman's flair for combining colors and textures that suited his personality. He left having purchased two suits, a sport jacket and five new shirts, not to mention two pairs of shoes, a silk sweater and a raincoat with a zip-out liner. Hong Kong, he had noted, can be chilly in the winter. Fortunately, Mark was one of those males, whose measurements coincided exactly with those of the manufacturers. Thus, he never encountered any problems buying things off the rack. Not surprisingly, more than a few of the coeds and young females on the faculty at Marshland State referred to him behind his back as the 'Model Administrator'.

Room service dinner, featuring poached grouper, Basmati rice, a vegetable medley and a bottle of white *Bordeaux*, was light and satisfying. Mark laid out his clothes for the next morning. After catching the news on two English-language channels, he spent a few minutes watching part of a Chinese opera. While reading in the *Financial Times*, he fell asleep. He had been more tired than he imagined.

* * *

It was the second ring of the alarm clock the next morning that succeeded in summoning him back to the living. The sun shone brightly outside. Clean shaven and the very picture of a modern English gentleman, Mark was poring over the telephone directory. Under the rubric 'schools', he spotted the *Paulian Sisters School for Girls*.

He found the address in the street guide. It was in a lane off Lockhart Road in a section of the island called *Wan Chai*. Mark decided to walk there. The walk was exhilarating. His nose was slightly red. The streets turning off Lockhart Road were teeming with life. It was the antithesis of *the Vyhorlatské Vyrchy* in Eastern Slovakia. No white-washed huts and wooden churches here. Instead, multi-story apartment buildings flying flags of undergarments and laundered bedding from balconies perilously attached to the sides of structures devoid of architectural appeal. Mark dodged a child pouring kitchen waste into the gutter. On one of the buildings he saw an ornate arched sign identifying the '*Paulian Sisters School for Girls*', beneath it several Chinese characters.

As had become second nature, like a robin preparing to swoop down from a limb to snatch a tasty morsel from the grass, he looked in all directions, secretly hoping to discover that no one had followed him. Gratefully determining he had not been tailed, he walked through the school entrance. It was open. An inner courtyard presented a pleasant picture of young girls from six to sixteen gathered in twos and threes, some intently watching a ping-pong match in a corner of the yard; the others talking, giggling or engaged in jump roping, making calculations on an abacus, or munching on a snack. A pretty girl, barely in her teens, came over and asked if she could be of any help. Mark was impressed with her English and her manners. She directed him to the headmistress' office. It was across the courtyard. A bell rang signalling the end of a recess. Mark waited until the tide of dark blue skirts and white blouses had receded, then knocked on the door of the headmistress. It was half past nine.

What sounded like a friendly command answered his knock. Mark assumed it must be Chinese for 'Come in'. It was, in fact, Cantonese. The distinction was unimportant, because the desired outcome was achieved. No sooner than he showed his face inside the door, came the surprised gasp, "Mark! Professor Davidson. I had no idea you were in Hong Kong!" Sister Catherine was sitting behind a large teak desk covered with file folders and stacks of papers. She was wearing a head cover. A grey tunic with a white sash completed her outfit.

To Mark she looked older, more tired, than she had some four months earlier in New York. Her smile and her voice betrayed a weariness that seemed so unlike the vivacious nun, so full of optimism, who had sat next to him on the flight from Charleston to New York and again at the Met.

"Sister Catherine. I arrived here yesterday. I have some business with an old university classmate. I wouldn't feel right, if I hadn't come by to say hello. Are you well? Has the challenge been everything you anticipated?"

"I wouldn't be honest, if I didn't admit to being rather worn out. I'm well enough. The Order here and the school have many problems. I'm afraid my reputation as a problem solver is destined for reassessment. Soon, at that."

"Please tell me about it. I may be able to help."

"We're just about beyond help already. I appreciate your offer. I know you're earnest, but this is truly a major, major problem." Knowing the complexity and gravity of her situation made Sister Catherine sceptical of casual offers of help however well-intentioned.

"May I sit down?"

"Please forgive me. It seems I'm beginning to forget even common courtesies."

A Chinese nun brought cups of hot green tea and a few rice biscuits. Sister Catherine, with an air of resignation, explained in detail the predicament, the crisis in which her assignment had embroiled her.

Essentially, the building housing the school and a couple of the neighboring buildings stretching to the corner of the street belonged to the *Paulian Sisters*. Well, not quite, it turned out. They have six more monthly payments to cover before receiving the deed. Enrollments are down. Contributions have fallen off. It was probable that the Order wouldn't be able to meet the payment schedule. She went on to say, "The investors who own the buildings want to raze them and construct a new high-rise multi-purpose building with a hotel, shops, luxury apartments. They will not grant us an extension or ease the terms of our lease." The once modest area, it seemed, had increased exponentially in value in recent years. Poorer residents were being forced into more outlying 'estates', shorthand for crowded concrete creations accommodating thou-

sands of people under one roof, in other words, a modern slum development. Sister Catherine, bravely stifling her tears, admitted to being at her
wits end. Nothing she had attempted in an effort to resolve the difficulties had met with any favorable response.

Mark clenched his teeth. He was a novice here. He had no expertise
where real estate was involved. He sat silently for a few moments, sensing
Catherine's growing despair. He might not have a solution for Sister
Catherine, but perhaps Gordon could help. Mark took Sister Catherine's
hand in his. He stood; she likewise. He started to speak: "I don't know
how, not yet, but you and your girls will be helped. I am as sure as I
stand before you, that your prayers will be answered. Trust me." Sister
Catherine looked in his eyes and knew it would be so, at least she wanted
with all her heart to believe it would be so. Mark glanced at his watch.
"Oh my gosh! I'm going to be late for an appointment. I'll be in touch
tomorrow. Good-bye."

Chapter Nineteen

On the street again, Mark half jogged to the corner. Dodging street cars, taxis and the unrelenting onslaught of automobiles, bicycles, motorbikes and pedestrians hell bent on getting somewhere, he made it to the other side of *Gloucester Road* unscathed. A trolley pulled away before he reached the curb. The first three taxis he attempted to hail were occupied. The next one pulled over, but rolled ahead about twenty-five meters to get closer to the sidewalk. Mark ran up, the rear door opened, he gave an address on Connaught Road, jumped in and the driver sped off, nearly hitting a cyclist, who shook his fist angrily, while uttering in Cantonese what was surely unsuitable for delicate ears.

Observing that Mark, who continually looked at his watch, was in a hurry, the taxi driver urged his diesel *Nissan* forward and landed in front of a tall specimen of modern architecture: concrete, clad in glass. Gordon's office, it turned out, was on the fourteenth floor and claimed a spectacular view of *Victoria Harbor*, truly a visual gem. Mark was ushered without delay to Gordon's spacious, well-appointed office by a lovely Eurasian secretary.

The ubiquitous green tea materialized instantly. "I've got Coke or Pepsi, if you'd rather, Mark," said the breathless host, just arriving from a meeting on another floor.

"Thanks, I find the tea very soothing. Say, your office is very impress-ive. Back home, mine used to be a bedroom in a patrician manor house. It's hot in the summer, cool and drafty in the winter and the Palmetto bugs think it belongs to them. I might be envious, except that I've seen lots of places I consider far less desirable than mine. Especially these past few weeks."

"Where have you been? You gave me a synopsis on the phone from Switzerland. Now we have time for the long version."

Mark proceeded, as succinctly as he could, to relate the events of the past four months. He began with his conference in New York, detailed his meeting with Zdeněk Székely, the first phase of his quest for the account numbers in the Carpathians, the attempt on his life, the death of Aja, the close call on Lake Garda, and the hair-raising chase in *Lausanne*. Avoiding specifics of a personal nature, Mark described the remarkable women, without whose aid he would not have survived his arduous journey. As he did so, his subconscious was analyzing these fortuitous encounters. All three women, Aja, Toni and Elli were strong, confident women of accomplishment. They exhibited unusual courage and daring. The brevity of his relationships with them stood in startling contrast to their willingness to take risks for, well, a complete stranger. Yet, somehow, for some reason he could not comprehend, a special connection had developed. Of the three women, Elli came closest to being a true soul mate. He wished she were present. His train of thought was interrupted by Gordon.

"Did you sleep well last night?"

The message, subtle as it was, penetrated the involuntary trance. "I'm sorry, my mind was wandering a bit. There is an important matter I learned about only this morning. I hope you can help me."

"I'll try. You know that."

The dilemma facing Sister Catherine, the *Paulian Sisters School* and the students being nurtured there was not totally unfamiliar to Hui Chen-Li, some of whose prowess in financial circles stemmed from his well-publicized real estate dealings.

Gordon Hui stared out the window for a moment. "Oh, look, there goes the hydrofoil. It's flying to *Macao*." Then, checking his Rolex, "Right on time at that." Walking pensively back and forth for a couple of minutes, Gordon circled his huge desk and pressed the intercom button.

"Jasmine, please call Prakesh Bhindi. Ask him if he could come down to the office for a quick chat!"

"Yes, sir."

"Prakesh is an Oregon State grad. He's fourth generation in the Colony. His forebears came from Goa. They've been active in business and legal circles here ever since. Prakesh has an import-export business, dabbles in precious metals and has an immaculate reputation in Hong Kong real estate. I have an idea I'd like to bounce off him."

Jasmine buzzed her boss to report that Prakesh was on his way down from an upper floor. Mark and Gordon chatted quietly about the *Paulian Sisters School* and Sister Catherine. Gordon had never met her, but knew of her and her efforts to return the school to its former glory as a top elementary-secondary institution.

Prakesh Bhindi was a charmer. Tall, handsome, with smooth dark skin, glistening black hair, blinding teeth, twinkling eyes and a smile as cheerful as his handshake was firm. As soon as he entered the room he was the center of attention. Mark felt comfortable right away. Bhindi's knowledge of the principals and the circumstances in the case showed him to be a master of details. He convinced Mark and Gordon that the owners of the land and current buildings on it, were absolutely determined to evict the school if it defaulted on its scheduled payments and fully expected that that would indeed happen.

"What if," Mark interjected, "what if the school made its final payments on time. How would the picture change?"

Prakesh nodded. "That would take the pressure off... for a while. The fact remains, that particular location is one of the more commercially viable sites for expansion and development on the north shore of the island. The school, I've been there, incidentally, is crowded in a neighborhood desperately in need of revitalization. Enrollment has dropped, partly because many of the girls come from Kowloon side and the travel takes up too much of their time."

"I've had a thought while you were talking, Prakesh." Gordon stood with a finger on his chin, making some mental calculations. He walked to a large framed map of Hong Kong island on a side wall. "What if the School paid off its loan and then, instead of merely selling their building, they were to trade it for a larger, better piece of land somewhere else?"

"What do you have in mind?" Mark was excited and pushed to prod his new partners to throw some suggestions on the table.

Prakesh interrupted. "There's a good-sized parcel of land near Shek-O, that's on the east side of the island, Mark. It would be a hilly site requiring excavation. It might work out. And I've heard it's on the market." He seemed pleased he had been able to keep the ball rolling.

"That would involve a prohibitive commute for the students. Some are rather young." Gordon hated to be the one to pour cold water on the idea.

Mark jumped up. "Is a residential school, one with dormitories, out of the question here?"

Gordon's face lit up. "By George, I think you've got it." Before anyone else could get a word in, Gordon launched his imitation of Professor Higgins. "The rain in Spain stays mainly in the plain! By George, you've got it!"

Mark chuckled. "Sometimes I long for the good old days of the red and white, the parties in Gordon's room. Those lazy, hazy, crazy days. Hard to believe it was ten years ago. Rex Harrison would applaud your rendition. But, tell me, this Shek-O property. Is it really available?"

Prakesh took the floor. "The group that wants to build where the School is located is actually a consortium of five or six partners. If I'm not mistaken, two of them own the place I have in mind. As I said, it's a hillside location. They probably have options on enough adjacent land to do a swap. Should I contact them, put out a couple of feelers? I am personally acquainted with three of the heavy hitters in the consortium. A deal could favor the School."

Mark clapped his hands. "Do it! Prakesh, Gordon! You have been immensely helpful. I'm going to talk with Sister Catherine tomorrow. I am going to arrange for the School's debt to be erased. If the deal goes through, I'll also cover the cost of constructing the new school." He flushed ever so slightly. Mark was feeling for the first time what it was like to exercise the power of money. It felt good. Nevertheless, he reminded himself, humility, not bluster and bravado, would travel farther in his new situation. He also ran through his gray matter the fact that the money on which his fortune was based actually came from an entirely different part of the planet. *Is it right to use the sum this project would require in far off Hong Kong? Well, when you think about it, the accounts, as they now stand, are the result of global investing. I can justify this as an investment in people. If just a few of the students in this school achieve something that benefits others, it will have been worth it.*

For one, Prakesh's eyebrows leapt to attention at Mark's matter-of-fact pronouncement. He shot a glance to Gordon, whose facial expression left no doubt; Mark was a man of his word. The three parted, each having agreed to pursue various aspects of the arrangements they had discussed. Early the next day, they would confer by telephone to report on their progress.

Mark walked back towards the *Mandarin Hotel*. He needed some air and a few moments by himself to digest the content of the morning's proceedings. At a time like this the solitude of the snow-covered mountains would have been most welcome. Solitude was not in the vocabulary of Hong Kong's thoroughfares, however large or small they might be. Mark headed first to *Des Voeux Road*. He found a pedestrian crossing and followed a throng of people to *Queen's Road*. Making a left, he stared at the windows, apologized a few times for being in someone's way and finally ventured down some of the lanes connecting *Des Voeux* and *Queen's*.

Brimming with activity would be an understatement. He had often heard Gordon brag about his hometown, claiming one could find anything his heart desired there, or have it made to order. Mark was now willing to accept that notion categorically. The sights and smells, the din created by the hordes of men, women and children throbbing up and down the streets, hawking priceless antiques, exquisite carpets, convincing copies of Swiss watches, faux jade jewelry and a myriad other items, real or imitation, all tantalizing to every sense organ, combined in his mind and reemerged as two words: Hong Kong. It was a human kaleidoscope, the likes of which he had only imagined. Human enterprise personified by a restless quest for progress. And, of course, wealth!

At one point, suddenly in the midst of a cluster of waifs, each holding out a hand, Mark had made the mistake of giving each a coin from the change he had collected in his jacket pocket. That act of charity only served to attract still more children. Ultimately forced to retreat, he slipped back onto the main street from the labyrinth of never ending stalls. Soon he was at *Chater Road* and entered the hotel. He thanked the doorman. Something didn't click right.

The mass of mobile humanity, the signs, the constant stream of colors, fast moving bodies, cars, the shadows. *Yes, that was it. The shadows.* His peripheral vision had picked up a strange movement in the shadows on the opposite side of the street, just as he had stepped into the hotel. He walked back nonchalantly to the revolving door, pretending to be looking for something he might have forgotten. His eyes strained to filter out the nonessential, as he peered into the crowd across the way. *I guess I'm imagining things. Zdeněk warned me never to underestimate Gregor and his ilk. As far as I know, he's still out there. But here in Hong Kong? Hmmm. I don't see how.*

In the mezzanine, Mark had noticed the café the day before. He found a seat at an empty table. A plateful of scrambled eggs, a rasher of bacon, a huge helping of fried potatoes, a green salad and a cool *Tsingtao* later, he had overcome his hunger pangs and solved the problem of where to have dinner. He continued on to his room.

Before departing from Zürich, once Mark had made his naïve promise to Zdeněk, he had asked Judge Willinggate, Marshland's president, for a temporary leave of absence. At the time, Mark assumed he might need at most thirty days, or thereabouts. It was a false assumption. From Vienna he had asked for an extension. It had been granted without question. Much had changed since then. It wasn't just about money, Mark tried to convince himself. But, really, it was all about money. Today he had felt the power of wealth. He had gained insight into the potential for change and help for worthy causes and worthy and needy people. Tibor, and Zdeněk, too, had wanted this. While he might never truly understand how or why destiny had singled him out to become one of the world's wealthiest men, he would follow his conscience. He would use the modest gifts he had to see this through.

The call to the Low Country went well. The Judge, without knowing the particulars, accepted Mark's explanation of 'new challenges', although he thought the fact the call was coming from Hong Kong a touch 'mysterious'. "I won't be coming home for a few weeks yet. In the morning I'll fax you my resignation. If Mattie would continue to water my house-plants, I would be most appreciative. She might want to cover my furniture with some sheets and check my mail for any bills. I'll send a money order to cover them." He suggested a couple of colleagues as potential temporary replacements until a formal search for his successor could be conducted.

In a call to Sister Catherine, Mark proposed lunch the next day at the *Peninsula Hotel*. He set the time at noon. Gordon and Prakesh he invited for 1:00. Before retiring for the night, Mark looked out his window, straining unsuccessfully to see if anyone was lurking in the shadows across the street. There may have been fewer people on the streets now that most businesses were closed. Mark couldn't judge. It still seemed quite busy to him.

It should be right after lunch in Vevey. I must call Elli. Mark dialed the bank. "Mlle d'Entremont, s'il vous plaît."

"Dr. Davidson, is that you?" inquired a saccharine voice, that had immediately recognized Mark's.

"Yes, Mme Chounard?"

"*Oui*, I mean yes. Just a moment, Elli, Mlle d'Entremont, that is, just entered the elevator. She's going up to her office. I'll transfer the call." It seemed like an eternity to Mark. *What if she doesn't pick up?*

"Hello, Mark, is that you?" The sound of Elli's voice immediately elevated his spirits.

"Yes, I'm doing fine. No snow here. It was nearly seventy degrees Fahrenheit today. Are you all right?"

"I'm fine too. I've been very cautious. Everywhere I go I keep watching for your friend Gregor. I may be getting paranoid. I'll have to send you a bill for my psychiatrist."

Mark visualized Elli with a wry smile on her face. He enjoyed people with a good sense of humor. "Stay alert. You never can tell. I even thought I saw something unusual today. A false alarm, I guess."

"Please be careful, Mark! How long will you stay in Hong Kong?"

"My friend here thinks a lot like Jean-Luc. They would make a good pair. A team of auditors is combing through the materials Jean-Luc sent. I have more papers to sign tomorrow. A project is under discussion that may delay my departure for several days. Then I'll probably fly back to the States. I have lots to tell you. When does your vacation start?"

"Dani and Roland are coming back at the end of the week. Next Monday, I'm off to Aspen. Oh, dear, I have a call coming in, please wait a moment." After a few seconds, "A client with an emergency, Sorry I've got to go. I miss you, *Au revoir!*"

"I miss you too. *Au revoir!*"

The following morning, Mark ordered up breakfast from room service, while he showered and shaved. On the way out of the hotel he picked up a map of the island from the reception desk. Adapting to the local pace, he dashed out onto the sidewalk, gave the doorman a tip and promptly left in the next taxi. His destination was Shek-O. *I've got to see this myself. If what Prakesh and Gordon have suggested is practicable, I'd like to get the project launched straight away.*

The taxi took a route that passed to the west of *Mount Collinson* then made a sharp left onto a road that separated *D'Aguilar Peak* from some high hills south of *Mt. Collinson*. The land he was shown on the map in Gordon's office actually looked out onto *Big Wave Bay* and was north of Shek-O. Mark stopped the taxi. He stepped out and attempted to get a feel for the site with the naked eye. *This has genuine possibilities. I like it.* After a few minutes of looking about, Mark returned by the same route.

He was occupied making notes in a small pad he carried in his pocket. The driver let him out in front of the *Peninsula Hotel*. Mark checked his watch. Two hands straight up. *Mr. Punctuality. That's me.*

A buffet lunch was being served on the veranda. Mark spotted Sister Catherine as she entered the hotel from *Salisbury Road*. She was wearing the same type garment as the day before. She appeared more vigorous than the previous day. Mark suggested the buffet. Sister Catherine said that she had been so busy since arriving in Hong Kong, she'd never been to the *Peninsula Hotel*. Whatever Mark suggested was fine with her. Once seated, Mark revealed his motive for the luncheon meeting. He outlined a plan that would begin with the completion of the School's purchase of the building presently occupied. The School would sell it to the consortium, which would pay for it in part with a building site near Shek-O. Then, a foundation that Mark was associated with, would grant the School sufficient funds to construct a whole new campus. Sister Catherine was excited and enthralled. Although intrigued by the plan, she raised some of the same objections and questions that had come up when Mark, Prakesh and Gordon had developed the solution. Mark said that he had also had reservations at first. In the meantime, he had visited the site and refined the plan. He had an answer for every objection. Sister Catherine's face flushed slightly. A great weight had been lifted from her heart. When asked, whether her Order would be likely to agree, she was enthusiastically affirmative.

A few minutes after one, Gordon and Prakesh arrived. It was an odd looking foursome. Lively discussion followed between main courses, dessert and tea. The conversation ended on a positive note. Everyone was very excited about the plan that evolved. Most of the luncheon customers had already left. Service staff were clearing the buffet tables. The few diners still on the veranda looked up and smiled upon seeing the disparate four high-five each other.

Sister Catherine was confident the leadership of her Order in New York would ratify the plan that emerged from the meeting of four fertile minds this afternoon. *The Paulian Sisters School for Girls* would move to the Shek-O area. Students would live on campus in a series of residential cottages. They could live there full time, or just during the five-day school week. Athletic fields would be included in the campus, along with a small chapel, a dining hall, an auditorium that could be used for community events and a hotel facility primarily for short stays by parents of students. Students and their parents would receive a transportation allowance. Additionally, the Sisters would operate a medical clinic there and add a nursing curriculum.

Gordon recommended a graduate of *Georgia Tech* and *MIT*, Alice Leung, who had apprenticed in Los Angeles and Berlin with award winning architects, to meet with Mark, Sister Catherine, Prakesh and himself to come up with the overall design for the campus. Prakesh was certain his contacts on the consortium would agree to the arrangement and that construction could begin by late spring.

Mark saw Sister Catherine off in a taxi in front of the hotel. She looked in his eyes. She admired him greatly. Was she wondering what might have been? Mark returned her smile. In his heart he was overjoyed that it had been possible to help engineer this project. Never one to waste time, Gordon had called Miss Leung's office from the hotel and set up an appointment for Sister Catherine, Mark and the architect for the next afternoon. Things were moving fast.

* * *

The following morning passed quickly. Mark was eagerly looking forward to the meeting with the architect. Architecture had always been an interest and he thought he might be able to contribute to the planned project. The handiest way to reach Miss Leung's office in *Tsim Sha Tsui* was to take the ferry to Kowloon. Mark left early. He strolled through the lobby of the *Hong Kong Hotel* and meandered aimlessly in the *Ocean Terminal*. Leung and Co. occupied the fourth floor in the *J. Hotung House*, a stone's throw from the *Peninsula Hotel*. Mark was ahead of schedule. He passed some time gawking like a tourist in the shop windows on *Hankow* and *Peking Roads*. By accident, he sauntered into a cavernous space in a neighboring building, only to discover he was in a cafeteria-style Chinese restaurant. *Well, why not? The dim-sum displays are very enticing.* This opportunity to visit the famed *Oriental Palace Restaurant* satisfied an appetite his musings had concealed. The egg rolls and other delights proved to be deceptively filling. Mark hoped no one heard him belch as he entered the office building on *Hankow Road.*

Sister Catherine, once again, arrived shortly after Mark reached the fourth floor. Alice Leung was dressed casually in jeans and a sweatshirt emblazoned with a gold GT and Yellow Jacket logo. The three exchanged pleasantries. The floor, except for support beams in the center, was open. Work spaces were defined by low partitions that formed cubicles. Two rows of these, one on either side of the floor, were filled with large tilted drawing tables. Staff were seen conferring in small groups, often engaged in spirited conversation. The natural light coming through the windows was augmented by bright florescent fixtures in each work space. On the walls were drawings and photographs of what Mark assumed were current projects. They were functional structures. Plain and functional. *Very plain and very functional,* thought Mark. He was beginning to have some reservations about the choice of Miss Leung. He had hoped to see some imaginative creations, inspirational architecture. Boxes of aluminum, prestressed concrete, and a profusion of glass wouldn't cut it, as far as he was concerned. Sister Catherine's angelic countenance failed to suggest her feelings.

At the far end of the large room, Miss Leung led the way into a partitioned section that contained her office and a gallery. The walls were tastefully hung with more photos, hand-colored sketches of elevations, interiors, and architectural and engineering details of a wide variety of buildings. The captions showed that they could be found in Europe, the Middle East, Africa, Latin America and North America, as well as here in East Asia. Mark examined the illustrations from several angles. He found them fascinating.

"Do you like them?" Miss Leung asked, seeing how carefully Mark was studying the illustrations. "I apprenticed for three years with Professor Luungulla, the Finnish architect, in Berlin. I was responsible for the engineering aspects of several of his most famous projects. In Los Angeles, I was an associate in an architectural firm in which Hidaki Kasamura was the principal. There, I devoted most of my time to leading the design team."

Speaking as one, both Sister Catherine and Mark expressed simultaneously, "These are so exciting. I like them!" They laughed. A pleased Miss Leung laughed too.

"I'd love to see the site you've chosen. I haven't been to that part of the Colony for years." Miss Leung looked expectantly at Mark.

"Let's go right now. Sister Catherine, would that suit you?" Mark was brimming with enthusiasm.

"Oh, yes. I cleared my afternoon. I would love to hear what Miss Leung thinks about the location."

"My driver is waiting outside." Miss Leung gave whispered instructions to an aide and the three headed for the elevators.

* * *

Miss Leung walked around the lower part of the site, unconcerned about getting dirty. She found some surveyors' marks and a place where some soil samples had been dug, probably by the site's current owner. She stopped occasionally to register an observation on her notepad. At times, she appeared to be making rough sketches and entering numbers. Mark helped Sister Catherine over some piles of stones and dirt that had been left by previous activity. They all met back at the limousine.

"How much money do you have available? We'll need a budget, you know?" Miss Leung didn't mince words when it came to cost estimates. She didn't want to make any suggestions or proposals without first ascertaining whether the School could afford them.

"I'm from a frugal background." Mark said, thoughtfully. "I don't like to waste money. On the other hand, I have a grand vision for this undertaking and I do not want to skimp on the scope or quality of the concept or the construction. Let's hear your ideas. We'll approach them with common sense. If Sister Catherine approves, I'll… ahhh, the money will be available. You can count on it."

Miss Leung and Sister Catherine said nothing. Their hearts were pounding so loudly, they worried that Mark might notice. This could be a signature project for the young architect. Done well, her reputation in the region would be established. Sister Catherine, meanwhile, had received the blessing of the Order's leadership in New York, albeit with the caveat that local decisions would be entirely her responsibility. There would be no recourse to financial help from other sources. She saw how confident and resolute Mark looked and acted. She prayed her school would once again flourish and attain its former prominence and distinction. For his part, Mark was concerned not to seem overbearing and imperious. *I had better watch how I use that first person singular pronoun,* he thought.

Leaving the Shek-O site and returning to the north shore of the island, the limo detoured past the *Paulian School*. Sister Catherine got out. Mark also stepped onto the pedestrian walk, after thanking the young architect, who assured them she would have a preliminary plan and an estimate of costs in about three days. They agreed mutually that Miss Leung would arrange a meeting for Friday. The limo pulled away from the curb. Sister Catherine entered the passageway that led to the School's central courtyard. Mark followed. Classes were in session and the area was silent.

"I'd better get back to my hotel. I may have some messages. I hope you are as pleased with our progress as I am." Mark's admiration for this remarkable woman, who pursued her goals with such single-minded tenacity and never lost her composure, was boundless. She looked so much happier than when he had first visited her in her office. He was inwardly grateful for the inexplicable quirk of destiny that was enabling him to serve her and her students in their hour of need.

They stood facing each other in the dim light of the passageway. To one side, the muffled noises of constantly moving pedestrians, hand-drawn carts and motor vehicles; on the other the quiet of the vacant courtyard. After a pause of seconds that seemed an eternity to both, Sister Catherine broke the silence. "I've been neglecting my duties. I don't need to attend the meeting with Miss Leung on Friday. It should suffice, if you, Mr. Hui and Mr. Bhindi attend. I can drop by Mr. Hui's office next week to sign any necessary papers. Let me say thank you from the bottom of my heart for everything you are doing for us." She bent forward, embraced him and kissed him. Mark had a lump in his throat. No words came forth, although he had much in his heart to say. She turned and walked to the door leading to her modest office. She did not turn to look back. A forlorn Mark slowly exited the passage. On the sidewalk, he looked pensively in both directions. A page had been turned. One chapter in his life had just closed. Another had begun. He recalled the night in New York. Sister Catherine had initiated a new phase in his life. He kicked a piece of orange peel on the sidewalk into the gutter. He muttered, "Love. Its levels, degrees, nuances. I think I understand now. Yes, I do!" An old woman carrying a live chicken in her shopping basket walked by. She looked perplexed, thinking Mark might be addressing her. He smiled and loped across the main street to catch a cab. Back at the hotel, the *Mandarin* staff now recognized him on sight. He was a 'regular'. They opened doors; catered to his every whim. This was his home away from home. A new chapter had indeed begun.

In *Vevey*, it was early morning. Mark's brain was nearly consumed by the tempest within. He had so many questions, concerns, and ideas competing for attention and dominance, that half were muddled or lost before he could jot them down in a little notebook he found on the desk in his hotel room. In spite of the unfortunate time, he had to call Jean-Luc Renard at home. This couldn't wait, shouldn't wait. "Jean-Luc, Mark here in Hong Kong. Sorry about the early hour. I hope you and your family are all well...... Great! That's good to hear. I've been wracking my brain about the best way to deal with my... ahh, new circumstances. I need your help. I want to set up an eleemosynary foundation. Geneva would be an excellent home for it. I intend to name a

Board of Advisors, people I know and trust. I would be honored to have you chair that Board."

There was a pause in the conversation. Monsieur Renard was still combing the cobwebs out of his grey cells.

"Look," Mark went on, "you can continue at the bank. We'll have a small staff to deal with the paper work. If the details can be worked out, I'd like to have everything set up and ready to roll by May. As I see it, the Board we create would meet two or three times annually. The foundation's *raison d'être* would be to promote health and education, particularly as the issues involved impact children."

Mme Renard had come to her husband's rescue with a mug of *café au lait*. As his metabolism kicked in, Jean-Luc bought into Mark's vision; a vision that would have the foundation provide the seed money without which many worthwhile projects would never make it off the table. He agreed to serve. Mark proposed a tentative meeting, in *Vevey*, in late March, to work out details of organization and a timetable and agenda for the remainder of the year. Thus was born *La Fondation Székely*.

"Jean-Luc, there's one more thing on my mind. I don't quite know how to put it, I... I... Look, I think I'm in love with Elli, Mlle d'Entremont, that is. I think she likes me too. This is strictly confidential, but I can't help wondering if it's the..."

Renard interrupted. "The money! Isn't that what you're thinking?"

"Well, sort of. I'm just beginning to realize what an attraction it is."

"If she likes you and I rather suspect it's more serious than that, the money plays no role. Monsieur d'Entremont, her late father, was extremely well off; a millionaire himself. He left both his daughters a very substantial estate. I hope that sets your mind at ease."

"It sure does. Thank you. See you in Geneva." A relieved Mark set the receiver down, smiled broadly and began to make plans.

When Mark hung up, his cheeks glowed pink with excitement. *Sister Catherine, in Aja's absence perhaps Tomáš, Jaroslav, Toni, Luigi, Gordon, certainly Prakesh too.* In the next few weeks he would add others to his projected Board of Advisors. *Plenty of time to think it through some more before I start contacting them.* Satisfied that this had been a truly banner day, Mark freshened up, substituted a light sweater for his suit jacket, and took the elevator down to the lobby. He was more tired than he realized. He stopped by the concierge desk. A white-haired Chinese was on duty. Mark got directions to a restaurant nearby, where he could indulge his yearning for a juicy steak. He had, as he said under his breath, '*a hankerin' for beef.*'

The temperature was still mild and the walk up *Ice House Street* to *Queen's Road Central* and then over to the *Hilton Hotel* was pleasantly relaxing. His steak and lobster dinner, while a rather lonely affair without anyone to share it with, was delicious. The three glasses of wine accompanying his meal affected him enough that he was more generous with his tip than he was accustomed to being and walked much more slowly than usual down the stairs to *Garden Road.* A bit confused, he took an extra few seconds before realizing he was around the corner from the entrance he had used to reach the restaurant. It was not very late and the pedestrian walks were full. He ended up behind a large group of senior tourists who were so spread out laterally across the pedestrian walkway on *Queen's Road* and on the *Battery Path* adjacent to it, that he had no choice but to stay behind them at a snail's pace.

Upon reaching *Ice House Street*, Mark turned right and proceeded to return to the *Mandarin.* Most of those who had been blocking his way thus far chose the same route and, boxed in thus, he resigned himself to maintaining their casual gait. He hadn't the foggiest notion of a shadowy figure that had been seated on a bench amidst the shrubs and trees on the *Battery Path.* Rather tall, jacket collar up, the figure had hoped his quarry would be entirely alone. Muttering oaths in a Slavic language passersby did not understand, the frustrated figure abandoned his hunt and skulked away.

In his room a few minutes later, Mark draped his clothes over a chair, nearly brushed his teeth with shaving cream and, within seconds of sliding between the sheets, was oblivious to everything.

Chapter Twenty

The following morning, Mark rose very early. He ordered up a continental breakfast. It arrived while he was showering. Between bites and gulps, he dressed. The morning news program predicted a pleasant day. Before he was finished, a call came in from Gordon suggesting he come by to go over the arrangements the banker had made regarding Mark's deposits.

A short while later, seated behind his desk, Gordon began by praising Renard. "My auditing team and I have reviewed the records he sent me at your request. This guy Renard is a genius. The management group he assembled is truly exemplary. His predecessors were also incredibly sharp. The funds in the accounts you transferred were exceptionally well managed. It's like they had a crystal ball. They placed all the investments to earn the maximum percentage of interest possible, in good times and some that were not so good. Based on yesterday's market data and our analysis of the holding company's portfolio, the figures he gave you are the best approximation we can come up with. Would you like to sit down? Your total worth is between 36 and 37 billion dollars. I'd hire Renard in a heart beat!"

Mark swallowed hard. "It's going to take a while for this to sink in. I don't know Renard well, but I found him very likeable and his competence was apparent from the outset. I have asked him to establish a charitable foundation. I hope you'll accept a position on the Board of Advisors. I value your judgement highly."

"You know, I'll be happy to serve." Gordon pointed to a large box of files on the floor next to his desk. "We've got to work through this pile. It should take about two hours. There are some items to sign, much to read, a few to discuss. When we're finished, you'll know how the money was put to work and where it is."

* * *

Daunting, tedious, other worldly might describe Mark's reaction to the documents he and Gordon spent over two hours thumbing through. There was a lot to absorb in a single sitting. Mark suspected there were few individuals in the world who could match his wealth. He felt his head, when Gordon's attention was distracted. He wanted to be sure it was still the same size it had been when he woke up in the morning.

"Gordon, this has been a sobering exercise. You know me. I'm an educator from a small public college. I live pretty comfortably. I pay my bills. I have even been able to contribute to a retirement plan. I have modest medical coverage. Or at least I did. I feel a bit uneasy with this money. I did nothing to earn it. I don't want it to spoil my life. I think my blood pressure has gone up a few points this morning alone."

"Look, old buddy! There's no question, controlling this kind of massive wealth is probably known to just a few people on the planet. You're right. I do know you. I honestly think you are the most grounded person I have ever met. Your head is screwed on right. You'll be able to handle it. By the way, the foundation is a super idea. It will help you maintain a reasonable degree of anonymity."

"I hope so. I truly hope so."

"Would you mind, if Prakesh and I looked over the site in Shek-O? We want to verify a few things."

"Not at all. I don't think I need to go back there again just yet."

* * *

Gordon Hui and Prakesh Bhindi arrived in Gordon's *Jaguar*. They had requested that Miss Leung join them. A certain amount of imagination was necessary in order to envision the final product. The two men had questions for the architect. She fielded them well, occasionally stopping to pencil a note into her ever-present sketchpad. Earth moving, she reported, would not be a problem. Soil tests on record show that little or no blasting will be required. The extensive landscaping roughed into her plan pleased them both. Mark had suggested a swimming pool. That would be no problem, Miss Leung declared. A little more than half an hour later, the three of them, thrilled with the project as outlined, were motoring back in the direction of the Central District. Gordon would arrange for legal documents to be drawn up. Mark had already signed a power of attorney so that Gordon could supervise construction in Mark's absence.

* * *

Upon arriving back at the hotel, Mark had a message to call Renard in *Vevey*. Mark was relieved to learn there was no urgency attached to the message, merely Renard's wish to confirm he was aboard and that the foundation documents were being processed by the powers that be. They agreed on meeting dates in the spring. When Mark inquired about Elli, Renard told him, she had left early for Aspen to spend a couple of days there with her sister and Monsieur Denis-Breuer before their return to Europe. Mark was surprised, but drew no attention to it. Saying simply he hoped she would have a pleasant holiday.

After he had hung up with Renard, Mark paced back and forth in his room. He was restless. *I've done just about all I can here. There's no point in staying on. I kept a sharp eye out for any sign I might be followed. Maybe I was being hyper. I didn't see anything suspicious today. Gregor is probably back in Zürich trying to find another free meal ticket. I hope he had the decency to give Zdeněk a fitting funeral. I'll definitely check on that.*

The English-language television news emphasized, as news programs often do, the negative and nasty, at home and abroad. Two stabbings attributed to Triad feuds, violence in the Middle East, a kidnapping in California.......... *By God, I hope and pray every penny the Foundation spends will somehow become an investment in something positive and uplifting. My most important function will be to steer the Foundation uncompromisingly in the right direction. I hope I'm up to the task. Some-times I have my doubts.*

Ruminating on his inadequacies, Mark's thoughts wandered back to Sister Catherine. She was a person worthy of emulation. Including her on the Foundation's Board of Advisors was a wise move, he thought. The manner in which they had parted, however, constituted a reality check for Mark. They had reached the frontier of their relationship and it was labelled: friendship. He understood her commitment. Her selflessness stemmed from her religious conviction. The selflessness he sought to summon now was inspired by his admiration and respect for her.

This crazy winter odyssey held a key to his future. *Had there been some divine intervention as the strange concatenation of events of these past three or so months unfolded?* He concluded, it wasn't just the money, although he could not deny that it had a major role to play. Besides Sister Catherine, he had befriended three other women. Each had accepted him readily, had made sacrifices to help him, had exposed herself to danger and had demonstrated a brand of courage and bravery, that he, a stranger, had had no right to expect. *I truly liked and admired each one*, he recalled.

Aja's rescue and her ultimate sacrifice would remain forever in his memory. He remembered Toni's daring plan to divert attention away from him so that he could flee *San Vigilio*. If he had lost his heart to any one of them, it had to be Elli. Theirs was a special connection. From the instant their eyes met in the café in Zürich to the tender moments together in *Lausanne* to the tearful send off at the pier in *Ouchy*, there had been an emotional tie that he could not deny, did not want to deny.

It was with full cognizance of the irony involved, that Mark ordered from room service a bowl of chicken soup and a grilled cheese sandwich in a place with hundreds of outstanding restaurants, many within walking distance. Restless, Mark had difficulty falling asleep. He flipped on the radio and caught the tail end of a classical music program. A pleasant sounding soprano, he didn't catch her name, was singing '*un bel di vedremo*'. The ensuing discussion was... well, Chinese to him. He turned the radio off. *I won't abandon you. Pinkerton-Linkerton will not abandon you!* With those words in his mind, he finally began his nightly rest.

* * *

Upon arising, Mark first threw his suitcase onto the bed. He laid out the clothes he figured would be appropriate to wear. The rest he packed as neatly as possible into the suitcase. He left the raincoat hanging in the closet. The cashmere pea coat didn't fit in. While the day's expected temperature in Hong Kong wouldn't require it, Mark wanted to return it to Monsieur Denis-Breuer, and he might well need it where he was going. The rucksack, to which he had a strong sentimental attachment, had been abandoned in Switzerland. *Just as well. It's a break with the past. Of course, I can afford the luxury edition now.* Shaved and showered, Mark went down to the café for breakfast. He returned to his room temporarily to use the facilities. Before leaving, he called the desk to prepare his bill.

On the way down to the lobby, Mark detoured to the Thomas Cook Agency wedged in among the boutiques. He bought a ticket for the States, departure at 3:58 pm. It was silly, he chided himself, to check out now. He had hours to wait before his plane was scheduled to depart. Yet, he felt driven to get moving. An uneasiness overcame him. He needed to get out of the hotel and head for home. The Reception staff, the bellhops, the doorman, all fell all over themselves trying to help him. *Could the word be out about my financial status?* Mark speculated silently.

Because the *Star Ferry* was so close, Mark declined any assistance and walked over to the terminal. His luggage was not heavy. The usual lines were thinner than on workdays. Since this would be his last passage for some time to come, Mark opted to find a quiet seat on the open lower deck. He moved aft to the stern section, surprised to find he had it all to himself. *I guess most passengers prefer the enclosed upper deck, when the wind acts up.*

He chose a seat in a long center section of benches roughly two rows from the aisle that traversed the stern. He leaned his suitcase against the bench to his left. The pea coat he laid on the bench to his right. He loosened the buttons on his suit coat, but left it on. The wind was blowing cool damp air from his left to his right. It was refreshing. He felt good.

Mark's thoughts drifted off. He wondered, whether there was a reason why Elli hadn't contacted him about her change in travel plans. Could it be a question of pride? She was one of the few who knew how incredibly wealthy he was. He was certain, she liked him. Well, fairly certain. *She wouldn't want to be thought of as a gold-digger*. He would have to make the next move.

Without warning, a strong arm swung under his chin and he felt an unbearable pressure on his wind pipe. He grabbed for the arm with both hands. The grip tightened. He gasped, attempted to call out, but no sound came out. His back was hurting. He was being pulled tightly against the firm wooden back of the bench. A cold object was pressed hard against his left temple. A menacing voice from the past, forced through teeth clenched by hate and anger, "***Du, Schwein!* You took the money that should have been mine! You won't get away with it!**"

Mark gasped. *Gregor! I should have been more careful*. Thoroughly adrenalized, he planted his feet against the bench in front of him, arched his back, pushed himself up and, remembering some old wrestling moves, reached back vigorously with his right arm. He caught the back of Gregor's head and jerked it forward violently. Simultaneously, with all the force he could muster, he rammed the back of his own head into Gregor's nose. "**Arrgghh!**" Gregor's grip relaxed for an instant as he dealt with the pain of a broken and now profusely bleeding nose. Mark wrenched himself partially free, but Gregor, with his superior strength, managed to fling him down hard onto the deck. Mark's head grazed the edge of a bench. He was dazed and incapacitated. Lying sprawled on his back, his vision blurred in the fall, Mark couldn't see the barrel of a *Beretta* aimed right at his head.

The ferry was just meters away from its berth on the Kowloon side of the harbor. The passengers above were shuffling for position in that extraordinarily smooth exodus that occurred many times in the course of a day. The captain had reversed his engines. "**Gregoorr!**" A hoarse shout in desperation emanated from the vicinity of the bulkhead. Startled, Gregor looked up. A shot rang out. Gregor fired reactively in the direction of the flash. As he did so, he reeled backwards, holding one hand covered in blood against his chest. He stumbled over the foot of the last bench and fell against the railing. He rose, tried to steady himself, dropped his gun, then fell backwards once more, rolling over the rail and plummeting into the frothing, oily, debris-strewn waters below.

Mark, on his knees and holding his throat, looked forward to the bulkhead that housed the crew stations. His vision was still blurry. A figure was sitting on the deck leaning against the wall. Still shaken and wobbly, Mark stumbled forward. A couple of crewmen were gesticulating in a frenzy. A few passengers, curious to a fault, had started to come aft to see what the commotion was about. The crewmen waved them back. Mark knelt. The blood ran from the victim's head. It was Zdeněk Székely! "Herr Székely, you're wounded. Help is on the way. Hang in there!" *He's supposed to be dead. I saw them taking his body away in an ambulance.* Mark laid Székely down, rolled his own jacket and placed it under the wounded man's head.

"Mark. I am so sorry, so sorry. You are a good man. A good man." His weak voice trailed off. His voice was barely audible. Mark wanted him to remain silent in order to conserve his energy. "I am so sorry. So sorry. Gregor and his cronies faked my death and forced me…" Zdeněk was beginning to choke on his own blood. His voice barely a whisper. "…and forced me to tell them where you would be going." He coughed again. "They found the credit card numbers I had given to Runzli and had them traced to follow your movements." His voice was raspy, gurgling. Zdeněk continued, "Thank God, you are all right. I bribed the men Gregor hired to guard me and flew here. I had to stop Gregor. My father…" His breathing was labored. His lips moved, but no sound came out. An emergency medical team was running up the gangway. The crewmen pushed back the crowd that had developed. Mark, too, was pushed away. Zdeněk's eyes rolled back. His arms slid off his chest and hit the deck.

The medics checked the victim's pulse. Nothing! They tried three times to resuscitate him. No response! They placed him on a stretcher and covered him with a sheet. As the medics left, a police officer, following the pointing fingers of some of the spectators, approached Mark. He was asked for his identification. A plain clothes officer, Choi Kwan-Tung, asked a few questions. Mark identified Gregor as the assailant who attacked him and named Zdeněk as the person who had saved his life. Mark gathered his belongings and was escorted to a waiting police car. He was driven to the closest precinct station in Kowloon. Enroute, Mark was asked for local references. When Hui Chen-Li's name was mentioned, the Assistant Inspector got on his radio and spoke animatedly with headquarters. Arriving at the police station, Mark was met courteously by Trevor Atherton, a British subject. He identified himself as a Senior Inspector. Mark was asked to write a report describing what happened. He learned that two men in a passing *sampan* had fished Gregor's body out of the oily waters. He had no I.D on his person, but a hotel receipt corroborated Mark's information. A short while later, Gordon showed up. After a brief conference, Mark was told there was no reason to hold him in custody. His head wound was superficial. It was cleaned and dressed. Gordon volunteered to arrange for Mr. Székely's body to be repatriated to Switzerland for cremation and interment.

Mark told Gordon he had been planning to call from the airport. He needed to go home for awhile. They spoke for a few minutes, embraced and parted. Mark's clothes had been brushed off for him. He requested a taxi, but Gordon's driver took him to the airport. Mark checked in. He had a little more than an hour before boarding. Seated in the waiting area, the adrenaline rush that probably saved his life, had long since subsided. Now he felt creeping exhaustion beginning to dull his thinking. His head throbbed. His right arm was aching. Gregor had put all his energy into it, when he slammed Mark to the floor. The medical personnel had given Mark an envelope with two aspirin tablets. He got up, swallowed the aspirin and drank voraciously from a fountain in the waiting room. He returned to his seat, walking slowly, taking measured breaths to help relax his muscles and relieve his headache. After a few minutes he felt calmer. It was time to say good bye to Sister Catherine. He walked over to a bank of telephones.

* * *

"This is Mark. How are you today?"

"I'm fine. We've written to the parents of our students to give some notice of our tentative plans. The feedback is enthusiastic and mostly positive. When our plans firm up, I'm certain of their acceptance. This is such a wonderful step for us to take. I am so happy. We've had calls from other schools wanting more details."

"I'm happy for you. Look, you may hear my name mentioned in the news in conjunction with an incident on the *Star Ferry* today. Two men died in an exchange of gunfire. One was the man who has been stalking me for several weeks; the other was the son of the man who amassed the fortune that is our blessing and, quite possibly, our curse. I sincerely hope it's the former."

"Oh, Heavens!" Sister Catherine gasped. "You're not hurt, are you?"

"A scratch or two. I'm OK. I just wanted you to know before you read it in the papers or saw it on television. Please say a prayer for Mr. Székely. If he had not intervened on my behalf, I might not be making this call."

Another hushed gasp at the other end of the line, as the gravity of the circumstances became clearer. "Where are you going? What will you do?"

"I'm going to take up a friend's offer of free snowboarding lessons."

"Something in your voice makes me think this offer was made by a lady friend. I think she's a very lucky woman. God bless you in everything!"

"I'll be in touch soon about the Foundation and some organizational meetings in the spring. I look forward to your participation."

A British accented voice came over the loudspeaker announcing the boarding of *Northwest Orient Flight Number 46* for Seattle and Denver. Mark threw the pea coat over his shoulder. He missed his old rucksack. As he took his place in line, a broad smile appeared on his face. *I hope there's still a lot of snow in Colorado.* His shoulders straightened. He stepped onto the plane, ready for the future. Ready to fulfill his destiny.

THE END

A Mark Davidson Story

LOVE AT FIRST SIGHT

PART II:
KIDNAPPED !

Hellmut Edelmann

Kidnapped!
1995

Day 1, Saturday, 22 April

April, a fickle month at best, had arrived in Paris with cold showers during a short business trip on which Elli had accompanied Mark. Now, some three weeks later in Cannes, the Mediterranean sun shone brightly and spring fashions were as welcome as the flowers sprouting in the warm, fertile soil. The Davidsons had flown down from Geneva the previous night to participate in the Saturday breakfast and silent auction that had attracted so many celebrities to *La Bastide Blanche*, a tennis complex on the *avenue Michel Jourdan*. The event had gone well and Mark noted with pride the admiring eyes of the audience as his wife announced a special gift to the regional youth sports program from the *Foundation*. She was absolutely stunning in her cornflower blue skirt and white silk blouse, a surprise from him on her recent birthday. Except for her sister Dani, who had joined them, no one knew Elli's sparkling presence and gorgeous glowing smile might be attributed, at least in part, to the fact that she was four months pregnant with their first son, a welcome addition to the charming two-year old twins, Mireille and Sylvie, who were safely at home with their governess.

This morning's treat was an exhibition match between Bjørn Borg and his younger countryman, Mats Wilander. All even at a set apiece, the clay court warriors were resting before the third set and Elli had taken advantage of the opportunity to visit the facilities in the club house, indicating as she left, that she might also browse through the festive rows of tented booths in search of souvenirs for friends back home in Yverdon-les-Bains.

Dani, at 32, just two years older than her sister, was busy glancing at her watch between points. "Mark, Elli's taking a long time. I'm going to see if I can catch up with her in one of the bargain tents. Do you want anything?"

"Well, I could use a bottle of cold water, if you happen to see one. Hurry back. This set may not take long."

Enigmatic as ever, Borg moved his opponent back and forth, firing crisp forehands and backhands into the corners from the baseline. Almost equally unemotional, although periodically showing a graceful smile to the audience, Wilander made a few too many unforced errors and the set seemed certain to favor the elder of the two wily court combatants.

Mark, too, started to glance frequently at his watch. *Seems like they've been gone a long time. I tell ya, get two women together where there are sales…"*

During a changeover on court, Dani came rushing up and slid into the chair beside Mark, who was located in a sponsor's box at center court. Whispering loudly into his ear, a concerned look on her face, Dani blurted out rapidly, **"Mark, I can't find Elli anywhere. I'm worried. Please come and help me!"**

Like a *premier danseur* Mark rose, wheeled and vaulted the two steps to the passage separating the boxes from the general stands. Dani was behind him, both loping to the exit. They checked the clubhouse, some temporary toilets arranged in a row behind the club, and carefully scoured the tented bazaar, including the refreshment café next to the main parking lot. There was no sign of Elli anywhere. Telling Dani to stay put on the clubhouse porch and to keep her eyes open, Mark raced back to the stands and charged up to the announcer's booth. On a piece of paper on the announcer's desk, he scribbled a note and handed it to the young man with the microphone. Less than a minute later, during another changeover, the young man opened the public address system. In French, and in English he read: "*Will Mme Michèlle Davidson please report to the clubhouse, where her sister is waiting.*" He repeated it again in

192

both languages. Mark thanked him and departed like a snowman in a heat wave.

When he reached the clubhouse again, Mark found Dani in an animated conversation with one of the security guards. She was frantically trying to explain the situation and describe her sister. For his part, the guard was attempting to calm her, to slow her down so that he could understand. He was one of eight security personnel on duty. They were not policemen, just volunteers recruited to help direct traffic, watch the ticket booth during rush periods and to regulate movement in the stands while play was underway. They didn't seem to comprehend the urgency that Dani, then Mark, were conveying. The latter sensed something serious might have happened. Because they were unconsciously beginning to add a tone of belligerence to the discussion, one of the guards who had approached to see if he could help his colleague summoned the police.

The first policeman to arrive, Patrol Officer Philippe Martin, listened patiently to Dani and Mark, made notes in a pad he carried. and asked a few routine questions, as if quoting verbatim from a text book. Mark's patience was not without limits. His voice grew noticeably louder. Finally, he exploded, demanding more police to assist in the search. Martin detected a slight American accent in Mark's French, which he had improved steadily since taking up residence in Yverdon on Lake Neuchâtel. Martin did not especially like Americans and his disdainful attitude was all too transparent.

Mayhem was avoided when a cook from the clubhouse ran out with two slightly bloody, grossly disheveled young men, shouting that they had been beaten, tied and gagged, then locked in a pantry in the rear of the kitchen. Their catering van was missing. From the crowd of attendees that had gathered to satisfy their curiosity, a boy came forward to say he had seen the catering van drive off. Two men, he claimed, were helping a lady who seemed a bit drunk into the rear of the van. Another woman was also there. He couldn't remember exactly when he witnessed the incident and hadn't noticed which direction the van took when it left the grounds.

A police vehicle, its annoying siren wailing until it screeched to a stop, delivered the well-liveried Chief Inspector, whose polished metal name tag identified him as one Jérôme Pouillnac. He arranged for Dani, Mark and Officer Martin to meet in the club manager's office.

Pouillnac must have been Martin's mentor, for he was cut from the same cloth. He was not so obvious with his anti-Americanism, but was excruciatingly methodical. When he suggested that married women sometimes run off with an admirer, Mark was ready to punch him, but thought better of it. Mark wanted action. Pouillnac was eager to display his amateur psychology theories. This was going to be an intellectual inquiry. Was there really a kidnapping? Why would this woman be considered a desirable victim? Did she have any enemies? Had there, perhaps, been marital difficulties? When Mark insisted some roadblocks be established, Pouillnac ridiculed the request. Straightening his *kepi*, he pontificated, "It would be premature to involve police throughout the entire Côte d'Azur, when there was no proof that a crime had actually been committed." At this comment, Dani excused herself.

At a desk in the main office, Dani took a deep breath. Using her cell phone, she contacted her husband, Roland. He was at home in Lausanne. Hurriedly relating the events of the day as best she could, Dani asked Roland if there was anyone he might call to overcome local inertia and incompetence. Roland, who was an honor graduate of one of the influential Grandes Écoles in science and engineering, had earned his doctorate in Grenoble. A fellow graduate and good friend currently occupied a corner office in the Ministry of Justice in Paris. By some miracle, he was in his office on a Saturday afternoon. Five minutes later, the tension in Pouillnac's headquarters was at its apex, when a conversation between Paris and Cannes dramatically changed the tenor of the meeting. The crimson on Mark's face was transferred, as if by magic, to that of Pouillnac. Criminal Inspector Henri Rinaldi was summoned and put in charge of the investigation. His manner defused the tension. Moments after his arrival an area-wide search for the catering van was instituted. Meanwhile, the clubhouse manager at *La Bastide* called to report a purse, unfortunately empty, had been found near the parking lot, as well as a small syringe. It would be held for the police to retrieve.

Interviews with the catering employees developed only sketchy descriptions of the two probable kidnappers. Rinaldi advised against announcing the case to the media. Requests for information from reporters who had heard rumors of a problem at the tennis tournament were declined.

* * *

Jean-Luc Renard, Director of the *Banque sociale de Léman*, where the Székelys had hidden their secret accounts for nearly five decades while they multiplied in value many times over thanks to the astute management of Renard and his predecessors, normally did not drive into town to his office on a Saturday afternoon. This Saturday was different. Shortly before noon, he had received a most unusual, and startling call just after returning home with his family from a visit to the Vevey municipal farmers' market. Unusual because it was anonymous; startling because it conveyed some negative and derogatory information, expressed as fact, about Hein van Hoek, one of the newest members of the *White Cross Holdings'* Advisory Board. According to the mysterious caller, van Hoek, who was principally responsible for WCH's insurance portfolio, was siphoning off funds and arranging for false claims that defrauded the organization of thousands of dollars. Jean-Luc recalled how he had personally invited van Hoek to join the Board, based largely on a very strong recommendation by van Hoek's countryman, the late Frans Aalster, a long-time Board member in whom Jean-Luc and his late mentor and uncle had the utmost confidence. Trusting absolutely Aalster's judgement, Jean-Luc had skipped the customary vetting procedures for new members. Something that he now feared might have been a most unfortunate oversight on his part. In the privacy and numbing silence of his office, Jean-Luc pondered what to do. First, he contacted an investigator he knew. A discreet check on van Hoek was a priority. Hard, cold facts were required. Strict confidentiality. And, of course, speed. That arranged, the Director took a deep breath. He would have to tell Mark.

Theirs was a relationship built on complete openness and honesty. It could wait until Monday.

As he was about to close up and return to his family, Jean-Luc noticed two old messages were on his secretary's answering machine. The first was an urgent request by an older Board member to contact him about some important matter. The second was a most perplexing and disturbing demand expressed in a calm, deliberate voice in German, a demand for ten million dollars for the safe return of Mrs. Davidson. A crank call? A joke? A sick joke? Neither he, nor Mark knew anyone given to stupid pranks. This was serious.

Mark's cell phone rang. Renard inquired, whether everything was going well.

"Jean-Luc, Elli is missing. Kidnapped! At least, that's what we, what the police think."

"Mark, I'm in the office. There was a message on Marie's answering machine. A demand for ten million dollars for Elli's return. The call was in German, not a Swiss accent. Another call will be made, it said, with further instructions."

"Thanks for calling right away. I'm going crazy here. Dani got Roland to pull some strings in Paris. Otherwise, we'd still be arguing with the local police about some arcane matter. The kidnappers have had a big head start. I'll keep in touch, either at the bank or at your place, as soon as something develops. Please call Roland and tell him about the ransom message."

* * *

Rinaldi was a big, tall, rather gaunt looking chap, but impressively professional. He quickly obtained a detailed description of Elli, made note of the observations of the catering crew and other witnesses, while ordering an all points bulletin for two couples, possibly driving in a white van with a red and blue catering logo on both sides.

Autoroute A8 running east-west along the coast was a logical escape route. The possibilities, especially with a head start, were not encouraging. They might have driven east towards Nice and beyond, or perhaps headed north on N202 towards Isola and Avron. There was also a small highway that hugged the coast in the direction of Juan-les-Pins. N85 north to Mougins and Grasse was usually busy and could provide some cover for fleeing kidnappers. A8 west and N7 led to St.-Raphaël, St.-Tropez and Toulon. To the south was the Mediterranean; another route that couldn't be ignored. Mark and Dani looked at each other, somewhat bewildered by the profusion of escape routes, hoping beyond hope for a lucky break. They were advised to return to their hotel to await further word. Rinaldi promised he would keep them informed.

* * *

In his room at the *InterContinental Carlton*, Mark, a reverent man, though not openly religious, sank to his knees and prayed to the Almighty that the woman he had fallen in love with at first sight be protected during her ordeal. He called home in Yverdon and talked to Mlle Longet, the governess, to inform her of the situation and to talk to his two daughters briefly. He decided to pack Elli's things, just in case he had to leave suddenly the next day. As he did so, he recalled their first brief, actually only seconds-long meeting in Zürich. The wild drive through Lausanne in her GTI was a prelude to a night of ecstasy at the Denis-Breuer villa north of that charming lake-side city. It was in Aspen, where Elli shared her love of winter sports and her new-found prowess on the snowboard, that Mark proposed. The low-key wedding in Vevey, the honeymoon in the Bernese Oberland, and the ultimate joy of twins in the Spring of 1993 had been part of his idyllic existence these past three and a half action-filled years. The *Foundation* he had formed with the billions left to his care by the Székelys was a brilliant success. Elli's sister and her husband, as well as Jean-Luc and his family and the many marvelous men and women on the WCH's Board had all contributed to his happiness, to the sense of satisfaction he experienced in his work. And now, he, or more accurately, his wife had become a target, in spite of the quiet life-style he and Elli consciously chose. They avoided ostentation, lived in a renovated farmhouse outside Yverdon they had bought from Roland, pursued, in most respects, very ordinary, unobtrusive, low-profile lives. It was becoming quite clear that his wife's abduction had been carefully and elaborately planned. *By whom?* Mark wondered.

* * *

The narrow, winding streets of St.-Tropez were not crowded. The tony boutiques on the Place des Lices had used the winter months well to spruce up and prepare for another busy tourist season. The pastel-colored houses glistened in the late morning sun. Most of the pedestrians were locals out to buy essentials for the evening meal. A scene of tranquility greeted a 7-series BMW as it motored nonchalantly into town. The vehicle made an unobtrusive stop on a popular thoroughfare. Jörg Stumpf and his girl friend, Dorthe Steinhammer, called Tati, helped an attractively attired but wobbly young woman to a bench along the Quai Jean-Juarès. They sat down, the woman with the blue skirt and the white blouse between them. Behind them a most impressive array of yachts temporarily lulled to sleep by the gentle, rhythmic ebb and flow of the tide. The driver eased away and continued for five or six hundred meters, then turned right, drove on a couple of blocks and parked in a small lot reserved for shoppers. He slipped out from behind the wheel, closed the car door gently and sauntered back towards the quai, as if looking for a place to catch a bite to eat. After rejoining his companions, he and Jörg, walked along the quai for several minutes, stopping finally at a stairway leading down to a floating wooden dock and a small hut next to which was tied up a handsome 45-foot cabin cruiser, *"La Reine de la Côte"*, a trim vessel sleeping four comfortably in two well-appointed cabins. An afternoon cruise along the coast towards Nice was negotiated, with a hefty cash bonus for the captain, who was induced to serve as the skipper. The boat actually belonged to a group of friends, who alternated use whenever they could interrupt their constant quest for fame and riches. When they were not in town the captain charged with its maintenance was free to take it out for short local runs. A mate was on call to help with the boat and to serve as a waiter, should meals and drinks be required.

Jörg convinced the captain he was capable of assisting with the handling of the boat. He returned to fetch Tati and Elli. Meanwhile, Klaus Uebel, well dressed in gray slacks and a long-sleeved knit maroon shirt, who was readily perceived to be the leader and spokesman for the group, explained that his "wife" had partied a bit too much the evening before and was still recuperating from her excesses.

The Vieux Port faded into the background; sleek, gleaming yachts bobbing up and down from the cabin cruiser's wake. Elli had been hustled below while the captain was distracted. She was resting on a padded bench. Jörg, who had grown up in Stralsund on the Baltic Sea and had worked on fishing boats as a teenager, was busily observing Captain Rosser, who with his seaman's cap pulled down firmly against the wind coming from the west, was a movie director's dream of a salty, leathery-faced man of the sea. The twin inboard diesel engines droned reassuringly as the vessel cut gently through the waves on an easterly heading. The shore was still visible, although a haze obscured the hills beyond. Dark clouds obscured the sun as they approached from the west.

* * *

As his long day as manager of KaDeWe's toy department drew to a close, Rudi Deuffel's feet were killing him. He had been on his feet all day; mostly providing guidance for his sales staff on the selling floor, but also in the sub-cellar storage and work facility, a large space enclosed by a two-meter high chain-link fence and containing three windowless locked work areas, where the most delicate and costly toys were kept. Inside the fence, many toys, still in their shipping cartons, were stacked more than two meters high on sturdy pallets, among which a labyrinth of passageways led like a maze to the largest of the three work spaces, Deuffel's office. The day's only interruption had been a short lunch break that took him up Tauenzienstrasse to the Europa Center from which he had made an important telephone call from one of the phones in a bank of booths on the ground floor; a call to Vevey, Switzerland, where he knew he could leave a message for a man reputed to be incredibly wealthy. Deuffel's sympathetic, kindly façade fooled even his closest associates.

Brought into the post WW II world and christened Gustav Horst von Pyritz, the scrappy youth grew up hearing his parents complain constantly about losing the family estate in what is present-day Poland. His father had been pressed into service defending Berlin as it gasped its last breaths in 1945. By a miracle, he escaped to the countryside with minor wounds. Eventually, he adapted begrudgingly to life in the Soviet Zone and learned to control his dissatisfaction with the bumbling, but brutally repressive totalitarian state that evolved there. Wisely, he dropped the 'von' in his name. He and his wife both died in their fifties from lung cancer.

Gustav was a survivor. He had street smarts and saw the state apparatus as a means to a comfortable life. A cold ruthlessness characterized his general attitude. For a brief period he was a border guard. By accident, he drifted into clandestine activities. Having learned some English, he was recruited to accompany sports figures and government officials on overseas trips; to insure their "safe" return. His career in the *Staatssicherheitsdienst* occasionally involved violence. Few who knew him realized that behind the benign countenance lay a successful hit man. Enemies, dissidents and others who failed to accept the state's persuasive arguments often had "unfortunate" accidents followed by quiet funerals.

Clever Gustav, a great keeper of secrets in a system that was eager to know everyone's private peccadillos, used the inside knowledge gained in his work to completely change his identity. Thus was created Rudi Deuffel, the master bureaucrat. That his new moniker, a play on Ruddy Teufel, or Bloody Devil, was the ultimate inside joke, tickled him whenever he heard someone call his name. Rudi had lots and lots of secrets.

The former Stasi operative, who had worked his way into a choice desk job, was ideally situated to remove and destroy his personnel file when the Ministry of State Security began to crumble in the late eighties. Together with the Uebel brothers, Jürgen, who died in an auto accident in Italy, and Klaus, with whom he had a special relationship, he had masterminded a band of burglars, thieves, smugglers and pimps in a criminal organization, whose annual take from break-ins in German communities along the Czech border was sufficiently substantial to provide for a number of amenities and acquisitions. Following reunification of the two Germanys, Rudi's position at KaDeWe was the perfect cover. At first, they dealt in car radios, CD players, and tires, then late model cars, both for their parts and for the whole vehicle, many of which disappeared into Eastern Europe, only to emerge in the Middle East and Africa, where they brought a premium price. Smuggling American cigarettes, handling drug transportation, dealing in oil, raking in a small fortune, literally on the backs of attractive prostitutes and from porno films made in Hungary, Serbia, Rumania and Bulgaria, all using his solid job at Europe's largest department store as a front, had been lucrative; lucrative, but highly dangerous. Deuffel had made many enemies along the way. The layers of subordinates designed to shield his identity notwithstanding, he was beginning to feel that he was becoming a target for jealous accomplices and rivals alike. Competition with groups in pursuit of alternative agendas had turned ugly. His carefully layered protection was slowly being peeled away. Profits were falling. It was time to find a means of leaving, for, shall we say, a life of well-deserved "retirement".

Rudi and Klaus had met at a bar in the Prenzlauer Berg section of Berlin, when both were employees of the sinister Stasi. It was love at first sight. Ostensibly, they were "on duty", informing on homosexuals in government and other circles. They never reported on each other. The friendship they forged was strong. Both realized that now was the time to score big and "disappear".

Klaus had been engaged by his brother's crony, Gregor Mukhachevo, to guard Zdeněk Székely in Zürich, while Gregor pursued Mark Davidson to Hong Kong. Having heard of his brother's untimely and violent demise, Klaus, who had no reason to be loyal to Mukhachevo, jumped at Székely's offer of money "to look the other way".

While Klaus stepped out of the apartment to stop by a pastry shop

down the street, where he had found some of the most delicious Florentines he had eaten since his mother died, Székely had slipped out of town
and flown to Hong Kong. The short obituary in the back pages of the
Zürcher Tageszeitung mentioned not only the deaths of Székely and his
former aide, Mukhachevo, in a strange shoot out on Hong Kong's Star
Ferry, but also referred to a Dr. Mark Davidson, an American academic.
Rumor had it that a fortune worthy of Midas had fallen into Davidson's
hands. Klaus had not forgotten. Subsequent research revealed Davidson
was married and living in Switzerland, purportedly heading up a foundation worth many, many millions of dollars. Rudi, connecting the dots,
developed a plan to obtain a sizeable chunk of that money. Enough for
the two of them to "retire" to a remote, sparsely-populated island where
they could live their lives in luxury. Rudi was literally thinking of an
island, perhaps in the Andaman Islands. Winters in Berlin were not pleasant.

His office had its own private bathroom; a room that was strictly off
limits to staff members. Tired as he was, Rudi had an errand to run and
he felt the urge to go dancing. He stood for a good twenty minutes in
front of the mirror in his bathroom. A transformation quickly took place
under his practiced hand. The light was extinguished. Taking a purse
from a locked drawer in his desk, Rudi Deuffel, also known in a number
of bars and dance clubs in Berlin as Trudi Valentin, exited from a sel-
dom-used emergency door in the rear of the building and entered the
sultry world of nighttime Berlin.

Trudi was actually quite pretty. She attracted more than a few admiring glances on her way to the Wittenberg Platz U-Bahn Station. In the
subway station, several men did a double take, as it were, ogling the tantalizing gait of the sexy blonde passing by. Finding an empty telephone
booth, she entered, closed the door, deposited several large coins and
dialed from memory a number in Vevey, on Lake Geneva. So complete
was the transformation, that Trudi spoke in such a convincing falsetto
whenever she was in drag, virtually no one had ever detected her true sex,

based on her voice alone. She anticipated correctly that only an answering machine would be on duty.

"Be prepared," she said in even tones, "to deliver a large black leather Louis Vuitton garment bag filled with one million, I repeat, one million American dollars, in accordance with instructions you will receive soon. In addition, nine million dollars must be deposited in a numbered account in an off-shore bank whose details will follow." She hung up, looked about in the station, and proceeded to the subway line that would take her to the Mehring Damm and *Die Hasenfalle*, her favorite coffee bar.

* * *

Waking slightly, Elli's arms were hurting. They had been tied together behind her back. She remembered having been bumped by strangers at the tennis tournament. Her thigh was sore. Something had pricked her there. The rest was fuzzy. She peeked about furtively, sensing accurately she was in danger. The bench she was on was swaying. She could see gray sky through a stairway to the deck of a small craft. There were people arguing. Loud voices, angry words. A man with a captain's cap cocked slightly to the side was distracted by someone. Another man grabbed him from behind, jerked his head back sharply. Elli winced. The man fell over. A few minutes later Elli heard a splash. The sky was heavy now; the sun obscured by clouds. The waves were capped with white. She felt hungry. And scared.

A nattily, if casually dressed man came down into the cabin. He addressed a woman sitting on the opposite bench, who was holding a basin in her hands. "Mein Gott, Tati, are you going to be sick again? A storm is coming from the west. It's going to get a lot worse."

"I can't help it." The woman responding was about Elli's height. Not unattractive, but apparently cold. She was buttoning a sweater around her neck. "What's happening?"

"Jörg has 'taken care' of the old man. We're heading for Corsica. Jörg has charts and he can handle the boat. It's going to be a little rough, but the storm will prevent anyone from finding us. There's something to eat and drink in the locker up front. Give something to our "guest" when she wakes up. Should be soon now. If she causes any trouble, we'll give her another dose."

Dorthe Steinhammer, still looking woozy and pale, got up, rinsed her face in cool water from a container on a shelf behind her and reached for a bottle of Evian, nestled in a rack beneath the shelf. She helped Elli sit up and was about to open the bottle and hold it to Elli's mouth, when she decided it was safe to untie Elli's hands and let her drink by herself from the plastic bottle.

Everyone who knew her called her Tati. Steinhammer was her mother's name. Her mother had been a prostitute. Her 'steady' was a Russian officer. He named their illegitimate daughter Tatiana, after his grandmother. The girl's mother named her Dorthe. After her lover returned to his home and family in Russia, she never heard from him again. She insisted on calling her daughter Dorthe, but friends dubbed her Tati. It stuck and most everyone knew her by that name. Tati was blonde, quite buxom, rather attractive, although there were hard lines in her face. She adored Jörg. Theirs was a relationship of mutual dependency. In spite of his background in crime, Jörg was terribly insecure. He had never really known his father. That was one point of commonality between him and Tati. The other was their appetite for passionate sex. Jörg, principally an enforcer for Rudi, was like a mastiff, whose organ of procreation stood permanently at attention. Tati was like a bitch in perpetual heat. She was about five years older than Jörg. In one sense, she was a replacement for his mother, who had died, while he was working at sea on a fishing trawler. He always had a pocket full of cash and spent it freely on the woman who doted on him and satisfied his most basic needs.

Elli feigned waking up. In answer to Elli's questions: "Where are we? Where are we going?" Tati gave no answer. She hurried up on deck instead. Over the howling of the wind, Elli heard her retching and, finally, vomiting.

The small craft was buffeted by the wind and waves. Rain pelted the cabin roof. Jörg and Klaus, both of whom had put on rain gear they found in a compartment in the aft of the cabin, had taken to shouting at each other, in order to be understood over the churning sea and the fierce wind. They hoped the worst would pass as quickly as it had arrived.

* * *

The glorious April sun that had greeted the day in Cannes had turned to nasty spring showers by late afternoon. Rinaldi called Mark to say that a van spotted in Menton turned out to be a false alarm.

"Police chemists, however, have been able to identify the substance in the syringe found near the tournament's shopping bazaar as 3-Quinuclidinyl Benzilate (QNB, BZ), an anti-cholinergic agent, a so-called "date rape" drug. Roughly 10 to 12 milligrams can incapacitate a person for from four to eight hours. It induces sleep, affects coordination, causes confusion and serious lapses in attention." A terse and disturbing message from Rinaldi. He continued, "The boy who thought he saw a drunken woman being helped into the van probably saw your wife. The mild stupor the drug causes could easily be interpreted as a state of intoxication."

At the words "date rape", Mark's heart took an extra beat. He felt so utterly helpless and wanted to do so much to find her, help her, protect her.

Sensing from the slight gasp he heard that Mark was sinking into despair, Rinaldi, who had three daughters himself, said; "Be strong. If the kidnappers expect a ransom, they won't harm your wife. At least, not right away. If you should be contacted directly, insist on talking to her, just to verify she is all right."

"Thank you. I'll come down to the station early in the morning. I'll go crazy, if I stay here at the hotel. I'm sending my sister-in-law back to Geneva on the first flight."

"Very well. I'll probably be here all night. Try to rest."

* * *

Trudi Valentin, her mind brimming over with plans for Sunday, danced her not so little feet into exhaustion, before catching the subway home to the fourth floor apartment she normally shared with Klaus. There was much to be done in the coming days. Reviewing the plan, detail by detail, her make-up removed, she drifted into dreamland once again as Rudi Deuffel.

Day 2, Sunday, 23 April

Jean-Luc was not himself. His wife noticed as they arose earlier than usual on Sunday morning, that he was distant, apparently lost in troubling thought.

"I had three calls yesterday. Two, coincidentally, anonymous. There was always something about Hein van Hoek that grated in the back of my mind. However, with his countryman Aalster's glowing recommendation, I went ahead and got him on the Board. The caller painted a rather dark picture of van Hoek. I am the one who extended the invitation to him and if he's tainted somehow, I am the one who must get to the botom of it. I put Georges Salber on the case. We'll see if there's a problem."

"I hope it works out. Did you tell Mark?"

"No, once I listened to the second message, the one about Elli, and passed it on to Mark, I just couldn't add another problem. I had one more call on the answering machine. I tried to return it, but there was no answer. I'm going in to the office to try again. Roland is going to contact me there to see what we can do about Elli."

"I won't cook for dinner. Let me know when you're coming home." Madame Renard understood this was not to be an ordinary Sunday.

* * *

"Did Dani make the first flight out of Nice?" Jean-Luc was solicitous.

"Yes, she took a taxi from Geneva to Yverdon. She's going to stay with the girls and the governess. I've hired around-the-clock security for the house. They should be O.K." Roland was talking, but his mind was traveling.

Roland Denis-Breuer, in Mark's view, was a 'gift from God'. He possessed that unique combination of dreamer-inventor and practical entrepreneur. He had a special talent for attracting like-minded individuals to his employ. Roland's ideas and Mark's often coincided. They seemed to communicate intuitively with one another. Often a thought begun by the one would be completed by the other. It was uncanny. In addition to creating and manufacturing precision medical instruments and bio-medical devices, Roland's companies were designing unique prosthetics, many with state-of-the-art electronics and computer controls. The *Foundation*, of which Roland was an important member, helped place new facilities, together with hospitals and trained staffs, in locations in the Middle East, Africa and South Asia, in particular where land mines and on-going armed struggles had injured and maimed significant numbers of innocent civilians. Wherever possible, the *Foundation* hired and trained men and women who had been victimized by these insidious instruments of death and destruction to help design and create medical aids of all kinds to assist in alleviating and ameliorating the human physical damage wreaked on those caught in the middle of conflicts in which they often had no part.

Mark was especially proud of these endeavors of the *Foundation* and the way in which the financial resources of *White Cross Holdings* were being used to bolster *Foundation* objectives and projects. Simple things like helping to provide drinking water and food to those deprived of access to such necessities due to circumstances and situations beyond their control was an obvious goal. Often, creative solutions were required. Likewise the movements to eradicate common debilitating diseases which the *Foundation* spearheaded in multiple locations, relied on the expert input of Roland and his energetic staff. Mediating political disputes was another area in which Mark and Roland had devoted considerable time and effort. While *White Cross Holdings* continued to manage and grow the accumulated wealth so carefully husbanded by Tibor Székely, the

Foundation's Board was continually busy identifying and assessing global needs that fit its philosophy and objectives.

Jean-Luc continued his concise explication of recent events. "This morning I returned a call made to me yesterday by Carl Sorterup in Copenhagen. This van Hoek is contacting some of the newer WCH board members, badmouthing Mark and urging some sort of action to oust him from his chairmanship. The guy must be crazy. He doesn't seem to understand that Mark *is* *White Cross Holdings*. You probably didn't get a call because you're related to Mark."

"Right. I haven't heard a thing."

"This is strictly confidential, but I've had to initiate a secret investigation of van Hoek, because of serious charges against him, unfortunately, via an anonymous call. But I can't simply overlook the matter."

"Jean-Luc, I've been wondering how anyone could have known Elli was to attend the tennis tournament in Cannes. It wasn't in the papers and we did our best to keep it under wraps. You know how cautious Mark is."

"That is curious. I hadn't thought of it. From what Mark says, the kidnapping appears to have been pretty well planned. Say, listen to these telephone tapes. I had one call yesterday. This morning there was another call on the machine. The first was a man's voice; the second a woman's voice."

Jean-Luc and Roland listened to the recording twice.

Roland was cogitating at warp speed. His mind had been to Mars and back in the space of a couple of seconds. "Let me take these to Hermann Weidinger. He's the chief of our audio research lab, an outstanding speech scientist. I'd like to have him subject these to his latest spectrographic speech identification techniques. Do you record all telephone conversations at the bank?"

"As a matter of fact, we do. For security and training reasons."

"How long do you keep the tapes?"

"Generally, sixty days."

"Give me all the tapes from the past two months. Maybe Hermann can turn up something interesting."

* * *

The phone was ringing in Mark's hotel room. "Monsieur Davidson, here is Inspector Rinaldi. I have news you can interpret as good... or bad. I prefer to see it in a positive light."

"What is it?" Mark was apprehensive.

"It's a breakthrough of sorts. The missing catering van was located this morning by a security guard on a routine patrol. It was parked behind a warehouse about two miles from *La Bastide Blanche.* There was no evidence of any significance in the van. Aha, but in St.-Tropez the local police found a BMW sedan that had been stolen three days ago in Nice. Two items of interest are in the report. First of all, there was a gold earring on the back seat. You mentioned, I believe, your wife was wearing something in her ears. Also, a broken piece of a Florentine was wedged between the driver's seat and the center console. Are you familiar with this pastry item?"

"Yes, I happen to like them. What has that to do with the investigation?"

"The owner of the BMW does *not* like them and is allergic to chocolate. So we have our first interesting clue. One of the abductors, probably the driver of the stolen car, was eating a Florentine. We also found some crumbs from a Florentine on the seat of the catering van. The caterers claim their cargo included no such item."

This was not the sort of breakthrough Mark had hoped for. His glum reply, "Let's hope it helps."

* * *

The sea was calm again. The storm had gradually abated at sunrise. Jörg navigated the cabin cruiser, which still had ample fuel, through the cerulean blue waters to a stretch of white sand in a hidden lagoon on the craggy northeast coast of Corsica. The turbulence, the huge swells of the evening before now only an unpleasant memory, Jörg tossed out an anchor and the weary passengers waded a few feet to shore; jagged rocks and dramatic cliffs not far above them. Klaus led the way up a winding path to an outcropping of large granite boulders. The view ahead was captivating. Towering mountains, deep valleys, vine-clad hills. Rather enchanting!

Jörg stopped for a few moments. From his map, he was certain a small town and tourist center they had hoped to find was about a mile to the north. Elli was tied and gagged. Jörg studied her with undisguised sexual arousal. With Tati remaining behind to watch her, both were leaning against tree trunks in the shade of a group of Laricio pines while the two men strode into town. Rudi had arranged by internet, using a forged credit card for payment, for a two-week rental of a remote vacation cottage. Now they needed transportation. Two 4-wheel drive Subaru wagons were rented from a sleepy agency that never imagined such pre-season business so early on a Sunday morning. Each required a substantial security deposit. No problem! Klaus had lots of cash; French, Swiss and German currency.

He and Rudi understood, it might require some expenditures, an 'investment' if you will, in order to reap a really big profit. Klaus helped Elli onto the rear seat of his wagon. Tati sat next to Jörg in the front of the other. Jörg led the way. The major roads were good. After twenty minutes they turned inland following a dirt and gravel road that twisted and turned, climbing higher and higher. The further they drove, the bumpier the roadway, which had more than its share of potholes. They passed a small farmhouse with what looked like a working distillery under a shed covered with corrugated steel panels. Jörg told Tati it was probably an artisanal enterprise producing aromatic oils and ointments from the natural herbs, flowers, roots, and other botanical materials found in the *maquis*, the dense shrub-covered expanses that lined either side of the road. There were signs of some terrace cultivation on an adjacent hillside. A sweet chestnut forest gave way to fields with a mixture of lavender, arbutus and juniper bushes growing in heaps near myrtle and heather.

Finally, in a clearing amidst orchards of apple trees, cork oaks and a few olive trees, there was a cottage of stone with a lean-to carport. Both drivers backed their vehicles into the parking area, one behind the other. The cottage was small. Indoor plumbing was a plus. The kitchen corner was strictly utilitarian. It had a typically small European refrigerator. The pantry, as requested, was stocked for a two-week stay, all paid in advance. Linens were on the beds. There was one bedroom, an open living-dining space, the kitchen and pantry tucked into one corner and on the opposite side a spiral staircase leading to a sleeping loft with a double bed. The latter was claimed immediately by Jörg, who dragged his "woman" up behind him. Elli was tied hands and feet to the bed in the bedroom. Klaus chose to sleep on the sofa in the living area. Looking out one of the rear windows, Klaus thought he saw a wild pig running into the bushes. In the distance were several peaks and what Klaus thought was one of the alpine volcanic lakes found on Corsica. They all hunkered down. Rudi was to contact them on the cell phone in the evening. Klaus plugged his phone into a wall outlet to be sure it was adequately charged. He considered how lucky they were, that there were so few people on the roads on Sunday.

* * *

The earring found in the BMW arrived in Cannes. Mark was at the police prefecture to identify it. It was definitely Elli's. Mark had picked it out himself. Rinaldi had gone to the morgue in Nice to check a body that had washed ashore early in the morning. It was a male, late fifties or early sixties. Hands and feet bound with rope. Apparent trauma to the neck. They would have to wait for an autopsy to determine the exact cause of death. Foul play was obvious. From St.-Tropez there was a missing person report. The captain of a charter boat, a 45-foot cabin cruiser, had not returned from a cruise along the coast Saturday afternoon. His office log book noted that he was taking two couples out for a two-three hour cruise. The boat was not in its usual slip.

* * *

Rudi Deuffel liked to sleep late on Sunday mornings. Lately, he had had so much on his mind, that the Sunday sleep-in was essential to his health. Learning that the call which jolted him like a bolt of lightning so early on his day off was from that Jew, Moshe Jutz, irritated him no end. His irritation was obvious when he spoke to the short, shapeless, pink-faced gnome with the long nose and the thick glasses. He might have been far to the left of ugly, but he was an absolute genius, whom no one respected more than Rudi, who had dreamed of owning a magnificent model railroad since his childhood. For, at Rudi's insistence and with his full support, Jutz had taken an elaborate concept and created a genuine masterpiece.

This cross between Merlin and Alberich kept a delightful model railroad layout in the basement of his apartment building in Steglitz. Every Channukah/Christmas he allowed neighborhood children to view the trains as they ran in and out of the tunnels and over the bridges that he had constructed in his magical, whimsical landscape; a Never-Never-Land of wondrously executed miniaturization. N-scale was his favorite, his ideal. All his train stock, his houses, barns, stations, figures, everything was exactingly made to the scale of 1:160. Herr Jutz' "Putz", as his layout was called, was an annual delight. The occasional *Mark* or fifty-cent coin grateful parents and children gave him for the privilege of viewing the "Putz", was scarcely just recompense for the long, tedious hours and the extraordinary skill invested in his creation.

Rudi, who often referred to himself as a "trainiac", first met Jutz at KaDeWe, where the latter would come to see some of the new commercial trains on the market. Once he had visited the Putz, Rudi's brain worked overtime, trying to figure out how he could get a similar train display. Not for the store necessarily, but for himself. In a moment of pure inspiration he challenged Jutz, who enjoyed the adulation, to create "Die Vierjahreszeiten", The Four Seasons; four train layouts, each representing the identical imaginary landscape in each of the four seasons,

Spring, Summer, Autumn and Winter, in a typical Piedmont or sub-alpine geographic area, as true to the colors and features of nature as pos-sible.

Providing Jutz with modest financial help and store discounts, Rudi followed the shy, careful craftsman's progress patiently for an entire year, as he assembled the highly detailed, complex landscapes. Deuffel encouraged Jutz by proclaiming he could sell them through KaDeWe for an enormous sum, which he would share equally between the creator and the store.

A true triumph of diligence and artistic dexterity on Jutz' part, the finished products, displayed prominently in the store, had been a record-setting draw in the store's toy department for two months. Deuffel exulted in their detail and realism. He often played with them before and after store hours. Toy sales had been boosted to new highs. Rudi lusted for "Die Vierjahreszeiten" as an avid art collector for a rare Van Gogh, a Modigliani, an original Renoir. Each of the hand-carved, hand-painted figures, whether of lead, pewter, wood, or plastic, many movable on electronic stimuli, required hours of intense labor. The highway traffic, the farm scenes, the ski lifts and aerial tramways, all to scale, could be actuated from a master control board through a unique system of computer chips, switches, solenoids and relays. The waterways, tunnels, bridges, switchbacks, buildings, lighting systems and rail yards all functioned with perfect realism. Six separate trains could operate simultaneously; two electric commuter trains; four diesel locomotives for freight and long distance passenger hauling. The junctions and crossings were programmed to stop, start or slow trains so that no accident could occur. It was, indeed, an ideal world. Each "Season" was constructed in such a manner, that its four two by three meter sections could be separated and safely packed into a huge crates for shipment or storage. Two additional crates carefully protected a wide array of rolling stock; many were well-known European locomotives built from scratch according to the originals. The asking price was 500,000 *Marks* for each season, including a complete set of the rolling stock and computerized control panels.

The "Seasons" display had been carefully removed from the selling floor of Europe's largest department store. Rudi had told Jutz an oil baron from the Middle East was the purchaser. Upon safe receipt of the layouts, prompt payment would be made and Jutz would get his share. Jutz called to arrange a meeting with Rudi and was planning to bring his mother along. Deuffel, who despised the aggressive and demanding Frau Jutz, dissuaded his friend from subjecting his mother to the rigors of sub-way travel, even on a Sunday, and, instead, arranged to meet with him privately, letting him in to the sub-cellar through a rear door. Jutz loved to ride the freight elevator. A simple enough thrill Rudi was happy to provide. As it turned out, the visit was not entirely pleasant. Jutz was get-ting impatient for his money, even asked for an advance. He became rather insistent. Rudi had to be a bit abrupt. Getting rid of him by prom-ising the money at the end of the week. Jutz, grumbling under his breath in Jiddish, departed.

"*Hmmm, things are beginning to come together,*" thought Rudi. "*Tim-ing is everything.*"

* * *

At Roland's suggestion, Jean-Luc drove over from Vevey to the Denis-Breuer estate north of Lausanne. Hermann Weidinger, one of Roland's top research scientists was already there.

"Jean-Luc, we think we've found something interesting. Hermann and his staff have taken the analog recordings from your telephone sys-tem and re-recorded them digitally. Several expert linguists were involved. They listened to the accent, the inflection, syllable groupings, breath patterns and other speech habits from the two ransom demands. Comparison of the psycholinguistic features of the speakers' voices has led them to the conclusion, that they are one and the same person, albeit a person with a dual personality, possibly with issues of sexual identity. The dialect is definitely from Berlin. We examined the telephone records. Both calls originated there. The initial contact was from a phone booth in the Europa Center; the second call emanated from a booth in the Wittenberg Platz U-Bahn Station. If there are further calls, we'll trace them. There was also something else we noted in a review of all calls made the past sixty days. You have a very courteous and helpful staff, truly professional. One exception, however, came to our attention. Mme Chounard has had several calls from a M. Van Hoek. They usually speak in French, although he, I believe, is Dutch. They have become rather cozy. He has apparently been pushing her for confidential information about Mark and Elli, especially Mark. Another thing, a stranger managed to get from Mme Chounard details of this weekend's trip to Cannes, including flight schedules, hotel information and other particulars of their stay."

"Well, that explains how someone could plan an abduction so carefully, doesn't it?

* * *

Hein van Hoek had managed to get Mme Chounard's home phone number from her while probing for information on one of his shmoozing expeditions. Having learned by chance on one of his earlier calls that she was celebrating a birthday today, he had taken the liberty of sending a floral bouquet to her home. His follow-up call was yet another rather transparent attempt to further ingratiate himself with this useful inside source of information. An unexpected dividend flowed easily from the busomy divorcée's mouth as she revealed that Dr. Davidson's wife had apparently been kidnapped while on her visit to Cannes. It could not be said that van Hoek was happy to learn of Elli's unfortunate circumstance, but in a purely pragmatic sense, he thought leaking the information to the media might somehow benefit his case for dumping Mark from WCH leadership. A tip to a friendly reporter got the ball rolling. No matter, it jeopardized the intense search currently underway. No matter, it deeply angered Mark and his friends.

* * *

That the abduction was now in the news troubled Mark. Although he did not want to appear paranoid about his family's privacy, he had nevertheless gone to great pains to avoid publicity about himself, his wife and his children. He did this in part out of modesty and a general desire to pursue the *Foundation*'s objectives quietly, and partly to protect his loved ones from those who might be attracted to his wealth as a result of excessive public scrutiny. To his neighbors he was a devoted husband and father, who, in the true Swiss tradition, was an internationally-oriented business executive, often required to travel abroad. His personal charitable activities were conducted anonymously, wherever possible. Elli and the girls were rarely photographed. The exception being quiet family functions.

How could this information have leaked out? The police themselves had recommended a media blackout, hoping to encourage the kidnappers to negotiate directly. Everyone at the bank and at WCH headquarters had been cautioned to keep the matter hushed. How had a reporter gotten the details? Who could have been so thoughtless and reckless with this information? Mark's concern for Elli's precarious situation and the health of their unborn child was elevated a couple of notches as he pondered this new development.

* * *

Breaking in the late afternoon on some television and radio stations, Rudi Deuffel, too, was angry upon learning that his caper was now in the public domain. A cool evening breeze was blowing and a few rain showers dampened the streets of Berlin as an attractive woman, estimated by passersby to be in her late thirties or early forties, took the subway to the Augsburgerstrasse U-Bahn Station. Assuming that Klaus and Co. didn't have access to a radio or television receiver, Trudi Valentin first called Klaus' cell phone and told him to be wary, lay low, because news of the kidnapping was now public. Her second call was picked up by a security guard on duty at the bank in Vevey.

Sounding somewhat like a spinster condemned by society to live a solitary existence of all work and no play, Trudi, showing her irritation, agitatedly scolded the clueless guard about the disclosure of the kidnapping and threatened bodily harm to Elli, if further details were broadcast. The guard immediately contacted Jean-Luc to report the call.

* * *

In the loft, Tati had dozed off following a session of passionate sex with Jörg. Klaus, still exhausted from the strain of the turbulent passage to Corsica, was conked out on the sofa. Jörg descended the circular staircase and padded in his socks to the main bedroom. Elli lay still, her hands tied to the metal headboard, her feet bound to the foot rail. Before she could vocally protest, Jörg deftly covered her mouth with his hand. She was groggy, but awake. Jörg climbed on the side of the bed. He touched her cheek, then bent and kissed her forehead. As he fondled her breasts, he whispered, "I've got something here, that's going to give you the treat of a lifetime." He touched his crotch with one hand; then he started at her right knee and slowly moved up the inside of her thigh, squeezing her firm flesh. As he progressed, Elli's eyes were full of revulsion and defiance, her muscles tensed. She squirmed.

"Jörg, what the hell are you doing? Get out of the room! You know Rudi insists she not be mistreated!" Fortunately for Elli, Uebel was a light sleeper. He needed to maintain control. Too much was a stake to allow an oversexed pervert to screw it up.

Klaus' obvious irritation miffed Jörg. "Hey, what good is she, if we can't have some fun with her?" He resented the scolding.

Tati, awakened by the loud voices below, had rushed down the stairs and stomped across the floor to the bedroom. Jörg was hers, she felt, and she was not going to let him stray, if she could help it. Somewhat sheep-ishly, he followed her back up the stairs.

Klaus helped Elli to sit up and gave her a few swallows from a glass of water. He knew he had to keep her alive. For now. He was fully aware that she had seen all their faces. He had nothing personal against her, or any other woman for that matter, but he knew what eventually had to be done. He left the room and shut the door.

* * *

Elli longed for her farmhouse in Yverdon, for her two lively little girls; constantly, impishly mischievous, but still such lovely darlings. Meeting Mark had changed her life. She was blessed with an adoring husband, two wonderful children, a challenging position as liaison between the bank and *La Fondation Székely*, the charitable entity Mark had created to deal with the billions that had sprouted from illicit wartime loot, whose origins were shrouded in the ashes of history. How could she escape? What if there was no escape? She was overcome with a sense of helplessness. She understood the menace in the eyes of her captors.

* * *

Mark, trying to rest, found his thoughts wandering back through the three years since he met Elli. Fate had always seemed to smile on him. Often, when he least expected it, or when the future was unsure, some interesting twist of fate picked him up and carried him along for a splendid ride. His decision to move to the Carolina Low Country had been fortuitous. His election to the deanship was the work of fate. So, too, was the unusual encounter with Sister Catherine. He had made an immediate connection with her, whom he greatly admired, was inspired by and with whom he had been infatuated for months. Random dorm assignments, casual acquaintances from college days, involving men that chance had thrown together, had evolved into enduring friendships. And these had freely offered support and help during his quest for the secret numbered accounts that were the key to securing the funds old Tibor Székely wanted so much to use to help mankind.

It all seemed like some crazy fantasy now; an impossible dream. To look for an instant into a woman's eyes and to know you were destined to be with her. Subsequent events had demonstrated how fate and the efficacy of positive thinking could converge to achieve the most sublime dream. The inner voice that dictated his flight to Colorado, the wedding soon after and the glorious three years that followed, all capped by the birth of two angels that warmed his heart and lifted his spirit whenever he thought of them.

In the bargain he had gained a loving sister-in-law, her brilliant husband, whose participation in the *Foundation*'s activities had already generated wide acclaim. Jean-Luc, the quintessential banker, was a rock. As a principal in both the *Foundation* and the holding company, he had played a masterful role in pursuing the details that led to recent completion of the Aja Lasková Regional Medical Center in eastern Slovakia. Old buddies, Luigi Nardini, who assisted in the creation of a movement to establish hospices for persons suffering from AIDS, cancer and debilitating diseases like Alzheimers, and Gordon Hui, who oversaw the construction of the Paulian Sisters' Girls College complex in Hong Kong, together with Sister Catherine, were truly remarkable.

Fate had been good to him, Mark reminded himself. Still, he had had a prophetic moment in Hong Kong, when he expressed the hope that the multi-billions he had suddenly come into, would not have a negative side. Elli's kidnapping illustrated in a most personal manner, how evil, a constant in a world of humans, could rear its ugly head and thumb its nose at those seeking to do good. *The indomitable spirit of avarice. The thirst for easy riches that blinded Gregor and moved him to show his benefactor the ultimate ingratitude.* Fate, *in toto*, had been decidedly good to him. He needed desperately for it to be good once more. With that on his mind, he drifted off to sleep.

Day 3, Monday, 24 April

Klaus is up early. He makes coffee and checks on Elli. During the night, as the temperatures dropped, probably because of the altitude, he had given her an extra blanket shortly after Tati finished supervising a bathroom break. The urbane Klaus, shaved and showered, is mumbling about the *biscotti* he is dunking in his coffee. "*When we requested provisioning the cottage, we should have specified a good supply of Florentines.*" The thought crosses his mind, that if he and Rudi move to the Andaman Islands, he'll probably have to bake his own. *Not likely to find a German Konditorei there.* So as not to upset his nervous accomplices, Klaus decides not to discuss further the fact that the kidnapping and the search for Mme Davidson is now a public matter, something Rudi had communicated on a call from Berlin.

* * *

Klaus' most vivid memory of his mother, was one in which she was busily baking in their small third-floor walk-up apartment's kitchen. Baking delicious pastries, her way of compensating young Klaus for the absence of a father in the home and a somewhat abusive older brother, a brother with a mean streak. Her specialty was *Florentiner*, a delightfully chewy concoction rich with butter, cream, and honey, loaded with candied orange peel, or, sometimes, apricot marmalade, finely slivered almonds and, on certain occasions, topped with a candied cherry. He loved the first one he ever ate. As an adult, Klaus had become something of a connoisseur. Whenever he saw a *pâtisserie*, a *konditorei* or a pastry shop, he checked to see if there were any fresh Florentines. If there were, he was seldom able to resist sampling them. He was partial to those baked like cookies, usually round, and, more often than not, glazed on the bottom with chocolate; bitter chocolate being preferred by far to milk chocolate. He especially enjoyed the Florentine he bought in Cannes. This one, he recalled nostalgically, had been baked in a pan, then cut into triangles. One corner had been dipped in an icing of dark, half-bitter chocolate. It was, he remembered, slightly crisp and the delicately sliced almonds were perfectly baked to a golden brown. His eyes began to moisten, when he visualized the sudden stop he had had to make driving to St.-Tropez. Luckily, he had avoided an auto accident, but in the confusion he had dropped a corner of his Florentine beside the driver's seat.

* * *

A gendarme, whose beat was the section of Corsica's northeast coast where Jörg had beached the cabin cruiser, was alerted to its presence there by some boys who discovered it while fishing. Word of the discovery reached police headquarters in Bastia not long after a fax was received describing a charter boat missing from St.-Tropez. Claude Doucette, an inspector in the department, contacted St.-Tropez and was told to phone Special Inspector Rinaldi in Cannes.

"Have you had an opportunity to inspect the boat yet?" Rinaldi, masking his excitement, seemed fairly calm.

"No, but the officer who reported the incident is at the scene right now. I have him on a portable phone. Should he look for anything in particular?"

"Can he determine anything about the occupants? Any sign where they might be now?"

Doucette queried the officer, who was looking the cabin cruiser over. "He says it's a bit of a mess. Looks like more than one person on board was seasick. Otherwise nothing left behind."

"Don't let this go beyond your office. We think a kidnapped woman was on board. If she's not there now, she may have been taken some-where. I suspect the kidnappers did not stray too far from the area. Begin checking on local hotels, car rental agencies and the like. I will be flying into Bastia with an aide and the woman's husband within the next two hours. This is a serious case. Please keep it quiet. No press."

"*Bien sûr*! I'll have a police car meet you at the airport."

* * *

Taking the elevator to the sixth floor, Rudi Deuffel strolls swiftly through KaDeWe's famed food counters. He opts for a *currywurst* and a tall glass of *Berliner Weisse*. Consumption takes almost less time than placing the order. The lunch hour crowd is bustling and boisterous. No one notices the balding Rudi, as he leaves the store and catches the subway at Wittenberg Platz, alighting minutes later at the Kurfürstendamm Station. Strolling casually, Rudi peruses the shop window displays for a good ten minutes, then inconspicuously steps into an unoccupied phone booth. Using coins, he dials a now familiar number in Vevey.

Jean-Luc Renard picks up at the other end. "*Ici* Renard."

"Renard, Listen carefully! I'm calling about Mme Davidson. If her husband wants to see her alive, he must pay ten million dollars. One million cash in twenty, fifty and hundred dollar denominations in a manner I will describe. Nine million deposited in a numbered off-shore account. The details have been mailed to you. Any tricks and the woman will die! Do you understand?" Rudi's tone was harsh.

"Yes, yes, of course!" Renard didn't want to be cut off and hoped he might enable a solid trace, if he could prolong the conversation. "Dr. Davidson is willing to pay. However, he needs proof his wife is all right. He insists on talking to her. You must arrange it." Renard tried to be firm, insistent, without antagonizing the caller.

"I'll see what I can do." There was an abrupt clicking sound and the line went dead.

* * *

Perpignan, southern France. Dr. Med. Jules Picone was listening to the noon news review in his office, while munching on a lettuce and tomato sandwich and sipping a glass of rosé his wife had delivered just after his morning consultations. After a brief 30-minute nap, his routine would take him to a retirement home he owned, where twenty well-to-do elderly patients awaited his doting, if expensive ministrations.

Picone intended to retire early to a life of ease. His goal was to amass an investment portfolio that would guarantee him and his wife long years of comfortable leisure living. The retirement home, a nursing facility, was part of his portfolio. In addition, he owned beach properties on the Costa Brava, two condos outside Sète and one near Antibes. He also had two condominiums for rent on Mallorca and had recently bought rental properties in Corsica. His web site was beginning to pay off. One of the Corsican rentals had attracted a German client from Berlin who paid in advance for two weeks sight unseen.

Picone's ears caught the word Corsica. He turned up the volume: A pleasant woman's voice was reading a bulletin. "*A female Swiss citizen visiting Cannes Saturday is believed to have been kidnapped there by two men and a woman, possibly German. A small cabin cruiser chartered by the group was found off the northeast coast of Corsica.*" There it was again. "*A search is underway to locate the missing woman and her captors.*" Picone did not listen to the announcements that followed. He pursed his lips. Thought for a moment, then shook his head in an expression of disbelief and departed for the nursing facility.

* * *

Inspector Doucette had nothing very encouraging to share with his mainland colleague and the earnest-looking young man who was with him. They had arrived by charter plane within the hour. However, by late afternoon an officer reported that a car rental agency had rented for an extended period two Subaru wagons capable of off-road travel. The two men who rented them paid a substantial cash deposit and intimated they were going south towards Ajaccio, possibly all the way to Bonifacio. One had hiking boots and a rucksack. Between themselves they were discussing some climbing or hiking objectives. Apparently, no details were noted.

Doucette, a thoughtful, professional-looking policeman, regretted not having more to go on. A bulletin had been issued to look for the two vehicles. Mark, who had been slightly up-beat upon arriving in Bastia, now looked pretty glum. He studied a map of the area mounted on a wall in Doucette's office.

* * *

Roland Denis-Breuer, engineer, research scientist, a great admirer of Mark and Elli, was a natural detective. He had barely slept since learning of the kidnapping. Aside from concluding that the male and female voices recorded on the bank's telephone screening system belonged to one person, the knowledge that the caller was a Berliner was truly significant. Roland and his voice identification specialist, Weidinger, arranged for incoming long distance calls to be automatically traced. The latest call showed clearly that the calls were placed from subway station phone booths within a relatively short distance of each other, all essentially with the Europa Center as a hub.

"If I had to guess," Roland rubbed his chin thoughtfully, "I'd say the person making the calls probably works nearby. He makes the calls either during his lunch hour or, in his female *persona*, some time after the end of the work day. What do you think?"

Weidinger, a clean-shaven, tanned fellow in his late twenties opined, "It sounds highly plausible to me. I've spent some time in Berlin. There are, of course, many, many thousands of people passing through the subway stations in question each and every day. Tourists alone constitute, together with the foreign panhandlers who gather there, an enormous chunk of humanity in or near the Europa Center, a building, by the way, that has lost much of its earlier glitter, and the open space next to the Kaiser-Wilhelm-Memorial-Church, if my memory serves me. Government offices, private businesses, all kinds of commercial establishments abound in the area. How can we possibly narrow it down?"

"I have a contact in Bern, a relative, as a matter of fact. With his help, we'll have the authorities in Berlin show us how technologically advanced they are. We're going to place these telephone banks under video surveillance and see what develops. Call Jean-Luc and let him know what's up. I'm going to my office to twist some arms."

* * *

Schinkenwurst, Blutwurst, several slices of flaxseed bread and a small wedge of *Brie* were consumed by a restless Rudi Deuffel. He was drinking hot tea because of a noticeable chill in the April air. The streets were damp again. Every few bites, he jumped up, opened another drawer and dumped a variety of items into a sack he would later leave in the trash receptacles behind his apartment building. He had also begun to separate in his closet the clothes he planned to pack later in the week and those he intended to abandon. He switched on his little television set and turned the dial to ZDF for an evening news review. Nothing of great import. It occurred to him that he had never heard any news on TV emanating from the Andaman Islands. Interesting! A brief item about some celebrity's divorce was followed by an odd interview. A young female reporter was holding a microphone in the face of a uniformed policeman, equally as young, and obviously thrilled to be asked something on camera. At first, he protested he was not able to discuss the case being investigated. The reporter, nonetheless, tricked him through her line of questioning, into revealing that a tip from an absentee French landlord might lead to the kidnappers. A surprise was being organized for the next day. Rudi's eyes bulged noticeably.

Disembarking from the subway car in the Uhlandstrasse Station, Rudi, clad in jeans, a leather jacket and blue baseball cap, found a booth empty and placed a call to Klaus on the latter's cell phone.

"Klausi, listen carefully. The police may be on to your location. You need to leave before dawn. There might be a raid. We talked about contingencies before. Austria, the Alps, maybe Bavaria. They'll be watching airports, ship departures, major highways, railroad terminals. I'm counting on you. The money is due on Friday. Viel Glück!" Before Klaus could get in a word, his partner hung up.

* * *

Tati was watching Elli, who had been allowed to shower. Klaus pulled Jörg into the kitchen corner and began talking in a low voice. "The kidnapping has made the news, if not the headlines. There's a good possibility, a search may be launched near here. They have found the cabin cruiser. I have a plan. We'll be leaving here in the middle of the night. Pass it on to Tati quietly. Get your things together and catch forty winks."

"Where will we go? How will we get there?"

"Stay cool! I'll tell you in the morning."

* * *

Feeling sore all over from having been tied to the bed, Elli's mind struggled mightily to connect her random thoughts. She was aware that she was being drugged. She worried about her two little girls. An escape seemed impossible. *This lethargy. I keep drifting away. My poor babies! Why am I here?* She was concerned about the one called Jörg, an arrantly evil man whose lascivious glances sent a chill of revulsion through her being.

* * *

Mark lay in bed. He knew he needed rest in order to contribute 100%, however, once again, his mind involuntarily recapped the past three amazing years. Always somewhat hectic, yet incredibly fulfilling, rich and varied, their breathless pace could be attributed to Mark's insistence on being heavily involved in the *Foundation's* work. He averaged only 3 or 4 days a month in his office at Geneva headquarters. When he wasn't running the overall operation from the old farmhouse in Yverdon, he was in the field researching proposals, meeting with project managers, reviewing plans, scrutinizing budgets, developing and signing contracts. He could be in Latin America, in Asia, in Africa, somewhere in Europe, even back in the States. Often, Jean-Luc or Roland came along.

His travel, among other things, was managed by Samantha Willis, a quadriplegic, for whom the headquarters building had been substantially renovated. A new entrance was constructed, a special elevator installed, sophisticated voice-activated controls invented and made available throughout the building. Sam was an organizational genius. Her steel-trap mind was ever busy and she never forgot a detail. The *Foundation*'s directors relied on her. Her staff was a model of efficiency and Sam, herself, generated an immense sense of pride and commitment that infused all with whom she came into contact. She had become, in a word, indispensable. She was fiercely loyal to Mark and Elli.

Whatever satisfaction he felt when thinking of the *Foundation*'s accomplishments and the marvelous people it had been his good fortune to attract to work with him, he could not deny the central role in his existence played by Elli, the love of his life, a woman with as many brilliant facets as the finest diamond. *I bless the fate that brought us together, and curse the fate that now separates us.*

A wonderful wife and an exemplary, loving mother, Elli's background in business and economics had proven itself a tremendous asset on numerous occasions. She was great fun to be with and often accompanied Mark, to his delight, on extended trips abroad. With his encouragement, Elli had continued her interest in music and the theater, garnering accolades wherever she performed. He especially remembered a local production of *Die lustige Witwe* in Basel, in which she played Valencienne. In Montreux, her Susanna in *Le Nozze de Figaro* was a smash hit. Together with Jose Carreras and a distinguished international cast, Elli had sung arias from Traviata, Fledermaus, Carmen and a selection of Schubert songs for a benefit gala in Neuchâtel that had received rave reviews. Her acting and singing brought boundless joy to Mark, a self-proclaimed incurable romantic. He fell in love with her over and over again.

Elli's fellow performers had no idea that she was, in her own right, a millionairess, much less that she was married to one of the world's richest men. And now, in spite of their constant efforts to avoid public attention,

Elli, somehow, had become a target for ruthless criminals. What could he do? How could he help his precious Elli in her hour of need? Worry finally brought on the fatigue that induced sleep.

Day 4, Tuesday, 25 April

The Honorable Dr. Picone's conscience prevailed. By late afternoon Monday, just after leaving his private nursing home, he called the police in Cannes. He had, he said, recently rented a mountain cottage he owned in a relatively inaccessible northern Corsican location to a party from Germany. The transaction took place on the internet and full payment, with authorization for an additional sum, should there be physical damage to the property, was accomplished with the renter's EuroKarte. While he had no reason to believe the kidnapping reported in the news was in any way related to his vacation rental, he felt it was something the police might want to check out. He provided directions from Bastia.

* * *

The Commissar, considering this development a potentially important career-advancing coup, directed Inspector Doucette to organize a squad of his best men, with the intention of conducting a surprise early morning raid. The Inspector was advised to inform his officers that use of firearms must be avoided, unless the officers were in mortal danger. "We don't want any innocent parties to be harmed!"

The Commissar didn't need to remind the Inspector that a loose cannon on the force had recently overreacted in a raid on a band of Corsican separatists and one of the suspects was killed, causing an enormous political furor in the region.

Mark sat next to Doucette, who was driving the lead vehicle in a convoy of three off-road utility vehicles. Rinaldi was accompanying as an observer in the last vehicle. The climb up the rough, winding road challenged the four-cylinder engine. They stopped on the side of the dirt and gravel road about a hundred meters short of the deeply rutted driveway leading up to the cottage. It was well before dawn and clouds obscured a weak moon. At least one vehicle, which looked like a Subaru, was under the car port. The cottage was enveloped in darkness.

Officers fanned out quietly, effectively surrounding the house. Doucette saw a faint light flicker on and off in the building. Using a bull horn, he announced the presence of his force, exaggerating its number by a factor of three. He demanded the occupants exit through the front door, without weapons, and with their hands held high. The raiders squatted in total silence. Doucette thought he had seen a head pop up in one of the two small windows in the front of the structure. His bull horn raised again, he repeated his demand. Some of the younger officers, eager for action, shuffled their feet, a sign of restlessness. There was no further indication of activity in the cottage. Doucette and his men waited patiently, silently. A new summons to vacate the building with hands held high was issued over the bullhorn. If the circumstances hadn't been so serious and compelling, Mark would have let the stray thought about Keystone Cops take its course. Here he was in the middle of nowhere and he felt helpless, lost.

A voice in the dark near Doucette suggested using tear gas or a concussion grenade. Rinaldi, squatting next to Mark, temporarily forgot he was out of his jurisdiction and stated the obvious; that might endanger Mrs. Davidson. Doucette agreed. He ordered the vehicles to be moved up within twenty meters of the house. With high beams directed at the front and sides of the cottage and officers placed at both front and rear exits, the bullhorn once again, more resolutely than before, demanded the occupants leave with hands folded behind their heads.

Suddenly, the front door opened meekly. Multiple fingers began to press lightly against rifle and revolver triggers. The officer next to Doucette and Mark played the beam from a long olive-green military-style flashlight on the figure slowly emerging sheepishly from the door. Two officers who had been crouching on either side of the entrance, grabbed the figure, actually a rather frail, shaggy looking male, and flung him to the ground.

The two officers entered the cottage; Mark on their heels. The interior lights were flicked on. Empty! Completely empty! Mark was dumbfounded. Outside, Doucette was interrogating a frightened homeless man. He had been camped nearby in the woods. Noting the departure of the occupants, two couples, a few hours earlier, he had crept in through an unlocked window to scavenge for food and valuables. He was scolded and released on the spot. He scampered into the trees like a startled fawn. The house was scoured for evidence. Elli's white blouse, rather soiled, was on the bathroom floor. Otherwise, nothing useful.

The three off-road vehicles returned down the steep incline. The unpaved upper section of the road was rocky. As they approached the ramshackle farm house closer to the valley floor, Doucette stopped. An old woman wearing a kerchief was plucking greens from her garden.

In response to the Inspector's inquiry, she replied, "We didn't see anyone go up the hill, because we've been working some fields a couple of kilometers further down the valley, but very early this morning, maybe around two o'clock, I heard a car or truck roll past the house. I think the driver was intentionally trying to avoid waking us. Very thoughtful, I felt."

"Thank you. Have a nice day!" The Inspector tipped his cap. The convoy sped off, heading back towards Bastia.

* * *

Initially, Klaus considered leaving the island by boat. Then, he realized they would be too vulnerable to observation from the air. Faster boats could easily overtake them. He liked simple plans. However, he was not averse to enhancing them or tacking on an embellishment that might gain them extra time, might confuse the "enemy". Whenever he could, he bore right, aiming in the direction of the rising sun. There it was. The coast. A roadside sign with a couple of bullet holes in it announced the community of Soretta. It was virtually asleep, with the exception of a few hardy souls who either had a job to report to, or were compulsive early risers. The paved road dipped down towards the beach. A wharf lay ahead. The Subaru stopped. Klaus had an idea. Taking a fistful of French francs from Jörg's rucksack, he sauntered down to one of the figures on the concrete and weathered-wood finger jutting into the blue sea. His crude French skills sufficed for him to identify one of those he was addressing as the skipper of a motor launch anchored just off the wharf.

For a week's pay in advance, Jacques DesRoches, seaman-for-hire, agreed to leave immediately for Elba off the Italian coast, where three German tourists would be waiting to be picked up and brought to Corsica. A Herr Schultz, his wife and small son could be counted upon to provide a very, very generous *pourboire*. They were to be taken to Rogiano on Cap Corse, where they would be met between 8 and 9 o'clock in the evening. The lucky seaman could be seen counting and recounting his largesse, as the Subaru found its way back towards the inland.

* * *

"Do you remember the small private airfield we saw somewhere the day we arrived?" Neither Jörg, sitting in front, nor Tati, seated in the rear next to a sleeping Elli, her head resting uncomfortably against the window, knew which one was being asked the question.

Jörg responded first. "Ja, I remember. It was perhaps three kilometers outside town on our right."

"Correct. That's where we're heading." Klaus was excited.

He didn't need to mention, he was a licensed pilot. The Pommersche Segelflugklub used a field in the low farm country northeast of Berlin near his boyhood home for its weekend flying activities. An adventurous youth, Klaus had managed to wangle a few free rides as a passenger. By his mid-teens he had qualified to solo. A rusty VW was used to tow the slender gliders until they were sufficiently airborne to drop the towline and continue on unaided. Those silent flights over the marshes and lakes of his homeland were always very thrilling and pleasant. To assure himself a chance to fly real airplanes, Klaus had been an active member of the

Russo-German Friendship Corps, had taken part in the socialist youth programs of his community and had even joined the SED. He was trusted enough to gain a substantial number of hours in single-engine, usually fixed-gear aircraft. Someone, unfortunately, nixed his application for military flight training. No matter! He knew what he needed to know for the next phase of his kidnapping caper.

"We're going to charter a plane. Our cover story is that we are scouting for investment land for a European consortium that wants to build an exclusive resort on Corsica. Is that clear?"

"Clear. But we don't want to stay here. They're on our trail."

"Naturally. We're heading north." Looking off to the left, where there was a cluster of shops getting ready to open, Klaus saw a *pâtisserie*. "I've got to stop for a couple of minutes. I'll grab a couple of baguettes. Anybody want something else?"

Tati spoke up. "I could use some coffee, or at least a bottle of juice." Pointing to Elli, she said, "We need a beverage for her, too."

Klaus pulled in between two buildings and parked beside a Renault, using it to shield the Subaru from scrutiny from the highway. He bought four bottles of Orangina, two baguettes and two fresh Florentines, the round kind. The delicacy had been coated on the bottom with a rich, dark chocolate icing.

* * *

Doucette's task force pulled into the parking area of a small roadhouse now serving breakfast. Mark stifles his anger. *I guess we have to eat sometime. But the kidnappers are out there somewhere with my wife.*

"What's your next move, Inspector?"

Doucette, although trim and slender, was a man who placed inordinate value on eating well and regularly. He screwed his face into an odd shape. "I believe they may attempt to leave the island. Possibly for Italy. Probably by boat. We'll have to hold a press conference. We desperately need citizen input."

"Do you have an organized air patrol that is ready to start a search?"

"We have only one aircraft in our district. I regret to say, it is in a hangar waiting for repair parts."

Mark's frustration was quickly approaching 100 degrees Celsius. He struggled to maintain his composure. As soon as they reached Bastia, he planned to contact Jean-Luc and Roland for advice. Rinaldi, too, was less than impressed with his Corsican colleagues. He suspected more than one of the officers along today was probably a member of the popular separatist movement here.

* * *

Before he accepted a commission with the Stasi, Uebel had been a minor functionary in the Ministry of Education. He had studied three years at the Humboldt University, knew a smattering of French, which he had to rely on once again. He was fairly articulate in his mother tongue, spoke Russian well, but was only barely able to communicate in the romance language. Using his hands helped.

From afar, Klaus spotted the telltale windsock holding gently perpendicular to the ground. It was a grassy field, but did have a suitable strip of hard-packed gravel down the middle. There was only one hangar. Three single-engine planes, whose manufacture he couldn't identify, were lined up on one side of the field, still tied down to protect them from the weekend's gusty winds. The Subaru was observed approaching. Klaus parked next to the hangar. He and Jörg walked over, peeked in the only window. Seeing no one inside, they assumed the two men working on a nice looking low-wing plane that was big enough to hold four people, were alone on the field.

With their biggest smiles and least menacing manner possible, Klaus and his compatriot tried to talk the two men, both pilots, it turned out, into flying them and their wives down the east coast of the island and back up the west coast. They represented land developers from Switzerland, they claimed, businessmen, who wanted to inject massive sums into the Corsican economy. The immediate objective was to find enough suitable, available land for a golf – tennis country club with beach access and room for a huge resort hotel. The two men, who had completed their check of the aircraft and had already fueled it, had other plans and regretfully, but politely, declined Klaus' generous offer.

Jörg caught the wink from Klaus. It was their prearranged signal to get physical. Jörg, the barroom brawler, cold-cocked the bigger of the two men, pulled off the man's belt and tied his hands behind him. He was so fast he didn't need the pistol in his side pocket. Klaus, an amateur kickboxer, knocked his target onto the turf, punched him on the side of the head and also used his belt to secure his hands. The two men were dragged to the hangar. Jörg wanted to kill them. Klaus imposed his will, tied their feet together and found some utility tape to gag them with. The motionless bodies were pushed awkwardly into a tool shed at the rear of the hangar, which was then locked on the outside.

Grabbing their rucksacks, the daring duo, together with Tati and Elli, who had to be half carried to the plane, climbed aboard. Klaus performed a standard check of the instruments. He noted they would be flying in an EADS Socata TB9 Tampico. The gear was fixed. The fuel, he determined, should be adequate for a flight well into Italy. He taxied without further ado to one end of the runway, warmed his engine another couple of minutes and started rolling for take-off.

The lift-off was smooth; a text-book manoeuvre. Among his passengers, Jörg and Tati were most impressed. Elli was in a semi-delusional state and not talking. The Socata flew easterly for about fifteen minutes, banked south and flew again for roughly a quarter hour, then completed a 180 degree turn and, now comfortably over the turquoise waters of the Mediterranean, continued at about 9000 feet on a northerly heading.

Holding the controls steady, Klaus perused the charts he found in the map pocket. The sleek aircraft, powerful enough to carry four or five, fly to 11,000 feet and with a range of at least five hundred miles, was precisely the transportation they needed. The heading was adjusted. It was just after 8:00 am. They were aiming for the Alpes Maritime between France and Italy. Klaus descended to about 5000 feet. Once he spotted the coastal city of Imperia, he flew at just 3000 feet and tried to make it appear his was a tourist flight along the fabled coastline. Almost over the small town of Loano, the plane darted inland flying at about 2000 feet following some of the valleys between high points in the coastal range. Spotting the *Belbo*, Klaus used the river as a guide and headed for Alessandria, as inconspicuously as he knew how.

* * *

Georges Salber's call was put through to Jean-Luc without delay.

"Jean-Luc, I've been using my business contacts to dig up the dirt, as they say, on your Hein van Hoek. The going is much easier than I anticipated."

"What have you found, Georges?"

"Van Hoek travels frequently. That's not unusual. However, his favorite destinations are. If he's not heading to Monaco or Baden-Baden, it's Las Vegas, Atlantic City or Macao. What do they have in common? Gambling, of course."

"Are we talking about some kind of addictive behavior? Is he a compulsive gambler?"

"And then some. I'm compiling the details. When I have more, I'll check back in. Prepare yourself for the worst."

* * *

The Italian Consul in Ajaccio, at Mark's urging, had been in touch with naval and coastal protection forces in his country. An air search of the waters between Corsica and Italy had been initiated. Meanwhile, on a hunch, a local gendarme, who had heard of the case and was intrigued by it, discovered while talking to seamen along the coast east of Bastia, that a friend was on his way to Elba, having received a very generous payment to pick up some tourists and bring them back to Corsica. It was not actually clear, whether anyone was aboard the boat in question for the outbound portion of the voyage. The appropriate forces had been alerted and their attention focused on the sea lanes likely to be used.

Around noon, an Italian patrol boat flagged a small cabin cruiser heading to Elba, boarded and found only a much surprised skipper, who was made to repeat his story several times to various investigators before he was released.

Doucette was shouting, "**Merde!**" and pounding on his desk. Embarrassed and angry, he told Mark they had apparently been duped. The boat had been nothing more than a trick, a diversion. He had no idea where the kidnappers had gone.

Reading the thought, "incompetent fool!" from the expression on Inspector Rinaldi's face would have been incorrect. Rinaldi, accompanying Mark into the office, understood that investigations often hinged on plain old good luck. While the three were brainstorming, an officer came in to report two pilots were attacked early in the day at a private airfield near Morado. They were beaten and locked in a shed. They eventually managed to free themselves and escape through a small window. Their prized possession, a used French Socata, was stolen. They heard it take off. Sounded like it was flying east, they guessed. It has a range of over 500 miles, was fully tanked and in perfect working condition.

Within half an hour authorities in France and Italy had received details of the missing aircraft and were asked to alert appropriate agencies to intercept and seize the plane.

* * *

An old air chart in his map pocket showed a tiny service field about nine miles south of Alessandria. The location appealed to Klaus, because several highways crossed in the vicinity and he liked the plethora of escape options that presented. The Socata was a nimble performer. Klaus summoned all his flying skills, fueled by a burst of adrenaline, and brought the elegant bird home with a smooth, bump-free landing. He taxied over to a small building that served as the control tower and office. Klaus was unaware that Tati and Jörg had perspired more than he had.

A teen-aged boy stepped out of the office to greet them. His father had left him in charge, as no flights were expected, either in or out, during the week. There was no time to waste. Claiming engine problems,

Klaus inquired about the availability of a mechanic. None was on duty. The boy was suspicious. Jörg, in a burst of anger, pistol-whipped him. He was tied and left on the floor behind the desk. Keys for a small dark green Fiat were found in the boy's jacket. It was a tight fit for the four travelers, who didn't appreciate the oversized speakers mounted behind the rear seat. Now traveling without a prescribed plan, the foursome, staying on secondary roads, aim for Piacenza. In the parking lot of a large shopping mall, Jörg swaps the Fiat for a Mercedes diesel. The swap requires all of three minutes.

Brimming with pride, Jörg bragged that he had never met a motor vehicle he couldn't steal, adding, "And I learned that before I started working for Rudi and Klaus."

To gain more time, they risk the *Autostrada* and arrive in quick order on A21 in Cremona. Respecting the speed limits, they continue to Brescia. The fuel gauge is on empty. At the railroad station, Jörg again works his magic and shows up in an Alfa Romeo that still has the new car smell. He figures the owner is probably away for the day, so the theft is not likely to be reported for several hours. Klaus suggests they can probably blend in better in Germany and starts checking the road atlas he finds in the glove compartment.

A gas station close to one of the Autostrada interchanges accepted from Klaus the German Marks he offered for a tank of gas, tacking on a hefty charge for the bank exchange. Prepared sandwiches and hot coffee for the driving crew, apple juice for the ladies made everyone feel better. Tati gave Elli another shot and the latter quickly lost consciousness.

The drive north on secondary roads, some busy, some mostly empty, all narrow, hilly and winding, becomes arduous. New car or not, the passengers are sore from sitting and take an occasional fresh air break to stretch. Elli, waking groggily on occasion, gets car sick twice. The drive on Highway 42 along the eastern shore of Lake Iseo is lovely, though the driver and passengers are too tired to enjoy it. At Édolo, they switch to Highway 39, then back to Highway 38, following the severely serpentine roads to Highway 40. Jörg insists on doing all the driving. The air is significantly cooler. A hasty peek in the trunk reveals a large sheepskin throw. Tati claims it. She shares it with Elli. Elli slips in and out of consciousness; is never fully cognizant of her whereabouts or the current circumstances.

Finally, the Alfa reaches the Kajetansbrücke on the Inn River and crosses into Austria near Pfunds. The route taken thus far has been genial; no police sighted, relatively little traffic, and no mechanical problems. Pfunds is a blip on the map. Only the most perfunctory of checks is performed at the border, especially after dusk on a rather cool, damp April evening. Jörg readily locates Highway 180, then the *Autobahn* in the direction of Innsbruck. At the first rest stop he pulls in to tank up, buys himself coffee, tea for the ladies and Klaus. He spots a somewhat stale-looking Florentine wrapped in plastic. Saying, "My buddy is crazy about these things," he takes it and a package of butter cookies back to the car. Not even the caffeine can overcome the general feeling of exhaustion. A catnap in the Alfa, parked inconspicuously behind three tractor trailers, evolves into a two-hour sleep-fest.

* * *

Everything pointed to a flight towards Italy. Once a report was received about a plane landing near Alessandria, alert detectives connected some of the auto theft information and it was deduced that the kidnappers were going east towards Verona. No firm sightings of the Alfa, the vehicle stolen in Brescia, had been reported. Other car thefts were being analyzed to see if they could be significant. Mark flew to Milan and awaited further information. He kept in touch with Jean-Luc and Roland; talked also with Dani and the girls. They tried to be supportive and to bolster his flagging morale. He wished his purpose for being in Italy again was to show Elli and his children some of the lovely sights around Lake Garda, where his old college roommate, Luigi Nardini, lived. Now that the kidnappers were on the run, being hunted like animals, they might become desperate. That had to be his concern. Elli was in more danger now than before. Mark prayed for her.

* * *

The call of nature prompted Klaus to suggest a short break to stretch. Jörg left the *Autobahn* temporarily and soon found a decent minor highway west of Innsbruck. In a town named Zirl he silently rolled to a stop outside an inn in the pre-dawn darkness. Klaus walked past a few parked cars and stepped into a clump of oaks to relieve himself. Upon his return he wondered aloud, if it wasn't time to ditch the Alfa, or at least to swap the license tags. Jörg, who had spied a fairly new Audi A6, told them to count slowly to one hundred, and then to walk slowly with Elli and the sheepskin throw towards the Audi. They would push it down the sloping drive to the roadway, then start it and resume their journey.

It was now approaching 6:00 am. The Audi handled beautifully. Klaus checked the weather on the radio. News of the on-going kidnap investigation was scant. Whether contemporary in nature or 'golden oldies', a genre known generally as Volksmusik seemed to dominate where entertainment was concerned. There was a surprising number of cars and trucks on the *Autobahn*. Assuming the "liberation" of the Audi might have been noticed by this time, Jörg exited on a convenient off-ramp leading into Kufstein. He headed north on a steep, winding road that still had snow along its edges where the sun had difficulty penetrating the tall, stately evergreens. The road itself was clear. On most curves there was a good deal of sand and salt residue. Tired and hungry, they bypassed Bayrischzell, "the Wendelstein Dorf", according to a sign alongside the highway. Klaus took the wheel after a short break. They had to make some decisions. This was Germany. They urgently needed a place to hole up for a couple of days. Rudi had indicated he expected to collect the ransom on Friday. A few rays of sunshine shone on the snow-capped Wendelstein, a handsome 1800 meter high landmark north of Bayrischzell. There were a couple of modest hotels on the highway. Klaus wanted to find something fast, but something where they would not attract undue attention. On their left they spotted signs for a Gasthof and vacation apartments. This had to be it. The Audi made a right angle turn to the left past a number of rustic farms. A herd of cows ambling to their pastures had exercised their priority for the narrow stretch of asphalt. Klaus and his associates waited patiently. The road clear, they proceed slowly, trying to read all the signs carefully. The *Postgasthof Rote Wand* looked inviting, but there were too many cars parked outside. Klaus wanted anonymity. A half-dozen houses later, they found their refuge.

Haus Schönblick had a garage that had been converted into a small, but tidy guest house that would easily sleep up to six persons. It was rented on the spot. Klaus withdrew a week's rental from his cache. The foursome crashed almost immediately, in spite of their hunger. Elli, was given water and some cookies, then tied to a bed and gagged, to prevent her from creating a disturbance, should she wake before the rest of them. She was beginning to look the worse for her ordeal. Tati declared they were going to eat well later. They all needed a decent meal.

Day 5, Wednesday, April 26

The Alfa Romeo sedan that had escaped detection on its tour of northern Italy was not an acceptable trade for the Austrian salesman from Vienna. When he couldn't find his beloved Audi, he became unbent and created a scene in the lobby of the inn where he stayed whenever he had business calls to make in Innsbruck and beyond. The local police were duly notified. They had come and gone, showing, much to the salesman's chagrin, more interest in the Alfa than in his car.

The discovery of the Alfa helped Mark and Roland, who had flown in on a charter flight in mid-morning, to trace the suspected route of the kidnappers through Italy to Innsbruck. Now the news media were asking police and the general public to keep an eye out for a black A6 with Viennese plates. Roland, who regularly travels the alpine regions in pursuit of skiing thrills, guessed that the kidnappers might be seeking to return to Germany, but not likely to Berlin.

"My gut feeling," Roland's brain cells were computing at blinding speed, "is that they have 'crashed' somewhere in Bavaria. They are undoubtedly pretty tired, maybe a bit scared. They know the heat is on. They can listen to the radio bulletins as easily as we can."

"Roland, I trust your judgement. But look, they could have gone over the hills to Garmisch. They may also have continued east, or, who knows, they might have backtracked into western Austria. They've demonstrated a penchant for avoiding the obvious."

"I have a hunch they'll begin to make some mistakes. I can't do much here. I'm returning to Lausanne. This person calling from Berlin appears to be the brains, or the spokesman. He's got to keep in touch with his

243

buddies. I expect he's contacting a cell phone. Maybe we'll get lucky and get a big clue soon. Hang in there. We all want this to end well. I'll give the girls a hug for you. Dani brought them to our place. It's more secure, she says. She's also worried about Elli's medications and the supplements the doctor gave her. She hasn't had them for close to a week."

The two shook hands. Roland gave Mark a hug. They parted.

* * *

Tati had agreed to walk up to the *Rote Wand*, a handsome traditional inn with a thriving restaurant, if the cars constantly parked in front were any indication of popularity, to see if she could get some food to take out. Everyone was starving and Elli looked pale and weak. Hesitating until she was sure Klaus was awake and in a position to keep Jörg away from their 'prize', Frau Steinhammer, made herself as presentable as possible. She had given Elli her last clean shirt. The one she had on now was wrinkled, both from the long, uncomfortable drive and from having slept in it most of the morning. She covered it with a nylon rain jacket. She applied some lipstick and combed her hair again. She put a wad of 20-Mark bills in her purse.

The short walk to the inn was invigorating. The air smelled fresh and spring-like. In Berlin, it was no longer likely that one would have to tread with care when crossing the street to avoid stepping in cow dung. Some-how, she didn't mind. It had its wholesome aspect, she thought. She counted only about a dozen houses and farms in the village. For a big-city girl this was a most unusual venue. She walked gingerly up the stairs to the main entrance.

The peak dinner traffic had subsided. There were a few couples scattered throughout the three dining rooms. Small groups of old men, half hidden by cigarette smoke, nursing the remaining beer in their mugs, were looking to settle up and go back about their business. A local with a salt and pepper beard sat on a bench playing folk songs on a zither sur-rounded by several couples. Tati spoke quietly with a waitress, looked at the menu and ordered enough *sauerbraten*, potato dumplings, and red cabbage for four. Thinking ahead, she also got four ham and cheese sandwiches. They'll come in handy for later, she thought, hoping to be able to stay inside the remainder of the day. Beverages were not needed. There was a case of beer in the apartment. She left balancing several large disposable containers of hot food that smelled so good her feet covered the distance to their refuge in half the time it had taken to reach the inn.

Jörg ate with a thin blanket draped over his shoulders. He had showered. His sweater was hanging on a clothes line behind the apartment, where the car had been parked. Tati liked his tattoos, especially the one on his right arm, the heart with a ribbon banner beneath it with TATIANA inscribed in red. Elli was untied and allowed to eat by herself in a corner. She still appeared confused. In fact, she was desperately trying to formulate a plan to escape.

* * *

Mme Chounard escorted a Monsieur Salber to Renard's office. Her curiosity about the bank visitor prompted a few aggressive questions. She was more than a trifle obvious in her attempts to discover why he was calling on the bank's director and why the boss' schedule had been instantly rearranged to greet him. Salber was no dunce, he recognized immediately that he was being pumped for the reason for his visit. He adroitly parried every thrust and at Renard's office door politely thanked the frustrated and flustered matron.

After a traditional French greeting, Renard and Salber got right down to the subject of the day: Hein van Hoek. The Dutchman had been seeking to garner support for a move to effect a chairmanship change on the *White Cross Holdings* Board. As nearly as Renard could tell, the effort had been wholly unsuccessful. Salber opened his briefcase and withdrew a sheaf of documents.

"These tell the story that will curdle your blood. Your Monsieur Van Hoek is nothing more than a bold-faced thief. I have several signed affidavits. I have copies of cancelled checks. I have business documents, letters, e-mail messages, in short, a damning paper trail. The bottom line:

WCH has been taken for several hundred thousand dollars. That's the part I'm sure of. I suspect there's more."

"How was he able to do this?"

"Insufficient oversight played a role. Mix in the fact that van Hoek is an extraordinarily clever operator, has an extremely addictive gambling habit, is a pathological liar and it all adds up to big time crime."

"I'm aghast. You know, I was instrumental in putting him on the Board in the first place?"

"I'm aware of that. Looks like you'll have to straighten it out."

"Thanks for the outstanding work and for the incredible speed in assembling this information."

"It's iron-clad, absolutely irrefutable, and it's all in black and white. Good Luck!"

"I'm flying to Rotterdam in the morning to confront van Hoek."

An envelope for Salber was waiting on Marie's desk. He shook Renard's hand and departed via the rear exit, not wanting to be subjected to the inevitable barrage of prying queries from Mme Chounard.

* * *

Calling in the early afternoon from a booth in the Zoologischer Garten subway station, coincidentally just after the kidnappers had completed their heavy dinner, Rudi was surprised by a huge belching sound, for which Klaus apologized. Rudi was told the group was holed up in a vacation apartment and had just had their first solid meal in days. At the caller's request, Klaus stepped out behind the apartment to continue the conversation. He was warned not to name the location.

"Klausi, I'm sorry things didn't work out on the island. Keep strong. Matters have taken an earnest turn. We *are* going to pull this off. I know it. We will follow our timetable. It's full steam ahead to the *Endstation*. Listen carefully. This has to be quick. I'm setting up the "delivery" for Friday. As soon as it's made, I'll call you. You remember what we decided about the others when we developed the plan two months ago at the big fair in Nürnberg? Don't forget the items I gave you. There can be no weak links left behind."

"I understand. I'm ready." Klaus sounded resolute.

"Find another safe haven tomorrow. When you are leaving arrange for the woman to speak a few words to her husband or her sister at a number I'll dictate. Don't use your cell phone, Liebling. This guy Davidson wants to be certain his wife is still alive before any payment is made."

"*Verstanden.*"

Rudi read off a Lausanne telephone number. Klaus repeated it as he jotted it down on a scrap of paper. The line went dead.

* * *

As Deuffel departed, losing himself in the midday throng of transients in the centrally located station, Roland Denis-Breuer was already listening to a recording of the call. At his side was Hermann Weidinger. With the help of Deutsche Telekom investigators and the Berlin police, calls from all the subway station phone booths clustered around the Europa Center were being monitored. Technicians were seeking to obtain the precise location of the cell phone using GPS data. The call hadn't been quite long enough for the kind of precision needed, but the general area was clear.

A grim Roland looked at his associate. "I believe I detected an ominous message hidden in some of the remarks emanating from Berlin."

"Absolutely. I think you should pass that information on to your brother-in-law and the police. Did you catch the caller referring to *Klausi*? He also used the term Liebling."

"Strange. Wasn't it? What do you make of that tone of endearment? *Klausi?*"

"I can't claim any expertise on the subject, but I'd say they might be lovers."

"Exactly my impression. There was some kind of railroad jargon there too. Wonder what that's about? I'm going to call Mark right away."

"The fellow in Berlin mentioned a fair in Nürnberg, in February. If I recall correctly, that's the site of the *Spielwarenmesse*, one of the world's largest annual toy expositions. It's always held in February. I'm going to get someone on that immediately."

* * *

There were no direct flights from Geneva to Rotterdam on Thursday morning. Jean-Luc booked a flight to Amsterdam and arranged for an auto rental there. He had read through the documents Salber had left with him three times. His blood boiled each time. Such perfidy was inexcusable. The instrument on his desk rang. He reached for the phone. "Hello, Mark, tell me you have good news."

"Hello, I just spoke with Roland. He thinks the kidnappers are under great pressure. They seem to be on the verge of some critical step. They're also becoming prone to errors and their calls are helping investigators to develop some useful profiles. Roland and his staff are collaborating with the police in Berlin. As we speak they are installing some devices on phone booths in certain U-Bahn stations that may help them identify and track a key member of the kidnapping team. We're paying most of the cost as part of a research project in the security field."

"Sounds good. We've got a problem here, too. If it could wait, I'd say it might be a job for you. It's simply too urgent so I'm going to handle it myself. It's van Hoek. He's got to leave the Board without delay. I plan to terminate his seat tomorrow. I won't take time now to enumerate the many, many instances of fraud he has perpetrated. WCH has lost a substantial amount of money. I plan to seek restitution, but his personal wealth is greatly diminished. This could be a write-off situation. I'll keep you informed."

"Thanks, Jean-Luc. Do what you have to. Say, I met the Commandant of the Tyrolean branch of the Austrian State Police today in Innsbruck. They've been pretty helpful. The Bavarian State Police have also assigned a couple of officers to the search and have other resources on call, in case something develops in their neck of the woods."

"Mark, I don't have to remind you, time is so important. Elli must be under great stress. Urge them on."

"Doing it, Jean-Luc. Doing it. Pray for Elli. My regards to your family and good luck tomorrow."

* * *

Elli's beautiful blue skirt revealed a pair of shapely legs, especially when she lay tied to her bed. Klaus never gave any sign of being attracted to them. Tati observed, on the other hand, that her Jörg's blood pressure started to rise every time he looked at Elli and began to undress their captive in his mind. Maybe his pure animal and not so subtle lust was understandable. Yet it irked Tati that he wasn't better able to mask his feelings, however involuntary they might be. She borrowed a bicycle that had been offered to them for use by the landlord, and rode about four kilometers on a paved bike path that paralleled the highway in the direction of Schliersee. At a crossing she saw the equivalent of a country store behind a gas station. She bought two pairs of regular jeans and two oversized sweatshirts, one each for herself and one each for Elli. *Maybe these will blur his overactive imagination*, she thought to herself.

* * *

Rudi, resting at home, went over and over his plan for the final stages of the kidnapping. He called one of his part-time workers, Kemal Kodoglu. Kemal was a small-time crook. He was one of the children of the many, many Turks who had come to Berlin as guest workers and never returned home, except for periodic trips, when they were heavily laden with the material things so often taken for granted in the West. Kemel spoke Turkish, but could neither read nor write it. He had started the Volks High School curriculum, but never finished it. Unable to get and hold a steady job that he was willing to do, he made ends meet by engaging in petty crime. He had actually become a successful pick-pocket. His skill as a shop-lifter, however, failed the test one day, when Rudi caught him red-handed in his toy department. Seeing a use for someone who was not terribly bright, eager for occasional cash and reasonably loyal, Rudi had offered him odd jobs, mostly as a courier. He also helped with stock and was generally able to follow instructions well, provided they were not overly complicated.

Kemal was free. He would come by the next day for an assignment. He was free Friday as well. A smile crossed Rudi's face. *"Alles einsteigen! All aboard,"* he thought. *"This will be a ride to remember. Now, if that damned Moshe Jutz and his nagging mother will just hold off until next week, everything will be fine."*

Day 6, Thursday, 27 April

The cow in front was in charge. She seemed to know where to go as she passed the black Audi waiting to pull out of the drive next to the white stucco garage with the varnished clear pine trim. Klaus mumbled a curse. A young boy dressed in *Lederhosen* like the ones his ancestors may well have worn centuries before, used a long pole to nudge a couple of stragglers back in line. When they had completely passed, the Audi rolled out and slowly drove ahead a mere fifty meters, where it stopped next to a free-standing outdoor telephone booth, which was positioned adjacent to the *Gasthof Rote Wand*. Luckily, the telephone, from which it was possible to place international calls, accepted coins as well as phone cards. Klaus got out of the car, opened the rear door and pulled Elli onto the street. He pushed her into the booth, popped some one-Mark coins in the slot, took out a piece of paper with the number he was to call, and told her sternly she was only to state she was well. He dialed Lausanne, the Denis-Breuer villa.

"*Ici* Denis-Breuer!"

"Herr Breuer, as agreed, Frau Davidson is going to say a few words." Klaus spoke slowly in German.

"Elli, are you all right? Where are you?" Roland's voice was full of anxiety mixed with hope. He spoke French.

Klaus grabbed the receiver and held the speaker against his chest. Addressing Elli, he said, "Just tell him you are well. No tricks!"

Elli's mind was fairly clear. Stepping out of the car she had noticed the peak of a mountain jutting prominently into the morning sky slightly southeast of the inn. In French, intentionally hoping to confuse her captor, Elli said, "I'm well. So, too, are the Bavarian and the Scot."

Klaus tore the receiver from her hand and pushed her from the booth, where Jörg rushed her roughly into the back seat. "You will never hear from her again, if you fail to follow the instructions you will receive later today." Klaus' tone was icy and ominous. He slammed the receiver on the hook.

Behind the wheel again, he moved away smoothly, but swiftly. He wasn't familiar with this part of his reunited country. Typically, Berliner consider their country cousins in Bavaria to be slow and dull of intellect. Klaus wondered. Discussing their next move while loading the car, Klaus and Jörg had decided to stay somewhere in the mountains. They were going to head west and try to find a remote rental for another day or two. Both were getting nervous, but tried not to display any weakness. Tati also was eager to finish the matter so she and Jörg could set up house-keeping somewhere with their share of the ransom.

The sandwiches with Prague ham and Emmentaler cheese had been washed down with lots of beer the night before. Elli drank water. Now new hunger pangs were announced by growling stomachs. From the main highway Klaus detoured to the right, seeing a little town ahead where there would surely be a bakery already open.

Fischbachau was reluctantly showing signs of life. A tractor had just turned off the highway and was heading for a day in the fields. A pair of elderly Hausfrauen, heads under kerchiefs, ankle-length skirts rustling, were carrying their market baskets and sharing gossip from the previous day. Down a side lane Klaus saw the words he had hoped for, *Bäckerei – Konditorei Meyer*. He stopped, backed into a driveway and turned around to drive down the narrow lane where the bakery was located. Inside, he bought eight crisp, fresh rolls, three apple turnovers and four gorgeous Florentines, freshly baked and neatly arranged on a large baking sheet. These, he could tell at first sight, not only had slivered almonds, but also chopped hazel nuts. *Exquisite*, he thought, his taste buds already shifting into high gear. He bought a small jar of raspberry preserves, and from a refrigerated display case, a plastic-wrapped package with 250 grams of sliced salami and another with 200 grams of Tilsit cheese. Two four-packs of spring water seemed the best beverage choice.

"I hope your friends enjoy the Florentines. They came out of the oven within the hour." The baker's wife was clearly proud of her husband's products.

"The Florentines are for me!" Klaus, without intending to do so, laid definitive claim to these delectable treasures. "They get the apple turnovers," he added, waving his hand to indicate someone outside.

Klaus had spoken quite forcefully. The middle-aged baker's wife, was surprised by his possessive tone. Klaus left hurriedly and the Audi retraced its route back out of Fischbachau to the main road. The baker's wife watched pensively, as the car pulled away.

* * *

The bank director rose early for the drive to Geneva and his flight to Amsterdam. For him money was a commodity, a tool. He was well paid, had the necessities of life and his family enjoyed good health. The thought of stealing, of illicitly taking even a penny from the funds entrusted to him, was abhorrent. Yet, he was a realist and understood that avarice was one of man's more common weaknesses. Still, for a person he trusted to betray him, Mark and the other Board members had been a blow that left him both very sad and very angry.

The flight was smooth. The arrival on time. Renard picked up his rental car and accomplished the drive to Rotterdam on a good highway in record time. He did not relish the task it was his duty to perform today. It had to be done.

Van Hoek's forte was marine insurance, although he was acknowledged by experts in the field to be a strong player in all forms of insurance. Rather garrulous, he had many contacts throughout the industry. His firm occupied the top two floors in a modern office building with an excellent view of the harbor. Renard's secretary had scheduled a call she implied was routine the day before. Van Hoek intended to be in town all week, so it was no problem to set up an early meeting. Renard was ushered into a large carpeted office with tinted glass windows on two sides. The walls were finished with Brazilian rosewood panels. Van Hoek's impressive desk was made of stainless steel, with rosewood accents and a dark brown leather top.

The host directed his visitor to a corner where there were two plush leather chairs and a modern round pedestal table with a glass top. Prominently displayed on a wall-mounted shelf was a handsome model of a four-masted sailing vessel. A stainless steel floor lamp, a designer creation, and numerous potted trees completed the decor.

"Can I offer you something to drink?" Van Hoek's welcome showed the touch of a master salesman. He had placed his left hand on Renard's shoulder while vigorously shaking his right hand. His general ebullience and ingratiating smile, however, did not deter the sober Renard.

"Mynheer van Hoek," he began, "my purpose in calling upon you today brings me no joy." He opened his briefcase and laid on the table the papers Salber had gone over with him the day before. Renard summoned all his self control. He continued, "These documents are irrefutable proof of gross malfeasance on your part with respect to your responsibilities as a member of the Advisory Board of *White Cross Holdings.*" He paused, swallowed hard, and resumed sternly. "You have committed fraud, perjured yourself and have diverted many thousands of dollars into your personal accounts. The exact amount of your theft is still being determined."

Van Hoek's jaw dropped. His voice shaky, his face flushed, he protested, "This is not true. I can explain!" He articulated the lie easily and with conviction.

"Dr. Davidson, who is, in fact, the sole proprietor of *White Cross Holdings*, and I, both placed our complete trust in you to help manage the company's investments in the insurance field. **You betrayed that trust!**" Renard's voice rose in volume. He regained control and continued with appropriate modulation. "The documents you see before you, all copies of the originals which are now in the hands of our legal counsel, reveal with great clarity your despicable activities. Your colleagues are disgusted and disappointed. I have been authorized to terminate your participation in *White Cross Holdings* forthwith. It is our intention to prosecute you and to seek full restitution through the courts. Dr. Davidson has personally asked me to urge you to pursue drug and gambling treatment and rehabilitation without delay. I should like to add that Mme Davidson, who, as you know, has been kidnapped, may well be in even greater jeopardy due to your thoughtless and clumsy interference." Renard collected the documents and inserted them in his briefcase.

His misconduct exposed, his future buried in the murk of an interminable legal quagmire, his business subject to annihilation as a result of the bankruptcy he now believed he could not possibly avoid, a broken van Hoek sat in his leather executive chair staring glassily at the expensive pictures adorning his rosewood panel walls. Renard took his leave and departed.

* * *

Dani was playing on the floor with her two nieces, when Roland came into the living room. "*Chérie*, what do you make of Elli's remark, you know, about the Bavarian and the Scot? Does it make any sense to you?"

"I've been racking my brain. It must be some kind of clue, probably about the kidnappers? It's simply not logical that a Bavarian and a Scot would team up to kidnap a little known Swiss citizen. It has to be something else."

"Could it possibly be a hint regarding her location?" The doorbell rang, interrupting the conversation.

Herr Weidinger, the young audio engineer and voice ID specialist entered, shook Mme Denis-Breuer's hand and squatted on the carpet to greet the twins.

Addressing his associate, Roland asked, if the phrase "a Bavarian and a Scot" had any particular meaning to him.

"Odd combination, isn't it? Yodeling and bag-pipes don't usually end up in the same sentence." A quizzical look appeared on his face. "I think there's a contemporary folksong, a novelty song, if I'm right, about a Bavarian and a Scot meeting on the Wendelstein. Something about bag pipes and a zither. The Wendelstein, as you know, is a tourist attraction and landmark near the town of Bayrischzell."

"That's what Elli was trying to impart to us!" Roland's thought processes began to make multiple connections. "I hope she didn't suffer for the attempt." Roland started for the telephone.

Dani picked up the girls and headed upstairs. "You'd better get in touch with Mark and contact the State Police in Bavaria. I'm putting the girls up for their nap."

* * *

Berlin, the capital of a nation of over eighty million people, is a busy metropolis. Its economy is driven not just by the needs of its citizens for goods and services, but to a large extent by the move of so many government agencies from Bonn, Beethoven's peaceful hometown on the Rhine, to the whirlwind milieu of a world-class city full of excitement twenty-four hours a day, seven days a week.

Stores and shops of every persuasion abound throughout the commercial centers of the city and its suburbs. At Roland's insistence, the police acted on a hunch of his. To their surprise, in spite of the numerous toy retailers listed in the city directory, the only significant toy seller within the circle bounded by the subway stations from which the kidnappers had contacted Mark Davidson, was in the KaDeWe department store.

* * *

Emmi Fischer volunteered for a special assignment. A five-year veteran of the police force and recently promoted to the plain-clothes division, Fischer was a resourceful, talented, and attractive representative of Berlin's finest. Her assignment, arranged with the aid of top management, was to start today as a stock clerk and merchandise display assistant in the sporting goods and toy departments at KaDeWe, the Kaufhaus des Westens, continental Europe's premier department store.

Since the sporting goods staff had already completed their summer displays days earlier, Rudi Deuffel, of toy department fame, was asked to find work for Fräulein Fischer. She seemed cooperative and willing. Deuffel indicated he would send some items up to the selling floor via the freight elevator. He showed her where they might be stacked and left it to her to make an attractive and appealing presentation. He reminded her that the sub-cellar storage area was off limits.

Before engrossing herself completely in her task, Fischer walked the toy department to check on other displays. In the process she overheard a noisy conversation between Herr Deuffel and a stooped, pot-bellied and agitated man who was wearing thick glasses. Deuffel had his arm around the man and gave the impression he was assuaging his companion; somewhat condescendingly reassuring him about something. The visitor finally crept off like some kind of roach given a reprieve by a large shoe that had been poised to crush it.

Herr Jutz may have left, but he remained unconvinced by his friend's entreaties to be patient. He hoped his mother would not berate him the rest of the day because he had acquiesced to Rudi's appeal for one more week. International bank transfers were being made, he would tell her. They always required more time than one might think, didn't they?

A short time later, Detective Fischer sent a Turkish male, approximately five foot five, late twenties, dark, drooping moustache, full head of black hair, redolent of garlic, to a clerk she noticed in the aisle featuring dolls. He was asking for the manager. The clerk told him to go on down to the storage area; he was expected. Fischer thought that was very interesting.

* * *

Sitting on a chair near the ovens in the bakery's huge kitchen, the baker's wife was putting her feet up on a stool for the first time since early in the morning. She drank tea from a large mug and took a big bite from a whole wheat roll smeared with lots of fresh cream butter. The radio was on low volume. Nevertheless, she listened intently to the latest news regarding the kidnapping of a wealthy Swiss woman the preceding Saturday.

"One of the suspects may have a sweet tooth, not for chocolate, or bonbons, but for Florentines." The reporter continued in a monotone to indicate police had traced the kidnappers to Oberbayern. Nearly dropping the rest of her roll, Frau Meyer jumped up, told one of the apprentices about her customer of the morning and was advised to pass it on to the police right away. There's a reward, the apprentice said. The call was made. A detective from Schliersee dropped by the bakery an hour later and obtained more details from the baker's wife.

* * *

Klaus had wanted to slap Elli for saying more than she was told. He figured the call was probably too short in duration to be traced. Elli was tied hand and foot. She had no gag, but had been sternly warned by all three car mates to remain silent. More injections were threatened, if she tried anything stupid. She tried to see if she could tell where they were going. Occasionally, Jörg turned to check on her. He smirked, his peculiar lascivious smirk. Elli's loathing of this man and everything he conjured in her mind was bottomless. Her thoughts turned to Mark and the twins. Oh, how she missed them. They would be terribly worried. It pained her to think that they, and her sister, and Roland would be beside themselves in their concern for her.

* * *

Mark had been advised by the Austrian State Police in Innsbruck to drive east on E45, the *Autobahn* to Kufstein and Salzburg, and to take exit No. 39. From there it was suggested he head for Germany, stopping at Achensee to call for any updates. If no new information had come in, he was to proceed to Bad Tölz. The police official to contact there was a fellow by the name of Mosch, Karl Mosch.

At Achensee, Mark called back to Innsbruck, learning that police were now almost certain the kidnappers were in southern Bavaria. The police in Innsbruck, the Federal Border Police in Germany, and Bavarian State Police stationed in Bad Tölz were collaborating. Bad Tölz was temporarily in charge. Mark sensed new developments. If he hadn't already known how much he loved his wife, this frightening episode had shown him how completely she had become part of him. Their hearts were one.

* * *

Klaus tanked up at a self-service station. No one paid any attention to him. At a traffic signal he checked his map and noticed a strange finger of land along the border that was part of Austria, yet accessible by road only from Germany. Buying a tent and some camping gear had crossed his mind as an option. It was already afternoon and the sun was heading west in a hurry. It was imperative that something be done while there was still light. Jörg found the place on the map and declared it was worth trying.

Once on the right road they reached the valley, Engtal by name, in forty minutes. The approach road was flat, paved and didn't look like it was going to a specific destination. The Audi approached a small shack, a kind of glorified sentry post at the entrance to the valley proper. A man was washing the window and sweeping out the structure. A sign attached to the side of the building indicated there was a five-*Mark* toll. There was also a freshly lettered sign on the front of the building advertising the *Ahornalm Gasthaus und Restaurant*. Klaus pointed to the sign.

The man in the building, who continued to do his chores, paying little attention to the driver in the Audi and his passengers, said, hardly looking up, "There is no toll today. The Gasthaus is closed until the first of the month. The floor of the valley is still very wet from melting snow. There's a lot of debris on the ground; winter storm damage that hasn't been cleaned up yet. If you plan to camp, you'll have to find a dry spot, maybe the plateau just behind the Gasthaus."

Klaus could already see a fair cover of snow at the edges of the valley and on the higher elevations in the surrounding mountains. An SUV with skis clamped on the roof rolled by in the opposite direction. The driver waved to the man.

"Is there any place around here, where we could stay for a few days? We like this area very much." Klaus found the apparent isolation appealing.

The man put his broom down and a smile emerged on his blank countenance. "As a matter of coincidence, I have three cabins for rent up ahead on the right side of the valley. They're pretty simple. Propane gas heat. Electricity. Small refrigerator. Quiet. Very quiet. They are about halfway between here and the Gasthaus. You'll see a narrow drive veering off to the right. If you take one for three nights, I'll include linen rental free of charge. This is still the off-season. The rate is very reasonable."

His mind already made up, Klaus spoke with a sense of relief. "We'll take all three for a week. We'll even pay in advance. The bed linens and towels will be appreciated." The deal closed; three occupants breathed freely. This was the perfect spot. Elli, all but her head covered by a throw blanket, feared there was trouble brewing in the shadows. She contemplated saying something the man could hear, but refrained from doing so out of concern for his life.

Klaus decided they would stay in the largest of the three cabins. The Audi was left close to the side of the building. An old tarp was found lying on a pile of wood stacked behind the cabin. Jörg threw it over the car. It effectively concealed it from prying eyes. The layout was traditional. A narrow central hallway connected a kitchen and sitting room in the front half of the building and two bedrooms, separated by a bath, in the rear half.

The previous occupants had left a few bottles of beer, a two-liter jug of bargain wine, a tin of sardines, a box of crackers, some canned peaches and an unopened bag of gummibears. The cabin had plates, glasses, cups and eating utensils. A new bar of soap and a full roll of toilet paper was found in the bathroom, as well as a half-empty plastic container of laundry detergent. Home, sweet home!

* * *

The bank's staff had left for the day. At Renard's request, Mme Chounard had remained behind. As she entered his office, she entertained thoughts of a possible raise, maybe a promotion. Such was not to be the case. He knew her personal life had had more downs than ups and he was not unsympathetic to the plight of a woman in her middle years with two children and a husband who had dumped her for, of all things, a circus performer. Nevertheless, she had tread beyond the bounds he expected in his key employees. Because of her long years of service, this was after all, the only place she had ever worked, he would not fire her.

"Mme Chounard." She noted he did not use her given name. "We are beginning a series of periodic shifts in assignments within management at the bank. Effective tomorrow, your responsibilities will involve providing direction to our maintenance personnel, managing all bank supplies and generating a complete inventory of our technological and mechanical equipment. I'm confident, you will do a great job for us. Your salary and benefits remain as they are. Thank you."

Complaining, protesting were out of order. Renard's authoritative tone and the dismissive "Thank You", left no doubt about that. Mme Chounard left quietly. She would have much to ponder this evening.

* * *

The sub-cellar was silent. It was actually two floors beneath the building's basement and in addition to the large area dedicated for the exclusive use of the toy department, it was shared with a fully enclosed section with refrigeration and moisture control occupied by the store's fur department, and tucked away in the far corner was the walk-in vault maintained by the jewelry department. The latter two departments shared a freight elevator. The toy department had its own elevator.

Tomorrow was usually a slow day and the rest of the giant department store was virtually vacant. Of course, the cleaning crews were busy and the night shift of stock staff were racing about to restore the glut of wares that made shopping there so enticing. Rudi was grateful for a few moments of peace. The next forty-eight hours would see the end of his working days and the beginning of a life of sand and surf with his lover in a place where they would never be found.

Merely because his Klausi was out of town, didn't mean there should be no fun, no dancing, no chatter in the bars full of interesting people. Soon he would be leaving Berlin forever. The make-up went on as usual. The wig was ready. From a locked closet, he chose an appropriately pro- vocative dress for a weeknight on the town. In a matter of minutes, clutching a discreet purse, Trudi Valentin emerged from the toy depart- ment stock facility, locked the gate, took the freight elevator up to street level and sashayed like a wispy model on the runway to an unused side emergency entrance, for which only she had a key.

Late April often felt more like winter than spring in Berlin. It was cool. A shower had left the streets damp, The sidewalk had enough puddles that it was difficult to walk in a straight line. For no logical reason she could express, Trudi had walked to the Augsburgerstrasse U- Bahn station. All the phone booths were in use. She strolled about for a few minutes gawking at fashions in the shop windows. Upon returning, there was a vacant booth. The number in Vevey generally was unattended at this time in the evening. Bankers have great hours, Trudi thought. The phone rang four times. The answering machine came on.

"Listen carefully!" she began, "Tomorrow, Friday, at precisely 11:50 am, local time, a large black leather Louis Vuitton garment bag with one million dollars is to be set down and left unattended at Berlin's Kurfür- stendamm U-Bahn Station approximately two meters from the edge of the platform on the northbound side of subway line U9. There is a police call-box there, above it an ad for *Camel* cigarettes. If there is any attempt whatsoever to interfere with the person who claims the suitcase, or to fol- low the person, Frau Davidson will be killed." A tone of finality. "By midnight Friday, nine million US dollars must be deposited electronically to a bank account identified in a letter you will receive in the morning." A gloved hand replaced the receiver.

The instructions were explicit enough, she thought, as she opened the door of the booth and joined the busy throng heading home from work or from shopping or, perhaps, looking for big city excitement, not unlike the attractive woman, who hadn't noticed a tiny light flash from the top of her phone booth the moment she had connected to those eight digits in far off Switzerland.

* * *

Hugo Leupoldt, rolled up the newspaper he had been studying on the bench opposite the bank of telephone booths, put it under his arm, and keeping his eye on the woman a few meters in front of him, set out to fulfill this evening's assignment. He didn't care for night duty anymore. He was a couple of months from retirement. He would rather have gone home to his family, a beer and the television. Fußball on tonight. Budget restraints, however, had left the department with too few choices. There were simply too many banks of telephones to cover. *If the guy in Lausanne is right. We might make a big catch tonight.*

Trudi, initially not actually cognizant of her tail, was, nonetheless, a cautious and prudent person by nature. She left the station. At the traffic signal, she crossed the street and immediately went back down an escalator into the very same subway station. A criminal's sixth sense was operative. Frau Valentin hopped a train going north. At Kurfürstendamm she got off the train, started to light a cigarette, sensed all was not as it should be and leapt back through the closing door, nearly getting an arm jammed as the door brushed her body. A plain clothes officer, surprised by his own agility, managed the same stunt one car back.

The cat and mouse game continued as the resilient Trudi switched from the subway to the streetcar and back to the subway going in the opposite direction, trying to shake someone who was obviously following her. In the Prenzlauer Berg section she rode from Senefelder Platz to the Schönhauser Allee Station, exiting once at Dimitroffstrasse and suddenly hopping back on again. This was her old bailiwick. These were her streets, her alleys. She walked energetically to Gleimstrasse. Whoever was following her was a pro. A lesbian bar, *Der Biberpelz*, was a favorite hangout in the section of Berlin known as Mitte, nearby was a sultry new establishment, *Tropische Nächte*, Tropical Nights, where gays and lesbians, 'Die Schwülen', reigned supreme.

Trudi didn't see anyone on the street behind her. *Tropische Nächte* had a street-level vestibule and cloak room. Two burly bouncers were on duty. A short stairway the width of the vestibule led up to the main floor. There was a door on either side, both entered the same large, dimly lit, smoke-filled room. In the center, extending back perhaps sixteen meters, was a huge horseshoe-shaped bar with slightly undulating lines that created interesting seating arrangements. The section to the right had a wooden floor, a small semi-circular band stand and a polished dance area. On the left side of the club, the space was divided by cleverly placed walls into a large number of cozy, private dining areas abounding in corner seating options. This side was carpeted. The lighting was in modernistic style; lamps with pastel-colored shades, providing a mildly erotic-exotic overall appearance that was sufficient illumination for those dining, but made it nearly impossible to see from table to table with any clarity. Artificial palm trees and generously placed South Seas decor in profusion set the stage for secluded gatherings.

In a strategically placed mirror, Trudi saw her tail entering from the vestibule. She went, as if joining two friends by arrangement, to a table for three in a shadowy corner. She immediately began an animated conversation with the couple seated there, who had been enjoying an intimate tête-à-tête, while throwing her coat over her chair back. If startled or shocked, the two females she joined, seemed merely amused and fascinated. Trudi appeared to ask where the restrooms were. One of her table-mates pointed to a sign: ZU DEN DAMENTOILETTEN. The man who had followed her was wiping the perspiration off his forehead as he noted a similar sign on the other side of the bar: ZU DEN HERRENTOILETTEN. He felt the urge, but decided to wait.

Trudi walked steadily with her large purse to the ladies' lounge. The cop sitting at the bar ordered a tonic water. A middle-aged man took the stool next to him and tried to generate a conversation. Officer Leupoldt had never been propositioned by a man before. He muttered some excuse and turned away, slightly embarrassed. Several minutes went by. *Where is that woman?* he wondered. Two women brushed by him on their way to the Damentoiletten. A man with a black turtleneck sweater, a green apron, and a visibly receding hairline coming from the opposite direction with a tray of glasses, stepped aside to let the ladies pass, then continued to the front of the building. Leupoldt was so completely absorbed in the entrance to the Damentoiletten that he didn't notice the man set his tray down on an empty table, together with his apron, and quietly pass through the vestibule to the street. Shortly afterwards, the bouncers were called to eject a "weirdo" from the ladies' lounge; some guy claiming to be a police officer.

Rudi Deuffel walked hastily through familiar streets until he spotted a taxi, hailed it and had it drop him off a couple of blocks from his apartment. He hated leaving his coat and that beautiful dress in the restroom. Heck, he could buy himself a dozen in a couple of days. He went to bed thinking about Kemal and what he expected of him the next day. The big day!

Day 7, Friday, 28 April

Gott sei dank, es ist Freitag! The thought repeated itself frequently in Rudi Deuffel's busy mind. *This is going to be a big payday, THE biggest ever. To hell with the petty thievery and the disloyal associates who had muscled in on his and Klaus' mini-empire so painstakingly built in the months and years following the collapse of the Soviet Union and its East European satellites.* For all he cared, they could continue to eke out their grimy existences, stolen TV by stolen TV, forever bitching prostitute by forever bitching prostitute. *Today is a new beginning.*

At the Europa Center, Rudi approached an empty phone booth and slipped in discreetly. He got Klaus, who was up, had made coffee for himself and the others, and who had been pacing back and forth in the cabin's efficiency kitchen, cell phone in hand waiting for this call.

"Wir sind da, Klausi, die Endstation. Tomorrow we begin a new life. I will be able to enjoy the four seasons all year long. You know where to rendezvous. Be careful. Take good care of our friends." The last sentence was rendered with a strong layer of irony. They had concluded at the outset, there could be no witnesses. None!

"In Ordnung! I'm O.K. Leave it to me."

"*Gut*! Once I'm clear, I'll ring you three times, hang up, then ring you again three times. That's your signal arm. Got it?"

"*Richtig! Bis dann*!" There were no sugar-plum fairies dancing before Klaus' face; perhaps a Florentine or two. Normally cool and calculating, Klaus was experiencing some butterflies and struggled to curb any sense of panic.

Rudi, thus reassured, put the receiver on the hook and walked casu-

ally out of the Center and down Tauenzienstrasse to his place of employment, whistling to himself as he went.

* * *

Jean-Luc Renard heard it while shaving. The words were still echoing in
his soapy ears: *"Hein van Hoek, a popular Dutch business mogul, holding
memberships on several prestigious directorial boards, was found shot to death
in his office near the waterfront in Rotterdam late last night. Police have
determined it was suicide. Van Hoek is said to have incurred huge gambling
debts and his company is believed to be facing bankruptcy. Stay tuned to our
midday broadcast for further details."*

Renard stopped shaving and looked at himself in the mirror. He
reasoned that he had done what was appropriate. He was sorry to learn of
this drastic turn of events. He felt no guilt. He continued with his morning toilet.

* * *

Several German citizens had been roused from their feathers during the
night to answer questions from police investigators. The descriptions of
Klaus provided by the landlord of the vacation apartment in Geitau and
the baker's wife who had sold him the Florentines were almost identical.
These were further corroborated by the toll collector at the mouth of the
Eng Valley. He had also recollected the make and model of the car the
kidnappers were driving.

* * *

In a large, covered picnic facility outside the village of Hinterriss, Austria,
a diverse group had assembled. Mark, sitting at a picnic table on which a
detailed relief map of the area was spread, was pondering possibilities
suggested by the rugged terrain. Karl Mosch, a major in the Bavarian
State Police had introduced everyone to Mark. Andrea Schmidt, a Senior
Ranger in Austria's Karwendel National Park, was sitting beside him. She
was tracing with a pencil the narrow dead-end asphalt road that went into

the Eng Valley. She pointed to the location of the three cabins. It was already known which one the kidnappers were occupying.

Schmidt, speaking softly, said, "From their vantage point, they are able to watch every movement into the valley. If they are armed, and we presume they are, they have a huge advantage."

Hans Höflich, a senior officer in the Austrian National Police, ostensibly in charge of whatever police action was to be taken, pointed to a hefty-looking armored vehicle that had just rolled into the line of cars and trucks in the field next to the picnic area. "That's one option. If necessary, we can storm the cabin."

"They might kill the woman they're holding, if we do anything rash like that." The bass voice that grabbed the attention of all seated or standing around the table, belonged to Sepp Lindner, Captain in the German Federal Border Patrol, a mountaineer, champion mountain biker, hunter and avid camper.

"What's the name of this valley?" pointing to the map. "It parallels the Eng Valley." Mark looked at Andrea Schmidt for a response. He held his finger on a spot on the map.

"That's the Laliderer Valley. At the moment the floor of the valley is snow free. In several places on the trails leading to the Ochsenjoch, a yoke along the crest of the mountain separating the Eng and Laliderer Valleys, there is still considerable snow. In the higher elevations in the mountains, the rain we have experienced here nearer sea level has fallen as snow. The older, more exposed snow cover has a granular quality. Movement up there is treacherous."

Mark continued. "I want to find a way to take the kidnappers completely by surprise. They should have no advance warning, should be shocked by our sudden presence. I don't want my wife to be harmed. And, I should add, I don't want any of the rescue team to be harmed either. How can it be done?"

Marta Rauchfuss, a lieutenant from the Innsbruck division of the Austrian National Police, moved forward from behind Mark to make a suggestion. "I think one thing we might do is to establish a presence in the Eng Valley, preferably today. I volunteer to lead a group of four or five women. We can enter on bicycles, pretending to be school girls on an overnight outing. Any weapons can be hidden in our rucksacks."

Three hands were raised immediately. Marianne Schoedel, Bavarian State Police, a medical doctor, well known amateur athlete, and marksman, Hilde Mödling, an instructor at the German Defense Force's Mountain Training School in Garmisch, and Silke Braun, a SWAT team marksman and outdoor enthusiast from Bad Tölz, were joined a minute later by Suleika Neubacher, another Austrian National Park ranger and guide.

It was decided the five, dressed in schoolgirl attire, would enter the park in the early afternoon, cycle towards the dead-end of the narrow valley, which dog-legged to the right, and set up camp. They would have sniper rifles and maintain contact by radio.

Intensely studying the relief map once more, Mark asked Herbert Hofer, a local climber with a lifetime of experience in his 40 years in the Bavarian and Tirolean Alps, if it would be feasible to paraglide into the valley from either the Ochsenjoch or the Gamskopf, which formed the pinnacle of the giant and daunting vertical wall of granite shooting into the sky directly behind the location of the three cabins.

"Sure," was the quick answer. "If you're totally crazy." A few among those around the table chuckled at Hofer's response. Hofer, whose initials pronounced in German, were Ha Ha, turned deadly serious. "Actually, it could be done, can be done. It would require a person with plenty of training and practice." Hofer was well known for his paragliding time and distance records.

"Well, I've got a few hours before I take off, let's train and practice!" Mark's tone said it all. He was determined. He was confident. The time had come for him to act. His Elli was in the greatest danger he could imagine and he had no intention of letting her down.

* * *

Kemal shows up in the toy department shortly after the store opens. Rudi is waiting. They take the freight elevator down to the sub-cellar. An attractive female colleague, placing signs at strategic places on the selling floor for the weekend specials, notes the time of Kemal's arrival in a notepad in her apron pocket. She dusts a display of building blocks.

The toy department storage area is as quiet as a morgue. "Kemal, I have a very important job for you today. Make a mental note of everything I tell you. It is extremely important. There is no room for even one mistake. Is that clear?"

"I'm listening." The Turk had never seen Rudi with such a serious look on his face.

"This is so important, I'm going to pay you five thousand *Marks*. Here's half. The rest I'll give you one week from today. Understood?" Kodoglu, nodded. Five thousand *Marks* definitely got his attention. Rudi had a subway system chart. "You must be on the northbound platform of Line U9 in the Kurfürstendamm U-Bahn Station a couple of minutes before 10:50 this morning. Be sure you have the same time on your watch as you see on my wall clock."

"What do I have to do?"

"You'll see the police call-box mounted on a huge metal post. There's a *Camel* poster hanging over it. Someone is going to set a black leather garment bag next to it at 10:50. As soon as the train stops, prepare yourself to grab the bag and leap onto the train just as the doors close. Got that?" Kodoglu nodded. "At Zoologischer Garten, get off the train, walk upstairs. Enter the men's toilets adjacent to the Kant-Strasse exit." He hesitated a moment, looking intently at Kemal to be certain he was taking in every detail. "Step into the first toilet booth on the left. You will see another black leather garment bag sitting on the toilet. Take it and leave yours in its place, count to fifty, and reenter the subway. You may be followed. Don't worry. Take line U2 west to the Olympia Stadion. Exit there, but leave the bag under the seat. Here's a bundle of subway and bus tickets and a hundred *Marks*. Spend the afternoon riding all over the city. Remember, come here next Friday for the rest of your five thousand *Marks*."

"I can do it. See you in a week." Kemal the Willing departed for a busy day on the streets of Berlin where he felt right at home.

* * *

Mark and Herb Hofer put their heads together. A plan evolves quickly. A local enthusiast lends the pair his light-weight gliding chute. It weighs about 40 pounds. Mark wonders to himself how much a normal chute weighs. The enthusiast, his left leg in a cast, vouches for the condition of the chute and shows the two where the best trail is to the take-off point that has been recommended. A jeep takes them up from the Laliderer Valley to a ski hut at close to 500 meters. The remainder of the climb must be accomplished on foot. The climb is arduous, mostly because of the heavy packs, the loose rocks, and the ice and snow. Every twenty to thirty minutes the two adventurers change loads, swapping the chute for the tent and sleeping sacks. The plan is to sleep on the mountain overnight. With help from Hofer, Mark intends to take off and guide his chute to a landing between the granite wall and the three cabins at first light in the morning.

Drawing diagrams on a pad of paper, Hofer illustrates how Mark is to manipulate the risers to steer his chute. Due to the weight limitations, there is to be no emergency chute. It will be just Mark, a nylon jump suit, likewise on loan from the hobbled enthusiast, and a two-way radio strapped to his epaulet.

* * *

Saying he had a brief errand to run, Herr Deuffel, manager of KaDeWe's top-notch toy department, strolled out of the gigantic merchandise emporium's main entrance. Over his shoulder hung an empty, over-sized duffel bag, dark red in color. He arrived at the Zoologischer Garten U-Bahn Station according to the schedule etched in his memory.

At 11:03 the northbound train from the Ku'damm Station pulled into the Zoologischer Garten Station, a vital crossing in Berlin's subway system, a station throbbing and pulsing with human traffic spraying out in multiple directions from early morning until late at night.

Less than two minutes after slipping into a stall in the men's toilet nearest the Kant-Strasse exit, Rudi heard the door of the end stall, the one next to his, open and bang against the partition. He could hear the garment bag he had just placed straddling the toilet seat being slid off and replaced with the "thunk" of another. The stall door banged again. Approximately twenty seconds after that, a strange voice said, "Sorry, excuse me!" Someone had apparently bumped into someone or something in the doorway to the restroom.

Rudi slipped out of his stall. There were three men standing at the urinals; all staring straight ahead at the alternating white and gray wall tiles. He slipped into the now vacant end stall, locked the door and swiftly transferred handful after handful of greenbacks into his oversized duffelbag. Upon exiting the stall, he used a tool in his pocket to turn the knob to "Occupied". He followed two men back into the station, went to the escalator up to Hardenberg-Strasse, hailed a taxi, told the cab driver to take him to Tempelhof Airport. There, he entered the ticketing hall, sat quietly on a bench for several minutes, studied the people there carefully, exited, and took the first cab in line to the KaDeWe store on Tauenzienstrasse. Home again, so to speak, he walked to the employee's entrance in the rear and took the freight elevator to his office behind the chain-link fencing in the eerily quiet sub-cellar.

* * *

Five girls wearing heavy sweaters or ski jackets, some with caps, all in jeans or ski pants rode noisily on the narrow road into the Engtal. They raced one another, sang naughty songs favored by girls on a same-sex spree, and played tag, laughing and joking along the way. Jörg watched with interest through a pair of binoculars.

* * *

There was no time to lose. The "Four Seasons" were sealed and marked with the international symbol for fragile goods. The addressee was stenciled on one side of each of the rather large specially built crates. On Monday, a moving company was scheduled to pick them up for shipment.

Rudolf Deuffel
c/o Duty Free Transit Warehouse
International Wharf 22
Manama
Kingdom of Bahrain

Two additional steamer-sized crates in front of Rudi's desk had been designed by Jutz to hold the rolling stock, some spare parts and the electronic control boards. Rudi had modified the design to accommodate false bottoms. Filling one with about half of the ransom, he used an electric screwdriver to close it tightly. He had almost finished stuffing bills into the second crate, when someone behind him, in an irritatingly squeaky voice he immediately recognized as that of Moshe Jutz, was screaming, **"That's my money! My mother knew you would cheat us!"**

Panic was not a word in Rudi's vocabulary. "Moshe, Moshe, it's not what you think. You'll get your money. But, **verdammt, noch einmal! What the hell are you doing here? You were told to be here next week.**"

Jutz was in a state of agitation reading the address on the huge crates holding the "Vierjahreszeiten". He only wanted what had been promised to him, his fair share.

Rudi's criminal gene directed him to anticipate the worst. He always had an alternative plan or two for contingencies. Jutz was one of those he had guessed might accidentally throw a wrench into the machinery. He had always intended to skip out without paying. While Jutz was engrossed in touching and feeling his precious "Vierjahreszeiten", Rudi noiselessly extracted what appeared to be a wire with heavy oak dowels on either end from the bottom drawer of his desk. Tip-toeing up behind Jutz, he suddenly looped the wire over his head and, using his well-muscled arms, jerked them violently apart.

Garrotting was not a pleasant way to die, but, done properly, it was virtually instantaneous. There wasn't even a gasp. Jutz, his head, partially severed, lay slumped on the floor in an expanding pool of blood.

Two more wooden crates, casket sized, were standing on end against another wall. No one should be shocked to discover the one Rudi dragged over to the corpse on the floor was a perfect fit for his unfortunate victim. The crate was lined suitably, in black plastic about ten millimeters thick. Inside the plastic were ten-centimeter thick foam panels cut to make a snug fit on all interior sides of the crate. Jutz' body was lifted with difficulty and squeezed into place in the crate. Deuffel rolled an insulated barrel on a hand truck up to the crate. Wearing gloves, he scooped out handfuls of dry ice and filled all the spaces around the still-bleeding body. He placed another sheet of the foam material on top, pulled the black plastic over the package, sealed it, and was in the process of screwing the wooden top on, when a loud gasp of disgust and horror sounded behind him. Kemal, impatient for the rest of his earnings, had come to the store after all. The gate was not locked and seeing the sliver of light from inside Rudi's door, which Jutz had left ajar, he ventured in.

"**Idiot! Du verdammtes Schwein! I explicitly told you not to come until next week!**" Rudi exploded. His plan was unraveling. He went ballistic.

Kemal's jaw was hanging. His complexion was snow white. He had seen a dead man! There was a pool of blood on the office floor! Rudi, who was at least six inches taller, grabbed Kemal's shirt below his neck. The toy department manager was livid with rage. He shoved the Turk onto the desk, knocking a few catalogs stacked there onto the floor. The Turk tried to defend himself. He saw out of the corner of his eyes an air-line ticket on the desk with today's date on it. He realized he was being duped, possibly being used as a scape goat. Rudi, meanwhile, looking at the other crate standing against the wall, now had a stiletto in his right hand. Kemal couldn't move. Rudi's right knee was pressing against his crotch and the pain was intense.

"Stop! Hände hoch! Drop the knife! Get on the floor... fast! Spreadeagle!"

Kemal had fainted. Rudi turned quickly towards the voice, only to face a service revolver clutched firmly in both hands of a woman with a determined, menacing look that directed him to get down fast.

Emmi Fischer had been forced to shoot before in self defense and she didn't plan to hesitate in this situation. Deuffel complied, protesting vociferously that the Turk was trying to rob him.

Fischer radioed for back-up. Three officers burst into the storage area within a minute and a half. Deuffel was taken away. Alternately whimpering and blurting out his story in half sentences, Kodoglu, assisted by the police, walked with difficulty to the waiting police van, and was also driven to the police revier as a material witness.

There would be no call to Klaus tonight,...... or tomorrow.

* * *

A turbid sunset was the prelude to a cold, dark night on the barren peak. Temperatures on the Ochsenjoch dropped to the mid-twenties. Mark was grateful to the anonymous forest ranger who had lent him a new fleece pullover and fleece inserts for his boots. He genuinely liked Hofer, a modest chap, he thought, a good person to work with. Hofer set his wristwatch alarm. Both men did their best to get some rest. The wind howled nearly all night. It may have been heavier to carry, but the double-walled tent provided the protection they needed.

Mark's thoughts were of Elli and his daughters. He had no choice, but success. Failure was unthinkable. In the dream that followed he saw Elli again for that first time in Zürich. He recalled the heart-stopping drive to the Denis-Breuer's villa. He saw again those incredible brown eyes looking up at him as he held her in tight embrace beneath the cascading shower. He knew then he would always be putty in her presence. She was sweetness and light personified; the most exotically, erotically beautiful woman he had ever known; intelligent, talented, loyal, passion-ate, caring... There weren't adjectives, nor superlatives enough in any language to describe her adequately? A marvelous wife, a wonderful mother, there could never be another woman quite like her.

* * *

Lying on one's back with hands and feet tied to a bed for hours on end is not conducive to healthy rest. Elli, her mind nearly clear of residual effects from the drugs, tried to swallow. Her mouth was parched, her throat raw. She had no gag, but realized yelling would be fruitless. She had observed the isolated nature of her present location. She tried to recount the days since the tennis tournament in Cannes. Everything was jumbled, confused. Her sense of time was distorted. She thought she had read a sign when the Audi passed Bayrischzell, but couldn't be absolutely certain. She hoped her clue about the Wendelstein had helped. She prayed for her children, for the fetus in her womb, and for Mark. She knew her captivity had reached a critical juncture. She noticed the tension in the faces of her captors. She braced for the worst.

Her thoughts were not for herself. Whatever happened, she felt she would have no input. Her concern was for her two girls, their unborn brother, for her husband, her sister, her friends. Weak and emotionally and physically exhausted, she was overcome by sleep. As she drifted off, she knew Mark would come for her. Somehow.

Day 8, Saturday, 29 April

While it was still dark in the Eng Valley, the cyclists broke camp. They were deployed to assist in the rescue of Elli Davidson. Lieutenant Rauchfuss set up her command post behind a rock outcropping in the vicinity of the prospective landing zone. Two of the women were on their bellies in the swampy ground about forty meters from the front of the three cabins. The remaining two officers, both with sniper training, were positioned on either side of the lone road in and out of the valley. Two helicopters loaded with uniformed members of a joint Austro-Bavarian special forces team were ready for lift-off on a farmer's field north of Hinterriss.

Klaus, concealing it as best he could, was even antsier than Tati. Jörg seemed subdued. "Why hasn't your friend Rudi contacted us?" Tati was irritated, anxious, worried that something had gone wrong. "You know, he could take the money and run."

Klaus stood up for Rudi. "He would never do anything like that." The same thought had been on his mind all night. Klaus went outside into the cool air to smoke a cigarette, a sign he was getting a case of nerves. Weighing on him, too, was the knowledge that he was supposed to "eliminate" his cronies and their captive. The smoke from his *Marlboro* was carried off quickly by a gust of wind.

Tati went back down the hall to the bathroom. When she emerged, following a sponge bath, dressed only in her underpants and bra, Klaus was back in the hall, having checked on Elli. Tati brushed past Klaus, who had seen her thus attired on a couple of other occasions.

"How come you never show any interest in me, you know, sexually? Or in her?" pointing to the bedroom, where Elli was tied to her bed.

Taken aback by her blunt questioning, Klaus blurted out testily, "Sex and business don't mix!" He walked back to the kitchen.

On his way to use the bathroom, Jörg, who had utilized the night in this secluded venue for an orgiastic tryst with Tati, overheard the exchange. He looked at his lover, stuck a finger in his mouth, and, pretending to touch Klaus, went, "Tzssst!" Tati's eyes widened.

* * *

Berlin police had contacted the task force assembled in Bavaria about the arrest of Rudi Deuffel and the recovery of the ransom. The information was passed to Mark on the mountain. The general assessment by the officers in charge, was that the three kidnappers, should they discover what had happened, would be loathe to capitulate, and, instead, might become emboldened to try and fight their way to safety, possibly using Frau Davidson as a hostage, as a shield.

* * *

Hofer, a survival trainer, was a performance paraglider with a cabinet full of medals to prove it. Mark's previous airborne experience dated back to his sophomore year in college, when, on a dare, he had gone tandem skydiving twice. Over some canned meat, a few slices of nearly frozen bread, a chilly banana and a cup of hot oxtail soup, (the person who packed their supplies had accidentally omitted the coffee), Herb gave Mark a much condensed version of the customary one-week introductory course in paragliding. Fortunately, Mark, being a good student and accustomed to storing lots of data in his memory bank, asked good questions and quickly grasped the essentials. Before their gourmet breakfast, Hofer had stuck a small flag between a couple of rocks on a rocky shelf that would be the launch pad. The wind was coming steadily from their right. With this information, Hofer drew on a piece of paper a sketch of the valley and the surrounding mountains, giving the location of the three cabins, marking also where the supporting cast below was hiding and outlined the line of flight Mark should attempt to follow. Peering into Mark's eyes, just inches from his own, Hofer said, "There is no room to abort the flight. Once you are airborne, that's it. There will be no second chance. Are you ready?" Before Mark could reply, Hofer picked up a baseball-sized rock and threw it over the edge of the take-off area. Both listened intently. There was no sound. "You see. If you make a mistake, you'll fall a thousand meters before you hit the rocks below. God speed!"

Mark was helped into the harness. The helmet fit perfectly. A two-way radio was attached to his collar. With the earphones in the helmet he could communicate with Hofer and the forces in the valley. They laid out the chute in a neat semicircle. It was a little over three meters wide. The lines were sorted out. No tangles. Mark went through his checklist: chest strap and cross straps – OK, A-lines and braking toggles – in order, leg straps and boots – OK.

Plunging off a mountain top into the frigid void that waited below was not an act Mark had ever truly contemplated. There was something absurdly irrational about the whole thing. If he were honest, he would have to admit he was very scared. There was no time now to mull through this anymore. Saving Elli was paramount. He couldn't ask anyone else to do it. It had to be him, the man who had said to himself countless times, he would gladly give his life for the woman he had loved since he first saw her. He waved to Herb and pulled gently on the lines.

The cells inflated; the canopy lifted off the ground. Mark ran about four steps forward. He lifted off and up into the air. A rustling sound, even a short snapping noise, indicated the canopy was fully deployed straight above him. The chute immediately caught a light updraft and Mark swung momentarily like a pendulum. The wind hitting his face was icy cold. Behind him, equally cold and gray in the dim pre-dawn light, was the impenetrable handwork of an ancient glacier. Somewhere below, still shrouded in a layer of fog, was his target, the valley floor with its maple trees, many from four to six hundred years old. Mark made a concerted effort to marshal all his physical strength and mental acuity to focus on this critical flight, the most important role of his life. He fought to control his craft. Swinging out in wide circles to avoid being dashed against the masses of crenulated, castellated rock shooting out of the stark vertical face of the cliff from which he had just leapt. Myriads of fantastic, angular forms made more menacing yet by the deep shadows and craggy out-croppings of ice and snow held hostage from the sun, stood in stark contrast to the fresh, green emerging faintly through the snow and fog in the valley floor stretching out below. The arc he formed cut gently through the veil of feathery clouds fleeing before the new day.

On one particularly wide swing Mark strained to see if he could spot any of the volunteers who had entered the Engtal the previous afternoon. Unable to make out any sign of them, he could only hope they were in position and he focused on mastering the enormous surge of adrenaline he felt and his growing anxiety regarding Elli's well-being after a harrowing week in the hands of ruthless criminals.

Three chamois on a promontory he swept past, stopped to stare at the crimson wings of a strange new bird. The wind allowed him to glide out well past the jagged cliffs below his launch site. Now he turned, slowly, carefully shifting his weight to help control the chute. After he had made an approximate 270 degree turn to his left, he straightened his canopy. He needed to get down relatively fast, so as not to overshoot his goal, a smooth, grassy knoll behind the three cabins. The novice paraglider felt like a noble eagle, swooshing by cliffs, their cracks and crevices unwilling to release their hold on winter's ice and snow. He adjusted his steering toggles; performed a deep spiral maneuver that Herb had described to hasten his descent. A bit of vibration developed. Probably not a good sign, Mark suspected. He used his risers to reestablish stability.

He executed the circling maneuver several more times, constantly wary of striking the ever-present wall of unforgiving stone. Gradually, he descended towards his objective. As he drew closer to the valley floor the ground fog dissipated. He made out the location of the cabins. A minor directional alteration to leeward was accomplished with a leg crossing trick. Close to the sheer wall of the mountain, some extra turbulence was felt. The air was suddenly gusty and bumpy. Mark looked up. The leading edge of the canopy was directly above. He prepared for his landing. At about four meters above the marshy soil Mark pulled on his braking toggles to slow his forward speed. Seconds later, he made a beautifully controlled landing. *Herb would be proud.* Loosening his harness and simultaneously gathering his chute, he jogged away from the pile of nylon. He could collect that later. A figure in a camouflage suit to his right waved. Lt. Rauchfuss whispered the location of the others. She planned to circle around behind the cabin.

* * *

Hearing Tati in the kitchen getting a bite to eat, Jörg silently opened the door to the room where Elli was being kept. She was startled to see him and became all the more apprehensive as he closed the door behind him. She was about to scream, when he straddled her and slapped her sharply. She grimaced in pain. He bent forward and kissed her. If she could have, she would have spit in his face. He pulled his pants down to his knees. Next he unbuttoned her jeans. She twisted and squirmed to the extent her bonds allowed. "Good, I like it best when they struggle." He thought he heard someone outside the door and stopped for a moment to listen.

* * *

Outside the cabin, dispirited and wary, Klaus had pulled the tarp off the Audi. He checked the gas gauge. Half empty. He was turning to reenter the cabin, when he was suddenly tackled hard from behind. In a flash, two male figures were sprawling on the gravel in front of the entrance. Klaus, ever nimble, rolled over and leapt adroitly to his feet first. The *Stasi*-trained fighter kicked Mark in the stomach. Mark, the wind knocked out of his gut, fell backwards. Another kick to the kidneys and Mark was unable to regain his footing. Reaching into a musette bag that he had hung on the door handle, Klaus' hand came out with an object that could have been mistaken for a huge pear. He pulled a pin, counted to three and hurled it into the hall between the kitchen and sitting room.

The dull explosion that followed jolted Mark back to full consciousness. Klaus raced for the Audi as the front of the house spewed flame and smoke. It had been an incendiary device of some kind. Fearing Elli would be trapped inside, Mark, turned his attention away from Klaus, shook the cobwebs out of his brain, summoned his wits, overcame the pain, gathered his strength and dashed through the front door, now unhinged and charred. He knew the layout of the building. Rushing past the kitchen, he didn't notice in the smoke-filled interior a moribund woman's body crushed beneath a burning table. Bright tongues of flame, crackling and quivering, sated themselves greedily on the wooden furnishings and the dry lumber of the floors and walls. At the rear on the left, Mark, holding his knit cap over his nose and mouth, tried to survey one of the bedrooms for signs of life. He called for Elli. No response. The dry wooden floor was audibly hissing and sizzling. The opposing bedroom's door was closed. No, locked. Three superhuman blows with his heavily-booted right foot broke the lock and sent most of the door jam flying across the floor.

Jörg, who was tugging on Elli's jeans, jumped off the bed half naked. The same booted foot that had made kindling of the door, struck Jörg's groin with a thundering thud. The recipient doubled up and fell to the floor, shrieking in pain. Mark took the wooden stool next to the bed and smashed the window, glass, frame and all. Dark smoke was billowing into the room. Strapped to Mark's left calf was a leather sheaf holding a six-inch hunting knife. Using it carefully, he freed Elli from her bonds. He gently lifted her from the bed with one arm. With the other he laid the pillow over the shards on the sill, covered it with the comforter and helped his wife out of the cabin. As flames and black smoke roiled across the smouldering floor of the room, Mark made his escape, diving headlong through the open hole in the wall.

With Elli in his arms, he ran a good thirty meters from the blazing skeleton of the cabin. The propane tank behind the house exploded in a gigantic ball of flame. A pile of firewood began to burn. The heat was too intense to attempt to go back. Mark kissed Elli's parched lips. He whispered, "Now I'm whole again."

* * *

Lieutenant Rauchfuss, who had followed Mark to the cabin, was on her walkie-talkie, giving orders for the ambulance to enter the valley as soon as the suspect in the escaping vehicle was apprehended. A firetruck was asked to stand by.

* * *

With both rear tires destroyed by sharpshooters' bullets, Klaus abandoned his vehicle and made a run for the woods. A helicopter landed, disgorging six special forces agents. Klaus tripped on some of the debris from trees that had lost branches during the past winter. He was taken into custody and transferred later to Innsbruck to be held for trial.

* * *

The medical team arrived. Following a doctor's examination, Elli was given a clean bill of health for herself and her baby. She and Mark first thanked all those on hand for the help they had so selflessly provided, then flew home on a charter flight to a happy reunion in Yverdon. Mark kept his arms around Elli all the way.

Epilogue

In Berlin, Moshe Jutz, the genius of miniaturization, his bewildered mother tearfully watching, was laid to rest in accordance with his people's tradition, a photograph of 'Die Vierjahreszeiten' clutched in his folded hands.

Mark purchased the four exquisite N-Scale model railroad layouts from Frau Jutz for a generous sum. At his suggestion, and with her appreciative concurrence, Mark made arrangements for a special permanent display to be housed at the German Museum in Munich. Until a suitable structure is complete early in the 21st century, this unique technological and artistic creation can be seen in the lobby of White Cross Holding's Geneva headquarters.

The End

A Mark Davidson Story

REMEMBERING

Hellmut Edelmann

Chapter One

Within a few minutes and a few kilometers of each other three vehicles and three men whose lives would forever be intertwined were knifing through the moonless black of a stormy night heading west on a quiet highway in eastern France. Dark, heavy clouds were intermittently belching showers of wind-driven rain and hail punctuated by an occasional heavy roll of thunder and flashes of lightning that illuminated the steep inclines and sharp curves of the asphalt ribbon etched in the hilly rural landscape of the Vosges Mountains.

A massive low pressure system had settled over broad northern and central sections of France. The strong winds and pelting rain might be welcome to the farmers whose main crops had recently been harvested. Lightning brought nitrogen. Drivers, however, especially those for whom travel this night was more an option than a requirement, dreamed of a good meal and a warm bed in the comfort of home or a cozy inn. Autumn in Western Europe had been more like Indian Summer. Warm, sunny days had prevailed. Few complained about the weather. Now, finally, a taste of fall and a portent of winter was manifesting itself.

Mark Davidson, Secretary General of *La Fondation Székely* and Chairman of *White Cross Holdings*, positions of great influence that qualified him as one of the world's richest men, had been especially busy today. Following a breakfast meeting in Basel, he met with industrialists and toured manufacturing plants from Mulhouse to Colmar, investigating innovative new techniques that might help introduce useful technologies into remote parts of the globe thirsting for opportunities to spur economic development. He had been especially impressed by advances in prefabricated housing that would permit storage of materials in key centers throughout the world, from which rapid deployment and erection of modular structures would be relatively simple in the event of natural disasters.

Mark normally enjoyed driving and had opted to continue on his journey to Nancy, then Paris for further meetings and conferences the next two days in spite of forecasts predicting inclement weather and dangerous storms along his intended route. At the last minute, he had adjusted his itinerary to a more southerly highway in order to avoid detours due to extensive construction projects further north that had been delayed by the downpours and a few resulting floods.

The small Citroën four-door sedan from the WCH motor pool was fairly comfortable. It certainly wasn't a luxurious model. Its four cylinders, however, performed reliably and had sufficient power to negotiate the rugged hills through which he was driving. The car's operating costs were reasonable and Mark thought it important to set a modest example for his colleagues.

He chided himself for allowing his new cell phone to run out of power and for forgetting to bring along the automobile charging device. Perhaps there would be an opportunity when he tanked up next to call home again. Traffic was extraordinarily light. Visibility was terrible. Keeping within the lines on the highway required Mark's full attention. He questioned his apparent failure to exercise more prudence when choosing to press on to his next destination right after a delightful dinner at a small country inn outside Colmar. The roast duck was superb and the local wines of surprisingly outstanding quality.

Spotting a sign advising of a highway rest area 1000 meters ahead, Mark decided it might be an appropriate time to relieve the discomfort under his belt before continuing further. Gently applying the brake pedal, he slowed down, pulled into the semi-circular drive that arced into a level wooded area at the apex of which was a neat stone building providing toilets and a covered battery of coin-operated snack and beverage dispensers. The building was about 40 meters in from the highway.

The Citroën rolled a few meters past the structure. The rain had abated considerably, allowing Mark to make a dash for the entrance designated for "Les Hommes". A rather weak mercury-vapor lamp was the solitary light source above each of the entrances.

Moments later, another vehicle approached the same rest stop, but merely pulled over at the beginning of the arced drive. Behind the wheel was a bosomy blonde. Her passenger, his features obscured somewhat by a dark beard and mustache, was one Abbas al Khalid, a French citizen born of a refugee couple from Morocco. Abbas was raised in some rough neighborhoods near the docks in Marseille. He was an angry young man who had difficulty, not entirely of his own making, fitting into French society. When it suited him, he allowed his emotions to run amok and had, as a result, become familiar to police in a number of jurisdictions where he had sought to practice his trade as a journeyman plumber. Abbas' 'chauffeur' this evening had not volunteered her services, not as a driver, that is. He had paid for her feigned affection in a boarding house in a small town further east. Their tryst was marred by Abbas' ingrained misogynous attitude and his penchant for gratuitous violence. Had we been able to look more closely, the scratches and bruises on her body would have been obvious. She was being forced to drive him to another town where he claimed to have a friend he wanted to visit. Whenever he dozed off, the driver checked her black eye and fat lip in the visor mirror. She was scared to death of her passenger. As well she should be.

Abbas Khalid had ordered the car off the road because of an urgent need to urinate. He slid the large satchel containing his plumbing tools onto his seat as he slipped out the door. Leaving the door open, he stepped back onto the grass a couple of meters, unzipped and immediately unleashed a furious stream. Suddenly, the blonde shoved his tool bag out the open door and stomped on the accelerator. The car lurched forward. The driver gained the highway in an instant and disappeared into the dense dark void. Abbas, caught in mid-stream, tried to grab the door handle while simultaneously screaming curses in French and Arabic at the top of his lungs. In his rage he hadn't noticed he had badly soiled his trousers. A clap of thunder and a sudden burst of rain effectively drowned out his vulgar tirade.

As the taillights of the car were quickly swallowed by the dark, the enraged Abbas' gaze caught the dim reflection of the mercury-vapor lamps on a vehicle parked ahead just beyond the service building. The blonde's deception had left him fuming. He grabbed his satchel and jogged up to the vehicle. It was empty, but the driver's door was unlocked. He yanked on it and was fishing about on the dash for the keys, when Mark came up, saw someone bent over in his vehicle, and shouted at him to get out. A startled Abbas reached into his tool bag, wrapped his big fist around a large object, a heavy pipe wrench, swung around in a flash and struck Mark soundly on the side of the head. Abbas then continued to unleash his pent up fury with more savage blows to Mark's face and head.

Mark fell unconscious to the wet pavement. Abbas kicked his victim hard twice to turn him over. He knelt quickly. Immediately, he found Mark's wallet in his jacket pocket and located the car's key in his right-hand pants pocket together with a cell phone. Looking about, Abbas was pleased to note that the parking lot was absolutely desolate. He reached down, grabbed Mark by the jacket and dragged his limp body across a concrete walkway, then dropped it in the muddy grass adjacent to a trash receptacle. Before rushing to the car, Abbas slid Mark's watch off his left arm. Why not, he thought. He won't need it.

The Citroën moved smoothly towards the exit as the new driver searched frantically for the light switch and the windshield wipers. The headlamps lit the caution sign at the end of the arced drive and the Citroën sped off into the night. The surveillance camera, out of order for over a month, was impotently aimed in the right direction.

Anyone familiar with Mark Davidson, Ph.D., knows the role he often ascribed to fate in his journey from a small town boy in the American Midwest to the Deanship of a growing Carolina Low-Country college to the beneficiary of the vast financial holdings of the Székelys in Switzerland. Following a strange winter odyssey in Central and Southern Europe,

Mark was able to lay claim to the fortune resulting from secret accounts presumably established by war criminals in the late 30's and early 40's in parts of what is now eastern Slovakia and Hungary.

It was the earnest wish of both Tibor Székely and his son Zdeněk that the funds derived from these accounts be used for humanitarian purposes. Mark Davidson, together with trusted friends and colleagues, had made that wish come true. He had pursued his responsibilities selflessly and with great energy and passion. And now, fully twelve years hence, Dame Fortune had seemingly abandoned one of her favorites. The one who had so carefully nurtured and guided this remarkable human being to the peak of his maturity was guilty of gross neglect. Mark Davidson, his face and head covered with mud and blood, lay forsaken and dying next to a garbage can along a remote stretch of highway in the French countryside. A bizarre, tragic and undeserved end to a life filled with unspent promise.

Also hurtling along this forlorn byway is a faded gray Peugeot station wagon. At the wheel, humming along to a cassette tape of Pavarotti arias, is the eccentric and brilliant Dr. Med. Jean-Pierre Baumann. Baumann, mid-seventies, his tall, stately frame relaxed against the faded fabric of the driver's seat, is as strong as the proverbial ox, an unlikely violinist and propagator of prize orchids, and an avid collector of international postage stamps featuring exotic flora. Incongruously, he pursues a very reclusive lifestyle on a large, 2100 acre estate left to him by his wealthy parents, while enjoying world-wide acclaim for his innovative research into the mysteries of the human brain.

A renowned neurosurgeon and psychiatrist, Baumann converted the château he inherited into a world-class clinic and treatment center, specializing in brain damage and extraordinary psychiatric cases. The château sits in the midst of the estate that contains substantial wooded areas, rolling hills, lush meadows and pastures, extensive vineyards, an arboretum, two small ponds, a park, barns for his horses, kennels for his dogs and sumptuous gardens, in which much of the food for the patients and staff is raised. Baumann's timely arrival on the scene may represent an attempt by Dame Fortune to make amends for a tragic lapse in oversight.

The doctor resides with his wife in the central portion of the secluded château, while the large right wing houses his modern treatment center, the left wing his research laboratories and a small hospital containing the ultimate in technologically advanced equipment.

Perhaps it's the rain, but Dr. Baumann, too, feels the urge to ease the pressure of a distended bladder, coincidentally as he spies the rest area sign. The sign represents in no way a surprise for the doctor, as his estate is actually located in an isolated region less that a quarter hour away. Since the rain had abated substantially, at least temporarily, he decided he would assuage the discomfort under his belt at one of the urinals so conveniently placed to receive the three bottles of beer he had consumed following a specialist seminar in *Guebwiller* earlier in the evening.

Stopping right in front of the rest rooms, Baumann turns off the engine, slides off the well-worn seat and enters the building. A quick look in the stainless-steel mirror substitute, while he rinses his hands, a hasty move to brush his hair back with his fingers and, his business completed, he steps out into the damp air, glides back over the smooth, shiny fabric, turns the key and his engine leaps to attention, ready to complete the day's travel. As the vehicle slowly aligns itself with the curb, the headlamps catch an odd bundle off to the right. Strange, thinks Baumann. He is ready to roar off into the night, eager to get home and relax, when he applies the brake to see exactly what is piled up in the grass just a meter or so away.

Leaving the engine running, Baumann walks over to the pile of undetermined nature. The "pile" assumes the outline of a person, rolled up in a modified fetal position. Baumann bends quickly, feels a weak pulse and senses a faint breath on his cool, damp hand. *"Mon Dieux!"*

Looking closer at the face in the dim light, Baumann recoils and winces upon noting the brutally damaged countenance of the once handsome victim. Rushing to the car, Baumann lowers the rear seats, opens the fifth door and runs back to the unconscious body. Although Mark weighs about 175 pounds, the doctor easily lifts him with tender strength and lays him in the rear of the station wagon.

The closest trauma facility equipped to deal with this kind of injury is a good half hour away in decent weather. The nearest emergency ambulance service would require an additional thirty minutes to respond, possibly longer on a night like this one. Baumann makes a decision to take the man to his own hospital. The Peugeot is pushed to the limit. Within ten minutes the wide automatic gates open to receive the doctor's car. Moments later, at the end of a long tree-lined lane, the car stops smoothly at a side door, Baumann races inside, shouts a command to the orderly on duty to bring a gurney, to summon Madame Baumann and Helga, the head nurse, and to switch on all power to the operating room and its equipment.

Almost immediately, Helga, who had been in the adjacent study reading a medical journal, pushes the gurney into the operating theater, where she and Baumann transfer the patient to a special table. At once she begins to cleanse the wounds of the naked male lying on the operating table. She also recoils upon viewing the hideous cuts, gashes and the severe bruising.

The patient, breathing labored, is comatose and feels no pain.

* * *

Even if driving conditions had allowed Abbas to enjoy the beauty of the Vosges Mountains, a scenic delight, whose lofty vistas offer panoramas of nature that attract visitors in all seasons, his negative attitude would be unlikely to permit the wondrous landscape to register amid his dark thoughts.

Abbas, still incensed and muttering choice invectives over his betrayal by the blonde, presses on towards Paris. Mindful of the possibility that she had alerted the police regarding his threats of violence and forcing her to drive him westwards, Abbas tried to be as inconspicuous as he could, keeping to the speed limit and staying off the major *Autoroutes*. The further west he drove, the better the weather. He tanked once, catching a petrol station shortly before closing time. Mark's wallet had nearly 600 Euros in bills, some change and two credit cards. Abbas decided to get rid of the credit cards. Too dangerous he thought. Too easy to be traced. He tossed them, together with the wallet, the dead cell phone and Mark's driver's license into a trash bin. The cash payment for the fuel, the stale fish sandwich and the bottle of Orangina raised no eyebrows, as a sleepy clerk quickly locked the door and pulled down the 'FERMÉ' sign.

Although growing more tired with every kilometer, Abbas resisted sleep and between three and three-thirty in the morning he approached Paris from the east passing through *Marne la Vallée*. A hasty search of the map pocket produced a recent edition of a fold-out map of *Paris* and its environs. Acquaintances in *Marseille* had given Abbas the name and address of a contact in *Clichy sous Bois*, a suburb populated with many Arabs. The streets were relatively quiet at this hour. Abbas found his destination, but decided to ditch the vehicle. Nearby was a rather large park, *le Forêt Régionale de Bondy*. On one of its paved roads Abbas parked the car. He left it unlocked and tossed the keys into a small pond. The walk back to call on his contact was invigorating.

Response to the two short and two long rings on the doorbell of a dingy apartment in a block crammed with shabby and uninspiring clones, led to a brief vetting, followed by coffee, pastries and some fruit for the road. Instructions for reaching his party in *Rotterdam* were verbal. Abbas looked forward to serving Islam. Hugs and traditional kisses preceded Abbas' quiet departure. Clutching his tool bag, he walked onto the street and started looking for new wheels. He grabbed a bus to *Bobigny*, another suburb. Alighting there, he strolled a couple of streets with lots of cars parked at the curb. Finally, a few blocks away he hit pay dirt. The driver's window had been left open just enough for Abbas to reach in and unlock the door. He hot-wired the ignition and had it running in an instant. The gas gauge was full. Although far from being a new model, it ran well and its dust-covered exterior rendered it definitely nondescript. Perfect, thought Abbas. Following the signs, he was soon caught up in the heavy traffic on A1 (E 15) heading for *Lille* and France's industrial northeast.

* * *

Mark's Citroën had cooled down in the early morning air for nearly four hours when it was discovered in the park by a band of Arab youth disinclined to attend school or pursue gainful employment. With minimal effort, the engine was purring and the boys took turns at the wheel, driving finally into the heart of Paris for sport with no particular goal in mind. Ultimately, the fuel gauge slipped past the 'low petrol' light and the engine gasped a final breath on a side street in *Neuilly sur Seine* just a block from the river. Before being found there three days later by a police patrol, it had become a mini-playground for an indeterminate number of street urchins pretending to be Michael Schuhmacher at the Nürburgring. No one knew how or when the car had arrived there. There were no retrievable fingerprints. It was definitely the vehicle Mark Davidson had been driving. Of that there was no question. However, there were no clues whatsoever. None. Had Mark made it to Paris? Where was he now? What had happened to him? The only witness, an abused hunk of metal, glass, rubber and plastic, offered no help.

Meanwhile, Abbas had made good time to *Lille*, where he stopped for lunch, washed down with a couple of glasses of wine. Outside *Ghent* in Belgium, he became confused about the route and made a wrong turn. While trying to get back on track for *Rotterdam*, he made an illegal U-turn and was broadsided by a huge tractor-trailer rig. He died on impact in the vicinity of a small town named *Lokeren*. In his pocket was a fake driver's license, 450 Euros and no other identification. His tool bag was given a cursory glance by a local patrolman, then tossed into the evidence room at the station house. Two days later Abbas' unclaimed body was buried at public expense in a communal plot reserved for indigents.

A fancy Swiss timepiece for which the deceased obviously had no further use, made its way into the pocket of an emergency medical attendant. He later pawned it without noticing the fine engraving on the back of the case: *Mark, with love, Elli.*

Chapter Two

In *Yverdon-les-Bains*, Mark's home of choice, an easy commute to WCH's headquarters in *Geneva*, his wife Elli, the former Michèlle d'Entremont, having read a bedtime story to the twins and their younger brother Theo, was reviewing the lyrics she would sing in an upcoming operetta concert in *Lausanne*. The showers in *Yverdon* had been light and moved swiftly eastward after giving the meadows and flower beds around the Davidsons' farm a good dousing. The Davidsons had spoken earlier following Mark's dinner. At the time, he had assumed he would travel a different route, but had learned subsequently of the construction detours and altered his plans. Elli was unaware that the cell phone in his jacket had run out of juice and that he had forgotten to bring a charger for the automobile. When he reached *Paris*, he thought, he would call home and tell Elli about the change in plans and the miserable weather conditions.

Mark and Elli were still deeply in love. Their twelve years of life together had flown past. In spite of Mark's busy schedule and extensive travel, he always made time for holidays in nearby areas with Elli and the children. With her degree in Economics and her MBA in International Finance, Elli had become a most able advisor and partner in his humanitarian work. Mark encouraged her to further develop her artistic talent. She was now in considerable demand for her acting and singing skills, appearing often in charity concerts.

* * *

For her part, the blonde, nursing her bruises safely back in her apartment near *Colmar*, thanked her lucky stars that she had been able to escape from the mad Arab's clutches. No telling what might happen when you're with a moody brute at war with the world. It was very late when she changed into her nightgown, took a pill for her headache and finally fell asleep.

* * *

Baumann, or rather his parents, had never chosen a fancy name for their château. It was simply Château Baumann. Actually, in spite of his acknowledged artistic sensitivity, the good doctor had been too occupied with other interests to properly furnish and decorate his home until he had proposed to his wife, Anni, at a medical conference in *Prague*, three years ago, approximately 18 months after their first meeting on a charity medical mission in the Balkans.

Anni was over 30 years her husband's junior. Born and brought up in Finland, her hobbies were portrait painting, sculpture, and horses. She brought new life into the château and enlivened the doctor's existence with her passion for living, her love of the out-of-doors, equestrian competition and the potential for developing the château's extensive vineyards. She came, regrettably, with a certain amount of unfortunate baggage that hung over her like a dark cloud.

In her native Finland she had studied dentistry, becoming an oral surgeon, then medicine. After five years of residency she had become a qualified plastic surgeon. Actually, one of the youngest in Scandinavia. Her reputation for outstanding results in difficult and complicated surgeries grew. When a nurse administered an incorrect amount of a medication prescribed for post-operative treatment, and the patient died, Anni was held accountable. Not long after, an anaesthetist involved in one of her operations made a tragic mistake and another patient suffered a serious debilitating condition. Anni was again held accountable and her medical license suspended. Baumann's proposal at a medical convention in Prague had come at a juncture in her life where the alternatives were unacceptable. At Baumann's hospital she served as his surgical aide and performed nursing duties. Her petition to have her license reissued was

298

still under consideration, deeply imbedded in some obscure governing board's tedious process.

When her medical services were not required, Anni read voluminously in the literature of her field, trained and cared for her three Trakehners and consulted with the men in charge of rehabilitating the vineyards her husband had neglected following his parents' deaths a few years before. The emergency buzzer in her library brought a rapid response. Carefully scrubbed and gowned, she entered the operating room and approached the patient. She choked back a gasp. Only once before, in the case of a motorcycle accident in Finland, had she seen such extensive damage to a human face. She wondered who he was, how this had happened.

* * *

Guillaume Nabholz, fiftyish, Chief of Rehabilitation Services, a licensed Physical Therapist and nurse, also an expert nutritionist, who on previous occasions had assisted in the operating room, had been roused from his bed to help in dealing with what all present realized was a race to save a human life.

Ordinarily, operations performed at Baumann's clinic were elective procedures scheduled well in advance, allowing for extensive preparation, for some were rather complex and risky. The difficult surgical procedures tonight, also complex and definitely filled with risk, were strictly of an urgent nature.

Baumann, cool and in command, issued short, clear instructions. Each member of the team did his or her part quietly and expertly. A blood test showed that Mark had type AB+, relatively rare. Once again, Dame Fortune smiled. Anni had the identical type. Helga and Guillaume managed to obtain a pint of Anni's blood on Baumann's instruction, for it was obvious a transfusion would be necessary, even though the patient had not actually lost too much of his own blood. Guillaume noted that one of the patients in the psychiatric ward, who was nearing release, also had type AB+ blood, in the event more was required before replenishment could be obtained from Strasbourg.

The doctor performed an emergency tracheotomy, inserting a tube to make breathing easier. Mark was then attached to a ventilator. Guillaume, with Helga's aid, monitored all the mechanical equipment. The swelling of Mark's head required prompt relief. While Mark was being hydrated intravenously and receiving antibiotics, Baumann prepared to relieve the hydrochephalus condition by draining off the fluid build-up using a shunt terminating in his third ventricle.

Keen on research, always eager to acquire state-of-the-art equipment, to investigate new and experimental protocols and procedures, Baumann had a hospital boasting the best and latest equipment. An MRI and computerized three-dimensional tomographic scan reveal the extent of Mark's injuries. Both Baumann and his wife understood the complexities and danger of what they were about to undertake.

Virtually all of Dr. Baumann's patients were the subjects of thoroughly detailed, long-range studies. Everything from the food they consumed, the various therapies: speech, games, creative projects, reactions to animals, outings on the estate, were carefully documented. Video tapes of their activities and personal sessions with the doctor were available. Likewise, any medical procedures.

Dr. Baumann and his staff routinely reviewed everything for its effectiveness. Staff input was regularly solicited. Adjustments were made as deemed desirable. Much would eventually be incorporated into an article or book outlining the clinic's research efforts. Fortunately, the highly trained and experienced staff, along with Anni's available expertise, allowed the good doctor to engage, additionally, in a lecture and seminar series which often took him abroad.

* * *

Elli had seen the report of inclement weather on the evening news and was not overly concerned for her husband, who was expected to be traveling in the area on his way to the French capital. He had discussed the possibility that he might go north from *Colmar*, then head west via *Nancy* to *Paris*. Generally, he called to check on the girls and young Theo whenever he was out of town. Maybe the business meetings had taken longer than he had anticipated and he would call or e-mail a message later, she thought.

She sat for a while at the piano studying the libretto for Lehar's *The Merry Widow*. She had agreed to sing excerpts from the role of Madame Glavari together with Rolando Villazón, the talented young Mexican tenor, who was to assume the role of Count Danilo, in a benefit concert operetta for a charity in *Basel* in two weeks. The irony involved would only become apparent to her in time.

She dozed off, not waking until shortly after midnight. No message from Mark. "Hmmm, highly uncharacteristic". She called her sister, Dani, in *Lausanne*, who sought to reassure Elli that there was no reason for concern, but agreed to contact her husband, Roland, who had opted to stay in *Geneva*, where he had scheduled breakfast meetings with several East European medical instrument manufacturers. Roland suggested that he would contact French highway patrol officials to see whether there had been any accidents reported. The reply: None involved any fatalities. None involving a Monsieur Davidson. Roland's advice was simply to wait for the morning. Mark would surely call by then.

By eight-thirty the following morning, the children had finished breakfast and were engaged in English lessons with their new American governess, Kristin Reed. Not having heard from Mark, Elli contacted the *Foundation* offices in *Geneva*. Samantha Willis responded personally.

It had been Mark, who recognized the enormous intellect, the indomitable will and the extraordinary potential of a quadriplegic most had written off as a useless cripple. At great expense, the *Foundation*'s headquarters building had been thoroughly renovated to allow complete access for Miss Willis' hi-tech wheel chair. The investment had proven its value many times over, as Willis' contributions had improved efficiency, and accountability, and effected countless savings in operational efficacy. Willis sensed immediately that something was wrong. Something grave had occurred, her intuition told her. She did not want to alarm Mark's wife and family unnecessarily.

Her unflappable, practical, reasoned approach to the problem helped calm Elli. When, by evening of the same day, no word from Mark was forthcoming, Ms Willis decided on a course of action. She alerted the entire staff. Everyone went into overdrive. Telephone and internet contact was established with every public and private hospital in a 200 kilometer wide swath from the Swiss-German border to *Paris* and beyond. Result: there were no admissions of any males corresponding to Mark's description. Further queries directed to police departments in the same areas failed to reveal any automobile accidents of any nature involving a person resembling Mark. Willis set up two websites: *www. lacasMarkDavidson.fr* and *www.markdavidsonsearch. com*, in the hope that keeping the subject before the public would eventually produce clues leading to information about his fate. She wanted to be as proactive as possible.

No one realized, of course, that the good doctor, Jean-Pierre Baumann's medical facility was officially known as the *Justine Marie Baumann Research and Rehabilitation Institute*. It was named after his dear mother, whose financial legacy enabled its creation.

Posters were printed with a handsome color photograph of Dr. Mark Davidson and particulars of his person that might aid in his identification. A substantial reward was offered for information leading to his return. There were a few crank calls in response. Nothing solid resulted from either effort. The authorities were baffled. At Jean-Luc Renard's suggestion, Georges Salber, the private investigator who had assisted the *Banque sociale de Léman* on occasion, was called in and given *carte blanche* to locate Mark. Salber and an associate conducted intensive investigations of all the logical routes from eastern France to Paris. The fruitless outcome of these myriad attempts to find Mark cast a pall over the lives of all who knew or worked with this unique, unselfish and caring man. Special security measures were instituted at Roland's insistence to protect Elli and the children. You never know, he claimed, what might be happening.

Once before, ten years earlier, Elli had been targeted for abduction and a ransom demand. Something like that could be in play again.

Weeks passed. It was as if the earth had opened up and swallowed Dr. Mark Davidson, husband, father, teacher, philanthropist. For the authorities the "All-American Boy" was as good as dead. However, his friends and family in *Yverdon* and in *Geneva* refused to accept that conclusion.

Chapter Three

Jean-Pierre Baumann, at 75 years of age, considered himself merely to be approaching the epitome of his professional knowledge and skills as a neurosurgeon. Whether propagating rare and exquisitely beautiful orchids in his greenhouse or working on his valuable philatelic collection of floral postage stamps from around the world, anyone who was even remotely acquainted with him, understood that he was the quintessential, consummate and most passionate practitioner of anything he undertook, be it a hobby, a sports activity or his medical calling. He demanded of those around him the same dedication and precision he expected of himself. Nothing less.

His team moved about the operating chamber like agile dancers in an intricate ballet. Authoritative, orderly instructions came from the doctor. Everyone present had participated on numerous occasions in serious operations. None, however, held the drama and urgency of the one before them. The unidentified patient, in a deep coma, was fighting for his life. The team wanted desperately to save him, but also to restore his very existence as a human being by undoing the damage to his face at the savage hands of a vicious and wanton attacker.

The tracheotomy was a success. The patient was on a ventilator and breathing steadily. Dr. Baumann was alternately checking the heart monitor and reading the results of the MRI and the three-dimensional computerized tomographic scan.

No expense had been spared in equipping the operating chamber and no one was more grateful than Dr. Baumann, that he had had the foresight to acquire the very latest diagnostic aids available. The patient had been stabilized as well as possible. In his mind Baumann quickly ticked off items in the Glasgow Coma Scale to determine the degree of severity of the patient's comatose condition that resulted from his head and facial trauma.

As the patient was being prepared for surgery and treated simultaneously for shock, everyone noticed how youthful and strong he was. His musculature suggested a male of barely thirty years. He was well proportioned, obviously took good care of himself, ate sensibly, exercised on a regular basis and frequently engaged in vigorous physical activity. The callouses on Mark's hands were those of a happy gardener.

The scans performed thus far indicated there were only two or three skull fragments exerting pressure on the brain. Though fractured, the patient's skull would need relatively little in the way of repair. The blunt force that caused the damage to the patient's face was partly to blame for the hydrocephalus that Baumann absolutely had to bring under control before any facial repair could be considered. He decided on an endoscopic third ventrilostomy, a procedure he had witnessed first hand while visiting Johns Hopkins Hospital in Maryland the year before. All the necessary tools were ready. Anni and Helga assisted. Baumann's superior recall played a key part in assuring the success of this complex technique.

The vital signs were good and all present felt blessed by the outstanding physical shape of their unconscious patient. On the negative side, the various measures employed indicated that the engram, the site of memory in the brain, had been seriously disturbed. Probably from multiple heavy blows with a blunt instrument. The room temperature was lowered. Baumann and his wife stepped to the side to confer. Both knew the ordeal was just beginning, for them and for their helpless patient.

Anni's confidence in her skill as a plastic surgeon had never been shaken. She was disappointed and dismayed by the unbelievably slow bureaucratic nonsense that prevented her from regaining her suspended medical license. It was all the more frustrating because the negligence of others had placed her name and professional reputation in jeopardy. For the support of her husband and the pleasant distractions of her equestrian activity and her sculpting she was most grateful. She had continued to attend medical seminars and meetings in her specialties. During the preceding month she had viewed and reviewed countless times several videotaped craniomaxillofacial surgeries, including reconstruction of damage to the naseothmoid area.

With the help of her husband's deep pockets Anni had recently spent two weeks at a small factory in Italy where a unique line of micro and mini plates crafted from titanium formed a ductile and pliable system enabling surgeons to correct facial anomalies resulting from birth or trauma. Anni had ordered and received a wide selection of the titanium plates, together with titanium screws and some cobalt chrome alloy parts guaranteed to be bio-compatible.

Baumann had no doubts or reservations about his wife's ability. They had worked side by side in difficult situations abroad, as well as in his state-of-the-art operating theater. Her argument for early open repair, allowing for precise reduction and stabilization of bone fragments and prompt treatment of the blunt and penetrating trauma to soft tissues was detailed and succinct. She had the MRI and CT scan results, as well as color photographs of the injuries she and Guillaume had just taken. Convinced that definitive repair so soon after the injury was indeed the only appropriate course of action, Baumann agreed that Anni should make preparations to proceed. While the patient's brain waves were slow, his heart and lungs showed strength.

"Anni, what you are suggesting will require several hours to complete. Can you handle it? Do you feel all right?"

Having just finished donating a pint of blood, Anni had consumed a glass of an electrolyte mixture and was now gulping down a half liter of her favorite beverage, chocolate milk. "I'm fine; ready to go. Helga is doing an EEG and should have the results in a few more minutes."

As soon as Dr. Baumann was able to remove the bone fragments from the brain, which he could accomplish, fortunately, through two holes drilled in Mark's skull, Anni took over.

* * *

Both Baumanns resembled creatures from outer space as seen in science fiction flicks. Strapped on over their mint green medical caps and face masks were bands of high intensity lights and powerful microscopic glasses. Closer physical examination indicated there was some damage to the patient's hearing in the left ear and potential long-term problems with vision in the left eye, whose socket was fractured.

Upon Mark's arrival at the medical facility, Guillaume, assisted by Helga, had removed his clothing and wrapped him in a warm shock blanket. Antibiotics and fluids were introduced intravenously. A routine search of his clothing revealed nothing but a clean handkerchief in his rear pants pocket. Guillaume removed a plain wedding band from Mark's left hand, placed it in an envelope with the date written on it and then put the envelope in a cubby hole in Dr. Baumann's desk in the adjacent office. The patient had no observable scars, tattoos or other identification marks. He had no driver's license and carried no pictures of any kind. What he really looked like was not readily discernible when looking at a face that was grossly discolored and badly swollen and misshapen from the merciless beating he had suffered.

In spite of her earnest and practiced intention to remain professionally detached and objective about any patient under her scalpel, Anni Baumann, D.D.S., M.D. was already experiencing an emotional attachment. It was unconscious. It was involuntary. He would soon have her blood coursing literally through his veins. There was simply something at work that she could not control. A magnificent body like his had to be matched to a handsome face. It was up to her to make that a reality. In the back of her mind was the realization that she might sacrifice her medical license forever, if it became known she had operated while suspended. But a man's existence was at stake. It was a risk that had to be taken.

Anni's careful assessment of damage reckoned on repair of the cheek bones, the chin, where an implant and bone grafting would be required, the nose, and the left ear. Fine, supple titanium mesh would be inserted in the left eye socket. That would also require grafting with a miraculous adhesive that had just been approved for use. Blepharoplasty to repair the eyelid would follow the otorhino corrections to the left ear and the patient's nose. The titanium micro plates worked wonders. All vital signs were within acceptable parameters. After nearly three hours of intense work, Baumann tapped his wife on the shoulder and suggested a two-minute break for stretching and fluid intake. Meanwhile, Guillaume double-checked all monitors.

Satisfied that all fractures had been effectively treated by bone grafting or reinforcement with the plate systems, Anni addressed the contusions and then grafted skin from the patient's buttocks on his forehead and on the right cheek. She accomplished the suturing with patience and precision, seeking to minimize any scars.

Several teeth would obviously need replacing. For that it would be desirable to implant the screws that would eventually support new caps. The remainder of the procedure would wait for his gums to heal. Dealing with the teeth would be delayed for a secondary operation. That is, if the patient survives. Somehow, no member of the team had made any reference to his survival chances. Comas from anatomic causes that disrupt the normal physical structures of the brain responsible for consciousness generally last two to three weeks, according to Baumann. He admitted, however, it might take longer. The coma might endure indefinitely. Science and medicine had their limitations.

The patient was tenderly transferred for intensive post-operative care to a special hospital bed. Heavily bandaged, his eyes covered, tubes extending from his trachea, his arm and elsewhere, Mark Davidson, lay still, presumably resting and, hopefully, recuperating.

Luck, be a lady tonight!

A large clock on the wall showed five-thirty. A brilliant orange glow was rising gradually in the East. The forecast was for warm sun, drying out the landscape drenched the previous night. Helga checked on the patient. The Baumanns cleaned up and changed into fresh whites. Dr.

Baumann helped his wife to a cot in a corner. She was exhausted. Within seconds, she lay there deep asleep, a furrow on her brow, a faint smile on her lips. The Doctor thanked his two assistants and ordered them to bed. He would take the first watch. Anni would spell him in a couple of hours.

Baumann wondered for the first time who this poor soul might be. As he fingered the photos that had been made automatically by the overhead camera and reviewed the video tape, he started to dictate his notes into a tiny recording device resting on a table next to his chair. The monitors and other devices hummed quietly in the background, while the doctor recalled in his soft voice a minute-by-minute playback of the entire procedure.

It seemed terribly impersonal to refer to the patient as "the patient", "the victim", or simply to employ a personal pronoun. Anni's favorite relative was her mother's father, Matti, a fun-loving, good natured fellow, who was the backbone of the family. Anni, for whom the man on the operating table before her had already become a son, or brother, or lover, named him 'Matti'.

The Baumanns were so completely engrossed, not only in this most unusual case that fate had unexpectedly placed almost literally on their doorstep, but also in an unusually full roster of patients in their long-term treatment center, that they had little time for themselves. Their hobbies offered them brief but welcome moments of relaxation. Being naturally somewhat reclusive and esoteric in their interests, neither doctor read a newspaper or followed the news on the radio or television.

In fact, Jean-Pierre did not allow televisions or radios in the treatment center as a precaution to avoid unwanted emotional stress among some of his more extreme psychiatric cases. Staff members, most of whom resided on the estate in pleasant quarters provided by the Baumanns, similarly contented themselves with refreshing pursuits available on the estate: gardening, tennis, a putting green, swimming, fishing and hiking, as well as sledding, skating and skiing in the winter.

It was possible, not long after the surgery, to remove Matti from the ventilator. His life signs were acceptable and improving. His severe coma, however, continued, even after the drugs used to ensure he suffered no pain from the multitude of medical procedures, had been eliminated. He was monitored constantly.

It was Three Kings' Day, when finally, during a body massage, Matti opened his eyes briefly, said something no one present understood and resumed his trauma-induced sleep. It was, of course, a precursor to a full awakening. This occurred a few days later. By this time most of the band-ages had been removed.

Matti's recovery could now begin in earnest. A protocol of therapies was begun. At first slowly, then, as he responded favorably, with greater intensity. Weeks passed swiftly. Winter crept away. Spring brought the promise of new life.

There was a gym on the estate. It was located in the basement of the château. Reserved for patients during the day, staff used it evenings and weekends. Matti had a carefully prescribed regimen of exercises. He undertook speech therapy. Gradually, he was allowed to walk outdoors, to play with the Baumanns' dogs, which he enjoyed immensely, and to groom their three Trakehners in the horse barn. He delighted in garden-ing.

During his all-night emergency surgery, Anni had prepared for the eventual insertion of tooth implants on the right side of his damaged jaw. Now that Matti was up and about, she scheduled the completion of the implant process. He was fitted, as well, with corrective glasses for reading. Some microabrasion was necessary to refine the plastic surgery work on his face, neck and head. For the memory loss, only time and Mother Nature could tell his future status.

After a few weeks, Anni decided that a special protective helmet designed especially to help prevent damage to Matti's face was no longer required. Matti's strength and balance were considered normal. He was advised to be cautious with regard to his face and skull. However, they were healing quite well. Both Drs. Baumann were extremely pleased. Anni was tentatively planning follow-up surgery, providing the patient's general condition continued to improve and they were able to avoid post-operative infections.

Chapter Four

Mark/Matti, after several months of recuperation and three subsequent minor surgical procedures, still persistently amnesic, ventures forth on a lovely early summer day together with Anni, Dr. Baumann's wife, on their huge estate with the intention of camping out overnight on a hill in the northwest corner, which happens to look down on a quiet country road. Dr. Baumann, has been called by *Médicins Sans Frontières* to assist on an emergency basis as team leader for three months in operations in East Africa.

Arriving rather early in the morning after a refreshing hike, Matti fishes in a small stream nearby, catches a couple of fish, builds a fire and prepares breakfast for himself and Anni. He grills his catch and they eat some bread and fruit they have brought with them. After cleaning up and putting out the fire, Matti lays back in the grass to ponder his situation. He suffers from substantial retrograde amnesia and has frequent bouts of anterograde amnesia as well. Dr. Baumann has attempted to explain his situation, encouraging him to reflect on his past whenever any stimulus comes along that might open up his memory.

The hike to their camping spot has tired Anni somewhat and she too relaxes in the soft grass. During Matti's stay with the Baumanns Anni has become increasingly more attached to him. While in his coma, she spent hours daily tending to him. Her extraordinary skills helped create a new face for Matti, although, since he has no memory of the past, neither he, nor Anni, nor Dr. Baumann are aware that his present countenance actually nearly resembles his former appearance. Those who had known him before, might agree that his new face was even more handsome than the one he was born with. Matti likes Anni, too. They are approximately the same age and have been in close proximity for many, many weeks.

The air is warm and slightly humid. Lying next to him, Anni suddenly rolls over and kisses Matti. Somewhere in the deep recesses of his memory he senses that he owes someone, a woman, his loyalty, his fidelity. Without rebuffing Anni, whom he does not wish to hurt in any way, he shows he has no desire to allow amorous advances to interrupt his train of thought. The message received, Anni proposes a walk to a neighboring hill with a view of a small pond. Matti accepts.

They walk together, silently, then engage in small talk, mostly about the beauty of the landscape and the perfect weather. Upon their return to the tent they had erected, Anni claims she had forgotten some important reports she needed to finish. She asks forgiveness for spoiling their outing, but suggests Matti might like to remain alone. He can return to the château for breakfast the next morning. Matti agrees to stay.

Feeling a bit restless, Matti decides to walk the perimeter, part of which has been fenced. In a remote corner of the estate grounds, much of it forested with hardwoods, Matti, from an elevated position, notices two round-topped green wagons parked at roadside. Nearby four horses were grazing in the sweet tall grass along an extra wide shoulder of a rarely traveled country byway. This mode of travel was new to Matti. While he wondered what this was all about, two men, one probably a teenager, the other gray-haired and weathered, came out of the woods. Matti looked over to the horses and came to the conclusion that each man was driving a wagon with two horses. When he looked back towards the spot were he had seen the two men, only one was visible. He was running to a place in the tall grass a few meters away. He bent over a figure lying in the grass and seemed concerned; wailing in distress.

Matti ran down the hill, slipped over a section of low fence and raced towards the two men. The elder had apparently collapsed. It was a seizure of some sort. Matti pushed the boy aside, speaking calming words in French. Lifting the unconscious form, he instinctively tried mouth-to-mouth resuscitation. Observing that the unresponsive male had a very weak pulse he applied intermittent pressure to the chest area. After a few minutes the old man began spitting up and Matti turned him to help clear his throat. The boy ran to get some water and a bottle of tablets. These he gave to the old man. In about fifteen minutes he was sitting up, leaning against a wheel of the first wagon. In heavily accented French, he thanked Matti, holding his hand to reinforce his gratitude.

Matti soon learned that the two wagons were part of a small caravan. The other wagons had continued on to their intended destination for the day. These two had stopped to rest the horses. In the process they discovered one horse needed a new shoe. The old man was not in condition to undertake the task, although a new shoe was on hand. The boy hadn't much experience in such matters.

Under Anni's tutelage, Matti had spent a lot of time in the horse barns, grooming, cleaning and, even shoeing some of the horses. The Baumanns often wondered where Matti had acquired his way with animals. Their dogs and horses loved him and he loved them. He played with them, fed them and showed them great affection. All of this they returned in kind.

Matti helped the boy shoe the horse. They brought water from a nearby mountain pond, gave the horses a welcome drink and checked all the harnesses. The old man was putting on a brave face, but was clearly in no condition to drive his wagon. Matti told the boy to lead the way. He climbed onto the wagon, took the reins with some authority and, with the old man sitting next to him, off they went. Matti had completely forgotten about his camping, about breakfast the next day and about the Baumanns. He had just joined a band of gypsies.

By nightfall, after many kilometers and a number of turns they arrived at a large meadow outside a small village. Several green wagons, like the two he drove until his arrival in a cloud of dust, were drawn up in a classic circle. Lanterns illuminated the doorways. A spit had been erected over a fire. Potatoes were roasting in one corner, chickens were being rotated by hand on the spit. Bottles of wine stood nearby. The two men Matti had encountered in distress explained hurriedly to their compatriots the afternoon's adventure and Matti was invited to break bread with them.

The lanterns failed to provide enough light for Matti to see clearly the many new faces present. There was a certain amount of movement that persisted throughout much of the evening. Children playing, visiting, men fetching second helpings, filling glasses. Talking. Smoking. Tending the fire. Joking and taunting one another. These were happy people, thought Matti, though he sensed a pervading note of melancholy.

The women, dressed for the most part in long, colorful skirts and heavy blouses covered with warm sweaters against the cool night air, quietly went about their chores, cleaning the campsite and washing the utensils carefully on one side of the site. Matti noticed a kind of stage constructed of wood, no larger than four meters square. Four men, one a muscular, young, swarthy fellow in his mid-twenties, two much older, the fourth, and youngest barely into his teens, pulled up stools and produced their instruments, two guitars, a concertina, and a fiddle and began playing. It had become dark outside. From the shadows a young woman, maybe twenty or so, stepped forward, carrying a guitar, and commenced to sing. Everyone grew quiet.

A sizeable crowd of local residents, possibly responding to posters hastily distributed in the village, appeared. A low, portable fence had been placed in such a way that visitors were herded through a gate next to which was a booth. One of the older gypsy women collected money. The spectators either sat on the ground or on folding chairs they had brought with them. Many of the younger men sat cross-legged surrounding the stage.

The singer, tapped gently on a tambourine and hummed a tune while the guests slowly made themselves comfortable. A few of the young gypsy girls circulated among the crowd selling red wine they poured into plastic cups from large ceramic decanters. The singer moved gracefully about the stage, her skirt flaring out saucily as she turned and twisted to the rhythmic clapping of the men behind her and the melodic refrain from the musicians.

That her name was Leila, Matti learned the following day, when he saw her in better light and realized she was a woman of uncommon beauty. Her black curls, glistening in the spotlight, hung down loosely around her neck. Her eyes were dark, her skin olive. Her figure excited every male present. In the reflected campfire, most noticeable was her extraordinary voice. Matti listened intently. He was as captivated by her voluptuous voice, as the lecherous young males, who would dream that night of seducing such a gorgeous and fiery woman, were inspired by her sensuous movement.

Accompanying herself, Leila sang songs in French, Spanish, Italian and in a language Matti had never heard before. Some of the songs were obviously from the group's history. Others appeared to be extemporaneous in nature; the composer and lyricist creating sultry, moving sounds on the spot. There was a strong emotive aspect to her performance. Shouts of appreciation punctuated the responses. Finally, acquiescing to repeated calls to dance, Leila put down her guitar and began to undulate on the tiny stage. Castanets and the clapping hands of the musicians behind her established a moderately fast beat. Leila sang. She started to dance, swishing her long skirt and punctuating her steps with clapping hands. The music and her movements were sinuous and hypnotically gorgeous. The swarthy musician named Carlos also put down his instrument and joined the dance, a kind of *sequidilla*. The rhythm increased gradually in tempo. The passion of the dancers was intense. They challenged each other, their heels creating a rapturous beat on the wooden stage. Never touching, it seemed the two were alternately tempting and rejecting each other. The clapping and clicking of heels reached a crescendo. Four other young gypsy woman joined the couple. A chaos of whirling, stomping, spinning color and emotion enthralled the onlookers. It reached a fever pitch, totally absorbing both the dancers and the spectators, before ending abruptly. The audience went wild, cheering noisily for several minutes. Bowing briefly, the dancers withdrew from the stage and disappeared.

One of the guitarists took the stage and played and sang in French and the tongue Matti could not understand. Behind the musicians Matti could see Leila in the shadows, smoking a cigarette. Then, Aleta, neither old nor young, maybe 45–55 years old, Leila's mother, came and the two went back to their wagon. After a few more songs and group instrumentals, the crowd realized the performance was at an end for the night and it dispersed quietly, many walking or cycling back into town.

Matti slept in a wagon with three other men. One of them was Bruno, the young boy he had helped. Bruno was sixteen. The old man who had skipped his medicine and thus caused a medical problem, was Tito, Bruno's grandfather. Clothing, a pair of jeans, a couple of T-shirts, some new underclothing, and a few toilet articles, including a razor, soon found their way to a table next to Matti's bed.

* * *

"Young man, you did a brave thing – saved your friend's life. He could have drowned, but he'll be O.K. We're taking him to the hospital for a check-up." Matti was sitting bolt upright in bed. His head and torso were damp with perspiration. The others sleeping in the wagon rolled over. He had not awakened them, but his rest was broken by the strange dream. A vivid image of an ambulance receding down the highway from the lakeshore remained fresh. His mind wrestled with this snippet of memory that had to be from his past. But it was gone.

Rising early the next morning, Matti had no solid recollection of his overnight camping plans of the preceding day. He ate bread and drank coffee for breakfast. He went with Bruno to check on the horses and spent much of the morning doing the things he had learned at the Baumanns, and, before that, with the beautiful black pony he had bought for the girls, Mireille and Sylvie and their little brother, Theo.

The remainder of his first full day kept him fully occupied. He and Bruno, occasionally helped by another member of the traveling group, changed three tires. One wagon had sustained slight damage, perhaps having been driven too close to a tree. Spare lumber was produced and Matti and Bruno made repairs, then painted. Tito came by every hour or so to check on them. He seemed very pleased. He liked Matti, even though he was rather quiet. For Bruno he was a good mentor, he thought.

"Are you feeling well today?" asked Matti.

Tito nodded his reply.

"Have you taken all you medicine?" Matti was genuinely concerned, since no doctor had been involved the day before. That he even recalled the incident was a positive sign in his own recovery.

"I am following my daughter's instructions," replied the old man, stuffing tobacco into a well worn pipe and lighting up.

While Bruno stowed tools and the leftover paint in a trunk in the wagon behind them, he listened quietly to the conversation between his grandfather and Matti. Matti was unable to give his family name. He apparently had no specific job skills, no trade. Without seeking to be deceptive, Matti could not recall where he had been or where he called his home. His responses were short. He offered no explanations, appearing to be sad and bewildered by his inability to provide such basic information. Bruno thought aloud, "He has no shadow. How strange to have no past."

Within the gypsy encampment whispering began and spread with lightning speed. Matti picked up references to the *gadje*, the non-Roma. Combined with glances in his direction, he assumed people were talking about him. Generally, he was treated with respect. The respect was earned through his diligent, non-complaining attitude and willingness to tackle whatever he was asked to do. He was pleasant and no one had any reason to doubt his honesty or decency. In no way had he ever uttered or demonstrated any disparaging thoughts regarding his hosts.

Some among the group obviously felt pity. Not to have a past, even a negative past, was most unfortunate. A few, when discussing the matter amongst themselves, offered reasons for such a calamity: an accident, an injury to the head, a defect of birth, perhaps. With others, a sense of alarm sounded. Leila belonged to the first group. She arranged to pass near him daily, exchanging pleasantries. Carlos, whose feelings for Leila were never well disguised, fell into the latter group. He voiced negative thoughts about the *gadje*, whose presence represented a threat to them all. He was unclean, not Roma, and would ultimately contaminate them, he said. Some nodded agreement. That Maxim, the group's acknowledged leader, shared some of Carlos' views was clear, though he made no immediate effort to act on them.

On the following days, Matti joined Emilio, one of the musicians, and Alejandro, Leila's uncle, on a daily drive in an old van that belonged to the troupe. They went into residential sections of the nearest two towns. There they parked unobtrusively on the side of the road and rolled out of the van a heavy table with rubber wheels that supported a peddle-driven grinding wheel. Saying he would return to the same place in the late afternoon, Alejandro drove off.

Matti, the only one in the group without a thick, wide, black moustache, perhaps because he was so handsome and his general appearance non-threatening, went from door-to-door asking if there were any knives, scissors or tools to sharpen. Matti delivered the items for sharpening to his co-worker, then returned them to the housewife, who was probably staring admiringly at him from behind the house curtains, collected the modest cost in cash, and moved further down the street. Business was rather brisk until the noon hour. Around 2:30 in the afternoon, it once again attained a pace that held until it was time to rendezvous with Alejandro. Emilio was quite satisfied with their earnings. Although he did not mention it to Matti, Emilio was also glad that the police had not bothered them.

After a few days or a week at a location, the gypsies packed up and quietly moved away. Their travels had them criss-crossing Alsace and Lorraine. The troupe's forays into local communities to earn money continued almost daily. Occasionally, local police came by and made a point of checking on the strange travelers, who were often accused in rumors of engaging in theft and fraud. There were, of course, always empty fields or other areas where they could stop and conduct their business. This mode of living seemed to suit Matti.

He was never completely accepted by the others. Yet, neither was he rejected. He kept to himself. His continued presence was supported by Tito and his family; still grateful for Matti's kindness and life-saving assistance. Almost daily, Leila, in the company of some of the other young girls, would arrange to come by the place where Matti was working in the camp. She stopped, initiated some small talk and did her best to avoid an appearance of flirting. Matti was always polite. He never showed any overt romantic interest. He did love Leila's singing. Perhaps he was also flattered by her interest. Carlos watched. Carlos was concerned.

One evening, already in their fourth location in three weeks, a short while before the nightly performance, Emilio, and a young woman who answered to the name Tsura, whom Matti had seen frequently talking to Leila, sat next to him as he was sipping the last of his wine. After a few attempts at conversation based on his impressions of their particular lifestyle, they asked if he would like to have his fortune told.

"Why not?" Looking at Tsura, an attractive woman in her early twenties, he asked, "Are you going to look into my future? Can you tell me about my past, as well?" He was serious.

"Come with us," Emilio and Tsura spoke in unison. "We'll take you to Ilona."

The air was balmy. It was already dark and every wagon's entrance was lit by its lantern. Additional lighting was set up to illuminate the small stage for Leila and the musicians. Because the group planned to pull up stakes and move on, locals were coming in greater numbers, not wanting to miss their last chance to see and hear the beautiful gypsy about whom the entire region was buzzing. The threesome went to a wagon parked in the rear. A young couple, smiling and giggling, was exiting the wagon as they arrived. Whatever their fortune, it had left them in a good mood. Emilio knocked on the door. A muffled "Entrée!" was heard. Emilio opened the door, stuck his head in and, speaking the language Matti could not understand, he explained they brought the *gadje* to have his fortune told.

Matti understood that the pointing finger was his signal to enter the wagon. His escorts melted back into the darkness. Slowly, his eyes adjusted to the dim interior lighting. Sitting several feet away behind a table on which there was a calendar, a pencil, a deck of cards with strange figures showing and what appeared to be a bear's claw, was an older woman, her head covered by a dark cloth. He responded to a motion to take a seat. The woman, who leaned towards him across the table, was obviously old, but still quite beautiful. Her eyes were bright. Black curls hung below her head scarf and covered much of her forehead. Her face was smooth and wrinkle-free. She reached out and grasped his left hand in her hands. Her touch was warm, gentle, soothing. He relaxed almost immediately, in spite of a feeling of apprehension. Learning one's future was, after all, a revelation not without a potential negative aspect.

Speaking softly, with a slight rasp, she inquired, "What is your name?"

"I am called Matti."

"Do you have a family?"

"I don't know."

"You speak French well enough, but I believe it is not your native language. Where are you from?"

"I, I, I don't really know." Matti felt a bit uncomfortable making this admission. Other people knew where they had come from. Why was he different?

"When were you born?"

"I don't know."

"How old are you?"

"I don't know."

"Where were you before you joined us?"

"I have tried to recall it, but it doesn't come into the thing called memory. It was a huge house, I think."

"Let me see your hand."

Matti extended his left hand palm up. Ilona studied it, feeling the fingers, closing the fist, holding it closer to the dim lamp on her table. She looked then at his face, examining his features closely, touching his chin and cheeks. When she looked into his eyes, her gaze was one of sympathy and benevolence.

She turned again to his hand, tracing the lines with her index finger. Slowly, Ilona released his hand and lowered her head slightly for a few moments, gathering her thoughts. The French she spoke had an accent with which Matti was not familiar. "You are a man of learning. You have come here by a circuitous path from a great distance. You know pain. Your travels are not over yet. I believe you will reach the destination you seek. The way will be shrouded in mist; the path strewn with obstacles. An abundance of joy awaits you. Persevere. Be true to yourself. You shall achieve your destiny with the aid of many. Go now, my son, I see for you a long life, one that will bring peace and good to others."

Matti was speechless. He wanted to believe Ilona, whose words were spoken in an ethereal voice so softly he barely understood them. It was as if the earth, the sky, the trees and spirits alive in the woods and fields around them had pronounced his future. It crossed his mind that she might say positive things to all her customers.

Ilona stood. She was barely five feet tall and extremely slight of figure. She pointed to the door. Matti thanked her several times in parting. He opened the door and walked out into the night.

The performance by Leila, the musicians and other young women, who had danced was over and the guests were leaving, engaged in animated conversation, lauding the power of the songs, the haunting music and the emotion-laden dances.

Ilona's words paraded through his sleepless head all night. "…man of learning…… from a great distance… abundance of joy…… will reach your destination… long life… peace and good." What did it all mean? Why couldn't he remember who he was? His name? His home?

Rain fell before dawn. The ground was damp. Most of the group ate breakfast by themselves in their wagons. Matti had heard mention of moving on to a new location soon. Gradually, the men set about their chores. Matti sat on a short wooden stool, leaning against the wheel of a wagon. Rope strung between a couple of wagons was filled with drying laundry. Matti had observed how fastidious the women were about cleaning.

Leila, Gina, Sara and Tsura were throwing a ball and catching it. On the opposite side of the mini-arena formed by the circle of wagons, some of the men: namely, Carlos, Bruno and Emilio were talking loudly about something. Maxim was huddling with Tito and Alejandro near the group's two vans.

The scene was suddenly transformed by a shriek. Leila had caught her foot on a rope on the ground and fallen hard. Matti was closest. He ran over. A rapid assessment revealed a twisted and possibly sprained ankle. Without hesitation, Matti picked Leila off the ground, told the children to run to Aleta and open the door to her wagon. He walked firmly to the wagon carrying Leila, surprised to find she was so light in his arms. They gazed at each other and a look of recognition smothered what would have been a loving smile. Her lips formed the unspoken words, "Je t'adore!" Ahh, l'amour. Cupid's arrow often strikes when it is least expected. This, both sensed subconsciously, would be a forbidden love. Matti laid Leila on a blanket spread on a couch in the center of the wagon. A bit embarrassed by the looks on the faces of those who had assembled to see what had happened, Matti said something to the effect that he hoped she would soon be able to dance again and left.

Carlos had studied with dismay and a tinge of anger and jealousy the look exchanged by Leila and Matti. Carlos had always assumed Leila would one day be his wife. She had probably assumed as much herself, but was never able to produce any natural affection for him. He possessed a huge ego. His consuming interest was the image he saw in his mirror when preparing for a performance. Others joked behind his back about his constant preening. From the moment Matti had entered their camp, Carlos looked upon him as a potential rival. Now he would have to act.

Leila's father had died in an accident when she was a young girl. His brother Alejandro helped Leila's mother raise her. Aware of his influence, Carlos had cultivated Alejandro, though he was not especially fond of him, anticipating that a strong male ally in the family might be welcome if he were to seek to marry Leila. During the morning hours Carlos approached Alejandro and suggested it was time, before moving to a new location, to rid themselves of the non-Roma, the *gadje*, the man without a shadow, Matti. Alejandro agreed.

Maxim and Tito were consulted later. Tito liked Matti and did not view him as a threat. He was a worthy person who contributed much to the welfare of the group, he claimed. Maxim, on the other hand, whose decision it would be to allow Matti to stay or to sanction his expulsion, was deeply concerned about *bibaxt*. A non-Roma could bring bad luck. While he could not say that Matti caused Leila's fall, or that he didn't like Matti or that he had intruded in any fashion on their customs and beliefs, a possible relationship, not to mention an eventual marriage with a prize such as Leila, would be detrimental to the Roma way of life. "He must go," spoke Maxim firmly. "There is no alternative. Tito, you arrange it in the morning. Take him into the town. You will think of the words to use. We wish him no harm."

Tito struggled to hold back his tears. He nodded in agreement and went directly to his wagon. Over night the rains returned, accompanied this time by whistling winds, thunder and lightning.

Chapter Five

Dr. Anni Baumann, née Pakkula, wife of the distinguished medical researcher, brain surgeon and psychiatrist, Jean-Pierre Baumann, was confused, even mildly distraught. Matti had not returned to the château for breakfast as she expected. By mid-morning she worried that her blatant amorous overture of the previous day had upset him in some way and that he was hesitant to return. She was embarrassed. Guilt feelings dampened her mood until well past the noon meal. How would she explain this to Jean-Pierre. He was so trusting. She had done what doctors should avoid. She had fallen in love with a patient and had violated her personal rule not to become emotionally involved with a person under her care.

Inexplicably, she waited impatiently another night. Still no sign of Matti. Oh, God. If something has happened to him, I'll never forgive myself, she thought. I've got to find him. Around eleven in the forenoon she went to the barn and the stables. On her favorite steed, she cantered out to the place where, together with Matti, she had helped set up their tent and had built a small fire. The fire was out and the site had been cleaned up. The tent had been prepared for an overnight stay, but had not been used. There was no sign of Matti. No indication of any struggle. There was no note. He was simply gone. When she was in daily contact with Matti, she had lost sight of the fact that his memory loss might include bouts of anterograde amnesia that allowed even new events to be deleted from memory much as a message might be removed from a list of emails. It was still not completely clear to Jean-Pierre whether Matti's memory would eventually be totally restored or whether some persistent impairment would develop. Because his health was returning to something that could be termed 'normal', both Anni and her husband ruled out a prognosis that would assign their patient's mind to a bottomless abyss of oblivion. That was a term Jean-Pierre had once used in describing someone admitted to the treatment center for evaluation following severe brain damage resulting from extreme drug abuse.

The possibility that Matti might be suffering from a *fugue*, a state of psychological amnesia where apparently rational behavior masks a condition that obscures events that occur during a temporary flight from reality, troubled Anni. Could her reckless behavior cause such a condition?

Anni tied her horse to a tree and walked a good distance in all directions from the camp site. Soon she reached the perimeter of the estate and found herself looking down on a quiet country road she couldn't recall seeing before. On the wide grassy shoulder she saw what looked like tire tracks. Further on, a racing cyclist had stopped to stretch a cramped left calf contracted on a stiff uphill climb.

Hailing the cyclist, Anni jogged to the fence and crawled over, calling out a need to talk with a trim-looking male of around thirty. She was slightly out of breath when she arrived and took a few seconds to address the cyclist. "Is your leg all right?"

"Just a cramp. I used the wrong gear coming up the hill over there and strained my left calf. It'll be OK in a couple of minutes."

"Do you cycle here often?"

"Actually, I do. I live in the village up ahead about 10 kilometers and this is a regular training ride for me. I cycle about 80 kilometers a day now. I'm trying out for a sponsored team next month."

"*Bon chance*! If you came by two days ago in the afternoon, do you recall seeing anyone here, a camper?"

"Hmmm! Well, it's interesting that you ask. The day before yesterday I rode past two *tsigane* wagons in almost this same spot. I think they were having trouble with their wheels. Three men were here doing something to the wagons and the horses that were pulling them. Much more than that I didn't notice. Hope that helps."

"Yes, thank you! Eat some bananas. They'll help with the cramps."

The cyclist mounted and disappeared surprisingly swiftly in the distance. Anni walked pensively back to her horse, collected the camping gear and returned to the barn behind the château.

* * *

Tito was waiting alone in his wagon when Matti arrived. Bruno had awakened the man without a shadow well before the sun was prepared to greet the day. Dreams of a joyful future had been interrupted. A breakfast of coffee, rolls, fruit and figs was spread on the table.

"Some day," Tito began, his mien serious, "you will read the history of the Roma in Europe. It will reveal to you our troubled journey, the constant wandering, the incessant harassment, the endless hate and persecution our people have suffered, wherever we have been. I hope you will come to understand why we feel such compulsion to protect and preserve our way of life, our culture, our blood. Please to know, in this family you are liked and respected by everyone. Still, we look upon you as *gadje*. You can never truly be one of us. Our elders have decided we must part our ways. I will drive you to the next town. Bruno has collected your belongings." His head spinning at this abrupt change in direction, Matti was dumbfounded. He could not comprehend, why he was being cast out. He had no quarrel with Tito, whom he dearly loved. He sat quietly in the passenger seat of the dusty Peugeot van, looking straight ahead, trying to relate this event to Ilona's vision of his future.

Tito drove to the east side of the town. He said there might be better opportunities to work here, as this was a more affluent or upscale part of the community. At a gas station, he stopped. Both men dismounted. Tito, holding a large plastic bag, handed it to Matti. "In the bag are your clothes, two new pairs of jeans, 3 shirts, new underwear and socks, and your cap. This envelope is from me and Bruno. It is only 200 Euros. It is all we had." Then, reaching into his jacket, Tito extracted a small velvet purse. A heart-shaped amulet of polished red agate emerged. Tito pressed it into Matti's outstretched palm. "Leila sends this to bring you good luck and as a remembrance of her. *Zhan le Devlesa tai sostimosa!* Go with God and in good health!" He slipped behind the wheel, backed up and retraced his drive to the circle of wagons, where everyone was packing, preparing to resume their travels.

Matti watched Tito drive away. Somewhat forlorn and confused, he looked around and spotted a bench in a grassy plot of land framed in flowers off to one side of a rather new looking gas station. He slumped onto the hard metal bench. Stunned by the completely unexpected events of the day, he absentmindedly fondled the amulet in his hand. He raised it to his lips. Without realizing it, his heart had found a place for Leila, whose beauty and gift of song had given him much pleasure. He was fond of her. She must have felt it too, he thought. Others had noticed it as well. That's what provoked his rejection from the group. The more he thought about it, the clearer this conclusion became.

The sun was rising and growing substantially warmer than on the previous day. Matti focused his thoughts on Leila. She would marry Carlos. Their fate, he guessed. He understood that the group traveled only in the warmer months. By autumn they would return to Southern France, where they had permanent homes. There, children would follow and she would soon forget him, an interloper, one of the "unclean", a man without a shadow. Matti remembered how beautifully Leila could sing. She was entirely self-taught. Her repertoire was extensive. Not only did she sing songs passed down through the ages by Roma in Europe, she had added folk music from all the areas her family had roamed since she was a child. Additionally, she mimicked classical singers and had a rich, lusty voice that encompassed soprano and mezzo soprano roles easily. He had heard her sing the *Vilja-Lied* in German from *Die lustige Witwe* one evening. At the time, he was absolutely mesmerized. His brain went into high gear seeking a special connection, until a headache forced him to abandon the effort at recall.

It was a song Elli was often requested to sing when giving charity recitals. Could Dame Fortune be testing the water?

A priority now was finding a place to stay for a couple of nights and, of course, some kind of temporary employment. The 200 Euros would not last long.

Behind the gas station on the *rue d'Alsace* Matti saw neat rows of single family homes, each carefully separated by tidy fences. On the other side of the station, *l'avenue Schweitzer*, were three-story apartment buildings fading into infinity. The parallel street beyond that appeared to have buildings of equal height, but with a variety of shops at street level. Matti concluded the latter would be more likely to have tourist rooms to rent, perhaps even work possibilities. He headed in that direction, his plastic bag firmly in his right hand; his left holding the amulet in his pocket.

* * *

At this juncture, it is not yet a matter of certainty that Dame Fortune has overcome her ambivalence towards Mark/Matti and his plight. Can there be a reason for her equivocation?

Matti, his mind still a quagmire of miscellaneous electrons getting in each other's way, thought for a moment about the fortune teller, who had prompted considerable reflection. Matti recognized that as a sign he might be on the threshold of regaining the thing called memory. The hurried expulsion from the wandering group of gypsies was hurtful. He had done them no wrong. Leila's smile and her gift of the talisman he was holding in his pocket counted among the good things he remembered. Shelter for the night required his attention. Something to eat would also be welcome. He had 200 Euros. His plan: He would go past the shops on the street two blocks over and find a snack bar. Negotiating the traffic was not taxing. Matti enjoyed looking in the windows. Each presented new and colorful sights. It was as if he were discovering the material world for the first time.

The baskets full of bread and rolls in the windows of the *Boulangerie Baudelaire* were very tempting. During the day, small snacks were available. No customers were in the shop. Matti entered. Monsieur Laurent, the current proprietor, responding to the tinkle of the bell attached to the door, emerged from the back room. Matti ordered *un croissant au jambon et un jus de pomme.* Laurent, accustomed to sizing up his clients, pegged Matti as a transient. Perhaps it was the plastic bag he was carrying. Or maybe he just looked different. Matti was about to pay for his ham sandwich and apple juice, when Laurent, acting on a hunch, asked if he would like a job. With little hesitation Matti's answer was affirmative. He never asked what was involved.

Laurent refused any money for the snack, which Matti consumed while listening to his new boss. Monsieur Laurent's wife, who normally waited on customers, Laurent explained, was away caring for a sister who was ill. The apprentice had quit without giving notice. The Laurents' only son, a teenager, left early every day to play computer games with his *copains* and expressed a reluctance to working in the shop, actually to working at all. Matti, good looking and clean, was a gift from heaven.

It was normally his wife who stood all day in the bakery dealing with the customers, most of whom she knew on a familiar basis, and with whom she regularly exchanged neighborhood gossip. The baker himself, usually arising in the dark of night, and completing his primary task of transferring a variety of breads, rolls and croissants from the mixing bowls to the stainless steel counters to the hot ovens to the cooling racks before the first newspapers arrived on his doorstep, wanted badly to sit a spell over his *café au lait,* devour a *croissant au chocolat* and doze for a half hour or so in the kitchen of the family apartment above, but opted instead to wait on customers, while his new hire handled the clean-up in the baking area.

Matti had an orderly mind, something instinctive that his amnesia could not obscure. In no time at all, he had thoroughly cleaned and scrubbed the premises to withstand the scrutiny of the most stringent white glove examination. Laurent strove to control his approbation. Knowing he had struck gold today, the baker promptly offered Matti the use of a spare back bedroom, three meals a day and a modest weekly wage, if he would stay. There was also mention of a bonus, if he stayed a month. Matti was relieved. He would have a roof over his head, board and a little spending money, at least while he was sorting out his future direction.

Three days later, Matti was providing serious help. His passivity was waning. With more responsibility, he asserted himself more. His confidence was growing. He grasped the routine in the production end and, more importantly, proved himself to be a superior salesman in the shop, charming the female customers with his handsome looks and gentlemanly manners. On more than one occasion Laurent could be seen crossing himself and gazing heavenwards. Business was booming.

On the sixth day, Madame Laurent returned. It may have been the trying, stressful atmosphere that pervaded the sick room at her sister's house, or the arduous travel and loss of sleep, whatever the cause, she exhibited considerable hostility towards the new assistant her husband had hired without consulting her. She soon found fault with a number of things Matti was doing, which she considered contrary to her own time-proven methods.

About half way through the next day, while her husband was making a delivery to a restaurant across town, Madame Laurent, checked a small compartment in the back of her cash drawer for the 200 Euros she kept there for emergencies. They were missing! Certain that her husband would have mentioned it, had he removed the money, the only possible culprit who came immediately to mind was Matti. She confronted him in the back room. He denied any knowledge of the money. Madame allowed herself to become overwrought, even furious. She summoned the police, who, finding 200 Euros in his bag, arrested Matti and took him to jail. When he returned from his errands, M. Laurent was flabbergasted. He had thought Matti to be thoroughly honest and reliable. He would have bet his reputation on it.

At the police revier, Matti was questioned repeatedly. A young officer was searching local records to determine whether similar crimes had been committed in the area. The accused was fingerprinted, a DNA sample was obtained, a requirement for every person booked, and front and pro-file photos were taken. Matti, quite perplexed and dejected, sat in a locked room, where he would be held until arraigned before a magistrate.

A stunned Monsieur Laurent, unable to enjoy his *café au lait*, sat hunched over the cup and saucer on the table before him suffering sub-stantial verbal abuse from his irate wife. He had always thought himself an above-average judge of character. He did not want to believe that Matti had stolen money from him. He was concerned that his wife might have jumped precipitously to a convenient conclusion.

The sun set on another day. The bakery closed at the stroke of six. Young Monsieur Laurent returned to partake of some evening sustenance consisting, of course, of bread and cold cuts. He set his backpack down next to the kitchen table before washing his hands and taking his custom-ary end seat. As he moved his seat, the backpack, open at the top, tipped over and some of its contents spilled out on the floor. The father bent to help pick up the items and noted that most were new, unopened com-puter game cassettes. They still had their price tags. They struck the father as being rather expensive. Forget the typical good cop, bad cop interrogation, the scene that followed was strictly bad cop, worse cop. The truth came out, albeit reluctantly. Young Monsieur Laurent earned himself a hefty cuff on the ear and a harsh lecture from both parents. Restrictions were enumerated. Unavoidable chores were spelled out in great detail. Stealing money from the bakery cash drawer was inexcusable.

Tomorrow was a Sunday. It was decided that three Laurents would appear early at the police revier to undo the terrible wrong visited on an innocent man.

Chapter Six

Frans Albers, police Sergeant in Lokeren, a town slightly northeast of Ghent in East Flanders, limped about the station house trying to ignore the cast on his leg, the result of an attempt to block a goal kick in his club's loss to the eventual soccer champion of the region. His family treated him like a hero for his valiant effort. His fellow officers complained that if he had been a bit faster on his feet he might have won them the champion's cup. Whatever, Albers was relatively new to Lokeren, having joined the force a mere two months earlier. The assignment to a desk in the station house until his leg mended was not a joyful option for a self-styled 'man of action', an officer who preferred to be on the streets. He had quickly reduced the pile of papers on his desk to the scratched surface of its long-abused walnut top. Needing more to take his mind off the three-week recuperation period specified by the police physician, he wandered into the cramped storage space in the back of the station that served, among other things, as the police evidence room.

Housekeeping was certainly not a strong suit in the Lokeren police revier. A variety of items, mostly in small cartons or clear plastic bags, had dusty, dated tags. In the cartons, hidden from view, or awkwardly placed in each plastic bag and thus, partly concealed by the objects whose details they described, were typed identification tags. Confiscated firearms were kept in the adjacent armory.

Albers read off the dates. Some had been occupying space on a shelf for at least 12 years. One item, catalogued a few weeks earlier, lay squeezed in between a few other pieces long overdue for a culling sweep.

A crumpled black leather valise caught Albers' attention. Its date went back to the preceding November. The contents were listed merely as 'hand tools'. About to move up the aisle to check containers on another shelf, Albers thought it might be interesting to see what the tools actually consisted of and to learn about the circumstances of their addition to the collection. The information enclosed in the valise indicated the presumed owner died suddenly when his vehicle, attempting an illegal turn on a major inter-European highway located within the town limits was T-boned by a fully laden tractor trailer registered in Turkey. The deceased had no personal identification and the vehicle, a VW Vento, had been stolen the previous day in a Paris suburb.

The deceased was assumed to be of Arab background on the basis of his appearance. "DNA samples are on record in the unidentified victim's file for the date on the slip." Hmm! One by one, Albers removed the tools and laid them on a counter. Well used, he counted three different screwdrivers, a rubber mallet, a carpenter's claw hammer, a huge pipe wrench, two files, part of an acetylene torch and a small container of plumber's putty. The pipe wrench seemed much dirtier than the other pieces. Looking more closely, Albers saw matted hair stuck to the business end of the wrench on what could be dried blood, perhaps even a trace of skin.

His curiosity aroused, Albers pulled up the unidentified victims' files on the computer and discovered the victim's DNA record and a reference to the fact his unclaimed body was buried in a communal plot for indigents and others without proper papers and insurance.

Although laboratory budgets were thin, Albers felt it unlikely that the material he observed on the wrench was that of the victim. To whom did it belong? He would find out. He wrapped the wrench appropriately and sent it to the regional crime lab for analysis. His wife picked him up at the end of his shift and they drove home.

* * *

Several months had passed since Mark's mysterious disappearance. Elli refused to believe he was dead, as many suggested, both among some of their acquaintances and in the press. She and Roland and Dani had reviewed *ad infinitum* all the facts they knew. There were damned few, they admitted. No body had been found. There was never a ransom note. No attempt had ever been made to use the missing credit cards. No one had apparently seen the man whose face was on so many posters, in newspapers and on television, not to mention Samantha Willis' ambitious websites.

The car had been located in Paris. Abandoned on a side street near the *Seine*, it was utterly devoid of any usable clues. Exhaustive checks of police records, hospital admissions, auto rentals, hotel registrations around the time of Mark's disappearance and virtually every other possible link that might lead to information about a loving husband, and father and a foremost world citizen had been pursued countless times. In the belief that hope springs eternal, not one of Mark's family or friends was willing to admit defeat.

Prudence dictated, however, that certain information should be readily at hand, in the event an identification had to be verified. A dossier lay on Samantha Willis' desk. It contained a selection of photographs, all Mark's vital measurements, his fingerprints, dental records, blood type, details of his most recent physical examination and a printout of a report on his DNA. As stressful as this episode in her life was, Elli continued to maintain an attitude of guarded optimism. She fostered positive thinking in her children. Their schooling progressed. They seemed to understand. It was the dogs, alas, poor McGregor, the Yorkie, and Sampson, the Belgian Shepherd, who failed to comprehend that their master could remain away from home for such a protracted period of time. Whenever a strange vehicle drove up the drive to the house, they waited with breathless anticipation to be greeted with the warm affection Mark always showered on them. They missed sitting at his feet on cold evenings when a fire crackled in the large country fireplace. No amount of explanation, regardless of the language, could assuage their restless longing for a dear friend.

Chapter Seven

Professor Doctor Jean-Pierre Baumann, whose idol as a young man was Albert Schweitzer, had given much of himself in the past few months. His ongoing research, together with satisfying the needs of the patients in his brain-injury and psychiatric treatment center, would be taxing enough for a young surgeon, but for one who was 75 going on 76, it might be coming close to the limit. He was tired. The flight from *Maputo*, his last station in Africa, had left him very tired. Now, a two-hour stopover in Nice was like salt on an open wound.

In the adjacent waiting area, out of Baumann's earshot, a large-screen TV, dozens of pairs of bleary eyes staring at it from various angles, was in the midst of a news update. A 30-second clip from a cultural program broadcast the previous night throughout much of Western Europe, showed a costumed Michèlle Davidson portraying Cherubino singing a poignant "*Voi che sapete che cosa è amor...*" from Mozart's *Marriage of Figaro*. The excerpt was followed by an appeal, filmed earlier by a representative of *La Fondation Székely*, for any information that might lead to the whereabouts of Dr. Mark Davidson. His photo was flashed briefly on the screen.

After slumping into a cushioned chair in the waiting room for twenty minutes, Dr. Baumann grew restless and began wandering from shop to shop along the concourse. He should buy Anni a souvenir, he decided. He was irritated and disappointed when he first heard of Matti's unplanned departure from the estate. Anni had called to explain how Matti had disappeared. Jean-Pierre understood that 'things happen'. In a purely emotional and professional sense the doctor had invested heavily in the collection of data on Matti's case. While he was away Guillaume was responsible for maintaining meticulous records of Matti's progress and his test results. Guillaume's trained observations would be important for judging the next steps in orchestrating Matti's recovery. He had wanted to follow it closely to determine when and how Matti's memory would return. In his estimation, Matti would eventually be able to recall most, if not all of his past life. Remembering the events subsequent to the brutal attack that left him in a dangerous coma was more problematic. In any event, careful monitoring of the patient was critical.

Baumann relied on the suggestion of the enthusiastic clerk and purchased a conservative cashmere twin set consisting of a sleeveless pullover with a crew neck and a button-down cardigan in a delicate light blue. It was gift wrapped and he, who detested shopping, departed the boutique happy that it had been a painless exercise.

More time to wait. Ah yes, the bookstall. If it wasn't a medical periodical or a new work on a topic directly connected to his field of expertise or one of his hobbies, Dr. Baumann generally showed no interest. He saw nothing among the music CD's that he didn't already have in his collection. Next came several racks with lurid looking tabloids. If one were to believe all the headlines and covers, *homo sapiens* was devoid of any ethical and moral scruples. One cover caught his eye. It was an appeal for information about someone, obviously a person of importance, who had disappeared several months before. Mark Davidson, an American living in Switzerland, had failed to reach his destination, Paris, on a motor trip the preceding November. His facial photo and numerous details, not only of his physical self, but also of his personal background were included. After reading the article Baumann knew instinctively that Matti and Mark could very well be one and the same. He bought a copy and tucked it into the bag with the sweater. The flight to Strasbourg was now boarding.

* * *

The temporary "visitors" in the police lock-up were not an especially attractive bunch. A man who beat his wife, the lover, who failed to exit via the fire escape in time, three males who had yet to judge correctly the quantity of alcohol they might consume without losing control over their reflexes, a bicycle thief, a prostitute who compounded her misery by seeking to buy drugs from an undercover cop, and Matti. In their various states of alertness, all glanced towards the front desk when the Laurents arrived. Monsieur Laurent, visibly mortified by the transgressions of his son and his wife, admitted that a mistake had been made. The man called Matti was completely innocent and they were present to drop all charges.

Matti was given his plastic bag. A separate envelope held his 200 Euros. In the police revier's small lobby, Monsieur Laurent begged Matti's forgiveness for the egregious misjudgement on their part, the rush to brand a stranger a criminal. Young Laurent, with a firm push from his father, came forward and admitted he was to blame for taking something without first asking. Madame, her face flushed crimson, was uncharacteristically subdued. She said she was sorry. Most of the time she looked at the floor, angry with herself for providing her husband with ammunition to use in the event of future disagreements.

An offer by Laurent to continue Matti's employment with an increase in wages, was politely declined. Not because he was ungrateful or unforgiving, but rather because he felt the need to move on, to try to recall his past. Laurent understood. He slipped some paper money in Matti's pocket, hugged him warmly and each party went its way. Madame Laurent, given to prejudicial thoughts, turned to watch Matti walking in the opposite direction, carrying his plastic bag. Under her breath she muttered, "*Tsigane!*"

* * *

Months long, Samantha Willis, who believed with all her might that she owed her very life to Mark Davidson, spent part of every day thinking, researching, contemplating how she could find out what had happened to her boss, the individual who epitomized all that was good about *La Fondation Székely* and *White Cross Holdings*. Mark's compassion and understanding had created her independence, had allowed her mind, trapped as it was in a fragile and broken body, to grow and make her contribution to society. Virtually every effort undertaken thus far had met with failure. The web site had increased awareness of the missing man and his family's plight, but had also attracted weirdos. Sightings were reported, almost as if the goal was to locate an unidentified flying object. Police investigators were stymied. Without any clues whatsoever, there could be no progress.

Samantha had learned that a national data collection point had been established in Paris for the identification information garnered from all persons arrested for crimes, or involved in incidents where the perpetrator or victim had died. Since the cost for assembling the information had to be born by localities, compliance was slow and spotty.

Sergeant Albers in the Belgian town of Lokeren knew of the law in France. When the DNA report from the pipe wrench found in the tool bag of an unknown accident victim returned, and it was not that of the accident victim himself, Albers thought the only possible course of action – the car in the accident did have Paris plates – was to submit it to the data collection center.

When Willis' most recent request for any possible matches to Mark's DNA was processed, lo and behold, a positive result emerged. She was notified by telephone. In turn, she got in touch with the police in Lokeren. Albers read off the details contained in the pertinent accident report. The date was of great significance – just two days after Mark's disappearance. Samantha called Roland, who then passed it on to Elli.

A forensic expert was dispatched by *La Fondation* and the Geneva police. His conclusion was that the material on the tool, arrived there by having made violent contact with Mark's head and face. The question was – where did it happen? How badly was Mark hurt? Did he survive the attack? If so, where was he now? Simple questions. No easy answers.

The autopsy report on the unidentified male who ostensibly owned the tool that was involved in Mark's injuries had revealed nothing. Probably a vagrant. A random attack. No particular relationship between alleged perpetrator and alleged victim. Back to Page One.

While this was going on, Dr. Anni Baumann, looking forward to her husband's return in a few weeks, had instituted an intensive search of her own. Her aim was to find Matti and bring him back to the château where his professional treatment could continue. She had sensed Jean-Pierre's aggravation upon hearing about the interruption in Matti's treatment. Fortunately, Jean-Pierre was totally engrossed in his charitable medical labors in East Africa and barely had time to eat and grab a wink, much less converse at length with his wife about Matti. Perhaps Anni could set everything right before Jean-Pierre came home.

After an excruciating week's delay, Anni finally traced Matti to the gypsy encampment. By the time she had done that, they had picked up and shifted locations. The caravan meandered about Alsace and Lorraine. The gypsies had no special itinerary or schedule. At first, no one knew where they might have gone. Following numerous inquiries to towns north and east of the château, Anni learned where they were currently enjoying considerable success. It was just a few hours by car. She took a day off and drove there. Yes, she was told, the person whose picture she showed them, had spent a few weeks in the camp. He worked hard and was well liked, but had decided to continue on his way alone. Anni gave the reporters the benefit of the doubt. Neither she, nor they had any idea which direction to travel next. She declined an offer to have her fortune told.

Chapter Eight

With the money he had been given by Tito and a generous contribution from the remorseful Monsieur Laurent, Matti toyed with the idea of traveling to a new location, possibly a larger town where he might find employment. He felt a need to work, to keep himself busy. He had heard some of the men in the gypsy camp talk about Strasbourg. As he walked, somewhat aimlessly near where he had been dropped off by Tito, he spotted a tobacconist shop that advertised itself as a bus stop. A major destination, if the posters in the window were any indication, was Strasbourg. "Well", he thought, "maybe that's where I should go."

The ticket agent gave Matti the price of the ticket, indicated there was one change of bus, quite a few intermediate stops, and arrival would be in mid-afternoon. The next bus was expected to come on time in about an hour. Matti was pretty certain that he would go to Strasbourg, but wanted to think about it over something to eat and drink. The morning's events had cost him considerable emotional energy and he was famished.

Known simply as *Le Snack-Bar*, Matti liked the bright, cheerful, modern furniture and the polite service provided by an attractive younger woman in her mid-twenties. Seeing some of the ingredients in the open kitchen behind the counter, Matti's appetite for fresh garden produce took charge. He ordered a huge green salad with carrots and tomatoes and cucumbers. He could visualize himself caring for the vegetables in a small home garden, harvesting them with pride and sharing them with others who also appreciated wholesome fare guided with love and respect from seed to the plate. Staring vacantly at the table before him, Matti envisioned himself seated at a dining table spread with wonderful food surrounded by a family and friends.

"Is everything all right, Monsieur?" The pretty girl from behind the counter had brought some rolls and butter and the tea Matti had requested.

"Ohh,… yes, everything is fine. Thank you. I think I was daydreaming."

"The roast duck, the potato dumpling and the peas will be ready shortly. Can I bring you anything more to drink?"

"Thank you, I'm fine." While he appreciated the waitress' solicitous attitude, he was in a pensive mood. He felt that he was close to remembering something. Something important. His train of thought was lost. It would return. Later, perhaps. His main course arrived and he attacked it with relish.

"May I?" a rotund fellow, possibly fortyish, was asking, in European custom, if he might join Matti at his table. With a wave of his upturned right hand, Matti offered his self-invited guest a place opposite him at the table.

Looking about, Matti saw that the bistro was approximately three-quarters full. There were a few empty tables. Apparently the pleasant-looking man, suddenly engaged in arranging his plate and eating utensils, did not want to eat alone. Undoubtedly, Matti seemed like a compatible type. "It's a lovely day outside. I'm off on a trip this afternoon and I decided I'd better have a bite before I'm trapped behind the wheel for a couple of hours. I saw you coming out of the bus station. Are you traveling, too?"

Uninhibited and very inquisitive for a stranger thought Matti, who wanted to be a bit wary. However, his curiosity had been aroused. Besides, the outgoing fellow just two feet away seemed non-threatening, a happy, talkative sort, who craved company. His charm was infectious. "I believe I'll ride south to Strasbourg. I've never been there."

"Really? That's where I'm heading, soon as I finish my lunch and tank up. The company I work for is buying machine parts there and they need me to verify that they're the right ones." He ate a couple of bites, then drank from his glass of mineral water. "I don't suppose you'd like to drive along, would you? I wouldn't charge anything and I hate to drive alone. Afraid I might fall asleep."

The pink-faced, almost cherubic table mate, was very trusting. Matti felt the same way. Why not? Besides, he could save the money for the bus fare. "Sure, I'll be glad to keep you company. Are you going right into the city?"

"Yes. The parts are at a warehouse downtown. I can let you out near a couple of inexpensive hotels, if you want."

"Great. I'm ready when you are." Matti stood, then extended his hand. "By the way, I'm Matti, Matti...... Laurent."

"Matti, huh? My name is Gervais. Carl Gervais. Pleasure."

"Here, too."

Matti had begun to realize that family names were expected. Not to have one created problems. The first one he could remember was Laurent. He couldn't recall his real family name. He assumed he must have one.

While Gervais excused himself to use the men's room, Matti went next door. The ticket clerk had been helpful and informative and Matti thought he owed her the courtesy of letting her know he had changed his plans.

"Thank you for your help. I've made a new acquaintance and have accepted an offer of accompanying him into Strasbourg, where he has a business call." As Matti turned and strode to the door, the clerk added a cheerful, *"Bon chance!"*

Gervais brought the vehicle from a parking space behind the bistro to the spot where Matti was waiting. There was but a single traffic signal before the beckoning open road. The light turned red and Gervais rolled to a stop. Waiting for the crosswalk light to turn green was a young woman holding the hands of two girls. The latter were probably about ten, thought Matti, as he studied them carefully. They were so similar in appearance they might have been twins.

"Do you know them?" Gervais had watched as Matti stared at the three pedestrians.

"No. It's odd, but they do seem familiar."

The light changed again. The mini-van moved out of town without delay and followed a number of secondary roads that twisted and turned, climbed and descended. It dodged cyclists and small trucks that seemed to have difficulty staying on their side of the road. The ride was fairly comfortable and the scenery very beautiful. Matti's thoughts returned several times to the image of a young mother with her two daughters. He didn't understand why.

Matti's powers of observation were not as well organized as they had been in his previous persona. He couldn't recall the name of the town he had just left. Tired of trying to remember, he settled down and enjoyed the curves, the fields and forests and special views of the countryside afforded by the drive with Gervais, who, by the way, talked constantly, not really caring whether Matti was listening.

The capital of Alsace has always been an important regional city. Now Strasbourg plays an important role in a unified Europe. Drawing closer to the city, Matti noticed signs for *Rosheim, Molsheim* and *Entzheim*. The number of large buildings, warehouses, small factories and transport garages grew exponentially the closer they were to the heart of the city. Matti was looking left, then right, attempting to drink in the ambience of a large city. On the right he saw a billboard. Gervais, caught up in the rhythm of the inbound traffic, was moving along at 85 – 90 kilometers an hour. The billboard had a man's photo and a question: *Connaissez vous cet homme?* Matti thought it gave the person's height, weight and age, and a telephone number to call. There was also something about a… *Récompence*. Unfortunately, Matti couldn't read all the particulars, but he thought it a novel way to try and find someone.

Gervais, glancing frequently at his watch, knew he had a narrow window left to pick up the parts he had come for, and to head back to his office before dark. He suggested dropping Matti off near the *Cathédrale*. The passenger agreed. Gervais jotted on a piece of paper the names of two hotels he would recommend. The telephone numbers would be easy to come by, he said. Expressing his gratitude, Matti alighted from the van and probably stood on the very spot where a soon to be famous student from Frankfurt am Main had admired the cathedral nearly 250 years earlier.

Matti succumbed to the entreaties of a young university student who was hustling tourists for a tour bus company. On the bus Matti relinquished his window seat to an elderly lady who claimed she was from London. Matti didn't actually realize it until they had conversed for a few minutes; he understood and could speak English quite well. He was even asked if he came from the American Midwest. His seat mate was an English teacher whose hobby was dialect studies.

L'Ancienne Douane and *le Petite France Quartier*, *Mont Sainte-Odile*, the Rohan Palace, Strasbourg's lovely bridges, the astronomical clock, virtually all the sights worth seeing on an afternoon, were squeezed into the itinerary. Thus oriented, Matti took a local bus to a section he thought had one of the hotels Gervais had told him about. *Robertsau*, an extension of Strasbourg to the northeast, was definitely not where Matti wanted to be. It was actually out of town, partly rural, partly residential and partly industrial. Stumbling upon an inn, *L'Auberge Papillon*, Matti was shown a single room. The price, 65 Euros with breakfast, seemed reasonable. He had a simple supper at the inn. Tired from his busy day, Matti Laurent, according to his registration form, fell asleep after a quick shower. His dreams were populated by an affable companion, an unusual billboard appeal, two girls crossing a street with their mother, and a quaint elderly teacher, who suspected he had come from the American Midwest. Strange are the ways of Dame Fortune.

* * *

By a strange coincidence, Matti and the man who saved his life, unbeknownst to one another, would be in the same city on the same day. Dr. Baumann's visit was extraordinarily brief. Minutes after disembarking from his flight from Nice he was seated in a limousine taking him to his beloved *château*.

Matti overslept, but did make it to breakfast before it closed down. Afterward, he decided to check out. In a nearby luggage shop he acquired at a bargain price a plain-looking backpack. With his gear stowed in its largest compartment, he was able to get about hands-free. The air was warm, but not unduly so. One foot followed the other and soon Matti had put a considerable distance between himself and the *Auberge*. He lunched in a *Biergarten* with a delightful view of the Black Forest on the opposite side of the Rhein. More walking. Another great spot to indulge in a soothing liter mug of foamy *Fischer La Belle*. Time passed. The sun was setting. A restful afternoon was being transformed into evening to the accompaniment of a brilliant display of glorious hues of crimson and orange in a sky with a few wispy clouds far to the west.

Signaling that it was time to dine once more, Matti's stomach growled. Slightly tired from the walking, Matti headed back to the *Biergarten Hagenauerhof*. It lay in the vicinity. Matti noticed on his initial visit that there were tourist rooms to let there, too. Along the street were large semi-trailers parked at the curb. Matti had seen some earlier neatly lined up on a massive meadow on the fringe of *Robertsau*. These had printing on the side: WEINSTEIN und Co. "Fahrendes Vergnügen für Jung und Alt – Traveling Amusement for Young and Old."

While he may have forgotten it, and given the circumstances, it is understandable, both Drs. Baumann had warned Matti to avoid any activity that could expose his head and face to possible physical injury. Matti was not a confrontational type and would never intentionally engage in a battle of flying fists and flailing feet. However, Matti had another side, for neither would he ignore a call for help. His response was automatic.

Dusk. Twilight. Even at close range shapes and faces are often slightly obscured. As he strolled back towards the *Hagenauerhof* on the left side of the street, he passed a few rows of shops with a wide array of goods and services to offer. The retail venues, mom and pop enterprises, were already closing. The eateries were, on the other hand, just preparing for the evening's expected visitors: unhappy housewives, tired factory workers, transient truck drivers, thrill-seeking *lycée* students putting off home assignments in favor of flirting, and an assortment of regulars eager to share local gossip and express their political opinions. All, of course, over a mug of beer or a glass or two of wine.

An alleyway between two groups of four or five shops was wide enough for delivery trucks to gain access to loading docks in the rear. Looking up the alley, Matti saw two figures silhouetted in the fading light. One was larger than the other and had adopted a threatening position *vis-à-vis* the other. The smaller, in a female voice, uttered loudly in disgust, *"Va t'en! Crétin! Je te déteste!"*

Matti halted in his tracks. Staring up the alley, the larger figure appeared ready to strike the smaller one. A male voice boomed forth, *"Je te veux! Du gehörst mir! Verstehst?"* The tone was dripping with lust and anger.

The language he heard left the distinct impression the male figure was intent on forcing his affection on the other, now attempting to retreat. Matti was approaching at a run. In French, Matti told the male in a firm, business-like voice to back off and leave the woman alone. As he did so, he saw out of the corner of his eye two men coming towards them quickly from the rear of the shops. He didn't know whether they were planning to help him or join the male threatening the young woman. Losing his eye contact momentarily with the male with the abusive tongue, Matti received a strong push and fell backwards bumping his head on a trash can that was next to an emergency exit. Stunned, seeing stars that were not part of the firmament, Matti started to get up. One of the men grabbed him and helped him. He started to brush the dirt off Matti's clothes with his hand.

The second man had subdued the would be attacker, who was moaning, his hands behind him in shackles. A third male joined them panting breathlessly, sucking air to regain his ability to speak. He thanked Matti profusely. The girl hugged the new arrival, weeping tears of gratitude and contrition. After calming her with a hug, the third man, somewhat older, slightly heavy set, extended a hand to Matti. "You are a brave man," he said in a deep voice, "and I thank you for coming to the aid of my foolish daughter. The man you stopped is a brute, who preys on young girls. He sweet-talked my Rebecca into a *rendez-vous* and would surely have harmed her if you had not intervened so quickly."

Feeling the back of his head, Matti ascertained the bump had drawn no blood. His mind working at hyper speed, he accepted the thanks gracefully, but retorted, "Everyone has an obligation to help when someone is in distress. I am glad she is safe."

Matti's backpack had absorbed much of the shock of falling backwards. Nevertheless, he felt different. He couldn't explain it exactly. Something was different.

The third man was finally breathing normally following his exertion. "Ich heiße Weinstein, Max Weinstein. Hinten auf dem grossen Feld sind 48 Wagen. Ahh, pardon, I should probably speak French." He hesitated again, shifted gears and resumed *en Français.* "There are 48 wagons on the huge field behind us. They are part of our traveling carnival. We are in the process of regrouping. We will divide into two shows for our journey east into Germany. Come, have dinner with us. That is the least we can do. You are, I trust, not too modest to accept my humble invitation?"

Feeling better, Matti said, "*Andiamo!*" An expression he often heard among the gypsies. They all walked to the rear of the shops, where a BMW 700 series sedan, lights on, doors open, awaited them. The thug had been taken away by the first two men while Herr Weinstein was speaking to Matti. Weinstein had a firm grip on the hand of a red-eyed young woman who had received a valuable lesson.

The dinner, prepared and served by a German-speaking chef dressed in a white jacket and a chef's cap in Weinstein's modern *Wohnwagen* featured *escaloppe de veau* and *spätzle.* It was punctuated at key points by delicious wines. After a large piece of *Schwartzwälder Kirschtorte and Kaffee,* Weinstein and Matti walked up and down some of the rows of wagons ready to pull out the next day for engagements in Germany.

There were to be two groups. Each had a small one-ring circus, a carousel, a Ferris wheel, booths with a variety of games of chance and skill, a fleamarket, various thrill rides, food stalls, a magic theater and animal acts with horses, jungle cats, dogs, and chimpanzees. There were a few clowns and *animateurs* to help generate pace and excitement. One group was going to a large space with good parking facilities near *Tübingen* and *Reutlingen,* still accessible for visitors from *Stuttgart;* the other group was scheduled for *Freiburg im Breisgau.* Following another one week stand, both groups would rejoin near *Zürich* for an 'Oktoberfest-style' gala.

Weinstein was proud of his organization and Matti proved to be an enthusiastic listener. Having learned that Matti had no current job, no apparent roots, and finding him bright and very personable, an offer to learn the ropes as his assistant was extended and accepted before the evening was over.

A smaller *Wohnwagen,* older too, but well maintained and outfitted with all the necessities, was located with the aid of a strong flashlight. Matti was told where to report at 6:00 the following morning and given the key.

Chapter Nine

Lay observers often refer to 'sudden' or 'miraculous' cures or recoveries of a medical nature in a most casual manner. While they may indeed seem to represent a miracle in light of the potentially negative outcomes that also lurked among the possible end results, it is likely that they were achieved in virtually imperceptible units of improvement over an extended period. Even Matti himself scarcely noticed how his vision was improving. His hearing, too. That most magnificent of human organs, the brain, taken for granted by most, was ever so gradually healing itself and striving incessantly to make its owner whole.

Pieces and chunks of memories returned at the oddest times and intervals to tantalize Matti. He wondered if the little bump he had received when he was pushed backwards while trying to help Weinstein's daughter had anything to do with his new ability to recall. Would, per chance, Dame Fortune know?

Rising to the challenges of helping to operate the diverse and exciting world of a traveling carnival was exhilarating. Matti's self-confidence increased as Weinstein praised his efforts and gave him more freedom to make decisions. Studying the traditional layout of the booths, the rides, the mini-circus, the other ancillary profit centers of the carnival, Matti developed a few new approaches. He was given an opportunity to test them. Grumbling by some of the individual operators at the inconvenience and 'meddling' subsided when receipts and net profits increased. Matti had a flair for marketing and merchandising that worked. His skill at negotiating with suppliers helped improve profits. Attention to detail aided in upgrading safety measures. New product ideas brought more sales. Matti's willingness to step in and spell an attendant or operator when the latter's absence was necessary for legitimate reasons made him even more popular. Settling down a dangerously skittish white stallion that starred in one of the animal acts burnished Matti's reputation further. Even the horse's owner found it amazing that someone could gain such quick control over a huge, powerful animal by merely touching and talking to it.

Weinstein und Co. had been outbid earlier in the year for a featured role in the panoply of entertainments at Munich's Oktoberfest. Ever resourceful, however, Herr Weinstein pursued another possibility and had won significant backing for it. Thus, his and one other traveling carnival, in cooperation with three large Swiss breweries were establishing their own Volksfest, lasting three full weekends in September and October.

It was to be located outside the Swiss city of Winterthur where it was expected to draw large crowds of revelers from Zürich and as far away as St. Gallen, Konstanz, Schaffhausen and from many smaller nearby communities. A week in early September was set aside for staging the combined resources of all participants, hiring part-time help, refurbishing some of the booths and rides and laying out the grounds and parking areas. Totally involved along side Herr Weinstein was the master's protegé. Matti was so busy he decided to forego shaving regularly and within days he had a handsome mustache. He allowed his hair to grow longer and fuller as well. In spite of some good-natured ribbing about his hairy countenance, he opted to keep it. Even if trimming the facial hair became more of a chore than merely shaving it all off.

As night fell and operations closed down, Matti's memory began processing the day's images and the stray thoughts that popped up unannounced. Lake Constance, which Matti had admired on the trip to Winterthur, was considerably larger than the Lac de Neuchâtel, whose southern tip he had happily shared with other residents of Yverdon. It seemed familiar. Being near a lake. Living or working within view of a large body of water. Swimming. Saving a drowning man. Riding on a ferry. Befriending a nun. Teaching a class of students. Yes, it was a link to his past. The nice man in the white coat had explained, had he not, that the past would probably return eventually. He remembered the fortune teller had talked about a long path 'back to myself'. It was important to remember. Matti finally fell asleep.

* * *

Dr. Anni was in Strasbourg coordinating the efforts of the three investigators she had hired to help locate Matti. From the gypsy, Tito, they had found the town where Matti had been let out after his expulsion from the traveling tribe of *Manouche*. Showing a photo of Matti taken after his recuperation from the reconstructive plastic surgery jogged the memory of a woman who remembered seeing such a man in a local bakery. "*Boulangerie Baudelaire,*" she exclaimed.

At the bakery, Monsieur Laurent told the story of the missing money and the rush to judgement that led to Matti's overnight incarceration. The police were induced to share a photo they had taken, a DNA report and fingerprints. More information was not available. However, a chance visit to the tobacconist's revealed that a man resembling Matti had inquired about bus fares to Strasbourg. The clerk remembered that he had been considerate enough to inform her of a change in his plans. He was going to get a ride from an acquaintance who had business in Strasbourg. Unable to find the person who had offered Matti the lift to Strasbourg, the trail hit a big bump. Dr. Anni decided to go to Strasbourg and to try and retrace his steps there.

Jean-Pierre, in touch daily with his wife, encouraged her to continue the search. He had read and reread the article from the tabloid. He had studied his information on the patient they had named Matti. The date of the incident at the highway rest stop, and, more importantly, the general location, all pointed to the undeniable reality that Matti and Mark Davidson were one and the same.

Jean-Pierre dialed the contact number in Geneva.

"*La Fondation Székely, Si vous téléphonez de le cas Dr. Davidson, pressez numéro un; sinon attendez l'operateur.*"

Jean-Pierre pressed one. A pleasant female voice responded. "*Bonjour, ici* Samantha Willis."

"Hallo, Mlle Willis, my name is Jean-Pierre Baumann. I am a surgeon with a private clinic in a relatively remote area in the Vosges Mountains. I regret that I have buried myself so deeply in my work, that I only recently saw an article in a news magazine about your Dr. Davidson's disappearance. On the night that he went missing I found a seriously injured man at a highway rest stop near my clinic. He had no identification whatsoever. He required immediate and extensive emergency medical treatment. My wife, also a surgeon, and I were able to help him physically and I am happy to report that he survived his misfortune. He is alive and, as far as we know, in good condition."

"What wonderful news. What do you mean, when you say, 'as far as you know'? Do you have any data to verify this before I pass word on to Mrs. Davidson? Blood tests, a DNA report, dental x-rays?"

"I recall well that he was AB+. I do have a DNA print out and will be glad to fax it to you immediately. What I cannot do, is tell you where Dr. Davidson is. He had, and undoubtedly still has, a severely aggravated amnesia. He wandered away from our property several weeks ago. My wife has investigators tracking him down. They are temporarily stymied, I regret to add, but we are hopeful that he can soon be found."

"Do you have a current photo?" Samantha was ready to increase the intensity of her search.

"Yes. We have one taken a few weeks after his bandages had been removed. I have it before me now. I will also fax that. Let me warn you first. His face was heavily damaged as a result of savage trauma. He will be happy with his appearance. However, his appearance has changed. It will probably be noticeable to his family, his friends and colleagues."

Willis was trying desperately to absorb the information. She loved the Davidsons and had been at the family's side throughout the ordeal. A change in appearance? Trauma?

"Miss Willis." The speaker hesitated a moment. Jean-Pierre was not a heartless, unemotional person, cold to the plight of his patients and their families, though he exerted considerable self-discipline and restraint in order to serve as a tower for them to lean on in times of tragedy. "May I have Madame Davidson's telephone number? I wish to call her to provide more details and to reassure her that her husband's amnesic condition will most likely correct itself, given patience and understanding."

Samantha agreed and gave him the number, requesting only that she be allowed to contact Mrs. Davidson first, after receiving the faxes. Dr. Baumann had no objections.

Approximately 20 minutes later Baumann heard from Ms Willis and he made his call. "Bonjour, Madame Davidson?"

"*Oui, bonjour! Vous avez dire ma collègue que vous avez l'information importante de mon mari.*"

"*Oui. Je m'appelle Baumann, Jean-Pierre Bauman. Je suis chirurgien et J'habite à une ville trés petite dans les Vosges.*"

Silence at the Swiss end.

Continuing in French, Baumann got right to the heart of the matter. "I know your husband and I have every reason to believe he is safe and well."

"Dr. Baumann, I have had many calls reporting sightings of my husband. Some, unfortunately, were cruel hoaxes, some well intentioned, but not one has shed any light on my husband's disappearance. Can you offer me any proof?"

"I have sent to your Miss Willis, a DNA report and other information. I understand your cautious attitude. I have no desire to add to your misfortune. However, would a gold wedding band with the initials *M + M 1990* engraved inside convince you?"

A gasp in Yverdon. "Yes! Yes! Have you seen such a ring? How did you get it? This is the most convincing evidence in nine months!"

"Madame Davidson, The story is long and complicated. Your husband was apparently the victim of a random and serious criminal attack by an unknown assailant. He was given emergency treatment at my private clinic. He survived a long period of coma, complex surgeries, and intense physical and mental recuperation and rehabilitation. His survival, in my humble view, was nothing short of miraculous." A pause, while Jean-Pierre collected his thoughts and his breath. "He emerged from his ordeal, however, with a severe case of amnesia."

"Where is he now? I want to see him and bring him home."

"I understand completely. In an unguarded moment he slipped away from us. He probably could not remember enough to effect his return without help. My wife is tracking his whereabouts as we speak. She has the help of three experienced investigators. Recently, they placed him in Strasbourg. They have picked up his trail there. May I please make a suggestion? Could we meet tomorrow or the next day in Basel? I can give you his medical records and a photograph."

"Oui! I'll come with a colleague and my brother-in-law. Do you know the Grandhotel Les Trois Rois?"

"Of course, in the Blumenrain on the river. Let's meet at one o'clock. I'll book a private meeting place. Look for an old man with a beard."

"*D'accord! Merci beaucoup, Monsieur le Docteur. À bientôt!*"

Chapter Ten

A slightly rumpled, but still uniquely distinguished looking gentleman, whose erect stature and salt and pepper beard commanded the bellman's attention, climbed nimbly from behind the wheel of his very ordinary vehicle. It was moved off posthaste to the valet parking area, where it suffered somewhat when compared to the upscale motorcars patiently awaiting their masters there. Baumann had reserved a private sitting room off the lobby of the five-star Hotel Drei Könige, as it is known in German.

About a half hour earlier Madame Michèlle Davidson, her brother-in-law, Roland Denis-Breuer, and Samantha Willis, at the controls of her specially equipped wheel chair, had arrived and had been escorted to the beautifully appointed room, served finger food and beverages, and had begun the mercifully short wait for Dr. Baumann.

Baumann arrived, a portfolio in his left hand. He immediately approached Elli, kissed her hand and introduced himself. *"Je suis Jean-Pierre Baumann. S'il vous plaît, Jean-Pierre."*

Kneeling next to Ms Willis' chair, Baumann, lifted her hand gently and kissed it as he had Madame Davidson's. He greeted her warmly. She felt truly welcome. She thanked him for the telephone calls that had brought them together this morning.

Roland stood. "Denis-Brauer, Je préfère Roland." The two shook hands. "I understand you speak English quite well and I suggest we continue in that useful international language, if you have no objections?"

"None. Of course. Please accept my sincere and profound apology for the long and difficult interval between Mr. Davidson's disappearance and our meeting today. It is entirely my fault. I will not hide behind my unusually reclusive lifestyle. In some matters, I see now, I have shut myself off very selfishly from the world about me. You have been harmed. Your husband, your children and your friends have been harmed. Members of my own family and my circle of associates have suffered as well. I do intend to change."

Having made his personal confession, Baumann felt he could continue. "I will relate the part of the story that only I know. One evening late last November, I was returning by car from a meeting in *Guebwiller*. The weather was miserable. In the hilly and mountainous area where I live, the temperatures were falling and a very slow-moving storm hovered over the steep hills and abundant curves in the highway. When it rained, it poured. The thunder and lightning were reminiscent of a war zone. I stopped to use the facilities at a rest stop in a quiet and remote section not far from... my home. As I was driving off, something that was out of place caught my eye. I pulled up to the curb and, with the car in neutral, I went over to inspect what seemed at first to be a large bundle that did not fit into the trash container next to it. When I was nearly upon it, I realized it might actually be a person. I rolled the body slightly to the side as I felt for a pulse and looked for signs of lung activity. It was a male. His face had been struck several times with a heavy instrument. His life signs were very, very weak." Baumann paused to swallow. He looked carefully at his small audience.

Elli and Samantha, as strong as they were, cringed slightly upon hearing Baumann's description of his discovery.

"I will spare you the exact nature of his injuries at this time. In my judgement he was in imminent danger of dying. In my medical work I have had to watch many men and women die under similar circumstances. Some fifteen minutes from the rest stop I own a private clinic that boasts of some of the most advanced medical equipment available. Cutting-edge equipment it is frequently called. Without reflecting more than an instant, I moved him to the rear of my van and rushed him to the clinic." Looking at Ms Willis, he continued, "We refer to the facility as a 'research institute'. As such, it undoubtedly fails to appear on lists of emergency hospitals. My wife, a physician and surgeon, was on duty, as were two of my most experienced technicians."

"Had he lost much blood? He has a rare type, I believe." interrupted Madame Davidson.

"Surprisingly, he had not lost an excessive amount of blood, as far as we could determine. My wife has the same type and she made an on the spot donation for an emergency transfusion, if needed." Baumann, cleared his throat slightly and took a sip of water. "The patient, who had no identification whatsoever, save for the wedding ring that a technician removed, recorded and placed in an envelope, which was moved to a safe place in the office, was treated immediately for possible shock. As in most cases of severe head trauma, a hydrocephalic condition was developing. This was effectively dealt with. We prepared him for surgery by first performing a tracheotomy and placed him on a ventilator."

Roland indicated he had a question. Dr. Baumann nodded. "Your clinic appears to be exceptionally well endowed in terms of highly trained personnel and advanced life-preserving equipment."

"Indeed it is. We have had remarkable successes, although we are generally afforded more time and planning for our major surgeries."

"Was there brain damage?" Elli's inquiry, spoken in a soft voice, expressed her desire to know the worst so that she could begin to deal with the consequences. Her plaintive manner touched Baumann.

The doctor hesitated, searching for the best way to explain Mark's dilemma at the time. "As a result of the trauma to his head, your husband was in a coma, a coma so deep, more than six weeks passed before he regained consciousness." Elli's face turned white. "Our brain scans showed possible damage to his vision in the left eye, to hearing loss in the left ear, and a few small skull fragments that were applying pressure on the brain. His face had received substantial frontal damage. My wife is a reconstructive plastic surgeon. My specialties are psychiatry and brain surgery. I don't know whether you believe in God, or Luck, or Fate. I am a modest and humble man. It is for situations such as this that I have trained for some fifty years. My wife is a preeminent practitioner in her field. I honestly believe Mr. Davidson would not have survived the night had the great, inscrutable forces in nature not collaborated to place him almost literally on my doorstep at the moment they did."

Baumann's audience was hushed. He sipped from his glass of water and continued. "To answer your question simply. Yes, there was brain damage. I did not think it would necessarily be permanent. Your husband was exceptionally fit. The brain is a most remarkable organ. It is capable, over time, of adjusting to deficiencies. It can undertake certain internal repairs."

"How did you deal with the fragments?" Roland was fascinated.

"Because they were close together, we were able to employ special techniques to remove them without disturbing any brain functions."

Samantha Willis posed the question her compatriots had been reluctant to broach. "What was the nature of the reconstructive plastic surgery? If there was no picture ID available, you really had nothing to guide you."

"It is important that I tell you first, that Mr. Davidson's surgery was a tremendous success. Physically, he recovered gradually, but fully. If you considered him handsome before, your judgement will not change. However," here Bauman paused. "His features may not be exactly as you knew them."

Elli looked quizzical, but all three, who had listened intently to Dr. Baumann, shared a sigh of relief.

Baumann continued. "Here is the situation. Mr. Davidson's facial injuries were not unlike some I have witnessed in warfare. He suffered a brutal battering. In such cases immediate open face surgery is dictated. Mrs. Baumann, whose homeland is Finland, is an oral surgeon and is also EU certified in all types of maxillofacialcranial reconstructive surgery. Due to a legal case pending in her homeland, in which she was merely an innocent bystander, her license in France was temporarily suspended. It has since been reissued. At the time, I took it upon myself to authorize the life-saving procedures."

"Is that why no report of an operation on an unknown victim was ever made?" Samantha was curious.

"No. I suppose I should have been more aggressive on that matter. Remember, Mr. Davidson, my wife named him Matti by the way, after her grandfather; Mr. Davidson was completely comatose for an extended period. Once his consciousness returned he was severely amnesic. Months were devoted to complex therapies and rehabilitation. Until the time that he slipped away from our control, his retrograde amnesia, memory of his past, was dominant. He had serious bouts of anterograde amnesia as well and would struggle to recall events since the accident. He learned to communicate in French again. On a couple of occasions he used fluent English, once in a great while he would use or recognize some German expressions."

Roland asked, "What were the circumstances of his disappearance from your clinic?"

"I was away at the time on an assignment for *Médicins Sans Frontières*. Part of our therapy involved extensive work outdoors with our dogs and our horses. Mr. Davidson seemed to thrive on this. He loved the animals and they responded to him in a most uncanny way. He seemed to communicate with them on a special level. We restricted any riding for a long time, not wanting to place him in jeopardy of further brain damage. He routinely exercised the horses and played with the dogs. Walking in our forests and on the many paths around the estate was very appealing to him and his health grew ever more robust the more time he spent in nature. One day, he was planning a night of camping in a remote corner of our estate. He and my wife went there together. They set up a tent. He fished in a pond and, after catching an edible fish, prepared an early breakfast.

"My wife had forgotten an important matter at the clinic and returned briefly to attend to it. Matti asked if he could camp out alone. My wife agreed. When she went to fetch him the following day, he was gone. Apparently, he never actually stayed the night."

Elli interjected, "Didn't you try to find him?"

"Mrs. Baumann made immediate inquiries in the neighboring villages. These were without success. About two days later she saw a bicyclist in the vicinity who had come upon three gypsies repairing a wagon and treating a horse near where Matti had been. With the help of an investigator, the band of *Manouche* were eventually located, but not until after they had moved further away. They claimed that one of the woman in their tribe had displayed some personal interest in Matti. This, many of them felt, put the 'purity' of their clan at risk and Matti was invited to leave them. They actually liked him very much, but were obliged to transport him to the next town, where he was left with a small amount of money. They referred to him as a 'man without a shadow'."

"Have you been able to pick up the trail again?" Samantha Willis was eager to find out where he was now.

Handing Elli a large envelope, Baumann spoke, "This contains a photograph, fingerprints and a DNA report on Matti that was part of his arrest file in a mountain town further north in the Vosges."

"Arrest file!" Elli looked shocked.

"Please do not worry. It was a mistake. The matter was clarified, but the good thing is that a record was established that proves he is alive and well." Handing Elli another, considerably thicker envelope, Baumann continued. "These are copies of his records with us. I have withheld a picture of his face prior to the operation. Perhaps he will choose to share it with you someday. A complete video record has been made, but I will not release it without Mr. Davidson's considered permission."

"On the phone you said you might have a surprise for us." Elli assumed it was a pleasant surprise and wanted to pursue it.

"My wife has invested much of herself in Mr. Davidson's recovery. She personally regrets that her brief absence gave him an opportunity to venture into a world he was not completely ready to deal with. From Strasbourg our three investigators have traced him to a traveling carnival. Thus, the good news. The carnival is a German entity that is currently engaged in a joint venture near Winterthur, a giant Volksfest. I propose that we meet here in the morning, or tomorrow afternoon in Zürich, and

361

drive together to Winterthur. Not being absolutely certain of the progress he has made regarding his amnesia since leaving the clinic, I want to be present should any special counseling be desirable."

"Would you advise having our children present? They miss their father so and constantly ask about him." Elli obviously would go to Winterthur.

"I think it would be all right. Don't forget, his appearance will not be exactly the same as they remember him."

Roland offered, "Dani could collect the girls and Theo and drive to meet us in Zürich tomorrow."

"Great! Let's get started early. I'll take care of the room reservations. I have some affairs to attend to in town. Please be my guests in the dining room tonight at 20:00." Baumann was relieved that all was going well.

"Wonderful!" Roland spoke for them all.

* * *

Max and Matti. Matti and Max. If ever two individuals thought and acted as if they were Siamese twins, it was these two. For his part, Weinstein, who was a good twenty years older, admired Matti's total honesty, his diligence, personal integrity and the positive attitude that quickly infected everyone attached to Weinstein and Co. Matti developed great respect for the boss, who treated his workers fairly and rewarded them generously. He had the feeling that he was part of a huge family. In quiet moments, of which there were relatively few, Matti and Max each revealed to the other a great deal of their personal lives. Max had lost his wife years ago, when his daughter was still very young. Never remarrying, he sought to be both father and mother to his beautiful offspring. With the usual problems arising from generational differences, guiding Rebecca to maturity had become an enormous challenge.

Matti told as much as he could recall about living on a large estate, where he recovered from what he was told was a 'terrible accident'. The struggle to recall had thus far met with bits and snatches of memory, all disjointed and incomplete. Matti felt that, as his general health improved and as he grew stronger and was required to use his brain more, the impulses he was receiving were growing in intensity and frequency. He was optimistic. Both Max and Matti were thriving on the Volksfest project that had as many facets as a finely cut jewel. To them the successful amalgamation of the two carnivals and the participating breweries was a work of art, a jem to be admired.

A friendship had also developed between Matti and *Gurke-Nas*, a clown, both clever and versatile, readily identified, quite obviously, by his large 'pickle-like' proboscis. Tim McKeil hailed from Glasgow. Ironically, an unhappy youth, spent largely serving as the butt of cruel jokes about the unusual size and appearance of his natural nose, had led to the conclusion that his 'liability' could be an 'asset', if he were to transform it into a key feature of his clowning *persona*. In his early forties, *Gurke-Nas* had been a fixture with Weinstein and Co. for a dozen years. He had a circus act that involved sliding rapidly head first down a pole and stopping inches away from crushing his cucumber-length nasal prosthesis. Tim toured the grounds greeting children, he juggled, balanced spinning plates on poles, rode a unicycle, took pratfalls, engaged in simple magic tricks and, in general, injected a spirit of fun and frivolity into the carnival experience.

Matti had met Tim at breakfast one day in the staffers' dining tent. Without makeup Tim's nose was a magnet for a stranger's eyes. He had learned to deal with it by employing self-deprecating humor. Matti got into the spirit and joked about his lost past, his flawed memory, his lack of a shadow.

They conversed in English, Matti struggling to decipher Tim's brogue; Tim, who had roamed the forty-eight contiguous States for years with a small circus, trying to place Matti's accent. Without realizing it, he came incredibly close. Matti couldn't confirm it because he didn't know where he was from. Their conversations always seemed to give Matti much food for reflection. Tim probed and probed, honestly hoping to jolt some connection with the past that would help his American friend.

"What happened to your wedding band?" inquired Tim one morning.

Matti was slightly perplexed by this question right out of the blue. "What do you mean?" was his response.

"Well, look! See how the coloring on your right hand is different? Except for this light-colored strip, where a married European might wear a ring, your fingers are rather well tanned."

"I'd never really noticed. Never given it a thought. Do you suppose I was... am married?"

Matti seemed lost in thought trying to answer his own question.

"You're a good looking chap. It's logical to think some bonnie lass would have considered you a good catch. Let's see. You're probably in your late thirties, possibly slightly older. You could have been married for ten to fifteen years."

Silence from Matti. Somehow Leila came to mind. He remembered the striking gypsy woman, actually just a girl. He had felt attracted to her. She was quite pretty. Her eyes flashed. Her skin was dark. Her hair was a lovely black. She sang. She danced. She liked him and, well, he found her congenial, even alluring. Yet, he never thought about marrying her. He reached in his pocket. The amulet was there. He fingered it for a while. *What was the basis for her appeal to him. Did she resemble someone he had known? Did she remind him of a woman he loved?*

One of the roustabouts interrupted the conversation. Matti had to leave and render an opinion about some technicality. *Gurke-Nas*, wondering what thoughts were obviously marching through Matti's mind, went back to his trailer to check on his costume.

* * *

Mark is beginning to remember more and more of his past. Like some huge jigsaw puzzle, images from the past couple of months are falling into place to form recognizable portions of a larger picture. He wakes up frequently at night recalling places: college classrooms, hometown sights, crowded streets in a far-away land, marshes in the Carolina Low-country;

events: graduation exercises, meetings with the governor, a visit to Zür-
ich, a shoot-out on a ferry; people: Gordon Hui, the Székelys, Gregor,
Jean-Luc Renard, Sister Catherine, a woman with a hole in her forehead.
There seems to be no specific chronology, no particular pattern. He asks
in his dreams, "Who are these people? How did I get to these places?
What was my role in these events?" He strains to recall every thought, to
acquire more detail. Most of his thoughts slide away into a strange void.
Lost. He awakens. Tantalized. Angry. Frustrated. Confident his memory
will ultimately return.

Recurring often is the image of a beautiful, dark-haired woman, walking with three small children. A black horse, a pony, appears again and
again in a favorite dream. He envisions demonstrating how to rub down
the horse, how to reward it with an apple for cooperating and following
commands well. Children watch intently.

The first weekend in October was accompanied in Winterthur by
glorious autumn weather. The sun shone brightly. The air was crisp and
invigorating. Weinstein and Co. were ecstatic with the success of their
joint venture and had already agreed with the other participants to dupli-
cate the Volksfest effort the following year, each promising to make it
even greater.

Dr. Baumann had spoken by phone with Herr Weinstein earlier. He
related to him the history of the Davidson case from his perspective and
indicated that he and Dr. Davidson's family were planning to pay a visit
on Sunday, the final day of the Volksfest. Baumann's concern centered
on the effect a sudden meeting with the past might have on Matti/Mark.
He knew also that seeing a husband and a father after such a long time
might very well be traumatic for Mrs. Davidson and the children. Not to
mention the effect on Matti. He didn't know precisely how the situation
could best be handled. He requested that Weinstein, who had apparently
developed a special bond with Matti/Mark, be available to help.

Anni, who had finally traced Matti to Winterthur and the Volksfest,
called her husband from Germany and left a message to inform him that
she was close to making contact and would attempt to bring Matti "home".

Dr. Baumann arranged to meet Elli and Roland, as well as Samantha Willis at a small hotel in town. Dani joined them with Sylvie, Mireille and young Theo. The dogs, McGregor and Sampson, were also along for the ride. The children were not told in advance about the possibility that they might see their father. For them it was simply a fun outing. After a snack, mainly to fortify the young ones, Baumann, who had rented a Mercedes mini-bus, loaded up and departed smoothly for the Volksfest, occupying a huge meadow a couple of kilometers east of the city.

Elli was excited, and nervous. Dani tried to calm her, without giving away to the children the fact that their father might be a short distance away.

"Mommy, why did we have to come so far to visit a Volksfest? There's one in Neuchâtel this week." Mireille was the more curious of the twins.

"This Fest, we've been told, is supposed to be very big, very special. It has lots of rides, a small circus and much, much more." Elli hoped Mireille would not push the matter too far.

A virtual sea of automobiles, buses and other means of conveyance greeted the mini-bus on its arrival at the fair grounds. With the aid of parking attendants, the bus found ample space.

"I want to hold Mac's leash." Sylvie laid claim to her favorite dog. "You can take Sampson, Mireille."

Theo didn't mind. He saw the ferris wheel ahead and that's what he wanted to do. Besides, Roland had promised him a big wiener and a sip of his beer.

Herr Weinstein had lingered near the main entrance. He spotted the mini-bus and its contents. The "tall man with the beard" (Dr. Baumann) was conclusive proof he had found the right party. He approached them, introduced himself, then conferred quietly off to one side with Dr. Baumann and Madame Davidson.

Matti/Mark was sharing substitute duty with some assistants due to an illness that prevented the owner of a traditional booth from participating this afternoon. The booth was a standard in most carnivals: "throw a ball, knock over a target and win a stuffed doll for your sweetheart." Matti's hair came down to his collar in back. His mustache was dark and full. It could have used a trim, but still looked neat. He wore a red jacket, blue pants and a white straw hat with a red ribbon. He was rather dashing in appearance and obviously relished the role he was playing.

"*Herrreinspaziert! Meine Damen und Herren! Versuchen Sie es! Gewinnen Sie ein herrliches Püppchen für Ihren Liebling!* Step right up, sir. Is your aim good enough to win a prize for the apple of your eye?"

Potential customers stopped, looked, and a couple of young men with dates tried their luck. One was successful. The other better practice more.

Gurke-Nas, by chance, stopped the children as they strolled down one of the lanes between the booths. The crowd was thick. He made balloon figures for Theo and the girls. As he left he intrigued Theo by reaching up and squeezing his over-sized nose. The resulting **honk-honk** startled the youngster, but he responded with a hearty laugh.

"Come here, young man," Matti confronted Theo, "Try your strong arm. Knock over a bottle and win a pair of dolls for your lady friends." He handed Theo two balls to use.

Partly in protest and partly to set the record straight, Theo spoke to the mustached attendant behind the counter covered with a striped cloth that also formed a skirt for the counter. "They're not my lady friends! They're my sisters."

The adults had caught up to the children. Roland was now in charge of the dogs. Suddenly, McGregor started barking. Uncharacteristic for his behavior away from home. Sampson also began to bark, expressing considerable excitement. Both dogs proved too much for Roland. They pulled away, dove under the skirt of the counter and started to pull at Matti's pant legs, begging for attention. Elli was embarrassed at first and called the dogs back. The children, especially the twins, stared at the man and listened again to his voice. Meanwhile, Matti, who loved dogs, was alternately vigorously petting them and being kissed by them.

"Daddy!" Mireille was the first. He looked different, but in almost a year children can forget exact features.

"Yes, it's Daddy! Mom, it's Daddy!" The girls crawled under the counter and embraced their father. He was in tears. He called them by name and looked helplessly across the counter, first at Elli, then at Roland and Dani.

A crowd of onlookers gathered. They had no clue. It was a reunion of sorts. That was clear. The circumstances were baffling. Herr Weinstein and a couple of helpers tried to break up the throng. Tried to move them away from the booth. Elli and Mark were embracing. Samantha Willis was shedding tears of sheer joy.

Dr. Baumann, looking at the faces in the mob that had been glued to the ground in front of the booth, saw his wife. She had come upon the scene, realized that Matti had recovered his memory and that he had been reunited with his family. Baumann worked his way through the mass of the curious. He put his arms around Anni. She hugged him. They walked away, holding hands. Neither saying a word. They had done their work. They were together.

Weinstein managed to get the Davidsons and Dani, Roland and Madame Willis to his trailer. He opened two bottles of champagne for the adults, some sparkling apple juice for the children and left them with a toast to a happy future. Saying he'd be back in less than an hour, he departed.

Later, walking to the mini-bus parked on the east side lot, Theo walks in front with the dogs. The rest follow. Mark is carrying a duffle bag with his belongings. The setting sun warms their backs. Theo teases his sisters by jumping on their late afternoon shadows. "Look! Daddy has the biggest shadow," he says.

Mark looks ahead at the bouncing shadows. He smiles and squeezes Elli's hand. Remembering.

Epilogue

The Davidsons did not stop hugging, kissing, talking for three days. There was much to cover, almost an entire year's worth of activities. Mark's return to the office was an event of unbridled jubilation. Samantha Willis was named to the WCH Board.

Within the month, Mark and his family visited the château. Mark underwent a thorough physical and mental examination. Elli sat in on the discussion of the results. Mark was given a clean bill of health. Mark and Elli expressed their gratitude to both Baumanns for their acts of heroism. The Baumanns would accept no money for their services. Mark gave them permission to publish his case study and to distribute their video tapes to medical institutions for training purposes.

The Baumanns were invited to serve on the *Foundation*'s medical and scientific advisory board. A substantial donation was made to *Médicins Sans Frontières*.

Mark and Herr Weinstein spoke frequently on the telephone or emailed each other.

Gurke-Nas was invited to the château for a consultation. Not long afterward he vacationed in Italy while recuperating. He was extremely proud of his new nose.

McGregor and Sampson waited faithfully near the gate to the Davidson farm to greet their master whenever he was away on a trip or just in to the office. It was easy to gauge their devotion; they began to bark as soon as they heard the sound of his Renault's motor and didn't stop until he embraced them both.

In the lobby of a modern office building in Colmar, proudly holding her diploma, a neatly dressed blonde graduate of a comprehensive course in Microsoft Computing had just received a job offer, an opportunity for a new beginning. Her mind wandered for a moment to a wet and dreary night in the mountains nearly a year ago. Remembering what might have been.

THE END

A Mark Davidson Story

A DEATH AT SEA

Hellmut Edelmann

CHAPTER ONE

Monday Afternoon

Members of the Advisory Board had first suggested, then insisted on it. Mark and Elli deserved a vacation. Indeed, they needed one. This time without the children. Dani, Elli's sister, loved the idea and immediately volunteered to look after the fourteen-year-old twins, Mireille and Sylvie, and young Theo, who was eager to become a teenager.

The Davidsons were initially somewhat reluctant to take what was probably their first real holiday alone. The more they thought about it, however, the greater the appeal of a "second honeymoon". They decided on a cruise. The agreed-upon destination: the Eastern Mediterranean.

The flight from Geneva to Barcelona was brief and uneventful. Now, holding hands like two young lovers, Mark and Elli stood on the starboard deck high above the pier observing the preparations for the embarkation scheduled for late-afternoon. Mark's thoughts traveled back two days to the Zürich Opera, where the whole family had attended a Saturday evening performance of Verdi's *La Traviata*. Although they had seen and heard the work numerous times before, they had experienced again the exhilaration and excitement that was part and parcel of a live production: the cacophony of instruments being tuned, the parade of men, women, and children entering the theater, taking their seats, whispering their impressions and observations, wondering, hoping that the new staging would live up to expectations.

The house lights dimmed. Everyone awaited with baited breath the arrival of the conductor, his acknowledgment of the audience's appreciative applause, the raising of the baton, the spirited overture, and then, the solemn parting of the huge curtain as singers and dancers filled the stage with glorious sound and an energetically moving tableau of colorful costumes, carefully nuanced gestures, and, last not least, the meeting of Violetta and Alfredo.

The scene before him, thought Mark, was definitely analogous. The air was filled with electricity. Limousines and taxis, arriving dockside in a stream of yellows, whites, reds, stripes and roof-mounted signs and lights, disgorged an array of colorful characters, all bent, presumably, on pleasure and relaxation. Their luggage took every shape, size and hue. Passing through the embarkation hall, each of the fellow travelers received his documentation and prepared to enter the vessel by the huge gangway just a meter or two above water's level. Pairs of eyes on the promenade deck, or watching from balconies on several of the decks with outside cabins and suites, were all occupied with their personal assessments of nationality, economic status and fashion consciousness as the remainder of nearly two thousand passengers filed on board.

A small music ensemble on the dock, dressed in blue and white, played lively Greek folk dances and Catalan favorites. The well-practiced crew hustled to complete the weekly miracle of a total turn-around of passengers and supplies in a few short hours. On the bridge above them, Captain Mario Lucchini, a *Marebella Lines* veteran, was reviewing weather data and conversing with his First Mate, the Chief Engineer and the Purser about *The Venetian's* ten-night itinerary from Barcelona to Istanbul and return, with visits to Sicily, Malta and one of the popular islands in the Cyclades, where white-washed homes and brilliant blue roof-tops covered the hills and promised day-long sunshine, incredible sunsets and evenings full of pleasures for every palate.

The Davidsons were truly warming up to the idea of a cruise. A break from their overly busy schedules would do them both good. *All work and no play*, thought Mark, *is... what is it they say...?* His dreamy mood was interrupted by a squeeze on his hand by Elli. With her head she directed his gaze to a woman pushing a man in a wheelchair across the gangway.

Three crewmen followed, wrestling with more than a half dozen bulky suitcases. Other priority passengers among the late arrivals followed: a young couple with an infant, two families with toddlers in tow, a woman struggling with crutches, twins cradled in their mother's arms.

Elli glanced at her watch briefly. It was almost time for their coffee date with Captain Lucchini. *White Cross Holdings*, of which Mark was Chairman, owned approximately 80% of *Marebella Lines*, whose ships, staffed by a highly regarded international crew, were registered in Liberia. The Davidsons had never met the Captain before, but his professional competence and personal charm were legend at headquarters. Tipped off in advance about the Davidsons' cruise choice, Lucchini intended to start off on the right foot by extending an invitation for a glass of champagne followed by coffee and pastries in his cabin prior to the departure from the capital of Catalunya. Checking his watch, Mark turned slowly and guided his lovely wife through a nearby door back into the ship. *The captain shouldn't be kept waiting*, he thought, *this is bound to be a busy time for him.*

Meanwhile, after an elevator ride to Deck 10, Lurene Johnson, obviously much younger than her spouse, was steering her husband's wheelchair down the narrow hallway towards their spacious luxury outside cabin, one with a generous balcony affording them marvelous views of the sea and the many islands they would pass during the next ten days. To avoid a collision with a steward rolling a cart full of fresh linens from the opposite direction, Lurene accidentally bumped a protruding emergency alarm box.

"Dammit! Watch where you're going," barked her passenger, turning slightly and glaring at her, obviously unhappy about her clumsiness maneuvering the wheelchair.

"Sorry, sweetie." The term of endearment was merely a habit she had picked up in her days as a waitress. She was actually irritated by her passenger's constant complaining and often unpleasant attitude. "We're almost there. We're looking for Number 1012. Oh, there it is. I've got the card that opens the door." *The Venetian*, just christened three months before, sported all the latest technological wonders for its passengers, including the now ubiquitous keyless entry.

Lurene backed up the wheelchair a couple of feet to facilitate a turn that would help ease it through the cabin door. "Ooops! Sorry!" In the process of proceeding through the door, she made contact with the right side door frame and jolted her testy charge once again.

"For Christ's sake! Can't you steer this thing any better?" Mr. Johnson's gravelly voice was audible the length of the hall. He continued to mumble until the door closed and muffled his rough language.

Lurene shrugged it off. She was determined to be patient. In one of her 'Just you wait, Henry Higgins' moments, Lurene's inner voice spoke. *You old bastard. One of these days I'll be free, and then….* Her thoughts trailed off, disappearing in a fantasy world, where her burdensome husband's wealth would help her forget the misery she experienced every day he was in her face.

Not unlike many in her generation, Lurene was the product of a dysfunctional home. She abbreviated her secondary education to join the work force. Lacking many of the skills the modern workplace has established as a base for more specialized training, she found waiting tables in a local eatery provided at least a minimum income and a modicum of independence. Her physical attributes and out-going personality masked her less than perfect command of English. Encounters with members of the opposite sex whose interests and objectives revolved principally around sharing certain animal pleasures was life's on-the-job training. Her street smarts helped her to apply the lessons learned to advance her station in life and to achieve an ever-improving standard of living. Marrying Robert Chamberlain Johnson had seemed a significant triumph. Time and subsequent events were rapidly altering that assessment.

* * *

Many decks below, in the cramped crew cabin Bobbi Johnson shares with Suzanna Rodriguez, Bobbi is enjoying a fifteen-minute break before returning to the kitchen, where she is a Sous-Chef specializing in dessert preparation. Now 30, Bobbi is a petite five-foot-two bundle of charm. Cute as a button, full of energy, and very popular with her fellow crew members, Bobbi, like many of them, hails from the Philippines. Named Roberta Felicia Johnson by her mother, she graduated from a culinary institute in Manila and worked in Hawaii, Chicago and Rome, prior to joining *Marebella Lines* at the beginning of this year's cruising season.

Suzanna, also from Manila, is an attractive and unattached, career-oriented, young woman of 27. She is an Assistant House-Keeping Manager responsible for all hotel services on Decks 9 and 10, where the majority of the superior and luxury accommodations are located. She and Bobbi met on the first cruise this year and formed an immediate friendship. They have freely shared their past histories and their dreams for the future.

Holding a sheaf of papers in her hand, Suzanna, rather breathlessly says, "Look at this! I just got a copy of the passenger list. I always check to see if anyone named Rodriguez is sailing with us", she chuckles. "No luck, but… there are eight passengers named Johnson. And…" She waves the papers in the air. "Ta, dah… one of them is ROBERT CHAMBER-LAIN JOHNSON and his wife Lurene!" She hands the list to Bobbi, who reads and rereads the names several times.

"Do you think it's him? The combination Robert Chamberlain Johnson has to be fairly unique. I remember seeing it on a letter my mother kept in a small container on her dresser. I wonder if it's really him. I wonder what he's like."

"Well, the Johnson's are in the largest stateroom on Deck 10. It's the Royal Suite. He must have piles of money. That's one of mine. I'll check him out as soon as we head out of the harbor. I know one thing. I already hate him."

Bobbi was silent. She stared at the list. Her mind wandered back to her childhood, a time in her life that brought no special joy, no positive memories. She had heard the story numerous times. Oddly, never from her mother. Always from strangers who knew her background.

Bobbi's mom, Seraphina Malagan, came from a prominent upper

middle class family. Seraphina's father was strict; a devout Christian whose moral values where shaped in the eighteenth and nineteenth centuries and passed on to him by the missionaries whose schools he attended. Bobbi's mom was very social and artistically inclined. She loved dancing and often went to a non-commissioned officers' club at an American military post on the outskirts of her hometown near Manila. It was there that Sergeant Robert C. Johnson met and squired the pert, lively woman, who succumbed to his charming personality and handsome appearance. He proposed. They became intimate. Bobbi's mom was pregnant. Her parents were livid. The family honor was irreparably damaged.

The Marine Corps shipped Sergeant Johnson back to the States, where, nearing completion of his service, he was honorably discharged a couple of months later. He wrote one letter to his lover. In it was five hundred dollars and the suggestion that she get an abortion. Bobbi's mom never heard another word from him. Disowned by her family, disgraced, lacking job skills, and emotionally scarred, she eked out an existence as a domestic. Letters to Bobbi's father were returned unopened. When Bobbi was nine, her mother died. Her broken heart had apparently never recovered. Bobbi, rejected by her grandparents, was taken in by a Catholic orphanage. At eighteen she left to seek her fortune.

For her mother she felt deep sorrow. For her biological father she felt disappointment and, at first, disgust. How anyone could act in such a heartless manner baffled her. Nevertheless, she was inclined more towards lenity than enmity. Sister Esmeralda had taught her forgiveness and the love of God. Bobbi was a receptive pupil. If ever a negative outlook on life were justified, thought Suzanna, Bobbi had a right to be bitter and angry. It became clear as their relationship developed, however, that Bobbi's was a truly kind heart that knew only love and forgiveness.

Suzanna, on the other hand, to whom Bobbi had revealed her unfortunate past, had been deeply moved by the tragic circumstances in Bobbi's childhood and had developed a strong sense of antipathy towards the man whose cowardly betrayal and unfeeling cruelty had wreaked such misery on a dear friend.

Johnson, who in his military days had been known familiarly as Bob, now preferred to be called RC by family and associates. At fifty-six he had never completely outgrown his 'love 'em and leave 'em' attitude with regard to women. The shapely, physically well-endowed, stylishly attired Lurene, with an intellect that adhered to that often unfairly ascribed to natural blondes, was considerably younger than her husband, by twenty-two years as a matter of fact, and was his third wife. Wife number one and their two-year-old twins had died in a car accident many years ago. Wife number two had given him a son, Herb, now 26, a lazy, oversexed, college dropout, hot for his step-mom. Herb's own mother was a Chinese born in California. Cancer claimed her when Herb was just eleven. As an Asian-American, Herb struggled with identity issues. He had most of his father's negative characteristics and too few of his mother's positive qualities. She had been ambitious and hard-working, had a college degree and was capable of making sacrifices for her child's sake. The 'good life' attracted Herb. He felt that his well-to-do father should loosen up the purse strings so that he could indulge himself without necessarily having to earn it.

Upon his return to civilian life, Robert C. Johnson soon took over his father's construction business. His practice of using others to further his own objectives was not restricted to women. He proved himself a rather ruthless business man and achieved considerable success, if lots of money and obvious material wealth, the expensive foreign cars, the ostentatious houses and the free-spending vacations were the principal measures involved. Investment in a pest control firm had led to ownership of three such regional businesses and a string of franchises in four states. A cabinet manufacturing company and part interest in a lumber distributorship followed. His 'stable' of business enterprises expanded continuously.

A careful examination of Johnson's life reveals that he has virtually no real friends, but many silent enemies. Even his family despises him. Hurting others, inflicting mental and psychological pain is Robert's secret pleasure. He is a vengeful, vindictive person. To attract and hold sway over those he needs and has come to depend on, he uses his money and the vague, yet frequent and subtle hints that this one or that one might be in line for his largesse when the grim reaper has claimed his soul.

Introspection has come to occupy much of Johnson's daytime hours now that he is confined to a wheelchair. At first, it was the unfortunate, if suspicious, 'accident' when a load of building materials fell on him and several surgeries were required to make him nearly normal again. Not long after, a debilitating, often painful disease combined with the residual affects of the accident to render him unfit to carry on his business alone. Ever since he has had to rely on others to handle the day-to-day responsibilities, both for the operation of his growing construction empire and his daily life. This phase of his life has witnessed a sharply magnified intensification of his negative characteristics. Life's experiences have served to intensify his mean and confrontational nature.

By nature or inclination a party-boy and ladies man, Mr. Johnson sought to obviate an inferiority complex and shallow intellect and their concomitant vulnerabilities by being mean-spirited, by expressing his hyper-critical views clothed in verbal abuse. He tried to manipulate the lives of those around him. His hateful, wicked tongue spits out venom in every direction. He finds pleasure in bullying, in diminishing the worth of others. His comments aim at embarrassing, humiliating and denigrating. And why do those around him tolerate such behavior? Each believes he or she will be a significant heir and come into a sizeable fortune upon his demise, which, based on his precarious health, they calculate to be sooner rather than later.

Johnson is well aware how others view him. He enjoys the knowledge that they are being deceived. After much reflection, he has conceived a plan, a means to inflict more hurt after his death. Assuming that most would revel in his departure from a life that no longer offers the pleasures he relished, Johnson decided to keep a secret diary containing his true thoughts and personal assessments of family, friends and business associates. He finds private time each day to make extensive entries.

Periodically, he sends the most recent additions, duly sealed, to his bank for inclusion in his private safe deposit box. This action is not known to his lawyers, nor to his secretary/accountant of many years. His family has no idea. Johnson's impossible wish: to see their faces when they read his diary. His contempt for others is boundless.

The Davidsons' visit with Captain Lucchini was followed by a tour of the inner workings of the luxury liner conducted by none other than the jolly, affable Captain himself. Having revealed details of his own background over coffee and exquisite samples from the ship's bakery, Lucchini's curiosity soon had Elli and Mark sharing similar biographical tidbits extending from their quite different childhood years to their meeting in Zürich, Elli's kidnapping and rescue, and Mark's 'lost' year as an amnesiac. A strong bond of mutual respect was formed. The Captain and his family were invited to visit with the Davidsons at their home in Yverdon. A tentative date was set for the late fall, when the cruise season took a break.

CHAPTER TWO

Monday Evening

The cabins located towards the aft on Deck 10's port side are *The Venetian's* most luxurious and most expensive. Johnson booked the opulent Royal Suite, over 1600 square feet, excluding the sizeable balcony. It has a king-size bed, a spacious bathroom large enough for handicapped access, a kitchenette, a well-appointed sitting room and a dining area. Mounted on one wall is a large flat-screen TV. For those who want it, there is a corner desk arrangement with internet access. Attractive oil paintings featuring Mediterranean landscapes add a tone of elegance. Its balcony offers marvelous views of the fabled sea, the islands, and the ship's ports of call.

Much of the late afternoon was spent organizing the suite, unpacking, sending a few items via the steward for pressing, setting up the bathroom for Johnson, and watching the east coast of Spain slowly recede over the horizon. Johnson insisted on the First Sitting, assuming that dining early would give his troublesome stomach more time to process the food, thus allowing him to sleep more comfortably. Room had been left, as requested, for his wheel chair to glide comfortably a short distance through a rear entrance in the dining room to a table for six.

This evening, Lurene, luckily, had maneuvered the wheelchair without incident to the dining room. The Johnson's table, not unlike those surrounding it, had its share of chatty people. Lurene struck up a conversation with a woman on the other side of her husband. This he found annoying, but stifled his urge to slap them both. It was difficult to hear because of the incessant chatter around them. Consequently, Johnson merely nodded and pretended to understand, as his table mates introduced themselves and made a few polite, if inane, remarks. Both Johnsons selected the seafood entrée, some ocean-going variety, poached and served on a bed of curried rice with a colorful vegetable garnish. Lurene drank a glass of White Burgundy; her husband contented himself with a glass of Evian. She devoured a rich, chocolate dessert and drank her coffee slowly. Although livid with irritation, he, rather uncharacteristically, mastered his desire to protest, endured with a pained expression the protracted good-byes until Lurene rose and guided his rolling chair deftly towards the exit.

Johnson was tired and planned to retire early. He couldn't resist first scolding Lurene sharply for making him endure his table-mate's silly remarks. Lurene, wearing a body-hugging, bright red pant suit, with expensive black, open-toed pumps and a matching belt, was feeling frisky. She announced her desire to get oriented, to walk the deck and to peek in the shops, perhaps stop by the casino for a few moments. Her husband's silence was tacit approval. He wanted to record some observations in his diary. Lurene mixed her husband's evening medicinal cocktail in a glass, surreptitiously diluting its potency and stirring in a small quantity of powder she had made by crushing two powerful sleeping tablets. She didn't want RC to be awake when she returned later. If he were asleep an ugly confrontation might be avoided. She left the concoction on the night table with the admonition not to forget it.

A moment after she departed, Johnson rose with obvious difficulty from the bed, where he had been resting, retrieved the milky-looking beverage from the night table, hobbled with the aid of a cane over to the bathroom and proceeded to pour it into the bathroom sink. "Ha! Think I don't know what you're doing? You bitch!" Bracing himself by grasping at furniture and supporting his weight against the stateroom's wall, he managed to move slowly, painfully back to the bed. On the way he fumbled about on his night table for his reading glasses. They slipped out of his hand onto the floor, where, from his reddened face he blurted out wicked curses as he retrieved them. Catching his breath with effort, he sat uncomfortably on his bed and wrote rapidly in his diary for about thirty minutes, then got up and locked it in his briefcase, which he kept in a corner of his closet. He felt a migraine coming and retrieved from a compartment in the briefcase a small tin in which he kept his strongest medicines. He removed several pills and washed them down with a glass of sparkling water. Old Doc Tribble back in Johnson's neighborhood in a North Atlanta suburb had described how the syphilis Johnson contracted in his military days would proceed, now that it had been definitely identified. His brain was affected. Late-stage syphilis inevitably provoked questions of mortality. Johnson knew his days were numbered. He was told bluntly by the good doctor that he should anticipate a painful end.

Meanwhile, Lurene made her way to Deck 6. There she headed for the Library/Reading Room. Sitting quietly in the corner was a well-built, attractive young man with Asian features. Lurene sauntered in, picked up a magazine and took a seat next to the young man. There was no one else there at the time. "I gave him his medicine with a sleeping potion to knock him out early. Sometimes I wish it would put him to sleep permanently. He's really getting to be too much to take on a regular basis. I'm tired of playing nursemaid to that bastard."

Herb nodded in agreement. "Hey, let's go down to my cabin. I need some action." Negotiating the two flights of stairs down to Herb's level, Lurene cautions Herb to always arrive late for the Second Sitting in the main dining hall in the evening. That way, she claims, he's not likely to bump into his father, who insists on the First Sitting. She adds, "Your father usually has room service for breakfast and lunch. I plan to push him around the aft deck on levels 11 and 12 for about thirty minutes beginnin' about 10:30. Otherwise, he's lookin' forward to sittin' on our balcony with a pair of binoculars. The Library is probably a good place to meet. Don't forget! He has no idea you're on board!" Once in Herb's cabin, the couple races to undress.

Half an hour later, Herb has dozed off; Lurene is fixing her hair in the bathroom. Returning to her suite after touring a number of the amenities areas and a stroll in the fresh air on the upper decks, Lurene is greeted in the hallway by Gustavo, the steward, who wishes her a pleasant rest. Gustavo, a native of Nicaragua, has been working cruise ships for eight years. His eyes widen slightly when he turns, looks back at Lurene, and confirms that her blouse is not completely tucked into her pants. *Well, well,* he thinks to himself. *So soon?*

Most passengers, overwhelmed by the intensive activities of the first day at sea, the life-boat drill, the excitement of meeting their dinner mates and watching the filmed cruise highlights with descriptions of upcoming excursions, gradually retire to their cabins for a well-deserved night of rest as the waves wash gently against the hull of their magnificent, gleaming white city at sea.

Pepino Maldonado, too, is ready to crawl into the sack. As soon as the theater emptied following the last film showing, Pepino and his fellow performers put the finishing touches on their performances scheduled for the next several nights. Rehearsing until after midnight, the stalwart troupe of singers and dancers, head quickly for their quarters and a night of pleasant dreams. Maldonado, a handsome, well-proportioned young man, like so many others in the crew, is a Filipino. At thirty-one years of age, he is an accomplished singer and dancer, a pianist, excellent guitarist, composer and choreographer, and was recently named entertainment director for the season's remaining cruises.

Pepino and Bobbi are an item. He is madly in love with her. He worships her. She is equally crazy about him. Moments after his head hits the pillow filled with thoughts of his soul mate, Pepino is sound asleep.

The Venetian is following a course towards Sicily. The first full day will be spent cruising eastward across a calm Mediterranean Sea. A sickle moon shines through a cloudless sky and dances lightly on the waves below. A senior officer checks the battery of gauges and dials on the bridge. Dawn is approaching at 18 knots an hour.

CHAPTER THREE

Monday Noon

Rather pale and wan, probably from sitting too long in front of her computer in Johnson's cramped back office in an industrial park on the fringe of one of Atlanta's northwest suburbs, Millie Austin, unmarried, late forties, RC's long-time secretary and bookkeeper and occasional lover, is staring at an invoice attached to a report she accidentally opened. Picking up the envelope, she reads more carefully, "Personal and Confidential". Sent from Peachtree Investigators, Inc., the contents were obviously intended for Johnson's eyes only. But now the secret is out. *He knows. And I know that he knows.* She read an excerpt: "Your bookkeeper has been siphoning funds from your accounts for several years. She has deposited money in five different banks with substantial sums diverted from your company's income."

Years before, it had become clear to Millie that she was not destined to become a Mrs. Johnson. That realization, in spite of her willingness to share his bed, saw the birth of a 'Plan B'. She would arrange for her own retirement fund by silently, secretly rewarding her devotion and dedication through regular contributions to her personal accounts from company receipts. Although she hoped her loyal endeavors for Johnson Construction would not be overlooked in the boss' will, embezzling was her insurance. After all, RCJ could be a real SOB.

Whispering to herself, she mouthed, "So that he won't know that I know he knows, I'll re-seal the envelope and leave it at the bottom of his inbox." Everyone else on the small staff had left for lunch. She walked to the adjoining office and slid the envelope under a pile of papers awaiting his return. She saw the coffee machine. Her inner thoughts took a dark turn. *If I could adulterate his coffee with arsenic, I would. That bastard! After all I've done for him.*

Millie felt sorry for Johnson's son. While he did not intentionally mistreat his offspring, Johnson largely neglected Herb for whom he provided a nanny in his younger years, prep school and college tuition as he progressed toward maturity. True love was lacking. When she could, Millie mothered young Herb. They became good friends, very good friends. If Herb was hurting for money, he knew he could count on Millie to slip him a few bucks.

Johnson had long suspected Millie of skimming for her personal benefit. The corroboration from the investigator would be superfluous. Reference to her in his will had long since been duly removed.

Tuesday

The Venetian's first port of call is Catania on Sicily's east coast. Cruising leisurely in calm seas, Captain Lucchini checks with the Purser regarding excursion plans for passengers and ascertains that all is prepared for the next day. Today will be a day for enjoying the ship's fabulous amenities. Johnson basked during the forenoon hours in the warm sun on his balcony. A coughing bout left him wheezing and generally out of sorts. After lunch Lurene had managed to take him via the elevator to the next higher deck for a turn around the aft quarter of the ship. With his cap pulled down over his eyes, Johnson dozed a while, then woke up with another gut-shaking coughing spell. He ordered her to return to the suite. As he rolled down the corridor to No. 1012, Ashoka Desai, lone occupant of one of the neighboring cabins approached. He appeared to be staring at Johnson.

Johnson stared back. "What the hell are you looking at? Haven't you ever seen a man coughing?" A throat-rattling cough is followed by a spate of unintelligible gurgling noises. "Hurry up, Lurene, that black bastard thinks I'm some kind of spectacle."

Lurene, shocked at the outburst, an apologetic look on her face, moves a bit faster. Mr. Desai, a wealthy Indian, shrugs his shoulders, a look of pity on his face as he glances back. He has heard worse insults before.

Johnson insists that Lurene contact the ship's infirmary. At first, Signora Piccolini, a heavy-set nurse with a no nonsense attitude arrives. She hears the complaint, inquires about existing medical conditions (dishonest response from Johnson), checks blood pressure, body temperature, and pulse, and listens to his lungs through a stethoscope. She advises Johnson to remain in bed and rest until Dr. Benotti is available.

Some twenty minutes later, Dr. Benotti himself knocks and is admitted. He reads the data from the nurse's note and also listens carefully to Johnson's lungs. "You have considerable congestion in the bronchi. Could be emphysema. Do you smoke? Or did you smoke?"

"Yes, I used to be a chain-smoker. Now, I rarely have a cigarette. What can you give me to control the coughing spells?"

Opening his black bag, Dr. Benotti took out a sample packet of a medicine designed to suppress the coughing and handed it to Lurene. "Have him take two in the morning and two at night with water. They are not a cure, but intended only to help control the urge to cough." Looking at Johnson, he said, "Once ashore I advise you to undergo a thorough medical examination. We are not equipped for the extensive help you may need. I would not delay getting an evaluation from a specialist." Benotti indicated his services would be added automatically to the charges collected by the Purser's staff. He excused himself and left.

The sliding glass door to the balcony was open. Johnson gazed somewhat vacantly at the broad expanse of blue-green water beyond. The serenity he imagined in the gentle waves contrasted markedly with the physical and mental turmoil rampant within his flabby, wheezing shell. He didn't need a ship's doctor to imply his condition was serious. He knew better than anyone just how precarious his health actually was.

Lurene's voice broke the silence. She noticed the pall of gravity that was expressed unconsciously by her husband's slouch, his ashen cheeks, the downward tilt of his graying head. "Let's order up some soup for lunch! A cup of tea with some honey might sooth your throat. You need some rest."

She actually seems concerned, Johnson thought to himself. "OK, good idea, soup and tea." He knew she was unlikely to shed a tear, if he were to drop dead on the spot. That observation notwithstanding, the note of sincerity in her voice caught his attention. The coughing abated considerably as Johnson began to drift off and his metabolism slowed. Lurene quietly left the cabin, for she had a spa appointment and the receptionist had indicated she should report on time as the schedule was very tight.

Two love birds, Bobbi and Pepino dined together in the crew's mess, a neat and tidy dining hall with several fewer degrees of decor and elegance than paying passengers enjoyed in the large formal restaurant above. Pepino ate only a green salad and settled for a cup of hot tea. Bobbi's eyes were fixed on his with unblinking intensity as he described the upcoming entertainment program. She was very proud of his accomplishments. Tonight was the première of a song and dance revue featuring his orchestration of a medley of Broadway hits. He had recorded the sound track in Rome two weeks earlier. He would play a feature role. The cast had heard a rumor that a famous Hollywood producer was traveling on the ship *incognito*. True or not, everyone was keyed for a stellar performance. A warm embrace and a kiss preceded their parting to pursue their respective duties.

In Suite 1012, Johnson pushed his empty soup bowl aside, wiped his mouth with the napkin, tossed it aside and pulled a surprised Lurene, who was clearing the table, into his lap. "Do you still love me, darlin'?"

"Of course, you dirty old man." Lurene tried to strike a light, teasing tone. "When you're feelin' right again, we're goin' to have a real party. Just like the fun we had in Bermuda, in Puerto Vallarta and Jamaica. Oh, let the gin, the tequila and the rum flow once more! Those were times!" Her laugh was forced and brief.

From the bathroom, where she was fine tuning her 'do' and checking her make-up, Lurene said she was going to the theater, then to an art auction. Exiting the bathroom, she said, "Your medicine is already mixed. I'll leave it on your night stand. Try to sleep." She swooshed out the door, closing it gently following a perfunctory peck on RC's cheek.

As on the night before, once Lurene had vacated the suite, Johnson managed with considerable effort to rise from his wheelchair and to stumble over to the bathroom sink to dump the vile concoction Lurene had prepared. From his briefcase he extracted a handful of pills, washed them down with a glass of lemon soda, and reclaimed his wheelchair. There he wrote for half an hour in his diary. Finally locking it away again in the briefcase. As he slipped into bed and flexed his aching knees his brow wrinkled and his jaw tightened, evidence of unwanted pain. Sleep came quickly once he reclined in bed. He slept soundly.

The reverie ended abruptly around one in the morning. Stumbling noisily through the door in an alcohol induced fog, Lurene turned on the brightest of the overhead lights, drenching RC in an incandescent glow that robbed his current dream of a pleasant conclusion. She accidentally knocked the lamp on her night stand to the floor, along with a glass of tea she had abandoned following lunch. Johnson was furious. "You dumb bitch! By God, you're drunk!" No one was present to establish an accurate decibel count, but Johnson had obviously awakened his neighbors. While Mr. Desai, snoring gently with ear muffs, slept on, his British neighbors on the other side in Suite 1014, Oliver and Muriel Hornsby, a working class couple from Liverpool, whose luck in the lottery was funding this first fling abroad, were most unhappy about having their peace so rudely disturbed. Ollie banged on the wall shouting, "Shut up!" Johnson's retort was a hail of short words mostly referring to bodily functions.

Mrs. Hornsby called the night attendant at the Cruise Director's desk to complain. A representative appeared shortly thereafter at the door to Suite 1012. He knocked gently. Johnson was still berating his wife. He called out, "What is it?"

"Is everything all right, sir?" came the query.

"Hell no!" The reply was definitely curt. The purser's aide listened at the door for a few minutes. Satisfied that an acceptable degree of calm had been restored, he returned to the Cruise Director's desk to report on his mission.

Lurene's stomach rebelled during her nightly toilet. She swallowed a sleeping aid and crawled under the blanket on her bed. In spite of her periodic snorting and snoring, both Johnsons were sound asleep as *The Venetian* made its wide turn northward past Cape Passero on Sicily's southernmost coast.

Less than an hour later, Syracuse, basking in the brilliant morning sun passed by on the port side. In another couple of hours the first port of call, Catania, would welcome them for a full menu of excursions offering opportunities for shopping, for adventurous visits to Mt. Etna, as well as for leisurely strolls through the streets of a city with a rich historic past.

CHAPTER FOUR

Wednesday Morning

Lurene, intellectually stimulated by the enthusiastic description of a planned excursion to Mt. Etna that had been distributed along with details of other activities ashore, opts to participate in an all-day visit to the edge of the volcano, coupled with lunch at a country inn. The designer jeans she has chosen to wear reveal the shapely contours of her *derrière*, but are not conducive to scrambling up the side of a mountain. A khaki windbreaker on her left arm, her purse slung over the right shoulder, she boards the first bus. And who should be seated in the fourth row holding a seat for her? Young Herb, of course. As soon as he learned his father had no desire to attempt the rigors of this shore excursion, he had arranged to accompany Lurene. For the moment, at least, he was totally preoccupied with the contents of her tautly stretched blue denim attire, and could care less about the geologic wonder that was the destination of the day's itinerary.

Once past the heavily sprung cabin door that was a challenge for the wheelchair-bound, Robert Chamberlain Johnson made his way to the nearest lobby, rolled across, then through the open door and made his way to the port deck. From his vantage point beside the railing he watched Lurene board the bus on the pier below, then he headed down to Deck 6, where the smokers' lounge and the card rooms were located.

The residual effects of jet-lag, he had concluded, were chiefly responsible for the intestinal discomfort that occupied his early morning hours. Then there was the long flight and the hassle of getting to the dock that had tired and upset him the day before. His medicine was beginning to kick in. The discomfort in his gut was slightly diminished. The blood in his urine he shrugged off nonchalantly. He still had a throbbing pain behind his eyeballs that wouldn't quit. He needed an activity that would divert his attention, help him avoid self pity and anxiety about the inevitable. His skill at cards and the raw luck that had made him the scourge of the barrack's all-night sessions of bridge, blackjack and poker during his stint in the military, had not won him any admiration from fellow Marines. On the contrary, his comrades, while silently envious of his purported success with the ladies, had nevertheless despised him.

Perhaps no one held him in greater contempt than Steve Bartram. Johnson and his father had known the Bartrams seemingly forever. After young Johnson had returned from military service and begun his climb to business success in his dad's construction company, Steve and RC bought a pest control company as partners. The enterprise was quite successful; made a profit from the beginning. Bartram developed a franchise program that expanded the company's reach into neighboring counties, even states. Well managed, the empire prospered. One night, however, after consuming prodigious quantities of expensive whiskey, Bartram and RC and two friends decided to play high stakes poker. Finally, thinking he had a winning hand, Bartram suggested they put their respective half shares of the business into the pot. RC agreed. He had a full house, kings over jacks. Bartram had a flush in hearts. The next day the company's locks were changed and RC's lawyers had the legal documents ready for signatures. Two weeks later, Bartram drove his pick-up into a tree and died instantly. RC didn't bother to attend the funeral. Johnson's cold-blooded, calculating nature, applied with relentless intensity to all his business ventures, brought considerable wealth. But not an iota of happiness.

In the Smoking Lounge several people were either reading or playing games. Johnson's lungs couldn't handle the fumes. He rolled past. Likewise, the adjoining billiard room held no particular interest for someone confined to a wheelchair. The next space was a well-appointed card room with several tables, good overhead light, comfortable chairs and plenty of decks of cards and racks of chips featuring the *Marebella* logo. Johnson maneuvered his wheelchair over to the corner of two tables that had been pushed together to accommodate eight players. Just as he arrived three players excused themselves. Apparently, they had lost all they could afford. From the size of the pot, Johnson surmised it was a low-stakes game. He asked if he could buy in. No problem. He was quoted an amount. He complied and the game began. After an hour, Johnson, who had struggled to give the impression he was somewhat inept at cards, having lost many more hands than he had won, wondered aloud if anyone would be interested in a strictly cash, no-limit, winner-take-all game.

Kelvin Hamrick, an American, who had played professional football for several NFL teams, excused himself. Farhad, an Arab from the Emirates, said he was interested. His full name was Farhad bin Abdul al Aziz. His daddy was an oil magnate. Money was never a problem. Two kibbitzers volunteered to join in. Rolf Detweiler, a German from Baden-Baden, the owner of a winery. Fine, purplish veins are prominent behind his plump, rosy cheeks that bulge whenever he emits the deep, throaty laughter that irritates his nervous competitors. Neville Easton, III, who had been standing behind Johnson observing his play, also wanted in.

Easton, unknown to the others, is a cruise-ship junkie. He romances attractive and wealthy widows inveigling them into investment deals from which he receives handsome commissions. He derives the bulk of his income, however, as a card shark and gambler. Easton is conservatively dressed. His garrulous sociability, proper manners and personal charm perfectly mask his true intentions, whether he is with the ladies, or seated at a card table. He smokes expensive Cuban cigars, prefers Port and Sherry, has a slight paunch, brags about his moneyed family and has the air of a successful aristocrat. The thin David Niven moustache that he constantly strokes adds to his suave and appealing image.

Although Easton's smoking, thanks to shipboard rules, is restricted either to the Smoking Lounge or the aft deck on Level 12, his clothes, unfortunately, carry the distinctive smell of his favorite Havana brand wherever he goes. Johnson's nose registers the smell. It seems vaguely familiar. Yet he cannot place it exactly. Could it be an odor that attached itself to Lurene's windbreaker, when, following an evening with Herb, she allowed the British charmer to grope her, while chatting intimately in a recessed doorway outside the Fitness Center on Deck 12?

Al Aziz suggests that they play 7-Card Stud, if everyone is familiar with that variation. All quickly agree. After two hours and several rounds, with modest pots in the low hundreds and no clear cut winner, al Aziz and Dettweiler beg off, claiming other obligations. The lunch hour is approaching. Johnson orders beer and pizza for everyone remaining. Afterward, Easton suggests that he, an enigmatic player by the name of Politovsky, and Johnson continue, but with a minimum ante of 1000 Pounds. They agree on $2000. An observer in the room agrees to deal.

The 3rd street begins. Johnson has the 2 of Clubs and the 9 of hearts in the hole and the J of Diamonds exposed. His British opponent has the A of Hearts and the K of Spades in the hole; the 10 of Hearts exposed. Politovsky, the Bulgarian, has the Q of Hearts and the 4 of Spades in the hole, the 10 of Diamonds exposed. Easton bets $800; Politovsky checks. Johnson calls.

Fourth street. The dealer places the 5 of Hearts face up in front of Johnson. Easton gets the J of Clubs. The Bulgarian gets the 8 of Diamonds. With a potential flush within grasp, Easton, his countenance betraying no emotion, bets another $800. Politovsky dreams of a flush. He throws $900 on the table. Johnson, his face an unreadable mask, hesitates, studies his cards and those showing on the table, appears to be deliberating whether to hang in or not, and finally calls again.

The 5th street begins with the 2 of Hearts on Johnson's pile; the K of Clubs on Easton's. Now the latter has a minimum of a pair of Kings. He bets $1000. Politovsky struggles to master a smile as the A of Spades appears before him. Johnson, with a pair of Deuces, stays cool and collected, showing no sign of weakness. He deliberately slows the pace, seemingly on the verge of dropping out. "Let's see who's got guts here," he says, intentionally taunting his opponents. "I'll raise you $1000." The

Bulgarian, sensing a bold bluff, raises it an additional $200. Easton, somewhat impetuously, calls.

The Q of Spades for Johnson, the 9 of Spades for Politovsky, and the 9 of Diamonds for Easton are all the 6th street brings. Easton recognizes that he has a chance for either an A-high or K-high flush. He bets $2000. The Bulgarian, hoping for aid from Lady Luck, still envisions a flush himself. Bluffing somewhat, he puts $3000 in the pot. Johnson, ever calm in spite of a splitting headache, throwing $4000 into the pot, raises him another $1000. Easton, who had won big in another game the preceding evening, checks his wallet. He has another $8000. He calls.

The 7th and final street will be dealt face-down. Johnson peeks quickly. The 2 of Spades. Politovsky's heart beats faster as he squints at the Q of Clubs in his hand. Easton involuntarily smiles upon seeing the A of Hearts. No flush for him, but two pairs, Aces and Kings. Politovsky realizes he is vulnerable with only a pair of Queens. He folds. With what Johnson has showing, Easton assumes he will beat the oddball in the wheelchair. He dawdles a bit, not wanting to come across as too eager. Sweat is trickling uncomfortably down his sleeve. He bets the $5000 remaining in his wallet.

Johnson hesitates. He stares at the table, studies his hand, then calls the bet, throwing $5000 onto the pot. "I think you're a wimp, just trying like an amateur to bluff me." Johnson glares contemptuously at Easton.

"Two pairs," says Easton smugly, with an air of triumph, revealing the Aces and Kings.

Johnson, matter-of-factly lays his three Deuces onto the space in front of him, one at a time. He slowly, casually, organizes the bills in the pot into one neat pile. "It's been a pleasure. Just luck, I guess. I've got to get ready for dinner. Have a good evening, gentlemen." Backing away from the table, Johnson rolls towards the entrance and disappears down the corridor in the direction of the elevator.

Politovsky mumbles audibly a few choice Slavic expletives, realizing he had been suckered. Easton's face is ruby red. *You bloody American bastard!* Four words he wants to shout are swallowed hard. Easton is furious with himself; mad as hell at the cards. Steaming inside in the knowledge that what should have been an easy mark has taken him for about $18,000. He suddenly bolts out of his chair and jogs down the hallway, catching Johnson as he is entering the elevator. He steps in behind him. There is a young couple also aboard. Through a forced 'friendly' smile, Easton, breathing rather heavily, addressing Johnson in an aggressive tone, says, "Say, I hope we can play again soon. I deserve a chance to even the score."

"Maybe in a couple of days. I'm not well and I'll need to rest up tomorrow." Adding with a tone of derision, "Sure you can handle another loss?" Johnson, a master of the disdainful, dismissive look, glances briefly at Easton, whose face is a bright pink. The elevator stops. Johnson rolls out. Easton, still panting slightly, is left trying to figure out the enigma that had just cast a shadow on what he had hoped would be a triumphant cruise. The other occupants, uncomfortable about the palpable tension, exchange a quizzical look.

Wednesday, Late Afternoon – Evening

Upon returning to the pier from their mountain excursion, Lurene and Herb exited from the bus separately. Herb pulled his cap down to cover his face and stayed behind to be the last to leave. Lurene mingled with the crowd passing through the security check, then hurried to her cabin. She planned to shower and change in a leisurely way before dinner. RC, slightly exhausted from his successful foray at the card tables, has enjoyed a nap on the balcony in his wheelchair.

Acquiescing reluctantly to Lurene's insistence that he dress up for dinner, RC dons a shirt and tie. The blue blazer he received for a recent birthday fits him well, although leaving it unbuttoned helps to conceal a few unnecessary inches around his waistline. Mrs. Johnson's *décolleté*, in medium blue chiffon, will impress the knowledgeable ladies, who will spend some time guessing at its price tag, and attract innumerable stolen glances from the males present, impressed no doubt by the cup size of her supportive undergarment.

By the time they arrive in the dining room the other guests at their table have been seated and have made their menu choices known. The customary polite greetings are exchanged. Chatter throughout the room has attained such a high decibel count that it becomes difficult to communicate even with a neighbor.

A young waiter, recently promoted from bussing duties, was dreaming about the generous tips often received by lead waiters and their assistants on this high-priced cruise. As he was about to pass behind Johnson to deliver a tray of beverages to a neighboring table, the wheelchair rolled backwards a few inches and caused the tray to tilt slightly. Rather agile, the waiter regained his balance. However, he was unable to prevent one glass of Chardonnay from losing most of its contents down the back of Johnson's neck. The wine had been well chilled.

With a heart-stopping shriek, Johnson unleashed a gutter full of offensive phrases that even had Lurene blushing and wishing she could crawl under the table and hide. The din in the room, as if by magic, was transformed into absolute silence. Embarrassed nearly to tears, she excused herself, backed the wheelchair away from the table and proceeded towards the exit. She told the waiter not to feel badly; it was just an accident. Her husband, she whispered to those within earshot, was quite ill and under extreme stress. Heads turned in her direction from some distance away. The many who were watching the Johnsons' hasty retreat felt pity for Lurene and utter amazement at the barroom vernacular that was so completely out of place in this otherwise so refined setting. Johnson's voice was still audible all the way to the nearest bank of elevators.

Mercifully, the *maître d'* reassigned the waiter to the kitchen for the remainder of the First Sitting. Having survived a similar incident early in his own career, he was sympathetic and wanted to avoid traumatizing his young colleague.

Johnson's off-color rant was soon exaggerated exponentially as it ran the gamut of second, third, and fourth retellings throughout the inevitable grapevine. The image that emerged was one of a veritable monster from America and his poor, unfortunate wife.

Silence prevailed in Suite 1012. Lurene, still mortified, prepared RC's medicine and retired. The monster likewise managed to slump onto his bed and there, totally in denial, he fell into a drug-induced slumber, wheezing gently, for several hours.

* * *

Mark had been to Messina and Palermo on business a couple of times, but never to Catania. For Elli, it was her first visit to Sicily. Both had looked forward to a pleasant, if brief stopover on this historic island.

The excursion to view Mt. Etna was conducted under a warm, brilliant sun. Both Elli and Mark, participating in the French-language tour, thought the guide very competent in terms of her scientific and historical knowledge of the volcano's often destructive course through ancient and modern times. They bought materials to help them share the experience with their children.

Walking up hill and over some rather rugged terrain had left the Davidsons feeling a bit scruffy. They returned to the ship, which was anchored at a pier in the port, freshened up, changed clothes and dashed off by taxi for luncheon with the director and staff of the *Teatro Massimo "Vincenzo Bellini"*, Catania's well known opera house. There was enough time to meet some of the singers, musicians and dancers who regularly performed at the theater, as well as Salvatore LoCicero, the recently appointed Artistic Director. Many of the artists were familiar with Elli from her numerous appearances on television. By late afternoon, the Davidsons were back on board. They retired early following a delightful eight-course candle-light dinner for two in the Ristorante DaVinci, a cozy gourmet venue aft on deck 14.

In the crew quarters, the moon-struck lover, Pepino Maldonado, listened intently to Bobbi, who related the principal events in her busy day emphasizing, as was her way, the happy and comical side of preparing first-class meals for over three thousand passengers and crew. Pepino modestly praised his troupe and the enthusiastic applause of two grateful audiences in the ship's huge theater. They kissed and retired to their respective cabins.

CHAPTER FIVE

Thursday Morning

A sudden spate of thunderstorms clears the decks on *The Venetian's* fourth day at sea. Tomorrow's destination is Mykonos where abundant sunshine has been promised. The ship's shopping arcade is throbbing with browsers checking out the pricey merchandise. Behind the counters the sales staff anticipates a banner day from the deluge of captive consumers clutching their credit cards. The slow-moving swell of humanity touched and squeezed the choice articles on display. If they were under glass, noses left marks there as ladies of all stations scrutinized carefully the exquisite time pieces, the shimmering stones set in rings and bracelets, and the gold and platinum chains and necklaces in a variety of lengths and styles.

With few exceptions, all but the early birds were relegated to standing room only in the ship's crowded bars and cafés. Adorned from head to toe with their seasonal acquisitions, the wealthiest among them drew satisfaction from the admiration and envy of those stealing glances at them. For the knowledgeable, a virtual catalog of designers was represented among the jostling jet-setters present. In addition, many wore deep, out-of-season tans. A small fortune in botox and silicone enhanced Mother Nature's gifts. Those who were not rich enjoyed immensely the titillation of pretense. The nicotine addicts among them suffered silently under Marebella's total smoking ban in the principal public venues.

Lurene conveniently scheduled another spa treatment and massage following a lengthy workout in the well-appointed Fitness Center. The instructor in charge was a handsome Italian. Lurene, the constant tease, enlisted his assistance as she sought to perform some hand stands. Her obvious enjoyment of a virile male in close proximity was evident to others nearby. They discussed among themselves later how brazenly she flirted.

RC, a persistent dull pain in his heavily medicated gut, found his way to the card room. A variety of games filled every available table. Today, one of the ship's younger officers was assigned to monitor activity, as reports of open gambling had found their way to the Purser. While small private bets might be tolerated, high stakes games were seriously frowned upon. A quick assessment of the new reality prompted RC to wheel close to Easton, who was playing at a table for eight. He had a sizeable pile of chips in front of him. "Interested in a Big Boy's game?" Having caught Easton's ear, RC continued in a whisper, "Let's play in my room. See if some of the same guys from the other day would like to join us." He rolled his vehicle off to one side, waiting for Easton, who was definitely interested, to ease away from his present activity and to round up a few more like-minded players.

Easton gathered up his chips, settled accounts and excused himself. He had done rather well, though the sum involved was modest. He approached a few others, including a woman, who volunteered to be a dealer. They slowly assembled in Stateroom 1012. Johnson's dining table could comfortably handle as many as eight players. He had one of the men grab a couple of bottles of Prosecco from the refrigerator. Glasses appeared from a wall cabinet and everyone started out in a happy mood. They were seriously impressed by the generous size and luxurious appointments in Johnson's stateroom.

After a few losing hands of Seven-Card Stud, the Spaniard, Escamillo Cardoza, begged off and left, poorer by a couple of thousand dollars. Gianni Stavros, a Greek passenger also left shortly thereafter. Kelvin Hamrick, the burly Black football star similarly caved and departed.

Four players were left. Johnson gave a new deck of cards to Rolf Dettweiler to shuffle. Olaf Jensen, a Dane who frequented the card room, had joined the group at Easton's invitation. He also shuffled the cards. "What'll we play?" inquired the Dane. "How about no-limit Texas Hold'em?"

"OK by me." replies Dettweiler. Easton nods approval.

"Texas Hold'em it is, gents. I say the sky's the limit. If you're a Cry Baby, this is the time to leave." Johnson stared at each of his three opponents. In situations like this he often assumed the air of a rough and ready barroom brawler. "If you ain't got the balls for serious bettin', you'd better go up on deck and learn how to cha-cha-cha with that cute little dance teacher."

Easton's reaction: he cut the deck. Johnson reached over and cut them again.

Giordana Flavia, the bosomy Italian woman, early thirties, with flame-red shoulder length hair who had committed to deal, was placing two cards face down in front of each player. Dettweiler anted $2000. Jensen threw $2000 into the pot. Johnson and Easton did the same. The results of the first round had RC with the 6 of Hearts and the 10 of Spades in the hole, Easton got the A of Spades and the K of Diamonds, Jensen peeked at the Q of Spades and the 7 of Diamonds, while Dettweiler received the 3 of Clubs and the 9 of Hearts.

RC had to put his cards down momentarily to deal with a prolonged bout of coughing. His fellow card players made involuntary grimaces as the unpleasant sound filled the room. Miss Italy got Johnson a glass of water. The game continued. Johnson peeled a few bills off a hefty roll and started the betting with $2500. In turn, each of the players called, bringing the pot to $18,000.

The Flop produced the Q of Hearts, the 4 of Diamonds and the 9 of Clubs. A slight smile flickered across Easton's otherwise benign countenance. Jensen was totally emotionless. His pair of Queens was a good sign. Dettweiler, too, already had a pair, albeit lowly Nines. Johnson was unfazed. There were two more cards to come. A lot can change with two more cards. He knew from experience.

Johnson pursed his lips slightly. He adopted a deliberative mien, then threw $4000 on the table. No one flinched. Three more donations in the same amount followed. $34,000 was waiting for someone. There was palpable tension in the room. Not everyone could afford to lose the amount he had already contributed.

The Turn called for a further card to be laid on the table face up. It was the J of Hearts. Johnson covered his mouth with a handkerchief and coughed a few times. Jensen turned away. Everyone waited to see if another would drop out. Dettweiler and Jensen certainly considered it. Easton nearly wet his pants anticipating a possible A-high or K-high flush.

Johnson bet $5000. No amount of underarm deodorant could mask Easton's perspiring body. He called, looking carefully at the rapidly diminishing stash of paper money he had brought with him. Dettweiler slammed his cards on the table in disgust. The Dane was less demonstrative. With a sigh of resignation he, too, folded.

The Italian dealer, whose cleavage was a real eye-stopper for those around the table, accidently showed the card to be dealt next, a 10 of Diamonds. Johnson immediately demanded that she 'burn' the card by putting it at the bottom of the deck, and deal a fresh card. Easton protested vociferously. The 10 of Diamonds would have given him a straight flush. He was furious. Johnson was adamant. The Dane and the German agreed the rules called for another card to be dealt. Miss Italy's contribution to the 'river' the K of Clubs.

Only Easton and his nemesis remained. Easton was not optimistic. He had only a pair of Kings. He put $2000 on the table. Johnson knew he was in the driver's seat. He quietly laid out $5000, raising Easton 3K. The latter had lost a couple of games earlier when he fell for Johnson's very convincing bluffs. "I'm calling!" He asked for a pencil and paper, which Signorina Flavia handed him. Easton wrote out an IOU for $3000.

Johnson slammed his fist on the table. "Hey, buddy! This is a cash game. If you ain't got the dough, you lose anyway. But, I'm going to give you a break. I'll give you 48 hours to bring me the $3000. If you know what's good for you, you'll get it to me on time." His voice had a gruff, unforgiving and menacing quality to it. He proceeded to lay out his straight, simultaneously organizing the bills on the table into a neat pile. He conspicuously placed the signed IOU on top, while reminding Easton there were three witnesses. The showdown was anticlimactic.

"You bloody bastard! You'll get your money!" Easton rose to leave. Under his breath, still audible, however, he mumbled he'd get even somehow.

Johnson shifted his weight to sit upright in his wheelchair. In his most condescending tone, he said, "You pudgy twerp. You're a bloody phony. Your Limey accent don't fool me! I suggest you stick to checkers."

The door slammed, drowning out the vituperative deluge, as a red-faced Easton departed. The other two players followed. As Signorina Flavia passed Johnson he reached out and pinched her buttocks. She turned to slap him. As she did so he caught her hand and gave her a bundle of 10 $100 bills he had just folded. She stared at him, smiled and slipped the money in her purse prior to exiting.

Placing an elastic band around the bills he had just won, Johnson opened his briefcase and slid the bundle in a side pocket. *Not bad for a 'friendly' little game,* he thought to himself. A sharp pain in his lower back caused him to clench his teeth.

As the party broke up, occupants of the adjoining staterooms appeared in the corridor, together with a representative from the Purser's office, who arrived in response to their complaints of excessive and intolerable noise. The uniformed young officer knocked on Johnson's door and Johnson, seated in his wheelchair, opened the door slightly and growled, "What do you want?"

Mrs. Hornsby exclaimed, "You made so much noise I was unable to take my nap."

"Why don't you just turn off your hearing aid?" was Johnson's fresh retort.

Mr. Hornsby would have punched him, but thought better of attacking someone in a wheelchair. Clearly, the lower-class they usually chummed with were much better mannered and more considerate.

Ashoka Desai, the Indian, his glasses hanging on the end of his aquiline nose, said nothing. It was obvious to him that Johnson was not a person with whom one could reason.

Johnson growled, "This is the most expensive stateroom on this ship and I'll make noise if I want to." The door closed. The conversation was over. The Purser's rep timidly apologized and returned to his office. Presumably, to deal with more pleasant matters. The neighbors retreated to their quarters.

Elli and Mark spent much of the day reading and working on photos taken thus far, hoping to have an organized album ready to share with the children and with her sister Dani and Dani's husband Roland when the cruise concluded.

Lurene lunched with Herb, spent two hours with him in his cabin, then hung out in the casino for a while. While pumping five Euro pieces into the slot machines she flirted with some of the men who watched her progress and stole admiring glances at her physical attributes.

Easton, the Brit, ever on the prowl, sauntered by later, struck up a conversation, rekindling the acquaintance initiated on the darkened deck their first night at sea, and invited her to his suite for a nightcap. Bored with her lack of luck with the slots, she gladly accepted. While mixing a couple of drinks, he suggestively fondled one of his Cuban specials. Although she had never studied Psychology 101, Lurene instinctively understood Freudian symbols. They proceeded to indulge in the twin boons of fermented grapes and carnal congress. Easton had no idea Lurene was Mrs. Robert Chamberlain Johnson.

Thursday Afternoon

The pizza did not digest without a struggle. Alone again, Johnson's body aches all over. His head is splitting, His mood is dark. The long months in a wheelchair have taken their toll in more ways than he expected. Old acquaintances avoid him. Conversations with employees, family, and business associates always seem abrupt, unduly brief. Johnson is lonely, feels imprisoned. He manages to leave his room and navigate to a section of open deck aft where dedicated walkers make their rounds, some even jog. It's warm and breezy. For a while he stops and stares, mesmerized by the constant movement of the undulating waves. After a few minutes, a tired and unhappy Johnson abandons the idea and returns to his suite.

During his absence the room has been made up by the steward. One of the towels, folded neatly to resemble a bunny rabbit, was on the bathroom counter top, rather than being hung on a rod to the side where it had been the preceding day. For some reason too obscure for the sane to comprehend, Johnson immediately rang for the steward, who came within two minutes.

Gustavo's solicitous smile was pounded into oblivion without warning by a barrage of invective laced with curses and punctuated by a threatening flailing of arms. The gist of the one-sided attack had something to do with an intentional plot, a conspiracy, to disturb Johnson's peace of mind by placing objects in the cabin in places where they were hard to find or impossible for an invalid to reach. Gustavo had encountered eccentric types before in his cruising career, but never anyone as volatile, as malicious and mean as Johnson. The poor steward was embarrassed by the commotion that soon involved passengers from neighboring cabins. Someone had called his supervisor, Suzanna. She first politely dispersed the onlookers and asked Gustavo to return to his station after he had explained the problem to her. She sought to assuage Johnson, who, turning his back to her, rolled his wheelchair onto the balcony. Overlooking his rudeness, she attempted to diffuse the situation and appease the disgruntled passenger. Johnson talked to the wind, addressed some unintelligible statements to the waves below. Suzanna chided him for claiming that Gustavo, one of the most frequently complimented stewards on the ship, had lied and was intentionally upsetting him.

"I've heard a lot about you, Mr. Johnson. I know more about you than you think. You have no right to treat Gustavo like a mendacious tramp. Your tirade in the restaurant last night has come to our attention. I am amazed that a single determined individual could disrupt the calm of an entire ship." Her voice began to rise perceptibly. Her face was a study in scorn. Thoughts of being diplomatic melted away in the heat of the moment. Before her was the man who had abandoned her dear friend's mother and had never showed any interest in his own child.

"Shut up and get out! You have no business talking to me this way. What the hell are you getting at anyway?" Johnson's blood pressure was surging upwards.

"Your daughter, named after you, works on this ship. She is my roommate. How someone so sweet and loving could have a father like you is incomprehensible." Suzanna blurted out the accusation without reflecting on the possible consequences and repercussions.

"Get out!" Johnson had the gaze of a bitter old man with galloping paranoia. He shouted again, "Get out! Get out!" His face was livid with anger... and confusion. An uncomfortable memory he had long since banished to the furthermost recesses of his mind had suddenly returned. He began to cough roughly.

The door was now slightly ajar. Suzanna was about to beat a quick retreat, realizing her job might be in jeopardy. She couldn't resist adding, "Her name is Roberta Johnson. We call her Bobbi. She checks on the desserts every night in the main dining room. You can usually see her near the front. A beautiful young lady a little over five feet tall." A defiant chin jutted out. A threat followed. "If you hurt her you will pay dearly!" The cabin door slammed shut as Suzanna left, agitated and trembling slightly. Two couples in the hallway, who had overheard the tail end of the conversation, turned and looked at her until she reached the corner leading to the stairwell. Gustavo, standing nearby in another cabin he was cleaning, was startled to hear Suzanna's threatening words.

Inside the luxury suite, Johnson threw a handy glass onto the floor, smashing it. He let out a stream of foul language. He strained to vacate his wheelchair, hobbled into the bathroom and spent a long time looking into the mirror. The image staring back was that of an old man, reddened with rage, ugly, grimacing, throbbing with pain. The eyes were jaundiced. His once vibrant skin and rosy complexion was sallow; crow's feet and hollow cheeks stared back. Sharp jabs in his lower back were more intense than earlier. He found some medicine in his briefcase, took two large tablets and washed them down with water. His pulse was surging and he felt his blood pressure rising further.

Twenty minutes later, the pain had subsided somewhat. Still, he knew from his doctor's prognosis the gravity of his situation. Metastasis was underway. His malignancy was spreading from one organ to another. He had been thinking, thinking about the past, thinking about the future. For him, the future was now. Sliding back into his wheelchair, he left his suite once more and managed to get down to Deck 5, where the Communications Center was located. He filled out a form and sent an urgent cable to Peachtree Investigators in Atlanta.

Later that afternoon, Suzanna, Bobbi and Pepino were chatting over coffee and pastry in a staff lounge. In the course of the conversation, Suzanna told of her confrontation with Mr. Johnson and the explosive exchange that took place. Bobbi was aghast. She didn't want her friend to expose herself to possible termination because of her. Bobbi had never known her father. To have strong feelings for him, to defend him was unnatural. Bobbi hugged Suzanna. She did not want her best friend to jeopardize her position on her account. Pepino, too, was concerned. And he was upset, even angry that this mean old man could upset his sweetheart and her friend. They decided mutually to let the matter rest and hoped it would not develop into a more serious issue. Bobbi, when asked if she would like to meet her biological father, was hesitant, but offered that she might seek him out before the ship docked again in Barcelona. In the meantime, she was simply too busy. Pepino, stifling his anger, voiced no comment.

CHAPTER SIX

Friday Morning

Johnson, arising early after a sleepless night, is first in the bathroom and notices blood in his urine again. This time it's a weak, dark-red stream. His jaw is clenched. Unusually grumpy, he complains constantly to Lurene, berating her for real and imagined lapses in attention. Room Service delivers breakfast. Lurene eats a half piece of toast and washes it down with her coffee. At the first opportunity she dashes off to the Fitness Center in her designer warm-up suit. Determined to stay out of her husband's way while he is so irritable, Lurene plans a brief workout, some touring on Mykonos, and after her return has a string of shipboard activities planned. On a ship this large, it's relatively easy to steer clear of those you prefer to avoid.

Johnson's body aches. A dull pain in his lower abdomen is growing stronger. His mood is dark. His head is splitting. He is left to his own devices. He is feeling lonely. Every movement is accompanied by considerable physical discomfort. His breakfast sits half finished on the table. A fit of coughing leaves him struggling for air. He feels helpless. His physical condition is deteriorating at a much more rapid pace than Doc Tribble had forecast.

Lurene manages to leave on the last tender going to the island. Johnson watches her leave from his balcony retreat. Finishing his morning toilet with difficulty (dressing himself is an ordeal), a particularly dour Johnson, alarmed by the yellowish tint of his skin, heads for the elevator bank nearest to his stateroom and drops down to the deck with the card rooms, the library and other game facilities. His reputation has preceded him and, if he were not so agitated, he would have found the myriad excuses for not wanting to play cards with him humorous. His disappointment in failing to find something to distract his consciousness of physical pain shows in his contorted facial expression. He decides to return to his suite. The other occupants on his elevator immediately become aware of his dwindling interest in personal hygiene.

Friday Afternoon

The merchants of Mykonos tallied the take from *The Venetian's* passengers. It had been a good morning. Two other cruise ships were anchored a few hundred meters off the landing dock. More travelers, more money. This was definitely going to be a good day for local vendors.

In order to allow for nearly a day and a half in Istanbul, the next port of call, it was important to head north by early afternoon. While many passengers busied themselves looking at the digital photos taken while ashore, others proudly showed their purchases to spouses and fellow passengers. A few were already packing their treasures away, looking forward to sharing their loot with friends back home.

The Davidsons were hosting an ice cream social in the ship's youth lounge and game room. It was real *gelato*, twenty different flavors of it. A few cartoons, some in English, others in French, Spanish, Italian, German and Turkish were shown on two large-screen TVs. Word had spread that Mrs. Davidson was a singer who had appeared on European TV screens on numerous occasions. Consequently, she was bombarded with requests for an autograph. Mark, his lovely wife's greatest fan, was perfectly happy to serve generous scoops of *gelato* as her silent partner. He responded to several challenges to play table tennis or one of the computer games available. Whether he was truly inept and uncoordinated or merely playing the gracious host may never be known, nevertheless, he succumbed in every contest, but never lost his smile or good humor.

Later, outside on Deck 12, he was soundly beaten in shuffleboard and mini-golf by his vivacious and skillful spouse.

Friday Evening

Lurene, attempting to show concern for her husband, was overly solicitous as she pleaded her case for skipping the first dinner sitting so that she might attend a fashion show in the Grand Salon. She asked repeatedly if he could manage to get to the restaurant unaided. When he insisted it would not be a problem and sent her off with an admonishment not to get carried away with her credit card, she quickly adopted an attitude of gratitude and agreed to exercise prudence.

For his part, Johnson was glad to be free. Suzanna's mention of Bobbi's regular appearances to chat with diners towards the end of the sitting had aroused his curiosity. He couldn't explain why after more than a quarter century of total indifference and neglect he should suddenly want to see his first offspring. But he did.

He waited until a few minutes before the Second Sitting to open the cabin door. His wheelchair rolled smoothly down the corridor. He found himself at the elevator bank just as the door on the elevator nearest to him opened wide in welcome. Upon reaching the dining room, he found diners were already filling their appointed seats in an orderly fashion. Cruising and healthy appetites seemed synonymous. By coincidence, the space he usually occupied at the First Sitting happened to be available. Johnson slid silently into the unoccupied place, merely nodding to acknowledge the obligatory greetings from his new table mates. Familiar with his misadventure through scuttlebutt shared with earlier diners, Johnson's unexpected arrival caused a few eyebrows to arch. They were obviously a tolerant bunch and set about ignoring him without being purposely offensive. Consensus opinion: Johnson was weird. His wife, a subject of numerous rumors, a little wild.

He picked at the beef dish he had chosen, after passing on the appetizers and skipping the salad. Oblivious to the multiple conversations ricocheting across the table, he kept staring at the area near the front of the the dining room. Suddenly, there she was. Rather petite, with a huge, infectious smile, lovely dark hair in a bun beneath her chef's cap, and beautiful dark eyes. Each night she worked a different section of the room. She was wearing her white apron. She moved smoothly from guest to guest, table to table, greeting diners, exchanging small talk and inquiring about the food, its quality, quantity, variety, presentation, and freshness. Johnson could not follow the conversations. His eyes were noticeably wide. He was absolutely mesmerized. She was the spitting image of her mother. A tear formed in his eye as Seraphina's image materialized in his consciousness. Clearly, Bobbi's visits had become an important and much anticipated feature of the evening meal. She radiated genuine charm and warmth. Johnson couldn't take his eyes off her. A member of the wait staff approached and whispered something in her ear. She finished talking to a young couple at the table she was visiting, excused herself and left for the galley, where she was needed.

Without a word, Johnson backed away from the table and his unfinished meal. Then he headed noiselessly for the exit. An elevator was waiting. He returned to his luxury suite. At first he failed to notice that he had rolled over an envelope lying on the floor just inside the door. Spotting it, he leaned over and scooped it up. It was a cablegram from the Communications Center.

TO: R.C. JOHNSON, ABOARD THE VENETIAN, MAREBELLA LINES

ROUTING: ATLANTA-PARIS-ROME-ATHENS

CLASSIFICATION: URGENT PERSONAL

RE: INVESTIGATION REQUEST MS R. JOHNSON

BIRTH/AGE VERIFIED STOP CERTIFICATE STATES MOTHER S.M. FATHER R.C.J. STOP RAISED CATHOLIC ORPHANAGE SISTERS OF CHARITY MANILA STOP EXEMPLARY STUDENT STOP CULINARY SCHOOL

GRAD STOP UNMARRIED STOP CURRENT
EMPLOYMENT MAREBELLA LINES STOP ALL
PERSONAL REFERENCES EXCEPTIONALLY POSITIVE
STOP SUBJECT AWARE BIRTH CIRCUMSTANCES STOP
PLEASE ADVISE RE FURTHER NEEDS STOP INVOICE
MAILED YOUR OFFICE STOP

MORTON, PEACHTREE INVESTIGATORS

* * *

His stomach was upset. He felt like vomiting. His illness was not to blame. A wave of self revulsion had pummeled his solar plexis and left his gut in knots. Fortunately, Lurene was still occupied with the other fashion-conscious females who were viewing the latest styles, oohing and aahing as the models strutted their stuff. Pulling himself up out of the wheelchair, Johnson used a cane to help him into the bathroom. A bilious taste formed in his mouth. He rinsed it with a small quantity of water. The mirror before him told no lies. He was old looking, terribly old looking for a man in his fifties. Many months in a wheelchair had left him pudgy and soft. His face was wrinkled and pasty. His hair was prematurely gray and thinning. There was nothing to admire about the exterior of the figure staring deeply into the silvered glass. Ugly is ugly, even when it's your own image.

His eyes closed involuntarily. In his mind he strained to call up a picture of the handsome, dashing young man that had once inhabited his jaundiced skin. There he was. He still had those small-town American virtues. He was honest and likeable. A buddy who was dating a local girl from the suburbs surrounding their base outside Manila introduced him to Seraphina. She was the most beautiful girl at the Non-Com Club's weekly dances. She floated on air. She was vivacious and full of charm. They became friends and steady dancing partners. Johnson was the envy of every red-blooded male on the base. He took a lot of ribbing. Most of

it with crude sexual innuendo attached. His tour was coming to its conclusion. The future looked bright. His father wanted him to return to
Georgia to help in the family construction business. Johnson remembered proposing one night at dinner in a fancy restaurant. Not long
afterwards, Johnson, promoted to Sergeant, pressured Seraphina to have
sex with him. She became pregnant about the time he was given early
reassignment to a base in Southern California. He promised to send for
her.

While waiting for discharge in San Diego, Johnson's new-found buddies, likewise ambivalent about returning to their hometowns, introduced
him to the bars and clubs where he soon indulged himself in booze and
easy women. Three-day passes made extended trips to Vegas and Tijuana
regular happenings. A self indulgent Robert Chamberlain Johnson, free
of familial and military constraints, established a reputation for both his
ability to handle alcohol and his appetite for the opposite sex. A few trips
to sick call seemed to clear up temporary problems stemming from lackadaisical use of contraceptives.

Once back home, he had fewer opportunities to satisfy his wild crav-
ings. Learning the ropes in the construction business came without strain.
His father had convinced him to dump Seraphina. Johnson married a
local girl. They had twin daughters. Two years later his wife and children
were killed in an accident with a drunken teenager. A year after burying
his family, Johnson married Mai Ling, a Chinese woman, who had
moved to Atlanta from San Francisco. Their son, Herb, was a good-looking boy with both Caucasian and Asian features. Ovarian cancer claimed
her life when Herb was just eleven. The loss of his second wife was devastating. Johnson devoted himself to his business interests. Money
became his new obsession and his wealth grew rapidly. He sent Herb to a
private prep school and saw him mainly during long holidays. Needless
to say, a father-son bond never developed.

When Herb was 14, Johnson had an affair with Lurene, a waitress at
a small eatery where he tended to go for lunch. Despite a substantial disparity in their ages they married. It was a mutually satisfying, loving

relationship at first. He was not, however, completely faithful. Respect for one another gradually deteriorated. Frequent arguments, recriminatory diatribes and distrust contributed to the evolution of a so-called 'open' relationship. Nevertheless, the couple lived together in relative peace. Following Johnson's 'accident', Lurene reluctantly became a virtual 24/7 nurse, an activity for which she expected an eventual payoff.

The irksome pain and internal discomfort, the occasional difficulty urinating, some intestinal problems, lesions on his skin, diabetes, an endless list of irritating maladies were attributed initially to the 'accident' and the months thereafter requiring a long period of bed rest, then confinement to a wheelchair. Only when the usual remedies failed to correct or ameliorate the conditions he experienced, was it discovered by his doctor, that improperly treated infections from unprotected sexual activity decades earlier had lain dormant for years, until now, in an advanced and irreversible stage, they were marching relentlessly towards their inexorable conclusion: death. Dr. Tribble could only promise to provide medications that would alleviate the worst symptoms. A cure was not available.

To Lurene's dismay, her husband abruptly terminated his amorous interest in her. She suspected infidelity. She was hurt. Actually, it was a decidedly rare unselfish act on Johnson's part, for he simply could not bring himself to knowingly infect her with syphilis. Without ever revealing his situation, he arranged for Lurene to have a thorough physical examination under the ruse of possibly allowing her to pursue some plastic surgery she had suggested. She was disease free. Eventually she gave up the idea of improving or augmenting her already generous attributes.

Assiduous reading of body language at home and at work, piecing together snatches of conversation here and there, decoding subtle messages in a look or facial expression, and other more blatant signs cumulatively revealed to Johnson the unspoken truth about family and associates, namely that his mortality was foremost in their thoughts. RC, an appellation Johnson had always associated with acceptance, even endearment, was now inherently connected to the wish for his hasty demise. This knowledge incessantly churned about in a mind warped by dark instinct and a disease that affected body and soul.

The cruise had been hinted at by Lurene on numerous occasions. Johnson quashed the notion out of hand each time. Then, one day, in a murky mood, Johnson had a vision. A cruise became an integral part of a plan of vengeance. He would arrange for many people to be considered suspects in a crime of violence against himself.

Tonight, fate had revealed to him a new and unexpected element. With extreme concentration, Johnson conjured up the image of the beautiful young woman, Bobbi, his namesake, who so closely resembled her mother. For a moment, he banished his previous thoughts and, uncharacteristically crossing himself, he vowed to honor this remarkable person, to give her what he had denied her mother.

He reached his wheelchair with considerable effort. Dull pains throbbed ominously in his abdomen and in the small of his back. He coughed. He sat down holding two documents he had retrieved from a hidden pocket inside his briefcase. While Lurene was frolicking, oblivious to the hour, several decks below, Johnson wrote feverishly in both documents. One his diary; the other a legal form with numerous blank spaces in which he made hand-written entries. When he had finished his work, he replaced them in the briefcase, took a few vari-colored capsules and washed them down with a glass of Perrier, before depositing his weary shell on the bed, soon to begin another fitful night.

CHAPTER SEVEN

Saturday Morning

Seminars begun the previous day by several distinguished scholars, continued to prepare interested passengers for their overnight stay in Istanbul. Fascinating lectures about the history of this great city and of Turkey and the colorful culture of its current inhabitants were conducted in several venues to full audiences. Most passengers would tour today, return to the ship over night, then go ashore the following day for more adventure.

Lurene had overslept. She wolfed her toast, slurped a cup of yoghurt and took a gulp or two of her coffee before rushing down to Deck 6 to attend a presentation on Islamic architecture with a couple of female acquaintances. Later they would join a large group of passengers going ashore to explore Istanbul's mosques, palaces, bridges and exciting shopping bazaars. RC saw the bus full of passengers pull away. He rolled over to the closet where he kept his briefcase. After extracting two bundles of papers he moved near the sliding glass door to the balcony to catch the strong natural light streaming down from a warm and friendly sun.

The first bundle consisted of entries to his diary made during the first four days of the cruise. He read them hastily, then placed them in a heavy duty brown envelope, before sealing it with some plastic tape. The envelope was pre-addressed to his bank and a cover letter directed the safe deposit box clerk to place them in his box together with similar materials he had deposited during the preceding 16 months. That done, Johnson began thumbing through the second document.

Fastened together as a unit in the upper left hand corner were over a dozen pages. They had been typewritten and prepared in conformity with the customary legal protocol for a last will and testament. A number of blank spaces had been left. These had been filled late the evening before in Johnson's neatest hand. He checked them carefully, appending a note which he had also written in longhand.

In response to a knock on the door, Johnson bellowed, "Come in!" The Purser and three members of the ship's crew, two stewards and a young lady from the Travel Desk, entered the suite. Johnson had arranged chairs for them at a table in the suite's lounge area. He greeted them and asked them to have a seat. The Purser was an authorized Notary official. Johnson explained that he wished to have his signature and initials on a legal document witnessed and notarized. The foursome nodded signaling their comprehension and willingness to participate. Johnson went through the document page by page, initialing his entries and obtaining the necessary witness signatures on each page. When they were finished, the Purser embossed his official seal on the final page and applied his personal stamp beside the signatures entered there.

Johnson thanked them and handed the stewards and the young lady from the Travel Desk small envelopes. Each had a €50 bill enclosed. He handed the Purser a check for $100, indicating it was for the Marebella Seamen's Relief Fund. The foursome thanked Johnson and departed. This sheaf of papers was inserted in its own brown envelope together with a cover letter addressed to Johnson's Atlanta lawyers and thoroughly sealed in a sturdy plastic envelope with the aid of waterproof tape.

Next, Johnson rang for Gustavo. He exaggerated feigned feelings of contrition and apologized profusely for the incident he had caused and asked if Gustavo would be going ashore in the afternoon hours. The response was affirmative. Gustavo was scheduled to be off duty for much of the rest of the day and had received clearance to leave the ship temporarily for some sight-seeing and personal shopping. Johnson arranged for his cabin steward to take the two envelopes with him and to send them by airmail to the United States. He gave him €100, and impressed on him the importance of careful handling. A sensation of great physical and mental relief came over Johnson. He took a sleeping pill and lay down on the bed to take a nap. In spite of a dull pain between his shoulder blades, the drug allowed him to sleep in relative peace.

Saturday Afternoon

The Venetian, proud and white, a true maritime gem, glistened in the warm sunshine as it lay moored all day at a choice pier on Istanbul's Golden Horn. Record numbers of passengers had opted to go ashore. Most participated in one or more of the several excursions planned for Turkey's largest city and its environs. Most were actually surprised to learn that Istanbul with its nearly 12 million inhabitants was considered the world's fourth largest city. Known earlier as Byzantium and Constantinople, the city, uniquely straddling two continents, boasts a rich history and a diverse and complex citizenry. Whether in their respective cabins, in the hallways, the large public rooms, or waiting impatiently in line for the beginning of the First Sitting for the evening meal, everyone was flush with sunburnt faces and an unlimited number of anecdotes relating to their escapades of the day. Some itineraries included many of the city's striking mosques. All told there are over 2500 mosques. Predominant among them: the Suleimanye and the Hagia Sophia. Topkapi Palace, familiar to many Americans as the site of a movie jewelry heist, was visited by hordes of tourists in the course of the day. While it was generally hot and humid, the high temperatures and glaring sun were insufficient to deter the dedicated shoppers who were well represented on the ship's manifest. The Grand Bazaar and the Mahmutpaşa Bazaar, as well as the Cevahir Mall did substantial business. The appeal of the great museums and architectural splendors of ancient and modern Istanbul left an indelible impression on all who went ashore.

Numerous conversations revolved around the fare at traditional Turkish restaurants, the *kebaps, the köfteler* (meatballs), the *sarma ve dol-malar* (stuffed vegetables), the *pilafs,* the *baklava* and other delicious pastries made from figs, coconut, sesame and poppy seeds or the marvelous dishes at some of the historic seafood venues. Calories had definitely been consumed and burned. Yet, the diners' appetites were huge. The mood was one of happiness and anticipation.

Robert C. Johnson chose to have Room Service deliver his dinner, but he insisted that Lurene go ahead and occupy their table. This, too, was to be a 'dress-up night' marking the beginning of the second half of the trip, and he knew she would be miserable if she couldn't show off some of the clothes she had purchased especially for the cruise. As she took a last look in the mirror, while reminding him to take his medicine, she thought he seemed unusually distant, lost in thought. Her observation was correct. Johnson, however, was also experiencing incredible physical pain. As soon as Lurene had left, he obtained from his briefcase a syringe and an ampule containing an unmarked fluid. This he injected, sat back, and took a deep breath.

While the ship had been anchored the previous day in Mykonos, a report circulated that a popular junior ship's officer, a Filipino, learned his family was seriously injured in a house fire in a small town in southern Luzon. The Captain had made arrangements for a charter helicopter flight to Athens, from where the officer was flown via Bangkok to Manila. Almost immediately a benefit concert had been arranged for this evening. Word got out that Alicia Baranova, a young Byelorussian ballerina, recently engaged by the *Opéra Comique* in Paris and now enjoying her honeymoon with her French husband, a software developer, would perform. Additionally, Michèlle Davidson, whom many knew from her appearances on European television screens, would sing opera and operetta favorites with an as yet unnamed male passenger. Members of the ship's own troupe of entertainers were also preparing to take part in what was shaping up to be a truly gala evening.

A veritable stream of passengers flooded the theater, claiming most of the seats in minutes. Bobbi, sitting in an end seat in the back so that she could depart quietly after Pepino had performed, scanned the freshly printed program to see exactly when he would appear on stage. Unfortunately, not until about mid-way through. She tried to relax. The seats were soon filled and even the stairs were jammed. Standees were so plentiful that most of the entrances were virtually blocked.

A chorus from the ship's complement of singers and dancers led off with a tribute to show business. A popular song of the day was well received, particularly by the younger members of the audience. Juggling, acrobatics, an accordionist, a Greek folk dance, a comedy routine based on linguistic differences and several other short acts followed in rapid order. The Master of Ceremonies then announced that Mlle Baranova would dance a *pas de deux* from the ballet *Giselle* with Señor Pepino Maldonado, the *Venetian's* Entertainment Director. A recording of Adolphe Adam's delightful score set the scene. There would be no idyllic peasant backdrop or props, no assisting *corps de ballet*. The wardrobe mistress, however, did have two appropriate costumes and both dancers had their ballet shoes.

Pepino, who played the piano and the guitar, had begun his artistic career at an early age studying classical ballet. He was strikingly handsome, a magnificent, virile, manly Albrecht, as he entered the stage. His well proportioned body and lithe, athletic movement helped establish his character. The audience watched breathlessly, even those who were unaccustomed to this form of dance, as he defied gravity, leaping effortlessly and landing like a leaf in a gentle breeze.

Exquisitely feminine, grace and beauty personified, Mlle Baranova displayed extraordinary technique as she pirouetted flawlessly across the stage. Only the most experienced critic might have noticed that more than the two hours of practice they had been afforded might have lent added polish to their coordinated movements on stage. The ballerina's near perfect facial expressions and hand and arm movements lent a superb lyrical quality to the duet that endeared her instantly to the audience. Pepino proved himself a generous and stalwart partner. The standing ovation was well deserved. Bobbi was intensely proud, even a bit jealous. Pepino, seeing her at the rear of the auditorium, blew her a kiss. While many women in the audience thought, even hoped, it might have been intended for them, others, witnessing Bobbi's blown kiss to Pepino, sensed a genuine romance afoot among the ship's staff.

Following the ballet sequence, a uniformed Marebella officer made a brief appearance on behalf of his colleague, requesting donations to a fund that would help cover the extensive rehabilitation costs for his wife and children. All had survived the accident, but faced a long period of recuperation. Containers were passed about the audience for several minutes. An additional collection point would be available at the Purser's desk, it was announced.

Elli had found enough music in the form of CD's and tapes in the ship's resource center to enable her to sing a few songs she thought the audience might enjoy. Frederic Washington, an African-American singer, who had just completed a year-long internship with the *Bayerischer Staatsoper* in Munich, was enjoying a holiday with his parents. He volunteered to participate and promptly teamed up with Elli for three duets. The drinking song from the first act of Verdi's *Traviata* was their initial offering. The predominantly Italian audience only stopped clapping, when Elli introduced their second number, a duet from Johann Strauss' *Eine Nacht in Venedig (A Night in Venice)*.

From the same operetta Washington sung to great applause Caramello's aria "*Oh, how magnificent to see all the charming ladies*", the so-called 'Lagoon Waltz'. His rich baritone was perfect for the Duke's aria "*Being faithful – that's not my thing*". From Strauss' *Fledermaus* Elli sang Adele's Second Act defense of her acting credentials. She later returned as Rosalinde singing the famous *csárdás* "*Klänge der Heimat…*", attempting to convince all that her Hungarian incognito was genuine. The audience wanted more, but the bell for the Second Sitting sounded and the house lights went up. From every point of view the benefit was a resounding success. Mark Davidson rushed backstage to congratulate his wife and the other performers.

CHAPTER EIGHT

Saturday Evening

As evening fell and passengers headed either to the theater for the benefit gala or to the main restaurant for the Captain's Dinner, RC held a cool, damp towel wrapped around some ice cubes against his forehead where a fierce migraine was forcing him to cancel plans to attend the feature event of the evening. As usual, Lurene mixed his medicinal cocktail, secretly doubling the sedative she added.

At the entrance to the darkened dining hall the *maître d'* and his assistants and members of the wait staff guided diners the length of the lanes on either side of the large room. When everyone had crowded in, a battery of subdued lights suddenly shone down a long row of cloth covered tables dissecting the dining room into equal halves. On the tables were colorful assemblages of fruit and vegetables, huge, gleaming ice sculptures and voluptuous floral displays. At the front of the restaurant festive flags surrounded the Italian tricolor. A chorus of ship's employees, accompanied by mandolins, guitars, accordions and trumpets, sang a song of joy and welcome. The diners, to put it mildly, were ecstatic in their spontaneous response. Battery-operated candles at every table were illuminated. The guests were invited to take their seats. *Spumante* was served to all who wanted it. Soon thereafter, orders taken, waiters streamed in with trays covered with the elegant and tasteful entrées of the evening. The Captain spoke a few words of welcome and introduced key members of his staff. He took the occasion to announce the promotion of Roberta Johnson to Assistant Chef-in-Charge. A huge round of applause followed. To claim the meal was sumptuous and unforgettable would have been an understatement. As soon as the last diner had departed, staff hurried to prepare for a repeat performance at the Second Sitting.

Solicitous inquiries about her husband, allowed Lurene, who was dining without him, to apologize again for RC's disruption of dinner four nights before. She ate every course offered and sampled three different wines.

Sunday

Armed with tips from fellow passengers, an energetic army of dedicated tourists went forth once again to savour the delights of the Turkish empire. Knowing where the best bargains could be had motivated the shopaholics. Culinary specialities at the city's finest restaurants became a goal for a host of travelers. Photographers had a beautiful day with ideal light. Temperatures soared, but did not dismay those who intended to make the most of this extended visit in a city with centuries of historic importance and many stories to tell.

By late afternoon the tourists were once again ensconced on their luxury liner. As the sun set to the west with a dazzling display of color, *The Venetian* was heading through the Dardanelles. Mother Nature had showered affection, mild breezes and abundant sunshine on the *Marebella* flagship, its stalwart crew and appreciative passengers for seven days. Now she had a surprise in store. The shipboard closed circuit channel brought the unwelcome news that a mass of frigid air would cross the ship's path during the night bringing showers, wind and dense fog. The forecast for the following day was, once again, for idyllic cruising conditions.

As Johnson was switching the TV off, he heard knocking at the door. Gustavo stopped briefly to say that he had mailed the two packages. He found Johnson's meek response, a quiet, distant "Thank you" somewhat baffling.

Guilt feelings were causing Gustavo distress. He had told a lie. His shore leave had been cancelled at the last minute due to an unscheduled safety seminar he was required to attend. He was promised time off in Valletta, Malta instead and planned to post the materials there. Because he was afraid that someone as rich and influential as Johnson might cause him difficulties on the job, he had decided to tell a 'good' lie. No harm done, he thought. The packages would be on their way just two days later than promised.

Feeling rather weak and unwell, Johnson lay doubled up on top of the bed to relax for a few moments. He soon dozed off. While he was sleeping Lurene stopped by, peeked in, and, finding him resting, took her checkbook out of a drawer in the kitchen and left quietly. Easton was waiting for her down the hall. He had since learned she was Johnson's wife. Also that Johnson hadn't had sex with her for months.

A check for $250 passed from Lurene's hand to the donation box in the Main Lounge. She had been touched by the tragedy visited upon the crew member. After a few drinks in two of the ship's bars, Lurene and her companion repaired to his cabin, where they remained for about an hour.

Young Herb, in the meantime, had met three American coeds cruising to cap a year of French study in Aix-en-Provence. One in particular had succumbed to his advances. They celebrated common interests in his cabin after allowing several slot machines to devour with impunity $150 in quarters. The absence of joy in the casino was duly compensated for between the sheets bearing the handsomely embroidered *Marebella* logo.

Monday, Early Morning

The unseasonably lower temperatures blowing down from the north and the warm waters combined to produce a moist fog pierced intermittently by wind-blown showers. Johnson awoke to near total darkness. The drapes covering the sliding glass door to the balcony were open. Still, little light came in. The moon was obscured by thick, fast-moving clouds. He slipped with difficulty into his wheelchair, sat quietly for a few minutes immersed in thoughts, mostly about himself, his past and what lay ahead. His body was wracked with pain. His parched throat emitted an involuntary moan. He rolled first to the bathroom. He felt the urge to urinate. He could not. His breathing was noticeably heavy. Next he reached into a compartment in his briefcase and extracted two small injectable vials containing a cloudy liquid. He held them in his left hand. He appeared to be meditating, collecting thoughts. It was unlike him to pray.

A loud knock at the door interrupted his train of thought. He managed to roll over and grab the handle, opening the door a crack. Easton, having left Lurene at one of the bars, had excused himself for a bathroom break. A raspy-voiced Johnson growled "You again! What the hell do you want?"

Easton, tall, dark and inconsequential, edged into the room. "Say, look Guv'nor." Easton was trying to strike a chummy attitude. "I'm having some money sent to me. Won't come until we get to Barcelona. I just wanted you to know I honor my debts. Sorry, it'll be a bit late."

Although the I.O.U. was totally alien to his current thoughts, Johnson instinctively switched gears. With energy summoned up from the depths of his being, he roared, "You bastard! I said I wanted it now, not after the ship reaches its final port."

"Look, I'm sorry, but that's the soonest my banker could wire it to me. Be glad you're going to get it at all."

Anger, and an innate dislike of the foppy Easton, got the better of Johnson, whose reflective mood had been rudely intruded upon. "You're a damn fraud!" Johnson's voice was now so loud, that Mrs. Hornsby pounded on the wall between her cabin and Johnson's. The knock was ignored. "Get out! Get out!" Johnson looked almost like he was about to emerge from his wheelchair to attack Easton, who backed out of the cabin, then, head bowed forward, slinked away in the direction of the aft staircase and elevator bank. The Hornsbys had recognized the voices and, while they could not make out exactly what was said, realized a nasty scene had disturbed their sleep.

The intrusion sapped Johnson's waning energy. His brain felt like it was afire. He rolled to the sliding glass door. In his lap were the two vials. His gaze was temporarily transfixed as he watched the tiny droplets of mist on the glass combine to form larger drops that slid noiselessly downward until they eventually became a thin pool on the floor of the balcony. Like life's experiences he thought. They accumulate, then rush faster and faster to an ignominious conclusion, finally mingling with the lives of those who have gone on before. He remembered how Mai Ling, who knew she was about to die, had talked about joining her ancestors.

Johnson recalled an old sergeant in his Marine outfit who frequently shared sage tidbits from his years studying humankind. Once he had said that men's minds dealt primarily with three topics: death, taxes and sex; and not necessarily in that order. Rummaging mentally through his teens and twenties, Johnson knew sex had been foremost in his thoughts then. As a businessman, tax issues that constantly threatened to suffocate his enterprises and overwhelm him in a maelstrom of paper and regulations had dominated. Now it was death's turn.

Having denied God, there was no place for thoughts of an afterlife in Johnson's view of human existence. Not that he had ever given it much weight in his infrequent reflections on the meaning of his life. Death was forever. It was darkness without end. What would it be like, he wondered? Would it come softly, painlessly? Would he simply stop breathing; enter a state of eternal sleep? He knew his bodily functions were shutting down. Would the end bring prolonged unbearable pain?

There was little wind noise outside his suite. The mist fell silently. The sea below was placid, passive, parting peacefully before the prow of the majestic *Venetian*. Johnson was alone. There would be no one at his side in his final moments. Little wonder, for he had rebuffed and rejected those who might have offered comforting words, even love. He wiped away a tear. The *Morphquell* was already taking effect. Numbness began to cloud his mind.

A long, silent pause ensued. Doc Tribble had said the *Morphquel* should be reserved for a circumstance where the other medications he had prescribed were no longer effective. He had said one vial would probably control the pain. Johnson had injected both into his right thigh. Finally, he opened the balcony door with some effort, and sat there in a kind of trance. Visibility was zero. Mini white-caps slapped silently against the white hull. Seemingly summoning strength, a determined look on his face, RC propelled his vehicle across the threshold. Gravity took the wheelchair to the railing. He inhaled the damp air. A veil of refreshing fog caressed his fevered brow, bringing a sensation of relief. Malaise and exhaustion ruled. He could just barely make out the waves below. The fog was cooling, comforting. The wind drowned out all the usual sounds. *The Venetian's* fog horn sounded the traditional warning.

* * *

Seeing that it was well after 2:00 in the morning, Lurene, who had been a popular customer in several of the ship's drinking spots and had finally left Easton in his cabin, was now a bit wobbly, having partaken of an additional couple of nightcaps with Herb, whom she had run into in the Grand Salon and who was now tagging along. She wanted to check on her husband. Herb stayed a few feet behind, ready to beat a hasty retreat, should his father be up and about. Lurene entered the suite on tiptoe. RC was not in bed, nor was he in the bathroom or sitting in the lounge area. The sliding glass door was open. She went out onto the balcony. Johnson was not there either, but... his wheelchair, tipped over on its side, was lying empty next to the railing.

"Oh my God! Oh, no!" Half in tears, filled with apprehension, Lurene, suddenly sober, ran into the hall and motioned for Herb to come quickly. They both surveyed the scene. Lurene continued, "Oh, God. Do you think he fell overboard? He couldn't really go far without the wheel-chair."

"Jesus! I don't know what to say. Was he suicidal? Do you think....? Crap! I'm gettin' outta here."

Lurene went back out on the balcony. She was dumbfounded. Herb, meanwhile, poked around in the closet, found his father's briefcase, saw the poker winnings in a bundle, stuffed them inside the loose sweater he

429

was wearing and told Lurene he was heading for his cabin. "Call the Security Office! Tell them what you found! Don't mention that I was here." So saying, he slipped out of the room and used the elevators at the end of the hall to reach his deck several levels below.

The flames of passion in the Johnson's marriage had been extinguished for some time. While Lurene's conjugal fidelity was seriously flawed, she, nevertheless, was a human being with feelings. After all, without Johnson she might still be waiting tables. When the security officer on duty arrived, she was still in shock, weeping uncontrollably, already convinced she would never see RC again.

* * *

Captain Lucchini was alerted by the security officer on duty. The ship's forward motion was stopped. A search effort was commenced. *The Venetian* was considered to be in international waters. Both the Greek and Turkish Coast Guard authorities were advised of a possible man-overboard situation and asked to investigate. The estimated time of the incident and the coordinates were given. The search parameters were discussed by radio. Several small ships were dispatched. Additionally, private sailing vessels, ferries, and fishing boats in the area were asked to assist. Marebella headquarters was also notified, as were the Greek authorities in Athens. Realizing the seriousness of the situation, the Captain promptly altered course to make port in Athens. Unfortunately, the stop in Valletta had to be cancelled. Thus, there would be a longer period of cruising to arrange to reach Barcelona on Wednesday morning. Captain Lucchini also personally contacted Mark Davidson, who was sleeping soundly. He immediately rose, dressed and joined the Captain in Suite 1012. Lucca Bruni, the Security Director met them there.

The cabin was temporarily cleared while two members of the Security Office dusted for fingerprints and took photographs of everything in the cabin. Other potential evidence was collected. A guard was posted. Mrs. Johnson was assigned another cabin. A stewardess was on hand to aid her. Signor Bruni also contacted his office to request that all video surveillance tapes be reviewed for the period from approximately 10:00 pm to 2:30 am, that is from Sunday night to Monday morning. Any containing anything suspicious either inside the ship or along the port exterior should be prepared for viewing in his office by 6:00 am.

CHAPTER NINE

Monday Morning

Early risers tuning into the ship's closed circuit news and information channel were greeted by a terse message read by Captain Lucchini. It also appeared as a printed bulletin in several languages on a second news channel.

"Buon giorno, Ladies and Gentlemen! This is your captain, Mario Lucchini, speaking. I am taking this unprecedented step of reporting to you an incident on board of which we became aware early this morning. I do so to quell the rumors and misinformation which have already been reverberating from prow to stern, from deck to deck.

Mr. Robert C. Johnson, an American passenger, was reported missing at approximately 2:30 local time this morning. He was occupying Suite 12 on Deck 10 together with his wife. A thorough search of our vessel was begun immediately. No trace of Mr. Johnson, who was confined to a wheelchair, has been found. There is reason to believe that he may have fallen overboard in the early morning fog and darkness. Greek and Turkish Coast Guard authorities are conducting a search.

Any passenger or crew member with any information that might clarify this case, is asked to contact Chief Bruni, Ship Security Director, by calling telephone number 701. You are asked to cooperate as well with Dr. Mark Davidson, a member of Marebella Lines senior management.

For legal reasons we are compelled to make port in Athens. Several excursions have been organized. They are described on Channel Three. Further details are available at the Travel Desk. We regret that we will not be calling on Malta as originally scheduled. Refunds for excursions planned there may be obtained from the Purser. Those crew members and passengers who are to remain on board to aid in the investigation have already been officially informed.

We extend our deepest sympathy to Mrs. Johnson, with the request that she be allowed to grieve quietly and privately. Thank You!"

* * *

The grieving spouse, aware that she was quite possibly a widow, was not listening very intently. Neville Easton III, whose British accent she "just loved to pieces", lay beside her on the bed in his cabin on Deck 8 slightly out-of-breath after a session of passionate love making.

Staring somewhat vacantly at the low ceiling, Lurene wondered aloud if perhaps her husband hadn't been pushed. "He had his charm, but basically he was a bullyin' bastard. Nobody liked him. Everyone, includin' me, who thought they might get a piece of his estate, tolerated a lot of crap, constantly kissed-up to him. I can't wait to find out what's in his will. He promised me the moon, he did. And I deserve it." She rolled over, kissed Neville and patted his flabby belly. "You need to exercise. If a little sex gets you huffin' 'n puffin' like you were, you ain't gonna last long with me. I guess I better start wearin' that black dress I bought in Barcelona." Easton remained silent.

Chief Bruni met around 9:00 with Captain Lucchini and Mark Davidson to discuss the steps they should take to collect evidence and, hopefully, solve the case of the missing passenger before returning to Barcelona. Bruni suggested that he and Mark divide the list of "persons of interest" and schedule interviews. The list included all the persons seen visiting the suite during the afternoon and evening hours. The surveillance cameras in which *Marebella Lines* had invested liberally constituted an invaluable investigative aid. The images were indisputably sharp and the exact times of entry and egress were carefully recorded. Regrettably, the fog had been so dense that the cameras mounted on the exterior of the ship failed to show any object falling over the side from the approximate location of Suite 1012.

Passengers in the neighboring suites had also been invited to meet with the investigators. Mark spoke with Mr. Desai. They met in a staff office off the main shopping concourse. Desai, a native of India from Hyderabad, was a Professor of Economics at the University of London. The author of several books on the subject and a well-traveled consultant with expertise in international banking, Desai had a number of observations regarding Mr. Johnson. From his brief encounters, Desai suspected Johnson might be psychotic with some sort of personality disorder. He repeated the things he had overheard Johnson say, specifically noting the negative tone and anger with which they were delivered. He thought Mrs. Johnson displayed incredible patience and calm in dealing with such an obnoxious person. Johnson, he noted, seemed intolerant and prejudiced. Desai attended the Second Sitting and had spent considerable time on deck reading or working on his laptop, when he was not participating in one of the shore excursions. He had not heard or otherwise noticed anything unusual on the night of Mr. Johnson's disappearance and had slept soundly during the period of inclement weather. Mark thanked him and indicated he might want to see him again at a later time.

Lurene was contacted by Chief Bruni regarding an interview. She begged off. She was so exhausted, she said, from dealing with the loss of her dear husband that even thinking about it now left her convulsing in tears. Bruni, although unconvinced by her protestations, said he would contact her again later, suggesting she rest in the meantime.

The Hornsbys, on the other hand, were quite eager to meet with Chief Bruni. Much of the conversation was dominated by Muriel. She had no kind words whatsoever for Mr. Johnson. He was a boorish, crude, loudmouth American. He was totally inconsiderate. Constantly upset her. Treated his wife very harshly, too. He had conducted meetings in his suite with at least a dozen men and frequently disturbed her naps with his raucous carrying-on. Neither she nor her husband would miss him.

Bruni, before meeting with the Hornsbys, had reviewed a videotaped encounter between Mr. Hornsby and Johnson. While no voice recording was available, it was clear from gestures and facial contortions that the exchange was not merely unfriendly, but insulting, especially to Mr. Hornsby. He plugged the portable video recorder into a wall socket and played the four-minute sequence for his surprised audience.

"You appeared to be angry when you were discussing Mr. Johnson's noisy behavior. It almost looked like you could have punched him." Bruni studied Hornsby's face.

A fairly muscular man in his late fifties, Hornsby thought a moment. "Yes, I was angry. If he hadn't been in a wheelchair, I probably would have popped him once or twice. He said unkind things to my wife and I was on the verge of retaliating." His right fist involuntarily doubled as he spoke.

"Were you angry enough to push him overboard, if you had been presented with the opportunity?"

Hornsby smiled. "No, we had already written him off as some kind of a kook. We felt sorry for his wife. She didn't hang around much. Always seemed to keep out of his way. I don't blame her. We decided to avoid them both."

Muriel added, "There was a quarrel of sorts the night Mr. Johnson disappeared. Actually, it was very early in the morning. We were awakened by shouting. We're sure it was Mr. Johnson and a countryman of ours, a Mr. Easton, I believe. We recognized his accent. It sounded like an angry exchange. After a few minutes the door shut noisily and everything was rather quiet. We wondered what it could have been about and couldn't get back to sleep for quite a while."

"Thank you for your thoughts. If I need to follow up, I'll get in touch." Bruni, who had met with the Hornsbys in their suite, rose and left with his recorder. Easton, he knew, had been one of Johnson's last visitors.

Mark and Bruni met in the Chief's office, compared notes and concluded that the Hornsbys' reference to a confrontation early Monday was highly interesting. Neither neighbor, however, was a serious suspect.

Their principal contribution was to reinforce an opinion about Johnson that was generally held by everyone whom he had encountered.

In the early evening, the two investigators met with Neville Easton III. The latter arrived at Bruni's office in his British casual attire, as if he were showing up at his club for dinner, brandy and a game of chess. His white shirt was open with a neatly arranged, conservative brown ascot tucked into the neck. A tweed Norfolk jacket and grey flannel slacks completed his wardrobe. He gave the impression he had spent much of his life in prosperous indolence.

Mark began. "Thank you for coming. We hope you can arrange to join your table for dinner. We don't intend to keep you long. Just a few questions."

"We understand," Bruni looked Easton square in the eyes, "that you knew Mr. Johnson, the gentleman who disappeared from his cabin, rather well, that you played poker with him on a couple of occasions."

"I'd hardly refer to him as a gentleman. He was a wily card player, shrewd and heartless. I thought of him as a low class slob from the Colonies, someone who'd had a lucky run in business, made a pile and flaunted it at every opportunity. He was the personification of the 'ugly American' so often in the news."

"Before you continue in this vain, Mr. Easton, I would like to point out that my colleague, Dr. Davidson, Secretary General of *La Fondation Székely*, Chairman and Chief Executive Officer of *White Cross Holdings* and the principal owner of *Marebella Lines*, is an American." Easton's complexion suddenly took on a ruddy tint. Bruni continued. "Information collected by my staff today indicates that you lost substantial sums of money to Mr. Johnson on more than one occasion while playing cards. A number of individuals have come forth to report that you were extremely angry as a result, that you demanded that Mr. Johnson give you a chance to "even the score", as it were. Your tone has been characterized as definitely threatening. Is that true?"

Slightly flustered and wondering who had volunteered such information, Easton said, "As an amateur at card games, I felt that this fellow

Johnson, obviously well versed in poker and other games, had taken advantage of me and others. I certainly deserved a rematch to recoup some of my losses."

"Our records and inquiries made to other cruise lines reveal that you have participated already this year in seven Mediterranean cruises of from five to ten days. You have a reputation for wining and dining single women, particularly elderly women, and of being what is often referred to as a "card shark".

"Well I do like life on the sea and am able to afford an occasional cruise or so." Easton seemed a trifle nervous. "I can't help it women find me pleasing company. A round or two of bridge or poker is a pleasant diversion."

Mark interrupted. "Did you, as reported to us, owe Mr. Johnson money?"

"Perhaps I did. That was something strictly between us." The statement by the Brit was made defensively.

Bruni continued. "Did you visit Mr. Johnson in his suite early this morning?"

Easton appeared about to deny that he had been there.

"Let me clarify something before you respond. One of *Marebella Lines'* foremost concerns is passenger and crew safety. There are literally hundreds of sophisticated surveillance cameras on this vessel that are monitored day and night. There is no significance to the number, but camera number 26 shows you entering Suite 1012 at 12:45 a.m. and exiting six minutes later. Until his wife reported him missing no one else entered or left that suite. We also have a report claiming that you and Mr. Johnson had a heated exchange during this visit. We have concluded there was no forced entry. Thus, Mr. Johnson, could have been thrown overboard during a visit, probably by someone he knew, or by someone who otherwise had access. Can you explain?"

Convinced lying would hurt him more than telling the truth, Easton said, "Yes, I did call on him last evening. I had given him an IOU for

$3000 and promised to pay by today. I wasn't able to arrange for the money so quickly and went to ask for an extension."

"What was Johnson's response?" Mark wanted to know.

"He was irritated. Cussed me and told me to 'bugger off', although those were not his exact words. I didn't argue. I just left while he was still shouting at me."

"Are you certain his remarks didn't provoke some sort of physical retaliation?"

"Look, I'm not a violent person. Frankly, I might have wanted to throttle him. He was an unbearable ass, that chap. However, I felt pity, not envy; sympathy, not revenge. I gave him my back and walked off."

"Do you know Mrs. Johnson, Lurene Johnson?" Mark posed the question.

Easton hesitated a moment to ponder his response. "Yes. I didn't know her last name at first. I probably wouldn't have gotten involved, if I had known she was Johnson's wife. I thought she was just a single woman out for adventure. She told me she wore the wedding ring to help her avoid men in whom she had no interest."

"Did you and Mrs. Johnson ever discuss her husband? He was more than just well-to-do, you know." Bruni waited for an answer.

"No. He never came up in our, uh, discussions. She didn't seem attached to anyone. I saw her a few times with a younger chap, Japanese or Chinese I'd say. They seemed rather chummy. I never mentioned that and neither did she."

"Thank you for your cooperation, Mr. Easton. We'll be in touch, should we need further information. Oh, by the way, unless notified otherwise, do not disembark with the other passengers in Athens or in Barcelona."

Mark and Bruni talked for a while about the day's schedule. They expected to be in Athens most of the day. The ship's normal routine would prevail. Potential witnesses were already advised not to leave the ship. A representative from the Greek Admiralty was expected, along with a prosecutor from the Piraeus Prefecture. While it was assumed that Captain Lucchini had jurisdiction because the incident occurred in international waters, Greek maritime officials had a few questions.

Responding in part to anonymous messages from both passengers and crew, Chief Bruni summoned Ms Rodriguez, Pepino Maldonado and Gustavo, Johnson's steward, for interviews. He saw them separately. Suzanna's parting threat to Johnson after blurting out the fact that his own daughter was a member of the crew, was of course, ill-advised, a spontaneous and intemperate eruption of anger that she immediately regretted. She admitted as much to Chief Bruni. It was, she volunteered, unprofessional, a momentary lapse in judgement, and she was sorry it happened. Perhaps the fact that Johnson recognized his guilt in abandoning his lover prevented him from reporting the incident himself. Bruni sympathized. Suzanna's remorse was genuine. There was no evidence that she was involved in the passenger's disappearance.

When Suzanna had explained to Bobbi her run-in with Mr. Johnson, Pepino was present. He was normally cool and even-tempered, If Pepino was angry at Johnson for causing his friend Suzanna unnecessary stress, he was doubly enraged by his unwarranted negative remarks about Bobbi. Within a group of fellow staff a remark slipped out to the effect that the Captain should make Johnson 'swim back to Barcelona'. A fellow crew member who had overheard the rash comment reported it to the Security Office once news of the disappearance was broadcast on board. Bruni satisfied himself that the remark, intemperate though it might have been, was actually intended partly in jest. It was quickly dismissed as a serious motive.

Gustavo, too, a stalwart in the housekeeping staff with years of satisfactory service to his credit, passed muster with Bruni and he was not considered a possible villain in the case.

Elli was a special guest of the ship's Chief of Cuisine. She had a cooking lesson and an in-depth introduction to procurement procedures, as well as food handling practices on a ship with over three thousand passengers and crew to feed several times each day.

The Captain, the Purser, Chief Bruni and the Davidsons lunched together in the Captain's quarters. Their conversation touched on a wide range of topics. It was a delightful meal. Everyone expected the rest of the day to be very busy.

Easton and Lurene met briefly in one of the bars. He recalled his interrogation. She gleaned tips for her interview the next day.

Herb and his new-found American friend had fun in the casino. Herb won a hundred Euros at one of the €5 slot machines. Feeling a bit giddy over the roll of bills he found in his father's briefcase, Herb bought his friend a few drinks and gave her the change. They decided to spend the night in his cabin.

CHAPTER TEN

Monday, Forenoon

From their breakfast tables in the main dining room and the snack bars further forward, diners could look out at Europe's largest, busiest passenger harbor, a jungle of smokestacks, cranes, sailing masts and heavy container lifting machinery. Neatly lined up were a dozen or more buses. Soon they would whisk passengers off for a wide variety of excursions to sights in and around Athens, approximately 12 kilometers away. The Travel Office had worked all night with local tour companies to arrange for what appeared to be a smooth operation planned months before.

Captain Lucchini, Security Chief Bruni and Mark had already greeted Lorenzo Ramazotti, a *Marebella Lines* legal counselor, who had flown down overnight from the company's headquarters in Genoa. Greek authorities had designated Stephan Anistopoulous, a maritime lawyer from the Piraeus Prefecture, as their representative. Captain Lucchini had requested the meeting to clarify his role in handling the case of the missing passenger. A continental breakfast was served in a board room adjacent to the Captain's quarters. Each person present introduced himself and made a brief statement based on his limited knowledge of the circumstances.

The Captain circulated a memorandum outlining the ship's geographic position at the assumed time frame for the passenger's disappearance. It showed that *The Venetian* was in international waters. He then reported that an extensive air-and-sea search by the Turkish and Greek Coast Guard had failed to find any trace of Mr. Johnson. He was officially presumed dead. In response to a question concerning sharks, the captain pointed out that although the Mediterranean was known to be home to dozens upon dozens of species of sharks, none was actually considered to be of the 'man-eating' variety that often made the headlines.

Ramazotti pointed out that although the ship was registered in Liberia, a precedent for jurisdiction in such cases had been established several years prior, when *Marebella Lines* was allowed to prosecute a similar case in Genoa. Mark proposed, that if there were no objections, based on information already gathered, he would suggest that responsibility for resolving the disappearance be left to the Captain's discretion. He noted that preliminary investigations had revealed only one possible suspect with a serious motive, an English passenger who had lost a large sum to Mr. Johnson playing cards. Should, however, the predominant initial suspicions that the victim might have accidentally fallen overboard, or even jumped of his own volition, tentative conclusions reached by Chief Bruni, his professional staff and himself, fail to be corroborated by subsequent investigative efforts, then the matter would be referred to the Italian maritime court in Genoa. A brief discussion ensued. Ultimately, all agreed on this solution and the meeting was adjourned after the Captain announced he would send each participant a transcript of the meeting.

Michèlle Davidson had tracked down Lurene Johnson and made a courtesy call to offer assistance and to convey the Davidsons' and the Captain's condolences. During the conversation she learned that Herbert Johnson, the victim's son, was traveling separately on the ship. She thought it odd, that the father had been unaware of his son's presence, but did not press the matter with Mrs. Johnson, who explained she was the boy's step-mother and had no children of her own.

An examination of Mr. Johnson's belongings had produced little that cast any light on his disappearance. There was one notable exception: his briefcase. It had contained, when retrieved from the suite by Chief Bruni's assistants, a few small plastic jars with various prescriptions, mostly pain killers, but also an array of substances in tablet or capsule form for maladies from diabetes to kidney problems to blood pressure altering medicines. Additionally, there were some writing instruments, a large pad, some business notes, a laptop computer, a battery-operated inkjet printer, a utility multi-tool, a small bottle of a substance for erasing ink, and three granola bars. The briefcase also had a secret compartment that was carefully sealed by velcro. The compartment was empty.

Noting that the prescriptions had been submitted by a Harlan Tribble, M.D. of Kennesaw, Georgia, an Atlanta suburban community, Mark decided to contact him by telephone. Because of the seven hour time differential, Mark said he would wait until about 3 p.m. local time to place the call.

Elli had set up an appointment for Mrs. Johnson to meet with her and Mark in their Suite, a more modest space than that enjoyed by the Johnsons, still quite comfortable and suitable for the interview. The meeting was set for 1:00 p.m. Chief Bruni was to see Herb, Johnson's son at the same time in the Security Center.

Not really hungry, perhaps because he was so involved in solving the mystery of Johnson's disappearance, Mark settled for a green salad and a ham sandwich served beside the larger of the ship's two swimming pools. Because virtually all the passengers had chosen to go into Athens or to participate in an excursion, the pool area was not well populated. A few families were playing ball in the bright blue water. Sunbathers occupied some lounge chairs on the opposite side. A remarkable lack of wind made it rather warm, but most suitable for dining *al fresco*. Elli, wearing a magenta halter top and white shorts was stunningly beautiful. Mark knocked on wood, thanking the day he had met her in Switzerland responding to Herr Székely's summons for help. Elli also chose a salad and a selection of fruit. Both opted to drink bottled water.

By 1:00 p.m. the Davidsons had returned to their suite on Deck 9. Lurene Johnson followed them by about five minutes. Mark thanked her for her promptness and her willingness to aid them by answering a few questions. He reiterated the message of sympathy conveyed earlier by his wife. He began by saying, "*Marebella Lines*, as you know, advises all passengers of its extensive surveillance arrangements via video cameras and other electronic and optical devices. These are designed, not to intrude on passenger privacy, but solely to assure the safety of all aboard. I regret to say that we do not as yet have an adequate means of penetrating dense fog with our lenses. Therefore, no usable images were retrieved that showed any object or objects falling from the balcony of your suite Sunday night or Monday morning after our passage through the Dardanelles en route to Athens. Of course, cameras inside the ship create a complete record of movement in the public areas and in the various passageways on all decks. This record shows your entrance to Suite 1012 a few minutes after 2:00 am Monday morning. It also shows you exiting to summon a companion, identified as Herbert Johnson, whom we have learned is your step-son and the biological offspring of the victim. You reentered the suite together with Mr. Herbert Johnson moments later. He then departed in haste alone at approximately the time you contacted Security to report your husband missing. Would you please describe in your own words what transpired. Please pay no attention to this voice recording device. We will provide you with a transcript later."

Lurene stared vacantly at the recorder, while she seemed to be collecting her thoughts. From her talk with Easton she realized that the ship's authorities were well informed about her movements on the ship. "Well, ya know, Herb, that is Herbert, he's my step-son, as you mentioned. His mother died when he was eleven. He was... I guess you'd call it... estranged, yes, estranged from his father. They didn't get along at all. As a child Herb... Herbert had a few nannies. He was sent away to schools and seldom spent much time together with RC... his father. I brought Herbert on board hopin' to help them to make up. I could see that RC... that's what we called him, was not well and gettin' worse. Look, he all of a sudden, one day came back from a visit to Doc Tribble, that's his regular doctor, ya know, and the passion we shared, his zest for life, went poof, like the air explodin' from a burst balloon.

"He never touched me afterward, ya know. Anyway, after Istanbul, hey that was some big town all right, we was... were partyin' and time

444

just flew by. RC had gone to bed early, but I figured I'd better peek in and see if he was O.K. I guess it was pretty late, after two a.m., you say? Well, he wasn't in bed. The bathroom was empty. He wasn't sittin' in his wheelchair or on the sofa. The balcony door was open. I couldn't see much it was so dark and foggy and rainin' a little. I didn't see RC, but I saw his wheelchair tipped on its side. I called him. He wasn't anywhere. Herbert was waitin' in the hall. I was concerned that somethin' awful had happened. Herb came quickly. We searched everywhere. There was no RC in the suite. He couldn't have gone off by himself. I called Security… and… and you know the rest."

"The security officer responding acknowledges your presence in the suite, but he did not mention Herbert. Can you explain that?"

"I thought he'd better leave. He was very concerned about his father. I checked the balcony again. When I came back into the suite Herb was gone."

Elli, who had read through Mark's notes and had gleaned some details about Mrs. Johnson's activities on board, was curious. "Aside from cataloging a number of visits by you to your step-son's cabin, the cameras also show you together with a Mr. Neville Easton, a British passenger. How would you characterize your relationship with Mr. Easton?"

"We were just acquaintances. We had a few drinks together."

Dismayed by Mrs. Johnson's lack of candor, Elli pressed on. "Most of your time together appears to have been spent in Mr. Easton's cabin. Some people might suspect that you were having an affair."

Interrupting quickly, Lurene interjected, "I wouldn't call it an affair, more like a fling. We had some fun together, ya know, nothin' serious."

Mark's turn. "Did you know that Easton visited your husband between 11:15 and 12:15 Sunday night?"

"No." Lurene's face had a puzzled expression.

"Well, he did. He spent several minutes there. When he left he looked furtively up and down the passageway before hurrying off to the aft elevator bank. He went from there to the casino, where he joined you.

Did you know that your husband had won several thousand dollars playing poker, and that a large part of that money was from Mr. Easton?"

"Neville, Mr. Easton, that is, did mention somethin' about poker in the card room. I got the impression he usually won."

"Actually," Davidson continued, "other participants, who also counted themselves among the losers, said Mr. Easton lost a substantial amount of money and even owed more that was covered by an IOU. A careful reading of the inventory made by our security investigators mentions neither the large roll of cash, possibly over $50,000, according to the other participants, nor the IOU they saw Mr. Easton give to Mr. Johnson. How do you explain that?" Mark hesitated a moment, then continued, "It seems logical to assume Mr. Easton had a motive... and the opportunity.... to harm your husband."

"Hell! Uh... Excuse me, I don't know. Maybe RC threw the money overboard. I didn't even know he had it." Her brain was racing to determine whether Easton, or Herb, or possibly the steward might have taken it from her husband. Herb was with her and he had only been alone in the suite for a couple of minutes. From what she had heard both Gustavo and Easton had been there longer. They might have pushed her husband over the side, searched and found the money and taken it for themselves. "If there was cash there, I didn't know about it. Besides I have no need to steal from my own husband. He pretty much gave me whatever I wanted. Easton is a wuss. He couldn't hurt nobody."

Elli picked up the conversation. "Does your husband have a will?"

"Yes, I'm pretty sure he does. I believe he even went to see his lawyers before our trip."

"Can we assume you are the principal heir?" Mark wondered aloud.

"Well, RC always said I'd be taken care of. I guess he meant I'd get most everythin'."

"Thank you for coming. We'll get back to you soon. Please do not discuss anything we've brought up here with other passengers. We are truly sorry about your husband's disappearance. It is not likely that he could survive if he went overboard. Please let us know if we can be of any assistance. Oh, by the way, witnesses have referred to a number of instances where your husband appeared to be engaged in abusing you verbally. Is that true?"

Lurene stopped momentarily, stared at the floor, then said, "Look, when we was… were first married he was attentive and well mannered. He never got cross with me. After his accident his attitude changed. His moods was… were up and down, real fast like. He could find fault where there was none. Usually I was the only one around and he tended to take out his frustrations and anger on me. I got used to it."

"Thank you again, Mrs. Johnson. You have our number. Please call if anything else that might be helpful comes to mind." Mark opened the door and Lurene left.

Several decks below in the Security office which housed the battery of surveillance monitors, Chief Bruni was part way through his interview with Herbert Johnson, the victim's son. Bruni and one of his assistants had completed the preliminaries, learning that Mrs. Johnson had invited Herb to join the cruise and that Herb and his father were not on the best of terms. No love had ever been lost between them. Herb's precipitous withdrawal from college had been a bone of contention. The son's dabbling in recreational drugs had also contributed to his alienation from his father. Mr. Johnson also resented his wife's meddling in what he considered a private matter.

"So, you really didn't like your dad, is that correct?" Bruni looked deep into Herb's eyes. The attractive young man sat opposite him at a small table.

"I get along with most people. My father was… different. He never really let me get close, especially when my real mom died. But, I would never hurt him. When he had the accident that eventually left him in the wheelchair I felt terribly sorry. He was always active. He lost his mobility and his independence. He went into a deep funk. Nobody could help him."

"Did your father cut your allowance when you quit school?" Bruni's assistant, standing nearby, was inquisitive.

"Yeh! He sure did. My step-mom and Millie Austin, she's dad's bookkeeper, helped me out with a few bucks now and then. It wasn't really fair."

"Were you angry with your dad?" Bruni wanted to probe further.

"I wasn't happy about it. Still I wouldn't hurt him to get even or anything."

Bruni, staring straight at Herb began again. "You saw the video we showed you. After your step-mother entered the suite and discovered your father missing, she called you in. You were only there about four and a half minutes. You said you checked the balcony, then looked in the bathroom. At that point, you mentioned that Mrs. Johnson went back onto the balcony. What were you doing at that time?"

"I guess, I was just dazed, confused."

"When you left the suite you first stuck your head out of the door to see if the passageway was clear, then you moved very quickly to the rear elevator bank and stairwell. Was there a reason for being so cautious, so secretive? Were you hiding something? Did you or your step-mother push your father over the side?" Bruni's voice had a distinctly accusatory ring to it.

"No!" Herb protested. "I just didn't want to become involved." Herb strained to retain his composure.

The assistant again spoke up. "Several parties who played cards with your father have told us he won thousands of dollars in cash gambling. One loser also gave him an IOU. None of these items were found anywhere in the room during our investigation. Do you have an explanation?"

Herb began to perspire. He had nothing to say.

A female assistant knocked and entered the room, giving Bruni a slip of paper. She departed quickly.

"Herb, you're not being candid with us." Bruni was looking at the slip of paper. His mien was serious. "Exercising our legal right, we have just conducted a search of your cabin. We have found a roll of American currency totaling some $48,000. We need the truth. Did you remove this money from your father's suite on Saturday night?"

Herb hesitated. "Yes. In case he's dead, I wanted to keep it safe. It belongs to Lurene and me."

"You've been seen with a young American woman. As a matter of policy *Marebella Lines* does not intrude on relationships between consenting adults. However, it seems odd that your account shows a sizeable increase in expenditures in the Casino, the gourmet restaurant, the bars, and the boutiques in the Shopping Arcade since your father went missing. There seems to be a disparity between the amount your father is said to have won at cards and the sum discovered in your cabin. Think about it."

"Can I go now?"

"All right. You may go now. You are not allowed ashore in Athens and you are not to disembark in Barcelona without the Captain's express permission. Italian law will be in force. You will be provided an opportunity to obtain legal counsel, should that become necessary."

Wondering what kind of a mess he had gotten himself into, a nervous Herb left and returned to his cabin. He called Lurene and they met in one of the snack bars, ostensibly to compare notes and ponder the future.

Meanwhile, Mark and Elli had tea in their cabin and discussed the several reports already available from the interviews conducted thus far. It was 4:00 p.m. local time. Mark tried to contact Dr. Tribble in Georgia from his cell phone. Several cell phone masts a short distance away in the port guaranteed a good connection. Tribble responded immediately; reception was clear.

"Hello, Dr. Tribble, this is Mark Davidson, I work with *Marebella Lines*, a major cruise provider. I'm calling from Athens, Greece. Can you hear me?"

"Yes, I can. How can I help you?"

"If I'm not mistaken, I believe you attended a seminar in Geneva sponsored by my brother-in-law, Dr. Roland Denis-Breuer, on the subject of computers and voice-controlled prosthetics last year. Is that correct?"

"It is indeed." replied a surprised Dr. Tribble. "What prompts this call?"

"A patient of yours, Mr. Robert Chamberlain Johnson, was a passenger on *The Venetian*, one of our newest ships, on an Eastern Mediterranean cruise from Barcelona to Istanbul and return."

"Oh, yes. He mentioned that. I hope he's having a good time. I actually advised him not to go. He's quite ill and needs to be close to good medical facilities." There was a short pause. "Did you say…'was a passenger'?"

"I regret to be the one to tell you that Mr. Johnson was reported missing early this morning shortly after we departed Istanbul. We fear he may have fallen overboard. Since we cannot rule out the possibility that he may have jumped overboard, I am calling to ask a few questions."

"I am so sorry to hear this. What can I tell you?"

"Several medications that you prescribed were in his belongings. We would like to know more about his medical problems, his prognosis and his state of mind when you last saw him. Can you share that information with us? I should mention that *Marebella Lines*, if it is unable to resolve the mystery surrounding Mr. Johnson's disappearance, will be obliged to refer the matter to the Italian courts for adjudication. This is so because we have not been able to determine what caused his disappearance. This is troubling due to the fact that several persons aboard ship may have had a motive to cause him harm." Mark felt it important to level with the doctor to encourage his cooperation. Divulging information obtained in doctor-patient relationships was tricky on both sides of the Atlantic.

"Mr. Davidson, hmmm. I recall meeting you at the seminar in Geneva. I have a salt and pepper moustache and goatee. Perhaps you remember. I interrupted a conversation you were having with that remarkable member of your staff, the quadriplegic in the high-tech wheelchair, to thank you for sponsoring the event."

"I do recall it."

"Look I'll be happy to share whatever you need to know. Mr. Johnson has been a patient of mine since his return to the area from military service a good twenty-five years ago. He is a rather successful businessman locally. Mostly construction oriented, I believe. He showed up every year for a general physical. A couple of years back he was injured in a work-related accident, spent time in the hospital, went through a period of rehabilitation, but had some lingering joint and muscle problems. Eventually, he decided against more surgery and relied on a wheelchair to get around. The net result was that he turned into an annoying grump. My nurse was always happy when his visits were over. But that's beside the point. Last year he began having internal problems that prompted a more extensive battery of tests and evaluation by some experts over at Duke University in Durham. To make a long story much shorter, Mr. Johnson was found to be suffering from late-stage syphilis. Specifically, his lungs are failing; his kidneys are beyond help. He could use a liver transplant. Diabetes has affected his pancreas. He relies on medication to control a rampant blood pressure anomaly. Frankly, he has virtually no chance of survival. He was fully aware of that. Our principal effort has had to focus on pain management."

"That would explain the numerous painkillers in his personal traveling apothecary shop."

"I advised him against going on the cruise. He needs to be close to a good medical facility. When he insisted on traveling, I prescribed two ampules of a drug called *Morphquell,* a very powerful agent often used in potentially fatal battlefield injuries. It is generally self administered with the aid of single-use syringes. I considered this a last resort medication. He insisted on having it."

"Would you say that Mr. Johnson was suicidal? Was he likely to take his own life?"

"Mr. Johnson and I estimated, based on details of his life in the military service and the life style he adopted as that service was ending, that he probably contracted syphilis at that time. The disease went dormant, as it will, if not effectively treated, and reemerged decades later. At that point

451

there is no cure. He knew the outcome was death. There was no date-certain attached to his prognosis. The only certainty was pain. Mr. Johnson never mentioned suicide, *per se*. It doesn't require much imagination, however, to assume he considered it an option. If he hasn't been found in those busily traversed waters by now, I expect he is no longer with us. Please convey my sympathy to Mrs. Johnson."

"Dr. Tribble, I am indebted to you for your assistance. I hope our paths will cross again sometime. Thank you."

"You're entirely welcome. I sincerely hope I have been helpful." With that the line went dead.

Monday Evening

The Davidsons were famished. They dressed for dinner and were about to leave their cabin when Captain Lucchini called and asked if he could stop by for a few minutes. Shortly thereafter he knocked, was admitted and began to share with them a new development. He went on to tell them that Ms Suzanna Rodriguez, a supervisor in the housekeeping department, and one of the stewards working the luxury units on Deck 10, Gustavo Ramos, had asked to see him immediately after the noon meal. Gustavo had been debriefed earlier in the day because the video cameras had captured a visit he made to Suite 1012 about 10:00 Sunday evening. He told the investigators that it was a routine stop to arrange the bedding for the night. Mr. Johnson was sitting in his wheelchair, said very little, and Gustavo had said he left almost immediately.

Resting on the end of their bed, the Davidsons listened carefully, as Captain Lucchini continued. "Later, he went to Miss Rodriguez and expanded on his story. She promptly brought him to see me. Sometime around noon on Saturday, Mr. Johnson, who earlier in the cruise had instigated a scene involving Gustavo over some silly, arcane matter, summoned the steward and apologized. He proceeded to inquire whether Gustavo would be going ashore in Istanbul. At the time that was something the steward was planning to do. Johnson asked whether Gustavo could mail two packages for him. Gustavo agreed and Johnson gave him these two envelopes." Captain Lucchini opened a bag he was carrying and handed the large envelopes to Mark. "Unfortunately, Gustavo's schedule was changed on short notice and his shore leave was cancelled. He figured, it would be acceptable to mail the envelopes in Valletta, when he would have an opportunity to enjoy the afternoon off. His purpose in visiting Mr. Johnson, he says, was to tell a 'good' lie, namely that the packages were sent as requested. Once he heard that the passenger was missing under mysterious circumstances, he became confused and failed to tell the security people the whole story. Realizing that was a mistake, he contacted his supervisor for advice. Thus, the matter came to my attention."

"Hmm, I see they're addressed to two parties in the Atlanta area; a bank and a law firm."

Mark studied the envelopes and the heavy-duty tape that enclosed them. "Johnson was apparently eager to mail them before he returned home. Why do you suppose he felt the need for such urgency?" It was an open question directed at no one in particular.

The Captain spoke. "Because they may materially help us reach a timely conclusion to the matter before us, I am authorizing you to open them, perhaps together with Chief Bruni and a disinterested witness. It's a bit late now. I will leave it to you to contact someone to assist you. You may meet in my conference room tomorrow morning between 9:00 and 10:00. Overnight you may want to take the precaution of locking them in the safe inside your closet. Thank you. *Buon appetito!*" The Davidsons thought they heard a sigh of relief as the Captain exited the cabin.

Mark and Elli tried to relax. It had been a hectic day. More of the same was the prospect for tomorrow. They enjoyed a delightful evening. Dinner was superb. They danced to a variety of music played by the ship's own band. They came in second in a fun-filled ballroom dancing contest. The prize was a gift certificate valid for use anywhere on *The Venetian's* shopping arcade. Elli said she planned to give it to a young woman whom she usually saw each morning working at the breakfast buffet. Both Mark and Elli were trying to think of someone who could help tomorrow when the two packages the Captain had given them would be opened and examined for any relevance to the investigation into Mr. Johnson's disappearance.

Elli broke a period of silence exclaiming, "I know who can help. Helga… Helga Hallstein, the German woman who sits at our dinner table. She's a Kindergarten-teacher. She seems very thoughtful and quite analytical. She'd be perfect. Let's call her now!"

"Great idea. Give her a ring. The Purser's office can give you her number. If she is willing, have her meet us in the morning… say around 9:30."

Fräulein Hallstein was receptive and readily accepted the invitation.

The Venetian moved south through gentle waters towards the Sea of Crete. Between the island of Kíthira and the southern tip of Pelepon-nesus the great white ship would turn westward towards the Ionian Sea and two days of sailing for Barcelona. The staff was prepared for a busy day of ship-board activities, lots of purchases in the boutiques along the Shopping Arcade, and many hungry and thirsty cruisers in all the dining venues. The Davidson's looked forward to an exciting day. They hoped the mystery of Mr. Johnson's disappearance would be resolved, perhaps with the aid of the packages he had intended to mail in Istanbul.

CHAPTER ELEVEN

Tuesday Morning

When breakfast had concluded on a full day of cruising at sea, Mark stopped by the Purser's office to chat with Marcello Reinhardt, a native of Merano and a twenty-year veteran cruise ship officer. Reinhardt succinctly related the visit to Johnson's suite with three crew members to witness and notarize a legal document. He had found Johnson pleasant, polite and appreciative. The passenger had been well organized and thoughtful in tipping the witnesses, even making a donation to the Seamen's Relief Fund.

Collecting the two packages from his cabin safe, Mark, ever the romantic, embraced his lovely wife and giving her his arm, the couple departed for the board room adjoining the Captain's quarters. Chief Bruni had already introduced himself to Fräulein Hallstein, when the Davidsons arrived.

Mark, using a pen knife, carefully cut through the thick layer of packing tape and the plastic outer envelope covering the first envelope to produce a bundle of eight hand-written pages. The envelope had been neatly imprinted with the address of a small community bank in North Georgia. The pages were not numbered, but each bore a recent date. Mark put them in chronological order and passed them to Bruni, suggesting he peruse the bundle page by page, then pass them to Fräulein Hallstein and so on until they had all had a chance to check the contents.

As Bruni read a page, then passed it on, he remarked, "These are diary entries. There are elaborate descriptions of a variety of people, some appear to be other passengers, members of the crew,... why he has a long passage here about Signorina Roberta Johnson... how curious, she has the same name... she's a charming young lady, who is making quite a name for herself in the kitchen, and he refers to some family members and, possibly, people he works with at home. From what I've seen so far, he is a highly critical person. Ahh, but here on the fourth page, he is writing a kind of confession. He reflects on his own life, talks about Manila, about California and the Marines. I gather he was in the military service at one time. Hmm! Miss Hallstein, you may want to skip the last two pages. He includes a string of personal details associated with some of his escapades. The language is a bit coarse, if I do say so."

"Signor Bruni, I may be a kindergarten teacher now, but I am well acquainted with life's seamier side. I started my working career as a probation officer. There is not much that shocks me anymore."

Elli finished reading all the entries. "The last page, where he catalogs all his medical troubles and describes the physical pain and mental distress he experiences, is touching. He also writes about his reaction to his medications. He obviously suffered greatly as his disease progressed and the various side-effects manifested themselves with increasing intensity. It's not a pretty picture."

Bruni and Fräulein Hallstein agreed. Mark, too, found it sad and morbidly engrossing. Next, Mark opened the second envelope. It was addressed to Buford H. Bowles of Bowles, Henderson and Kachinsky, Attorneys-at-Law, PLC, presumably his personal lawyer. This bundle contained thirteen pages. The first, was a loose page, hand-written, and was intended to serve as a cover letter. The remaining dozen pages had been typed on quality paper. Numerous spaces had been left for handwritten completion. The entries were appropriately spaced. Each had been initialed in ink "RCJ". There were two addenda, designated Addendum A and Addendum B. The pages were numbered and attached with a small removable metal device. The final page had been notarized by the Purser, Signor Reinhardt, who had also made an embossed impression with a special stamp. The whole was entitled "Last Will and Testament of Robert Chamberlain Johnson". It was a legal document.

Mark examined the sheaf of papers. He held them up for others to see clearly the condition in which they had been packed by Mr. Johnson. "I'll read these quickly, then pass them to you, Chief, then to Fräulein Hallstein. Elli will be the last to read them. Since they appear to be double-spaced, it should go without any delays. I ask you not to repeat anything you read. Because the beneficiaries happen to be aboard, I see no reason why we should not assemble the parties involved, all of them, that is, Miss Bobbi Johnson, Mr. Herbert Johnson, and Mr. Johnson's wife, Lurene, for a reading this evening."

The Davidsons had invited Bobbi Johnson to lunch on their veranda. Although she was fully occupied, Bobbi managed to slip away for about 45 minutes. In the process of arranging the luncheon Elli learned from Captain Lucchini that Bobbi was participating in a mentoring program designed to prepare her for advancement when an opening should occur. All of Bobbi's supervisors have consistently lauded her, not only for her culinary skills, but also for her leadership, management and public relations talent. By the next season *Marebella Lines* hoped to have her placed on one of their ships as an officer in charge of all food services.

Mark was amazed to see how Bobbi favored his wife. Their skin coloring, their brown eyes and deep brunette hair were strikingly similar. If that were not enough, both possessed in large measure a vivacity of spirit and magnitude of personal charm that was absolutely uncanny.

The three quarters of an hour had literally flown past when Bobbi politely excused herself to resume her duties. Later, Elli confessed it was like looking in a mirror. Knowing as they did the details of Johnson's will, both wondered aloud what Bobbi's reaction would be when she heard its provisions.

CHAPTER TWELVE

Tuesday Evening

To whom it may concern

I humbly request Buford Randall Bowles, Sr., my lawyer, to read this letter, a preamble to my Last Will and Testament, to those who have assembled to hear the terms of that document.

The illness from which I suffer can be likened to a dark tunnel, a tunnel without end. My life, too, has been a tunnel of darkness, a tunnel lacking an exit. I dug that tunnel myself. I have reflected carefully on my life. Whatever misery and pain I may suffer. It has all been self-inflicted. I realize now that the choices I have made were foolish, selfish and unwise.

This letter is intended for those who have long wondered what would be my final testament and what mention would be made of them. If you thought to find your sole salvation in my demise, you may be disappointed. If you have chosen to follow my nihilistic path, intending to gain great material benefit from that foolhardy association, you are in danger of reaching a point of no return.

My Faith was sacrificed to expedient, self-indulgent and transient wanton pleasure. Pain of a magnitude I never imagined has resulted and serves, ironically, to focus my vision on the eternal values that bring meaning to human existence. How 'philosophical' I have become. An angel guides my pen. An angel bearing my name, a child I denied a normal upbringing has appeared, seemingly by divine edict, to illuminate my final passage. The ways of Heaven are inscrutable.

As my rotting carcass is consigned to the waves, I urge you to search deep within yourselves. Learn your true identity. Heal yourselves before it is too late! Each day can be an eternity.

* * *

Mark looked up from his reading at the audience seated before him in a small private lounge reserved for senior officers adjacent to the Purser's office. Bobbi, blotting tears with a white handkerchief, was seated in the front row between her friends Pepino and Suzanna. The Purser, Signor Reinhardt, was next to them, at his side Chief Bruni. In the row behind them, experiencing both sadness and anticipation, were Lurene, playing the bereaved widow in her black 'Barcelona' dress, and Herb. Next to them were Captain Lucchini and Fräulein Hallstein. Elli was alone in the third row of seats.

"We have been informed by a reliable medical source that Mr. Robert Johnson was suffering from late-stage syphilis." Mark spoke softly. Lurene gasped audibly. "His condition had reached an acute level. He knew that he might die at any time. His pain, by his own admission, was extreme, virtually unbearable. Only powerful medications allowed him to undertake this cruise, an adventure from which several persons had sought to dissuade him. Among the unfortunate side-effects of his medications were the severe mood swings some of you witnessed first hand."

Mark took a sip of water from a glass on the table at which he was sitting. He continued, "Your cooperation in the investigation has been appreciated. Before I make known Mr. Johnson's bequests as outlined in his will, I want to share with you what we have learned from his diary entries. We know only the contents of the past several days covering this cruise. Mr. Johnson stated in the will that everything in his safe-deposit box, where his diary has been kept, should go to Miss Roberta Johnson, his biological daughter. Any further disclosures will be her prerogative." Another pause. Herb and Lurene looked at each other. Bobbi had a quizzical look. Suzanna clutched her friend's hand.

"We, Captain Lucchini, Chief of Security Signor Bruni, Mrs. Davidson, and yours truly, have carefully studied all the evidence available to us and have concluded that Mr. Johnson took his own life by going over-board during inclement weather at approximately 2:30 a.m. local time Monday following the ship's passage through the Dardenelles." A few gasps were heard. Lurene wiped her eyes and stifled a moan. Bobbi, who had intended to try and talk to the man everyone assumed was her father, once they reached Barcelona, was speechless. Suzanna was both relieved and apprehensive. Herb showed no emotion.

"I will spare you the legal verbiage in this document and provide the pertinent details of Mr. Johnson's bequests. Please note that a formal reading will be arranged in due course by Mr. Johnson's lawyer, Mr. Bowles, who is also named as his Executor. In a phone call I made earlier, he indicated he would arrange that as soon as he receives the official death notice and this notarized will.

"To Mrs. Lurene Johnson, her husband leaves the family residence on Captiva Island in Florida, its entire contents, and one half of the proceeds of his life insurance policy." When this information had worked its way through her brain and she realized that that was all she would probably receive, Lurene's face went pale. She was grossly disappointed. Mark continued, "To my son Herbert, I bequeath one half of the proceeds of my life insurance policy, the sum of which will be administered by the executor of my estate to assist him to complete his college education." Herb did not appear completely happy. He expected more. He grew restless and was on the verge of leaving, but remained in his chair.

"To Miss Roberta Johnson, a daughter I did not realize I had, from whom I beg forgiveness for my inexcusable neglect, I leave my country club estate in Atlanta, my mountain retreat in Tennessee and the firm of R.C. Johnson, Incorporated with all its assets, including all motor vehicles and boats. The entire contents of my personal accounts and safe-deposit boxes are hers as well."

Bobbi said, "Oh, my God! I don't know what to say. This can't be true! I never actually saw him. And he says I was his daughter." Pepino kissed her cheek. Suzanna, tears in her eyes, hugged her friend.

"By my calculation," Mark proceeded, "my poker winnings on this cruise as of Friday last were $52,312." Mark read on. "These I leave to The International Society for Sexually Transmitted Diseases. Further stipulations of this my Last Will and Testament are stated in Addendum B. Addendum A lists the principal business entities that comprise R. C. Johnson, Incorporated."

Everyone caught his or her breath. Elli was visibly overjoyed for Bobbi, who was so deserving of good fortune. Assaying that his audience was eager for him to wrap up the session, Mark pressed on. "Addendum A contains an impressive list of enterprises. I will be glad to share the information with anyone interested after the meeting. Addendum B is relatively brief. Among other stipulations Mr. Johnson points out that he would like his daughter to give Orin Babcock and Charlie Owens, two of his most loyal employees, both started, he notes here, as truck drivers with him when he took over the business from his father, any truck from current inventory either wishes. He further expresses the need to terminate Ms Millie Austin immediately for cause, namely embezzlement, full details should be forthcoming from Peachtree Investigators. Mr. Johnson recommends against prosecution, but believes she can not be trusted. Therefore, that she should not be allowed to continue working for the company in any capacity. He also notes that he does not consider it worth the effort to retrieve the funds she has taken. She may keep them in lieu of severance pay and company retirement benefits."

Mark moved his chair back and stood. "Thank you for coming. All the documentation regarding this matter will be assembled and forwarded to Mr. Bowles as soon as we land in Barcelona tomorrow. On behalf of *Marebella Lines* and the Captain and the staff of *The Venetian* I wish you a pleasant evening, a safe return to your homes and a happy future. I think we can all learn something valuable from Mr. Johnson and his life." The room emptied rapidly. While Captain Lucchini congratulated Mark and Chief Bruni, Elli was hugging Bobbi and offering her any help she might need. She also shook hands with Lurene and Herb, both of whom were noticeably subdued. The Davidson's adjourned to their quarters to prepare for the final dinner aboard. The others left for their usual stations, content and relieved that a death at sea had been successfully resolved.

Even for Elli and Mark the disappearance of Mr. Johnson had been the source of emotional and physical strain. The cruise was intended to be a carefree journey to pleasant places, a welcome break from the rigors of running a globally-involved foundation and its immense portfolio of commercial and charitable activities. The satisfactory resolution of the mystery surrounding the missing passenger permitted a period of relaxation after dinner that brought smiles to most of the faces of those caught up in the tragedy. Lurene Johnson, while relieved to be free of suspicion that she might have engaged in foul play, was now confronting a future without her husband. Herbert Johnson, reflecting on his relationship with his father, decided he might have tried harder to please him. Both he and Lurene had learned RC's life insurance policy was worth five million dollars. Bobbi was probably more perplexed than exhilarated by the sudden change in her life. Her friends Suzanna and Pepino, while happy for Bobbi, knew that major changes were lurking around the corner. They were concerned for her future.

Lingering at their dining table to converse with their table mates, the Davidsons shared as much of the incident and its outcome, as they thought appropriate. Questions arose about Bobbi's new circumstances that also prompted Mark and Elli to feel some concern for Bobbi. Seeing that the staff was eager to complete their clean-up operation, everyone departed with hugs and kisses and best wishes for a safe return home. The Davidsons repaired to their cabin where Elli had already begun some preliminary packing. A telephone call home revealed that Uncle Roland had taken the girls and Theo to Leysin for the day. There, Sylvie and Mireille, both avid equestrians, spent the day attending a dressage class and a tour of the stud farm owned by one of the Denis-Breuer clan. Theo, who loved all animals, shadowed the farm's veterinarian as the latter pursued his daily rounds.

Less than half an hour after the Davidson's had drifted off to sleep, Elli whispered, "Mark, are you sleeping?"

Mark rolled over and leaned on his elbow. "I guess I slept for a few minutes, but I've been thinking a lot about Bobbi Johnson. She has a lot on her plate, if you'll pardon the pun. I'm worried about her. She's about to enter a whole new world and she's probably not too well prepared. I think we need to help... and we're going to land in a few hours. There's not much time available.

"We need to get on the phone. It will be too early for some and too late for others, but you're right, we have very little time to get organized."

Tuesday Night

On their feet again, dressing casually, Elli and Mark managed to reach Bobbi by phone in her cabin. They decided to meet in the Grand Salon, where they found a quiet corner table. Suzanna also joined them there. Mark outlined the matters Bobbi would have to deal with in the coming weeks. Bobbi hadn't had time to think everything through, but acknowledged that she was entering unfamiliar territory and that help would be appreciated.

Mark proposed a plan of action. Bobbi gratefully accepted. Several calls to Atlanta led to the following: Mr. Bowles would schedule the formal reading of the will in three weeks. Bobbi would take a week off to attend and also meet with a colleague of Mark's who was active in the business consulting arena in the American Southeast. Bowles, already in possession of Johnson's power of attorney, would immediately fire Ms Austin and hire an auditor to check the books of all the enterprises under the R.C. Johnson umbrella. Mark's colleague would set up interviews for Bobbi with three qualified persons to serve as general manager of the company until such time as she would be able to take over, or pursue another course of action. Lurene and Herb would be offered an opportunity to take any furniture or memorabilia they wished from the Johnson's Atlanta mansion. The structure would likely be offered for sale, with Lurene and Herb having the right of first refusal. Dates and times were established. Elli and Mark indicated that they would be amenable to further consultation at Bobbi's convenience, if she would like.

"I'm overwhelmed. You hardly know me and you have been so kind." Bobbi, with Suzanna nodding agreement, was deeply grateful for the incredibly generous help offered so readily by the Davidsons. "I plan to complete my current contract. Next season I have been offered the position as Head of Food Services on a slightly smaller ship with a home base in Venice. We'll do Adriatic ports and some of the Greek islands. After that, I don't know. I've always wanted to have my own restaurant… maybe in Los Angeles. Now, of course, I have to share my plans with someone else. Last week Pepino asked me to marry him." Holding out her left hand with a modest engagement ring, she went on, "We want to locate somewhere that allows us both to pursue our careers, at least until we start a family."

"Congratulations!" Speaking in unison, the Davidsons hugged Bobbi again. "Whoops! It's after midnight. You must be tired." Mark looked at his watch. "Let's all get some rest. Tomorrow will be a busy day, especially for you, Bobbi."

"Thank you. I am tired… and so excited."

"What a day! I am amazed and so happy for Bobbi." Suzanna was truly excited. "No one deserves a day like this more than Bobbi."

Before heading off for their cabin and a good night's sleep, Elli turned to Suzanna. "And everyone could use a good friend like you, Suzanna. Sleep well."

CHAPTER THIRTEEN

Wednesday Morning

During the night, as weary passengers snoozed peacefully rehashing their experiences and embellishing them with hyperbole for consumption at home, stewards and stevedores wrestled the luggage so carefully stacked outside their cabins down to Deck 4. Sorted by alphabet, it would be off-loaded upon arrival and organized in neat rows in the giant hall where disembarking passengers could claim it before rushing to the long-term parking facility, the railroad station or the airport.

Security Chief Bruni was busy editing his official report for the Captain's signature. It would be filed in Genoa, *The Venetian's* home port. Copies would be made available to the appropriate authorities in Athens and Barcelona, as well as to the American Consul in Barcelona for transmission to the Coroner in Johnson's county of residence and to the District Attorney there.

Somewhere aboard, Neville Easton III, chatting up an attractive widow, was maintaining his affable veneer of casual charm. Elli and Mark were standing outside at almost the same spot on the deck from which they had observed the Johnsons' entrance ten days earlier. They breathed in the crisp, salty air. The great blue sweep of the morning sky was clear. The pall cast on their spirits by Johnson's mysterious disappearance had been lifted.

Bobbi was engrossed in her responsibility to receive the fresh produce and other supplies for the next passage east to the Greek islands. Suzanna was directing her staff as they cleaned the cabins and suites and arranged them for those who would board in the afternoon. The entertainers, under Pepino's watchful eye, were rehearsing a new routine. The benefit concert had been so popular that Pepino hired two young opera singers and a ballet duo to rendezvous with the ship enroute for a special "high brow" performance.

Fräulein Hallstein, the owner of a spacious condo in Kitzbühel, invited the Davidsons to pick a week next winter to stay rent-free for a skiing holiday. She also extended an invitation to Lucca Bruni, who she learned was a bachelor, an excellent dancer and only a year older than she.

* * *

A final item. Church sacraments for a person who, according to the official death certificate, had taken his own life, were doubtful. Bobbi's dilemma found a happy compromise in Elli's suggestion of a non-sectarian remembrance service in Atlanta during the week Bobbi would be there to meet with Mr. Johnson's lawyer. Mr. Bowles had agreed to arrange it. This was a time for endings and beginnings. All agreed; looking ahead was more important than looking back.

THE END

A Mark Davidson Story

COLLABORATION

Hellmut Edelmann

Chapter One

The red BMW 3-series convertible deftly negotiates the open gate of *União Bebida e Distribuiçao Companhia do Sul*'s headquarters not far from Campinas in São Paulo State in southern Brazil. Dressed in natty light blue designer slacks and a knit white silk polo shirt open at the neck, Henrique da Serra, a recent Ph.D. in Chemistry from a prestigious Brazilian university, reaches into the rear seat, grabs his briefcase and walks confidently towards the main entrance of the handsome, stucco-faced building that houses the company's administrative and sales offices. The BMW, a serious expression of status in Brazil, is left to cope with several hours of direct sun and high humidity without the protection of its custom canvas top.

Less than a year before, when da Serra first joined the edgy, aggressive staff of the up-coming beverage manufacturer and distributor, his transportation was a well-used Taiwanese motor scooter, his clothing was Wal-Mart-chic. He had shared a small apartment in an older section of Campinas with his parents and a younger brother. Some colleagues wondered among themselves how their young counterpart was able to afford a flashy new car and a modern apartment in a choice neighborhood after just a few months of employment. The answer, although da Serra wasn't about to share it, was relatively simple. Unfortunately, as in similar circumstances, what appears simple in the onset often garners complications as time progresses.

União Bebida is a member of *White Cross Holdings'* growing family of Latin American enterprises. The world market has shown an affinity for metabolically-stimulating, fresh-tasting sports drinks. Young people, in particular, appear to crave products that can enhance performance, and are low in calories, as well as relatively sugar-and fat-free.

Da Serra's area of expertise, developed during his graduate studies, focused primarily on the production of foods and beverages based on Brazil's enormous Amazon resources in tropical and semi-tropical fruits and exotic herbs and flora, many of which have proven medicinal value. A stellar, rather driven student, da Serra was showered with scholarships. He became a department darling, as evidenced by his numerous awards, not to mention the glowing letters of commendation that appealed to potential employers.

While conducting a series of experiments aimed at producing new "sports beverages" with exotic tropical flavors, da Serra, working with protein molecules from a rare tuber found only in the bio-diverse rain-forests in the northwestern corner of South America's largest country, accidentally discovered a previously unknown enzyme with unusual prop-erties. From several extracts brewed from a stew-like concoction that contained a combination of the enzyme and other rare roots, leaves and flowers there arose a strange, yet oddly pleasant odor. He fed a few drops to each of three mice. They promptly began to move about their cages erratically, stumbling after a few seconds of frenzied movement. Unable to stand, they died, dark blood oozing from their mouths and anal regions. Further analysis of the compound that had contributed to the unintended demise of his four-footed assistants led to the conclusion that the new enzyme had accidently attached itself to bacteria present in the mice cages. The potent concoction had apparently invaded vital cellular structures causing instantaneous large-scale uncontrollable hemorrhaging. The infectious bacteria had somehow leap-frogged several developmental stages and brought about a fatal conclusion. Da Serra, who regretted the loss of his tiny 'associates', saw no immediate application for his discov-ery. Nonetheless, although its significance and potential were not clear, da Serra, imbued with the academic spirit, wrote a short article in an obscure local professional publication. He proudly, if conceitedly, named his discovery *Henserrase*. After all, it will look good in his resumé, he thinks.

That was in January, in the midst of a hot Brazilian summer. Within a relatively short time, the article is referenced in *The East Asian Chemistry Journal*, whose editor, Endo Kiriguchi, is an opportunistic entrepreneurial-type with few scruples. Kiriguchi suspects there may be commercial benefits to be reaped by exploiting the discovery. From his perspective, further experiments are essential. Funds from a recently deceased bachelor uncle would serve as seed money.

Kiriguchi's initial approach occurred online. A follow-up personal visit in Rio, where he lavished the young scientist with a stay at one of Rio's finest hotels, opulent restaurant dining and expensive gifts, easily found a vein of raw ambition and da Serra, naïve in the ways of the world, made a pact with the devil. After convincing da Serra that their collaborative initiative ought best to remain strictly a private matter between the two of them, da Serra begins to receive regular payments in return for his detailed notes and for continuing his experiments 'on the side'. During the summer and early fall in the southern hemisphere da Serra concentrated on his experiments. The company, meanwhile, impressed by his diligence and the modest but continuing progress towards his assigned objective, gave him a raise and virtual *carte blanche* to explore further for a 'winning formula'. The gifted biochemist had wasted little time upgrading his lifestyle.

The receptionist greets the young scientist cheerily. His rich dark hair, sun-tanned masculinity, handsome smile and jaunty step are generally met with appreciative glances from fellow staffers. The women are especially grateful for any sign of recognition. Exiting at the rear of the building, da Serra continues another thirty meters to the manufacturing and bottling division, passes through the side corridor, swaps greetings with a half dozen white-coated associates and enters the restricted section of the building containing the laboratories. Those on the left are for checking product samples. On the right is the sanctuary of the creative who toil tirelessly to generate the new wave of foodstuffs and beverages all hope will help União Bebida forge to the front of the industry and establish itself with a major share of the market for energy drinks.

Having made it plain to colleagues that he prefers to work without assistance, da Serra, while working concurrently on several company-assigned projects, manages to devote a substantial effort towards learning more about 'his enzyme'. Dozens upon dozens of unsuccessful attempts later, he succeeds in synthesizing the enzyme. Kiriguchi is delighted and proposes several tests to help determine how the enzyme might best bring about an increase in their personal fortunes, while, of course, contributing to man's knowledge of the universe. Da Serra was sympathetic to the note of altruism so smoothly sounded by Kiriguchi. The possibility of significant wealth creation as a result of his work was equally appealing.

The widely accepted principle that 'discoveries' made in company facilities on company time are the intellectual property of the sponsoring firm had escaped da Serra until one night while reflecting on his situation he suddenly realized he had unwittingly become an accomplice to a crime. At the very least it was a serious breach of professional ethics.

It was common knowledge that enzymes are proteins that can catalyze up to several million reactions each second. *Henserrase*, his studies showed, could increase the rates of chemical reactions by over one hundred million per second. After it was learned that the new enzyme's principal characteristic was its function as a truly super accelerant in other chemical processes, a substance that materially increases the velocity of certain chemical reactions, Kiriguchi's train of thought began to reveal a dark side to his interest for possible applications. After a few weeks Kiriguchi decided communicating in the clear was 'unwise', as he put it. He arranged for appropriate encryption software.

Unbeknownst to either collaborator, intelligence personnel in the U.S. and other Western countries had stumbled upon random internet transmissions with a variety of 'trigger words', such as, 'hyper-reactive speed', 'highly contagious', 'destructive power', 'method of dispersal', 'quick death', and the like in messages sent by Kiriguchi to a few correspondents in Eastern Europe and the Middle East. The participants in these exchanges were traced and identified. Some were known terrorist organizations; a few had not previously been on watch lists. Switching to encrypted messages had the effect of further concerning analysts, who wondered why innocent scientists would require such secrecy.

When da Serra began to realize the potential for harm connected to his enzyme and started to question Kiriguchi's motives and his negative orientation, his reaction was to intentionally put the brakes on his research. He had a gut feeling that Kiriguchi was up to no good. He manufactured excuses for delays and attempted to disparage the potential of the enzyme and to complain about its inherent instability. When pressed to hurry up his efforts, the young scientist began to balk, an attitude to which his Japanese benefactor was certainly not blind. The publisher/entrepreneur determined da Serra's usefulness was waning. Claiming the project unworthy of further investment and suggesting it was a failure, Kiriguchi backed away and ceased providing financial support. His actions were merely a ruse to throw da Serra off balance and to obscure a change in direction.

The young Brazilian was relieved. He realized himself that he had strayed afar from his original noble intentions. Colleagues had begun to inquire about his long hours; asked why he always locked up all his work in special cabinets; commented aloud about possible conflicts of interest. In the meantime, Kiriguchi had decided he needed to identify another 'helper'. The Japanese publisher was also actively testing the waters for potential partners, partners with deep pockets.

* * *

In a middle-class Baltimore suburb two men passed each other in the restroom of a popular lunch-time eatery. The elder of the two, frail-looking and grey-haired, had just entered; the taller and younger, notable for his five-o'clock shadow and receding hairline, was leaving. The former took a neatly folded paper towel from the counter and stuffed it in his pants pocket before proceeding to the urinals, where he disposed of the cigarette stub that was dangerously close to burning his lips. Shortly afterwards both exited the restaurant, heading in different directions.

Chapter Two

Two south-facing corner offices on the top floor of the Sunshine Assurance Group Building had a great view of the St. John's River flowing past central Jacksonville into the Atlantic Ocean. There was but a single entrance next to which was a modest brass sign with the engraved name: Agrar Imp-Ex, S.A. The gravelly voice emanating from behind the bushy gray moustache and the well-kempt heavy beard of Clark Willette resonated clearly in the larger space where the entrance was located. "Come and look at this!" The person to whom this directive was addressed had little choice. When the boss called, Dr. Gayle Beckmeister understood her presence was not optional. She strolled into the space cluttered with piles of boxes, each stuffed with papers many would be surprised to learn contained important and highly sensitive intelligence.

"What have you got?" She plunked down in the chair next to Willette's desk and immediately took possession of the sheet of paper thrust into her hands. Although Willette was the boss, Beckmeister, known for her keen intellect, considered herself an equal.

"…difficulties… contamination of specimens…" Her eyes consumed the printed sheet in a flash. "Doesn't sound like much. From the same source?"

"Yup. It seems innocuous at first glance. But this Japanese fellow appears to have a more serious interest, a proprietary interest perhaps, in certain experimental activity than one might expect of the editor of a professional publication. He ought to be impartial and objective. His online correspondence with contributors is not entirely straightforward. There's a devious quality to some of the messages he receives and some that he sends. What do you think? Oh, by the way, his messages are now transmitted in encrypted form."

"Any further reference to *"a devastating virus"*, the expression picked up on a phone tap recently?"

"No. That line has gone dead. By the way, it was used just once." Willette combed his mustache with his fingers, a habit that usually indicated he was deep in thought. "Top Dog," his euphemism for the nation's nervous leader, "has signaled we should get on this 'big time'. No telling what might be behind it. Since other intercepts of a similar nature have led to solid results, there's reason to be worried about this one."

"Have the Japanese or the Brazilians been alerted?"

"Un-huh.! This has to remain our baby until we've got an iron-clad case."

"Guess I'll start with that scientific article from Brazil. My feminine intuition tells me it might have started there."

"Keep in touch. And for Christ's sake, be careful!"

Beckmeister nodded in Willette's direction as she closed his door. She checked her email account, stuffed a couple of folders in her briefcase, and headed out the door. Jacksonville's temperature and humidity indices were high and rising. She drove south on I-95, turned east on Butler Boulevard and set a course for Ponte Vedra Beach, where she had a comfortable ocean-side condo in an exclusive club neighborhood.

Gayle Beckmeister, graduate of a premier private woman's college, spent a year at the University of Tübingen, then earned a law degree from Yale and a Ph.D. in International Law from Columbia University. Earlier in her career she taught law at Emory in Atlanta, served in a few Washington agencies and had done a stint in a large private practice that concentrated on maritime issues. Smart, well-spoken and attractive, she had come to the attention of Willette through her expert handling of several highly sensitive international legal matters. He liked her superior intelligence, her ability to deal with complex issues and personalities, as well as her personal integrity and strong loyalty. He often wondered why such an attractive and desirable woman had not caught the eye of a potential mate.

Willette, a Ph.D. in Psychology from Cornell, had a checkered background. He spent a couple of tours as a junior diplomatic officer, survived a shadowy career in the CIA, and was a partner in a security firm with ties to leadership figures in the legislative and executive branches. Along the way he earned a reputation as a loyal and competent operative who delivered the goods. While Beckmeister was on her way to the beach, Willette exchanged encrypted messages with someone at the highest level in the nation's capital. Fingering his beard again, Willette wondered to himself if the effort to investigate these references wasn't rather late in coming. *Damned if we're not way behind in dealing with this potential threat. Why isn't 'Top Dog' more concerned? Hmmm!*

* * *

With the help of a contact in Miami, Beckmeister did a careful search of União Bebida's business activities and research programs. The company was well run and generally respected for its business practices. Investors considered the company one with excellent prospects for future growth. The only unusual item was the scientific article by an employee. Unusual because he gave no credit to the company whose resources he used for his experiments. The discovery of a hitherto unknown enzyme didn't strike the investigator as earth-shaking. The fact that da Serra's financial circumstances improved markedly not long after his article made the rounds of scientific circles, did, however, raise eyebrows. It appeared to Beckmeister that getting inside the company for a first-hand look was a priority. Who better to help than The All-American Boy, Mark Davidson. She wondered to herself, *How has time changed her former college acquaintance?*

* * *

Mark Davidson, his small, wheeled suitcase at his side, waited patiently for the female behind the Reception counter at Atlanta's Ritz-Carlton

Hotel to process his credit information. He had decided, partly due to reported airport delays, to remain in town overnight, before resuming his itinerary westwards. He thanked the comely young lady, who had no idea she was dealing with the hotel chain's majority stockholder, and began to roll his suitcase away, his room card firmly in hand. As he looked up to check the location of the elevators across the lobby, he stopped momentarily to determine the identity of a very lovely, very professional-looking woman waiting for her turn to register. The face was familiar. She looked up. A mutual jaw dropping occurred, expressing genuine surprise on Mark's part, feigned surprise on hers.

"Mark, Mark Davidson, is that really you?" She appeared to have been totally unprepared to bump into an old acquaintance from college days on a rainy night in Georgia's capital city.

"Gayle!" Her name rolled off his tongue immediately. "Well, what brings you to this fair city? Gosh, it's been quite a while since we last saw each other. How have you been?"

Gayle Beckmeister, J.D., Ph.D., a demure expression on her face, had relinquished her place in line, her similarly small rolling luggage in tow. Slightly embarrassed, Mark thought to shake her hand, but abruptly, however smoothly, switched to a friendly embrace and a token peck on Gayle's cheek. Both subconsciously calculated the dozen years since their last meeting. It had been an inter-collegiate debate contest. Gayle and Mark, both leaders of their respective college teams, were involved in a season-ending challenge debate between their conference and a similar all-star team from the Big Ten. David had bested Goliath in a close decision. The conquerors celebrated enthusiastically in a marathon beer bust that terminated in a nearby motel. No enduring 'relationship' developed. There were a few phone calls and an occasional letter. Mark went on to graduate school. Gayle spent a year at a university in Germany, then returned and pursued studies at Yale Law School. The correspondence faltered and ceased by default as both pursued their respective careers.

"Time has been kind to you, Gayle, you're lovelier than ever." Mark didn't intend to flirt. He merely stated the obvious. She was, indeed, attractive, expensively, but tastefully dressed. And still wearing the low-heeled shoes she had always preferred. Her bright complexion reflected the vibrant energy and enthusiastic curiosity he always associated with her.

"You don't look so bad yourself. Here on business?" Dr. Beckmeister knew full well what had brought Mark to Atlanta. Her office had briefed her thoroughly. Clark Willette, her boss, believed in careful preparation.

Looking at his watch, Mark figured the time differential quickly and realized he had promised to call the office in Geneva while his staff was still there. "I've an idea. Let's have a drink around six. Perhaps dinner afterwards, if you have no plans, of course."

"I was going to spend the evening with some dreary papers. I'd prefer dinner with a handsome escort. I'll meet you in the bar at six. See you." She rejoined the line. An elderly gentleman, recognizing that she had been ahead of him earlier, motioned for her to step in front of him. She acknowledged with a smile and soon completed her arrangements at the Reception counter.

Davidson called home, spoke with his office, then chatted with his wife Elli, relating his activities of the day and informing her of the change in plans that would have him in Atlanta for another day. He closed his cell phone. Somewhat pensively, he thought to himself, *Hmmm, Gayle Beckmeister. Still single and still quite a looker. Her voice and her language were rather flirty. Interesting. Some people you never forget.*

* * *

At a small corner table, two glasses of the house Merlot before them, a casual blue blazer-clad man with handsome features engaged a neatly coiffed woman in a Chanel-style tweed suit in cozy conversation. Although the woman had been briefed in detail about Mark's recent history, Mark was learning much that was new regarding Gayle's activities since graduating from college. They were both suitably impressed with their respective table mate's accomplishments. Mark, ever the modest college professor, gave no sign whatsoever that he was one of the world's wealthiest and most powerful men. Gayle, while equally modest and unassuming, was, in Mark's estimation, quite a woman, with a list of accomplishments few of her sex could match. Dinner followed. The All-American Boy indulged in a beef steak with a perfect baked potato and a medley of vegetables. Miss World enjoyed fresh Alaskan salmon, rice and peas. Both passed on dessert, and retired to their rooms after saying good-byes and expressing wishes to meet again sometime.

Chapter Three

Already in office two years, America's first woman president, Clarissa Barton-Howell, an attractive, childless widow, celebrated her 64th birthday together with her two public relations advisors and her Chief of Staff, Manfred Scharffenberger. As usual, Madame President spent several minutes discussing her daily poll numbers. Her approval rating was well up in the fifties. She planned some photo ops with a view towards assuaging veterans organizations unhappy with her budget cuts, and influencing gays and lesbians not totally satisfied with her commitment to guarantee marriage rights for same-sex partners. The former Senator from North Dakota, who began her career as a journalist and made most of her fortune, not to mention her generous inheritance from Wally Howell, as a result of her highly successful radio and television talk show, had a world-wide female following that was immense. She was also popular with liberal ethnic groups. Owning her own cable TV and radio network certainly proved to be an advantage when running for office.

President Barton-Howell was by and large a 'big picture' person. She delegated liberally. Sticky details were left to her Chief of Staff, her former campaign manager. She especially found dealing with security matters "a dirty affair" she would rather leave to others. Where the President's love of big, expensive parties and her penchant for real estate acquisitions, including homes in Southern California, Upper Michigan, a luxury penthouse in New York City, a ski lodge in Idaho, resorts in the Florida Keys and the Caribbean, were the grist of tabloid writers and gossip columnists, Manfred Scharffenberger studiously maintained a low public profile. His material needs were modest. His home in a Baltimore suburb was notoriously unspectacular. He preferred to bury himself in his work, letting others appear before the press. Getting credit for the President's smooth transition and early appointments was not important to him. During the first half of the President's term he had quietly consolidated virtually every important presidential function in his office. He had hand-picked most of the Cabinet and a significant number of secondary players. They all understood where their true allegiance lay. Members of Congress capitalized on every opportunity to curry favor with him. The daily CIA, FBI, Homeland Security briefings were made to him. He filtered out what he felt the President had little real interest in and spoon-fed her an easily digestible menu of froth. He also controlled the President's discretionary budget and routinely decided whom she would see and who would have to settle for him. Scharffenberger either penned or edited virtually all the President's speeches. Fortunately, as an accomplished actress, the President always read her prepared texts with great aplomb, her verbal skills made her appear entirely believable, knowledgeable, honest and sincere.

The President considered herself a multi-tasker. While getting a news briefing she often had her staff manicurist in the Oval Office, or a dress designer measuring her for a new outfit. She put her telephone on loud speaker while simultaneously talking to foreign leaders, checking fabric swatches and texting her celebrity friends. Scharffenberger made it known within the White House that no mention should be made of the President's frequent consultations with her 'personal astrologer', a Bulgarian émigré, whose gift of a miniature white poodle called 'Snegelpod' was headlined in the tabloids for months. He had also threatened *Vanity Fair* with serious tax problems if it pursued a story about Barton-Howell's latest yoga vacation at an Indian guru's 'wellness' ranch outside Phoenix. Part of her morning routine involved carefully combing her hair to cover the nearly invisible scars left by the cosmetic surgeon's scalpel. The staff of the White House spa complex and the President's Hungarian-born cosmetologist labored daily to keep the Nation's leader the envy of her sex everywhere.

The President found it somewhat annoying when confronted with issues carried over from previous regimes. Currently, government officials were engrossed in the latest of a series of health care scandals. The National Union of Physicians and Health Professionals was threatening a new strike for an additional increase in fees. Seniors for Suicide, an off-shoot of the defunct AARP, was planning a march on Washington to demand expansion of existing assisted suicide laws to all fifty states. Barton-Howell generally referred contentious matters of this nature to her loquacious Vice President, LaRon DeMario Lincoln, a dapper Angelino, who was the darling of certain late night talk shows because of his charm, racy wit, and appeal to younger voters.

Scharffenberger's self-penned official biography indicated he was 45 years old, married to his college sweetheart, now a municipal judge in a Maryland community bordering on the nation's capital, and the father of three teenage girls. Good teeth, horn-rimmed glasses and a professorial appearance lent him credibility. His ever present five-o'clock shadow was a negative. His black hair had thinned to the point where he was quite bald. His prominent nose was slightly arched. He was a man of few words. A smile was rare. Dark eyes constantly surveyed his surroundings. His penetrating stare left many a target uncomfortable, somehow violated. He had an advanced degree in political science from a state university better known for its sports successes than its academic standing. He was a long-time supporter of liberal political groups and causes, and had impressed Barton-Howell sufficiently early on to become her confidante and principal political strategist. His only hobby was sailing.

When it came to his childhood the facts were somewhat murky. The most prevalent story revolves around his adoption by a Jewish couple from an orphanage in Romania when he was very young. While he occasionally attended temple, neither he nor his adoptive parents were particularly religious. The unfortunate couple died in an automobile accident shortly after Manfred earned his bachelor's degree. Scharffenberger assiduously avoided questions about his background and youth. Generally, he was effective at deflecting inquiries. Reporters, caught up in the heat of current events, allowed Scharffenberger's past to languish in the haze. He was never pressed for more information.

Following her early session, Madame President was hustled off to meet with a number of Hollywood supporters who were requesting additional funds for increased wildlife refuges in the Rockies. Scharffenberger devoted a full half hour to a conversation over his secure phone to a small office in Jacksonville, Florida. "You simply must ramp up your efforts. We need to know what this Japanese guy is up to. Do you understand?"

"Yes sir, we're on it and expect to have more information soon."

"Let me know, if you need more money. I'll check back at the end of the week. The President wants results." Scharffenberger's tone was firm, demanding. He hung up the phone.

On his way home early in the evening, Scharffenberger stopped his Mercury Mariner in front of Acme Produce, a mom and pop enterprise specializing in organic fruits and vegetables. George Labbani, an Iranian-born US citizen, was just beginning to carry inside the store a few of the boxes of fresh produce that had been displayed during the day on the wide sidewalk in front of the shop. Scharffenberger greeted Labbani, asking if the melons were ripe. Assured that they were perfect for dessert this evening or breakfast in the morning, the President's Chief of Staff asked Labbani to pick one out for him. He did. They exchanged a couple of "for men only" jokes. Then Scharffenberger left with his melon after handing the shopkeeper three new one dollar bills. Anyone watching would probably have been moved to note how comfortably a Jew and an avowed Shiite from Iran could get along in a free society.

Scharffenberger's wife was attending her neighborhood book club meeting. The children were engaged in after-school sports programs. He entered the kitchen from the garage, set his bulging briefcase on the counter, found a long knife in a drawer and proceeded to cut the melon open. First, however, he removed the grower's label that had been stuck over the place where the stem had been. Scharffenberger then carefully removed a small plug before halving the melon. Inside was a thin plastic capsule. This he retrieved, pulled it apart and unrolled an encrypted message.

While Scharffenberger read the note passed to him from his control, the busy green grocer, seated at his desk in the back room of his shop puffing away on the stub of a foul-smelling cigarette, removed from one of the dollar bills a microdot, placed it in a magnifying reading device, read the contents of the President's security briefing and then, moving to the large sink along the rear wall, slipped the dot into the disposal together with some lettuce leaves he was discarding. Since there was nothing warranting further action on his part, he proceeded to finish preparing to close up for the day. He would summarize the contents in tomorrow's report. He sucked hard on the remaining cigarette, then stomped it out vigorously on the floor as he slowly exhaled a cloud of yellowish smoke.

The President's Chief of Staff included knowledge of German and French on his resumé, but failed to note that he was also fluent in Hebrew, Arabic and Farsi. The Orioles' baseball fan and avid sailor with access to the country's most sensitive secrets was born Reza Falani in Qum, Iran. He attended a Shiite-run *Madrasah islamiyyah* until it was decided at the age of nine, that because of his extraordinarily high IQ and exceptionally mature poise, not to mention his single-minded devotion to the faith, he would be sent to the United States as a mole; a mole who would surface at the right time and do the bidding of his mentors.

* * *

Endo Kiriguchi exited the elevator in the Sheraton-Hong Kong's main lobby. He moved quietly and energetically through the hallways to the Jade Ballroom, where exhibitors at one of Asia's largest scientific congresses had their booths. Earlier in the morning he had dismissed his escort, Ken, following a night of sexual magic during which the youthful Chinese had shown his mastery of a variety of techniques well worth the extravagant price the Japanese had paid for his ministrations. Now, the focus had to be on searching for a new bio-chemist to assist with the enzyme research Kiriguchi believed had huge promise. Unfortunately, he realized he would also need an investor, or, perhaps, investors, who could help meet the high cost of perfecting the enzyme's strange potential.

While Kiriguchi loved his homeland for its food and culture, it was not a country that showed much compassion to homosexuals like himself. This, he understood, was why he enjoyed frequent foreign travel, where he could usually avoid the scrutiny of the prying eyes he disliked at home. Visits to the United States confirmed his view that it was a decadent land with relatively few redeeming features. Both his grandfathers had died in WWII. One, a kamikaze pilot, was consumed by flames when his Mitsubishi fighter dove into an American destroyer. The other, while operating a machine gun from a hillside cave, was reportedly the victim of a flame thrower on a forlorn Pacific island liberated by US Marines. That terrorists would want to target America was perfectly logical and acceptable to Kiriguchi.

Copies of the current issue of *The East Asian Chemistry Journal* Kiriguchi handed out at his booth contained a box on the back cover soliciting resumés from biologists and chemists interested in finding new and exciting employment opportunities. On each of the four days the Congress was in session Kiriguchi interviewed from two to four persons who responded to his ad. They usually met in his suite in the late afternoon. The host provided light refreshments and beer or wine. Kiriguchi had in mind an arrangement similar to the one with Henrique da Serra, that is, an ambitious young male, with strong academic credentials and solid lab experience, eager for a big increase in income. Unlike da Serra, however, Kiriguchi was looking for a person for whom scruples were not likely to be an impediment to risky experimentation. He wanted someone over whom he could gain total control.

The first three days Kiriguchi met and spoke with eight candidates, mostly middle-aged men stuck in a career rut who were interested in a change that would elevate their status and income. None had the qualities Kiriguchi felt were imperative. None had the circumstances that would allow them to continue their present responsibilities while concurrently pursuing Kiriguchi's enzyme research. During the mid-day break on the Congress' final day Kiriguchi left the hotel to arrange for another tryst that evening. Upon his return a nice-looking, youngish man with black hair and smooth dark skin was filling out a questionnaire and was about to leave it in a tray designated for that purpose at the *Journal's* booth. The Japanese introduced himself to Taufik Susila, an Indonesian. Although Kiriguchi realized immediately that Susila was straight, the two struck up a pleasant conversation and bonded readily.

Susila's work situation was nearly perfect. He had considerable autonomy. His laboratory was new and his background in biology and chemistry was ideal for the project Kiriguchi envisioned. Susila, who enjoyed considerable success with the opposite sex, had managed to develop long-term relationships with two women. In the ensuing conversation Kiriguchi discovered that both of them, living in opposite ends of the island of Java, were high-maintenance lovers. Satisfying their taste for luxurious living had plunged Susila into debt. The Japanese publisher couldn't have found a better collaborator. An arrangement was spelled out that each party considered fair and reasonable. They departed with plans to meet in Surabaya, Susila's place of employment, the following week. By a strange coincidence, of which Kiriguchi was totally unaware, Susila's employer was a science-oriented enterprise also functioning under *White Cross Holding's* firmament. Small world. The handsome Indonesian returned home with a sizeable bonus in his wallet. The Japanese had more than one reason to smile as he boarded an Air Japan flight to Tokyo.

* * *

Two men from the Middle East and a fellow Asian, all attendees at the Congress, had their 'antennas' extended constantly as they moved inconspicuously about the meeting rooms and exhibitions, alert for ideas and products that might defeat the defenses erected by anti-terror forces in America and Western Europe. All three had found Endo Kiriguchi of special interest. All three sat not only on huge financial resources, but also controlled extensive covert assets fired by radical ideologies urgent for a mission, hungry for deployment against their perceived enemies, the Infidels. The Korean was the first to make an overture to Kiriguchi. The latter played coy at first. He was, however, no match for his ruthless Pacific neighbor. A deal was proposed not long after Kiriguchi outlined the frightening potential he foresaw for *Henserrase*. Mr. Goh Il Wan was suitably impressed. He, in turn, reached out to the Iranian and the Saudi agents his spies had been following at the Congress for it was their bottomless pockets he would need to develop the enzyme's evil promise. Goh was especially happy that the experimentation would be conducted in Indonesia, far away from the satellite-mounted cameras aimed 24/7 at his North Korean homeland. If he had any reservations, they were about the Brazilian scientist, whose discovery might now be helped to a frightening application. Were he to contact the authorities, the trail would lead to Kiriguchi... and beyond.

Chapter Four

Munich was basking in the glow of a bright early spring sun with daytime temperatures in the high fifties. Mark usually walked when he had an opportunity to visit one of his favorite cities. Besides, parking was a problem and he could get about on foot nearly as fast as by taxi. *Lodenfrey* had just what he wanted: two lovely plaid woolen skirts for the girls and a woolen cardigan for Theo. They'd surely be pleased. For Elli, Mark planned to wait until they visited Paris later in the month. There, she had a couple of boutiques she favored. Crossing Maffei Strasse and proceding along the Promenadenplatz, Mark took the passage leading to the *Kleine Komödie*. He wanted to see what was playing this week. He read the notice on the box office window. *Too bad, temporarily closed for vacation*. From there he entered the side entrance to the Hotel Bayerischer Hof.

"Mr. Davidson, you have a message." The clerk, recognizing a frequent guest by sight, handed Mark his room key and an envelope. It was hotel stationery.

"Thanks, Karl." Mark pocketed the key, looked at a display window with gold necklaces, then sat for a moment in one of the lobby's rich brown leather arm chairs. He thought he could smell the faint fragrance of a delicate perfume. Opening the note, he was surprised to find it was from Gayle Beckmeister. *Strange*, he thought. He read, 'Heard the porter mention a Dr. Davidson, checked and learned it was the Dr. Davidson I know. How about lunch or dinner? My treat this time.' A cell phone number followed an artistic signature.

It was only 10:30 and Mark's next appointment wasn't until 2:00.

He checked his cell phone for messages. None. He called and left a message: *'Dallmayr's* at 12:30. Expect it to be crowded.' Stopping by the Reception desk on his way to the elevator, Mark asked Karl to call and reserve a table for two at the popular gourmet restaurant.

Where many a man with Mark's wealth and influence might be expected to act like a power player in virtually every circumstance, Mark, handsome and healthy-looking, studiously assumed the role in public of the pleasantly inconspicuous everyman, humble, casual, and friendly, the guy next door. He neither expected, nor wanted special attention or privileges. Exposed as he was in his frequent travel to danger of all kinds, he had felt fairly comfortable with his personal safety since Elli's kidnapping had begun to fade in his memory. He considered the days of constantly looking over his shoulder for the likes of Gregor Mukhachevo to be ancient history. However, his staff and friends insisted that certain measures be taken. And they were. Back in his room to freshen up for lunch, Mark stopped for a moment to mentally retrace his morning. He began to sense that he might have been followed. *Unusual,* he thought. *There were at least two people, both men, yes, they must have been tailing me. The middle-aged man in a... a gray suit, no gray trousers... and a tweed jacket who crossed the Sendlinger Tor behind me was the same fellow who was shopping later at Lodenfrey's. A coincidence? I wonder. I'll check on it later.*

From the hotel to Diener Strasse was not far. Mark walked briskly and arrived at his destination in time to peruse the marvelous displays of choice foods, coffees, baked goods and meats in the street-level gourmet shop. He was checking some of the wine offerings when Gayle Beckmeister showed up. They exchanged greetings, then Mark escorted her upstairs to the dining area. They found a corner table, ordered quickly and engaged in small talk: the weather, travel hassles, and college days. Still subconsciously suspicious of the 'coincidental' nature of their presence in the same city and the same hotel so soon after their 'coincidental' meeting in Atlanta barely a week earlier, Mark's busy mind was mulling a myriad possibilities. He needed to know more about his hostess' occupation. *Why, after all these years, has she suddenly and inexplicably reentered my life?* He was subconsciously fascinated by her beauty and charm. She was alluring and had an aura of mystery about her.

By the time Mark and his college acquaintance had finished their lunch, almost all the tables were full and several guests were waiting impatiently for early diners to depart. "I've an idea," said Mark, leaning slightly across the table to obviate the need for speaking too loudly, "Let's skip dessert and continue our conversation across the street. The sun is pleasant and there are some benches in a small park there."

"It is getting a bit noisy. Good idea." Mark jumped up and helped her with her chair. She grabbed a jacket she had draped over the back of the chair and both exited smartly. More than a few pairs of eyes looked up to notice the departure of the attractive couple.

Looking about carefully to avoid the cars and bicycles moving aggressively in the high noon traffic, the two visitors managed to reach the *Marienhof,* a small grassy plot behind the *Rathaus,* unscathed. An empty bench beckoned. En route, Mark had surveyed the area and thought he might have seen a figure familiar to him from the previous day's forays into the bustling inner city's pedestrian melee. The early autumn day was especially mild.

"Gayle, I have a couple of questions for you."

"And I for you. You go first."

"As part of my responsibilities for the, ah… company I work for, I travel rather extensively. Every once in a while, I happen to cross paths with someone I used to know. Such occasions are, however, actually quite rare. Now, within just several days' time, we have met twice in the same city, and the same hotel. Am I following you, or are you following me?"

"Well, you were here first, so I suppose it's the latter." She had a sexy smile.

Mark turned towards Gayle and looked her straight in the eye. "You mentioned in Atlanta something about consulting on international legal issues with an obscure government agency. Frankly, that sounds vague and evasive. Could you expand on that."

"Before I answer that, I have done some research on you. You keep saying things like 'the company I work for', 'the group I represent', 'I've been assigned to...' I know for a fact that you are the Secretary General of the famous philanthropic *Fondation Székely*. You are also the Chairman and CEO of one of the world's largest and most powerful holding companies. You answer to no Board of Directors. I've heard you do have an outstanding panel of advisors and often delegate authority to some of them. What I'd like to know is, how someone so rich and powerful can wander around a city like Munich like some happy-go-lucky tourist. Don't you believe in taking some precautions?"

"Looks can be deceiving. I'm not as naïve as I may appear." Nodding to his right, Mark spoke softly, "I believe that fellow studying our reflection in the shop window on the other side of the street is one of yours. Am I right?"

"O.K." Her expression indicated she had been caught. "I'm sorry, but I can explain."

"Wait a minute! See the elderly lady with the dachshund sitting on the bench facing us on the other side of the fountain?"

"Yes."

"She's going to wave to you."

A surprised Dr. Beckmeister reflexively waved back. Perplexed, she mumbled, "I don't understand."

"A few years ago my wife was kidnapped and held for ransom. Out of concern for her and our children we engaged a security firm to protect them. Later, following an accident, I wandered around parts of France and Germany for nearly a year as an acute amnesiac. That prompted the people around me to insist that we create a special department to provide discreet surveillance wherever I go. Since I travel to Germany quite often, we have a resident team here. The woman with the dog is one of them. The dog's collar and little coat are actually a hi-tech directional antenna. Miryam was listening to our conversation. She's actually 32, a champion kick-boxer, expert marksman, and qualified in both helicopters and multi-engine aircraft. The cyclist who just parked his bicycle near the phone booths over there on the left is armed and ready to assist me, if necessary."

"Well, I am impressed. I had no idea. And I do hope it won't be necessary."

"That's how it's supposed to work. I regret the necessity for such measures. I sincerely do. But we have to deal with realities. O.K. It's your turn. Why are you following me? What is this all about?"

"Although you live abroad, I know you're as American as apple pie. What I am about to tell you is not to be shared with anyone. And I mean anyone." Mark nodded assent. His mien was serious. He nodded to the lady with the dachshund, who turned off her earpiece. "The FBI and CIA are increasingly subject to Congressional and, therefore, public scrutiny. For partisan political reasons, dangerous leaks are all too frequent. Obviously, that is highly detrimental to the kind of covert operations required to combat those who work relentlessly to undermine and destroy the peace and tranquility for which most peoples and nations strive." Gayle paused. "Pardon me, if I sound like a college lecturer. I will get to more specifics." She looked around, surveying the area for any obvious threats.

"Within one of the cabinet offices whose portfolio, on the surface at least, seems rather bland and primarily domestic in nature, a very small secret agency was formed to deal with issues of the highest sensitivity. As a cover I am officially charged with responsibility for international legal matters relative to foreign shipments of perishable foodstuffs. Our agency is tiny, literally only a handful of specialists. We report through my boss directly to the President via her Chief of Staff."

"But where do I fit in? Based on what little you've said, I am already concerned about the integrity of the *Foundation* and *White Cross Holdings*. We have worked diligently and constantly to establish our credentials as a global philanthropy, totally impartial and free of politics. As the manager and steward of an incredibly diverse empire of business ventures with a footprint in every continent I am adamantly adverse to jeopardizing our standing in any way."

Looking about once again, Gayle moved closer and lowered her voice even more. "Recently, we became aware of a potential plot to foment enormous unrest, death and destruction through the possible use of biological agents. Because employees of companies under the *White Cross Holdings* umbrella may be involved, we urgently need your assistance."

"My God! What sort of evidence do you have?"

"It's not well defined at this point. Wire taps. Internet hints. A careless email message. Keywords. A name or two. We wouldn't involve you if it weren't held to be of the utmost importance."

Mark thought for a moment. He leaned back against the bench. "All right, I'll give it serious consideration, but I've got to know more. Who else is in on this?"

"Only the agency I mentioned. The President apparently has considerable disdain for the FBI and CIA. We'll need someone in your headquarters who is intimately acquainted with everything about your various companies and philanthropic activities."

"Elli, my wife."

"I'd advise against that. It would be better for you, for her, and for your children if she is left out of it."

"O.K., then, Samantha Willis, one of our senior directors. She's a genius. Knows everything about us, and she is absolutely, one hundred percent loyal and trustworthy."

"Isn't she the severely handicapped woman who helped track you down while you were suffering from amnesia?"

"That's her. She's not handicapped. Challenged, maybe, but one of the most creative and resourceful people I know."

"I'm sold."

Mark checked his watch. "I have a meeting coming up in a few minutes. Let's continue our conversation at dinner this evening. The *Ratskeller* is behind us and the crowds there usually guarantee a fair amount of privacy. How about 7:00?"

"See you there." She rose and left, heading into a crowd moving towards the throngs shopping on Kaufingerstrasse.

Mark, still pondering this unexpected development, watched quietly as she blended smoothly into the stream of tourists and locals. He thought, *Very professorial and serious, and kind of sexy and captivating at the same time. Better be careful.*

* * *

Dr. Gayle Beckmeister, lawyer, former law school professor, well-known counsel on international legal issues, drew little attention from those passing her as she waited in the lobby of the *Ratskeller* on Munich's *Marienplatz*. Mark, also known for his punctuality, appeared moments later, arriving directly from his meeting with an advisory group that worked closely with the *Fondation*.

"Hope you haven't been waiting long." Mark, giving Gayle a polite hug, found her outfit quite attractive. Her perfume was subtle, understated. She dressed well, but conservatively, seeking intentionally to be relatively inconspicuous.

"As a matter of fact, I just arrived." She noted that Mark must have changed before his meeting. His jacket was a beautiful Bavarian-style leather, soft brown, with tasteful trim. His trousers were a medium gray flannel. Looking every bit the native, he fit into his surroundings rather well. Both ordered beer and chose *a pair of Nürnberger Bratwürste with Sauerkraut*. Caught up in the restaurant's ambience, they both spoke in German for a few minutes, then gravitated to English. In hushed tones, Beckmeister outlined her mission: to determine exactly what was behind some potentially ominous bits and snatches of information that was obviously intended strictly for the eyes and ears of a select group.

"How could one of the companies we control have possibly become involved? As far as I am aware, *White Cross Holdings* includes no entity that produces anything that could be remotely connected to a 'weapon of mass destruction'. And that's what you're implying, right?"

"I must admit, our information, which has been pieced together from several sources, is a jumbled mess, an amorphous blob of disjointed, yet highly suspicious tidbits that can't be ignored. We believe it may have begun with a scientific article in Portuguese written by a biochemist at one of your plants in Brazil. The synopsis, in English, speaks of a new enzyme with unusual characteristics. The enzyme, as reported, functions as an accelerant that easily and quickly invades cells. If true, some of our experts have concluded that when combined with bacterial or viral material, there is a possibility such materials could be spread uncontrollably among dense populations."

"What in the world possessed someone to conduct such an experiment? I am no chemist, but I fail….."

Gayle interrupted, "The discovery, it seems, was accidental. The person who wrote the article is a minor staff member of a small beverage producer and bottling company in São Paulo state in southern Brazil. It's located outside *Campinas*. Apparently, there is substantial competition to develop sports and health drinks based on herbs and medicinal plants unique to the Amazon. The company in question has a large enough lab facility to undertake foodstuffs, pharmaceutical and even pesticide testing for other companies in the region. ***União Bebida*** is the company's name."

"I haven't visited that company, but I do know of it. Unfortunately, I am not familiar with any particulars. What do you want me to do?"

"Firstly, we'd like you to conduct a very discreet inquiry into the matter of the article. Presumably, any discovery made in the course of conducting company business becomes the property of the sponsoring company. Has this employee, his name is Henrique da Serra, reported his findings? Has anyone determined whether or not to seek a patent? What further experimentation, if any, is being conducted? Has the scientific community expressed any special interest in the article, and, consequently, in the discovery?"

"That should be easy enough."

"Remember, this must be done in such a way that no undue suspicion is aroused – at any level."

"Gotcha!"

Thanking Mark for the meal, Gayle stood, they embraced politely, and saying she'd be in touch, she slipped quickly out of the restaurant and departed. A fascinating scent remained. Mark paid the bill. After walking back to the hotel, he inquired about a Dr. Gayle Beckmeister at the reception desk. No such person had been registered.

This is curious, thought Mark. *Shades of the Székelys. More cloak and dagger stuff. Ughh!*

* * *

Overcast skies greeted Mark the next morning. He had a single meeting with a member of the *Foundation's* advisory board. It was scheduled for 9:30. He sat in the dining room over breakfast and read the *Süddeutsche Zeitung* until 9:00, then set out on foot. A short cut led him to the *Frauenkirche.* He then joined the early morning shoppers on *Kaufingerstraße,* continued past the *Marienplatz,* turned right just past the *Peterskirche,* strolled through the *Viktualienmarkt,* tarrying a minute or two here and there to check the offerings, and eventually crossed the *Frauenstraße,* following *Reichenbachstraße* past the east side of the *Theater am Gärtnerplatz.* Checking his watch, he slowed in front of a nondescript office building. A glance ahead to the next corner revealed an elderly woman holding a dachshund on a leash. She demonstrably threw a folded newspaper into a trash receptacle. Mark knew the coast was clear, entered the building and took the stairs to the third floor. It was exactly 9:30.

Hubert Scholl was an architect, engineer and art historian. Slender, pale and white-haired, he was the kind of person you might pass a dozen times on the street and barely notice. There was a wispy quality about him. He had the ability to appear inconsequential and insignificant wherever he happened to be. Mark and Scholl hugged briefly. The latter greeted his guest warmly. His voice was firm and clear. Among friends the public *persona* disappeared and an individual with a sharp intellect and keen powers of observation stepped forward. While photographing famous churches in Eastern Europe, including Russia, for a new publication he was preparing, Scholl also collected invaluable close-up insights into political and social trends that could guide both the *Foundation* in its charitable efforts, as well as *White Cross Holdings*, which was considering further major investments in the region.

The assessment was thorough and objective. Dealing with a government that had not completely abandoned the totalitarian concepts of previous decades would be problematic. True freedom did not exist. Mark left after 90 minutes of discussion with the impression that the matter of large-scale financial infusions should best be deferred. Scholl gave him advanced copies of three new photographic calendars his publishers had assembled. The photographer gave the profits to local human rights groups.

* * *

Upon his return to Geneva, Mark took Samantha Willis aside for a private conversation in her conference room. He laid out the scenerio presented by Gayle Beckmeister, impressed on Willis the high degree of security required and asked her to set up a quiet inquiry into an employee by the name of da Serra in União Bebida's laboratory. She noted the urgency and went to work on it.

Afterwards, Mark drove home to Yverdon and enjoyed a warm reunion with Elli and the children. The next morning they inspected the vineyard they shared with Elli's sister, Dani, and her husband. Conclusion: a very good crop seemed a certainty. The children loved their gifts from *Lodenfrey* and Elli was looking forward to Paris. She already had tickets for the *Opéra* and a ballet performance.

The next day, Mark and Elli motored west to Geneva after first dropping the children off in Lausanne for the weekend with Dani and Roland. It was raining slightly, mostly showers that came and went quickly. In Geneva, Elli consulted with her staff and spent some time reviewing mail, looking over account records and visiting with various department heads. Mark and Samantha Willis met again in her conference room. There, ostensibly discussing plans for *Foundation* activities in the Middle East, the two locked heads and Mark related his ideas for ferreting out information regarding the alleged terrorist plot.

Willis suggested checking out da Serra in Campinas with the aid of private investigators. They could ascertain who his contacts were, determine whether he had income unaccounted for by his salary and any other legal activity, and make discreet inquiries of friends, acquaintances and neighbors under some plausible ruse to learn about his lifestyle. Mark approved. Sam made all the appropriate contacts, obtained assurances of discretion, secrecy and privacy, and set in motion a thorough vetting of Henrique da Serra. This was to be a priority investigation. Prompt responses were guaranteed.

The Davidsons then flew to Paris for the weekend. Friday night they enjoyed a performance of Mozart's *Le Nozze di Figaro* at the *Théâtre du Châtelet*, following an early dinner at a friend's villa outside the city. Saturday, Mark devoted himself patiently to a shopping tour with Elli. Her birthday was imminent and Mark wanted to help her buy something special. Gorgeous weather the following day called for a walking tour of the city, lunch in an outdoor café and a leisurely drive to the airport. Their French-based security detail was totally unobtrusive. Mark made a note to congratulate them.

In Switzerland once again, the Davidsons, at Dani's insistence, spent the night as guests of the Denis-Breuers and enjoyed a marvelous dinner made all the more delightful by some of Roland's exquisite wines. Mark recalled his first visit to the villa and his and Elli's harrowing escape from Gregor Mukhachevo. Monday's drive home to Yverdon was uneventful and pleasant.

Checking his email before retiring Mark had an encrypted message from Sam Willis. *"Problème en Brasil. Conseil nécessaire. Mardi matin."* Mark deleted the message, thinking, *What could be the matter?* Mark decided the matter was serious enough that he should support the local and regional directors involved by personally going to Brazil.

The Davidsons' relationship was one of absolute trust and honesty. Consideration for his family's safety and the knowledge that Elli's expertise in international finance and wireless communication would be enormous assets in combating the enemies Gayle was referring to, prompted Mark to explain the matter to his wife as he saw it, and to solicit her input. She readily agreed to help.

* * *

At the office, sequestered in Willis' conference room, Mark and Elli raced through the communication from the private investigative agency in São Paulo. Looking up at Willis, Mark wondered aloud, "Good Lord! Completely disappeared. Reported missing only one week ago by his family after failing to report for work or to show up at his apartment. This looks bad, really bad. What could have happened to him, Sam?"

"I received a second report. He seemed to be living somewhat beyond his means. We paid him well, but not so much that he could afford the lifestyle he adopted recently." She paused for a few seconds. "His sports car has not been found. The local police surmise his automobile has probably been dismantled and sold for parts. My guess, for what it's worth, is that he might never be found."

"Anything else?" Mark was genuinely concerned about the fate of the young scientist, although he had never met him.

"There's evidence he used his company computer occasionally for private communications. He sent encrypted messages to a computer based in Japan. We haven't traced them yet. The last message sent was a few weeks ago."

"Do what you can to track it down. Elli's people can assist."

"Too bad. This fellow was creative and curious. He wrote an article about an enzyme he discovered. Even got it published in a professional journal."

"About an enzyme, you say? Interesting. I'll pass that on to Tweed Suit." Tweed Suit being Gayle Beckmeister, who seemed to have a preference for attractive tailored outfits made from tasteful tweed fabrics.

"In the two reports from our affiliate in Campinas, União Bebida, it was reported that Henrique da Serra had failed to show up for work three days in a row. A colleague who went to his apartment building reports he had not been seen there for at least four days. His car was gone. He still had mail in his mail box. A private investigative firm later found the license plate to da Serra's sports car for sale in a flea market in São Paulo. An unidentified male body is awaiting identification by means of DNA there, too. Detectives speculate that da Serra's car has already been dismantled and the parts resold to dealers. Their assumption: foul play. Motive: unknown." Willis turned her special mobile chair towards a map on the wall and her laser light focused on São Paulo.

Mark sent an email to an address Beckmeister had given him. Not much to do but to wait for her reply.

Chapter Five

In a beautiful display of color the sun had set to the west. The evening air was muggy. Only a sliver of moon provided natural illumination. There was a small public park off to the left of the Hotel Nieuw Amsterdam in a rather rundown suburb of Jakarta, Indonesia's bustling capital. Taufik Susila, a scientist at Batavian Laboratories, a minor subsidiary of Pan-Pacifica Pharmaceuticals, was sitting quietly on a wooden bench facing an expanse of poorly maintained grass, surrounded by chaotic, yet colorful flower beds. These were difficult to appreciate, for there was but a single lamp on a post near the center of the meager landscaping. The light was weak; the shadows dominant.

Susila found this cloak-and-dagger business annoying. However, his Japanese contact insisted on it. Since it was his money that now played a major role in Susila's lifestyle, the micro-biologist, always apprehensive at such meetings, cooperated. It was difficult to see. Susila checked his watch. 21:30. He was on time. The air was still heavy with humidity. He wiped his brow and neck with a handkerchief. His thoughts drifted off for a moment to the rendezvous he had arranged for later with the lovely Sujata.

"Don't turn around! Keep looking ahead!" The voice was masculine, sounded Asian, maybe Chinese. Definitely not the voice he was accustomed to hearing. The tone was gruff. *Definitely not Kiriguchi*, thought Susila. "Are the experiments finally underway?"

A rather slender, dark-skinned, handsome man in his mid-thirties, Susila, his hair reflecting an oily tonic in the dim light, responded nervously in Bahasa. "Yes, I have acquired much of the equipment I will need. I must still have a few items that are available from European man-ufacturers. I have maxed out the amount I can reasonably expect to divert from my company's budget. I'll need another $330,000 to deal appropri-ately with the 'subjects' and to take the experiments to the level you have requested." He was planning to use monkeys and mice for the more com-plex and dangerous experimentation demanded by Kiriguchi. It required more sophisticated and more expensive equipment. When he was through with his 'subjects', it would be necessary to eradicate the evidence. A form of cremation seemed best to Susila.

"Can't you do with less?" The speaker's voice showed considerable irritation.

"No, once contaminated and evaluated the 'subjects' will pose an extreme threat to me and my assistant if they are not destroyed. The system I have developed requires exposure to ultra high frequency micro-wave radiation, followed by super-heated cremation and disposal of the ashes. Because the 'subjects' are small, I am able to employ equipment whose installation should attract no special attention. Precision spectro-graphic equipment is essential for other aspects of the work you have outlined." Susila hoped his explanation would be accepted without criticism.

There was silence for a moment. "Very well, it will be authorized. You may pick up the sum you request at the usual place tomorrow even-ing."

"When will we have our next meeting?" Susila was wondering when he might be returning to Jakarta where he was often summoned for such meetings. He waited for an answer. Silence. No response. He turned slowly. He was alone again. After waiting fifteen minutes, as per standing instructions, he got up. Folding the newspaper he had placed next to him on the bench, he walked slowly to the car park on the opposite side of the hotel. The street was empty. Susila struggled to free his mind of the meet-ing. His rental car made its way, passing a noisy, smelly shanty town, through heavy traffic across the city to Sujata's small apartment, where a passionate dalliance would temporarily allay his insatiable craving for pleasures of the flesh.

The city was crowded. Traffic congestion was at a peak in the evening. Susila was not fond of the sprawling slums and the shabby neighborhoods. The streets were richly scented. Jakarta was a melting pot, a hot, smoggy mixture of beauty and chaos. There was, of course, something appealing about the decadent night life, the hectic clubs, the *gamelan* music and the easy women. Jakarta was home to Sujata. Susila's mind wandered to thoughts of her soft, taut skin, the smell of her hair, and the warmth of her embrace.

* * *

Early the next morning, a tender parting, a drive to the airport, a flight to Surabaya on Java's east coast, and in less than two hours Susila was home in his studio apartment south of the city. He called Soraya to chat for a while and to set up a date for two nights hence. He tried to relax. Tension kept him awake for a couple of hours.

A wave of exhaustion overcame Taufik. He stretched out on a sofa to nap awhile. As he lay there hoping for sleep, a feeling of foreboding clouded his mind. Taufik knew it was his fascination for Soraya and Sujata that was to blame for allowing himself to become so involved with the Japanese publisher, whom he had met by chance at a science convention in Hong Kong months earlier. If he didn't need so much money to satisfy his two 'girls', he would never have acquiesced to Kiriguchi's offer and subsequent demands. There was something sinister about the fawning Japanese that he instinctively disliked. Susila's busy mind finally turned to more pleasant thoughts.

Fortunately, the 'girls' were not acquainted with one another. Taufik was determined to keep them apart. He felt strangely blessed to have at his beck and call two of Java's sexiest, most nubile, voluptuous and amorous young woman; both just turned twenty. Their appetite for jewelry, the latest fashions, and expensive dining was as boundless and voracious as their lust for Taufi's 'one-eyed monster'. Between satisfying his desire for the 'fiery pit' and maintaining his demanding laboratory schedule, Susila was gradually beginning to fall victim to extreme mental and physical stress. How would it end? He often wondered.

It had begun innocently enough. Intrigued by a chance to help develop a 'new enzyme', Susila had agreed to spend part of his working hours on a 'private' project that would earn him a healthy supplement to his regular Pan-Pacifica paycheck. Pan-Pacifica, at the time, had just been acquired by *White Cross* Holdings. New management was engaged in extensive consultations with officials in Geneva. The Batavian Laboratories subsidiary was inadvertently treated as an orphan in the transition period. A major reorganization of WCH enterprises in the Pacific rim had become more complex than anticipated. The vacuum in solid oversight allowed Susila to essentially hijack the new labs recently added in a field not far behind the existing structures that housed operations and warehousing facilities. Batavian Laboratories manufactured generic drugs and served as a huge distribution center for various pharmaceuticals in South Asia.

Regular staff, including mainly chemists and pharmacists, oversaw the purity of the generics, while Susila and an assistant focused on the development of new drugs. With data from Kiriguchi, Susila was able to reproduce the synthesized form of the 'new enzyme'. Since it was obvious from the start that one of the enzyme's principal properties was its ability to function as a powerful accelerant in conjunction with other substances, the thrust of the first round of experiments, was to determine whether various medications could be made to work faster, thus increasing their efficiency and ability to bring about cures or improvement in certain medical conditions. The outlook was positive. Kiriguchi hinted broadly at huge profits for himself and Susila. The latter was enthused and dreamed of great riches.

* * *

In the intervening period since Susila first met Kiriguchi, the editor/ entrepreneur's quest for capital to fund his plans for the 'new enzyme' had attracted the interest of a mysterious Korean, whom Kiriguchi first encountered in Hong Kong. Subsequent meetings occurred in Tokyo and Pyongyang. Eventually, a joint venture, a collaborative effort, was proposed to which there would be mutual benefit, but the financial risk would fall principally on the shoulders of the Korean partner. Kiriguchi jumped at the offer, little realizing that he would almost immediately sacrifice control. It was now the agents of the mystery man from north of the 29th parallel who met secretly with Taufik Susila. This alteration in Susila's relationship with his benefactor was concealed from him. However, the new mission for his research was both puzzling and perturbing. Employing the 'new enzyme' with the highly contagious virus, Zeta-Qb8, cast a sinister pall over the entire venture.

At the time, perhaps no one anticipated that the North Korean viewed himself more as a broker, than a financier. He would unite an idea and a product with enormous wealth and ideological myopia. He foresaw a managerial role for himself and a position of power within his government. His own hatred of America and Europe was mirrored in the attitudes and actions of certain Middle Eastern groups. It was there that he sought support. He foresaw a collaboration whose appeal would prove irresistible to the fanatics whose religious zeal recognized no bounds.

* * *

Batavian Laboratories was part of a conglomerate of all-Asian enterprises originally assembled by two Indian brothers. The parent firm, Pan-Pacifica Industries, had its headquarters in Singapore. The sales and marketing arm of Batavian Laboratories was located in an industrial park outside Jakarta. The labs were part of a large complex constructed two years earlier on reclaimed land on the East Javan coast south of Surabaya. The largest of three structures housed the firm's huge warehouse and distribution center. Behind it were a two-story building containing manufacturing facilities for generic drugs, and a separate building in the front quarter of which Batavian Laboratories maintained a well-equipped lab for testing the quality and purity of its drugs. The remaining three quarters of the building were thought to be empty, pending decisions on expanding the firm's R and D activities.

White Cross Holdings had acquired Pan-Pacifica several months earlier. Plans to integrate the various manufacturing and service ventures involved were under consideration. The manager of the Surabaya plant was playing a major role in working out a master plan and, consequently, found himself in nearly constant motion between Surabaya and Jakarta, Jakarta and Singapore, Singapore and Geneva. Mr. Susila, the Lab Director, as a result, was left largely to his own designs and operated quite independently.

Sujata and Soraya, the latter a resident of Surabaya, the former at home in her birth city, Jakarta, had no idea that they not only shared a keen interest in ladies fashion, shopping, dancing, American movies, international celebrity gossip, and a rather wanton night life, but also in a well-to-do, doting, and passionate business 'mogul', whose commercial activities demanded extensive travel and extended absences. That he should seek calming respite from the stress his work engendered was natural and understandable.

The physical and financial cost of Susila's fantastical double existence as a serious scientist and a 'playboy' with an insatiable sexual appetite was slowly emerging in his consciousness as an unsustainable dream. Satisfying his own proclivity for boundless joy between the sheets and keeping his strange harem duo content had forced him to compromise his professional principles and succumb to the demands of Professor Kiriguchi. The money was too good, but the nature of the work he had to perform in return was troubling. The longer he worked with the Japanese publisher and scientist, the more ominous his involvement seemed.

* * *

The gray Malibu Mark rented in Jacksonville moved steadily southward at the speed limit in the center lane of I-95 until just slightly past St. Augustine. There he turned off to the east and headed for A1A which hugged Florida's Atlantic coastline. Falling in behind tourist vehicles:

RV's, campers and rusty old pick-ups, Mark's pace slowed considerably. Not a problem. The Chevy passed Palm Coast. Traffic eased. He was to rendezvous for lunch with Clark Willette at *Aunt Tillie's Crab Bag* a mile or so north of Daytona Beach. Spotting the modest seafood outlet on the right, he pulled in and backed into a parking space off to the rear corner of the cinder-covered lot. Several other vehicles were parked there, including a few motorcycles. Most probably belonged to either tourists or local working class guys who knew today's special was 'all you can eat crab cakes and popcorn shrimp'.

The meeting had been scheduled at Mark's insistence. Signals from Gayle suggested Willette was unhappy with the quality and quantity of information he was receiving from 'Top Dog'. Mark needed to know what the score was. Whom could he trust? The matter seemed to him to be one of the utmost urgency. Gayle's off-hand comments implied there was a lack of cooperation and, perhaps worse, of faltering collaboration among the government agencies charged with collecting and analyzing threatening data. The unfortunate end of Henrique da Serra cast an ominous shadow on the matter. It had to be considered a serious turn of events.

Several tables were full. Leather jackets were hanging on the wall rack. Tattooed arms were engaged in heavy lifting. Serious eating was under-way. Recognizing Willette, whom he was meeting for the first time, was not difficult. The graying beard and mustache, well trimmed, and fram-ing a ruddy-complected male wearing a 'Save the Earth'-emblazoned T-shirt attracted Mark's attention as soon as he entered. He walked over, sat down and extended his hand. "Gayle sends her regards. I'm Mark David-son. It's good to meet you."

"Thanks for coming. The buzz here will enhance the cover. I didn't want to meet in Jacksonville. Someone might recognize me. Trying to be extra careful. Please call me Clark."

"Sure, Clark, have you ordered?"

"I took the liberty of asking for two orders of the daily special. What do you want to drink? I'm settling for iced tea. The waitress is bringing a pitcher."

"Suits me." Mark looked around. Everyone appeared to be engrossed in the business of devouring prodigious quantities of shrimp and crab cakes. "Let me get right to the reason I requested that we meet face-to-face. I have complete confidence in Gayle. She, in turn, vouches for you in the strongest terms. Somewhere in the chain of information we're getting there is a damaged link. It has to be fixed, and fixed in a hurry. I firmly believe we have fallen behind in dealing with this security matter. Any terrorist automatically has an advantage. We simply can't relax the pressure of our investigative efforts. What is your take?"

Willette also looked about discreetly. Leaning forward somewhat and fingering his mustache, his mien conveyed his personal concern. "Top Dog, my moniker for the party to whom I am ostensibly reporting, occasionally seems intentionally lacking in candor. Former buddies at CIA and FBI have independently reported certain information to the President, that either never reaches me or is passed down in corrupted form. I can't understand why this is so. It is a troubling dilemma. I feel that I'm being manipulated by my own boss." Looking around the dining room, Willette cupped his right hand so as to conceal his lips. "I received early this morning an anonymous note that I have since destroyed. According to the information in the note, we had a man on the inside in Teheran, deep inside. A reliable source reports he was arrested and secretly executed. To me, this means he was outed by someone on our side. It had to be a person with access to ultra high-level knowledge of our covert activities." A discreet glance to left and right satisfied Willette that no one seemed to be paying any attention to him or Mark.

"You're suggesting a serious breach of the highest order. As you undoubtedly know, through the *Fondation* and *White Cross Holdings* we have access to considerable confidential information from around the globe. As a result of my involvement in your efforts, we have upgraded our own intelligence activity in manifold ways, including via electronic means. Our intercepts, which, by the way, do not involve any domestic wire-tapping within the United States, are producing positive results. My wife is heading up an effort to track the flow of funds involving suspects thus far identified. Her banking expertise is already showing results. Now, you said, 'The party to whom I am ostensibly reporting'. Do you mean to say you're not sure whether the President actually gets your information?"

"The agency I head up is a top secret creation of the Office of the President. You are the only outsider to whom we've admitted that. I actually report to the President through Manfred Scharffenberger, her Chief of Staff. I have always had high regard for the man, although I must admit we do not have a long or close history together. Recently, however, I've had to question this blind loyalty."

Mark took a bite of the crab cake on his fork and drank from his glass of tea. "Look, this is how I think we should proceed. For your part, continue to report any information you develop independently as you've been doing. You, and Gayle, of course, and my people will share the leads were developing. Whenever circumstances dictate, we'll put our heads together and determine a plan of action. It is imperative that we stop what purports to be a potentially mortal blow to Western Civilization. We cannot allow incompetence or political dithering to undermine or thwart our efforts. Agreed?" Willette nodded assent. "Say, here's an idea. If you think there's some kind of breach in the flow of information from this guy Scharffenberger to the President, could you arrange for a reporter to ask a question that might reveal her lack of knowledge on some important issue? I know her press conferences are infrequent, but I believe she has set one for about a week from now."

"That could be arranged and it might prove helpful in assessing who knows what. I can do it." Willette reached across the table. Both men, looking each other square in the eye, shook hands. Their gaze was one of resolve. Mark slid two twenty-dollar bills under his plate, rose and quietly exited. Willette visited the restroom, then he, too, departed in his mud-splashed Ford 150. The government agent stayed on A1A all the way to Jacksonville. Davidson drove south, parked at the beach for half an hour, then, dodging a group of Harley enthusiasts throttling up nearby, he went west to I-95, before continuing to Orlando, where he caught an Air Tran flight to New York.

* * *

A long black sedan of Chinese manufacture pulled up next to the Airbus 320 that had just rolled to a stop at the end of a dimly-lit runway at a military airport several miles northwest of the nearly snow-bound city of Ch'ongjin on North Korea's Pacific coast. Goh Il Wan waited until his visitors had descended the mobile stairway before stepping out of his warm refuge to greet them. The stairway was quickly rolled away from the aircraft, whose engines came to life with a roar. The plane made a sweeping turn and raced down the runway, lifting off briskly and heading southeast to skirt the lower peninsula. It's green crescent insignia was barely visible in the weak illumination from the base of the control tower. The moon was obscured by clouds. Sunrise was hours away.

Khalid al Basra exchanged greetings without touching his host. He gladly entered the limo to escape the pre-dawn chill. His aide, likewise rubbed his hands and pulled his outer garment up around his neck.

Goh, First Deputy of North Korea's Intelligence Directorate, had been in communication with a Japanese scientist who had made a startling proposal. For a price, he could make available a deadly weapon that could be used to wreak havoc and panic among large populations, such as those in New York, London, Los Angeles and Paris. The results, he claimed, would be so devastating that the West would be brought quickly to its knees and rendered utterly impotent.

This weapon, in an advanced stage of development, was 'biological' in nature, easily transportable, and guaranteed to claim millions of victims within 48-72 hours. Perfecting it and developing a fail-safe delivery system would require a substantial investment. It was for this purpose that 'sources' in the Middle East were solicited for bids.

Goh's younger brother was a well-positioned general in Pyongyang. Secret discussions with like-thinking military officials had roughed out a plan to invade South Korea and create a Greater Chosen. For this to have any opportunity of succeeding it would be imperative to neutralize South Korea's support from the United States. A severely weakened United States would also impair Israel's ability to sustain its defense. Arab forces could soon squeeze it into submission from every direction. Al Basra, check book in hand, wasted little time in outlining his demands. Hard bargaining began. Poker faces predominated. An occasional forced smile was meant to ease tension and suggest congeniality. Goh held out for a sum more than twice what al Basra first offered. He also insisted on being consulted regarding the targets, as well as the timing. Al Basra dug deep into his pockets to satisfy his opponent's greed. Secretly, he had no intention of meeting the North Korean's demands about timing and targets. Eventually, as noon passed and sunset approached, an agreement was reached. The visitors enjoyed the guest facilities. Refreshed by warm baths and soothing massages, the visitors rested until well after dusk. Finally, night settled over an uninviting city. The mercury tumbled. The limousine moved swiftly through the gloom of empty streets and deposited Al Basra and his aide at a small government airport, where an unscheduled flight whisked them and a few other passengers away to Beijing, the first leg of the return trip to their sandy homeland.

Western intelligence, lacking human assets inside key agencies within North Korea, possessed few details of collaborative ventures being planned. Goh had learned of Kiriguchi and his 'project' through his network of agents blanketing Asia. Plying Kiriguchi with money and 'partners' had resulted in an arrangement whereby Goh would supply the funds for furthering the experimentation. Kiriguchi was to be the principal go-between, keeping Goh up-to-date on the development of the enzyme. The actual funding was coming from the Middle East, where particular interest lay in the potential for an unstoppable terrorist weapon that could be used in simultaneous attacks on multiple targets by a trained cadre of so-called 'suicide' operatives. The objective, as it evolved, was for a single, carefully coordinated event so overwhelming in its scope that it would forever change civilization on Earth. In the plan Korea would be spared, while China and Japan, suddenly forced to look inward, would be weakened and crippled. The United States and Europe, including Russia, would cease to exist as independent nations. It was held that the overwhelming chaos would lead first to anarchy, then, when the scourge had run its course, 'clean-up squadrons' would complete the destruction and facilitate rehabilitation of the conquered lands.

Goh was not totally sold on Kiriguchi's ability to complete the project and deliver within a reasonable period of time. His people conducted constant surveillance of the Japanese scientist. Soon they had a complete dossier on Susila, who, because of his pronounced proclivity for the opposite sex, was seen as an easily malleable subject. Should circumstances warrant it, Goh was prepared to work directly with the Indonesian chemist. Ultimately, eager to exert total control over the experiments and their outcomes, Goh's people had long since pushed Kiriguchi, whose participation had become superfluous, aside. Permanently.

Chapter Six

Thor Sundquist would probably qualify for treatment as a stereotypical ADHD patient. Without a doubt, he was an incurably restless young man brimming with energy and an insatiable thirst for knowledge. His curiosity was unbounded. This delighted his advanced secondary school students who were constantly amazed by the discoveries in physics and chemistry to which he so artfully guided them.

Two nights each week, Sundquist taught upper-level math and computer studies at a community tech school whose students were, for the most part, motivated adults that found Norwegian winters inside the Arctic Circle passed more pleasantly, when the marvels of the internet were dissected and explained by the popular, and ruggedly handsome instructor.

A native of Bardu, a valley town of some 4000 inhabitants in northern Norway, Sundquist never lacked for something to occupy his time. A bachelor, he skied, skated, hunted and fished at every opportunity. He loved to dance. His soccer team valued his ability as a striker, and the school track team benefitted from his outstanding coaching skills.

One of his strengths, his ever-wandering curiosity, might also be considered something of a liability. Having read somewhere about a powerful global holding company with a diverse empire of investments in all manner of businesses, Sundquist wondered what kind of security protected its master computer system. Completely without malicious intent, the young enthusiast was able within minutes to hack into *White Cross Holdings'* framework. Surprised by the relative ease with which he had penetrated the outer skin of what he suspected was a rather large onion, Sundquist was about to back off and prepare his evening meal, when a few additional clicks accidentally had him looking at files which included the current equipment inventory for a pharmaceutical lab located in Surabaya, Indonesia.

Sundquist had traveled extensively throughout Scandinavia. The previous year he had spent two weeks exploring Italy's Adriatic Coast. His dream was to go surfing in Hawaii and, perhaps, Bali. While his mind was busy wandering the globe, he read through the rather mundane list of basic lab equipment for the enterprise before extricating himself from the site. One of the items on the procurement list had been a subscription to an obscure Japanese professional journal devoted primarily to chemistry. Assuming he might find it of interest to his advanced science class, he noted the title and the appropriate website.

The pickled herring, boiled potatoes, bread and beer that constituted his supper were devoured in haste. Back at his computer, the muscular six-foot-two blond quickly found the journal's subscription details and the date of the next issue, including a few of the topics to be featured. He assumed English synopses of earlier articles might be available. A little innocent probing soon found him well past the elementary security of Professor Kiriguchi's publishing house. By coincidence, a folder containing information regarding shipments, covering the past few months, of sophisticated, hi-tech laboratory equipment to the very entity he had encountered while hacking before supper popped onto his monitor. *Well,* he thought, *what an unusual coincidence!* The academic publishing company was apparently also brokering the sale and delivery of lab equipment and supplies. Oddly, no other accounts were listed. How curious! Reading through the list, Sundquist was surprised, and undoubtedly, a bit jealous. Wouldn't it be great to have a budget that could afford such marvelous equipment? Everything had been shipped from Japan, or Hong Kong, or Singapore to a third party address, also in East Java.

Probing further, Sundquist noted that the billing details were omitted. In addition to commonly used retorts and other containers, raw chemicals, safety supplies and other ordinary items, there was a scanning electron microscope, several centrifuges, spectrographic equipment, animal cages of various sizes, special filtration equipment, three over-sized high-density microwave ovens, and miscellaneous supplies not usually found, so thought Sundquist, in pharmaceutical research laboratories. As he reflected on the list, he tried to imagine how they might be employed. It occurred to him that none of the items mentioned had been listed in the company's inventory. Nor had there been reference to their purchase in the company's financial report for the preceding quarter. "Strange. Indeed, very strange! But, after all," he thought aloud, "I really wasn't supposed to see this information, and it's none of my business. I might be liable for having invaded these sites without authorization." He exited, then checked the weekend weather forecast. He paused, his chin resting in the cup of his left hand. He gently rubbed his day-old blond whiskers. "Still, there seems to be something funny going on in Surabaya." Thor pulled out an atlas and studied the unusual nation of Indonesia.

* * *

A few days later, Sundquist could still not stop thinking about his unusual discovery. He realized that he faced a large dilemma. For him, hacking into computer systems was an innocent challenge, something akin to conquering a mountain peak. Achieving one's goal was exciting and immensely gratifying. He was not crazy, however, he understood that hacking, especially at his level of attack, was considered by most a crime. On the other hand, *isn't committing fraud by an employee a more serious crime? If hacking uncovers such activity, isn't it justified?* The more he thought about it, the stronger his feeling he had an obligation to call the situation he uncovered to the attention of the company involved.

His letter detailing his findings was addressed to the Chief Operating Officer, *White Cross Holdings*, Geneva, Switzerland. A friend leaving for a holiday in London was asked to post the letter there. It had no return address. It reached the desk of Samantha Willis the next day, setting in motion a chain of events that may have altered the course of history.

Several more days passed, when, while conducting a keyword search of names from his hacking memo, Sundquist was startled to come across

516

a news article about a Professor Kiriguchi whose body had been found with a broken neck in the kitchen of his Tokyo apartment. Police were investigating. Samantha Willis, herself something of an internet addict, made the same observation the same day. Instinctively, she suspected foul play and knew it was related to the matter with which Mark was currently dealing. She notified him immediately. He passed it on to Gayle Beckmeister.

Willis met with two of her own 'whiz kids'. Their assignment: track down the source of the hacking attack that produced the information in the letter from London.

Seated a few feet apart in a small, secure room at WCH's Geneva headquarters, Sol Benmaman, Moroccan by birth, and Hussein Daoud, a survivor of Saddam's cruel prisons, both grim-faced and determined, tirelessly pecked away at their computers. Expert programmers and considered outstanding all-round computer gurus by their peers, they were committed to learning the identity of the gifted hacker who had informed WCH of possible improprieties at one of their Asian properties. Both owed their present careers to Mark Davidson and Samantha Willis. For they were responsible for establishing the policies and practices that saved the two and helped each of them build a new career and a new life. Benmaman had lost his left arm and left eye to a hidden land mine. Hussein's right leg had fallen victim to gangrene that developed while incarcerated by the former Iraqi leader. Relentlessly, they employed their expertise to backtrack to the point of incursion at WCH's master terminal and also checked the breach of Professor Kiriguchi's publishing office. Slowly, methodically, an identification number for the rogue computer was produced. It had been manufactured for Siemens. A record check revealed the retail dealer, an electronics outlet in Oslo, Norway. From there to Thor Sundquist's apartment the trail was obvious.

* * *

Inge Halvorsen's discreet queries had acquainted her with Thor Sundquist's busy schedule. Upon his return from hockey practice on a cold Saturday afternoon, she was waiting near the entrance to his apartment. "Hallo, Mr. Sundquist! May I have a word with you?"

Sundquist turned suddenly, startled, surprised to be looking into the blue eyes of a strikingly beautiful blonde. Her smile, disarming, warm, and friendly, put the handsome teacher/athlete at ease. "Hey, come on in. I'm soaking wet and need to change my shirt right away." He held the door open. Ms Halvorsen shook his hand and entered. "Give me a couple of minutes to freshen up. There's hot tea in a thermos container on the kitchen counter. Cups are in the cabinet above the sink. Help yourself!" He moved smoothly into his bedroom, closing the door behind him.

Scanning the main room, a kind of bachelor's den, Inge noted the corner desk with a computer, monitor, printer, camera and speakers. She poured a cup of tea, sat down on an Ikea chair of varnished clear pine with a bright blue seat cushion, and waited for the virile and appealing reason for her visit to reappear. While she was subconsciously assigning Sundquist a high grade for his neat and tidy lodging, he returned, wearing a blue and white rugby shirt, gray trousers and the pink cheeks of a poster boy for some magical health elixir. "Please excuse me, my name, as you know, is Sundquist, Thor Sundquist, and yours?"

"Please forgive me for the unannounced call. I'm Inge Halvorsen. I work for a firm with headquarters in Switzerland. We have a few questions for you." She studied Thor's manly face. He didn't seem like an unscrupulous computer hacker intent on racking up millions at the expense of hapless victims in distant places who failed to properly secure their private financial information.

"Recently, an unsigned letter was received by our management, revealing details of transactions related to one of the firm's investments in Indonesia." Sundquist's complexion seemed suddenly pinker. "While the data, acquired illegally," (Here she stressed the adverb), "was vulnerable during a period when the firm was dealing with connectivity issues, it was improperly accessed. Our agents were able to trace the original hacker to your internet account."

"I can explain." Sundquist strove to appear calm.

"That won't be necessary." Halvorsen interrupted the embarrassed teacher. "You have done us a service and we have no intention of filing any charges. On the contrary, we have an urgent need of someone with your... ahh, special talent. We would like to offer you a short-term assignment at our headquarters in Geneva. Your school is on holiday for a week." Halvorsen's voice acquired an imperative tone. "I can give you an hour to arrange for any substitutes for your other obligations. While doing that, you can pack. A plane is waiting to depart as soon as we get to the airport."

* * *

Now, a mere four days later, a new colleague, fair-skinned and blond, had joined the high-priority investigative endeavor in Geneva. Additional computers and peripherals crowded the room whose area had been doubled overnight. Elli Davidson joined them for hours on end, probing with her staff for financial details regarding money transfers between known terror groups, especially between Kiriguchi and a secretive government entity in North Korea. Enough information was being collected and analyzed to indicate something big was brewing. And it wasn't *kim chi*.

Chapter Seven

The prospect of possibly patenting a formula together with Endo Kiriguchi, that, when leased to pharmaceutical companies and processed food manufacturers, might well be worth millions of dollars in royalties, had a powerful motivational effect on Taufik Susila's work ethic. He labored long hours testing the enzyme, eventually accumulating considerable insight into its potential. Not all he learned was positive in nature. Believing, or wanting to believe, he might have misread some of his results, he reported only the more promising information, keeping the negative or uncertain information to himself.

The primary thrust of Susila's investigations was to learn ways in which the 'new enzyme' could be employed to hasten the effectiveness of medicines frequently used to treat a variety of illnesses and ailments from the common cold to difficult-to-deal-with human immunity problems.

Deeply engrossed in the midst of his research, Susila was disturbed by a shift in focus insisted upon by Kiriguchi. He was now to try combining the enzyme with a variety of viruses, one of which was the dangerous Zeta-Qb8 virus. Susila wondered how Kiriguchi was able to obtain a sample, as it was thought the only strains of the deadly virus known to exist were locked away in the laboratories of two or three world powers.

Susila's stipend was increased. The money was welcome. His 'girls' had expensive tastes and were hinting about trips to New York, Los Angeles and Las Vegas. He had promised. He didn't want to disappoint them. He and his assistant instituted the most stringent protocols to avoid any possible contamination. Early experiments resulted in the deaths of innumerable mice, rabbits and several monkeys. Their carcasses were carefully reduced to ashes and disposed of. Susila and his assistant religiously followed a stringent decontamination protocol. No word of their work was shared with other employees.

One aspect of their experimentation required that both monkeys and rabbits be exposed to the enzyme-enhanced virus in the form of a mist-like spray. One day, after he had conducted such an experiment, Susila's assistant failed to report to work. There were no responses to phone inquiries. Concerned, Susila drove to the small house where his assistant lived with his wife, two children and his in-laws. They were all dead. Immediately, Susila suspected the virus. Since there were no other relatives in the area, Susila arranged for prompt cremation. He personally underwent the decontamination protocol three times in succession upon his return to the lab. The next day, following brief memorial services, the scientist returned to his apartment and spent much of the day buried in remorseful discontent about the predicament in which he was so completely immersed. He had already had growing qualms about his work. Contacting Kiriguchi was unavoidable. Susila wanted out.

Unbeknownst to the Indonesian scientist, control of his current project had since been usurped by the North Korean Intelligence Directorate. Kiriguchi's role was that of a puppet. News of the Japanese publisher's unfortunate and untimely death did not reach Indonesia. For some time, contact with Susila had occurred through North Korean agents, not Kiriguchi, who had long been considered dispensable by his Asian accomplices. Ruing the day he became involved in his insoluble predicament, Susila was coerced into hiring a new assistant, who was, indeed, a qualified chemist with laboratory experience, but also served his master, Goh Il Wan, with fervent loyalty.

* * *

Satisfied that preliminary reports confirmed that the Zeta-Qb8 virus, enhanced by combination with the 'new enzyme', was a lethal weapon, Goh pressed for manufacture of a quantity sufficient to create havoc in major urban areas in certain Western nations. It was determined that a little would go a long way. Small, easily-concealed water-soluble canisters of a special non-metallic material charged with a powerful aerosol-type propellant would be used to disseminate the virus. Susila's 'girls', about which his new masters had full details, were declared off limits. No play for Susila while there was work to be done. Production continued unabated for nearly three weeks. Finally, gently crated in specially coded crates, the deadly fog was transported to a rundown warehouse in a coastal town further south. From there it moved in a small motor launch past coastal islands out into the Madura Straits. A moonless night assured no witnesses. The cargo was gently transferred to a freighter that would later fly the flag of North Korea as it set course for the Indian Ocean and the Gulf of Aden.

* * *

Goh's researchers, an industrious lot, recklessly mixed fantasy with the relatively few hard facts about Zeta-Qb8 that had leaked out of tight-lipped government scientists in the handful of remote research labs where the virus was stored under the strictest security. Their consensus conjecture was that, once released into crowded areas, a sudden malaise would affect those that came into immediate contact with the virus. Full infection would follow swiftly; some deaths would occur within minutes, others in a few short hours. Contagion through contact with family and friends, co-workers, fellow pedestrians or passengers in subways, buses, trains and planes would guarantee that within 24 – 72 hours millions would fall victim to the uncontrollable scourge. Secondary and tertiary infection would occur in an expanding circle of horror. Health workers would suffer in great numbers. Additionally, as news of the deaths continued unabated, psychological despair would unleash mass torment. A wave of suicides could be expected. After a fortnight of intense medical terror, the virus would likely begin to lose its potency. At that point, with a crippling vacuum in national and international leadership and serious military decimation among the traditional world powers, cadres of trained personnel would swoop in to assume control. A rolling wave of sleeper groups, previously alerted by secret messages, would arise from strategic hiding places to assist them. A new world order would emerge. Collaborating forces would divide the spoils. Unfortunately, extreme vigilance would be essential, for even among the brotherhood of the 'striving peoples' differences existed that held the potential for treachery on a massive scale. The dilemma: which collaborator or collaborators could be trusted?

Chapter Eight

Landing in the darkness at Jakarta's Soekarno-Hatta International Airport on a flight with Cathay Pacific from Hong Kong, Mark Davidson was met by a junior executive from Pan-Pacifica Pharmaceuticals. Mirusia, a short, round-faced, rather bubbly young woman in her late twenties attached to the sales department, was supposed to take Mark and another person to the company Guest House a few miles outside the city. Mark, traveling light, had only a carry-on. He exchanged pleasantries with the personable chauffeur. Quickly checking his watch, while walking briskly to the Thai International gate where Gayle Beckmeister was due to arrive, he was already planning on an early start the next morning. The flight, he learned, was delayed about thirty minutes. Thanking the young lady who had extended her workday substantially to pick him up, Mark indicated he would grab a cab instead, and check into the Dharmawangsa Jakarta Hotel, where he asked Mirusia to meet him at about 8:00 the next morning.

Beckmeister's flight arrived from Bangkok forty-five minutes late and a slightly weary traveler relished the opportunity to stretch a bit and escape the confinement of the airplane. Mark's hotel suggestion sounded good to her. Both settled into spacious and luxurious rooms on opposing sides of a beautifully carpeted hallway. As Mark had told her en route that his company would pick up the tab, she graciously accepted, refreshed herself and had room service bring tea and fresh fruit. The room seemed rather warm. Attempts to adjust the temperature were unsuccessful. She picked up the phone and dialed Mark's room across the hall.

"Oh, hi. Mark, you're so good at everything else. I wonder if you could check my thermostat? I'm trying to cool the room and nothing seems to work."

"O.K. I'll be glad to give it a try. Are you decent?"

"Would you be unhappy if I weren't?"

Silence on the other end. Mark failed for words.

"Just teasing. C'mon over." *Such a fantastic place and my date is a straight arrow!*

Mark, who had been responding to about three dozen urgent emails, pulled on an ivory polo shirt, buckled up his light brown slacks and stepped over to Gayle's room. The door was ajar.

"I'm sorry. I think I just embarrassed you. I should feel guilty, but…"

"Don't. It was funny when I thought about it," interrupted Mark. "How do you like your room?"

"This redefines luxury. I'll give it a ten, if you can fix the thermostat."

The cover of the control panel snapped off easily. Mark looked inside and immediately noted that the color-coded wires were incorrectly connected. Using a microtool from his wallet, he rearranged them, pushed the cover back onto the unit and asked if 20 degrees Celsius would be acceptable. It was.

Gayle was examining a pile of international newspapers on a coffee table when Mark finished. As she turned to thank him her dressing gown caught on a chair, revealing most of her left leg right up to her thigh. Mark's gaze involuntarily traced the limb from her ankle upwards.

Their eyes met. He pursed his lips, smiled ever so slightly and retreated to his quarters to resume answering the day's accumulation of messages. His last email was to Elli, letting her know his schedule for the following day.

* * *

When he could arrange it, Mark loved a good breakfast. He and Ms Beckmeister met at the elevator nearest their rooms early the next morning. "Selamat Pagi, Dr. Beckmeister!"

"That must be Good Morning in Bahasa. You're a regular polyglob, Dr. Davidson."

"Unfortunately, that about exhausts my knowledge of the local language. Hey, I'm sorry, I guess I should call you Gayle. Mark suits me."

"I knew you were kidding. I'm hungry. Usually, I have a light breakfast, but today I'm famished. Hope this is a good restaurant."

"You won't be disappointed. It's one of the best in town."

Indeed, a marvelous spread awaited them at a buffet featuring Asian and European specialties. Both ate well. The conversation turned to family. Gayle, an only child, supported her parents. They lived in a retirement community in New Mexico. She usually visited for birthdays and major holidays. Occasionally, she joined them on cruises; mainly in the Caribbean.

Mark spoke warmly about his wife and children. He was clearly a devoted family man. He talked about his sister-in-law and her husband, about his staff and advisory board, a kind of extended family, about his dogs, and the horses his son and daughters cared so much for. He also revealed some of the *Foundation's* past successes, as well as a few vexing problems that still concerned him and his colleagues. Gayle was impressed by the richness of his personal ties. Similarly, hearing of the scope and depth of the affairs of the *Foundation* and of *White Cross Holdings* served to further her respect and admiration for him.

They met again in the lobby, each with luggage ready to go, for they planned to fly to Surabaya after meeting with Pan-Pacifica officials. From there they would continue their travels. Destinations and timing to be determined.

The flight was about half full. A father and son, both of whom checked large golf bags, conversed in English with a distinct clipped British accent as they showed their boarding passes to the attendant on duty. Seated in aisle seats further back in the Garuda International flight were two Chinese women, each with a stuffed purse. In the arrivals hall a uniformed driver held up a white sign reading: Dr. Davidson. Mark and Gayle saw him immediately, shook hands briefly and were escorted to a waiting limousine. The driver appeared unusually subdued as he motored south to the Batavian Laboratories complex. Not too distant behind them was a pair of taxis on the same highway.

Winston Shih, the ethnic Chinese Acting Manager of the company, waited with an aide in front of the neat, but plain entrance to the main building. His greeting was polite, yet noticeably somber. Ushering his guests into his office, he apologized first for the damp, humid climate and the fact that his ceiling fan was in the process of being replaced. His tone became more serious as he explained that Mr. Susila had been missing since the preceding day. Calls to his apartment, succeeded by personal visits by a member of the staff had failed to locate the employee, who was held in high regard by his colleagues. Mark and Gayle, exchanging glances, both suspected Susila's absence was involuntary.

It was decided to inform the authorities. A search was instituted. Within two days, press coverage in major news organs throughout Indonesia caught the attention of a pair of very lovely young women. They claimed to recognize the picture disseminated in newspapers and on television. The authorities treated them separately. The ensuing interviews provided a more intimate picture of the missing scientist's personal life and character, but were of minimal value in discovering his fate. Taufik Susila was nowhere to be found.

Although a conscious effort had been made to conceal anything unusual in the laboratory where Susila worked, investigators searched it scrupulously hoping for clues that might explain his disappearance. A number of papers had been removed from his files. Company officials were absolutely flabbergasted to see all the equipment Susila had acquired without their knowledge or approval. The new assistant had likewise gone missing. He, of course, was very much alive. Using false papers he was slowly returning to North Korea.

The fate of Taufik Susila, whose body had been consigned to the deep waters far out in the Selat Madura, would be the subject of conjecture for years to come. He was mourned by his lady friends. They missed his loving attention and generosity. His mother, a widow, prayed for him. Gayle and Mark considered the disappearance troubling.

The condition of the laboratory where Susila had labored so diligently revealed that he was highly concerned about his personal safety and that of his assistant. The place had been thoroughly sanitized on a regular basis. In the off hand chance they might come across notations or materials that would shed light on the nature of the bio-chemist's experiments, Mark and Gayle used the proverbial fine-tooth comb to no avail.

* * *

Back in Jacksonville, Gayle's boss, Clark Willette, had picked up from clandestine sources further tidbits that disturbed the veteran intelligence pro. Piecing together data from several sources, Willette was beginning to feel that they had literally missed the boat. From an old CIA colleague he learned that certain information regarding the matter had been given weeks prior to Manfred Scharffenberger at the White House. Willette felt uneasy, wondering why he had not been informed. He pondered his next move.

Little did Willette know that help was coming from an unexpected source. Susila's unnamed assistant, a North Korean agent who reported directly to Goh Il-Wan, was a red-blooded, horny guy. Having tasted the 'good life' beyond the confines of his desolate homeland, the virile young man decided a detour via Bali would represent suitable compensation for the risks and hardships endured on his recently completed assignment. A few days of R and R surely would not be denied him by his superiors. A raid by Indonesian Secret Police on an otherwise welcoming 'house of pleasure' brought about a dramatic change of circumstances. Unconstrained by ethical and moral issues that hamper the interrogation of suspected terrorists in some countries, harsh measures loosened the assistant's tongue in short order. Threatening to deprive him of his manhood was the clincher. He readily shared all he knew. Deadly biological materials were to be unleashed in several major American and European cities. Large-scale devastation and loss of life was expected. Specific targets were not known. A possible time line was developed. Fast action would be essential, if the plot were to be disrupted and halted. The focus was obvious : the homeland.

A report from Indonesian intelligence officials to the CIA in Washington was forwarded to Manfred Scharffenberger. He decided to notify the CIA that the President wanted the matter kept secret until more details could be collected. Personally, he was irritated that he had not been trusted enough to have been informed earlier of the impending action by his control.

Chapter Nine

Internet intercepts captured by Samantha Willis and the team of IT specialists she had assembled in Geneva were increasing in frequency. Deciphering the codes used was proving to be extremely frustrating. Success was limited. The nature of the dialog developing between North Korea and several sites in the Middle East, and, surprisingly troubling, transmissions to and from North American-based computers prompted Mark's return to Europe once it was concluded that Taufik Susila was probably no longer among the living.

Gayle Beckmeister stayed behind in Indonesia. She conducted separate, private interviews with both Soraya Suparmanputra and Sujata Wulandari, Susila's 'girls'. While she developed rapport with both, neither could contribute much, other than to note that Susila had become noticeably stressed in the weeks immediately preceding his disappearance.

* * *

The irony of fate never ceases to be a cause for wonder and occasional amusement. The President's latest task-force on domestic security met in week-long seclusion to review and revamp emergency plans designed to deal with natural disasters and terrorist attacks. A hefty volume containing critical actions, lists of resources, the names of responsible parties throughout the country and the means of communicating with them, the location of supplies, and countless other pertinent details was hastily reduced to a micro file in Manfred Scharffenberger's home office. Within a week, his control, who surprised his wife with a gift of a short

Mediterranean cruise, passed the information to a fellow passenger in a smoking area aft on Deck D somewhere between Athens and Kusadasi. Knowing the enemy's plans before mounting an attack would give the protagonist a remarkable advantage.

Scharffenberger, who practiced his religion in silent isolation, had taken pains to cultivate the culture of his early youth. He was able to conceal his personal interests from his family and associates. Still, he had matured in the West and had come to value a way of life that offered incredible freedom. He found he could sympathize with the martyrs who gleefully destroyed their mortal selves for a cause in which they apparently had an overpowering faith. For himself, however, Scharffenberger envisioned no such early departure for Paradise. Instead, he thought long and hard about a different sort of future. Major population areas would be targeted in any large-scale attack on the domiciles of the Infidels. Washington must, he thought, be high on the list. Consequently, it would be important to be elsewhere. Typical of Americans' indifference to matters of geography, none of the visitors to Scharffenberger's office bothered to ask why his atlas was frequently open, or why he was studying wind and weather charts. Perhaps some day they would.

* * *

Angelina, a 60-foot trawler, radioed a low-level alert, indicating motor trouble about 160 miles southeast of *Block Island.* It was 2:30 am Eastern Standard Time. The ship's current position was given, and repeated once. Ten minutes later a response was delivered by a fishing vessel of Danish registry. The *Star of Jutland* was less than an hour away and had a master diesel mechanic aboard. A rendezvous was arranged. The captain of the *Angelina* cancelled his request for assistance. With his crew of five, the captain set about insuring that the catch brought aboard thus far was properly iced.

The Atlantic was fairly calm. The weak moon was unable to penetrate the cloud cover. With radar and other electronic devices at their disposal, however, the two ships had no difficulty finding each other. While

Angelina, in need of fresh paint, readily showed its age, the Danish ship, had it been daytime, would have looked like an entry in a fancy regatta. A small boat was put over the side. Two men aboard the *Star of Jutland* carefully lowered a large cargo net that contained three dozen wooden boxes each thoroughly wrapped in heavy-duty waterproof plastic tarps. The vessel motored the few meters to the wounded trawler. The boxes were gingerly transferred to the trawler. One of the men in the motor launch gently bobbing up and down in the tranquil water waved to the *Angelina's* captain and proceeded to return to the mother ship. Shortly thereafter, as the *Star of Jutland* faded into the distance to the east, *Angelina's* husky engines rumbled to life and she headed for *Falmouth* on Cape Cod's southern coast. Farhad and Mahmoud Abbas, would ply an eastward route to their home port of Århus on the east coast of Denmark's *Jylland* Peninsula. They knew their first loyalty lay in answering the call of their Middle Eastern brothers. As devout *Jihadis,* delivering a special cargo to would-be martyrs in America was the least they could do. *"Death to the Infidels!"*

On successive days the following week, one box was transported by sailboat to Westhampton Beach on Long Island. A second box went by UPS to an address in Boston from which it traveled in a van via the Mass Turnpike to Albany, New York. A third box sat comfortably in the trunk of a sports convertible keeping well within the posted limits on I-95 through Rhode Island and Connecticut. The fourth winged its way westwards in a private jet bound for Las Vegas and the west coast. The remaining boxes were each sent similarly to specific addresses throughout the country. Captain Roberto Vargas of the *Angelina*, the only person who knew the ultimate destinations of the boxes, earned more for his little detour at sea than he had for his last four fishing ventures in the often fickle North Atlantic combined.

The boxes in question had begun their long journey in a similar fashion, albeit on the other side of the planet. Taken by a small fishing vessel out into the Madura Strait in the Sea of Java late one night, they were smoothly hauled aboard a North Korean freighter that showed up ten days later at a small port in *Yemen*. How they eventually reached Denmark is unknown. The fate of the other twenty four boxes prepared by Susila and his assistant and shipped by sea was not clear. Presumably, they found their way into eager hands throughout Europe.

Verbal instructions conveyed to recipients along the way included stern warnings against any tampering. The consequences, they were told, could be life threatening. A sign displaying the international symbol for breakable glass was pasted on all six sides of each box. No other markings were evident.

Satisfied that he had successfully completed his part of the deal, Vargas, once he had reached his bungalow, sat down at his desktop, pulled up his blog, *The Nor'easter*, and made the following entry: 'Great Catch Today. Thirty-Six Big Ones Shipped to Buyers.' As a rule, the second part of his payment could be expected by Fed Ex in two days. Vargas was planning a vacation in the Caribbean. He had no idea what the boxes contained; just that it was supposed to be a special cargo. On other occasions he had assumed his special cargo might involve drugs. Questioning the morality of his actions was an exercise he studiously avoided. He decided to get a bite and a pint at *Cantina Esperanza*, a Tex-Mex restaurant a few blocks from his rented digs. Tonight he could afford to buy drinks for a few of the 'regulars'.

* * *

Manfred Scharffenberger finished reading the last page in a speech he had prepared that the President was scheduled to give the next day at a meeting of cable and broadcast executives. It was fairly bland, designed to say something nice to just about everyone, and, consequently, ought to help boost her ratings prior to a campaign swing for the mid-term elections. It was after 7:00 p.m. and Scharffenberger was ready to head home for a dinner his wife was giving for some friends.

As Scharffenberger drove home in his Mercury Mariner, his thoughts were focused on the future, his future. *Say what you want about the United States, life here is good*, he thought. He was in a position to capitalize on a grand scale should there be an upheaval over which he might have some control. Provided, of course, that he survived. *Yes, how can I survive? Labbani needs to give me more details. After all my sacrifices, I deserve better treatment from that old bastard.* A horn sounded beside him, he was beginning to wander out of his lane. He moved over quickly and concentrated on his driving.

* * *

Before leaving his store George Labbani hit the internet button on his computer, clicked on his 'favorites' and pulled up a blog dedicated to the fishing industry in the Northeast. He read today's entry, smiled, and shut down his computer for the night. He looked forward to a cup of tea and a 'good night' smoke.

Chapter Ten

Instructions from George's superiors on the Persian Gulf may have pleased Mrs. Labbani more than her husband. The prospect of going on her first cruise, an anniversary surprise from her spouse, was joyful news. Labbani himself was somewhat apprehensive. He didn't know exactly what to expect. Something important was in the works. *Was it connected to the shipment from abroad?* He wondered.

* * *

Labbani's cruise headquarters, a Greek-flagged, refitted ship in gleaming white, routinely plied the Eastern Mediterranean, carrying bargain-hunting retirees and young families to the usual ports of call. The ship was well run, the cabins and common areas were clean, if uninspiring, and the food satisfying. All things considered, the passengers figured they were getting what they paid for. The itinerary had listed Kuşadasi as a destination, but the ship actually docked in Izmir, a thriving, modern port and commercial center on Turkey's Aegean Coast.

Most of the seven hundred passengers were either busy sight-seeing on excursions in and around Izmir, or, like Mrs. Labbani, had elected to join a bus tour to Ephesus, an archeological wonder of great significance for those interested in the history of Ancient Rome.

Carrying nothing that might identify him as a tourist, Labbani, who chose not to participate in the organized activities, leisurely strolled along the waterfront, occasionally staring in a shop window. In a tobacconists he bought two packs of Turkish cigarettes and immediately lit up, coughing a few times as he did so. It was warm and pleasant. A gentle breeze was coming in from the sea. At a bus stop, he waited patiently. Wearing a pair of gray slacks, a pale blue polo shirt and a thin khaki windbreaker hanging from his shoulders, he attracted no particular attention. He boarded the next bus heading for the *Kültürpark*. Once there, he ambled rather aimlessly about studying the crowd, his arms behind him, his cigarette dangling from his lips. He found a bench between two buildings that cast a cooling shadow and took a seat, puffing on his most recent cigarette. Another bench was behind his. It faced the opposite direction. Soon, an elderly gentleman, wrinkled, sun-tanned face, graying mustache and full head of gray hair, took a place on the bench behind Labbani. The new arrival opened a greasy paper bag and began to eat a sandwich. "*Salaam aleichem!*, Hello, old friend," he said softly. "The dog is well." Before Labbani could acknowledge the code word, the visitor continued, "Are you enjoying your trip?"

"It's all right, but I find it boring. You will be pleased to know the lions and falcons are ready." Labbani's reply was also given quietly. He looked about casually. No one was paying any attention to the back-to-back benches. Two women with head scarves passed in front of him. "What is so important, that I had to come here?" A cough followed.

"You do not sound well. You should be like the Americans; stop smoking, eh?"

"I must have at least one vice." He paused. "You used to smoke when we were together in SAVAK. Do your new bosses not like you to smoke?"

"I do what I like. But everything is different now. People in the Ministry of Intelligence and Security and the radicals in the Islamic Revolutionary Guard Corps do not always agree. Everyone is cautious. The Ayatollah has big eyes and bigger ears. The *Quds* have no tolerance for incompetence or treachery. With them death is preceded by extreme torture."

"All is going well with the seedling planted so long ago. It has grown and flourishes now in a favored place, as you know. Little hints have reached my ears of a bold thrust into the heart of all who do not believe. Am I to play a role in these plans?"

A group of tourists was approaching. The visitor rolled up his paper and threw it into a nearby receptacle. He took a string of beads from his pocket and began mumbling prayers. The group passed, engaged in noisy conversation. Without moving his head, a pair of alert eyes followed the group until it was well out of earshot. "We have been collaborating with many in the region who share our views. Through their dependence on oil, the Americans and West Europeans, ironically, are paying for their own destruction." The visitor's voice hardened. "Even the Russians will feel our wrath." He stopped, took a deep breath and quickly surveyed the area. "Because we are old friends and because you have masterfully guided the growth of 'our tree', you shall be rewarded with a great responsibility. We felt it necessary to speak to you in person to emphasize the gravity of what lies ahead."

"Can you tell me here?"

"No. Be prepared for an immense task. A recent distribution of special goods that was reported to you is part of the plan. Summoning forth our sleeping warriors and leading them into battle will require energy and concentration. Everything you need will be waiting for you upon your return to Baltimore. It has the highest security classification. You must not fail."

The visitor rose, uttered, "*Allah akbar!*" And wandered off, disappearing around a nearby building. He was gone before Labbani could process the thought. He, too, rose a few minutes later and walked towards the bus stop that would return him to the cruise pier.

* * *

'Big-boned' was the euphemism applied by family and friends to oversized girls like Estelle Charbonneau and Julia Ianuzzi. They really weren't fat, just considerably larger than the images of young women featured in the fashion magazines and on popular television. They bonded in their sophomore year at high school, depending on their mutual support to deflect the taunts and negative expressions of classmates. In fact, they were fun-loving, had good personalities and had ambitious plans for the future. For participation in the school clubs and other activities preferred by their peers, Estelle and Julia substituted after-school and weekend jobs as waitresses at *Cantina Esperanza.* They were saving for nursing school for Estelle and a course as a dental technician for Julia. Twenty-one now and enrolled in tech school, the inseparable twosome had endeared themselves to their boss, who valued their dependability, their honesty and their industry, as well as their ability to deal effectively with some of his raunchier customers.

While serving Captain Vargas and the moochers who were imbibing and eating on his tab, the girls parried the slew of suggestive remarks from the crude group that had assembled around Vargas' table. Working in tandem, they kept the beer flowing and quickly refilled the plates of spicy food and snacks. As they did so, they could not avoid overhearing the Captain's alcohol-induced slurred comments about the source of his sudden wealth. Neither girl smoked, and experimenting with any form of a prohibited substance would have been anathema to them. When they next found themselves alone in the kitchen they compared notes and came to the conclusion that Captain Vargas must be involved in drug smuggling.

The cash drawer was full and the *Cantina's* owner's eyes not so blurred by dollar signs that he lacked concern for a regular. He ordered a taxi for the Captain and three others clearly unfit to drive on their own. After closing, Estelle and Julia drove in Estelle's 1990 Dodge Caravan, a bequest from a deceased aunt, to the apartment they shared. The conversation revolved around the details they picked up during the course of the evening. They concluded that something really, really big had taken place, and, more importantly, that it might be a threat to the country. They resolved to call the FBI in Boston in the morning.

* * *

Jimmy O'Neill, the pride of the Francis X. O'Neill family of Quincy, Massachusetts, took the call the next day around 9:30 in the morning. Fondling the newly printed business card identifying him as an agent attached to the Boston office of the Federal Bureau of Investigation, O'Neill, who was assigned primarily to keep tabs on ethnic gangs in the area, jotted down key words, names, locations and other details provided by the young ladies from Cape Cod. As a teenager he had spent a summer near Barnstable working as a member of a landscaping crew at an exclusive golf resort. He knew the area well. Jimmy was a good listener. He took the girls' report seriously. After obtaining the pertinent names, addresses and telephone numbers, he thanked them, promising the matter would be looked into promptly. He also cautioned them not to take any independent action, nor to mention the matter to anyone else. For a while he sat at his desk and re-read his notes. While he was doing so, a colleague stuck his head in the door and asked if Jimmy would like to join him for lunch. A new member of the office, O'Neill knew it would be politic to go along and contribute to office camaraderie, but something told him he needed to digest what he had heard without delay. He asked for a rain check.

Only a week into his assignment to the Boston office, James R. O'Neill, B.A. Boston College and a new enrollee in a local evening law program, didn't want to make a fool of himself and, possibly, foul up his career before it had actually begun. Yet, there was something compelling about what he had heard and understood while talking to the young ladies from Falmouth. He picked up the paper with his notes and started for the door. The Special Agent in Charge was in. He'd know what to do. Before his hand touched the door knob, he hesitated, stopped and walked over to the window. Looking out onto an overcast sky, he sighed. "Dammit! This is what it's all about. Courage, boy, courage." He strode confidently towards the SAC's office.

Harold, "call me Hal", Wysocki, the SAC, was himself, rather new, having only been assigned some ten months earlier to the busy New England hub. A proud family man, the former college quarterback was nearly as popular in his Newton suburb as his wife, mother of two boys and two girls and the darling of her subdivision. She organized the local bake sales and was being encouraged to run for the School Board. No one was aware that she and Hal had meet at *Hooters*, where she worked to help cover the cost of out-of-state tuition.

"C'mon in", Wysocki called out as he hung up his phone and turned to the door. He liked the energetic young man who had just joined the agency. "Have a seat, Jim, what's up today?"

"I just had a call from The Cape. A couple of waitresses claim they overheard a local guy, who captains his own fishing trawler, talk about some kind of cargo that was transferred to his ship offshore. They implied it was some kind of hush-hush deal, maybe smuggling."

"I take it, you thought the girls were legit."

"Well, yeah. They sounded sincere and… troubled by what they heard. The guy was in his cups they said, and was talking about stuff he ordinarily would be keeping to himself. He was buying rounds for the house and seemed to have plenty of cash."

"You got his name?"

"Yeah. And I already pulled up a home address and a phone number too."

"O.K. We're heavy into a few investigations already. But let's query HQ and have someone see if this captain's on any of the usual watch lists. Check with Tom Pinkerton or Gabe Hansford. They'll know where to look."

"I'll get right on it. Thanks."

Wysocki smiled. *Probably a waste of time*, he thought, *but I don't want to discourage my new man.*

Chapter Eleven

Using a first name he had chosen for himself, Edward Lee, a North Korean by birth, wearing a suit borrowed from his brother, an engineer working on a civil engineering project in Egypt, spoke in broken English with Matthew Harrington, a high-ranking official in the United States Consulate in Alexandria. Both Koreans had risked their lives in a daring plot to escape to the West. Edward was a maritime officer whose cargo vessel had quietly taken on a contraband shipment one night more than two weeks earlier in the Bay of Madura off the east coast of Java.

Harrington, though sceptical, found the tale he was being told rather engrossing. Edward related how the ship, intentionally striving to appear inconspicuous, followed a round-about course that took it to the Red Sea. There, after lying off shore for a day, it docked briefly at a small sea-side Yemeni town, which Edward identified on a map as Al Luhayyah. The cargo from Java was lowered over the side. It was hastily loaded aboard a freight truck with Turkish identification. By pre-arrangement with his brother, Edward used the cover of darkness and some ineptness on the part of his crew to desert the ship. He took refuge in a warehouse until his brother arrived on a motorcycle. Further north along the coast, the two stole a small motor launch and crossed the busy waters to Egypt. Edward's absence was not noticed until the ship was through the Gulf of Oman and heading southeast in the Arabian Sea.

For sharing his information about the shipment, purported to be extremely dangerous and, according to ship-board rumors, intended to cause 'great mischief' in America, Edward and his brother hoped to obtain asylum in the United States.

Pretty far-fetched, thought Harrington, who enjoyed a good story and an inventive story-teller. Following further interrogation by Harrington and other intelligence personnel, Lee's information seemed credible. Regrettably, although Lee had gathered that the cargo was to be taken overland by long-distance trucks through Turkey and Eastern Europe, from whence it would be transported to the United States, he had not been privy to any particulars. Now, in light of his presumed defection, the original route might well have been altered.

After considerable discussion, it was decided that Homeland Security and customs officials should be warned without further delay. Because the brothers required more than a week to reach the fabled Egyptian port, it was assumed the mysterious cargo might already be in the United States, or wherever else it was intended to be sent.

* * *

"Acme Produce? You... ah Mr. Labbani?" The olive-skinned delivery man reading from a shipping notice mispronounced the name. His loud voice and the sharp snap of the spring-closing door woke the proprietor out of what was probably a pleasant daydream.

"Yeah. That's me. What you got?"

A second man, Black, was carrying a large, rather heavy carton with about six jumbo melons. "Where do you want these?" He wore jeans, a short-sleeved denim shirt and had a thin gold neck chain. A gold crescent moon pendant dangled at the bottom of it.

"I didn't order any melons!" Labbani, now fully awake, protested. "You sure you got the right address?"

"Says right here, Acme Produce. That's you, right? They look good, but not like the ones I used to raise back home."

Perusing the delivery ticket, Labbani noted that a PAID stamp in purple ink was smeared across it. "Where you come from?"

"I had a small farm south of Baghdad. My melons were so sweet. But these look pretty good. Sign here, please." The driver pointed to his copy of the delivery slip. His helper had set the carton down just behind the counter.

The truck pulled away while Labbani was looking at the melons. He tried to read the sign on the side of the small pick-up. It was a rental. He dragged the carton into the back room. He picked up one of the melons, thumped it with his fingers and determined it was ripe. Suddenly, he realized it was a 'special shipment', not an item for sale. He closed his shop early and began to open the melons. Beneath the labels pasted on each was a microdot. He carefully removed them and retrieved his magnifying reader from a locked closet. A full hour later he sat quietly, trying to absorb the enormity of his task, the detailed instructions, and the tight timetable from which he dared not deviate.

* * *

A few preliminary inquiries, particularly regarding Captain Vargas' income, the size of his catches, his general financial situation, as well as his personal life had served to increase curiosity about the man and his activities. Hal Wysocki invited Jimmy O'Neill and Keisha McWilliams, a new agent with a background as a detective in Los Angeles before joining the FBI, to discuss the case. Wysocki shuffled a bunch of reports, laid them in a pile on his desk blotter, and faced the two staff members across his desk with a troubled look. "No pun intended, there is something fishy about this subject. This guy Vargas appears to have financial resources well beyond what he could logically have earned as a fisherman. I want you to team up and employ every possible legal means to probe his activities. Come back in two days and convince me either to drop the investigation or to pull him in for questioning. Check out all his crew members as well. Discreetly!"

Without saying a word, the two agents left the Boston station chief's office and walked quietly down the hall, where they had adjacent offices facing the rear parking lot. McWilliams spoke first. "Let's sit down in my office and divide up the responsibilities."

In half an hour they had listed a large number of potential sources of detailed information on Captain Vargas. Brainstorming further, they agreed to use every imaginable electronic means to obtain a complete picture of the mysterious seaman. Having divided the tasks, they split up and got down to work.

* * *

On the other side of the Atlantic, Elli Davidson was sequestered with a special task force established by *White Cross Holdings* in its Geneva headquarters to attempt to track the movement of funds involved in the experiments undertaken by their employees in Brazil and Indonesia. Unfortunately, both of the key figures, da Serra and Susila, were missing and presumed dead. Using her extensive contacts in the fraternal global banking industry, it was learned that transfers of money to both former employees could be traced back to Professor Kiriguchi. He, too, however, was deceased. It was clear that the parties behind the activity played hardball, ruthlessly eliminating links they considered weak and expendable.

Information from a major private bank in Singapore linked transfers to Susila to a North Korean source. The same source had purchased a large lot of special canisters from a Chinese manufacturer of scientific equipment. Intercepts of internet contacts between another North Korean-based entity to a Saudi source via a Lebanese bank were also considered suspect because of the timing and sequence of transactions. The amounts being moved were substantial.

While Mark trusted Willette, he had much less faith in the reliability of Willette's 'boss', whether it was the American President, or her 'gatekeeper' Chief of Staff. As a result, he did not immediately share the data Elli and her electronic investigators had uncovered. Mark and Elli, together with Samantha Willis, WCH's Operations Manager, continued to press all divisions of the company to gather information and forward it to Geneva under strict confidentiality. The results rivaled the outcomes of several governments' intelligence agencies. All concluded that a large magnitude attack on the West was pending. Where? When? What was the nature of the assault? Many questions. No definitive answers.

* * *

The Boston-based FBI team enlisted assistance from Washington and the Falmouth, Massachusetts police. Vargas was tailed for a couple of days, as were his crew. Then, with evidence mounting that he was engaged in criminal activities, he was pulled in for questioning. Under rather intense interrogation at an FBI safe-house outside Osterville, he broke and revealed that he had smuggled ashore 36 wooden cases that he shipped shortly afterward to individual addressees scattered in fourteen or fifteen states. He had destroyed the address list given him, but could recall several of them. Those whose details escaped him were in places near major cities. Immediately, messages were sent to FBI offices to check the addresses and the possible recipients. Most of the addresses involved private mail boxes that had been abandoned. A few were phony businesses. A handful were identified and placed under twenty-four hour surveillance.

From Jacksonville, Clark Willette assigned two experienced members of his group to shadow Scharffenberger, taking great pains to be as discreet as possible. He did not want to tip off his employer. His gut told him something was just not right.

* * *

Sundquist and his cohorts, using a remotely-activated website in Morocco, finally managed to hack into the principal computer used by Manfred Scharffenberger in his White House office. The overwhelming majority of his transmissions were made using a very sophisticated code. Many were directed to what was determined to be a green grocery in a Baltimore suburb. A small number were clear transmissions, apparently orders for fruit and vegetable purchases. One referred to the coming weekend and inquired "please confirm next Friday to Sunday discontinued service." The response was merely, "Seek cover 48-72 hrs, Good-bye!"

Apprised of the exchanges, Mark, who was in New Orleans for a business meeting, contacted Gayle Beckmeister to inform her of his hunches about the person to whom Willette was ostensibly reporting. They agreed to meet in Dallas, where Mark would next travel on behalf of the *Foundation*.

In the meantime, Willette had discovered through an FBI contact that cases containing mysterious canisters had bypassed customs and had been distributed to suspected terror groups in over two dozen large cities in the United States; as many as three in Canada. It was concluded from other bits of information that similar materials had presumably been placed in the hands of terrorists throughout Europe.

* * *

Mark had reserved two rooms at the Four Seasons Resort in nearby Irving. Gayle arrived about an hour after he had settled in. It was Wednesday afternoon. He called WCH in Geneva and talked both with Elli and Sam Willis, getting the latest information. He also checked with Clark Willette, who was in Washington. Homeland Security had been fully briefed. The consensus view was that something really big was set for the weekend. Secret alerts went to counterpart bureaus in Europe. In the States FBI, TSA and emergency fire, police and medical services in the target cities thus far identified were notified of the impending danger. It was decided not to issue an alert to the general public. This was out of fear that mass hysteria might actually serve as a cover for the attack, as well as the fact that its exact nature was still unclear. There was some clarity, however. The type of target likely, that is, locales where large groups might gather, such as sports arenas, public transportation hubs, theaters, crowded waiting rooms, airport and railroad terminals, high-rise office buildings, schools, indoor shopping malls, hotel air-conditioning units, and similar venues. Additionally, sources of public drinking water were expected to be hit. If an attack occurred, authorities were prepared to broadcast pre-recorded advisories and to guide citizen evacuations of population centers.

Room Service delivered sandwiches and hot tea as Gayle was about to knock on Mark's door. He already had a dry-erase board set up. After a quick hug and a short exchange about their travel experiences, Mark reviewed actions taken in the past twenty-four hours. They concluded Dallas would definitely be one of the target cities. Mark listed a number of obvious places to attack. Gayle admired his organizational ability and insight into a field of activity so alien to his usual occupation. A conference call with local police and the FBI clarified who would be responsible for seeking to stop or contain attacks at the various expected venues. Mark and Gayle could now only hope to play a small role in preventing or thwarting an unfortunate outcome at a single place. Because of their proximity, they volunteered to join the plain-clothes police at Dallas Cowboys Stadium. They were assigned the upper concourse. Section 412 in front of the men's restrooms on the Cowboy's side was specified.

On Friday the stadium was hosting the annual Texas Interscholastic Marching Band Competition. There was a good crowd, but the stands were not full by any means. The intrepid duo encountered no problems. They wandered about striving for nonchalance, visited the food vendors, checked the restrooms, and otherwise kept an eagle eye out for trouble makers. The evening passed uneventfully and they returned to their hotel. They had a light dinner in the hotel restaurant.

Chapter Twelve

Soraya Suparmanputra, although she loved her parents and her younger sisters, and their mutual religious faith, considered herself a 'liberated' woman. She was self-supporting. The influence of her Muslim childhood still pervaded much of her daily routine. Her devotion to Islam, however, was tempered by her love of life, her desire for individual freedom, her well-developed sense of her own worth. Like many modern women in her country, she did not cover her beautiful, long black hair. In public, she was conscious of the need for modesty. Nevertheless, her wardrobe would have been right at home in Southern California, where the fashions and behavioral trends of the young female film and television stars she strove to emulate, were commonplace. She idolized Taufik and relished his company and the attention he showered on her when his busy schedule allowed. While she understood that 'good' Muslim girls were supposed to wait for marriage before having sex, she had succumbed to the physical and emotional call of nature. Now, Taufik was gone. He had disappeared. The newspaper reports showed that investigators had no clues. Foul play, they said, could not be ruled out. Most assumed he would never be found. Soraya mourned. Her life had changed. She neglected her chores. Her apartment showed the effects of lackadaisical and infrequent house-cleaning.

"*Allahu Akbar*." Looking into her mirror on a Sabbath morning after weeks of grieving, Soraya sought divine guidance. She looked around her small apartment and had her first answer. "I think I had better start by straightening out this mess." Talking, even to herself, and resuming her life through simple actions would prove to be a beneficial therapy.

To the accompaniment of light music from a CD Taufik had given her she set about dusting and cleaning, sweeping and vacuuming. In her bedroom she was so motivated that she bent and stretched to reach under her bed with the vacuum cleaner. The head of the vacuum bumped into something and she had to turn it off. She was on all fours trying to see what the obstruction was, when she noticed Taufik's briefcase. She pushed it through to the other side, then went around the bed to pick it up. There was something in it. She found a large heavy-duty envelope. It was sealed with packing tape. There was no address, only a note attached with a large paper clip. 'DELIVER THIS TO TRUSTED AUTHOR-ITY'. Soraya stared at the object. Her face had assumed a serious cast. She had never had any contact with local officials. All one heard or read seemed to mention corruption regarding public officials. Suddenly, Soraya recalled her interviews with the sympathetic American woman. On her dresser she found the card Gayle Beckmeister had left her. Beck-meister had been so understanding, so gentle and considerate. Yes, she would send it to her. As soon as her cleaning was finished, Soraya showered and changed into her street clothes. At the post office she sent the envelope to the Jacksonville, Florida address on Beckmeister's busi-ness card. Not accustomed to mailing packages overseas, Soraya opted for the least expensive form of postage. Her letter would proceed by sea to its destination. Satisfied that she had done her duty, she returned home, wondering what Taufik might have wanted to send in the envelope to a 'TRUSTED AUTHORITY'.

* * *

Normally calm and, to members of the minority party, irritatingly collected, Manfred Scharffenberger was having trouble sleeping. He covered his anxiety attacks well, but he was frustrated in the knowledge that he himself was not entirely in the loop. At least not where the plans Labbani had inferred were now in advanced stages of development were concerned. The CIA and certain military intelligence units had been reporting signs of increased and unexplained activity among and between known centers of anti-Western radicalism. Scharffenberger sought to blunt the implications of this reporting in his briefings for the President. For her part, she seldom pressed for more details, preferring to think that everything on the foreign relations front was under control.

On a Tuesday evening, after carefully reviewing assessments of present dangers reported both by the CIA and the FBI, the President's Chief of Staff motored homewards full of apprehension that whatever 'his side' was planning might directly affect him. He resented being kept in the dark. He drove past Acme Produce, continued around the block and parked at the curb around the corner from the store. Labbani was in the process of cleaning up, making notes for posters to advertise next week's specials: early New England McIntosh apples, Maine potatoes, locally-grown corn.

A woman with the ingredients for a great salad was exiting with her precious organic vegetables just as Labbani's protegé entered. He looked up. He read Scharffenberger's face like a familiar book, for he had nurtured him carefully throughout his youth and adolescence. "How can I help you, sir?" The shop door closed noisily in mid-sentence. Somewhat irritated, Labbani raised his voice slightly. "We have no meeting scheduled today. Has something come up?"

"Nothing startling, but our intelligence and agencies abroad are beginning to sense something in the wind. They're gearing up to crack down on security again… and substantially this time. I've tried to convince the President it's just hot air. So far she's buying it, but…"

"Don't worry. All is going well." As he spoke, Labbani moved to the entrance and locked the door. "Come into the back room."

Wiping some trash from a work table into a plastic bucket, Labbani sat on a stool and motioned Scharffenberger to do likewise. Speaking with visible pride, Labbani began solemnly, "The culmination of my career is fast approaching. It will be a moment of glory for me… and for you." He lit up a cigarette and took two or three puffs, inhaling vigorously. While his partner disliked tobacco smoke, he did not protest. "A collaboration between our country," continued Labbani, "especially

VEVAK agents, and several powerful and dedicated groups on the Arabian Peninsula, as well as important sources in Asia, has led to the creation of a weapon whose imminent deployment here in the States, and in Europe, will have a more profound effect than that of the atomic bombing of Hiroshima and Nagasaki."

Scharffenberger's eyes widened. He knew instinctively it involved more than flying aircraft into prominent buildings. "A biological weapon. That must be it."

"Indeed. I received notice recently that the material has been delivered here, even dispersed to our 'instruments'. In Europe, too, I presume everything is in place."

"Already that far along?" Scharffenberger could not completely disguise his disappointment in not having been informed sooner.

Having no reason to distrust the operative he had controlled from the time of his arrival as an adoptee in Pennsylvania, where as a concerned 'uncle' he managed frequent visits, to the present, when he expected his highly-placed mole to follow orders without question, Labbani decided to share some details of the impending catastrophe. His cough was accompanied by a rasping, wheezing noise as he extinguished his cigarette. "Reza," Labbani used Scharffenberger's true given name, "We of the Middle East whose great cultures and religion have been in temporary eclipse, will soon rule the world. The Infidels will become our slaves. Those that survive, I should say." Labbani's voice was filled with confidence. A tinge of megalomania eluded Scharffenberger's otherwise analytic mind. He was mesmerized by control's prophetic tone. "Simply put, a means has been devised to accelerate the ability of a deadly and contagious virus to infect all who come into contact with it. Our experts claim death follows exposure rapidly. Health care personnel will have no effective protection. An antidote does not exist. Devastation of the targeted areas will exceed everything in recorded history. Fortunately for us, the fires needed to dispose of human victims will leave valuable physical infrastructure in the affected lands intact for immediate occupancy. Residual toxicity is likely to be minimal."

"How is all this expected to take place?"

"In the thirty-four years since you came here, many hundreds more have followed. All carefully planted like little seedlings. They grow slowly. With time they become strong. Their dedication and commitment is rooted deeply. They wait patiently, resiliently bending with the wind, tolerating the rain and snow, reaching for the sun when it appears. They have been formed into small cells. Most are located in cities, both here and in Europe."

"Do you know where the attacks are aimed?"

"We have fourteen cells here; three of those in Canada will also be activated. I know the cell leaders, but for security purposes only the leaders know their members. Targets have been suggested. It has been left to cell leaders to make the actual choices. They will assign specific tasks following brief training sessions. In addition to municipal water supplies, where gas-fired crossbow devices propel water-soluble canisters up to one hundred meters into treated reservoirs, the majority of targets involve high occupancy sites where thousands can readily be infected: large stadia, covered shopping malls, railroad stations, subways, airport waiting rooms, high density pedestrian squares, entertainment centers, theaters, large office structures, and similar locations."

"Is Washington to be targeted, too?"

"Definitely! And important cities from New York to Los Angeles, Miami to Seattle and in between. We want all sections of the country to be affected. Likewise in Europe. Great Britain, France, Germany, Italy, Spain, the Low Countries and even Russia. No country that opposes us will be spared. *Allahu Akbar!*" Labbani's cheeks were red with excitement.

"*Inshallah!*" Scharffenberger feigned enthusiasm. Internally, he wondered what his fate might be. Perhaps the Palestinians and Arabs welcomed martyrdom. Past events had shown they placed little value on human life. Personally, Scharffenberger had come to enjoy the few pleasures he allowed himself. His double existence was stressful. Yet he had been able to deal with it successfully until now. What did the future hold? Was he also expendable? "When is the action to take place?"

Concurrently, his subconscious thoughts wrestled with the matter of where his loyalty stood.

"Soon. I expect it will be soon. The command will be given by an MOIS (The Islamic Republic of Iran Intelligence Ministry) agent embedded in our UN delegation. I understand he will first consult with an unidentified senior Arab official in New York. My role is essentially over."

"What about me?"

"My advice is to stay home this weekend. Do not leave your house… for any reason… maybe three or four days. We can expect pandemonium on the highways. Health care will be severely, if not totally disrupted. Chaos will rule. When the worst is over, you must emerge and use your knowledge and position to aid our takeover of the American government. Trained cadres will arrive to aid you."

Manfred Scharffenberger strained to avoid defecating in his pants. An event such as his control was describing had never occurred to him. He thought, *Could Allah really will the death and destruction of whole nations?* He stared vacantly at the wall behind Labbani. *What are the limits of religious faith? Are Christians and Jews and Hindus and Buddhists seeking **my** death?*

"Are you alright, Reza?"

"Oh yes. I was thinking about what I will say to keep my family at home Saturday and Sunday. Jessica mentioned some function at the Temple. I'll come up with something." He regained his composure and struggled to act normally.

Labbani casually lit up a cigarette, coughed a couple of times, and patted Scharffenberger on the shoulder with his yellow-stained right hand. He walked with his protegé, opened the front door and let him out. "*Inshallah,* Reza!"

Chapter Thirteen

The first full week of September brought glorious weather to virtually all forty-eight contiguous states. The sun shone brightly, the temperatures were perfect for short sleeves and light casual shorts and trousers. It was ideal weather for a nation of peace-lovers to be lulled into complacency about their security. The constant warnings of impending danger were beginning to wear down the populace. However, those in government whose responsibility it was to keep Americans safe in their homeland were doing their utmost to connect the dots. Indeed, a picture was beginning to form that seemed ominous to a few. At their urging the President scheduled a meeting to review the latest developments. Early Wednesday morning the heads of the NSA, the FBI, the CIA, the TSA and the intelligence chiefs of the various military services and representatives of the State Department convened in a crowded Cabinet meeting room. To the surprise of many, Manfred Scharffenberger was presiding. The President had decided to stay an extra day or two in Hawaii, where she was attending an Asian cultural conference.

The result of the discussion was unequivocal. Some sort of attack was possible during the next three or four months, perhaps within a few weeks. While some sort of 'dirty bomb', an often-mentioned option, was conjectured, intelligence appeared to point towards a biological weapon. Precisely what that might be no one could say with any certainty. Nevertheless, the consensus leaned sharply in the direction of a 'toxic' event. On the President's behalf, Scharffenberger urged all agencies to raise their alert level, but implored them to avoid generating unnecessary paranoia among the general population. The FBI was designated the coordinating agency for a domestic attack.

Later, when he reported on the meeting to the President, the Chief of Staff suggested that the intelligence people were exaggerating the problem and puffing it up prior to submitting next year's budget requests. Madame President tended to agree with his astute appraisal. She excused herself to rush to a meeting honoring Anya Slimnova, a visiting designer from Russia, whose evening gowns were the current rage in Paris and Milan.

Even with his knowledge of both sides of the equation, Scharffenberger still lacked some significant facts. Nonetheless, he understood that something terrible was set to take place, perhaps as soon as the coming weekend. He pulled out his desk atlas and studied it carefully, very carefully.

* * *

A group of plainclothes police and sheriff's office personnel met quietly with a couple of agents from the local FBI office and Mark and Gayle. They stood around in the front lobby of the Cowboy Stadium in Irving, Texas at 1:30 am on a pleasant Saturday morning. The crowds attending Friday's high school band jamboree had left. The parking lots, except for police vehicles, were empty. The food venues had closed and the clean-up crews had finished early. There were no reports anywhere of any terrorist activity. A suspicious group in Australia had been questioned about 'provocative' blogging activity. In Europe and in the US, however, evidence had pointed to something happening this weekend. One day had passed without a problem. The possibility for trouble now focused on Saturday or Sunday. One down, two to go. Mark and Gayle returned to their hotel.

Even Mark was tense. He checked with Elli back in Yverdon. He also contacted Sam Willis by email. Contact with local law enforcement and Homeland Security revealed that nothing untoward had happened on either side of the Atlantic. All was quiet. He invited Gayle to his room.

555

He ordered a beer and some sandwiches from Room Service. Gayle requested a martini. Both needed to unwind. Gayle stared out the window. There was no moon. Her eyes were met with a wall of darkness. She began to weep quietly. Mark picked up on her anxiety immediately. He approached and held her tightly. "Don't worry, Gayle, nothing has happened yet." He tried his best to sound reassuring. He understood that stress was mounting. He was not oblivious to the destructive force of the unknown.

Dabbing at her eyes with a handkerchief, Gayle turned and spoke, struggling to control her agitation. "I feel so helpless. So useless. We don't know what the hell is going to happen. And we have no idea what to do when it does. It's so damn frustrating." Her voice had risen a couple of octaves. Mark put his arms around her. She seemed reassured and calm.

Mark was in a quandary. Elli and the children were undoubtedly also unnerved by the nature of the threat facing them. Mark had felt compelled to keep them informed. Yet, here he was face to face with a woman whose facade of strength had slipped. She was really quite beautiful, he thought. Beautiful and vulnerable. They sat down on a sofa near the windows. "It's true that we're just fumbling around in the fog. In spite of the billions spent on security, there are dangers against which we really can't prepare. We try, of course, to prevent them. We try to anticipate them. Until they actually happen, we don't know what our response will be. Our job is to be on hand. To provide leadership. To determine from the capabilities available to us what the response should be. We have to direct the right assets, and hopefully we've got them, to the place or places where they can help the most. I guess you'd have to call us triage aides. Assuming we survive whatever it is that happens."

From Gayle's expression, he could see he hadn't truly assuaged her fears. She held his hand and sat silently, her arm touching his. Abruptly changing the subject, she asked, "What was it like suddenly becoming a billionaire?"

Mark looked at her for a moment, then replied, "I had always considered myself a billionaire… of sorts. I grew up in a loving home. I had the most wonderful parents. My youth was rich in positive experiences. My dreams and fantasies brought me untold joy and happiness. I welcomed every day in school and throughout college, for they brought me knowledge and the desire to learn more, to share it as a teacher, perhaps to help others experience the wonder of life as I knew it." Gayle was wide-eyed and could not take her eyes off Mark. She had known him off and on when they were college students, but realized she hadn't really known who he was.

Continuing, Mark, reflecting on his past, said, "I have such fond memories of my childhood and of my mother and father. School, too, in the little town where I was raised was a happy time in my life. I can even recall Lily, the cutest girl in my third grade class. She was always offering me part of her lunch. I liked her a lot. I guess I had a few crushes. Probably more than a few… every year. I even had a crush on you." Gayle smiled. "You were as beautiful then, as you are now. I envied you in our debates. You were so self-assured, so articulate and always better prepared than any other debater. I knew you'd be a big success in law school. Who knows, if fate hadn't taken us down different paths, our relationship might be quite different."

Perhaps it was simply female curiosity. Gayle took advantage of a tiny break in Mark's narrative to inquire exactly how he had met his wife. "What took you to Switzerland in the first place?"

"It's a long story. You may have surmised by now that I firmly believe in fate. So much in life is inexplicable. I see it as the work of some unknown, unknowable force. I call it fate." Looking at the ceiling, Mark gathered his thoughts. "I met a remarkable woman on a flight to New York for a professional meeting. She was a nun. We talked. And seemed to have a lot in common. At the time my work ethic had caused a form of burn-out. I actually invited this nun on a date. Her name was Catherine. I took her to see *La Bohème* at the Met. Walking back to my hotel on that rather cool fall evening I helped an elderly man whom I had come across in a confused state. I put him up for the night. He disappeared the next day. Several weeks later I received a note from him, inviting me to Zürich. He was asking for help. Well, I soon discovered that his father, a bank executive, had come across some unclaimed Nazi bank accounts. Unable to determine who the actual owners were or to whom the funds should be returned, he and a couple of like-minded friends secretly invested them. Their hope was to eventually find the true owners. Through the post-war years the investments grew and grew to become a rather astounding sum. Before death claimed him, the banker prevailed on his aging son to find someone who would realize his dream of putting these financial resources to use for the good of mankind. Fate chose me." Mark paused for a moment. "I agreed reluctantly to help and was charged with the task of finding the secret account numbers for the funds. This I managed with the aid of three women. They were all lovely, charming, accomplished and courageous. One of them literally died saving my life." Mark stopped again momentarily, a serious and pensive mien on his face. "The third woman appealed to my heart the very first time our eyes met. That encounter lasted mere seconds. I knew it was fate when I later met her again when I appeared at the bank where she was a senior officer to claim the accounts." Mark smiled and exhaled. "Fate had led me to her, and her to me. I have a sensation of absolute rapture when I think of her and our three wonderful children." Mark looked at his watch. It was nearly 2:30. "We'd better continue this conversation later. It's getting late and we need to be rested for whatever tomorrow brings."

Gayle would like to have heard more, but nodded assent and grabbed her gear on the way to the door. They embraced and she left.

Dead tired, though he had concealed it well, Mark sat on the edge of the bed. *Why has fate brought me to this place under these circumstances? If this threat materializes we're all toast. We can't possibly stop every attempt by this invisible enemy.* Kicking off his shoes, he lay down on top of the bed covers. He fell asleep almost immediately. Fortunately, he had set his alarm clock for 4:30 a.m.

Chapter Fourteen

An irritating buzzing sound jolted Mark in the midst of a dream whose thread he completely lost as he fumbled to reach the alarm clock next to his bed. His eyes not fully opened yet, he knocked the wireless device onto the floor. Swinging off the bed, he retrieved it and switched it to the off position. Early light penetrated the curtains. He had forgotten to close the drapes. Surprised to see that he was dressed, he stripped down, shaved and showered, then pulled on a clean shirt and a fresh pair of jeans. He called Gayle. She was already up and heading for the breakfast room. Mark joined her there.

"Mark, thanks for helping me get a grip last night. I'm O.K. today. I said a quick prayer this morning. I sure hope it'll help. I am very concerned though."

"Generally, or something in particular?" Mark interrupted.

"My boss, Clark, is not responding to any calls. Then, I heard on CNN that the President's Chief of Staff is away on an unannounced 'fact-finding trip' to an unknown destination. It's just not like Clark to totally ignore me, especially in a time of crisis like this. I'm worried, very worried. It's too weird."

"Let's check again after breakfast. The agent in charge here wants us to cover the same venue again today. Seems like they're spread even thinner than before because they came up with additional potential targets. Apparently, a couple of reporters who threatened to break a story about this emergency have been placed in 'protective custody' to reduce the danger of creating mass hysteria."

"You must be worried about your family."

"Of course, but the kids are safe at home. Elli is in Geneva at our communications hub, probing cyber space with our own intel team. So far, nothing new, just an uncanny and somewhat unnerving silence."

* * *

In an unprecedented action, European authorities imposed on news agencies a virtual total blackout of news about security activities. The move was not publicly announced. Nevertheless, vigilant private news sources, assembling tidbits garnered mainly by electronic means, were allowing news to trickle out regarding unannounced sweeps of public transportation facilities, sporting events and large-scale gatherings, such as parades, trade exhibitions, conferences and the like. Security personnel were conspicuous in substantially larger numbers than was customary in airports, subway and railroad stations. Border patrols were conducting more random checks than was normal. Persons suspected of illegal activity were rounded up for interrogation.

In America, ideal weather conditions coincided with a peak in athletic and sporting events in huge venues from coast to coast. Football games competed with baseball, early basketball, hockey, soccer, tennis and other outdoor and indoor activities for participants and audiences. The citizens of a great nation were en route or in place to enjoy Mother Nature's gift of sunshine, clear skies and moderate temperatures.

Of all the places they might be, fate had conspired to bring Mark and Gayle together at Cowboy Stadium, where literally thousands were assembling to watch their favorite professional team begin a season filled with dreams of getting to the Super Bowl. They saw no point in leaving for safer ground. It was their duty.

* * *

The national security apparatus of the United States, anticipating a truly unprecedented attack that threatened to surpass in size and scope previous attempts, had won from major European counterparts a pledge of strict censorship with regard to public pronouncements in order to help avoid public panic. Special secure communications lines were established at the national level. Similar arrangements had been rushed to completion for domestic communication to law enforcement agencies and security and emergency response directors in states, provinces and other viable political entities.

Early Saturday along the Atlantic coast, reports of problems in parts of Europe arrived in cipher messages. An exhibition football match in Wembley Stadium between Manchester United and F.C. Bayern München had been attacked by two four-person groups dressed as fans. They sought to discharge small canisters of an unknown material in the stands. Disgruntled fans incapacitated them. They are being held in custody. The stadium was temporarily quarantined.

At Heathrow Airport and at two London central subway stations unidentified persons successfully actuated spray devices among noonday crowds of transients. Paris likewise reported incidents at Charles de Gaulle airport and inside the lobby of the Louvre. A slow-moving vehicle on the Champs Elysées was halted by alert police when a passenger attempted to unload the contents of a small aerosol-charged cylinder aimed at throngs of tourists and pedestrians. In Rome, St. Peters was closed "to erect scaffolding". The Pantheon was closed for cleaning and minor maintenance. All police and Carabinieri furloughs had been cancelled.

In other locations in principal cities in Spain, Germany and Russia small canisters apparently molded from an unusual man-made substance were found abandoned in locales were traffic density would normally be quite high. The devices had plastic fittings consisting of a screw top and a nozzle not unlike those found on fire extinguishers. Thus far the only injuries reported involve minor scrapes and bruises suffered by persons seeking to flee police patrols. Some hospitals have admitted as many as two dozen persons complaining of breathing problems. None were considered life threatening. Hazmat crews and bomb squads were treating the mysterious cylinders as explosive threats.

Mark and Gayle were apprised of the reports. After being deputized, they took up their assigned posts at Cowboy Stadium. Uniformed and plainclothes officers of both sexes were everywhere. Many had been told the activity was a special drill to assess capabilities in the event of a real emergency. Mark knew it could potentially be a catastrophic blow, if it succeeded. He realized how truly insignificant he was in the grand scheme of things. How could he and Gayle possibly thwart a concerted assault by trained and determined forces. Especially if they possessed a weapon of unspeakable toxicity that they could easily deliver in a million different venues. There was no way the enemy could be interdicted wherever they might choose to attack. The aggressor had all the advantages. A feeling of futility and despair lurked below the surface in his psyche. He struggled to put on a brave face and to be vigilant in the tiny space he had been assigned. He was both relieved that no casualties were being reported from Europe, and confused by the apparent impotence and failure of what were clearly attempts to cause great harm.

More news: The final day of a special Picasso exhibit at Madrid's famed Prado was unexpectedly cancelled. Three cruise ships were diverted from Stockholm harbor on the basis of anonymous tips. Edgy Swiss officials closed the Great St. Bernard, Mont Blanc, Simplon, St. Gotthard Road and San Bernardino Tunnels for 18 hours to the consternation of mainly Swiss and Italian drivers. St. Mark's Square in Venice was cordoned off and closed to pedestrians. In Hamburg, the Hagenbeck Zoo was closed. An André Rieu concert scheduled to be televised from Schönbrunn Palace in Vienna was postponed.

From Maine to Florida superb weather reigned. Sun, moderate temperatures and only occasional gusts of 15–25 miles per hour were predicted for virtually the entire country east of the Rockies. Further west much needed rain was expected. The morning hours were calm. No activity of a suspicious nature anywhere. Yet, in accordance with their instructions, as issued in coded internet messages, individuals and small groups were quietly and inconspicuously assembling; some in suburban areas from which travel to target sites required less than an hour, others conveniently close to in-town 'places of interest'. Most of the participants, predominantly male, but also including a number of middle-aged women, assumed something huge was planned. They mumbled guesses, but only a few leader-types realized there was a potential for casualties among them, depending on the exact nature of the weapons they had received. Unquestioning loyalty was demanded of them. If lives were sacrificed, so be it. Thus, thought most. Here and there, however, doubters existed. *Americans are resilient. What good will killing people do? I'm happy. I don't want to die. No one here knows me.* Clearly, while some may have been eager to claim martyrdom, others, rational thinkers, realists, were wavering, looking for a way to exit.

* * *

At a secret airfield in the Saudi desert; in an underground room in an unmarked ministry building outside Teheran; in a suite of offices at a military base outside Pyongyang, nervous men were restlessly watching television news channels beamed via satellite from the United States and Europe. Busy fingers queried computers whose results appeared on oversized monitors mounted on walls, sitting on tables, or standing on the floor. Goh Il Wan, considered ruthless and unflappable, was biting his nails. In the Middle East there was head scratching and hand ringing. "Why are there no reports of deaths! We know the canisters have been discharged at many locations. Places where hundreds, even thousands of people should have been exposed to the virus." Nerves were on edge. Everyone was searching for someone to blame. Disappointment was turning perceptively into rage.

* * *

A strange misty fog was released in the Atrium at Atlanta's Hartsfield-Jackson International Airport. Several passengers coughed, complaining of a throat irritation. Three suspicious individuals were arrested at Turner Field, where the Braves were winning a National League playoff game. Detection devices helped intercept two males who had breached an electrified fence protecting the water supply for the Nation's capital. A jeans-clad woman and her 20-year-old daughter were apprehended by a guard on the fourth floor of the Mall of America in Bloomington, Minnesota. They were in the process of releasing the contents of a small canister from a railing above the Nickelodeon Universe. Similarly, a brief report from Boston indicated a man fell from the second-floor Rotunda at the Faneuil Hall Marketplace while engaged in a suspicious act. He broke both legs and suffered a severe concussion. Tunnels and bridges in and out of New York City were closed for 'inspection'.

All of these reports had one thing in common. No large-scale casualties. By mid-afternoon, Dallas Cowboys Stadium was full. This pre-season charity game featuring the challenging New England Patriots against a home team that had claimed last year's Super Bowl with a lop-sided victory was proving to be a record breaker. Almost every seat had an occupant. Mark and Gayle were patrolling the upper concourse. Mark walked the concourse in a clockwise direction; Gayle walked counter-clockwise. When they met at the opposite end they would reverse directions and make another tour. Everything seemed pretty quiet. The stadium basked in sunshine. Gentle breezes wafted from west to east. Mark and Gayle decided, for variety, to undertake the next round together. On the Cowboys' side, near Section 412, which was close to a Men's Room, they heard a commotion. Three burly-looking men wearing assorted logo-sweatshirts, were being questioned by a uniformed stadium guard. Several spectators had stopped to watch. There was a lot of yelling. Mark approached and confronted a man in a red sweatshirt. The man was holding a small canister that he aimed alternately at the guard and the open space above the stadium. Mark, identified himself as a sheriff's deputy and demanded the man put the canister down. A second sweatshirt, a blue one, stepped in front of his colleague and pointed a gun at Mark. A rowdy group behind the sweatshirts made threatening noises. Other curious bystanders behind Mark were approaching to see what was happening. The sweatshirt with the gun panicked and pulled the trigger just as Gayle struck Mark with a flying block, sending him sprawling on the floor. Mark hit the floor hard and rolled over. Three of the onlookers slammed the gunman to the ground and subdued his two buddies, Mark quickly shook off the cobwebs in his head. He rushed to Gayle's side. She had been stunned and knocked down when the bullet intended for him hit her shoulder. Yelling to the onlookers to hold the sweatshirt group and not to touch the canister or the gun, Mark used his walkie-talkie to summon reinforcements and medical help for Gayle. He used a scarf from a fanny pack she was wearing as a tourniquet.

A squad of sheriff's deputies arrived, cuffed the perpetrators, took statements from the onlookers and Mark, while an emergency medical crew checked Gayle. She was taken by elevator to an ambulance and transported to a hospital. Mark caught up with her there shortly thereafter. Following a medical examination, staff surgeons removed the bullet and treated the wound. As an extra measure, Gayle spent the night in the hospital.

* * *

Late the next morning, Mark picked Gayle up at the hospital. He had completed his report for the county sheriff. Arrangements for a flight to Paris, then Geneva were also ready. He had Room Service bring lunch to Gayle's suite.

"You look much better, Gayle. But you do seem to be concerned about something. Anything I can help with?"

"I had the strangest call this morning. A person referring to himself as 'a friend of Clark Willette' told me to clear out the office in Jacksonville, destroying all documents and any evidence of our activities. I was told a severance check would be mailed to me. Furthermore, the government would disavow any knowledge of the existence of the agency to which I was attached."

"Good heavens, Gayle, that's incredible. I heard that Scharffenberger is missing, possibly dead. Some deal in Africa. I think you've been abandoned. Your "agency" must have been some kind of rogue operation, not strictly legitimate, a bogus creation of the Chief of Staff."

"I just can't believe it. I had such faith in Clark. Now this! It's stranger than fiction." She thought a few minutes. "Well, I've got a fair amount saved. My bills are paid. I'll survive, even with an inexplicable gap in my curriculum vitae. I mean, how does one explain something like this?"

Mark held her hand. He knew she was a strong person, capable of coping with much adversity. "It has been a wild string of events that you've experienced. You're going to come out of this in great shape. Of that I'm certain. You know, I still can't understand why and how you risked your own life to save me. I was looking at the barrel of that gun and I figured I was a goner."

"The better I know you, the more I realize what a truly good person you are. You're too damn good to die. Not now. Perhaps it was just fate, like you say, but I had to act. The world needs people like you. Your Elli is a one helluva lucky woman."

"I'm definitely in your debt, Gayle. I'd be honored if you would join the advisory group that supports *La Fondation Székely*. Let me know how to contact you and I'll send the details."

They both stood. Gayle hugged Mark, wrapping her good arm around his neck. They kissed. She wiped a couple of tears with a handkerchief.

"By the way. The Reception Desk has information about your flight back to Florida, compliments of *White Cross Holdings*. It's a private jet. Just tell them when and enjoy the ride."

After leaving, Mark grabbed his bags across the hall, caught a cab for the airport and began the trip to his elective home.

Chapter Fifteen

Not unexpectedly, the print and electronic media managed to flood global communications with hundreds of exclusive stories pertinent to the events of the weekend. While a few may have contained some insight into the actual nature of the emergency, most were fanciful and brilliantly imaginative accounts that served mainly to add to the confusion. The stone wall of silence erected by security insiders world-wide did little to dispel the surfeit of surmise generated by a press whose sources now seemed to be in disarray. Cries for more manpower, better surveillance, upgraded equipment and increased budgets were officialdom's responses to calls for rapid improvement. Those whose responsibility it is to protect the public were equally awed by the audacity and scope of the plan and relieved that it had failed. Realizing that a likely error by the perpetrators prevented a cataclysmic disaster, the more thoughtful among security leaders remained intensely wary of further attempts. The dot-connectors of the world were engaged in a frenzied search for clues.

Except for his immediate family and some loyal customers, virtually no one noticed the brief obituary in the *Baltimore Sun* for a man named Labbani, a successful grocer and small businessman, who died of heart failure exacerbated by a previously undetected case of late-stage lung cancer. On the West Coast there had been altercations with participants in the 'attack'. Seattle's Space Needle had been temporarily closed. Sports venues in San Francisco, Oakland and Los Angeles had been closed briefly for sweeps by security forces. L.A.'s water supply was being tested. Hoover Dam, a possible target, had been protected by swarms of police.

Disneyland's surveillance cameras were monitored feverishly all weekend long.

A reporter for *The Washington Post*, stymied by her inability to obtain comments from the President's Chief of Staff, discovered that Manfred Scharffenberger, who had departed mid-week on an undisclosed mission to Africa, had failed to return as scheduled and was presently considered "a missing person". Across Europe and the United States, scores of persons arrested for conspiracy and for engaging in activities endangering the public were being questioned. Many more eluded notice and crawled back into their holes. Some had reneged on their commitments and hoped to regain their anonymity, having lost the will to participate in criminal acts against their fellow citizens. An infamous North Korean "Work Camp" gained several new inhabitants. Rumors from the Middle East suggest that in the constant game of "musical chairs" amongst terror groups, a few former power brokers had recently had their chairs jerked out from under them.

The so-called man in the street, Mr. or Mrs. Everyman, as might be expected, reverted to their daily routines. The topic of the day predominantly favored the results of the most recent sporting event: Major League Baseball, the beginning college and professional football seasons, hockey matches, soccer, the coming basketball season, the weather. Occasionally there was mention of the President's new Chief of Staff. It seemed fitting that the country's first woman president would feel comfortable with a woman in that important position. Maria Alicia Gomez had a long list of accomplishments. A former Miss West Virginia, Ms Gomez, who had come to the United States as a toddler from Nicaragua, graduated from Virginia Tech with a degree in Mechanical Engineering. Elected to the House for her second term, she was a frequent talk show guest and a well-known and respected commodity on the national scene. The newly elected Speaker of the House, Tovah Ginsburg, an Orthodox Jew from New York, promised close collaboration with the President on new social initiatives.

* * *

Still favoring a left arm and shoulder injured in the dramatic climax of the confrontation in Dallas, a tired and rather drawn Gayle Beckmeister, took a final look at the office she had shared with Clark Willette. It was empty of all but the desks and chairs, a couple of waste baskets and a shredding device that had done yeoman service these past two days. An exhilarating phase of her life had come to a close. She took the elevator down to the main lobby and surrendered her keys to the receptionist on duty at the Security desk, got a receipt and walked to her car in the parking lot behind the building. In her right hand was a shopping bag with a few personal items; under her left arm a large brown envelope addressed to her, postmarked Surabaya, Indonesia.

She still hadn't decided what she would do next. She might not be driving to Ponte Vedra Beach much more. It was time to move on. The intense pace of life dictated by the events of the past few months had left her more drained than she wanted to admit. It was a former CIA colleague who had told her confidentially of Willette's fateful mission to Madagascar.

Moments after the undeniable truth of Scharffenberger's treachery became known to Willette, he realized the enormous harm that would be done to the country he loved, should word of the President's Chief of Staff's perfidy leak to the press. Together with a man known only as P.C. Fisher, Willette's most trusted clandestine operative, the twosome had flown in a military transport to the Azores. From there, initially by chartered plane to Nairobi, then via another private flight to Tananarivo, Madagascar. Willette then traced Scharffenberger's route to a port town on Madagascar's west coast. In Mahajanga, Scharffenberger, an accomplished recreational sailor, had rented a twenty-four-foot sloop ostensibly for a week of sailing and fishing in the Mozambique Channel area. A storm and some strong winds had taken him to Dzaoudzi in the Comoros Islands. Willette and Fisher caught up with him there. Rumor has it a man with a beard and another wearing a New York Yankees baseball cap invited themselves onto the boat and all three set sail together. Four days later, the boat *sans* sailors was found floating about forty miles off shore. There was no evidence of a scuffle. Authorities assume the three men went overboard in extremely choppy seas and drowned. No bodies have been retrieved to date.

Sworn to secrecy by the three other people whose responsibilities had guided them to the awful truth of the ultra-covert agency set up by Scharffenberger, Beckmeister sat for a moment or two in her car, eyes closed, her lips mouthing a prayer for a true patriot.

In spite of it being autumn, the temperatures were holding in the low eighties in Northeast Florida. Beckmeister goosed the thermostat a notch, poured a light beer into a glass and seated herself out of habit at her computer to check for email. There was but a single message. "It's great to be home with my family again. I thank you once more for your extraordinary service to our beloved homeland. My personal debt to you for your bravery and sacrifice is boundless. If I can help you in any way, at any time, please call upon me or my family. At WCH we have ratcheted our security level down somewhat, but intend to maintain a suitable degree of surveillance for our own security and well being, as well as for the many entities we serve throughout the world. In the universe in which we live and operate it is a *sine qua non* that an organization such as ours cannot relax its vigilance ever. I hope you will take my advice and arrange for a couple of weeks of vacation. When you have an opportunity, do get your resumé updated. I have a feeling a prestigious institution of higher learning in New England is going to be looking to fill an important post soon. You would be the perfect candidate. By the way, we're renting a chalet near Davos for a couple of weeks in February. Elli and the children insist that we invite you to join us. Details to follow shortly. Love and warm regards, Mark, Elli, Mireille, Sylvie and Theo."

Gayle smiled, thinking how nice it would be to *schuss* down those gorgeous alpine slopes without a care in the world. Breathing in that crisp, cold alpine air; enjoying a hearty meal within sight of a crackling fireplace in one of the area's charming restaurants, poking around in the smart shops. Yes, a holiday in Switzerland sounds great. She made a mental note to keep February clear. Her gaze wandered to the space above her fireplace. The oil painting she had bought on a whim at a riverside art show her first weekend in Jacksonville intrigued her. It was not representational art, but rather a strange surrealistic *mélange* of swirling color and suggestive shapes. It might be an imaginary landscape, a battle of conflicting emotions, a vision of a deep hole on a distant planet, or a mysterious internal image of a troubled mind. Somehow, it seemed to reflect her existence during the preceding months. It could be a prescient view of the events that had unfolded so unpredictably in recent days.

Staring now out a window at the ocean lapping hungrily at the shore, Gayle was unable to satisfactorily explain why the most diabolic scheme she could imagine had simply fizzled into nothingness in virtually every instance where it was intended to wreak such devastation and havoc. Aggressive reporters had uncovered some details. The real story, however, was being closely guarded by a tiny group of insiders. They had no intention of causing global panic by releasing any particulars. A substantial number of the would-be perpetrators had been captured and arrested. It was claimed anonymously that they had been repatriated to their native lands. No one could corroborate the information. Some, it was assumed, had aborted the attacks to which they were assigned before the launch deadline. Apparently, they had learned enough about the event to find it too outrageous to participate. More than a few may have lost their zeal to act because they had become 'Americanized'. It was impossible to calculate exactly how many have resumed their 'sleeper' status, resigned to waiting for another effort at some point in the future. Ferreting them out will be difficult, perhaps impossible. But that's a task for others. Gayle felt she had done her share. Then, too, a degree of disillusionment had wormed its way into her psyche. Scaling the wall of skepticism she had erected would require time. A lot of time.

The glass of Sam Adams she had poured for herself when she reached home sat half full on her desk. It was now at room temperature. She took it to the kitchen and emptied it into the sink. On the counter was the brown envelope from Indonesia. She noticed the sender was Soraya Suparmanputra, and recalled having interviewed her at the address on the envelope. Opening it with a paring knife, Gayle removed a single sheet of paper covered with closely spaced lines of type in English that was less than perfect. A few words had been lined through.

*

To whom it may concern. My name is Taufik Susila. I am Laboratory Director for Batavian Laboratories, with place of work in Surabaya. Many months before I meet Japanese publisher name of Kiriguchi, Endo Kiriguchi. We make private deal for me to do researching on new enzyme called Henserrase This nobel enterprise take dangerous turn. Kiriguchi say investors want try experimenting with bad virus (Zeta-Qb8!).

Man from Korea help get much equipments. Threaten me to continue working. Idea to make virus very bad worser with aid of enzyme. Accidental death of assistant and family show evil result of combination. Korea man send new helper. We get from him special thermoplastic cylinders (strong, not heavy). Nylong valve and aktuator come with. Also three-component aerosol propellers. Make us work many hours, many days to fill over 600 cylinders. They think Henserrase make virus mutate so fast no vaccine can be make develop in time. Could be millions people die in few hours. I not tell about some character property of enzyme. It verry unstable. Could react so fast that it do suicide kill self. Helper not see I add Nogotrol – neutralize inhibitor I invent. I discover this destroy virus. I especk they kill me. Half money from car and house and bank to mother; other half for Soraya and Sujata. I am beg forgiving for involvement. Inshallah!

* * *

The page was signed with a defiant flourish – Taufik Susila. Gayle walked to the large ocean-facing window and gazed vacantly at the white caps punctuating the inexorable arrival of a high tide. *So. That explains why nothing came of an horrific plan to create a global holocaust. The little guy who was being used to manufacture an unstoppable pandemic unlike anything the world has known sabotaged the effort. Taufik Susila is the veritable 'unsung hero' whose name will not go down in history. I alone know of his bold and courageous deed.* The surf was beginning to ebb. The band of damp sand stretching along the beach was widening noticeably. Shouting at the waves, Dr. Gayle Beckmeister's voice was inaudible to mortals, "If there is a God in Heaven, I know she'll find a place of honor for this good man. May his soul rest in peace." She focused on a large wave that had formed at the limit of her vision and followed its path towards the shore where it dissolved meekly on the sand and receded leaving a line of froth. As she did so, the letter and envelope were reduced to a pile of tiny pieces between her busy fingers. As evening fell, a nondescript plastic bag containing the pieces was dropped in a trash receptacle outside the Fresh Market on Ponte Vedra Boulevard, where an attractive, unattached and unemployed lawyer purchased a head of Boston lettuce, a cluster of vine-ripened tomatoes, a cucumber, a wedge of brie and a baguette.

Dinner for one will be served on the veranda.

THE END

A Mark Davidson Story

DARK JOURNEY

Hellmut Edelmann

Dark Journey

"No, Mr. President!" Mark's voice was well modulated, firm, business-like, matter-of-fact. "The Foundation deals directly with its own staff or carefully selected, appropriately-trained partners, never through government agencies or bureaus." There was noticeable emphasis on the word 'never'. Mark looked deep into the eyes of the man sitting behind the expansive, well-polished desk, the centerpiece of a large, richly-appointed office, a work space befitting the leader of a major African nation. Mark continued, "We both know that the corruption and incompetence that plagues so many of your sister countries is as rife here as anywhere on the continent. I mean no disrespect. It is, however, a reality the *Foundation* encounters throughout the world."

This was to be the final stop on Mark Davidson's grand world tour. Renewing established ties, revitalizing programs, developing new opportunities, negotiating arrangements that would allow the respected *Fondation Székely* to continue and to expand its broad array of humanitarian services and charitable ventures was a mission the organization's founder and Secretary General approached with great zeal and passion. He had also made a few lightning visits to enterprises that played important roles within the global investment portfolio of *White Cross Holdings*, whose managing director he was. The whirlwind travel that had taken Mark to virtually every corner of the globe was a *tour de force* demanding enormous physical and mental energy. The stamina, fortitude and sheer will power nurtured on alpine hiking trips in the preceding several months had contributed much to his success thus far. His wife, Elli, had joined him while he was in Asia and the South Pacific. His trusted aide,

Samantha Willis, on loan for two years to Mark's brother-in-law, Roland Denis-Breuer's bio-medical engineering and pharmaceutical headquarters as Director of Research and Training, had flown down to join Mark on part of his African leg. Her task was to assess educational and training resources for a major thrust into Sub-Saharan developing nations. Mark hoped to improve medical delivery systems, create *in situ* manufacturing facilities and treatment centers for huge populations whose needs were currently being neglected.

Mark's dedication and determination notwithstanding, he was extremely exhausted. He continued to focus intently on the man sitting on the other side of the desk. Mark knew that the tide was changing. Opposition to the current regime was growing more vocal. New leaders were beginning to emerge. Holding on to power was a matter of importance to the man whose suit had been hand-crafted in Rome. His elegant footwear cost top dollar in Florence. The colorful ceremonial scarf draped around his neck, a clever touch to suggest his close ties to the poor masses, concealed the bitter irony that he had been skimming millions and millions from aid funneled to his country over the years by guilt-ridden donor nations in Europe and North America. While Mark was amenable to provisions in their proposed agreement that might burnish the ego of the President, he was absolutely adamant that every dollar provided by the *Foundation* be efficiently employed to ease the plight of the poor and to improve the health and welfare of the downtrodden and forgotten.

"I am certain that the best interests of your people are your foremost concern," Mark continued. "Our proposal provides for an extraordinary investment in the medical infrastructure of this great country. To be associated with it will undoubtedly prove to be a major facet of your legacy to your countrymen." Mark could almost feel his conscience hiccup as his words flowed. The President was presumed to have a fortune, taken from his own people, stashed in secret accounts in Europe and other off-shore havens. Mark's sources knew the presumption to be fact. Regrettably, it was often necessary in the pursuit of favorable outcomes through diplomacy to finesse the truth.

Finally, the President acquiesced. He agreed to the terms of the *Foundation*'s proposal, withdrawing in the process all the provisions he had hoped to insert. Provisions that would have resulted in financial benefits for him, his associates and followers. He secretly admired Mark. The Secretary General of the *Fondation Székely* was highly respected. He was incorruptible. Even thinking that word challenged the President's comprehension. Lacking a gene for avarice seemed almost inhuman to someone whose whole life had been dedicated to amassing political power and personal wealth at the expense of others. He looked at the documents before him, sighed internally at the lost opportunity, and put his gold Mont Blanc pen to the signature line. Mark signed too. They both rose simultaneously. Mark shook the hand of a man known to have caused the deaths of many innocent persons. The deal was done. He would wash the hand as soon as he got back to his hotel.

Samantha Willis, who had participated in earlier discussions with the President and his staff, had departed in her specially-equipped plane the preceding day. She intended to visit the *Foundation*'s training institutes in South Africa, Kenya and Morocco before returning to Switzerland.

Mark would like to have hopped on a plane immediately so much did he miss his wife and children. He was, however, extremely tired. It had been a struggle to maintain his focus on the negotiations and to appear alert and strong. His commercial flight was scheduled to depart early the next day. He had room service bring him a plate of rice and baked fish and a glass of wine. If he had been asked a few minutes later how the food had tasted, he would have lacked an answer. A few quick notes in his laptop, a vitamin tablet he promised Elli he would take daily, a warm shower and a fresh pair of sleeping shorts later, he slipped under a light blanket and rested a head bursting with details of his extensive travels on a soft pillow. He wondered how the despot he had just left would try to undermine the agreement and divert funds to his personal accounts. Mark had already selected a legal team to keep an eye on the greedy leader. Mere seconds later he was completely oblivious to anything and everything.

* * *

The English accent acquired during his university years in Great Britain, the perfect manners, and the gracious smile belied the reality set forth in the multi-paged dossier Mark had slammed down on the president's desk in disgust. Mark always prepared thoroughly when venturing forth on behalf of the *Foundation*. The man he was required to deal with on his final African stop was clearly a tyrant, an evil man, self-centered, greedy, even murderous when it suited his purpose. Now, face to face with his adversary, the sweet phrases from his opposite's mouth could not conceal the deceit at their root. Suddenly, Mark leaped out of his chair and grabbed his counterpart by the throat. He released his grip barely in time for the startled victim to draw a life-saving breath.

"You scumbag! You heinous criminal! I'll be damned if I'll let you get a finger on the charity we want to extend to your impoverished people." The President was about to press an alarm to summon help, when Mark slammed his fist on the outstretched hand, causing it to knock over an ornate desk lamp artfully carved from a dark native wood. The President, fearing for his life, stared at his fingers. They were bruised and swelling. Removing his gem-studded rings would be painful.

Hearing the scuffle, three burly uniformed guards burst into the room. With incredible agility and economy of movement Mark reduced them to unconscious lumps of flesh strewn on the expensive Persian carpets covering the handsome parquet floors. He turned to the President. "You bastard! I'm giving you 24 hours to resign and flee into exile!" Mark stomped out of the office, intense satisfaction registering on his face.

*

The classroom was filling slowly. Students tended to straggle in from the busy halls at the very last minute. Autumn temperatures were unseasonably warm. Shorts and tee shirts were experiencing an extended period of service. Mark took a seat in the front row. The noisy hall grew silent as Visiting Professor of History Rowena Smythe-Bagley, already the author of a popular new work on her field of specialization, Ancient Rome, walked briskly to the podium. She set her briefcase down on the nearby table and placed a sheaf of papers on the lectern. The overhead projector was switched on and the Roman Forum appeared miraculously on the screen at the front of the hall, now nearly full of bright-eyed young American college students.

Her academic treatise, a surprise best-seller, Ms Smythe-Bagley, at 26 years of age, stood on the threshold of a promising teaching career. Mark couldn't take his eyes off this unexpected ray of sunshine. She wore a delicate blue print chiffon dress that was rather low cut. It automatically drew attention to her well-developed figure. My God, thought Mark, *What a rack!* His gaze drank in the fullness of her body. Her auburn hair was cut short. Her complexion had a rosy freshness that screamed youth and vitality. Her smile was that of a freshman coed intent on befriending every male and female on campus. Involuntarily, Mark shamelessly undressed her in his imagination while pretending to take notes.

Professor Smythe-Bagley's review of the Punic Wars was presented with the necessary dates, the names of principal figures, with appropriate personal information obviously gleaned from extensive research, and the places and movements of warring armies. Mark jotted down the number of Hannibal's elephants (57), his horse mounted troops (9000) and his foot soldiers (ca. 50,000). As he did so, he began to sketch a shapely nude female figure and was beginning to add facial features, when Professor Smythe-Bagley, whose peripatetic style often had her moving about the classroom brought her close to Mark's seat. Her description of the Roman defeat at Cannae suffered a momentary pause as she noticed Mark's absent-minded doodling and found the image familiar. That Aemilius Paulus, a Consul, and 50,000 Roman troops were destroyed at that battle in 216 B.C. did not appear in Mark's notes.

During Mark's interview the following day in Professor Smythe-Bagley's office, ostensibly to choose a research topic, the attractive academic wondered aloud where students hung out in town. Mark mentioned a few places and offered to escort the comely single-woman on a tour of local hot spots the coming Friday evening. The offer was accepted. A surge of testosterone occurred.

The house special and two beers at *Bartoli's Villa Italiana* were followed by a drive to a secluded parking area on the town's lake in Rowena's leased Ford Mustang. Without warning, Row, as she suggested he call her, embraced Mark, planted a hot kiss on his eager lips and pressed her breast cage firmly against his chest. That she was determined to become intimate was a college student's dream come true. Then, another car, also a convertible, rolled up beside them. The parking brake was activated and the headlights were extinguished. Mark looked over. In the driver's seat, looking in his direction, was... his mother. He slid down in his seat until he was invisible.

*

With gloved hands, Mark had slid down from knot to knot on the thick climbers' rope dangling deep into the hole in the earth. From the roof of the cave's main chamber some thirty feet above, huge stalactites by the dozens hung in silence. Mark's heavy-duty flashlight played on them gently. Many were a dull, translucent milky white, others brownish or laced with shades of green. Much of the brownish expanse covering the cavern's roof, Mark understood, consisted of thousands of bats clinging together, resting for their next foray into the world outside, where they performed numerous feats that actually helped mankind. However useful they might be, Mark's countenance could not mask his subconscious squeamishness. With nightfall swarms of bats would exit through the very opening that had beckoned the would-be explorer.

He looked down. Viewed from the narrow ledge on which he was resting after a perilous descent by rope into the bowels of the cave, stalagmites of various lengths stood defiantly on the floor of the cave another twenty feet beneath his precarious perch. Mark was probably at the widest point of the cavern he had entered with the help of some spelunking friends. Looking off to the left and right he saw the cave narrow into dark passages. The next step was to figure out how to reach the cavern's floor without injury. Outside it was late afternoon. The light reaching through the nearly hidden opening in a grove of trees above was growing dimmer. He hoped his flashlight batteries would hold out. Rumor had it that the cavern and its myriad underground passageways had numerous exits, albeit well out of view to all but experts. Mark tied his rope around a sturdy-looking stalagmite and slowly lowered himself to the floor of the cavern, after testing it to ascertain if it could hold his 170 pounds. From this lower vantage point the entrance was no longer visible. Neither was the rope he had used to enter the cave.

What have I got myself into now? he thought. The silence was broken by an occasional drip-drip-drip, whose exact location he was unable to verify. To his right was a passageway large enough to offer itself as a possible way to another part of the cave system. Mark entered and felt his way carefully. Occasionally, he had to duck and crawl several feet at a time. Abrasions on his knees were sore. In a few spots it was necessary to remove his backpack and pass it through narrow places. In one of these he was almost stuck, until he finally managed to squeeze past. He paused in a small opening and tried to call out on his cell phone to the two friends who had accompanied him. There was no signal. None at all.

Ahead was a faint phosphorescent glow. He heard scratching. Half expecting to see a rabbit wearing a top hat, Mark pressed on silently. The scratching sound persisted. Spirits of the depths, he surmised. Lost souls condemned to live underground? The configuration of the tunnel in which he found himself required that he crawl on his knees again some fifty feet. Bleeding slightly, he emerged in a large chamber where there was sufficient light to illuminate a huge metal chest in the center. On it sat a bearded, peg-legged man with a patch covering his left eye. His grey beard was matted, scraggly. In his right hand was a gleaming scimitar. "Approach!" he shouted in a deep, gravely voice. "Come, let me see you closer!" Mark aimed the flashlight at him. There was no light. Damn! He dropped it and moved towards a shadow that could be an opening. He slipped on the floor and fell into a pool of cold water up to his armpits.

His backpack slipped out of his hand and floated away – out of reach. Although conscious, he was confused and full of apprehension.

*

Soaked to the skin, shivering and frightened, he sat on a blanket on the lake shore, a huge fireman's waterproof jacket over his shoulders, he reported to his parents. "Sorry, son," one of the senior rescue officials pronounced. "You were brave to try and save the man who fell into the water. We gave it our best, but couldn't bring him back. He was in the water too long. Are you from the university?"

The answer was affirmative He was unable to comprehend the loss of a dear college buddy. Totally stunned, he refused to believe Gordon was gone, dead, drowned. He was like a brother. Other boaters gathered around, watching as the medics moved the body bag into the ambulance.

"Chinese, I'd say, from the looks of him. Was he a student here too?"

Yes. He managed to mutter. To Mark he wasn't Chinese. He wasn't different. He was… a brother. He couldn't grasp that he had not been able to save him in time. The water was murky, but….

*

Looking out over the marsh that characterized so much of the Low Country coastline, the Governor and Frank O'Reilly, the State Representative from the college's district, listened intently. Both old pols, they knew instinctively that my idea was going to be good for the state, but more importantly, good for them. Both had aspirations beyond their current situations. All I needed was three million added to the college's budget this year and a commitment for ten more over the next two years. With that I could attract a top figure in environmental studies, especially one with wetlands' expertise, and I could begin developing a center for a first-class academic and research program that would really put the college and the state on the map. Lots of jobs would be created and the prestige would have an unbelievable ripple effect. The vital seed money would attract the remainder of the necessary funding. That day I could have sold an Eskimo tribe shares in an ice making plant. All my colleagues who had scoffed at my election as Dean of the College would be dining on humble pie this week. "Kiss my ring, guys! This campus is my Vatican now."

*

I admit it. I'm flirting. With a nun? I can't believe it. It's simply impossible. Hell, I'm not really religious, but this has to be a sacrilege or something. And I'll be damned, if she isn't flirting with me. Oh boy, the dangerous lives we academics lead. Mark was absolutely captivated by the beautiful woman sitting to his right. He could see her sparkling eyes and lovely complexion, all neatly framed by her headpiece, whatever it is they call it. She seems to be slender, but under that robe I can't tell. No matter. She's a real charmer. And she genuinely seems interested in me. How natural she is. Can this be real? It was the eyes. Yes, the eyes. Our hearts spoke to each other through our eyes. We recognized by some kind of magic that we were kindred souls. Boy, have I been working too hard! I've only known her a few minutes and my heart is aflutter. Who spiked my orange juice? Oh, please, don't let it stop here! Sister Catherine, did God send you to help me break out of this cocoon I seem to have built around myself?

"Catherine. May I call you Catherine, or Cathy, or Kate?" No one nearby seems to notice us. Mark continued, "Let's get married, buy a farm somewhere and have lots of children! It's your eyes. I can't help it. How do you do this?"

*

The old man ahead of him rarely looked back. He simply leaned forward and moved his skis, coordinated with the movements of his arms and ski poles. The wind blew freezing, blinding snow in his face. There was no turning back now. How did I get into this? I had a good job. It had many rewards. I was fairly comfortable. There were neat offers by word or mail to move on to larger, more prestigious institutions. My future was very

585

promising. But, instead of rearranging the furniture in a freshly painted office in an ivy-covered building, here I am slogging along on skis in a country I know nothing about. What quirk of fate brought this about? Have I lost my mind?

*

"Aja! Aja! Oh, please don't let her be dead!" Her body was limp. The blood oozed out of the hole in her forehead. A lucky shot? Fate? She was looking out for me. My guardian angel. I touched her cheek. The warmth of her body will dissipate quickly in the snow and wind. They might come back. I've got to get across the street and disappear in the woods. I must get a grip on myself, calm down. "Oh, God, why did this have to happen?"

The snow is making a crunching sound as I run through the woods, sometimes staying on the trail, occasionally looping off for several meters. This whole matter is cursed. Maybe I should... No, I've got to go on.

Someday, there will be retribution...... someday, somehow.

*

Leila's song had a melancholy ring to it. She looked sad. Was it the lyrics that recalled the plight of gypsies throughout history? Or was it her own personal situation? Mark/Matti might never know. He felt love. He felt pity. He was at once protective and aroused. Who was he? Why was he here? He had heard someone mention fate. When? What was fate? "If only I could remember my name! Did I have a home? There was a woman who helped me. Who was she?"

*

Maybe the rain is activating my bladder. Good thing this highway rest stop has a latrine. Lucky for me the rain is letting up. I probably should have stopped in the last town and stayed in an inn until the storms pass. Oh well. Things could be worse. Imagine, a flat tire in this weather? Oh,

586

look! Someone's poking around in my car. "Hey! What's going on? What are y......"

*

The voice was weak, faint. It sounded like a little girl's voice. Inquisitive, curious. "Jean-Pierre, do you have any idea who he is?" Anni's features mirrored the compassion she felt for the man lying on the operating table. While Helga and Guillaume were busied with the various tubes and sensors attached to the victim's chest and appendages, Anni studied the face that had been nearly destroyed by an unknown, but certainly merciless assailant. The patient was in a coma, yet he heard snippets of conversation as he struggled to regain consciousness. The anaesthesia dulled the sound of voices and dimmed the bright overhead lamps. Sleep, deep, restful sleep relaxed his muscles and slowed his brain waves as Anni and her husband studied the dials and gauges, attempting to assess the nature and extent of his injuries. Would he live to try and comprehend why one member of his own species would seek without provocation to rob him of his existence, while another would go to extreme lengths to restore his life and physical integrity? Men are such strange animals!

"We have no choice but to try. I believe we can help him. Are you ready?" The good doctor's presence was itself reassuring. His voice seemed to come from a huge void. He was calm and professional. While a larger staff might have been desirable under the circumstances, Baumann had his best people in place. They were skilled multitaskers and anticipated his every need. Mark was a lucky man after all!

A few hours later, Dr. Baumann threw his fourth pair of hygienic gloves into the bio-disposal receptacle. With a gentle clap on the backs of Helga and Guillaume and a hug for Anni, he said, "Now it's up to him and the Divine. He seems quite strong. We'll hope for the best."

Anni felt that God had worked through her eyes, her hands.

*

He leaned back, resting his head on the rounded rim of the tub. The

587

water had felt scalding hot when he had first tested it with the toes of his right foot. Now he was enveloped in soothing warmth. His muscles relaxed. He attempted to focus on a thought, but exhaustion took charge. His eyes struggled to stay open. Fatigue, warm water up to his neck, sleep overcame him.

A new life stirred within him. He had become a leaf. A green leaf. His home was on a branch of a sturdy limb reaching out from the trunk of a powerful tree; a tree that had stood on the same spot for at least a hundred years. He was not alone. Clustered about him were other leaves. Most were green like him. As a group, clinging to the branch, they exuded lushness, they were involuntary active participants in a verdant paradise stretching skyward with vigor and purpose. He liked his fellow leaves. They were colleagues in the process of photosynthesis.

Abundant sunshine, regular precipitation and distance from roads that bisected many forests contributed to his well-being and positive outlook. Perched near the apex of a magnificent tree that proudly exceeded the height of its neighbors, the leaf surveyed a kingdom so expansive it reigned from horizon to horizon. To the left were broad plains, then graying silhouettes of mountain peaks. To the right was a deep and broad valley, a band of water forming a ribbon of blue through several stands of trees and rolling hills. The leaf enjoyed the camaraderie. Gentle breezes tickled in the early morning. Occasionally, birds stopped briefly to rest and gossip or plan the resumption of their flight. Sometimes other birds joined them. Their chatter could get rather loud.

Refreshing rains mitigated the sweltering days of intense sun in summer. Once in a while powerful winds would wrench a friends's grip from the branch. They could be seen fluttering away. Most ended up near the trunk and slowly, inexorably began a pile. In time the pile turned brown. It was no longer possible to distinguish our friends. Eventually, the weight of other leaves, accumulated snow, rain and wind-blown detritus from the forest brought about the disintegration of our friends. Some were obviously from earlier generations of leaves.

The days grew cooler and cooler. The sun began to move slowly. The days grew shorter. The nights were longer. Somehow they all seemed less green. A few of them, especially the ones near the tip of the branch, started to turn yellow, then red. They were dry and scratchy. When the wind blew they made rustling noises. The leaves spread the alarm: Danger – hang on for your life! But they all knew, autumn would bring striking changes.

It was just past noon when the velocity of the winds became noticeably stronger. Besides, it was gusty. First one leaf, then another could no longer thwart the pull of gravity. Sudden blasts of air pulled a few leaves from a neighboring limb. They all began tumbling down. Nearby leaves gasped, witnessing silently the fate of others. Knowing their time was approaching. A few managed to float, while others appeared to be in a hurry to crash into the floor of the forest. He had clung as long as possible to his branch. His stem was weary. Suddenly, he was free, twisting and turning, descending slowly and gracefully, making unusual figures in the crisp air. Because his branch was on the edge of the forest overlooking a river valley, he had a superb view of the landscape he was about to join. An updraft wafted him higher, then in a swinging motion, now this way, now that way, he resumed his downward flight. A friendly leaf, a brother, as it were, raced silently past, eager to accept his destiny. He seemed like a rocket.

Winds from the opposite direction blew him closer to the still leaf-clad boughs nearer to the ground. Then, other winds, competing for sovereignty, created a whirlwind and the leaf climbed slightly, soaring wide over the valley, then zoomed toward the earth, where tall grass bent, and shivered, and lay silently on it's side. It was into one of these golden beds that the leaf landed, grateful for the soft cushion. Wind sweeping across the field carried the leaf for a considerable distance. It was dizzy from the somersaults and back flips. Before it could catch its breath, another blast whistled across the field and the leaf slid down a muddy bank, landing gracefully in the slow-moving stream at its base. The current received its newest conquest joyfully, gliding it past smooth stones, tree stumps and wild flowers as it flowed on to join a larger waterway downstream.

*

As he had anticipated, Wilma-Sue Cooper, a columnist for the local paper and wife of the Chairman of the Philosophy Department, had invited an unattached female to dinner, as well as Dr. Ashley, the Coopers' attorney, and his wife, Meredith, the 'queen' of the town's real estate agents. Rarely was Mark invited to dinner by the would-be matchmakers among the faculty wives, when a good-looking 'prospect' wasn't placed either beside or opposite him at the dining table. As a rule, little developed from these attempts to find the sought-after bachelor a winsome bride. The hostess' intentions were generally transparent. A concert date or dinner engagement could occasionally be traced to one of these events. Mark, however, was so tied to his responsibilities at the college, that such efforts had all proven thus far to be in vain.

Marcellina Mercurio was a notable exception. Her golden locks attributable to the artistry of her hairdresser, she was a voluptuous vamp, a seductress who took no prisoners. She never tired of dancing and knew all the latest steps. If you intended to lose graciously at tennis or golf, you didn't need to try hard, for she was a master of the putting green and could blister a backhand cross-court winner past almost any opponent. Fluent in five languages, well-traveled, a gourmet cook and much-envied couture hound, Marcellina, who found Mark charming and manly, gave a valiant effort, but ultimately lost out to Mark's single-minded pursuit of professional and academic excellence.

Following Marcellina's return to her native Italy, whenever Mrs. Cooper spied Mark in town or on the campus, she would often update him by reporting that Marcellina "says hi from St. Moritz", or "sends regards from Monte Carlo", or "Happy New Year from Vienna." Back in his office, Mark would wonder what life might have been like as Marcellina's companion.

*

"This is the most irrational thing I've ever done. Everyone agrees the kidnappers are bound to be so desperate by now that Elli's life is truly in danger." Mark would have preferred a civilized twentieth century solution. Like knocking on the door and demanding that the kidnappers come out with their hands up, surrender to the police, and release his beloved wife, an expectant mother. But no, in a machismo moment, a flash of courage that had taken him by surprise, he had proclaimed his intention to leap off a mountain and paraglide to his spouse's aid. Alas! The moment of truth had arrived. Was it a matter of stupidity, or stubbornness, or of pride and integrity? Mark knew only that he was scared half out of his wits. He was, however, absolutely determined not to show it. The man he had asked to help him explained the procedure. Hans Hofer, who understood the 'butterflies' of the novice about to undertake his debut solo flight, did his best to make it seem like a commonplace. His main concern was keeping his pupil far enough away from the craggy, and nearly vertical stone wall of the alpine mount from which Mark was perched to jump.

Freezing air boldly slapped his face as the chute opened fully and an updraft guided him away from the jagged face of the cliff that was his principal adversary. Following Hofer's oft-repeated instructions, he sought to master his fragile craft and maneuver carefully to his destination below – a patch of grass still partially covered by a lingering blanket of late spring snow. Suddenly, a gust of wind flipped his chute and, almost totally at Mother Nature's mercy, he crashed hard against the sharp rocks that defined the sheer surface of the alpine cliffs past which he had intended to descend. The chute lost air. Stunned by the force of the wind and the penduling thrust of his chute, he began an uncontrollable fall to the earth some 500 meters below. There was no time to pray or scream. The cool, soggy sod received him with an audible thump. He lay there, motionless, pain numbed by the cold, damp earth.

*

It was an unexpected jolt. "Your father passed sometime during the night." Mark held the receiver in his right hand. The words hung in the air like freshly washed laundry on a cool, but sunny November morning.

Mrs. Weingarten's voice was free of emotion. The elder Davidsons' neighbor of 25 years was in fragile health herself. Nevertheless, she sounded calm and objective. Like a reporter on the morning news.

Mark was engrossed in preparation for his mid-terms. His dad knew his heart was weak, yet he never made any concessions to the admonitions of friends, family and Doc Foster, his physician of many years. "Was he taking his medications regularly?" Mark wanted to know. "We'll have to set a time for the funeral? I'll have a friend, maybe Gordon, drive me down this afternoon. We'll need help with planning, Mary Klein would be a good choice. She's buried three relatives since last Christmas." Mark was trying to be helpful. The Kleins, frequent bridge mates, had the reputation of being people others often turned to for advice. They knew the routine. By the time Mark reached home, just three hours away, the shock would be setting in. He knew his presence would be welcome. He wanted to cry. Instead, he swallowed hard. Now he was alone in the world. The mantle had been placed on his shoulders. The King is dead! Long live the King!

*

"If I were a rich man, da divi divi divi divi dum." Not a truly natural singer, Mark had gargled before going on stage to soothe his throat. Perhaps it was the tremendous effort to overcome stage fright. At any rate, adrenaline, combined with a determination to succeed, coaxed his baritone to a creditable performance. He was pleased and surprised, as were his parents. Mrs. Feinberg, the drama teacher, was ecstatic.

The lyrics had materialized from his subconscious intermittently in the years since his meeting with Zdeněk Székely. His fate was full of irony.

*

Mark had often remarked that in a previous incarnation he had been born on an alpine mountain top. He and Elli and the children truly loved being in the mountains. Not to climb, but to hike along the seemingly endless network of trails, both easy and demanding, whenever they could get away for an afternoon, a weekend, or a longer period of time. The rigorous jaunts not only brought them together as a family, but also made them intimately aware of the wonders of nature. The glorious vistas from upland vantage points, the visible evidence of the incredible forces that squeezed and pushed the earth's crust to create great mountain ranges, and man's ability to adapt to life in terrain that frequently penetrated the clouds were wonders the Davidsons experienced first-hand. Their mutual interests and eager participation engendered a lifestyle that was reflected in the healthy glow each seemed to radiate in their everyday lives and activities. Mark carefully studied the hiking map before him.

*

As Mark managed to advance through a convoluted passageway to another huge cavern, he couldn't help but reflect on the joy he felt in the outdoors. He never thought of himself as claustrophobic, but the constricted entrance to the cavern and the lack of moving air or light were beginning to affect his mood. The threatening image that prompted his retreat from another section of the cave had not followed him. An eerie silence was interrupted intermittently by a thin ripple of moving water. Mark looked in vain in the darkness to try and locate its source. Gradually, his eyes adapted somewhat to the darkness and he noticed a dim, greenish-blue luminescence that helped him assess the size of the chamber. He judged it to be fifty meters tall, perhaps seventy meters long and thirty wide. It had a slight oval shape. There were a few stalactites. He assumed that some moisture must seep through from the earth above. Whenever he turned the sound of the water seemed to be behind him. Then, it stopped. He moved forward gingerly, testing each foothold before shifting his weight. He sought to traverse the long axis, hoping to find some way up and out, back to civilization. He forced a positive outlook on the darkest circumstances he had ever faced.

His amateur spelunker's sense told him he had been descending deeper into the maze of caverns. He stayed close to the side of the cavern.

It was not smooth, but was marked by numerous indentations, recesses that led nowhere. The air was damp. Some debris on the cavern's floor caused him to trip slightly. Thinking they were loose stones, he bent down to touch them. They were, he discovered, the crumbling bones of a skeleton that was partly fused to the floor. Mark shuddered involuntarily. His breathing was loud. It echoed off the opposite wall. The temperature was cool. Mark felt a chill. He was truly worried now about getting out. "Don't panic!" he told himself.

Returning to his starting point would be virtually impossible. Without food, sleep, support and appropriate equipment he doubted he could make it. Moving forward was his only option. Because his watch had been broken in a fall, Mark had no idea what time or day it was. Neither could he tell accurately how long it was taking to advance towards the far end of the cave. He guessed he could make it there in, say, fifteen minutes. He estimated when fifteen minutes had passed. Although he had moved haltingly, yet steadily, he appeared no closer to his objective. The greenish glow that offered some details of his surroundings was getting dimmer. He pressed on. Still, the end of the cavern struck him as even more distant, than when he had begun. Was it minutes or hours ago. Time existed no more. Space was a nonexistent dimension. He found a dry place to sit and rest. He prayed he would not meet the fate of the person whose remains now dominated his thoughts.

*

Mark watched with a mixture of confusion and amazement. He had had nothing to drink. So, he couldn't be drunk. But there he was, or there they were, one seated on the stone wall, the other leaning against the trunk of a giant oak. Two Marks! They looked alike. They sounded alike. But... somehow, they were different.

"Mark, you're not just naïve, you're plain stupid, dumb, ignorant! The money is yours. You don't have to share it, or give it away. You can actually spend every minute of every day doing whatever you want. Cost is not a factor. You can choose where you want to live. You can hire as many servants as you want. Don't you understand the power, the freedom and independence that totally liberates you from virtually all of the restrictions and obligations of the common man?" The message was delivered with some emotion. Dropping his arms to his sides, he drew a deep breath and stared at Mark, who had found a smooth place on the stone wall.

"Stop confusing me. You don't need to reiterate your argument again. Frankly, I'm deeply disappointed in you. Your point of view regarding the ungodly sum I received from the Székelys is repulsive. Never forget, while the senior Székely initiated the investments that so dramatically increased through the years to produce the immense treasure I now control, the source of that collection of secret bank accounts he found was undoubtedly the savings and possessions of countless persons, families and businesses that were wantonly destroyed in the Thirties and Forties. At this point, we can only begin to imagine the pain they suffered, the indignities they endured, the hopelessness and despair that accompanied their final hours. Are you so evil, that you cannot accept that hope must arise from those flames? The souls of those innocents so heartlessly consumed by greed, lust and hate cry out for retribution. Zdeněk was a good and decent man. He literally saved my life. I never met his father, Tibor, yet I am absolutely clear that their ultimate goal was for these resources to be used to make men and women reflect the very best of which our species is capable.

"My goal is to facilitate that process the best way my simple intellect and humble spirit will allow. I am fortunate to be surrounded with marvelous individuals who share that aim."

"You're a damned fool." The voice was full of exasperation. "However hard you try, there will always be efforts to steal your gifts, to circumvent your treaties and contracts, to cheat you, and ignore your lofty objectives. Some people probably don't appreciate what you're trying to do. You take a terrible beating racing about the globe to try and fix every problem. Charity, by any name, is a fruitless enterprise. I'm all for self indulgence. Give me wine, women and pleasure in every imaginable form!"

"Incorrigible, that's what you are. Don't you see, that true pleasure is achieved by helping others? I am not blind to the crime I encounter wherever I go. Still, the wonders of nature, the beauties of man's creations, and the soaring examples of man's triumphant spirit are pleasures even such a negative person as you can enjoy." Sliding gently off the wall, Mark approached the figure now slumped in a seating position at the base of the tree. He held out his hand. "Come, I'll not abandon you."

"Where do you go next?"

"This leg of my journey is completed. I'm heading home. I have a good wife who deserves my love. I gain incomparable pleasure from witnessing the exuberance and innocence of my children. I also have a duty to guide them towards responsible lives in a troubled world. Ah, reality! Formidable! Daunting! Challenging! Embraceable! Shall we go?"

*

"There's a sad sort of clanging from the clock in the hall." Elli and the children were singing to Mark, spread out on the living room floor with some of the photo albums from family outings during the year.

Taking turns, Mireille, Sylvie, Theo and Elli pretended to leave for their respective bedrooms. "So long, farewell, auf Wiedersehen, good bye…" They sounded so good.

"Adieu, bonne nuit! Come let me hug you all. You should be in the movies. I'm happy to see you have your mother's talent." Mark was immensely proud of his children. And, of course, of Michèlle, for whose love he would forever be indebted to the fates.

*

Why were they hurrying so? Mark's meeting had been in a monstrous Victorian building, a structure with endless rooms, hallways, stairwells, wings, added extensions. It was a curious place for a meeting. How he had found his way out was something of a mystery. So, too, was the call from Elli. She and the children were in town and wanted to have lunch, if he could manage it. Having excused himself from the working lunch meeting, he couldn't explain why his wife, twin daughters and son, Theo, had suddenly materialized in this huge metropolis. Weren't they home in Switzerland? I guess not. Mark was planning to take a taxi to the restaurant Elli mentioned.

There were no taxis. The streets were full of people, huge groups running or walking rapidly. Many looked back, worry, concern, fear on the countenances. Occasionally, some would stumble and fall. If they were lucky others would walk around them, possibly help them onto their feet. Some were trampled. Mark was swept up and rushed to maintain his footing. He looked for his briefcase, then remembered he had left it in a conference room. His cell phone was in it. The mob reached a large square. Other groups of people wearing every manner of dress, from pyjamas to evening clothes, were converging on the square from every direction. They mingled and continued, many reversing their direction and joining others who surged ahead.

"Mark! Mark!" He heard his name. Frantically scanning the crowds as best he could, he thought he saw Elli. She was waving. He pushed through the mob. Just as he was about to catch up, Theo's voice sounded from a group approaching from behind. He sounded as if he had observed Mark and was in need of help. Confusion reigned. Which way to turn? Strange, too, there were no cars, no trucks, no taxis!

Mark stopped, hugged a slight indentation on the side of a building, and searched for his son. "Theo! Theo!" He called as loudly as he could. There was no response. The group, actually a rather unruly mob, driven by fear, mostly running at jog speed, was moving towards a river. The main group proceeded onto a bridge. It had a steep incline and forward progress slowed visibly as the ascent took a toll on tired legs and strained lungs. A portion of the runners, resembling tales of lemmings, blindly followed a few leaders and veered left heading directly for the river. First, they slogged through mud flats, then plunged headlong into the swiftly moving waters. Many appeared to slip and fall under the water. Frenzied bodies turned the water muddy. Few attempts were made to assist them. Others started swimming. The opposite shore was some distance away. The size of the group diminished quickly. A large number floundered helplessly in the waters, wailing and pleading for help. There was none. Many apparently drowned.

Mark melded into a throng passing by. He continued to call out, "Theo! Theo! Elli! Sylvie! Mireille!" In the droning din of hundreds, now increased possibly to thousands fleeing the previously busy streets of the city, Mark's cries failed to carry far. They elicited no responses. The momentum of the hordes running in the direction of the suburbs was relentless. Attrition and exhaustion might eventually control the mindless movement. Mark finally stopped, out of breath, frustrated, totally con-fused, crying out in desperation for his loved ones. He ducked into a doorway. He had never felt so utterly helpless. The cause of the panic was a mystery. Mark was absolutely baffled by the mindless pandemonium that engulfed him. Whatever rules might have existed for public behavior were suspended. Men and women were hurdling the bodies of the fallen. Shrieks and shouts drowned out the wailing moans of the wounded and dying.

There was a slight break in the flow past his vantage point. Scattered about were lifeless bodies. A few writhed in pain. Mark's inclination was to dash out and try to help. A huge new surge of hundreds approached. They were yelling, crying, groaning, sucking air. A dense cloud of dust and acrid smelling particles hung above the stampeding mob and turned it into a sea of ghoulish figures. Was this the cataclysm that would end the struggle between good and evil? The latter would appear to be head-ing for victory. Just then Mark spied a small courtyard across the broad avenue. Behind a wrought iron fence a number of people were on their knees. They seemed to be praying. A lone figure stood. Back at the apex of the bridge large numbers were leaping into the river whose central channel was claiming victim after victim. A small boy joined him in the doorway. He looked up, a mask of despair frozen on his muddied face.

*

Luigi pleaded for help. Gordon and Mark looked at each other. Both had their own exams to study for. They were committed, however, to helping their buddy, although they often wondered why he signed up for advanced math classes, when his math skills, not to mention his interest, were nearly zilch. Gordon explained logarithms and their use in computer programming. Mark helped review Luigi's text on actuarial science. Luigi's brain was about to bust, he claimed. However, he thought he had a handle on it. They walked down to *Ianuzzi's Leaning Tower of Pizza*, where Luigi treated the trio. The cheese and tomato sauce were diluted with a few glasses of a respectable Rosso. They all knew this would be an enduring memory of college life.

*

Just below on the west side of the highway tracing the shore of Lake Garda the wind had picked up. Waves splashing on the rocky shore could be heard through the doors open onto the veranda. Seldom had Mark lusted so much for a woman. Toni, Luigi's cousin Antonia di Sogno, was an absolute dream. Bright and bubbly, exquisite features, gorgeous blonde tresses falling on her shoulders, a delightfully flirty attitude, and a figure string bikini manufacturers would die for. She was engaged. She was Luigi's cousin, and now, Mark's hostess. While Mark was totally unattached, his personal dream hinged on a chance encounter, a momentary exchange of glances in a Swiss coffee shop. It was the most fragile, the flimsiest of human connections. He had no idea who the woman was, or whether he would ever set eyes on her again. Only a true romantic, an irrepressible dreamer, and as he sometimes labeled himself, a naïve fool, could entertain the thought of ever connecting with such a fleeting vision. Mark and Toni talked animatedly on all manner of subjects. It was obvious to each that kindred spirits, alone together in a secluded haven, erotically aroused, could indulge their desires with little likelihood their secret tryst would wander beyond the confines of Luigi's retreat. Ah, but then there's that thing called conscience. Toni was deeply in love with her fiancé. Mark's sense of propriety and honor would not allow him to take advantage of his friend's relation. Both chose silently to cap this deliciously provocative instance with a simple '*Buona Notte!*' Their integrity tested, yet intact. A triumphant and satisfying moment for each.

*

Mom's friend, Becky Epstein, played a selection of piano pieces Mom enjoyed. Jim Mears, the flutist, who had sat hundreds of times next to his mother at concerts staged by the regional symphony to which she devoted so much time and effort, played two Telemann Fantasias, #6 in D minor and #9 in E major. She had been especially fond of Telemann. Mark and his Dad, who was seated beside him, had, of course, heard them many, many times. As well as she knew them, Mark's mother insisted on practicing over and over, discovering in the process, new nuances and variations that excited her musical soul. About fifty close friends, fellow musicians and neighbors had gathered for this memorial service. Both Mark and his Dad had shared with the gathering a few light and some serious memories, evoking both laughs and tears along the way. The funeral had been held at the end of the previous week. It was a small, very personal affair for a tight-knit group of his mother's inner circle. Her ashes had been interred in a niche in a memory wall at a private cemetery. She would be surrounded, hopefully for an eternity, by lush vegetation and fragrant roses. She had not felt well for some time when terminal cancer was discovered to be the cause. She lingered on through the late spring. Mark came home from the university every weekend to be with her. She managed to hold on until the summer holiday. Mark cancelled his holiday, work and travel plans to be with her and his father, who after over fifty years of marriage, was devastated by the prospect of losing his wife and partner.

When her energy allowed it, they talked about old times and things that would have to be done when she was gone. She listened almost constantly to music. Mark was the DJ. Her preference was for instrumental pieces, primarily from the baroque period. It was mainly music she had performed throughout her life: Scarlatti, Telemann, J.S. Bach, Boccherini, Vivaldi, Lully, Monteverdi, Rameau. She had always marveled at their virtuosity, their inventiveness, the remarkable energy, industry and devotion they displayed in an age absent the innumerable aids available to modern musicians. It had been a bright, sunny June afternoon, when Dr. Harris alerted Mark and his Dad to the approach of the inevitable. The sound was muted as Mom passed listening to a violin concerto by Johann Friedrich Fasch that had been recorded on a CD by a German pen pal just weeks before.

*

The black pony was supposed to be a surprise. Elli had taken the children shopping for groceries. Mark remained behind and was waiting at the end of the drive up to their farmhouse near Yverdon-les-Bains when the trailer pulled up and he took delivery of a lively pony. A stall had already been prepared in the barn not far from the house in the midst of a grove of chestnut trees. Theo had wondered aloud what the hay was for, as well as the new buckets, the brushes and a visit by the local vet. After dinner, at Mark's invitation the children walked out to the barn. Mireille was the one who decided he should be called Midnight. They hugged and squeezed and sat on the energetic equine wonder. It seemed equally as thrilled as its new owners. The children learned how to brush him, check his hooves, and fix his bridle. A feeding schedule was established. A paddock, enclosed by a freshly-painted white fence, had been hastily constructed a short distance away. It was the beginning of a great friendship. Never had a pony so many dedicated admirers. Mark and Elli were in seventh heaven. The children's joy was magnified a hundredfold in their parent's hearts.

*

The fullness of their outer garments, the white accents of their cuffs and cowls conveyed thoughts of penguins, a thought Mark knew was a bit unkind and of which he quickly disabused himself. They did appear to waddle slightly in their shiny flat-soled shoes. Mark couldn't help himself. He stared. There were rosy cheeks and smiles, stern, rather severe looks, benign countenances, strong chins, big noses, little noses, but not one resembled Sister Catherine. Why he thought he might see her among this particular group of nuns was not clear to Mark. Sister Catherine was, after all, thousands of miles away in Hong Kong. Her work there in the field of education had enjoyed considerable success. Her contributions to the work of the *Foundation* have been immensely helpful. What if she had not already committed herself to work in a religious charity before he met her? Yes, what if? One of those questions for which there is no answer. Idle, senseless conjecture? Perhaps.

*

The size and strength of the arm holding him in a painful headlock shocked an unsuspecting Mark Davidson, whose brief ferry ride from Hong Kong to Kowloon had been unusually serene. That is, until the sudden attack from behind. A split second was the length of time necessary for him to determine the immediate issue was life or death. The gruff voice, the malicious tone were familiar. Gregor Mukhachevo! But how? Driven by desperation and the need for an instantaneous response, Mark's head thrust back against the nose he sensed was millimeters away. Simultaneously, Mark's right arm stretched backward to its limit and forced Mukhachevo's head forward. The resulting severe blow to such a prominent feature of his assailant's face caused sudden pain and profuse bleeding. The burly brute's natural reflexes prompted a slight loosening of his grip on Mark's neck. Wrenching himself free, Mark was about to confront his foul-smelling opponent, when the latter regained his footing and flung Mark to the deck. In the process Mark's head struck one of the wooden bench seats and he was momentarily stunned.

As he relived the incident, Mark recalled next hearing shouts, two gunshots, then spotting a reclining figure forward. As he turned to see where Gregor was, he saw him stagger backwards holding his chest before tumbling over the rail into the harbor. Not until he raced forwards and approached the reclining figure did he see it was Zdeněk Székely. A revolver lay at his side. Unbelievably, the dying man had saved his life.

On the Northwest Orient flight east across the Pacific Mark had hours to recount the number of times his life had literally been saved at virtually the last moment by others. Was it his fate or theirs? Is there a God? Do I have a guardian angel? Or is there a Lady Luck, a force of nature that is watching over me, protecting me? Why? Yes, why?

*

"Dr. Mark Davidson!" Professor Delmar Henry Barton, a senior member of the Department of Fine Arts, the Faculty Secretary and himself a candidate for the Deanship on several of the earlier ballots, announced in a clear voice the name of the candidate gaining the Faculty's majority vote. The men and women in the small auditorium where the faculty meeting was being held were applauding politely, relieved that what had become an extended ordeal was finally over, and at the same time, wondering how their deliberations had produced such an unexpected conclusion. Most knew who Mark Davidson was, but really did not know very much about the man himself.

Mark rose in acknowledgment, stepped out onto the aisle and strode confidently towards the small stage. He was as surprised and perplexed by this unanticipated event as his fellow academics. He brushed back his hair and looked out onto the audience. He paused briefly, drinking in the scene before him. Turning to the gentleman who had made the announcement, he said, "Professor Barton," then, scanning the rows from front to back, he continued, "My dear colleagues. Whether you have just joined us this year, or you have devoted decades of loyal service to this institution, I thank you for this exceptional honor and I pledge to you that I will strive to earn your trust and support in our common endeavor to serve our students and the citizens of this great State. I move that this meeting be adjourned." Professor Barton rose and proclaimed the session at an end. The clever machinations of a handful of power seekers had back-fired. A colleague of a mere two years, an outsider, had been elected in a process that had strayed off the proscribed path. A new day was dawning at Marshland State College.

*

Feeling dizzy, Mark squatted for a few minutes. He massaged his toes. They felt numb from the dampness and cold. He closed his eyes temporarily. He was in trouble, deep trouble. He realized he was hallucinating. There are no flowers in this God-forsaken hole, he told himself. There was no music. No Elli. Mark did not intend to give up. His companions were certain there were several possible entrances or exits somewhere in the cavern system. But where? How far away were they?

Time for an assessment, he thought. He was reasonably certain that he had been going deeper into the cavern. He remembered the terrain above was hilly. Thus, even if his movement had been downwards, he might not necessarily be that far from the surface. There was a sound. Muffled, sure, but something like… a helicopter blade. Hovering. Maybe even searching for him. He stood. A bit shaky at first, he kept one hand on the wall and moved forwards tentatively, testing his footing. The cavern took a turn to the left. He followed it. A thin beam of light was visible ahead. It must be nighttime, he thought. Perhaps that's the moon. His pace quickened.

*

"Hallo! Hey! Is anyone here?" Mark's was the sole voice to break the uncanny silence. He studied his surroundings. A country road, rutted, dusty, void of all traffic. He was alone. As he looked back he saw no sign of the city where he had awakened that morning. Or was it yesterday morning? He was not sure. There were no birds singing in the copse of shrubs nearby. He walked up the hill before him to try and catch a glimpse of the environment. An aged man was sitting in the shade of a gnarled tree. "Have you seen a woman with three children?" Mark called out, as he approached the man. Drawing nearer, Mark watched the figure stand slowly. It was actually a woman. She wore a red bandana and held a crystal ball in one hand, a polished agate amulet in the other.

* * *

For the third time, the exasperated bell boy knocked loudly on the door. "**Hello, Misstah Davisson? Hello!**" His voice could be heard at both ends of the hall.

Mark sat up in bed. His brain reacted slowly. Finally, "**Yes, what is it?**"

"**You no respond to your wake-up call, Sah. If you flight leaves in 50 minutes, you may be late.**"

"Oh my gosh!" Looking at his watch, which he had laid on the bedside table, Mark saw that, indeed, his flight was scheduled to depart in less than an hour. "**Thanks. Send someone up in ten minutes for my bags and call a taxi, please.**"

"Yessah!" The bell boy dashed off for the concierge desk.

Fortunately, the hotel was at the airport. Mark splashed cold water on his face. Toweled off. Looking in the mirror, he said, "I feel as if I had traveled a million miles already today. Oh, my head! Can't wait to get home, see my family and sleep in my own bed."

The End

About the Author

The pseudonym, Hellmut Edelmann, is a somewhat conceited self-descriptor, that could as well be applied to his recurring character, Mark Davidson. Comfortably ensconced in a small North Georgia community, approximately half-way between his daughter in Charleston (SC) and his son in Birmingham, the author enjoys a peaceful existence with his "Lebensgefährtin" and principal critic. In good weather he tends his garden. Occasional travel takes him most frequently to Europe. His philosophical goal: to emulate Mark Davidson, face life's challenges with equanimity and pursue his destiny with compassion, grace and dignity.

www.ingramcontent.com/pod-product-compliance
Lightning Source LLC
Chambersburg PA
CBHW031019030726
47497CB00004B/926